John Kessel

JOHN KESSEL

This special signed edition is
limited to 1000 numbered copies.

This is copy __771__.

The

DARK
RIDE

The Best Short Fiction
of
JOHN KESSEL

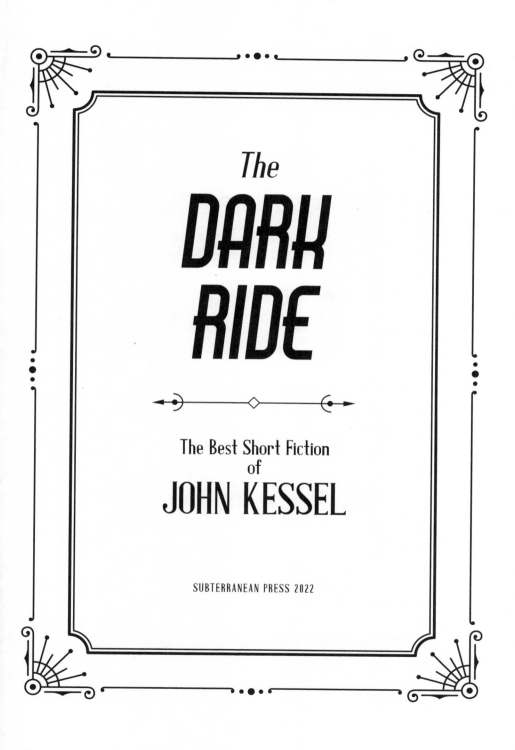

The

DARK RIDE

The Best Short Fiction
of
JOHN KESSEL

SUBTERRANEAN PRESS 2022

First Edition

ISBN
978-1-64524-058-7

Subterranean Press
PO Box 190106
Burton, MI 48519

subterraneanpress.com

Manufactured in the United States of America

Table of Contents

Introduction

by Kim Stanley Robinson

JOHN KESSEL comes out of the American science fiction community, as do I. It's a good home town, a little intellectual and artistic metropolis, semi-detached from the world, floating through space and time as in certain 1950s sf stories—Fritz Leiber's *The Big Time* is surely one portrait of it. Inside the town, after a clunky, naïve, and hopeful engineer's beginning, it developed by way of all the usual dynamics of ghetto culture, including countless intense esoteric internal exchanges, sharpening the arts and crafts involved to needlelike details of meaning not always visible to outsiders. Then in the second half of the twentieth century, when the whole world mutated into a vast science fiction story, this subculture's particular skill set proved to be the strongest art available for expressing our moment in history, and a remarkable flourishing of great fiction unleashed itself on the world.

Kessel has been part of that efflorescence. Over the course of his career he's been a leader in American science fiction, by way of his teaching, editing, organization of the Sycamore Hill workshop, close engagement with a large number of other writers, and most of all, his fiction. At the same time he's accomplished what is of course an important goal for any writer: he's stayed completely strange and idiosyncratic. His stories are singular experiences. They're also consistent among themselves, in ways that must simply be a matter of character. They're Kesseline stories, as recognizable as a fingerprint or a face.

I've been reading them for forty years. Now, surveying this Table of Contents, I feel happy for my friend. What a superb collection. Immediately

7

it joins the other great story collections in American science fiction—those of our brilliant New Wave predecessors, like Delany and Le Guin, Wolfe and Russ—also those of the wonderful generation that preceded them, writers like Sturgeon and Leiber and Emshwiller. The list could be greatly extended. This cluster of great story collections is what makes science fiction a highlight in modern American literature. If the community is considered as a Manhattan (I like to do that), this book is one of the big midtown skyscrapers, towering majestically among all the rest.

THERE ARE SOME genre questions concerning what kind of stories these are. They aren't the kind of science fiction stories that are realist-seeming accounts of more or less plausible futures for our world. Nor are they fantasies in the sense of stories about medieval worlds where magic works. They're more like fables, or parables—*fantastika* in the broader sense that has a prehistory in European folk tales, and informs the written literature of writers like ETA Hoffman and Kafka, and later, Borges and Calvino. In his introduction to an earlier collection, Kessel ponders this question of genre in a way that suggests he too is somewhat mystified by it, and at one point he mentions allegory. Allegory, he reminds us, is made of explicitly paired narratives, where a surface story expresses an understory that is connected to it as if by code. Story as metaphor, in other words. But Kessel then wonders what it would be like if the understory of an allegory were occluded or absent, remaining something to be guessed at. This made me think of New Criticism's terms for the two parts of a metaphor, the vehicle and tenor. And consider (I did): if only one part of this dyad were visible, then a vehicle without a tenor might be pictured as a never-ending car trip, as in "Not Responsible! Park It and Lock It!" And a tenor without its vehicle might be pictured as "The Lecturer," a man with a high voice, stuck in one place for lack of transport! Okay: joke. I doubt very much that the young Kessel was thinking in such terms when he came up with these ideas. But Kessel is a jokester, and also an English major, so hopefully this joke is okay here. And it's true that all these peculiar narratives, written in realist styles, while also carrying heavy but indefinite symbolic charges, do function in allegorical ways.

In the end I think it's probably best to set aside questions of genre, and just say these are non-realist stories written as if they were realist stories; or they are fables; or, better yet, that they are the kinds of stories that would get published in *The Magazine of Fantasy and Science Fiction* in 1963, when Kessel first encountered the field.

THERE ARE SOME descriptions of Kessel's writing as "savage," as if he were Jonathan Swift or some other angry satirist, but I don't think that's right. The impression comes perhaps from shocked memories of the narrator and protagonist of "The Pure Product," who in despair at the meaninglessness of his existence becomes murderously nihilistic. It's a powerful story, and maybe when combined with the forensic precision of Kessel's prose, and its insistent focus on existential concerns, such that nothing matters unless everything does, an impression of savagery is created—as in, savage honesty that won't be fooled or comforted. There are no sentimental stories here that pretend we are not on a sidewalk over the abyss. On the contrary—they have a tendency to point right at the drop-offs.

But this description, accurate enough as a start, misses entirely the warm sympathy suffusing almost all these stories. "The Pure Product" is a kind of limit case, about the moral failure of giving up hope, or forgetting that other people are as real as you, and in the same boat. That happens also in a few other stories here ("Invaders" comes to mind), but for the most part these stories are filled with a magnanimous, pastoral compassion for all the uncertainties, reversals and sorrows that people have to cope with. It's a kind of meta-attitude, a habitual state of mind, exhibited by almost all these Kesseline narrators.

Then there's also their humor. These stories are often slyly funny, spanning the whole reach from Groucho to Harpo. But also, concerned as they are with questions of meaning, or lack of meaning, they do put a very hard pressure on certain aspects of life. Can relationships sustain the pressures of existential solitude? Can any political action be meaningful if the universe itself has no meaning? These stories often seem to register great doubt on both counts. Often it's only the narrators' vivacity, eloquence and fellow feeling that save the stories from their inherent melancholy. So no, not savage; but very unrelenting, very skeptical. Very much in need of the narrators' focus on courage in solidarity, which is what these stories obviously admire and regard as the best way to deal with life.

THERE'S SOMETHING THAT happens in quite a few Kessel stories, it's a pattern in a body of work without that many patterns. A moment comes in many of them, a moment not difficult to notice, as it's often the crux of the story, when one character suddenly speaks to another in a hieratic way, in a pronouncement or revelation. Typically the protagonist runs into and is confronted by an insistent speaker, anything from a damaged robot to a animated statue to Captain Ahab. All these passages are remarkable. They burst out of their texts with news that is strange, mysterious, beyond reason or parsing—beyond Kessel himself, it seems, who must have been as startled as anyone to see such sentences appear on his page. They are uncanny. You can't get passages like these by wanting them, they come as a gift. Maybe it's a gift for story invention on the epiphanic model. And also a gift for listening closely and patiently to the story one is telling, so that when it suddenly rings like a bell, you can write down the sound of that ringing before it goes away. A moment of inspiration, caught on the fly. Kessel can do that. He has those gifts.

A LIFE'S WORK between two covers; that's an odd thing. The physical book you hold is made from a tree; and this particular book retains in itself, despite all the machinations of life and time and turning into paper, some of the strength and wholeness of a tree. Enjoy! Because the understory of the dark ride is a vivid flight.

Not Responsible!
Park and Lock It!

DAVID BAKER was born in the back seat of his parents' Chevy in the great mechanized lot at mile 1.375×10^{25}. "George, we need to stop," his mother Polly said. "I'm having pains." She was a week early.

They had been cruising along pretty well at twilight, his father concentrating on getting in another fifty miles before dark, when they were cut off by the big two-toned Mercury and George had to swerve four lanes over into the far right. George and Polly later decided that the near-accident was the cause of the premature birth. They even managed to laugh at the incident in retrospect—they ruefully retold the story many times, so that it was one of the family fables David grew up with—but David always suspected his father pined after those lost fifty miles. In return he'd gotten a son.

"Not responsible! Park and lock it!" the loudspeakers at the tops of the poles in the vast asphalt field shouted, over and over. For a first birth Polly's labor was surprisingly short, and the robot doctor emerged from the Chevy in the gathering evening with a healthy seven-pound boy. George Baker flipped his cigarette away nervously, the butt glowing as it spun into the night. He smiled.

In the morning George stepped into the bar at the first rest stop, had a quick one, and registered his name: David John Baker. Born 8:15 Standard Westbound Time, June 13...

"What year is it?" George asked the bartender.

"802,701." The robot smiled benignly. It could not do otherwise.

"802,701." George repeated it aloud and punched the keys of the terminal. "Eight hundred two thousand, seven hundred and one." The numbers spun themselves out like a song. Eight-oh-two, seven-oh-one.

David's mother had smiled weakly, reclining in the passenger's seat, when they'd started again. Her smile had never been strong. David slept on her breast.

Much later Polly told David what a good baby he'd been, not like his younger sister Caroline, who had the colic. David took satisfaction in that: he was the good one. It made the competition between him and Caroline even more intense. But that was later. As a baby David slept to the steady thrumming of the V-8 engine, the gentle rocking of the car. He was cooed at by the android attendants at the camps where they pulled over at the end of the day. His father would chat with the machine that came over to check the odometer and validate their mileage card. George would tell about any of the interesting things that had happened on the road—and he always seemed to have something—while Polly fixed supper at one of the grills and the ladies from the other cars sat around in a circle in front of the komfy kabins and talked about their children, their husbands, about their pregnancies and how seldom they got to drive. David sat on Polly's lap or played with the other kids. Once past the toddler stage he followed his dad around and watched, a little scared, as the greasy self-assured robots busied themselves about the service station. They were large and composed. The young single drivers tried hard to compete with their mechanical self-containment. David hung on everything his dad said.

"The common driving man," George Baker said, hands on the wheel, "the good average driver—doesn't know his asshole from a tailpipe."

Polly would draw David to her, as if to blot out the words. "George—"

"All right. The kid will know whether you want him to or not."

But David didn't know, and they wouldn't tell him. That was the way of parents: they never told you even when they thought they were explaining everything, and so David was left to wonder and learn as best he could. He watched the land speed by long before he had words to say what he saw; he listened to his father tell his mother what was wrong and right with the world. And the sun set every night at the other end of that world, far ahead of them still, beyond the gas stations and the wash-and-brush-up buildings and the quietly deferential androids that always seemed the same no matter how far they'd gone that day, Westbound.

When David was six he got to sit on George's lap, hold the wheel in his hands, and "drive the car." With what great chasms of anticipation and awe did he look forward to those moments! His father would say suddenly, after hours of driving in silence, "Come sit on my lap, David. You can drive."

Polly would protest feebly that he was too young. It was dangerous. David would clamber into his dad's lap and grab the wheel. How warm it felt, how large, and how far apart he had to put his hands! The indentations on the back were too wide for his fingers, so that two of his fit into the space meant for one adult's. George would move the seat up and scrunch his thin legs together so that David could see over the hood of the car. His father operated the pedals and gearshift, and most of the time he kept his left hand on the wheel too—but then he would slowly take it away and David would be steering all by himself. His heart had beaten fast. At those moments the car had seemed so large. The promise and threat of its speed had been almost overwhelming. He knew that by a turn of the wheel he could be in the high-speed lane; he knew, even more amazingly, that he held in his hands the potential to steer them off the road, into the gully, and death. The responsibility was great, and David took it seriously. He didn't want to do anything foolish, he didn't want to make George think him any less a man. He knew his mother was watching. Whether she had love or fear in her eyes he could not know, because he couldn't take his eyes from the road to see.

When David was seven there was a song on the radio that Polly sang to him, "We All Drive On." That was his song. David sang it back to her, and his father laughed and sang it too, badly, voice hoarse and off-key, not like his mother, whose voice was sweet. "We all drive on," they sang together.

"You and me and everyone
Never ending, just begun
Driving, driving on."

13

"Goddamn right we drive on," George said. "Goddamn pack of maniacs."

David remembered clearly the first time he became aware of the knapsack and the notebook. It was one evening after they'd eaten supper and were waiting for Polly to get the cabin ready for bed. George went around to the trunk to check the spare, and this time he took a green knapsack out and, in the darkness near the edge of the campground, secretively opened it.

"Watch, David, and keep your mouth shut about what you see."

David watched.

"This is for emergencies." George, one by one, set the things on the ground: first a rolled oilcloth, which he spread out, then a line of tools, then a gun and boxes of bullets, a first-aid kit, some packages of crackers and dried fruit, and some things David didn't know. One thing had a light and a thick wire and batteries.

"This is a metal detector, David. I made it myself." George took a black book from the sack. "This is my notebook." He handed it to David. It was heavy and smelled of the trunk.

"Maps of the Median, and—"

"George!" Polly's voice was a harsh whisper, and David jumped a foot. She grabbed his arm. George looked exasperated and a little guilty—though David did not identify his father's reaction as guilt until he thought about it much later. He was too busy trying to avoid the licking he thought was coming. His mother marched him back to the cabin after giving George her best withering gaze.

"But Mom—"

"To sleep! Don't puzzle yourself about things you aren't meant to know, young man."

David puzzled himself. At times the knapsack and the notebook filled his thoughts. His father would give him a curious glance and tantalizingly vague answers whenever David asked about them—safely out of earshot of Polly.

Shortly after that Caroline was born. This time the Bakers were not caught by surprise, and Caroline came into the world at the hospital at mile 1.375×10^{25}, where they stopped for three whole days for Polly's lying in. Nobody stopped for three whole days, for anything. David was impatient. They'd never *get* anywhere waiting, and the androids in the hospital were all boring, and all the comic books in the motionless waiting room he had read before.

This time the birth was a hard one. George sat hunched forward in a plastic chair, and David paced around, stomping on the cracks in the linoleum. He leaned on the windowsill and watched all the cars fly by on the highway, Westbound, and in the distance, beyond the barbed wire, sentry towers and minefields, mysterious, ever unattainable—Eastbound.

After what seemed like a very long time, the white porcelain doctoroid came back to them. George stood up as soon as he appeared. "Is she—"

"Both fine," the doctoroid reported, grille gleaming. "A little girl. Seven pounds, five ounces."

George didn't say anything then, just sat down in the chair. After a while he came over to David, put his hand on the boy's shoulder, and they both watched the cars moving by, the light of the bright mid-summer's sun flashing off the windshields as they passed, blinding them.

DAVID WAS NINE when they bought the Nash. It had a big chrome grille that stretched like a bridge across the front, the vertical bars bulging outward in the middle, so that, with the headlights, the car looked to be grinning a big nasty grin.

David went with George through the car lot while Polly sat with Caroline in the lounge of the dealership. He watched his father dicker with the bow-tied salesdroid. George acted as if he seriously meant to buy a new car, when in fact his yearly mileage average would entitle him to no more than a second-hand, second-rank sedan, unless he intended for them all to go hungry. He wouldn't have done that, however. Whatever else Polly might say about her husband, she could not say he wasn't a good provider.

"So why don't you show us a good used car," George said, running his hand through his thinning hair. "Mind you, don't show us any piece of junk."

The salesdroid was, like his brothers, enthusiastic and unreadable. "Got just the little thing for you, Mr. Baker—a snappy number. C'mon," it said, rolling down toward the back of the lot.

"Here you go." It opened the door of the blue Nash with its amazingly dexterous hand. David's father got in. "Feel that genuine vinyl upholstery. Not none of your cheap plastics, that'll crack in a week of direct sun." The salesdroid winked its glassy eye at David. "Hop in, son. See how you like it."

David started to, then saw the look of warning on George's face.

"Let's have a look at the engine," George said.

"Righto." The droid rolled around the fat front fender, reached through the grille, and tripped the latch. The engine was clean as a whistle, the cylinder heads painted cherry red, the spark plug leads numbered for easy changes. It was like the pictures out of David's school books.

The droid started up the Nash; the motor gave out a rumble and vibrated ever so slightly. David smelled the clean tang of evaporating gasoline.

"Only one owner," the droid said, volume turned up now so it could be heard over the sound of the engine.

George looked uncertain.

"How much?"

"Book says it's worth 200,000 validated miles. You can drive her out, with your Chevy in trade, for...let me calculate...174,900."

Just then David noticed something in the engine compartment. On either side over the wheel wells there were cracks in the metal that had been painted over so you could only see them from the reflection of the sunlight where the angle of the surface changed. That was where the shocks connected up with the car's body.

He tugged at his father's sleeve. "Dad," he said, pointing.

George ran a hand over the metal. He looked serious. David thought he was going to get mad. Instead he straightened up and smiled.

"How much did you say?"

The android stood stock-still. "150,000 miles."

"But Dad—"

"Shut up, David," he said. "I'll tell you what, Mr. Sixty. 100,000. And you reweld those wheel wells before we drive it an inch."

That was how they bought the Nash. The first thing George said when they were on their way again was, "Polly, that boy of ours is smart as a whip. The shocks were about to rip through the bodywork, and we'd of been scraping down the highway with our nose to the ground like a basset. David, you're a born driver, or else too smart to waste yourself on it."

David didn't quite follow that, but it made him a little more content to move into the back seat. At first he resented it that Caroline had taken his place in the front. She got all the attention, and David only got to sit and look out at where they had been, or what they were going by, never getting a good look at where they were going. If he leaned over the back of the front seat, his father would say, "Quit breathing down my neck, David. Sit down and behave yourself. Do your homework."

After a while he wouldn't have moved into the front if they'd asked him to: that was for babies. Instead he watched raptly out the left-side window for fleeting glimpses of Eastbound, wondering always about what it was, how it got there, and about the no-man's land and the people they said had died trying to cross. He asked George about it, and that started up the biggest thing they were ever to share together.

"They've told you about Eastbound in school, have they?"

"They told us we can't go there. Nobody can."

"Did they tell you why?"

"No."

His father laughed. "That's because they don't know why! Isn't that incredible, David? They teach a thing in school, and everybody believes it, and nobody knows why or even thinks to ask. But you wonder, don't you? I've seen it."

He did wonder. It scared him that his father would talk about it.

"Men are slipstreamers, David. Did you ever see a car follow close behind a big truck to take advantage of the windbreak to make the driving easier? That's the way people are. They'll follow so close they can't see six inches beyond their noses, as long as it makes things easier. And the schools and the teachers are the biggest windbreaks of all. You remember that. Do you remember the knapsack in the trunk?"

"*George,*" Polly said.

"Be quiet, Polly. The boy's growing up." To David he said, "You know what it's for. You know what's inside."

"To go across..." David hesitated, his heart leaping.

"To cross the Median! We can do it. We don't have to be like everybody else, and when the time comes, when we need to get away the most, when things are really bad—we can do it! I'm prepared to do it."

Polly tried to shush him, and it became an argument. But David was thrilled at the new world that had opened. His father was a criminal—but he was right! From then on they worked on the preparations together. They would have long talks on what they would do and how they would do it. David drew maps on graph paper, and sometimes he and George would climb to the highest spot available by the roadside at the day's end, to puzzle out once again the defenses of the Median.

"Don't tell your mother about this," George would say. "You know she doesn't understand."

EACH MORNING, BEFORE they had gone very far at all, David's father would stop the car and let David out at a bus stop to be picked up by the school bus, and eight hours later the bus would let him out again some hundreds of miles farther west. Soon his parents would be there to pick him up, if they were not there already when he got off with the other kids. More than once David overheard drivers at the camps in the evening complaining about how having kids really slowed a man down in his career, so he'd never get as far as he would have if he'd had the sense to stay single. Whenever some young man whined about waiting around half his life for a school bus, George Baker would only light another cigarette and be very quiet.

In school David learned the principles of the internal combustion engine. Internal Combustion was his favorite class. Other boys and girls would shoot paperclips at each other over the back seats of the bus, or fall asleep staring out the windows, but David sat in a middle seat (he would not move to the front and be accused of being teacher's pet) and, for the most part, paid good attention. His favorite textbook was one they used both in history and social studies; it had a blue cloth cover. The title, pressed into the cover in faded yellow, was *Heroes of the Road*. On the bus, during recess, David and the other boys argued about who was the greatest driver of them all.

To most of them Alan "Lucky" Totter was the only driver. He'd made 10,220,796 miles when he tried to pass a Winnebago on the right at 85 miles per hour in a blinding snowstorm. Some people thought that showed a lack of judgment, but Lucky Totter didn't give a damn for judgment, or anything else. Totter was the classic lone-wolf driver. Born to respectable middle-class parents who drove a Buick with holes in its sides, Totter devoured all he could find out about cars. At the age of thirteen he deserted his parents at a rest stop at mile 1.375×10^{25}, hot-wired a Bugatti-Smith that the owner had left unlocked, and made 8,000 miles before the Trooperbots brought him to justice. After six months in the paddy wagon he came out with a new resolve. He worked for a month at a service station at jobs even the androids would shun, getting nowhere. At the end of that time he'd rebuilt a junked Whippet roadster and was on his way, hell-bent for leather. Every extra mile he drove he plowed back into financing a newer and faster car. Tirelessly, it seemed, Totter kept his two-tones to the floorboards, and the pavement fairly flew beneath his wheels. No time for a wife or family, 1,000 miles a day was his only satisfaction, other than the quick comforts of any of the fast women he might pick up who wanted a chance to say they'd been for a ride with Lucky Totter. The solitary male to the end, it was a style guaranteed to earn him the hero worship of boys all along the world.

But Totter was not the all-time mileage champion. That pinnacle of glory was held by Charles Van Huyser, at a seemingly unassailable 11,315,201 miles. It was hard to see how anyone could do better, for Van Huyser was the driver who had everything: good reflexes, a keen eye, iron constitution, wherewithal, and devilish good looks. He was a child of the privileged classes, scion of the famous Van Huyser drivers, and had enjoyed all the advantages the boys on a middle-lane bus like David's would never see. His father had been one of the premier drivers of his generation, and had made more than seven million miles himself, placing him a respectable twelfth on the all-time list. Van Huyser rode the most exclusive of preparatory buses, and was outfit-ted from the beginning with the best made-to-order Mercedes that android hands could fashion. He was in a lane by himself. Old-timers would tell stories of the time they had been passed by the Van Huyser limo and the dis-tinguished, immaculately tailored man who sat behind the wheel. Perhaps he had even tipped his homburg as he flashed by. Spartan in his daily regimen, invariably kind, if a little condescending, to lesser drivers, he never forgot his position in society, and died at the respectable age of eighty-six, peacefully, in the private washroom of the Drivers' Club dining room at mile 1.375×10^{25}.

There were scores of others in *Heroes of the Road*, all of their stories inspiring, challenging, even puzzling. There was Ailene Stanford, at six-million-plus miles the greatest female driver ever, carmaker and mother and credit to her sex. And Reuben Jefferson, and the Kosciusco brothers, and the mysterious zen driving of Akira Tedeki. The chapter "Detours" held frightening tales of abject failure, and of those who had wasted their substance and their lives trying to cross the Median.

"You can't believe everything you read, David," George told him. "They'll tell you Steve Macready was a great man."

It was like George Baker to make statements like that and then never explain what he meant. It got on David's nerves sometimes, though he figured his dad did it because he had more important things on his mind.

But Steve Macready was David's personal favorite. Macready was third on the all-time list behind Van Huyser and Totter, at 8,444,892 miles. Macready hadn't had the advantages of Van Huyser, and he scorned the reckless irresponsibility of Totter. He was an average man, to all intents and purposes, and he showed just how much an average guy could do if he had the willpower. Born into an impoverished hundred-mile-a-day family that couldn't seem to keep a car on the road three days in a row before it broke down, one of eight brothers and sisters, Macready studied quietly when he could, watched the ways of the road with an intelligent eye, and helped his father and mother keep the family rolling. Compelled to leave school early because the family couldn't keep up with the slowest of school buses, he worked on his own, managed to get hold of an old junker that he put on the road, and set off at the age of sixteen, taking two of his sisters with him. In those first years his mileage totals were anything but spectacular. But he kept plugging away, taking care of his sisters, seeing them married off to two respectable young drivers along the way, never hurrying. At the comparatively late age of thirty he married a simple girl from a family of Ford owners and fathered four children. He saw to his boys' educations. He drove on, making a steady 500 miles a day, and 200 on each Saturday and Sunday. He did not push himself or his machine; he did not lag behind. Steadiness was his watchword. His sons grew up to be fine drivers themselves, always ready to lend the helping hand to the unfortunate motorist. When he died at the age of eighty-two, survived by his wife, children, eighteen grandchildren, and twenty-six great-grandchildren, drivers all, he had become something of a legend in his own quiet time. Steve Macready.

George Baker never said much when David talked about the arguments the kids had over Macready and the other drivers. When he talked about his own youth, he would give only the most tantalizing hints of the many cars he had driven before he picked up Polly, of the many places he'd stopped and people he'd ridden with. David's grandfather had been something of an inventor, he gathered, and had modified his pickup with an extra-large tank and a small, efficient engine to get the most mileage for his driving time. George didn't say much about his mother or brothers, though some things he let on indicated that his father's plans for big miles never panned out, and how it was not always pleasant to ride in the back of an open pickup with three brothers and a sick mother.

Eventually David saw that the miles were taking something out of his father. George Baker conversed less with Polly and the kids, and talked more at them.

Once, in a heavy rainstorm after three days of rolling hill country, forests that encroached on the edges of the pavement and fell like a dark wall between Westbound and forgotten Eastbound, the front end of the Nash jumped suddenly into a mad vibration that threw David's heart into his throat.

"George!" Polly shouted.

"Shut up!" he yelled, trying to steer the bucking car to the roadside.

And then they were stopped, and breathing heavily, and the only sound was the drumming of the rain, the ticking of the car as it settled into motionlessness, and the hissing of the cars that still sped by them over the wet pavement. David's father, slow and bearlike, opened the door and pulled himself out. David got out too. Under the hood they saw where the rewelded wheel well had given way, and the shock was ripping through the metal.

"Shit," George muttered.

As they stood there a gunmetal gray Cadillac pulled over to stop behind them, its flashing amber signal warm as fire under the leaden skies. A stocky man in an expensive raincoat got out. "Can I help you?" he asked.

George stared at him for a good ten seconds. He looked back at the Cadillac, looked at the man again.

"No thanks," he said.

The man hesitated, then turned, went back to his car and drove off.

So they had to wait three hours in the broken-down Nash as darkness fell and George trudged off down the highway for the next rest stop. He returned with an android serviceman, and they were towed to the nearest station. David, never patient at his best, grew more and more angry. His father offered not a word of explanation, and his mother tried to keep David from getting after him about his refusing help. But David finally challenged his father on the plain stupidity of his actions, which would mystify any sensible driver.

At first George acted as if he didn't hear David. Then he exploded.

"Don't tell me about sensible drivers! I don't need it, David! Don't tell me about your Van Huysers, and don't give me any of that Steve Macready crap, either. Your Van Huysers never did anything for the common driving man, despite all their extra miles. Nobody gives it away. That's just the way this road works."

"What about Macready?" David asked. He didn't understand what his father was talking about. You didn't have to run someone else down in order to be right. "Look at what Macready did."

"You don't know what you're talking about," George said. "You get older, but you still think like a kid. Macready sucked up to every tinman on the road. I wouldn't stoop so low as that. Half the time he let his *wife* drive! They don't tell you about that in that damn school, do they?"

"Wake up and look at this road the way it is, David. People will use you like a chamois if you don't. Take my word for it. *Damn* it! If I could just get a couple of good months out of this heap and get back on my feet. A couple of good months!" He laughed scornfully.

It was no use arguing with George when he was in that mood. David shut up, inwardly fuming.

"Follow the herd!" George yelled. "That's all people ever do. Never had an original thought in their life."

"George, you don't need to shout at the boy," Polly said.

"Shout! I'm not shouting!" George looked at her as if she were a hitch-hiker. "Why don't you shut up. The boy and I were just having an intelligent conversation. A fat lot you know about it." He gripped the wheel as if he meant to grind it into powder. A deadly silence ensued.

"I need to stop," he said a couple of miles later, pulling off the road into a bar and grill.

They sat in the car, ears ringing.

"I'm hungry," Caroline said.

"Let's get something to eat, then." Polly leapt at the opportunity to do something normal. "Come on, David. Let's go in."

"You go ahead. I'll be there in a minute."

After they left David stared out the car window for a while. He reached under the seat and took out the notebook, which he had moved there a long time before. The spine was almost broken through now, with some of the leaves loose and water-stained. The paper was worn with writing and rewriting. David leafed through the sketches of watchtowers, the maps, the calculations. In the margin of page six his father had written, in handwriting so faded now that it was like the pale voice of years, speaking from far away, "Keep your ass down. Low profile."

DAVID WAS SIXTEEN. His knees were crowded by the back of the car's front seat, and he stared sullenly out the window at the rolling countryside and the gathering night.

Caroline, having just concluded her fight with him with a belligerent "Oh, yeah!" was leaning forward, her forearms flat against the top of the front seat, her chin resting on them as she stared grimly ahead. Polly was knitting a cover for the box of Kleenex that rested on the dashboard, muffling the radio speaker.

"I'm tired," George said. "I'm going to stop here for a quick one." He pulled the ancient Nash over into the exit lane, downshifted, and the car lurched forward more slowly, the engine rattling in protest of the increased rpms. David could have done it better himself.

They pulled into the parking lot of Fast Ed's Bar and Grill. "You go back and order a fish fry," George said, slamming the car door and turning his back on them. Polly put aside the knitting, picked up her purse, and took them in the side door to the dining room. There was no one else there, but they could hear the TV and the loud conversations from the front. After a while a waitress robot rolled back to them. Its porcelain finish was chipped, and the hands were stained rusty brown, like an old bathtub.

They ordered, the food came, and they ate. Still George did not return from the bar.

"Go get your father, David," his mother said. He could tell she was mad.

"I'll go, Ma," Caroline said.

"Stay still! It's bad enough he takes us to his gin mills, without you becoming a barfly's pet. Go ahead, David."

David went. His father was sitting at the far end of the bar, near the windows that faced the highway. The late afternoon sun gleamed along the polished wood, glinted harshly from the bottles racked on the shelves behind it, turned the mirror against the wall and the brass spigots of the taps into fire. George Baker was talking loudly with two other middle-aged drivers. His legs looked amazingly scrawny as he perched on the stool. Suddenly David was very angry.

"Are you going to come and eat?" he demanded.

George turned to him, his sloppy good humor stiffening to ire.

"What do you want?"

"We're eating. Mom's waiting."

He leaned over to the man on the next stool. "See what I mean?" he said. To David he said, much more boldly, "Go and eat. I'm not hungry." He picked up his shot, downed it in one swallow, and took another draw on the beer setup.

Rage and humiliation burned in David. He did not recognize the man at the bar as his father—and then, shuddering, he did.

"Are you coming?" David could hardly speak. The other men at the bar were quiet now. Only the television continued to babble.

"Go away," his father said.

David wanted to kick over the stool and see him sprawled on the floor. Instead he turned and walked stiffly back to the dining room, past the table where his mother and sister sat. He stalked out to the lot, slamming the screen door behind him. He stood looking at the beat-up Nash in the red-and-white light of Fast Ed's sign. The sign buzzed, and night was coming, and clouds of insects swarmed around the neon in the darkness. A hundred yards away, on the highway, the drivers had their lights on, fanning before them. The air smelled of exhaust.

He couldn't go back into the bar. He would never step back into a place like that again. The world seemed all at once immensely old, immensely cheap, immensely tawdry. David looked over his shoulder at the vast woods that started just beyond the back of Fast Ed's. Then he walked to the front of the lot and stared across the highway toward the distant lights that marked Eastbound. How very far away they seemed.

David went back to the car and got the knapsack out of the trunk. He stepped over the rail at the edge of the lot, crossed the gully beside the road, and waiting for his chance, dashed across the twelve lanes of Westbound to the Median. A hundred yards ahead of him lay the beginning of no-man's land. Beyond that, where those distant lights swept by in their retrograde motion—what?

But he would never get into a car with George Baker again.

THERE WERE THREE levels of defenses between Westbound and Eastbound, or so they had surmised. The first was biological, the second was mechanical, and the third and most important, psychological.

As David moved farther from the highway the ground, which was more or less level near the shoulders, grew uneven. The field was unmowed, thick with nettles and coarse grass, and in the increasing darkness he stumbled more than once. Because the land sloped downward as he advanced, the lights ahead of him became obscured by foliage.

He thought once that he heard his name called above the faint rushing of the cars behind him, but when he turned he could see nothing but

Westbound. It seemed remarkably far away already. His progress became slower. He knew there were snakes in the open fields. The mines could not be far ahead. He could be in the minefield at that very moment.

He stopped, heart racing. Suddenly he knew he was in a minefield, and his next step would blow him to pieces. He saw the shadow of the first line of barbed wire ahead of him, and for the first time he considered going back. But the thought of his father and his mother stopped him. They would be glad to take him back and smother him.

David crouched, swung the pack from his shoulder, and took out the metal detector. Sweeping it a few inches above the ground in front of him, he crawled forward on his hands and knees. It was slow going. There was something funny about the air: he didn't smell anything but field and earth—no people, no rubber, no gasoline. He eyed the nearest watchtower, where he knew infrared scanners swept the Median and automatic rifles nosed about incuriously. Whenever the light in his palm went red, David slid slowly to one side or the other and went on. Once he had to flatten himself suddenly to the earth as some object—animal or search mech—rustled through the dry grass not ten yards away. He waited for the bullet in his neck.

He came to the first line of barbed wire. It was rusty and overgrown. Weeds had used it for a trellis, and when David clipped through the wire the overgrowth held the gap closed. He had to tear the opening wider with his hands, and the cheap work gloves he wore were next to no protection.

He lay in the dark, sweating. He would never last at this rate. He decided to take the chance of moving ahead in short, crouching runs, ignoring the mines. For a while it seemed to ease the pressure, until his foot slipped on some metal object and he leapt away, crying aloud, waiting for the blast that didn't come. Crouched in the grass, panting, he saw that he had stepped on a hubcap.

David began to wonder why the machines hadn't spotted him yet. He was far beyond the point any right-thinking driver might pass. Then he realized that he could hear nothing of either Westbound or Eastbound. He had no idea how long it had been since he'd left the parking lot, but the gibbous moon was coming down through the clouds. David wondered what his mother had done after he'd taken the pack and left; he could imagine his father's drunken amazement as she told him. Maybe even Caroline was worried. He was far beyond them now. He was getting away, amazed at how easy it was, once you made up your mind, amazed at how few had the guts to try it. If they'd even told him the truth.

A perverse idea hit him: maybe the teachers and drivers, like sheep huddled in their trailer beds, had never tried to see what lay in the Median. Maybe all the servo-defenses had rotted like the barbed wire, and it was only the pressure of dead traditions that kept people glued to their westward course. Suddenly twelve lanes, which had seemed a whole world to him all his life, shrank to the merest thread. Who could say what Eastbound might be? Who could predict how much better men had done for themselves there? Maybe it was the Eastbounders who had built the roads, who had created the defenses and myths that kept them all penned in filthy Nashes, rolling west.

David laughed aloud. He stood up. He slung the pack over his shoulder again, and this time boldly struck out for the new world.

"Halt!"

A figure stood erect before him, and a blinding light shone from its head. The confidence drained from David instantly; he dropped to the ground.

"Please stand."

David was pinned in the center of the search beam. He reached into the knapsack for the revolver.

"This is a restricted area, intruder," the machine said. "Please return to your assigned role."

David blinked in the glare. He could see nothing of the thing's form. "Role?"

"I am sure that the first thing they taught you was that entry into this area is forbidden. Am I right?"

"What?" David had never heard this kind of talk from a machine.

"Your elders have said that you should not come here. That is one very good reason why you should not be here. I'm sure you'll agree. The requests of the society that, in a significant way, created us, if not unreasonable, ought to be given considerable thought before we reject them. This is the result of evolution. The men and women who went before you had to concern themselves with survival in order to live long enough to bear the children who eventually became the present generation. Their rules are engineering-tested. Such experience, let alone your intelligence working *within* the framework of evolution, ought not to be lightly discarded. We are not born into a vacuum. Am I right?"

David wasn't sure the gun was going to do him any good. "I guess so. I never thought about it."

"Precisely. Think about it."

David thought. "Wait a minute! How do I know *people* made the rules? I don't have any proof. I never see people making rules now."

"On the contrary, intruder, you see it every day. Every act a person performs is an act of definition. We create what we are from moment to moment. The future before us is merely the emptiness of time that does not exist without events to fill it. The greatest of changes is possible: in theory you are just as likely to turn into an aimless collection of molecules in this next instant as you are to remain a human being. That is, unless you believe that human beings are fated and possess no free will..."

"People have free will." David knew that, if he knew anything. "And they ought to use it."

"That's right." The machine's light was as steady as the sun. "You wouldn't be in a forbidden area if people did not have free will. You yourself, intruder, are a proof of mankind's freedom."

"Okay. Now let me go by—"

"So we have established that human beings have free will. We will assume that they follow rules. Now, having free will, and assuming that by some mischance one of these rules is distasteful to them—we leave aside for the moment who made the rule—then one would expect people to disobey it. They need not even have an active purpose to disobey; in the course of a long enough time many people will break this burdensome rule for the best—or worst—of reasons. The more unacceptable the rule, the greater the number of people who will discard it at one time or another. They will, as individuals or groups, consciously or unconsciously, create a new rule. This is change through human free will. So, even if the rules were not originated by humans, in time change would ensue given the merits of the 'system,' as we may call it, and the system will *become* human-created. My earlier evolutionary argument then follows as the night the day. Am I right?"

If a robot could sound triumphant, this one did.

"Ah—"

"So one good reason for doing only what you're told is that you have the free will to do otherwise. Another good reason is God."

"God?"

"The Supreme Being, the Life Force, that ineluctable, undefinable spiritual presence that lies—or perhaps lurks—within the substance of things. The Holy Father, the First—"

"What about him?"

"God doesn't want you to cross the Median."

"I bet he doesn't," David said sarcastically.

"Have you ever seen an automobile accident?"

The robot was going too fast, and the light made it hard for David to think. He closed his eyes and tried to fight back. "Everybody's seen accidents. People get killed. Don't go telling me God killed them because they did something wrong."

"Don't be absurd!" the robot said. "You must try to stretch your mind, intruder; this is not some game we're playing. This is real life. Not only do actions have consequences, but consequences are pregnant with Meaning.

"In the auto accident we have a peculiar sequence of events. The physicist tells us that heat and vibration cause a weakening of the molecular bonds between certain long-chain hydrocarbons that comprise the substance of the tire of a car traveling at sixty miles per hour. The tire blows. As a result of the sudden change in the moment of inertia of this wheel, certain complex but analyzable oscillations occur. The car swerves to the left, rolls over six times, tossing its three passengers, a man and two women, about like tomatoes in a blender, and collides with a bridge abutment, exploding into flame. To the scientist, this is a simple cause-and-effect chain. The accident has a rational explanation: the tire blew."

David felt queasy. His hand, in the knapsack, clutched the gun.

"You see right away what's wrong with this explanation. It explains nothing. We know the rational explanation is inadequate without having to be able to say how we know. Such knowledge is the doing of God. God and His merciful Providence set the purpose behind the fact of our existence, and is it possible to believe that a sparrow can fall without His holy cognizance and will?"

"I don't believe in God."

"What does that matter, intruder?" The thing's voice now oozed angelic understanding. "Need you believe in gravity for it to be an inescapable fact of your existence? God does not demand your belief; He merely requests that you, of your own inviolate free will and through the undeserved gift of His grace, come to acknowledge and obey Him. Who can understand the mysteries of faith? Certainly not I, a humble mechanism. *Knowledge* is what matters, and if you open yourself to the currents that flow through the interstices of the material and immaterial universe, that knowledge will be vouchsafed *you*, intruder. You do not belong here. God knows who you are, and He saw what you did. Am I right?"

David was getting mad. "What has this got to do with car accidents?"

"The auto accident does not occur without the knowledge and permission of the Lord. This doesn't mean that He is responsible for it. He accepts the responsibility without accepting the Responsibility. This is a mystery."

"Bull!" David had heard enough talk. It was time to act.

"Be silent, intruder! Where were you when He laid the asphalt of Westbound? Who set up the mileage markers, and who painted the line upon it? On what foundation was its reinforced concrete sunk, and who made the komfy kabins, when the morning stars sang together, and all the droids and servos shouted for joy?"

It was his chance. The machine was still motionless, its mad light trained on him. A mist had sprung from the no-man's land. Poison gas? He had no gas mask; speed was his only hope. He couldn't move. He hefted the gun. He felt dizzy, a little numb, steeling himself to move. He had to be stronger than the robot! It was just a machine!

"So that is the second good reason why you should not proceed with your ill-advised adventure," it droned on. "God is telling you to go back."

God. Rifles. He had to go! Now! Still he couldn't move. The fog grew, and its smell was strangely pungent. Once past the robot, who knew what he could find. But the machine's voice exuded self-confidence.

"A third and final good reason why you should return to your assigned role, intruder, is this:

"If you take another step, I will kill you."

DAVID WOKE. HE was cold, and he was being shaken by a sobbing man. It was his father.

"Not responsible! Park and lock it!" For the first time in as long as he could remember, David actually heard the crying of the loudspeakers in the parking lot. He struggled to sit up. His mouth tasted like a thousand miles of road grime.

George Baker held his shoulders and looked into his face. He didn't say anything. He stood up and went to stand by the car. Shakily, he lit a cigarette. David's mother crouched over him. "David—David, are you all right?"

"What happened?"

"Your father went after you. We didn't know what happened, and I was so afraid I'd lose both of you—and then he came back carrying you in his arms."

"Carrying me? That's ridiculous." George wasn't capable of carrying a wheel hub fifty yards. David looked at the potbellied man leaning against the front fender of their car. His father was staring off across the lot. Suddenly David felt ashamed of himself. He didn't know what it was in his chest striving to express itself, but sitting there in the parking lot at mile 1.375×10^{25}, looking at the middle-aged man who was his father, he began to cry.

George never said a word to David after that day about how he had managed to follow his son into the Median, about what a struggle it must have been to make himself do that, about how and where he had found the boy, and how he had managed to bring him back, or about what it all meant to him. David never told his father about the robot and what it had said. It was all a little unreal to him. The boy who had stood there, desperately trying to get somewhere else, and the words the robot had spoken, all seemed terribly remote, as if the whole incident were something he had read about. It was a fantasy that could not have occurred in the real world of pavement and gasoline.

Father and son did not speak about it. They didn't say anything much at first, as they tentatively felt out the boundaries of what seemed to be a new relationship. Even Caroline recognized that a change had taken place, and she didn't taunt David the way she had before. Unstated was the fact that David was no longer a boy.

A month later and many thousand miles farther along, George nervously broached the subject of buying David a car. It was a shock for David to hear that, and he knew they could hardly afford it, but he also knew there was a rightness to it. And so they found themselves in the lot of Gears MacDougal's New and Used Autos.

George was too loud, too jocular. "How about this Chevy, David? A Chevy's a good driving man's car." He looked embarrassed.

David got down and felt a tire. "She's got good rubber on her."

The salesdroid was rolling up to greet them as George opened the hood of the Chevy. "Looks pretty clean," he said.

"They clean them all up."

"They sure do. You can't trust them as far as you'd...ah, hello."

"Good morning," the droid said, coming to rest beside them. "That's just the little thing for you. One owner, and between you and me, he didn't drive her too hard. He wasn't much of a driver."

George looked at the machine soberly. "Is that so."

"That is so, sir."·

"My son's buying this car, not me," George said suddenly, loudly, as if shaking away the dust of his thoughts. "You should talk to him. And don't try to put anything over on him; he knows his stuff and...well, you just talk to him, not me, see?"

"Certainly, sir." The droid rolled between them and told David about the Chevy's V-8. David hardly listened. He watched his father step quietly to the side and light a cigarette. George stood with Polly and Caroline and looked ill at ease, quieter than David could ever remember. As the robot took David around the car, pointing out its extras, it came to him just what his father was: not a strong man, not a special man, not a particularly smart man. He was the same man he had been when David had sat on his lap years before; he was the same man who had taken him on his strolls around the rest stops so many times. He was the drunk who had slouched on the stool in Fast Ed's. He was a good driving man.

"I'll take it," David said, breaking off the salesdroid in mid-sentence.

"Righto," the machine said, its hard smile unvarying. It did not miss a beat. Within seconds a hard copy of the title had emerged from the slot in its chest. Within minutes the papers had been signed, the mileage validated and subtracted from George Baker's yearly total, and David stood beside his car. It was not a very good car to start out with, but many had started with less, and it was the best his father could do. Polly hugged him and cried. Caroline reached up and kissed him on the cheek; she cried too. George shook his hand, and did not seem to want to let go.

"Remember now, take it easy for the first thousand or so, until you get the feel of her. Check the oil, see if it burns oil. I don't think it will. It's got a good spare, doesn't it?"

"It does, Dad."

"Good. That's good." George stood silent for a moment, looking up at his son. The day was bright, and the breeze disarrayed the thinning hair he had combed over his bald spot. "Goodbye, David. Maybe we'll see you on the road?"

"Sure you will."

David got into the Chevy and turned the key in the ignition. The motor started immediately and breathed its low and steady rumble. The seat was very hot against his back. The windshield was spotless, and beyond the nose of the car stretched the access ramp to Westbound. The highway swarmed with the cars that were moving while they dawdled there still.

David put the car in gear, stepped slowly on the accelerator, released the clutch, and moved smoothly down the ramp, gathering speed. He shifted up, moving faster, and then quickly once again. The force of the wind streaming in through the window increased from a breeze to a gale, and its sound became a continuous buffeting as it whipped his hair about his ear. Flicking the turn signal, David merged into the flow of traffic, the sunlight flashing off the hood ornament that led him on toward the distant horizon, just out of his reach, but attainable he knew, as he pressed his foot to the accelerator, hurrying on past mile 1.375×10^{25}.

Events Preceding the
Helvetican Renaissance

WHEN MY mind cleared, I found myself in the street. The protector god Bishamon spoke to me then: *The boulevard to the spaceport runs straight up the mountain. And you must run straight up the boulevard.*

The air was full of wily spirits, and running in the Imperial City was a crime. But what is man to disobey the voice of a god? So I ran. The pavement vibrated with the thunder of the great engines of the Caslonian Empire. Behind me the curators of the Imperial Archives must by now have discovered the mare's nest I had made of their defenses, and perhaps had already realized that something was missing.

Above the plateau the sky was streaked with clouds, through which shot violet gravity beams carrying ships down from and up to planetary orbit. Just outside the gate to the spaceport a family in rags—husband, wife, two children—used a net of knotted cords to catch fish from the sewers. Ignoring them, prosperous citizens in embroidered robes passed among the shops of the port bazaar, purchasing duty-free wares, recharging their concubines, seeking a meal before departure. *Slower, now.*

I slowed my pace. I became indistinguishable from them, moving smoothly among the travelers.

To the Caslonian eye, I was calm, self-possessed; within me, rage and joy contended. I had in my possession the means to redeem my people. I tried not to think, only to act, but now that my mind was rekindled, it raced. Certainly it would go better for me if I left the planet before anyone understood what I had stolen. Yet I was very hungry, and the aroma of food from the restaurants along the way enticed me. It would be foolishness itself to stop here.

Enter the restaurant, I was told. So I stepped into the most elegant of the establishments.

The maître d' greeted me. "Would the master like a table, or would he prefer to dine at the bar?"

"The bar," I said

"Step this way." There was no hint of the illicit about his manner, though something about it implied indulgence. He was proud to offer me this experience that few could afford.

He seated me at the circular bar of polished rosewood. Before me, and the few others seated there, the chef grilled meats on a heated metal slab. Waving his arms in the air like a dancer, he tossed flanks of meat between two force knives, letting them drop to the griddle, flipping them dexterously upward again in what was as much performance as preparation. The energy blades of the knives sliced through the meat without resistance, the sides of these same blades batting them like paddles. An aroma of burning hydrocarbons wafted on the air.

An attractive young man displayed for me a list of virtualities that represented the "cuts" offered by the establishment, including subliminal tastes. The "cuts" referred to the portions of the animal's musculature from which the slabs of meat had been sliced. My mouth watered. He took my order, and I sipped a cocktail of bitters and Belanova.

While I waited, I scanned the restaurant. The fundamental goal of our order is to vindicate divine justice in allowing evil to exist. At a small nearby table, a young woman leaned beside a child, probably her daughter, and encouraged her to eat. The child's beautiful face was the picture of innocence as she tentatively tasted a scrap of pink flesh. The mother was very beautiful. I wondered if this was her first youth.

The chef finished his performance, to the mild applause of the other patrons. The young man placed my steak before me. The chef turned off the blades and laid them aside, then ducked down a trap door to the oubliette where the slaves were kept. As soon as he was out of sight, the god told me, *Steal a knife.*

While the diners were distracted by their meals, I reached over the counter, took one of the force blades, and slid it into my boot. Then I ate. The taste was extraordinary. Every cell of my body vibrated with excitement and shame. My senses reeling, it took me a long time to finish.

A slender man in a dark robe sat next to me. "That smells good," he said. "Is that genuine animal flesh?"

"Does it matter to you?"

"Ah, brother, calm yourself. I'm not challenging your morals."

"I'm pleased to hear it."

"But I am challenging your identity." He parted the robe—his tunic bore the sigil of Port Security. "Your passport, please."

I exposed the inside of my wrist for him. A scanlid slid over his left eye and he examined the marks beneath my skin. "Very good," he said. He drew a blaster from the folds of his cassock. "We seldom see such excellent forgeries. Stand up, and come with me."

I stood. He took my elbow in a firm grip, the bell of the blaster against my side. No one in the restaurant noticed. He walked me outside, down the crowded bazaar. "You see, brother, that there is no escape from consciousness. The minute it returns, you are vulnerable. All your prayer is to no avail."

This is the arrogance of the Caslonian. They treat us as non-sentients, and they believe in nothing. Yet as I prayed, I heard no word.

I turned to him. "You may wish the absence of the gods, but you are mistaken. The gods are everywhere present." As I spoke the plosive "p" of "present," I popped the cap from my upper right molar and blew the moon-dust it contained into his face.

The agent fell writhing to the pavement. I ran off through the people, dodging collisions. My ship was on the private field at the end of the bazaar. Before I had gotten half way there, an alarm began sounding. People looked up in bewilderment, stopping in their tracks. The walls of buildings and stalls blinked into multiple images of me. Voices spoke from the air: "This man is a fugitive from the state. Apprehend him."

I would not make it to the ship unaided, so I turned on my perceptual overdrive. Instantly, everything slowed. The voices of the people and the sounds of the port dropped an octave. They moved as if in slow motion. I moved, to myself, as if in slow motion as well—my body could in no way keep pace with my racing nervous system—but to the people moving at normal speed, my reflexes were lighting fast. Up to the limit of my physiology—and my joints had been reinforced to take the additional stress, my muscles could handle the additional lactic acid for a time—I could move at twice the speed of a normal human. I could function for perhaps ten minutes in this state before I collapsed.

The first person to accost me—a sturdy middle aged man—I seized by the arm. I twisted it behind his back and shoved him into the second who took up the command. As I dodged through the crowd up the concourse, it began to drizzle. I felt as if I could slip between the raindrops. I pulled the force blade from my boot and sliced the ear from the next man who tried to stop me. His comic expression of dismay still lingers in my mind. Glancing behind, I saw the agent in black, face swollen with pustules from the moon-dust, running toward me.

I was near the field. In the boarding shed, attendants were folding the low-status passengers and sliding them into dispatch pouches, to be carried onto a ship and stowed in drawers for their passage. Directly before me, I saw the woman and child I had noticed in the restaurant. The mother had out a parasol and was holding it over the girl to keep the rain off her. Not slowing, I snatched the little girl and carried her off. The child yelped, the mother screamed. I held the blade to the girl's neck. "Make way!" I shouted to the security men at the field's entrance. They fell back.

"Halt!" came the call from behind me. The booth beside the gate was seared with a blaster bolt. I swerved, turned, and, my back to the gate, held the girl before me.

The agent in black, followed by two security women, jerked to a stop. "You mustn't hurt her," the agent said.

"Oh? And why is that?"

"It's against everything your order believes."

Master Darius had steeled me for this dilemma before sending me on my mission. He told me, "You will encounter such situations, Adlan. When they arise, you must resolve the complications."

"You are right!" I called to my pursuers, and threw the child at them.

The agent caught her, while the other two aimed and fired. One of the beams grazed my shoulder. But by then I was already through the gate and onto the tarmac.

A port security robot hurled a flame grenade. I rolled through the fire. My ship rested in the maintenance pit, cradled in the violet anti-grav beam. I slid down the ramp into the open airlock, hit the emergency lockdown, and climbed to the controls. Klaxons wailed outside. I bypassed all the launch protocols and released the beam. The ship shot upward like an apple seed flicked by a fingernail; as soon as it hit the stratosphere, I fired the engines and blasted through the scraps of the upper atmosphere into space.

The orbital security forces were too slow, and I made my escape.

I AWOKE BATTERED, bruised, and exhausted in the pilot's chair. The smell of my burned shoulder reminded me of the steak I had eaten in the port bazaar. The stress of accelerating nerve impulses had left every joint in my body aching. My arms were blue with contusions, and I was as enfeebled as an old man.

The screens showed me to be in an untraveled quarter of the system's cometary cloud; my ship had cloaked itself in ice so that on any detector I would simply be another bit of debris among billions. I dragged myself from the chair and down to the galley, where I warmed some broth and gave myself an injection of cellular repair mites. Then I fell into my bunk and slept.

My second waking was relatively free of pain. I recharged my tooth and ate again. I kneeled before the shrine and bowed my head in prayer, letting peace flow down my spine and relax all the muscles of my back. I listened for the voices of the gods.

I was reared by my mother on Bembo. My mother was an extraordinarily beautiful girl. One day Akvan, looking down on her, was so moved by lust that he took the form of a vagabond and raped her by the side of the road. Nine months later I was born.

The goddess Sedna became so jealous that she laid a curse on my mother, who turned into a lawyer. And so we moved to Helvetica. There, in the shabby city of Urushana, in the waterfront district along the river, she took up her practice, defending criminals and earning a little *baksheesh* greasing the relations between the Imperial Caslonian government and the corrupt local officials. Mother's ambition was to send me to an off-planet university, but for me the work of a student was like pushing a very large rock up a very steep hill. I got into fights; I pursued women of questionable virtue. Having exhausted my prospects in the city, I entered the native constabulary, where I was re-engineered for accelerated combat. But my propensity for violence saw me cashiered out of the service within six months. Hoping to get a grip on my passions, I made the pilgrimage to the monastery of the Pujmanian Order. There I petitioned for admission as a novice, and, to my great surprise, was accepted.

It was no doubt the work of Master Darius, who took an interest in me from my first days on the plateau. Perhaps it was my divine heritage, which had placed those voices in my head. Perhaps it was my checkered career to that date. The Master taught me to distinguish between those impulses that were the work of my savage nature, and those that were the voices of the gods. He taught me to identify the individual gods. It is not an easy path. I fasted, I worked in the gardens, I practiced the martial arts, I cleaned the cesspool, I sewed new clothes and mended old, I tended the orchards. I became an expert tailor, and sewed many of the finest kosodes worn by the masters on feast days. In addition, Master Darius held special sessions with me, putting me into a trance during which, I was later told by my fellow novices, I continued to function normally for days, only to awake with no memories of my actions.

And so I was sent on my mission. Because I had learned how not to think, I could not be detected by the spirits who guarded the Imperial Archives.

Five plays, immensely old, collectively titled *The Abandonment*, are all that document the rebirth of humanity after its long extinction. The foundational cycle consists of *The Archer's Fall*; *Stochik's Revenge*; *The Burning Tree*; *Close the Senses, Shut the Doors*; and the mystical fifth, *The Magic Tortoise*. No one knows who wrote them. It is believed they were composed within the first thirty years after the human race was recreated by the gods. Besides being the most revered cultural artifacts of humanity, these plays are also the sacred texts of the universal religion, and claimed as the fundamental political documents by all planetary governments. They are preserved only in a single copy. No recording has ever been made of their performance. The actors chosen to present the plays in the foundational festivals on all the worlds do not study and learn them; through a process similar to the one Master Darius taught me to confuse the spirits, the actors *become* the characters. Once the performance is done, it passes from their minds.

These foundational plays, of inestimable value, existed now only in my mind. I had destroyed the crystal containing them in the archives. Without these plays, the heart of Caslon had been ripped away. If the populace knew of their loss, there would be despair and riot.

And once Master Darius announced that the Order held the plays in our possession, it would only be a matter of time before the Empire would be obliged to free our world.

Three days after my escape from Caslon, I set course for Helvetica. Using an evanescent wormhole, I would emerge within the planet's inner ring. The ship, still encased in ice, would look like one of the fragments that formed the ring. From there I would reconnoiter, find my opportunity to leave orbit, and land. But because the ring stood far down in the gravitation well of the planet, it was a tricky maneuver.

Too tricky. Upon emergence in the Helvetican ring, my ship collided with one of the few nickel-iron meteoroids in the belt, disabling my engines. Within twenty minutes, Caslonian hunter-killers grappled with the hull. My one advantage was that by now they knew that I possessed the plays, and therefore they could not afford to blast me out of the sky. I could kill them, but they could not harm me. But I had no doubt that once they caught me, they would rip my mind to shreds seeking the plays.

I had only minutes—the hull door would not hold long. I abandoned the control room and retreated to the engine compartment. The place was a mess, barely holding pressure after the meteoroid collision, oxygen cylinders scattered about and the air acrid with the scent of burned wiring. I opened the cat's closet, three meters tall and two wide. From a locker I yanked two piezofiber suits. I turned them on, checked their readouts—they were fully charged—and threw them into the closet. It was cramped in there with tools and boxes of supplies. Sitting on one of the crates, I pulled up my shirt, exposing my bruised ribs. The aluminum light of the closet turned my skin sickly white. Using a microtome, I cut an incision in my belly below my lowest rib. There was little blood. I reached into the cut, found the nine-dimensional pouch, and drew it out between my index and middle fingers. I sprayed false skin over the wound. As I did, the artificial gravity cut off, and the lights went out.

I slipped on my night vision eyelids, read the directions on the pouch, ripped it open, removed the soldier and unfolded it. The body expanded, became fully three dimensional, and, in a minute, was floating naked before me. My first surprise: it was a woman. Dark skinned, slender, her body was very beautiful. I leaned over her, covered her mouth with mine, and blew air into her lungs. She jerked convulsively and drew a shuddering breath, then stopped. Her eyelids fluttered, then opened.

"Wake up!" I said, drawing on my piezosuit. I slipped the force blade into the boot, strapped on the belt with blaster and supplies, shrugged into the backpack. "Put on this suit! No time to waste."

She took in my face, the surroundings. From beyond the locker door I heard the sounds of the commandos entering the engine room.

"I am Brother Adlan," I whispered urgently. "You are a soldier of the Republican Guard?" As I spoke I helped her into the skinsuit.

"Lieutenant Nahid Esfandiar. What's happening?"

"We are in orbit over Helvetica, under attack by Caslonian commandos. We need to break out of here."

"What weapons have we?"

I handed her a blaster. "They will have accelerated perceptions. Can you speed yours?"

Her glance passed over me, measuring me for a fool. "Done already." She sealed her suit and flipped down the faceplate on her helmet.

I did not pay attention to her, because as she spoke, all-seeing Liu-Bei spoke to me. *Three men beyond this door.* In my mind I saw the engine room, and the three soldiers who were preparing to rip open the closet.

I touched my helmet to hers and whispered to Nahid, "There are three of them outside. The leader is directly across from the door. He has a common

blaster, on stun. To the immediate right, a meter away, one of the commandos has a pulse rifle. The third, about to set the charge, has a pneumatic
projector, probably with sleep gas. When they blow the door, I'll go high, you
low. Three meters to the cross corridor, down one level and across starboard
to the escape pod."

Just then, the door to the closet was ripped open, and through it came
a blast of sleep gas. But we were locked into our suits, helmets sealed. Our
blaster beams, pink in the darkness, crossed as they emerged from the gloom
of the closet. We dove through the doorway in zero-G, bouncing off the
bulkheads, blasters flaring. The commandos were just where the gods had
told me they would be. I cut down one before we even cleared the doorway.
Though they moved as quickly as we did, they were trying not to kill me, and
the fact that there were two of us now took them by surprise.

Nahid fired past my ear, taking out another. We ducked through the
hatch and up the companionway. Two more commandos came from the control room at the end of the corridor; I was able to slice one of them before he
could fire, but the other's stunner numbed my thigh. Nahid torched his head
and grabbed me by the arm, hurling me around the corner into the cross
passageway.

Two more commandos guarded the hatchway to the escape pod. Nahid
fired at them, killing one and wounding the other in a single shot. But instead
of heading for the pod she jerked me the other way, toward the umbilical to
the Caslonian ship.

"What are you doing?" I protested.

"Shut up," she said. "They can hear us." Halfway across the umbilical,
Nahid stopped, braced herself against one wall, raised her blaster, and, without hesitation, blew a hole in the wall opposite. The air rushed out. A klaxon
sounded the pressure breach, another commando appeared at the junction of
the umbilical and the Caslonian ship—I burned him down—and we slipped
through the gap into the space between the two ships. She grabbed my arm
and pulled me around the hull of my own vessel.

I realized what she intended. Grabbing chunks of ice, we pulled ourselves
over the horizon of my ship until we reached the outside hatch of the escape
pod. I punched in the access code. We entered the pod and while Nahid

sealed the hatch, I powered up and blasted us free of the ship before we had even buckled in.

The pod shot toward the upper atmosphere. The commandos guarding the inner hatch were ejected into the vacuum behind us. Retro fire slammed us into our seats. I caught a glimpse of bodies floating in the chaos we'd left behind before proton beams lanced out from the Caslonian raider, clipping the pod and sending us into a spin.

"You couldn't manage this without me?" Nahid asked.

"No sarcasm, please." I fought to steady the pod so the heat shields were oriented for atmosphere entry.

We hit the upper atmosphere. For twenty minutes we were buffeted by the jet stream, and it got hot in the tiny capsule. I became very aware of Nahid's scent, sweat and a trace of rosewater; she must have put on perfume before she was folded into the packet that had been implanted in me. Her eyes moved slowly over the interior of the pod.

"What is the date?" she asked.

"The nineteenth of Cunegonda," I told her. The pod bounced violently and drops of sweat flew from my forehead. Three red lights flared on the board, but I could do nothing about them.

"What year?"

I saw that it would not be possible to keep many truths from her. "You have been suspended in nine-space for sixty years."

The pod lurched again, a piece of the ablative shield tearing away. She sat motionless, taking in the loss of her entire life.

A snatch of verse came to my lips, unbidden:

> "Our life is but a trifle
> A child's toy abandoned by the road
> When we are called home."

"Very poetic," she said. "Are we going to ride this pod all the way down? They probably have us on locator from orbit, and will vaporize it the minute it hits. I'd rather not be called home just now."

"We'll eject at ten kilometers. Here's your chute."

When the heat of the re-entry had abated and we hit the troposphere, we blew the explosive bolts and shot free of the tumbling pod. Despite the thin air of the upper atmosphere, I was buffeted almost insensible, spinning like a prayer wheel. I lost sight of Nahid.

I fell for a long time, but eventually managed to stabilize myself spread-eagled, dizzy, my stomach lurching. Below, the Jacobin Range stretched north to southwest under the rising sun, the snow-covered rock on the upper reaches folded like a discarded robe, and below the thick forest climbing up to the tree line.

Some minutes later, I witnessed the impressive flare of the pod striking just below the summit of one of the peaks, tearing a gash in the ice cover and sending up a plume of black smoke that was torn away by the wind. I tongued the trigger in my helmet, and with a nasty jerk, the airfoil chute deployed from my backpack. I could see Nahid's red chute some five hundred meters below me; I steered toward her hoping we could land near each other. The forested mountainside came up fast. I spotted a clearing on a ledge two thirds of the way up the slope and made for it, but my burned shoulder wasn't working right, and I was coming in too fast. I caught a glimpse of Nahid's foil in the mountain scar ahead, but I wasn't going to reach her.

At the last minute, I pulled up and skimmed the tree tops, caught a boot against a top limb, flipped head over heels and crashed into the foliage, coming to rest hanging upside down from the tree canopy. The suit's rigidity kept me from breaking any bones, but it took me ten minutes to release the shrouds. I turned down the suit's inflex and took off my helmet to better see what I was doing. When I did, the limb supporting me broke, and I fell the last ten meters through the trees, hitting another limb on the way down, knocking me out.

I WAS WOKEN by Nahid rubbing snow into my face. My piezosuit had been turned off, and the fabric was flexible again. Nahid leaned over me, supporting my head. "Can you move your feet?" she asked.

My thigh still was numb from the stunner. I tried moving my right foot. Though I could not feel any response, I saw the boot twitch. "So it would seem."

Done with me, she let my head drop. "So, do you have some plan?"

I pulled up my knees and sat up. My head ached. We were surrounded by the boles of the tall firs; above our heads the wind swayed the trees, but down here the air was calm, and sunlight filtered down in patches, moving over the packed fine brown needles of the forest floor. Nahid had pulled down my chute to keep it from advertising our position. She crouched on one knee and examined the charge indicator on her blaster.

I got up and inventoried the few supplies we had—my suit's water reservoir, holding maybe a liter, three packs of *gichy* crackers in the belt. Hers would have no more than that. "We should get moving; the Caslonians will send a landing party, or notify the colonial government in Guliston to send a security squad."

"And why should I care?"

"You fought for the republic against the Caslonians. When the war was lost and the protectorate established, you had yourself folded. Didn't you expect to take up arms again when called back to life?"

"You tell me that was sixty years ago. What happened to the rest of the Republican Guard?"

"The Guard was wiped out in the final Caslonian assaults."

"And our folded battalion?"

The blistering roar of a flyer tore through the clear air above the trees. Nahid squinted up, eyes following the glittering ship. "They're heading for where the pod hit." She pulled me to my feet, taking us downhill, perhaps in the hope of finding better cover in the denser forest near one of the mountain freshets.

"No," I said. "Up the slope."

"That's where they'll be."

"It can't be helped. We need to get to the monastery. We're on the wrong side of the mountains." I turned up the incline. After a moment, she followed.

We stayed beneath the trees for as long as possible. The slope was not too steep at this altitude; the air was chilly, with dying patches of old snow in the shadows. Out in the direct sunlight, it would be hot until evening came. I had climbed these mountains fifteen years before, an adolescent trying to find a way to live away from the world. As we moved, following the path of a small stream, the aches in my joints eased.

We did not talk. I had not thought about what it would mean to wake this soldier, other than how she would help me in a time of extremity. There are no women in our order, and though we take no vow of celibacy and some commerce takes place between brothers in their cells late at night, there is little opportunity for contact with the opposite sex. Nahid, despite her forbidding nature, was beautiful: dark skin, black eyes, lustrous black hair cut short, the three parallel scars of her rank marking her left cheek. As a boy in Urushana, I had tormented my sleepless nights with visions of women as beautiful as she; in my short career as a constable I had avidly pursued women far less so. One of them had provoked the fight that had gotten me cashiered.

The forest thinned as we climbed higher. Large folds of granite lay exposed to the open air, creased with fractures and holding pockets of earth where trees sprouted in groups. We had to circle around to avoid coming into the open, and even that would be impossible when the forest ended completely. I pointed us south, where Dundrahad Pass, dipping below 3,000 meters, cut through the mountains. We were without snowshoes or trekking gear, but I hoped that, given the summer temperatures, the pass would be clear enough to traverse in the night without getting ourselves killed. The skinsuits we wore would be proof against the nighttime cold.

We saw no signs of the Caslonians, but when we reached the tree line, we stopped to wait for darkness anyway. The air had turned colder, and a sharp wind blew down the pass from the other side of the mountains. We settled in a hollow beneath a patch of twisted scrub trees and waited out the declining sun. At the zenith, the first moon Mahsheed rode, waning gibbous. In the notch of the pass above and ahead of us, the second moon Roshanak rose. Small, glowing green, it moved perceptibly as it raced around the planet. I nibbled at some gichy, sipping water from my suit's reservoir. Nahid's eyes were shadowed; she scanned the slope.

"We'll have to wait until Mahsheed sets before we move," Nahid said. "I don't want to be caught in the pass in its light."

"It will be hard for us to see where we're going."

She didn't reply. The air grew colder. After a while, without looking at me, she spoke. "So what happened to my compatriots?"

I saw no point in keeping anything from her. "As the Caslonians consolidated their conquest, an underground of Republicans pursued a guerilla war. Two years later, they mounted an assault on the provincial capital in Kofarnihon. They unfolded your battalion to aid them, and managed to seize the armory. But the Caslonians sent reinforcements and set up a siege. When the rebels refused to surrender, the Caslonians vaporized the entire city, hostages, citizens, and rebels alike. That was the end of the Republican Guard." Nahid's dark eyes watched me as I told her all this. The tightness of her lips held grim skepticism.

"Yet here I am," she said.

"I don't know how you came to be the possession of the order. Some refugee, perhaps. The masters, sixty years ago, debated what to do with you. Given the temperament of the typical guardsman, it was assumed that, had you been restored to life, you would immediately get yourself killed in assaulting the Caslonians, putting the order at risk. It was decided to keep you in reserve, in the expectation that, at some future date, your services would be useful."

"You monks were always fair-weather democrats. Ever your order over the welfare of the people, or even their freedom. So you betrayed the republic."

"You do us an injustice."

"It was probably Javeed who brought me—the lying monk attached to our unit."

I recognized the name. Brother Javeed, a bent, bald man of great age, had run the monastery kitchen. I had never thought twice about him. He had died a year after I joined the order.

"Why do you think I was sent on this mission?" I told her. "We mean to set Helvetica free. And we shall do so, if we reach Sharishabz."

"How do you propose to accomplish that? Do you want to see your monastery vaporized?"

"They will not dare. I have something of theirs that they will give up the planet for. That's why they tried to board my ship rather than destroy it; that's why they didn't bother to disintegrate the escape pod when they might easily have shot us out of the sky."

"And this inestimably valuable item that you carry? It must be very small."

"It's in my head. I have stolen the only copies of the Foundational Dramas." She looked at me. "So?"

Her skepticism was predictable, but it still angered me. "So—they will gladly trade Helvetica's freedom for the return of the plays."

She lowered her head, rubbed her brow with her hand. I could not read her. She made a sound, an intake of breath. For a moment, I thought she wept. Then she raised her head and laughed in my face.

I fought an impulse to strike her. "Quiet!"

She laughed louder. Her shoulders shook, and tears came to her eyes. I felt my face turn red. "You should have let me die with the others, in battle. You crazy priest!"

"Why do you laugh?" I asked her. "Do you think they would send ships to embargo Helvetican orbital space, dispatch squads of soldiers and police, if what I carry were not valuable to them?"

"I don't believe in your fool's religion."

"Have you ever seen the plays performed?"

"Once, when I was a girl. I saw *The Archer's Fall* during the year-end festival in Tienkash. I fell asleep."

"They are the axis of human culture. The sacred stories of our race. We are *human* because of them. Through them the gods speak to us."

"I thought you monks heard the gods talking to you directly. Didn't they tell you to run us directly into the face of the guards securing the escape pod? It's lucky you had me along to cut our way out of that umbilical, or we'd be dead up there now."

"*You* might be dead. I would be in a sleep tank having my brain taken apart—to retrieve these dramas."

"There are no gods! Just voices in your head. They tell you to do what you already want to do."

"If you think the commands of the gods are easy, then just try to follow them for a single day."

We settled into an uncomfortable silence. The sun set, and the rings became visible in the sky, turned pink by the sunset in the west, rising silvery toward the zenith, where they were eclipsed by the planet's shadow. The light of the big moon still illuminated the open rock face before us. We would have a steep 300 meter climb above the tree line to the pass, then another couple of kilometers between the peaks in the darkness.

"It's cold," I said after a while.

Without saying anything, she reached out and tugged my arm. It took me a moment to realize that she wanted me to move next to her. I slid over, and we ducked our heads to keep below the wind. I could feel the taut muscles of her body beneath the skinsuit. The paradox of our alienation hit me. We were both the products of the gods. She did not believe this truth, but truth does not need to be believed to prevail.

Still, she was right that we had not escaped the orbiting commandos in the way I had expected.

The great clockwork of the universe turned. Green Roshanak sped past Mahsheed, for a moment in transit looking like the pupil of a god's observing eye, then set, and an hour later, Mahsheed followed her below the western horizon. The stars shone in all their glory, but it was as dark as it would get before Roshanak rose for the second time that night. It was time for us to take our chance and go.

We came out of our hiding place and moved to the edge of the scrub. The broken granite of the peak rose before us, faint gray in starlight. We set out across the rock, climbing in places, striding across rubble fields, circling areas of ice and melting snow. In a couple of places, we had to boost each other up, scrambling over boulders, finding hand and footholds in the vertical face where we were blocked. It was farther than I had estimated before the ground leveled and we were in the pass.

We were just cresting the last ridge when glaring white light shone down on us, and an amplified voice called from above. "Do not move! Drop your weapons and lie flat on the ground!"

I tongued my body into acceleration. In slow motion, Nahid crouched, raised her blaster, arm extended, sighted on the flyer and fired. I hurled my body into hers and threw her aside just as the return fire of projectile weapons splattered the rock where she had been into fragments. In my head, kind Eurynome insisted: *Back. We will show you the way.*

"This way!" I dragged Nahid over the edge of the rock face we had just climbed. It was a three-meter drop to the granite below; I landed hard, and she fell on my chest, knocking the wind from me. Around us burst a hail of sleep gas pellets. In trying to catch my breath I caught a whiff of the gas, and my head whirled. Nahid slid her helmet down over her face, and did the same for me.

From above us came the sound of the flyer touching down. Nahid started for the tree line, limping. She must have been hit or injured in our fall. I pulled her to our left, along the face of the rock. "Where—" she began.

"Shut up!" I grunted.

The commandos hit the ledge behind us, but the flyer had its searchlight aimed at the trees, and the soldiers followed the light. The fog of sleep gas gave us some cover.

We scuttled along the granite shelf until we were beyond the entrance to the pass. By this time, I had used whatever reserves of energy my body could muster, and passed into normal speed. I was exhausted.

"Over the mountain?" Nahid asked. "We can't."

"Under it," I said. I forced my body into motion, searching in the darkness for the cleft in the rock which, in the moment of the flyer attack, the gods had shown me. And there it was, two dark pits above a vertical fissure in the granite, like an impassive face. We climbed up the few meters to the brink of the cleft. Nahid followed, slower now, dragging her right leg. "Are you badly hurt?" I asked her.

"Keep going."

I levered my shoulder under her arm, and helped her along the ledge. Down in the forest, the lights of the commandos flickered, while a flyer hovered above, beaming bright white radiance down between the trees.

Once inside the cleft, I let her lean against the wall. Beyond the narrow entrance the way widened. I used my suit flash, and, moving forward, found an oval chamber of three meters with a sandy floor. Some small bones give proof that a predator had once used this cave for a lair. But at the back, a small passage gaped. I crouched and followed it deeper.

"Where are you going?" Nahid asked.

"Come with me."

The passage descended for a space, then rose. I emerged into a larger space. My flash showed not a natural cave, but a chamber of dressed rock, and opposite us, a metal door. It was just as my vision had said.

"What is this?" Nahid asked in wonder.

"A tunnel under the mountain." I took off my helmet and spoke the words that would open the door. The ancient mechanism began to hum. With a fall of dust, a gap appeared at the side of the door, and it slid open.

THE DOOR CLOSED behind us with a disturbing finality, wrapping us in the silence of a tomb. We found ourselves in a corridor at least twice our height and three times that in width. Our lights showed walls smooth as plaster, but when I laid my hand on one, it proved to be cut from the living rock. Our boots echoed on the polished but dusty floor. The air was stale, unbreathed by human beings for unnumbered years.

I made Nahid sit. "Rest," I said. "Let me look at that leg."

Though she complied, she kept her blaster out, and her eyes scanned our surroundings warily. "Did you know of this?"

"No. The gods told me, just as we were caught in the pass."

"Praise be to the Pujmanian Order." I could not tell if there was any sarcasm in her voice.

A trickle of blood ran down her boot from the wound of a projectile gun. I opened the seam of her suit, cleaned the wound with antiseptic from my first aid kit, and bandaged her leg. "Can you walk?" I asked.

She gave me a tight smile. "Lead on, Brother Adlan."

We moved along the hall. Several smaller corridors branched off, but we kept to the main way. Periodically, we came across doors, most of them closed. One gaped open upon a room where my light fell on a garage of wheeled vehicles, sitting patiently in long rows, their windows thick with dust. In the corner of the room, a fracture in the ceiling had let in a steady drip of water that had corroded the vehicle beneath it into a mass of rust.

Along the main corridor our lights revealed hieroglyphics carved above doorways, dead oval spaces on the wall that might once have been screens or windows. We must have gone a kilometer or more when the corridor ended suddenly in a vast cavernous opening.

Our lights were lost in the gloom above. A ramp led down to an underground city. Buildings of gracious curves, apartments like heaps of grapes stacked upon a table, halls whose walls were so configured that they resembled a huge garment discarded in a bedroom. We descended into the streets.

The walls of the buildings were figured in abstract designs of immense intricacy, fractal patterns from immense to microscopic, picked out by the beams of our flashlights. Colored tiles, bits of glass and mica. Many of the buildings were no more than sets of walls demarcating space, with horizontal trellises that must once have held plants above them rather than roofs. Here and there, outside what might have been cafes, tables and benches rose out of the polished floor. We arrived in a broad square with low buildings around it, centered on a dry fountain. The immense figures of a man, a woman, and a child dominated the center of the dusty reservoir. Their eyes were made of crystal, and stared blindly across their abandoned city.

Weary beyond words, hungry, bruised, we settled against the rim of the fountain and made to sleep. The drawn skin about her eyes told me of Nahid's pain. I tried to comfort her, made her rest her legs, elevated, on my own. We slept.

When I woke, Nahid was already up, changing the dressing on her bloody leg. The ceiling of the cave had lit, and a pale light shone down, making an early arctic dawn over the dead city.

"How is your leg?" I asked.

"Better. Do you have any more anodynes?"

I gave her what I had. She took them, and sighed. After a while, she asked, "Where did the people go?"

"They left the universe. They grew beyond the need of matter, and space. They became gods. You know the story."

"The ones who made this place were people like you and me."

"You and I are the descendants of the re-creation of a second human race three million years after the first ended in apotheosis. Or of the ones left behind, or banished back into the material world by the gods for some great crime."

Nahid rubbed her boot above the bandaged leg. "Which is it? Which child's tale do you expect me to believe?"

"How do you think I found this place? The gods told me, and here it is. Our mission is important to them, and they are seeing that we succeed. Justice is to be done."

"Justice? Tell the starving child about justice. The misborn and the dying. I would rather be the random creation of colliding atoms than subject to the whim of some transhumans no more godlike than I am."

"You speak out of bitterness."

"If they are gods, they are responsible for the horror that occurs in the world. So they are evil. Why otherwise would they allow things to be as they are?"

"To say that is to speak out of the limitations of our vision. We can't see the outcome of events. We're too close. But the gods see how all things will eventuate. Time is a landscape to them. All at once they see the acorn, the seedling, the ancient oak, the woodsman who cuts it, the fire that burns the wood, and the smoke that rises from the fire. And so they led us to this place."

"Did they lead the bullet to find my leg? Did they lead your order to place me on a shelf for a lifetime, separate me from every person I loved?" Nahid's voice rose. "Please save me your theodical prattle!"

"'Theodical.' Impressive vocabulary for a soldier. But you—"

A scraping noise came from behind us. I turned to find that the giant male figure in the center of the fountain had moved. As I watched, its hand jerked another few centimeters. Its foot pulled free of its setting, and it stepped down from the pedestal into the empty basin.

We fell back from the fountain. The statue's eyes glowed a dull orange. Its lips moved, and it spoke in a voice like the scraping together of two files: "Do not flee, little ones."

Nahid let fly a shot from her blaster, which ricocheted off the shoulder of the metal man and scarred the ceiling of the cave. I pulled her away and we crouched behind a table before an open-sided building at the edge of the square.

The statue raised its arms in appeal. "Your shoes are untied," it said in its ghostly rasp. "We know why you are here. It seems to you that your lives hang in the balance, and of course you value your lives. As you should, dear ones. But I, who have no soul and therefore no ability to care, can tell you that the appetites that move you are entirely transitory. The world you live in is a game. You do not have a ticket."

"Quite mad," Nahid said. "Our shoes have no laces."

"But it's also true—they are therefore untied," I said. "And we have no tickets." I called out to the metal man, "Are you a god?"

"I am no god," the metal man said. "The gods left behind the better part of themselves when they abandoned matter. The flyer lies on its side in the woods. Press the silver pentagon. You must eat, but you must not eat too much. Here is food."

The shop behind us lit up, and in a moment the smell of food wafted from within.

I slid over to the entrance. On a table inside, under warm light, were two plates of rice and vegetables.

"He's right," I told Nahid.

"I'm not going to eat that food. Where did it come from? It's been thousands of years without a human being here."

"Come," I said. I drew her inside and made her join me at the table. I tasted. The food was good. Nahid sat warily, facing out to the square, blaster a centimeter from her plate. The metal man sat on the plaza stones, cross-legged, ducking its massive head in order to watch us. After a few moments, it began to croon.

Its voice was a completely mechanical sound, but the tune it sang was sweet, like a peasant song. I cannot convey to you the strangeness of sitting in that ancient restaurant, eating food conjured fresh out of nothing by ancient machines, listening to the music of creatures who might have been a different species from us.

When its song was ended, the metal man spoke: "If you wish to know someone, you need only observe that on which he bestows his care, and what sides of his own nature he cultivates." It lifted its arm and pointed at Nahid. Its finger stretched almost to the door. I could see the patina of corrosion on that metal digit. "If left to the gods, you will soon die."

The arm moved, and it pointed at me. "You must live, but you must not live too much. Take this."

The metal man opened the curled fingers of its hand, and in its huge palm was a small, round metallic device the size of an apple. I took it. Black and dense, it filled my hand completely. "Thank you," I said.

The man stood and returned to the empty fountain, climbed onto the central pedestal, and resumed its position. There it froze. Had we not been witness to it, I could never have believed it had moved.

Nahid came out of her musing over the man's sentence of her death. She lifted her head. "What is that thing?"

I examined the sphere, surface covered in pentagonal facets of dull metal. "I don't know."

In one of the buildings, we found some old furniture, cushions of metallic fabric that we piled together as bedding. We huddled together and slept.

Selene:	Hear that vessel that docks above?
	It marks the end of our lives
	And the beginning of our torment.
Stochik:	Death comes
	And then it's gone. Who knows
	What lies beyond that event horizon?
	Our life is but a trifle,
	A child's toy abandoned by the road
	When we are called home.
Selene:	Home? You might well hope it so,
	But—
	[Alarums off stage. Enter *a God*]
God:	*The hull is breached!*
	You must fly.

In the night I woke, chasing away the wisps of a dream. The building we were in had no ceiling, and faint light from the cavern roof filtered down upon us. In our sleep, we had moved closer together, and Nahid's arm lay over my chest, her head next to mine, her breath brushing my cheek. I turned my face to her, centimeters away. Her face was placid, her eyelashes dark and long.

As I watched her, her eyelids fluttered and she awoke. She did not flinch at my closeness, but simply, soberly, looked into my own eyes for what seemed like a very long time. I leaned forward and kissed her.

She did not pull away, but kissed me back strongly. She made a little moan in her throat, and I pulled her tightly to me.

We made love in the empty, ancient city. Her fingers entwined with mine, arms taut. Shadow of my torso across her breast. Hard, shuddering breath. Her lips on my chest. Smell of her sweat and mine. My palm brushing her abdomen. The feeling of her dark skin against mine. Her quiet laugh.

"Your leg," I said, as we lay in the darkness, spent.

"What about it?"

"Did I hurt you?"

She laughed again, lightly. "Now you ask. You are indeed all man."

In the morning, we took another meal from the ancient restaurant, food that had been manufactured from raw molecules while we waited, or perhaps stored somewhere for millennia.

We left by the corridor opposite the one by which we had entered, heading for the other side of the mountain range. Nahid limped but made no complaint. The passage ended in another door, beyond which a cave twisted upward. In one place, the ceiling of the cave had collapsed, and we had to crawl on our bellies over rubble through the narrow gap it had left. The exit was onto a horizontal shelf overgrown with trees, well below the pass. It was mid-morning. A misting rain fell across the Sharishabz Valley. In the distance, hazed by clouds of mist, I caught a small gleam of the white buildings of the monastery on the Penitent's Ridge. I pointed it out to Nahid. We scanned the mountainside below us, searching for the forest road.

Nahid found the thread of the road before I. "No sign of the Caslonians," she said.

"They're guarding the pass on the other side of the mountain, searching the woods there for us."

We descended the slope, picking our way through the trees toward the road. The mist left drops of water on our skinsuits, but did not in any way slow us. My spirits rose. I could see the end of this adventure in sight, and wondered what would happen to Nahid then.

"What will you do when we get to the monastery?" I asked her.

"I think I'll leave as soon as I can. I don't want to be there when the Caslonians find out you've reached your order with the plays."

"They won't do anything. The gods hold the monastery in their hands."

"Let us hope they don't drop it."

She would die soon, the statue had said—if left to the gods. But what person was not at the mercy of the gods? Still, she would be much more at risk alone, away from the order. "What about your leg?" I asked.

"Do you have a clinic there?"

"Yes."

"I'll take an exoskeleton and some painkillers and be on my way."

"Where will you go?"

"Wherever I can."

"But you don't even know what's happened in the last sixty years. What can you do?"

"Maybe my people are still alive. That's where I'll go—the town where I grew up. Perhaps I'll find someone who remembers me. Maybe I'll find my own grave."

"Don't go."

She strode along more aggressively. I could see her wince with each step. "Look, I don't care about your monastery. I don't care about these plays. Mostly, I don't care about *you*. Give me some painkillers and an exo, and I'll be gone."

That ended our conversation. We walked on in silence through the woods, me brooding, she limping along, grimacing.

We found the forest road. Here the land fell away sharply, and the road, hardly more than a gravel track, switchbacked severely as we made our way down the mountainside. We met no signs of pursuit. Though the rain continued, the air warmed as we moved lower, and beads of sweat trickled down my back under the skinsuit. The boots I wore were not meant for hiking, and by now my feet were sore, my back hurt. I could only imagine how bad it was for Nahid.

I had worked for years to manage my appetites, and yet I could not escape images of our night together. With a combination of shame and desire, I wanted her still. I did not think I could go back to being just another monk. The order had existed long before the Caslonian conquest, and would long outlast it. I was merely a cell passing through the body of this immortal creation. What did the gods want from me? What was to come of all this?

At the base of the trail, the road straightened, following the course of the River Sharishabz up the valley. Ahead rose the plateau, the gleaming white buildings of the monastery clearly visible now. The ornamental gardens, the terraced fields tended by the order for millennia. I could almost taste the sweet oranges and pomegranates. It would be good to be back home, a place where I could hide away from the world and figure out exactly what was in store for me. I wouldn't mind being hailed as a hero, the liberator of our people, like Stochik himself, who took the plays from the hands of the gods.

The valley sycamores and aspens rustled with the breeze. The afternoon passed. We stopped by the stream and drank. Rested, then continued.

We came to a rise in the road, where it twisted to climb the plateau. Signs here of travel, ruts of iron wheels where people from the village drove supplies to the monastery. Pilgrims passed this way—though there was no sign of anyone today.

We made a bend in the road, and I heard a yelp behind me. I turned to find Nahid struggling in the middle of the road. At first, I thought she was suffering a seizure. Her body writhed and jerked. Then I realized, from the slick of rain deflected from his form, that she was being assaulted by a person in an invisibility cloak.

This understanding had only flashed through my mind when I was thrown to the ground by an unseen hand. I kicked out wildly, and my boot made contact. Gravel sprayed beside me where my attacker fell. I slipped into accelerated mode, kicked him again, rolled away, and dashed into the woods. Above me I heard the whine of an approaching flyer. *Run!* It was the voice of Horus, god of sun and moon.

I ran. The commandos did not know these woods the way I did. I had spent ten years exploring them, playing games of hide and hunt in the night with my fellow novices: I knew I could find my way to the monastery without them capturing me.

And Nahid? Clearly this was her spoken-of death. No doubt it had already taken place. Or perhaps they wouldn't kill her immediately, but would torture her, assuming she knew something, or even if they knew she didn't, taking some measure of revenge on her body. It was the lot of a Republican Guard to receive such treatment. She would even expect it. *The order comes first.*

Every second took me farther from the road, away from the Caslonians. But after a minute of hurrying silently through the trees, I felt something heavy in my hand. I stopped. Without realizing it, I had taken the object the metal man had given me out of my belt pouch. *She would not want you to return. The freedom of her people comes before her personal safety.*

I circled back and found them again.

A flyer had landed athwart the road. The soldiers had turned off their cloaks, three men garbed head to toe in the matte gray of light deflection suits. Two of them had Nahid on her knees in the drizzle, her hands tied behind her back. One jerked her head back by her hair, holding a knife to her throat while an officer asked her questions. The officer slapped her, whipping the back of his gloved hand across her face.

I moved past them through the woods, sound of rain on the foliage, still holding the metal sphere in my hand. The flyer sat only a few meters into the road. I crouched, staring at the uncouth object the metal man had given me. I rotated it in my palm until I found the surface pentagon that was silvered. I depressed this pentagon until it clicked.

I flipped it out into the road, under the landing pads of the flyer, and fell back.

It was not so much an explosion as a vortex, warping the flyer into an impossible shape, throwing it off the road. As it spun the pilot was tossed from the cockpit, his uniform flaring in electric blue flame. The three men with Nahid were sucked off their feet by the dimensional warp. They jerked their heads toward the screaming pilot. The officer staggered to his feet, took two steps toward him, and one of the men followed. By that time, I had launched myself into the road, and slammed my bad shoulder into the small of the back of the man holding Nahid. I seized his rifle and fired, killing the officer and the other soldier, then the one I had just laid flat. The pilot was rolling in the gravel to extinguish the flames. I stepped forward calmly and shot him in the head.

Acrid black smoke rose from the crushed flyer, which lay on its side in the woods.

Nahid was bleeding from a cut on her neck. She held her palm against the wound, but the blood seeped steadily from between her fingers. I gathered her up and dragged her into the woods before reinforcements could arrive.

"Thank you," Nahid gasped, her eyes large, and fixed on me. We limped off into the trees.

NAHID WAS BADLY hurt, but I knew where we were, and I managed, through that difficult night, to get us up the pilgrim's trail to the monastery. By the time we reached the iron door we called the Mud Gate she had lost consciousness and I was carrying her. Her blood was all over us, and I could not tell if she yet breathed.

We novices had used this gate many times to sneak out of the monastery to play martial games in the darkness, explore the woods, and pretend we were ordinary men. Men who, when they desired something, had only to take it. Men who were under no vow of non-violence. Here I had earned a week's fast by bloodying the nose, in a fit of temper, of Brother Taher. Now I returned, unrepentant over the number of men I had killed in the last days, a man who had disobeyed the voice of a god, hoping to save Nahid before she bled out.

Brother Pramha was the first to greet me. He looked at me with shock. "Who is this?" he asked.

"This is a friend, a soldier, Nahid. Quickly. She needs care."

Together we took her to the clinic. Pramha ran off to inform the master. Our physician Brother Nastricht sealed her throat wound, and gave her new blood. I held her hand. She did not regain consciousness

Soon, one of the novices arrived to summon me to Master Darius' chambers. Although I was exhausted, I hurried after him through the warren of corridors, up the tower steps. I unbelted my blaster and handed it to the novice—he seemed distressed to hold the destructive device—and entered the room.

Beyond the broad window that formed the far wall of the chamber, dawn stained the sky pink. Master Darius held out his arms. I approached him, humbly bowed my head, and he embraced me. The warmth of his large body enfolding me was an inexpressible comfort. He smelled of cinnamon. He let me go, held me at arm's length, and smiled. The kosode he wore I recognized as one I had sewn myself. "I cannot tell you how good it is to see you, Adlan."

"I have the plays," I announced.

"The behavior of our Caslonian masters has been proof enough of that," he replied. His broad, plain face was somber as he told me of the massacre in Radnapuja, where the colonial government had held six thousand citizens hostage, demanding the bodily presentation, alive, of the foul villain, the man without honor or soul, the sacrilegious terrorist who had stolen the Foundational Plays.

"Six thousand dead?"

"They won't be the last," the master said. "The plays have been used as a weapon, as a means of controlling us. The beliefs which they embody work within the minds and souls of every person on this planet. They work even on those who are unbelievers."

"Nahid is an unbeliever."

"Nahid? She is this soldier whom you brought here?"

"The Republican Guard you sent with me. She doesn't believe, but she has played her role in bringing me here."

Master Darius poured me a glass of fortifying spirits, and handed it to me as if he were a novice and I the master. He sat in his great chair, had me sit in the chair opposite, and bade me recount every detail of the mission. I did so.

"It is indeed miraculous that you have come back alive," Master Darius mused. "Had you died, the plays would have been lost forever."

"The gods would not allow such a sacrilege."

"Perhaps. You carry the only copies in your mind?"

"Indeed. I have even quoted them to Nahid."

"Not at any length, I hope."

I laughed at his jest. "But now we can free Helvetica," I said. "Before any further innocents are killed, you must contact the Caslonian colonial government and tell them we have the plays. Tell them they must stop or we will destroy them."

Master Darius held up his hand and looked at me piercingly—I had seen this gesture many times in his tutoring of me. "First, let me ask you some questions about your tale. You tell me that, when you first came to consciousness after stealing the plays in the Imperial City, a god told you to run. Yet to run in the Caslonian capital is only to attract unwelcome attention."

"Yes. Bishamon must have wanted to hurry my escape."

"But when you reached the port bazaar, the god told you to stop and enter the restaurant. You run to attract attention, and dawdle long enough to allow time for you to be caught. Does this make sense?"

My fatigue made it difficult for me to think. What point was the master trying to make? "Perhaps I was not supposed to stop," I replied. "It was my own weakness. I was hungry."

"Then, later, you tell me that when the commandos boarded your ship, you escaped by following Nahid's lead, not the word of the gods."

"Liu-Bei led us out of the engine room. I think this is a matter of my misinterpreting—"

"And this metal man you encountered in the ancient city. Did he in fact say that the gods would have seen Nahid dead?"

"The statue said many mad things."

"Yet the device he gave you was the agent of her salvation?"

"I used it for that." Out of shame, I had not told Master Darius that I had disobeyed the command of the god who told me to flee.

"Many paradoxes." The master took a sip from his own glass. "So, if we give the plays back, what will happen then?"

"Then Helvetica will be free."

"And after that?"

"After that, we can do as we wish. The Caslonians would not dare to violate a holy vow. The gods would punish them. They know that. They are believers, as are we."

"Yes, they are believers. They would obey any compact they made, for fear of the wrath of the gods. They believe what you hold contained in your mind, Adlan, is true. So, as you say, you must give them to me now, and I will see to their disposition."

"Their disposition? How will you see to their disposition?"

"That is not something for you to worry about, my son. You have done well, and you deserve all our thanks. Brother Ishmael will see to unburdening you of the great weight you carry."

A silence ensued. I knew it was a sign of my dismissal. I must go to Brother Ishmael. But I did not rise. "What will you do with them?"

Master Darius' brown eyes lay steady on me, and quiet. "You have always been my favorite. I think, perhaps, you know what I intend."

I pondered our conversation. "You—you're going to destroy them."

"Perhaps I was wrong not to have you destroy them the minute you gained access to the archives. But at that time I had not come to these conclusions."

"But the wrath of the Caslonians will know no limit! We will be exterminated!"

"We may be exterminated, and Helvetica remain in chains, but once these plays are destroyed, never to be recovered, then *humanity* will begin to be truly free. This metal man, you say, told you the gods left the better part of themselves behind. That is profoundly true. Yet there is no moment when they cease to gaze over our shoulders. Indeed, if we are ever to be free human beings, and not puppets jerked about by unseen forces—which may, or may not, exist—the gods must go. And the beginning of that process is the destruction of the foundational plays."

I did not know how to react. In my naivete I said, "This does not seem right."

"I assure you, my son, that it is."

"If we destroy the plays, it will be the last thing we ever do."

"Of course not. Time will not stop."

"Time may not stop," I said, "but it might as well. Any things that happen after the loss of the gods will have no meaning."

Master Darius rose from his chair and moved toward his desk. "You are tired, and very young," he said, his back to me. "I have lived in the shadow of the gods far longer than you have." He reached over his desk, opened a drawer, took something out, and straightened.

He is lying. It seemed to me to be the voice of Inti himself. I stood. I felt surpassing weariness, but I moved silently. In my boot I still carried the force knife I had stolen from the restaurant on Caslon. I drew out the hilt, switched on the blade, and approached the master just as he began to turn.

When he faced me, he had a blaster in his hands. He was surprised to find me so close to him. His eyes went wide as I slipped the blade into his belly below his lowest rib.

Stochik: Here ends our story.
          Let no more be said of our fall.
          Mark the planting of this seed.
          The tree that grows in this place
          Will bear witness to our deeds;
          No other witness shall we have.
Selene: I would not depart with any other
          My love. Keep alive whatever word
          May permit us to move forward.
          Leaving all else behind we must
          Allow the world to come to us.

The Caslonian government capitulated within a week after we contacted them. Once they began to withdraw their forces from the planet and a provisional government for the Helvetican Republic was re-established in Astara, I underwent the delicate process of downloading the foundational dramas from my mind. *The Abandonment* was once again embodied in a crystal, which was presented to the Caslonian legate in a formal ceremony on the anniversary of the rebirth of man.

The ceremony took place on a bright day in midsummer in that city of a thousand spires. Sunlight flooded the streets, where citizens in vibrant colored robes danced and sang to the music of bagpipes. Pennants in purple and green flew from those spires; children hung out of second-story school windows, shaking snowstorms of confetti on the parades. The smell of incense wafted down from the great temple, and across the sky flyers drew intricate patterns with lines of colored smoke.

Nahid and I were there on that day, though I did not take a leading role in the ceremony, preferring to withdraw to my proper station. In truth, I am not a significant individual. I have only served the gods.

I left the order as soon as the negotiations were completed. At first the brothers were appalled by my murder of Master Darius. I explained to them that he had gone mad and intended to kill me in order to destroy the plays. There was considerable doubt. But when I insisted that we follow through with the plan as the Master had presented it to the brothers before sending me on my mission, they seemed to take my word about his actions. The success of our thieving enterprise overshadowed the loss of the great leader, and indeed has contributed to his legend, making of him a tragic figure. A drama has been written of his life and death, and the liberation of Helvetica.

Last night, Nahid and I, with our children and grandchildren, watched it performed in the square of the town where we set up the tailor's shop that has been the center of our lives for the last forty years. Seeing the events of my youth played out on the platform, in their comedy and tragedy, hazard and fortune, calls again to my mind the question of whether I have deserved the blessings that have fallen to me ever since that day. I have not heard the voices of the gods since I slipped the knife into the belly of the man who taught me all that I knew of grace.

The rapid decline of the Caslonian Empire, and the Helvetican renaissance that has led to our current prosperity, all date from that moment in his chambers when I ended his plan to free men from belief and duty. The people, joyous on their knees in the temples of twelve planets, give praise to the gods for their deliverance, listen, hear, and obey.

Soon I will rest beneath the earth, like the metal man who traduced the gods, though less likely than he ever to walk again. If I have done wrong, it is not for me to judge. I rest, my lover's hand in mine, in the expectation of no final word.

Pride and
Prometheus

HAD BOTH her mother and her sister Kitty not insisted upon it, Miss Mary Bennet, whose interest in Nature did not extend to the Nature of Society, would not have attended the ball in Grosvenor Square. This was Kitty's season. Mrs. Bennet had despaired of Mary long ago, but still bore hopes for her younger sister, and so had set her determined mind on putting Kitty in the way of Robert Sidney of Detling Manor, who possessed a fortune of six thousand pounds a year, and was likely to be at that evening's festivities. Obliged by her unmarried state to live with her parents, and the whims of Mrs. Bennet being what they were, although there was no earthly reason for Mary to be there, there was no good excuse for her absence.

So it was that Mary found herself in the ballroom of the great house, trussed up in a silk dress with her hair piled high, bedecked with her sister's jewels. She was neither a beauty, like her older and happily married sister Jane, nor witty, like her older and happily married sister Elizabeth, nor flirtatious, like her younger and less happily married sister Lydia. Awkward and nearsighted, she had never cut an attractive figure, and as she had aged she had come to see herself as others saw her. Every time Mrs. Bennet told her to stand up straight, she felt despair. Mary had seen how Jane and Elizabeth had made good lives for themselves by finding appropriate mates. But there was no air of grace or mystery about Mary, and no man ever looked upon her with admiration.

Kitty's card was full, and she had already contrived to dance once with the distinguished Mr. Sidney, whom Mary could not imagine being more tedious. Hectically glowing, Kitty was certain that this was the season she would get a husband. Mary, in contrast, sat with her mother and her Aunt Gardiner, whose good sense was Mary's only respite from her mother's silliness. After the third minuet Kitty came flying over.

"Catch your breath, Kitty!" Mrs. Bennet said. "Must you rush about like this? Who is that young man you danced with? Remember, we are here to smile on Mr. Sidney, not on some stranger. Did I see him arrive with the Lord Mayor?"

"How can I tell you what you saw, Mother?"

"Don't be impertinent."

"Yes. He is an acquaintance of the Mayor. He's from Switzerland! Mr. Clerval, on holiday."

The tall, fair-haired Clerval stood with a darker, brooding young man, both impeccably dressed in dove gray breeches, black jackets, and waistcoats, with white tie and gloves.

"Switzerland! I would not have you marry any Dutchman—though 'tis said their merchants are uncommonly wealthy. And who is that gentleman with whom he speaks?"

"I don't know, Mother—but I can find out."

Mrs. Bennet's curiosity was soon to be relieved, as the two men crossed the drawing room to the sisters and their chaperones.

"Henry Clerval, madame," the fair-haired man said. "And this is my good friend Mr. Victor Frankenstein."

Mr. Frankenstein bowed but said nothing. He had the darkest eyes that Mary had ever encountered, and an air of being there only on obligation. Whether this was because he was as uncomfortable in these social situations as she, Mary could not tell, but his diffident air intrigued her. She fancied his reserve might bespeak sadness rather than pride. His manners were faultless, as was his command of English, though he spoke with a slight French accent. When he asked Mary to dance she suspected he did so only at the urging of Mr. Clerval; on the floor, once the orchestra of pianoforte, violin, and cello struck up the quadrille, he moved with some grace but no trace of a smile.

At the end of the dance, Frankenstein asked whether Mary would like some refreshment, and they crossed from the crowded ballroom to the sitting room, where he procured for her a cup of negus. Mary felt obliged to make some conversation before she should retreat to the safety of her wallflower's chair.

"What brings you to England, Mr. Frankenstein?"

"I come to meet with certain natural philosophers here in London, and in Oxford—students of magnetism."

"Oh! Then have you met Professor Langdon, of the Royal Society?"

Frankenstein looked at her as if seeing her for the first time. "How is it that you are acquainted with Professor Langdon?"

"I am not personally acquainted with him, but I am, in my small way, an enthusiast of the sciences. You are a natural philosopher?"

"I confess that I can no longer countenance the subject. But yes, I did study with Mr. Krempe and Mr. Waldman in Ingolstadt."

"You no longer countenance the subject, yet you seek out Professor Langdon."

A shadow swept over Mr. Frankenstein's handsome face. "It is unsupportable to me, yet pursue it I must."

"A paradox."

"A paradox that I am unable to explain, Miss Bennet."

All this said in a voice heavy with despair. Mary watched his sober black eyes, and replied, "'The heart has its reasons of which reason knows nothing.'"

For the second time that evening he gave her a look that suggested an understanding. Frankenstein sipped from his cup, then said, "Avoid any pastime, Miss Bennet, that takes you out of the normal course of human contact. If the study to which you apply yourself has a tendency to weaken your affections, and to destroy your taste for simple pleasures, then that study is certainly unlawful."

The purport of this unusual speech Mary was unable to fathom. "Surely there is no harm in seeking knowledge."

Mr. Frankenstein smiled. "Henry has been urging me to go out into London society; had I known that I might meet such a thoughtful person as yourself I would have taken him up on it long 'ere now."

He took her hand. "But I spy your aunt at the door," he said. "No doubt she has been dispatched to retrieve you. I must thank you for the dance, and even more for your conversation, Miss Bennet. In the midst of a foreign land, you have brought me a moment of sympathy."

And again Mary sat beside her mother and aunt as she had half an hour before. She was nonplussed. It was not seemly for a stranger to speak so much from the heart to a woman he had never previously met, yet she could not find it in herself to condemn him. Rather, she felt her own failure in not keeping him longer.

A cold March rain was falling when, after midnight, they left the ball. They waited under the portico while the coachman brought round the carriage. Kitty began coughing. As they stood there in the night's chill, Mary noticed a hooded man, of enormous size, standing in the shadows at the corner of the lane. Full in the downpour, unmoving, he watched the town house and its partiers without coming closer or moving away, as if this observation were all his intention in life. Mary shivered.

In the carriage back to Aunt Gardiner's home near Belgravia, Mrs. Bennet insisted that Kitty take the lap robe against the chill. "Stop coughing, Kitty. Have a care for my poor nerves." She added, "They should never have put the supper at the end of that long hallway. The young ladies, flushed from the dance, had to walk all that cold way."

Kitty drew a ragged breath and leaned over to Mary. "I have never seen you so taken with a man, Mary. What did that Swiss gentleman say to you?"

"We spoke of natural philosophy."

"Did he say nothing of the reasons he came to England?" Aunt Gardiner asked.

"That was his reason."

"I should say not!" said Kitty. "He came to forget his grief! His little brother was murdered, not six months ago, by the family maid!"

"How terrible!" said Aunt Gardiner.

Mrs. Bennet asked in open astonishment, "Can this be true?"

"I have it from Lucy Copeland, the Lord Mayor's daughter," Kitty replied. "Who heard it from Mr. Clerval himself. And there is more! He is engaged to be married—to his cousin. Yet he has abandoned her, left her in Switzerland and come here instead."

"Did he say anything to you about these matters?" Mrs. Bennet asked Mary.

Kitty interrupted. "Mother, he's not going to tell the family secrets to strangers, let alone reveal his betrothal at a dance."

Mary wondered at these revelations. Perhaps they explained Mr. Frankenstein's somber manner. But could they explain his interest in her? "A man should be what he seems," she said.

Kitty snorted, and it became a cough.

"Mark me, girls," said Mrs. Bennet, "that engagement is a match that he does not want. I wonder what fortune he would bring to a marriage?"

IN THE DAYS that followed, Kitty's cough became a full-blown catarrh, and it was decided against her protest that, the city air being unhealthy, they should cut short their season and return to Meryton. Mr. Sidney was undoubtedly unaware of his narrow escape. Mary could not honestly say that she regretted leaving, though the memory of her half hour with Mr. Frankenstein gave her as much regret at losing the chance of further commerce with him as she had ever felt from her acquaintance with a man.

Within a week Kitty was feeling better and repining bitterly their remove from London. In truth, she was only two years younger than Mary and had made none of the mental accommodations to approaching spinsterhood that her older sister had pursued. Mr. Bennet retreated to his study, emerging only at mealtimes to cast sardonic comments about Mrs. Bennet and Kitty's marital campaigns. Perhaps, Mrs. Bennet said, they might invite Mr. Sidney to visit Longbourn when Parliament adjourned. Mary escaped these discussions by practicing the pianoforte and, as the advancing spring brought warm weather, taking walks in the countryside, where she would stop beneath an oak and read, indulging her passion for Goethe and German philosophy. When she tried to engage her father in speculation, he warned her, "I am afraid, my dear, that your understanding is too dependent on books and not enough on experience of the world. Beware, Mary. Too much learning makes a woman monstrous."

What experience of the world had they ever allowed her? Rebuffed, Mary wrote to Elizabeth about the abrupt end of Kitty's latest assault on marriage, and her subsequent ill temper, and Elizabeth wrote back inviting her two younger sisters to come visit Pemberley.

Mary was overjoyed to have the opportunity to escape her mother and see something more of Derbyshire, and Kitty seemed equally willing. Mrs. Bennet was not persuaded when Elizabeth suggested that nearby Matlock and its baths might be good for Kitty's health (no man would marry a sickly girl), but she *was* persuaded by Kitty's observation that, though it could in no way rival London, Matlock did attract a finer society than sleepy Meryton, and thus offered opportunities for meeting eligible young men of property. So in the second week of May, Mr. and Mrs. Bennet tearfully loaded their last unmarried daughters into a coach for the long drive to Derbyshire. Mrs. Bennet's tears were shed because their absence would deprive Kitty and Mary of her attentions; Mr. Bennet's were shed because their absence would direct Mrs. Bennet's attentions toward him.

The young women were as ever delighted by the grace and luxury of Pemberley, Mr. Darcy's ancestral estate. Darcy was kindness itself, and the servants attentive, if, at the instruction of Elizabeth, less indulgent of Kitty's whims and more careful of her health than the thoroughly cowed servants at home. Lizzy saw that Kitty got enough sleep, and the three sisters took long walks on the grounds of the estate. Kitty's health improved, and Mary's spirits rose.

Mary enjoyed the company of Lizzy and Darcy's eight-year-old son William, who attempted to teach her and Darcy's younger sister Georgiana to fish. Georgiana pined after her betrothed, Captain Broadbent, who was away on crown business in the Caribbean, but after they had been there a week, Jane and her husband Mr. Bingley came for an extended visit from their own estate thirty miles away, and so four of the five Bennet sisters were reunited. They spent many cordial afternoons and evenings. Both Mary and Georgiana were accomplished at the pianoforte, though Mary had come to realize that her sisters tolerated more than enjoyed her playing. The reunion of Lizzy and Jane meant even more time devoted to Kitty's improvement, with specific attention to her marital prospects, and left Mary feeling invisible. Still, on occasion she would join them and drive into Lambton or Matlock to shop and socialize, and every week during the summer a ball was held in the assembly room of the Old Bath Hotel, with its beeswax-polished floor and splendid chandeliers.

On one such excursion to Matlock, Georgiana stopped at the milliners while Kitty pursued some business at the butcher's shop—Mary wondered at her sudden interest in Pemberley's domestic affairs—and Mary took William to the museum and circulating library, which contained celebrated cabinets of natural history. William had told her of certain antiquities recently added to the collection, unearthed in the excavation for a new hotel.

The streets, hotels, and inns of Matlock bustled with travelers there to take the waters. Newly wedded couples leaned on one another's arms, whispering secrets that no doubt concerned the alpine scenery. A crew of workmen was breaking up the cobblestone street in front of the hall, swinging pickaxes in the bright sun. Inside she and Will retreated to the cool quiet of the public exhibition room.

Among the visitors to the museum Mary spied a slender, well-dressed man at one of the display cases, examining the artifacts contained there. As she drew near, Mary recognized him. "Mr. Frankenstein!"

The tall European looked up, startled. "Ah—Miss Bennet?"

She was pleased that he remembered. "Yes. How good to see you."

"And this young man is?"

"My nephew, William."

At the mention of this name, Frankenstein's expression darkened. He closed his eyes. "Are you not well?" Mary asked.

He looked at her again. "Forgive me. My younger brother, recently deceased, was named William. Give me a moment."

"Certainly," she said, dismayed at the contretemps. What Kitty had heard back at the ball in London must be true.

William ran off to see the hall's steam clock. Mary turned and examined the contents of the neighboring cabinet. Beneath the glass was a slab of rock unearthed in the local lead mine that bore the impress of the skeleton of some small fish. The lettered card beside it read: *Bones, resembling those of a carp, made of limestone.*

Eventually Frankenstein came to stand beside her. "How is it that you are come to Matlock?" he inquired.

"My sister Elizabeth is married to Mr. Fitzwilliam Darcy, of Pemberley. Kitty and I are here on a visit. Have you come to take the waters?"

"Clerval and I are on our way to Scotland, where he will stay with friends while I pursue—certain investigations. We rest here a week. The topography of the valley reminds me of my home in Switzerland."

"I have heard it said so," she replied. Frankenstein seemed to have regained his composure, but Mary wondered still at what had awakened his grief. "You have an interest in these relics?" she asked, indicating the cabinets.

"Some, perhaps. I find it remarkable to see a young lady take an interest in such arcana." Mary detected no trace of mockery in his voice.

"Indeed, I do," she said, indulging her enthusiasm. "Doctor Erasmus Darwin has written of the source of these bones:

> "Organic life beneath the shoreless waves
> Was born and nurs'd in ocean's pearly caves;
> First forms minute, unseen by spheric glass,
> Move on the mud, or pierce the watery mass;
> These, as successive generations bloom,
> New powers acquire and larger limbs assume;
> Whence countless groups of vegetation spring,
> And breathing realms of fin and feet and wing.

"People say such fossils offer proof of the Great Flood. Do you think, Mr. Frankenstein, that Matlock could once have been under the sea? They say these are creatures that have not existed since the time of Noah."

"Far older than the Flood, I'll warrant. I do not think that these bones were originally made of stone. Some process has transformed them. Anatomically, many resemble those of a lizard more than a fish."

"You have studied anatomy?"

Mr. Frankenstein tapped his fingers upon the glass of the case. "Three years gone by it was one of my passions. I no longer pursue such matters."

"And yet, sir, you met with men of science in London."

"Ah—yes, I did. I am surprised that you remember a brief conversation, more than two months ago."

"I have a good memory."

"As evidenced by your quoting Dr. Darwin. I might expect a woman such as yourself to take more interest in art than science."

"Oh, you may rest assured that I have read my share of novels. And even more, in my youth, of sermons. Elizabeth is wont to tease me for a great moralizer. 'Evil is easy,' I tell her, 'and has infinite forms.'"

Frankenstein did not answer. Finally he said, "Would that the world had no need of moralizers."

Mary recalled his warning against science from their London meeting. "Come, Mr. Frankenstein. There is no evil in studying God's handiwork."

"A God-fearing Christian might take exception to Dr. Darwin's assertion that life began in the sea, no matter how poetically stated." His voice became distant. "Can a living soul be created without the hand of God?"

"It is my feeling that the hand of God is everywhere present." Mary gestured toward the cabinet. "Even in the bones of this stony fish."

"Then you have more faith than I, Miss Bennet—or more innocence."

Mary blushed. She was not used to bantering in this way with a gentleman. In her experience, handsome and accomplished men took no interest in her, and such conversations as she had engaged in offered little of substance other than the weather, clothes, and town gossip. Yet she saw that she had touched Frankenstein, and felt something akin to triumph.

They were interrupted by the appearance of Georgiana and Kitty, entering with Henry Clerval. "There you are!" said Kitty. "You see, Mr. Clerval, I told you we would find Mary poring over these heaps of bones!"

"And it is no surprise to find my friend here as well," said Clerval.

Mary felt quite deflated. William returned, and the party moved out of the town hall and in splendid sunlight along the North Parade. Kitty proposed, and the visitors acceded to, a stroll on the so-called Lovers' Walk beside the river. As they walked along the gorge, vast ramparts of limestone rock, clothed with yew trees, elms, and limes, rose up on either side of the river. William ran ahead, and Kitty, Georgiana, and Clerval followed, leaving Frankenstein and Mary behind. Eventually they came in sight of the High Tor, a sheer cliff rearing its brow on the east bank of the Derwent. The lower part was covered with small trees and foliage.

Massive boulders that had fallen from the cliff broke the riverbed below into foaming rapids. The noise of the waters left Mary and Frankenstein, apart from the others, as isolated as if they had been in a separate room. Frankenstein spent a long time gazing at the scenery. Mary's mind raced, seeking some way to recapture the mood of their conversation in the town hall.

"How this reminds me of my home," he said. "Henry and I would climb such cliffs as this, chase goats around the meadows, and play at pirates. Father would walk me though the woods and name every tree and flower. I once saw a lightning bolt shiver an old oak to splinters."

"Whenever I come here," Mary blurted out, "I realize how small I am, and how great time is. We are here for only seconds, and then we are gone, and these rocks, this river, will long survive us. And through it all we are alone."

Frankenstein turned toward her. "Surely you are not so lonely. You have your family, your sisters. Your mother and father."

"One can be alone in a room of people. Kitty mocks me for my 'heaps of bones.'"

"One may marry."

"I am thirty years old, sir. I am no man's vision of a lover or wife."

What had come over her, to say this aloud, for the first time in her life? Yet what did it matter what she said to this foreigner? There was no point in letting some hope of sympathy delude her into greater hopes. They had danced a single dance in London, and now they spent an afternoon together; soon he would leave England, marry his cousin, and Mary would never see him again. She deserved Kitty's mockery.

Frankenstein took some time before answering, during which Mary was acutely aware of the sound of the waters, and of the sight of Georgiana, William, and Clerval playing in the grass by the riverbank, while Kitty stood pensive some distance away.

"Miss Bennet, I am sorry if I have made light of your situation. But your fine qualities should be apparent to anyone who took the trouble truly to make your acquaintance. Your knowledge of matters of science only adds to my admiration."

"You needn't flatter me," said Mary. "I am unused to it."

"I do not flatter," Frankenstein replied. "I speak my own mind."

William came running up. "Aunt Mary! This would be an excellent place to fish! We should come here with Father!"

"That's a good idea, Will."

Frankenstein turned to the others. "We must return to the hotel, Henry," he told Clerval. "I need to see that new glassware properly packed before shipping it ahead."

"Very well."

"Glassware?" Georgiana asked.

Clerval chuckled. "Victor has been purchasing equipment at every stop along our tour—glassware, bottles of chemicals, lead and copper disks. The coachmen threaten to leave us behind if he does not ship these things separately."

Kitty argued in vain, but the party walked back to Matlock. The women and William met the carriage to take them back to Pemberley. "I hope I see you again, Miss Bennet," Frankenstein said. Had she been more accustomed to reading the emotions of others she would have ventured that his expression held sincere interest—even longing.

On the way back to Pemberley, William prattled with Georgiana. Kitty, subdued for once, leaned back with her eyes closed, while Mary puzzled over every moment of the afternoon. The fundamental sympathy she had felt with Frankenstein in their brief London encounter had been only reinforced. His sudden dark moods, his silences, bespoke some burden he carried. Mary was almost convinced that her mother was right—that Frankenstein did not love his cousin, and that he was here in England fleeing from her. How could this second meeting with him be chance? Fate had brought them together.

At dinner that evening, Kitty told Darcy and Elizabeth about their encounter with the handsome Swiss tourists. Later, Mary took Lizzy aside and asked her to invite Clerval and Frankenstein to dinner.

"This is new!" said Lizzy. "I expect this from Kitty, but not you. You have never before asked to have a young man come to Pemberley."

"I have never met someone quite like Victor Frankenstein," Mary replied.

"HAVE YOU TAKEN the Matlock waters?" Mary asked Clerval, who was seated opposite her at the dinner table. "People in the parish say that a dip in the hot springs could raise the dead."

"I confess that I have not," Clerval said. "Victor does not believe in their healing powers."

Mary turned to Frankenstein, hoping to draw him into discussion of the matter, but the startled expression on his face silenced her.

The table, covered with a blinding white damask tablecloth, glittered with silver and crystal. A large epergne, studded with lit beeswax candles, dominated its center. In addition to the family members, and in order to even the number of guests and balance female with male, Darcy and Elizabeth had invited the vicar, Mr. Chatsworth. Completing the dinner party were Bingley and Jane, Georgiana, and Kitty.

The footmen brought soup, followed by claret, turbot with lobster and Dutch sauce, oyster pâté, lamb cutlets with asparagus, peas, a fricandeau à l'oseille, venison, stewed beef à la jardinière, with various salads, beetroot, French and English mustard. Two ices, cherry water and pineapple cream, and a chocolate cream with strawberries. Champagne flowed throughout the dinner, and Madeira afterward.

Darcy inquired of Clerval's business in England, and Clerval told of his meetings with men of trade in London, and his interest in India. He had even begun the study of the language, and for their entertainment spoke a few sentences in Hindi. Darcy told of his visit to Geneva a decade ago. Clerval spoke charmingly of the differences in manners between the Swiss and the English, with witty preference for English habits, except, he said, in the matter of boiled meats. Georgiana asked about women's dress on the continent. Elizabeth allowed as how, if they could keep him safe, it would be good for William's education to tour the continent. Kitty, who usually dominated the table with bright talk and jokes, was unusually quiet. The Vicar spoke amusingly of his travels in Italy.

Through all of this, Frankenstein offered little in the way of response or comment. Mary had put such hopes on this dinner, and now she feared she had misread him. His voice warmed but once, when he spoke of his father, a counselor and syndic, renowned for his integrity. Only on inquiry would he speak of his years in Ingolstadt.

"And what did you study in the university?" Bingley asked.

"Matters of no interest," Frankenstein replied.

An uncomfortable silence followed. Clerval gently explained, "My friend devoted himself so single-mindedly to the study of natural philosophy that his health failed. I was fortunately able to bring him back to us, but it was a near thing."

"For which I will ever be grateful to you," Frankenstein mumbled.

Lizzy attempted to change the subject. "Reverend Chatsworth, what news is there of the parish?"

The vicar, unaccustomed to such volume and variety of drink, was in his cups, his face flushed and his voice rising to pulpit volume. "Well, I hope the ladies will not take it amiss," he boomed, "if I relate a curious incident that occurred last night!"

"Pray do."

"So, then—last night I was troubled with sleeplessness—I think it was the trout I ate for supper, it was not right—Mrs. Croft vowed she had purchased it just that afternoon, but I wonder if perhaps it might have been from the previous day's catch. Be that as it may, lying awake some time after midnight, I thought I heard a scraping out my bedroom window—the weather has been so fine of late that I sleep with my window open. It is my opinion, Mr. Clerval, that nothing aids the lungs more than fresh air, and I believe that is the opinion of the best continental thinkers, is it not? The air of the alpine meadows is exceedingly fresh, I am told?"

"Only in those meadows where the cows have not been feeding."

"The cows? Oh, yes, the cows—ha, ha!—very good! The cows, indeed! So, where was I? Ah, yes. I rose from my bed and looked out the window, and what did I spy but a light in the churchyard. I threw on my robe and slippers and hurried out to see what might be the matter.

"As I approached the churchyard I saw a dark figure wielding a spade. His back was to me, silhouetted by a lamp which rested beside Nancy Brown's grave. Poor Nancy, dead not a week now, so young, only seventeen."

"A man?" said Kitty.

The vicar's round face grew serious. "You may imagine my shock. 'Halloo!' I shouted. At that the man dropped his spade, seized the lantern and dashed round the back of the church. By the time I had reached the corner he was out of sight. Back at the grave I saw that he had been on a fair way to unearthing poor Nancy's coffin!"

"My goodness!" said Jane.

"Defiling a grave?" asked Bingley. "I am astonished."

Darcy said nothing, but his look demonstrated that he was not pleased by the vicar bringing such an uncouth matter to his dinner table. Frankenstein, sitting next to Mary, put down his fork and took a long draught of Madeira.

The vicar lowered his voice. He was clearly enjoying himself. "I can only speculate on what motive this man might have had. Could it have been some lover of hers, overcome with grief?"

"No man is so faithful," Kitty said.

"My dear vicar," said Lizzy. "You have read too many of Mrs. Radcliffe's novels."

Darcy leaned back in his chair. "Gypsies have been seen in the woods about the quarry. It was no doubt their work. They were seeking jewelry."

"Jewelry?" the vicar said. "The Browns had barely enough money to see her decently buried."

"Which proves that whoever did this was not a local man."

Clerval spoke. "At home, fresh graves are sometimes defiled by men providing cadavers to doctors. Was there not a spate of such grave robbings in Ingolstadt, Victor?"

Frankenstein put down his glass. "Yes," he said. "Some anatomists, in seeking knowledge, will abandon all human scruple."

"I do not think that is likely to be the cause in this instance," Darcy observed. "Here there is no university, no medical school. Doctor Phillips, in Lambton, is no transgressor of civilized rules."

"He is scarcely a transgressor of his own threshold," said Lizzy. "One must call him a day in advance to get him to leave his parlor."

"Rest assured, there are such men," said Frankenstein. "My illness, as Henry has described to you, was in some way my spirit's rebellion against the understanding that the pursuit of knowledge will lead some men into mortal peril."

Here was Mary's chance to impress Frankenstein. "Surely there is a nobility in risking one's life to advance the claims of one's race. With how many things are we upon the brink of becoming acquainted, if cowardice or carelessness did not restrain our inquiries?"

"Then I thank God for cowardice and carelessness, Miss Bennet," Frankenstein said, "One's life, perhaps, is worth risking, but not one's soul."

"True enough. But I believe that science may demand our relaxing the strictures of common society."

"We have never heard this tone from you, Mary," Jane said.

Darcy interjected, "You are becoming quite modern, sister. What strictures are you prepared to abandon for us tonight?" His voice was full of the gentle condescension with which he treated Mary at all times.

How she wished to surprise them! How she longed to show Darcy and Lizzy, with their perfect marriage and perfect lives, that she was not the simple old maid they thought her.

"Anatomists in London have obtained the court's permission to dissect the bodies of criminals after execution," Mary said. "Is it unjust to use the body of a murderer, who has forfeited his own life, to save the lives of the innocent?"

Bingley said, "My uncle, who is on the bench, has spoken of such cases."

"Not only that," Mary added. "Have you heard of the experiments of the Italian scientist Aldini? Last summer in London at the Royal College of Surgeons he used a powerful battery to animate portions of the body of a hanged man. According to the Times, the spectators genuinely believed that the body was about to come to life!"

"Mary, please!" said Lizzy.

Kitty laughed. "You need to spend less time on your horrid books," she said. "No suitor wishes to speak with you about dead bodies."

And so Kitty was on their side, too. Her mockery only made Mary more determined to force Frankenstein to speak. "What do you say, sir? Will you come to my defense?"

Frankenstein carefully folded his napkin and set it beside his plate. "Such inquiries are not motivated by bravery, or even curiosity, but by ambition. The pursuit of knowledge can become a vice deadly as any of the more common sins. Worse still, for even the most noble of natures are susceptible to such temptations. None but he who has experienced them can conceive of the enticements of science."

The vicar raised his glass. "Mr. Frankenstein, truer words have never been spoken. The man who defiled poor Nancy's grave has placed himself beyond the mercy of a forgiving God."

Mary felt charged with contradictory emotions. "You have experienced such enticements, Mr. Frankenstein?"

"Sadly, I have."

"But surely there is no sin that is beyond the reach of God's mercy? 'To know all is to forgive all.'"

The vicar turned to her. "My child, what know you of sin?"

"Very little, Mr. Chatsworth, except the sin of idleness. Yet I feel that even a wicked person may have the veil lifted from his eyes."

Frankenstein looked at her. "Here I must agree with Miss Bennet. I sincerely hope that even the most corrupted nature is susceptible to grace. If I did not think this were possible, I could not live."

"Enough of this talk," said Darcy. "Vicar, I suggest you mind your parishioners, including those in the churchyard, more carefully. But now I, for one, am eager to hear Miss Georgiana play the pianoforte. And perhaps Miss Mary and Miss Catherine will join her. We must uphold the accomplishments of English maidenhood before our foreign guests."

ON KITTY'S INSISTENCE the next morning, despite lowering clouds and a chill in the air that spoke more of March than late May, she and Mary took a walk along the river.

They walked along the stream that ran from the estate toward the Derwent. Kitty remained silent. Mary's thoughts turned to the wholly unsatisfying dinner of the previous night. The conversation in the parlor had gone no better than at dinner. Mary had played the piano ill, showing herself to poor advantage next to the accomplished Georgiana. Under Jane and Lizzy's gaze she felt the folly of her intemperate speech at the table. Frankenstein said next to nothing to her for the rest of the evening; he almost seemed wary of being in her presence.

She was wondering how he was spending this morning when, suddenly turning her face from Mary, Kitty burst into tears.

Mary touched her arm. "Whatever is the matter, Kitty?"

"Do you believe what you said last night?"

"What did I say?"

"That there is no sin beyond the reach of God's mercy?"

"Of course I do! Why should you ask?"

"Because I have committed such a sin!" She covered her eyes with her hand. "Oh, no, I mustn't speak of it!"

Mary refrained from pointing out that, having made such a provocative admission, Kitty could hardly remain silent—and undoubtedly had no intention of doing so. But Kitty's intentions were not always transparent to Mary.

After some coaxing and a further walk along the stream, Kitty was prepared finally to unburden herself. It seemed that, from the previous summer she had maintained a secret admiration for a local man from Matlock, Robert Piggot, son of the butcher. Though his family was quite prosperous and he stood to inherit the family business, he was in no way a gentleman, and Kitty had vowed never to let her affections overwhelm her sense.

But, upon their recent return to Pemberley, she had encountered Robert on her first visit to town, and she had been secretly meeting with him when she went into Matlock on the pretext of shopping. Worse still, the couple had allowed their passion to get the better of them, and Kitty had given way to carnal love.

The two sisters sat on a fallen tree in the woods as Kitty poured out her tale. "I want so much to marry him." Her tears flowed readily. "I do not want to be alone, I don't want to die an old maid! And Lydia—Lydia told me about—about the act of love, how wonderful it was, how good Wickham makes her feel. She boasted of it! And I thought, why should vain Lydia have this, and me have nothing, wasting my youth in conversation and embroidery, in listening to Mother prattle and Father throw heavy sighs. Father thinks me a fool, unlikely ever to find a husband. And now he's right!" Kitty burst into wailing again. "He's right! No man shall ever have me!" Her tears ended in a fit of coughing.

"Oh, Kitty," Mary said.

"When Darcy spoke of English maidenhood last night, it was all I could do to keep from bursting into tears. You must get Father to agree to let me marry Robert."

"Has he asked you to marry him?"

"He shall. He must. You don't know how fine a man he is. Despite the fact that he is in trade, he has the gentlest manners. I don't care if he is not well born."

Mary embraced Kitty. Kitty alternated between sobs and fits of coughing. Above them the thunder rumbled, and the wind rustled the trees. Kitty shivered. Mary needed to calm her, to get her back to the house. How slender, how frail, her sister was.

She did not know what to say. Once Mary would have self-righteously condemned Kitty, but Kitty's fear of dying alone was Mary's own fear. As she searched for some answer, Mary heard the sound of a torrent of rain hitting the canopy of foliage above them. "You have been foolish," Mary said, holding her, "but all is not lost."

Kitty trembled in her arms, and spoke into Mary's shoulder. "But shall you ever care for me again? What if Father should turn me out? What shall I do then?"

The rain was falling through now, coming down hard. Mary's hair was getting soaked. "Calm yourself. Father would do no such thing. I shall never forsake you. Jane would not, nor Lizzy."

"What if I should have a child!"

Mary pulled Kitty's shawl over her head. She looked past Kitty's shoulder to the dark woods. Something moved there. "You shan't have a child."

"You can't know! I may!"

The woods had become dark with the rain. Mary could not make out what lurked there. "Come, let us go back. You must compose yourself. We shall speak with Lizzy and Jane. They will know—"

Just then a flash of lightning lit the forest, and Mary saw, beneath the trees not ten feet from them, the giant figure of a man. The lightning illuminated a face of monstrous ugliness: Long, thick, tangled black hair. Yellow skin the texture of dried leather, black eyes sunken deep beneath heavy brows. Worst of all, an expression hideous in its cold, inexpressible hunger. All glimpsed in a split second; then the light fell to shadow.

Mary gasped, and pulled Kitty toward her. A great peal of thunder rolled across the sky.

Kitty stopped crying. "What is it?"

"We must go. Now." Mary seized Kitty by the arm. The rain pelted down on them, and the forest path was already turning to mud.

Mary pulled her toward the house. She could hear nothing over the drumming of the rain, but when she looked over her shoulder, she caught a glimpse of the brutish figure, keeping to the trees, but swiftly, silently moving along behind them.

"Why must we run?" Kitty gasped.

"Because we are being followed!"

"By whom?"

"I don't know!"

Behind them, Mary thought she heard the man croak out some words: "Halt! Bitte!"

They had not reached the edge of the woods when figures appeared ahead of them, coming from Pemberley. "Miss Bennet! Mary! Kitty!"

The figures resolved themselves into Darcy and Mr. Frankenstein. Darcy carried a cloak, which he threw over them. "Are you all right?" Frankenstein asked.

"Thank you!" Mary gasped. "A man. He's there," she pointed, "following us."

Frankenstein took a few steps beyond them down the path. "Who was it?" Darcy asked.

"Some brute. Hideously ugly," Mary said.

Frankenstein came back. "No one is there."

"I saw him!"

Another lighting flash, and crack of thunder. "It is dark, and we are in a storm," Frankenstein said.

"Come, we must get you back to the house," Darcy said. "You are wet to the bone."

The men helped them back to Pemberley, trying their best to keep the rain off the sisters.

Darcy went off to find Bingley and Clerval, who had taken the opposite direction in their search. Lizzy saw that Mary and Kitty were made dry and warm. Kitty's cough worsened, and Lizzy insisted she must be put to bed. Mary sat with Kitty, whispered a promise to keep her secret, and waited until she slept. Then she went down to meet the others in the parlor.

"This chill shall do her no good," Jane said. She chided Mary for wandering off in such threatening weather. "I thought you had developed more sense, Mary. Mr. Frankenstein insisted he help to find you, when he realized you had gone out into the woods."

"I am sorry," Mary said. "You are right." She was distracted by Kitty's plight, wondering what she might do. If Kitty were indeed with child, there would be no helping her.

Mary recounted her story of the man in the woods. Darcy said he had seen no one, but allowed that someone might have been there. Frankenstein, rather than engage in the speculation, stood at the tall windows staring across the lawn through the rain toward the tree line.

"This intruder was some local poacher, or perhaps one of those gypsies," said Darcy. "When the rain ends I shall have Mr. Mowbray take some men to check the grounds. We shall also inform the constable."

"I hope this foul weather will induce you to stay with us a few more days, Mr. Frankenstein," Lizzy ventured. "You have no pressing business in Matlock, do you?"

"No. But we were to travel north by the end of this week."

"Surely we might stay a while longer, Victor," said Clerval. "Your research can wait for you in Scotland."

Frankenstein struggled with his answer. "I don't think we should prevail on these good people any more."

"Nonsense," said Darcy. "We are fortunate for your company."

"Thank you," Frankenstein said uncertainly. But when the conversation moved elsewhere, Mary noticed him once again staring out the window. She moved to sit beside him. On an impulse, she said to him, *sotto voce*, "Do you know this man we came upon in the woods?"

"I saw no one. Even if someone was there, how should I know some English vagabond?"

"I do not think he was English. When he called after us, it was in German. Was this one of your countrymen?"

A look of impatience crossed Frankenstein's face, and he lowered his eyes. "Miss Bennet, I do not wish to contradict you, but you are mistaken. I saw no one in the woods."

KITTY DEVELOPED A fever and did not leave her bed for the rest of the day. Mary sat with her, trying, without bringing up the subject of Robert Piggot, to calm her. It was still raining when Mary retired, to a separate bedroom from the one she normally shared with Kitty.

Late that night, Mary was wakened by the opening of her bedroom door. She thought it might be Lizzy come to tell her something about Kitty. But it was not Lizzy.

Rather than call out, she watched silently as a dark figure entered and closed the door behind. The remains of her fire threw faint light on the man. "Miss Bennet," he called softly.

Her heart was in her throat. "Yes, Mr. Frankenstein."

"Please do not take alarm. I must speak with you." He took two sudden steps toward her bed. His handsome face was agitated. No man, in any circumstances remotely resembling these, had ever broached her bedside. Yet the racing of her heart was not entirely a matter of fear.

"This, sir, is hardly the place for polite conversation," she said. "Following on your denial of what I saw this afternoon, you will be fortunate if I do not wake the servants and have you thrown out of Pemberley."

"You are right to chide me. My conscience chides me more than you ever could, and should I be driven from your family's gracious company it would be less than I deserve. And I am afraid that nothing I have to say to you tonight shall qualify as polite conversation." His manner was greatly changed; there was a sound of desperation in his whisper. He wanted something from her, and he wanted it a great deal.

Curious, despite herself, Mary drew on her robe and lit a candle. She made him sit in one of the chairs by the fire and poked the coals into life. When she had settled herself in the other, she said, "Go on."

"Miss Bennet, please do not toy with me. You know why I am here."

"Know, sir? What do I know?"

He leaned forward, earnestly, hands clasped and elbows on his knees. "I come to beg you to keep silent. The gravest consequences would follow your revealing my secret."

"Secret?"

"About—about the man you saw."

"You do know him!"

"Your mockery at dinner convinced me that, after hearing the vicar's story, you suspected. Raising the dead, you said to Clerval—and then your tale of Professor Aldini. Do not deny it."

"I don't pretend to know what you are talking about."

Frankenstein stood from his chair and began to pace the floor before the hearth. "Please! I saw the look of reproach in your eyes when we found you in the forest. I am trying to make right what I put wrong. But I will never be able to do so if you expose me." To Mary's astonishment, she saw, in the firelight, that his eyes glistened with tears.

"Tell me what you did," she said.

With that the story burst out of him. He told her how, completely bereft after his mother's death, he longed to conquer death itself, how he had studied chemistry at the university, how he had uncovered the secret of life. How, emboldened and driven on by his solitary obsession, he had created a man from the corpses he had stolen from graveyards and purchased from resurrection men. How he had succeeded, through his science, in bestowing it with life.

Mary did not know what to say to this astonishing tale. It was the raving of a lunatic—but what of the monstrous man she had seen in the woods? The earnestness with which Frankenstein spoke, his tears and desperate whispers, gave every proof that, at least in his mind, he had done these things. He told of his revulsion at his accomplishment, how he had abandoned the creature, hoping it would die, and how the creature had, in revenge, killed his brother William and caused his family's ward Justine to be blamed for the crime.

"But why did you not intervene in Justine's trial?"

"No one should have believed me."

"Yet I am to believe you now?"

Frankenstein's voice was choked. "You have seen the brute. You surmised, from your studies, that these things are possible. Lives are at stake. I come to you in remorse and penitence, asking only that you keep this secret." He fell to his knees, threw his head into her lap, and clutched at the sides of her gown.

Frankenstein was wholly mistaken in what she knew; he was a man who did not see things clearly. Yet if his story were true, it was no wonder that his judgment was disordered. And here he lay, trembling against her, seeking forgiveness. She prided herself on her Christian charity. No man had ever come to her in such need.

She tried to keep her senses. "Certainly the creature I saw was frightening, but to my eyes he appeared more wretched than menacing."

Frankenstein lifted his head. "Here I must warn you—his wretchedness is mere mask. Do not let your sympathy for him cause you ever to trust his nature. He is the vilest creature that has ever walked this earth. He has no soul."

"Why then not invoke the authorities, catch him, and bring him to justice?"

"He cannot be so easily caught. He is inhumanly strong, resourceful, and intelligent. If you should ever be so unlucky as to speak with him, I warn you not to listen to what he says, for he is immensely articulate and satanically persuasive."

"All the more reason to see him apprehended!"

"I am convinced that he can be dealt with only by myself." Frankenstein's eyes pleaded with her. "Miss Bennet—Mary—you must understand. He is in some ways my son. I gave him life. His mind is fixed on me."

"And, it seems, yours on him."

Frankenstein looked surprised. "Do you wonder that is so?"

"Why does he follow you? Does he intend you harm?"

"He has vowed to glut the maw of death with my remaining loved ones, unless I make him happy." He rested his head again in her lap.

Mary was touched, scandalized, and in some obscure way aroused. She felt his trembling body, instinct with life. Tentatively, she rested her hand on his head. She stroked his hair. He was weeping. She realized that he was a physical being, a living animal, that would eventually, too soon, die. And all that was true of him was true of herself. How strange, frightening, and sad. Yet in this moment she felt herself wonderfully alive.

"I'll keep your secret," she said.

He hugged her skirts. In the candle's light, she noted the way his thick, dark hair curled away from his brow.

"I cannot tell you," he said softly, "what a relief it is to share my burden with another soul, and to have her accept me. I have been so completely alone. I cannot thank you enough."

He rose, kissed her forehead, and was gone.

Mary paced her room, trying to grasp what had just happened. A man who had conquered death? A monster created from corpses? Such things did not happen, certainly not in her world, not even in the world of the novels she read. She climbed into bed and tried to sleep, but could not. The creature had vowed to kill all whom Frankenstein loved. Mary remembered the weight of his head upon her lap.

The room felt stiflingly hot. She got up, stripped off her nightgown, and climbed back between the sheets, where she lay naked, listening to the rain on the window.

KITTY'S FEVER WORSENED in the night, and before dawn Darcy sent to Lambton for the doctor. Lizzy dispatched an urgent letter to Mr. and Mrs. Bennet, and the sisters sat by Kitty's bedside through the morning, changing cold compresses from her brow while Kitty labored to breathe. When Mary left the sick room, Frankenstein approached her. His desperation of the previous night was gone. "How fares your sister?"

"I fear she is gravely ill."

"She is in some danger?"

Mary could only nod.

He touched her shoulder, lowered his voice. "I will pray for her, Miss Bennet. I cannot thank you enough for the sympathy you showed me last night. I have never told anyone—"

Just then Clerval approached them. He greeted Mary, inquired after Kitty's condition, then suggested to Frankenstein that they return to their hotel in Matlock rather than add any burden to the household and family. Frankenstein agreed. Before Mary could say another word to him in private, the visitors were gone.

Doctor Phillips arrived soon after Clerval and Frankenstein left. He measured Kitty's pulse, felt her forehead, examined her urine. He administered some medicines, and came away shaking his head. Should the fever continue, he said, they must bleed her.

Given how much thought she had spent on Frankenstein through the night, and how little she had devoted to Kitty, Mary's conscience tormented her. She spent the day in her sister's room. That night, after Jane had retired and Lizzy fallen asleep in her chair, she still sat up, holding Kitty's fevered hand. She had matters to consider. Was Kitty indeed with child, and if so, should she tell the doctor? Yet even as she sat by Kitty's bedside, Mary's mind cast back to the feeling of Frankenstein's lips on her forehead.

In the middle of the night, Kitty woke, bringing Mary from her doze. Kitty tried to lift her head from the pillow, but could not. "Mary," she whispered. "You must send for Robert. We must be married immediately."

Mary looked across the room at Lizzy. She was still asleep.

"Promise me," Kitty said. Her eyes were large and dark.

"I promise," Mary said.

"Prepare my wedding dress," Kitty said. "But don't tell Lizzy."

Lizzy awoke then. She came to the bedside and felt Kitty's forehead. "She's burning up. Get Dr. Phillips."

Mary sought out the doctor, and then, while he went to Kitty's room, pondered what to do. Kitty clearly was not in her right mind. Her request ran contrary to both sense and propriety. If Mary sent one of the footmen to Matlock for Robert Piggot, even if she swore her messenger to silence, the matter would soon be the talk of the servants, and probably the town.

It was the sort of dilemma that Mary would have had no trouble settling, to everyone's moral edification, when she was sixteen. She hurried to her room and took out paper and pen:

> *I write to inform you that one you love, residing at Pemberley House,*
> *is gravely ill. She urgently requests your presence. Simple human kindness,*
> *which from her description of you I do not doubt you possess, let alone the*
> *duty incumbent upon you owing to the compact that you have made with*
> *her through your actions, assure me that we shall see you here before the*
> *night is through.*
>
> *Miss Mary Bennet*

She sealed the letter and sought out one of the footmen, whom she dispatched immediately with the instruction to put the letter into the hand of Robert Piggot, son of the Matlock butcher.

Dr. Phillips bled Kitty, with no improvement. She did not regain consciousness through the night. Mary waited. The footman returned, alone, at six in the morning. He assured Mary that he had ridden to the Piggot home and given the letter directly to Robert. Mary thanked him.

Robert did not come. At eight in the morning Darcy sent for the priest. At nine-thirty Kitty died.

ON THE EVENING of the day of Kitty's passing, Mr. and Mrs. Bennet arrived, and a day later Lydia and Wickham—it was the first time Darcy had allowed Wickham to cross the threshold of Pemberley since they had become brothers by marriage. In the midst of her mourning family, Mary felt lost. Jane and Lizzy supported each other in their grief. Darcy and Bingley exchanged quiet, sober conversation. Wickham and Lydia, who had grown stout with her three children, could not pass a word between them without bickering, but in their folly they were united.

Mrs. Bennet was beyond consoling, and the volume and intensity of her mourning was exceeded only by the degree to which she sought to control every detail of Kitty's funeral. There ensued a debate over where Kitty should be buried. When it was pointed out that their cousin Mr. Collins would eventually inherit the house back in Hertfordshire, Mrs. Bennet fell into despair: who, when she was gone, would tend to her poor Kitty's grave? Mr. Bennet suggested that Kitty be laid to rest in the churchyard at Lambton, a short distance from Pemberley, where she might also be visited by Jane and Bingley. But when Mr. Darcy offered the family vault at Pemberley, the matter was quickly settled to the satisfaction of both tender hearts and vanity.

Though it was no surprise, it was still a burden for Mary to witness that even in the gravest passage of their lives, her sisters and parents showed themselves to be exactly what they were. And yet, paradoxically, this did not harden her heart toward them. The family was together as they had not been for many years, and she realized that they should never be in the future except on the occasion of further losses. Her father was grayer and quieter than she had ever seen him, and on the day of the funeral even her mother put aside her sobbing and exclamations long enough to show a face of profound grief, and a burden of age that Mary had never before noticed.

The night after Kitty was laid to rest, Mary sat up late with Jane and Lizzy and Lydia. They drank Madeira and Lydia told many silly stories of the days she and Kitty had spent in flirtations with the regiment. Mary climbed into her bed late that night, her head swimming with wine, laughter, and tears. She lay awake, the moonlight shining on the counterpane through the opened window, air carrying the smell of fresh earth and the rustle of trees above the lake. She drifted into a dreamless sleep. At some point in the night she was half awakened by the barking of the dogs in the kennel. But consciousness soon faded and she fell away.

In the morning it was discovered that the vault had been broken into and Kitty's body stolen from her grave.

MARY TOLD THE stablemaster that Mrs. Bennet had asked her to go with Darcy to the apothecary in Lambton, and had him prepare the gig. Then, while the house was in turmoil and Mrs. Bennet being attended by the rest of the family, she drove off to Matlock. The master had given her the best horse in Darcy's stable; the creature was equable and fleet, and despite her inexperience driving, Mary was able to reach Matlock in an hour.

All the time, despite the splendid summer morning and the picturesque prospects which the valley of the Derwent continually unfolded before her, she could not keep her mind from whirling through a series of distressing images—among them the sight of Frankenstein's creature as she had seen him in the woods.

When she reached Matlock she hurried to the Old Bath Hotel and inquired after Frankenstein. The porter told her that he had not seen Mr. Frankenstein since dinner the previous evening, but that Mr. Clerval had told him that morning that the gentlemen would leave Matlock later that day. She left a note asking Frankenstein, should he return, to meet her at the inn, then went to the butcher shop.

Mary had been there once before, with Lizzy, some years earlier. The shop was busy with servants purchasing joints of mutton and ham for the evening meal. Behind the counter, Mr. Piggot senior was busy at his cutting board, but helping one of the women with a package was a tall young man with thick brown curls and green eyes. He flirted with the house servant as he shouldered her purchase, wrapped in brown paper, onto her cart.

On the way back into the shop, he spotted Mary standing unattended. He studied her for a moment before approaching. "May I help you, miss?"

"I believe you knew my sister."

His grin vanished. "You are Miss Mary Bennet."

"I am."

The young man studied his boots. "I am so sorry what happened to Miss Catherine."

Not so sorry as to bring you to her bedside before she died, Mary thought. She bit back a reproach and said, "We did not see you at the service. I thought perhaps the nature of your relationship might have encouraged you to grieve in private, at her graveside. Have you been there?"

He looked even more uncomfortable. "No. I had to work. My father—"

Mary had seen enough already to take his depth. He was not a man to defile a grave, in grief or otherwise. The distance between this small-town Lothario—handsome, careless, insensitive—and the hero Kitty had praised, only deepened Mary's compassion for her lost sister. How desperate she must have been. How pathetic.

94

As Robert Piggot continued to stumble through his explanation, Mary turned and departed.

She went back to the inn where she had left the gig. The barkeep led her into a small ladies' parlor separated from the taproom by a glass partition. She ordered tea, and through a latticed window watched the people come and go in the street and courtyard, the draymen with their Shires and carts, the passengers waiting for the next van to Manchester, and inside, the idlers sitting at tables with pints of ale. In the sunlit street a young bootblack accosted travelers, most of whom ignored him. All of these people completely unaware of Mary or her lost sister. Mary ought to be back with their mother, though the thought turned her heart cold. How could Kitty have left her alone? She felt herself near despair.

She was watching through the window as two draymen struggled to load a large square trunk onto their cart when the man directing them came from around the team of horses, and she saw it was Victor Frankenstein. She rose immediately and went out into the inn yard. She was at his shoulder before he noticed her. "Miss Bennet!"

"Mr. Frankenstein. I am so glad that I found you. I feared that you had already left Matlock. May we speak somewhere in private?"

He looked momentarily discommoded. "Yes, of course," he said. To the draymen he said, "When you've finished loading my equipment, wait here."

"This is not a good place to converse," Frankenstein told her. "I saw a churchyard nearby. Let us retire there."

He walked Mary down the street to the St. Giles Churchyard. They entered the rectory garden. In the distance, beams of afternoon sunlight shone through a cathedral of clouds above the Heights of Abraham. "Do you know what has happened?" she asked.

"I have heard reports, quite awful, of the death of your sister. I intended to write you, conveying my condolences, at my earliest opportunity. You have my deepest sympathies."

"Your creature! That monster you created—"

"I asked you to keep him a secret."

"I have kept my promise—so far. But it has stolen Kitty's body."

He stood there, hands behind his back, clear eyes fixed on her. "You find me astonished. What draws you to this extraordinary conclusion?"

She was hurt by his diffidence. Was this the same man who had wept in her bedroom? "Who else might do such a thing?"

"But why? This creature's enmity is reserved for me alone. Others feel its ire only to the extent that they are dear to me."

"You came to plead with me that night because you feared I knew he was responsible for defiling that town girl's grave. He was watching Kitty and me in the forest. Surely this is no coincidence."

"If, indeed, the creature has stolen your sister's body, it can be for no reason I can fathom, or that any God-fearing person ought to pursue. You know I am determined to see this monster banished from the world of men. You may rest assured that I will not cease until I have seen this accomplished." He touched a strand of ivy growing up the side of the garden wall, and plucked off a green leaf, which he twirled in his fingers. In a softer tone, he said, "It is best for you and your family to turn your thoughts to other matters."

She did not understand. She knew him to be a man of sensibility, to have a heart capable of feeling. His denials opened a possibility that she had tried to keep herself from considering.

"Sir, I am not satisfied. It seems to me that you are keeping something from me. You told me of the great grief you felt at the loss of your mother, how it moved you to your researches. If, as you say, you have uncovered the secret of life, might you—have you taken it upon yourself to restore Kitty? Perhaps a fear of failure, or of the horror that many would feel at your trespassing against God's will, underlies your secrecy. If so, please do not keep the truth from me. I am not a girl."

He let the leaf fall from his fingers. He took her shoulders, and looked directly into her eyes. "I am sorry, Mary. To restore your sister is not in my power. The soulless creature I brought to life bears no relation to the man from whose body I fashioned him. Your sister has gone on to her reward. Nothing—nothing I can do would bring her back."

"So you know nothing about the theft of her corpse?"

"On that score, I can offer no consolation to you or your family."

"My mother, my father—they are inconsolable."

"Then they must content themselves with memories of your sister as she lived. As I must do with my dear, lost brother William, and the traduced and dishonored Justine. Come, let us go back to the inn."

Mary burst into tears. He held her to him and she wept on his breast. Eventually she gathered herself and allowed him to take her arm, and they slowly walked back down to the main street of Matlock and the inn. She knew that when they reached it, Frankenstein would go. The warmth of his hand on hers almost made her beg him to stay, or better still, to take her with him.

They came to the busy courtyard. The dray stood off to the side, and the cartmen were in the taproom. Frankenstein, agitated, upbraided them. "I thought I told you to keep those trunks out of the sun."

The older of the two men put down his pint and stood, "Sorry, Gov'nor. We'll see to it directly."

"Do so now."

As Frankenstein spoke the evening coach drew up before the inn and prepared for departure. "You and Mr. Clerval leave today?" Mary asked.

"Yes. As soon as Henry arrives from the Old Bath, we take the coach to the Lake District. And thence to Scotland."

"They say it is very beautiful there."

"I am afraid that its beauty will be lost on me. I carry the burden of my great crime, not to be laid down until I have made things right."

She felt that she would burst if she did not speak her heart to him. "Victor. Will I never see you again?"

He avoided her gaze. "I am afraid, Miss Bennet, that this is unlikely. My mind is set on banishing that vile creature from the world of men. Only then can I hope to return home and marry my betrothed Elizabeth."

Mary looked away from him. A young mother was adjusting her son's collar before putting him on the coach. "Ah, yes. You are affianced. I had almost forgotten."

Frankenstein pressed her hand. "Miss Bennet, you must forgive me the liberties I have taken with you. You have given me more of friendship than I deserve. I wish you to find the companion you seek, and to live your days in happiness. But now, I must go."

"God be with you, Mr. Frankenstein." She twisted her gloved fingers into a knot.

He bowed deeply, and hurried to have a few more words with the draymen. Henry Clerval arrived just as the men climbed onto their cart and drove the baggage away. Clerval, surprised at seeing Mary, greeted her warmly. He expressed his great sorrow at the loss of her sister, and begged her to convey his condolences to the rest of her family. Ten minutes later the two men climbed aboard the coach and it left the inn, disappearing down the Matlock high street.

Mary stood in the inn yard. She did not feel she could bear to go back to Pemberley and face her family, the histrionics of her mother. Instead she reentered the inn and made the barkeep seat her in the ladies' parlor and bring her a glass of port.

THE SUN DECLINED and shadows stretched over the inn yard. The evening papers arrived from Nottingham. The yard boy lit the lamps. Still, Mary would not leave. Outside on the pavements, the bootblack sat in the growing darkness with his arms draped over his knees and head on his breast. She listened to the hoofs of the occasional horse striking the cobbles. The innkeeper was solicitous. When she asked for a second glass, he hesitated, and wondered if he might send for someone from her family to take her home.

"You do not know my family," she said.

"Yes, miss. I only thought—"

"Another port. Then leave me alone."

"Yes, miss." He went away. She was determined to become intoxicated. How many times had she piously warned against young women behaving as she did now? *Virtue is its own reward.* She had an apothegm for every occasion, and had tediously produced them in place of thought. *Show me a liar, and I'll show thee a thief. Marry in haste, repent at leisure. Men should be what they seem.*

She did not fool herself into thinking that her current misbehavior would make any difference. Perhaps Bingley or Darcy had been dispatched to find her in Lambton. Within an hour or two she would return to Pemberley, where her mother would scold her for giving them an anxious evening, and Lizzy would caution her about the risk to her reputation. Lydia might even ask her, not believing it possible, if she'd had an assignation with some man. The loss of Kitty would overshadow Mary's indiscretion, pitiful as it had been. Soon all would be as it had been, except Mary would be alive and Kitty dead. But even that would fade. The shadow of Kitty's death would hang over the family for some time, but she doubted that anything of significance would change.

As she lingered over her glass, she looked up and noticed, in the now empty taproom, a man sitting at the table farthest from the lamps. A huge man, wearing rough clothes, his face hooded and in shadow. On the table in front of him was a tankard of ale and a few coppers. Mary rose, left the parlor for the taproom, and crossed toward him.

He looked up, and the faint light from the ceiling lamp caught his black eyes, sunken beneath heavy brows. He was hideously ugly. "May I sit with you?" she asked. She felt slightly dizzy.

"You may sit where you wish." The voice was deep, but swallowed, unable to project. It was almost a whisper.

Trembling only slightly, she sat. His wrists and hands, resting on the table, stuck out past the ragged sleeves of his coat. His skin was yellowish brown, and the fingernails livid white. He did not move. "You have some business with me?"

"I have the most appalling business." Mary tried to look him in the eyes, but her gaze kept slipping. "I want to know why you defiled my sister's grave, why you have stolen her body, and what you have done with her."

"Better you should ask Victor. Did he not explain all to you?"

"Mr. Frankenstein explained who—what—you are. He did not know what had become of my sister."

The thin lips twitched in a sardonic smile. "Poor Victor. He has got things all topsy-turvy. Victor does not know what I am. He is incapable of knowing, no matter the labors I have undertaken to school him. But he does know what became, and is to become, of your sister." The creature tucked the thick black hair behind his ear, an unconscious gesture that made him seem completely human for the first time. He pulled the hood further forward to hide his face.

"So tell me."

"Which answer do you wish? Who I am, or what happened to your sister?"

"First, tell me what happened to—to Kitty."

"Victor broke into the vault and stole her away. He took the utmost care not to damage her. He washed her fair body in diluted carbolic acid, and replaced her blood with a chemical admixture of his own devising. Folded up, she fit neatly within a cedar trunk sealed with pitch, and is at present being shipped to Scotland. You witnessed her departure from this courtyard an hour ago."

Mary's senses rebelled. She covered her face with her hands. The creature sat silent. Finally, without raising her head, she managed, "Victor warned me that you were a liar. Why should I believe you?"

"You have no reason to believe me."

"*You* took her!"

"Though I would not have scrupled to do so, I did not. Miss Bennet, I do not deny I have an interest in this matter. Victor did as I have told you at my bidding."

"At your bidding? Why?"

"Kitty—or not so much Kitty, as her remains—is to become my wife."

"Your wife! This is insupportable! Monstrous!"

"Monstrous."

With preternatural quickness, his hand flashed out and grabbed Mary's wrist.

Mary thought to call for help, but the bar was empty and she had driven the innkeeper away. Yet his grip was not harsh. His hand was warm, instinct with life. "Look at me," he said. With his other hand he pushed back his hood.

She took a deep breath. She looked.

His noble forehead, high cheekbones, strong chin, and wide-set eyes might have made him handsome, despite the scars and dry yellow skin, were it not for his expression. His ugliness was not a matter of lack of proportion—or rather, the lack of proportion was not in his features. Like his swallowed voice, his face was submerged, as if everything were hidden, revealed only in the eyes, the twitch of a cheek or lip. Every minute motion showed extraordinary animation. Hectic sickliness, but energy. This was a creature who had never learned to associate with civilized company, who had been thrust into adulthood with the passions of a wounded boy. Fear, self-disgust, anger. Desire.

The force of longing and rage in that face made her shrink. "Let me go," she whispered.

He let go her wrist. With bitter satisfaction, he said, "You see. If what I demand is insupportable, that is only because your kind has done nothing to support me. Once, I falsely hoped to meet with beings who, pardoning my outward form, would love me for the excellent qualities which I was capable of bringing forth. I was wrong. More than any starving man on a deserted isle, I am cast away. I have no brother, sister, parents. I have only Victor, who, like so many fathers, recoiled from me the moment I first drew breath. And so, I have commanded him to make of your sister my wife, or he and all he loves will die at my hand."

"No. I cannot believe he would commit this abomination."

"He has no choice. He is my slave."

"His conscience could not support it, even at the cost of his life."

"You give him too much credit. You all do. He does not think. I have not seen him act other than according to impulse for the last three years. That is all I see in any of you."

Mary drew back, trying to make some sense of this horror. Her sister, to be brought to life, only to be given to this fiend. But would it be her sister, or another agitated, hungry thing like this?

She still retained some scraps of skepticism. The creature's manner did not bespeak the isolation which he claimed. "I am astonished at your grasp of language," Mary said. "You could not know so much without teachers."

"Oh, I have had many teachers." The creature's mutter was rueful. "You might say that, since first my eyes opened, mankind has been all my study. I have much yet to learn. There are certain words whose meaning has never been proved to me by experience. For example: *Happy*. Victor is to make me happy. Do you think he can do it?"

Mary thought of Frankenstein. Could he satisfy this creature? "I do not think it is in the power of any other person to make one happy."

"You jest with me. Every creature has its mate, save me. I have none."

She recoiled at his self-pity. Her fear faded. "You put too much upon having a mate."

"Why? You know nothing of what I have endured."

"You think that having a female of your own kind will ensure that she will accept you?" Mary laughed. "Wait until you are rejected, for the most trivial of reasons, by one you believe has been made for you."

A shadow crossed the creature's face. "That will not happen."

"It happens more often than not."

"The female that Victor creates shall find no other mate than me."

"That has never prevented rejection. Or if you should be accepted, then you may truly begin to learn."

"Learn what?"

"You will learn to ask a new question: Which is worse, to be alone, or to be wretchedly mismatched?" Like Lydia and Wickham, Mary thought. Like Collins and his poor wife Charlotte. Like her parents.

The creature's face spasmed with conflicting emotions. His voice gained volume. "Do not sport with me. I am not your toy."

"No. You only seek a toy of your own."

The creature was not, apparently, accustomed to mockery. "You shall not say these things!" He lurched upward, awkwardly, so suddenly that he upended the table. The tankard of beer skidded across the top and spilled on Mary, and she fell back.

At that moment the innkeeper entered the bar room with two other men. They saw the tableau and rushed forward. "Here! Let her be!" he shouted. One of the other men grabbed the creature by the arm. With a roar the creature flung him aside like an old coat. His hood fell back. The men stared in horror at his face. The creature's eyes met Mary's, and with inhuman speed he whirled and ran out the door.

The men gathered themselves together. The one whom the creature had thrown aside had a broken arm. The innkeeper helped Mary to her feet. "Are you all right, miss?"

Mary felt dizzy. Was she all right? What did that mean?

"I believe so," she said.

WHEN MARY RETURNED to Pemberley, late that night, she found the house in an uproar over her absence. Bingley and Darcy both had been to Lambton, and had searched the road and the woods along it throughout the afternoon and evening. Mrs. Bennet had taken to bed with the conviction that she had lost two daughters in a single week. Wickham condemned Mary's poor judgment, Lydia sprang to Mary's defense, and this soon became a row over Wickham's lack of an income and Lydia's mismanagement of their children. Mr. Bennet closed himself up in the library.

Mary told them only that she had been to Matlock. She offered neither explanation nor apology. Around the town the story of her encounter with the strange giant in the inn was spoken of for some time, along with rumors of Robert Piggot the butcher's son and the mystery of Kitty's defiled grave— but as Mary was not a local, and nothing of consequence followed, the talk soon passed away.

That winter, Mary came upon the following story in the Nottingham newspaper.

GHASTLY EVENTS IN SCOTLAND

Our northern correspondent files the following report. In early November, the body of a young foreigner, Mr. Henry Clerval of Geneva, Switzerland, was found upon the beach near the far northern town of Thurso. The body, still warm, bore marks of strangulation. A second foreigner, Mr. Victor Frankstone, was taken into custody, charged with the murder, and held for two months. Upon investigation, the magistrate Mr. Kirwan determined that Mr. Frankstone was in the Orkney Islands at the time of the killing. The accused was released in the custody of his father, and is assumed to have returned to his home on the continent.

A month after the disposition of these matters, a basket, weighted with stones and containing the body of a young woman, washed up in the estuary of the River Thurso. The identity of the woman is unknown, and her murderer undiscovered, but it is speculated that the unfortunate may have died at the hands of the same person or persons who murdered Mr. Clerval. The woman was given Christian burial in the Thurso Presbyterian churchyard. The village has been shaken by these events, and prays God to deliver it from evil.

Oh, Victor. Mary remembered the pressure of his hand, through her dressing gown, upon her thigh. Now he had returned to Switzerland, there, presumably, to marry his Elizabeth. She hoped that he would be more honest with his wife than he had been with her, but the fate of Clerval did not bode well. And the creature still had no mate.

She clipped the newspaper report and slipped it into the drawer of her writing table, where she kept her copy of Samuel Galton's *The Natural History of Birds, Intended for the Amusement and Instruction of Children*, and *The Juvenile Anecdotes* of Priscilla Wakefield, and a Dudley locust made of stone, and a paper fan from the first ball she had ever attended, and a dried wreath of flowers that had been thrown to her, when she was nine years old, from the top of a tree by one of the town boys playing near Meryton common.

After the death of her parents, Mary lived with Lizzy and Darcy at Pemberley for the remainder of her days. Under a pen name, she pursued a career as a writer of philosophical speculations, and sent many letters to the London newspapers. Aunt Mary, as she was called at home, was known for her kindness to William, and to his wife and children. The children teased Mary for her nearsightedness, her books, and her piano. But for a woman whose experience of the world was so slender, and whose soul it seemed had never been touched by any passion, she came at last to be respected for her understanding, her self-possession, and her wise counsel on matters of the heart.

The Motorman's Coat

WHEN THEY opened the shop in Michaelska Street, Frantisek swore it would be the making of them. Veronika protested that the mortgage would leave them in penury, but he countered that a Staré Mêsto address was necessary to attract the clientele that would be interested in—and could afford—the merchandise they would have for sale. Veronika said they would just see tourists, not real monied people.

"Tourists have money, too," Frantisek would explain. He would be wearing a chef's jacket of nucotton twill with a double row of buttons down the front, or perhaps a Victorian cutaway with a red waistcoat, or even a synthetic denim shirt whose shoulders were embroidered with poppies.

"But will they pay a thousand euros for some old pitcher?"

"Tourists especially will pay."

She would only sigh, her dark eyes glistening so much Frantisek wanted to kiss her. Veronika was willowy, with long chestnut hair and a full mouth. "I hope you're right," she said.

Within a year she had left him.

As agent for InVirtu GMBH, Frantisek had established a large network of the most knowledgeable suppliers in Europa and the Caliphate. His shop, situated between a music store and a small restaurant, was full of exotic *objets d'art* dating from before the Die-Off. A seventeenth century astrolabe. Roman glassware. A functioning late-20th century Atari computer. Marlene Dietrich's hand mirror. A perfectly preserved tabla, with drumhead of genuine animal hide. The bicycle that had won the 2012 Tour de France. And

Frantisek's specialty: antique clothing of materials ancient and rare. Despite lanolin-resistant bacteria and the bio-engineered cotton smut, Frantisek could sell you a pre-collapse jacket in 100% genuine wool and put a 1950s sateen handkerchief into its breast pocket.

On the shelf behind the counter stood a photograph of Frantisek and Veronika from nine years before. Frantisek had had the photo done in the style of a century ago, in black and white. It was from early in their marriage, when they still thought they might have a child. The two of them were about to cross Zitna Street, on their way to the Museum Dvořák, leaning into each other, her face in profile smiling at him. A strong wind blew her hair back like a flag. He wore a polo coat; she had on the beautifully tailored redingote he had bought for her the day after they had first slept together.

Now Veronika was gone.

She was not able, she claimed, to handle the stress. She did not care about antiques, and never valued the things that he considered valuable. Frantisek had known that from the beginning of their relationship, but he had told himself that his love for her would overwhelm such matters of temperament. Instead, as their savings dwindled and their customers remained few, Veronika came increasingly to blame him for every thing that dissatisfied her.

As Frantisek dusted the row of vases at the rear of the store, he heard the bell of the shop door chime. He turned to find an attractive Black woman entering.

"Dobry den," the woman said, nodding to him.

"Dobry den," he said.

The woman idly circled the shop. Frantisek tried not to follow her with his eyes, letting her have her time. She possessed the lithe slenderness of a dancer. Had he seen her at the ballet? She stopped to examine a purple ceramic elephant, the product of some child's primary school class a hundred years ago. Beside it a Peruvian bird totem, fired red clay, glazed black, inscribed with intricate lines.

"You have interesting merchandise," she said.

"Thank you."

She turned to face him. "But your shop is not busy." She smiled.

"People do not always recognize quality," Frantisek said.

"Perhaps it would help if you had some item of transcendent interest. Something so rare as to attract even the purblind."

"Perhaps. Such items are hard to come by."

"I have one," the woman said. "A motorman's coat."

Frantisek laughed. "I don't believe you."

The woman laughed as well. Her laugh was light, sexy. "I don't blame you. Nevertheless, it is true."

"A motorman's coat? A Czech coat?"

"Praha Transportation Company, 1911, regulation issue, dark blue wool with solid brass buttons."

How did she know—did she know?—that Frantisek was a descendant of Frantisek Krizik, the engineer who in the 1890s established the second electric tram line in Praha. "Where did you find this marvel?"

Before she could answer, the door chime rang again and in came two young people. In halting Czech the man asked if he could buy some matches. The woman took a glance around the store with indifference and turned back to the front window. "These things are old," she said in English.

Frantisek gave the man a box of Kafkas and turned back to the black woman. "Is this coat for sale?"

"For the correct price."

"I would need to see it."

"Of course."

"Do you have any cigarettes?" the man asked.

Frantisek lost his temper. "Does this look like a tobacconist's shop?"

The man looked confused. He muttered something to his companion that Frantisek could not make out, then turned back. "You're right. It looks like a bunch of crap," he said in English. He took the woman's arm and they walked out the door.

The black woman had observed this calmly. Frantisek colored at her slight smile. "You should not have to deal with such people," she said.

"I have little choice."

"One always has choices," she said. She stuck out her hand. "My name is Carlotta Olembe."

"Frantisek Lanik. I would like to see this coat."

"Meet me tonight, Mala Xavernova 27, at ten PM." The elegant woman touched his wrist with her finely manicured hand. Her fingertips were warm. "Ciao," she said, and left.

Frantisek stood there wondering what had happened. The rest of the afternoon passed uneventfully, and unprofitably. At seven he closed the shop and went to his flat in Vinohrady. He washed, shaved, changed his shirt, and put on a jacket, then walked down to *Dert Dünyası*, a Turkish restaurant in his neighborhood. He wondered whether this coat could be what Carlotta Olembe claimed. He wondered if she had felt the same sexual charge from him that he had gotten from her. He had not thought of a woman in that way since Veronika had left.

Just past nine he took the tram south, then across the Vlatava. The buildings shortened as the tram climbed the bluff above the river. The address Carlotta had given him was in Smíchov, an industrial district in the mid-20th which had been renovated after the fall of the Communists, only to suffer another decline in the disasters that had depopulated the city in the mid-21st. Now it was coming back again. Biological buildings, edible ornamental hedges, brick walkways.

Mala Xavernova was a street of tree houses, underground clubs, new gardens. Frantisek wandered with groups of idlers out for the evening. Most of the people here were Czech, not tourists. Luminescents grew among the branches of fruit trees laden with fragrant blossoms. Number 27 was an organic building that must have been planted thirty years ago, in the aftermath. Between the building's massive buttress roots, beneath a neon sign announcing *Ne Omluva*, stood an open door. Frantisek heard the sounds of jazz as he stepped into the club. Smoke swirled over small tables in the crowded room. He spotted Carlotta sitting on a stool by the bar.

"Ciao," she said, kissing him on the cheek. She wore a tight green acrylic dress, a line of faux pearls dangling from its sleeve. She pushed a liqueur glass toward him. "Have a drink."

Carlotta did not look like a woman who indulged in emotigens. He sipped. Some sort of cocktail. It tasted like peaches and alcohol. "I would like to see this motorman's coat."

"Is that what you would like to see?'

"Among other things. If I can afford them."

"You can afford the coat. I am not able to tell you if you can afford any other indulgences."

"Is it all a matter of sale?"

"No. Some things are not for sale, at any price. Others are free."

If Frantisek had come to understand anything from his relationship to Veronika, it was that nothing came free. He plucked a cherry from the dwarf tree that grew out of the middle of the bar. "So, why do we meet in this club?"

"My flat is just below," Carlotta said, pointing down. "In the roots."

The jazz trio ground to a halt in a flurry of tortured sax triple notes. Polite applause. Frantisek finished his drink. He felt dizzy. "Let's see it."

"So businesslike." But Carlotta rose from the stool and wove through the crowd to a stairwell. He watched her hips swing as he followed her.

They descended into the roots of the building. The stairwell had been engineered out of the taproot, the spiraling treads shiny as mahogany. More luminescents gleamed from the organic surfaces of the walls. They might have been descending into the bowels of some animal. He was impressed with the condition of this building: no sign of the house blight that had destroyed whole neighborhoods as it swept through the city a decade before.

On the first landing, Carlotta took the polished faux-ivory handle of a door and opened it. Her apartment was elegant, sparely furnished. A false window showed a night scene of the Charles Bridge and the castle. In the soft light, beside a sofa, stood a mannequin with a blank silver face, wearing the motorman's coat.

Frantisek slipped past Carlotta and examined it. The sleeve was flawless, the stitching tiny and precise, a typical product of the first machine age. The hand that had formed the drawing-in stitches along the roll line of this collar had moldered in the grave now for close to two centuries. Yet the brass buttons gleamed. The worked buttonholes were in perfect condition. He ran his fingers along the lapel. On a cold night the man who had worn this coat would have been snug and warm, the fresh air on his face as the tram moved noisily through the stone city, on the electric magic carpet of his generation.

Frantisek had a vision of Praha as it had been, of elegant women, proper men, churches filled with believers while artists, con men, and prostitutes crowded the nighttime cafes under yellow incandescent lights.

"How much?" he asked her.

Carlotta named a large number. It was more than he could afford. He would have to borrow against his equity even to consider it. But with this coat in his shop he knew he could reverse his fortunes. It was a gift. An opportunity not to be passed by.

"Would you like to try it on?" she said. "It looks to be made for you."

It was true—the mannequin was precisely as tall as he. He touched the coat. "Go ahead," Carlotta said, putting her hand on his arm. He could smell her faint perfume.

Frantisek removed his own jacket. Carlotta took the coat from the mannequin and held it out for him. He turned his back to her, his face flushed, and slipped his arms into the sleeves. She lifted the coat toward his shoulders, and lowered it onto them. He pulled his shirt collar straight. The coat felt comfortable. Its scent, ancient but not unpleasant, filled his nostrils. He stretched out his right arm, slowly, feeling the weight of it, as if he were exercising tai chi.

"It's perfect," he said.

THE SHOP WAS crowded the day of the showing. He'd had the party catered, another expense, but by now he was falling free and money did not matter. A steady, cold rain dulled the street, but inside candles glowed, light piano music played softly, and the turnout made Frantisek giddy.

Many important people had come. Here was the actress Dusana Melk, and her director Javed Mostaghim. There stood industrialist and notorious collector of antiquities Josef Bondy, sliver-haired, elegant, and slender in black. The monk Vavrin Cerny, down from his Moravian retreat with two of his acolytes in white robes. The mayor herself, Nadezda Markovic.

Carlotta was there, dressed in red, a good color for her. Frantisek had sold his flat, cleaned out his bank account, and taken out a loan from the bank against the accumulated assets of the shop in order to pay her. In return he had the coat, which stood displayed, under a pin spot, on a mannequin in the center of the shop floor.

He had worn it all day the previous day. It was by no means a miracle of tailoring—it had been, after all, only a uniform, one of many manufactured in its time. It was not the coat of a rich man, not even as plush as the camel-hair jacket he had once worn for three minutes. But the destruction of most organic fabrics had left such items as this so rare as to give them an aura. When he wore the motorman's coat, Frantisek felt taller, handsomer, smarter, and more acute. He could discern the future with a knife's edge clarity and plot his course through it as agilely as a dancer.

Of course, Carlotta was the dancer. She approached him. "Are you happy with the turnout?"

"Very. Do you know Josef Bondy?"

"I have made his acquaintance."

"Why didn't you sell the coat to him?"

"You assume he wishes to buy it."

"Why otherwise would he be here?"

"Perhaps because I asked him?"

"You did?"

"Did I?" She touched her slender finger to the tip of his nose, then whirled away toward the table where a servant in a white coat poured champagne.

Frantisek lowered the music, then tapped his fingernail against the side of his champagne flute to get the people's attention. "My friends, and good people of Praha. I welcome you to my humble shop. Thank you for coming out on this wet evening. It does me honor to look around and see so many of the most discerning citizens of our great city.

"The city of Kafka and Rilke and Čapek, Havel and Klima and Kundera, beloved of the mystical Rabbi Loew and the brilliant Mozart and a dozen others too familiar to us all. It is a city of stories and of storytellers. And we tonight are here to continue a story. This coat that brings us together tonight—" he gestured with his glass to the motorman's coat, "—is a piece of history that persists, miraculously undamaged, into our quite different present. It provides us a way to connect with the past, and implies a future, both for me personally, and for all of us. We live in history, which is a tale we create out of events that happen—"

As he spoke, the door of the shop opened and a gust of wind flickered the candles. Through the door came Veronika.

She wore a long black coat over a blue dress cut to the knee. Her hair was loose on one side and pulled back with a comb above the opposite ear. Frantisek, disconcerted, stopped speaking, and a number of people, following his gaze, turned to see who had entered.

"—that story does not end," Frantisek continued. "That story takes what we know is real—our troubles, failures, mishaps—and transforms them into meaning. Our losses are put into a context that gives them purpose and proportion, so that, in the end, we are not overwhelmed, we do not despair, we are reconciled. That story creates joy."

A look of weariness and distaste flashed across Veronika's face, and Frantisek, though he had rehearsed this speech obsessively for weeks, forgot what he was about to say. Temporizing, he held his hand out to toward her. "Ladies and gentlemen, my wife. Herself a creator of stories."

Nervous laughter. Frantisek saw Carlotta, head inclined intimately, speaking softly to Josef Bondy. "And now, please enjoy each other's company, and the rebirth of our city."

The people applauded politely. Frantisek did not want to have to deal with Veronika, and she, thank God, after her abrupt appearance did not seem to want to speak with him. Perhaps she felt ashamed. If so, that would be the first time. She went over to the mannequin and examined the coat—reached out and fingered the lapel. He wanted to rush over and tell her to keep her hands off, but was interrupted by Mrs. Staegers, who complimented him on his redoing the décor of the shop.

By the time Frantisek had extricated himself, Veronika was leaning against a shelf, sipping from a glass of champagne. Frantisek decided to have a word with Mr. Bondy.

"Mr. Bondy, let me say how honored I am to have you visit my shop," Frantisek began.

"Call me Josef."

"Josef. I believe you are acquainted with Ms. Olembe? It was she who discovered this coat."

"Ms. Olembe obtained the coat from me."

Frantisek's hopes for a sale were dashed. He tried not to show it. "Ah. I am surprised that you would part with such a unique item."

"There is a season for everything, and then it passes. I have my eye on new things. This astrolabe, for instance. Did you know that I named my sons Tycho and Johannes?"

"I did not."

"Visionaries are my hobby."

"Well, if you are interested in the astrolabe, I can certify its provenance." And, thought Frantisek, perhaps get back some of the money that ended up in your pocket. Yet why had Bondy used Carlotta as his go-between?

Bondy smiled. "Not just a visionary, but an entrepreneur. You will excuse me?" The collector snagged another flute of wine from the tray of one of the caterers, and turned to speak with a very young woman in gray who was playing with a long beaded necklace than hung to her waist.

As Frantisek mingled with the others, gradually a heaviness settled over him. He could not say exactly what it was. Certainly he could not have asked for a better turnout. The fact that Bondy would not buy the coat, that he was in fact the seller of the coat, was a surprise and a disappointment, but he could not reasonably have counted on the industrialist's interest. Reason, of course, has little to do with desire.

He looked at the motorman's coat. It glowed in the lights, the brass buttons gleaming. It belonged to him now. If he wanted to, he could walk over, remove it from the mannequin and put it on.

Looking around the room of strangers, he realized that Veronika was not there. Had she come simply to discomfit him publicly, then run off without ever exchanging a civil word? He should have noticed if she had left.

Frantisek found her in the back room, bent over an open drawer in his desk. Her bateau neckline exposed her breasts. "What are you doing back here?"

She looked up, startled. She slid the drawer closed.

"I could not stand to watch you abase yourself to those people. Did you ever find my red scarf?"

Frantisek sighed, and sat on the edge of his desk. "Veronika, I'm glad to see you, but as usual, I can't fathom your behavior. You know how hard I have worked. All that happens here tonight is for your benefit as much as mine. So have some wine, meet these people, and please, please, do not hurt me any more."

"Frantisek, I am not hurting you. I'm trying to keep you from making a pompous ass of yourself. You hang your entire future on a coat?"

"This venture will save me. It could save us both, if you loved me."

"I don't need saving."

She had always needed saving, from the moment he first saw her overdosed on theostimulants in the nave of St. Vitus', her pupils as large as saucers as she stared at the stained glass image of the blessing of St. Cyril. How that trembling girl had turned into this judgmental bitch was beyond him. He took her by the hand and pulled her to him, pressed his face to hers and crushed his lips against hers. She did not resist. He felt her nerveless body beneath the sheath of her dress. But, passive as a martyr, she did not kiss him back. He let her go.

"When all this ends, call me," she said. She took her coat and walked out.

It was several minutes before he could make himself go back to the front of the store. The crowd of people had thinned. Carlotta was leaning forward, examining the coat from a few centimeters away, as if she were hypnotized by the weave of the fabric. She looked up as he approached. "Has this gone as well as you hoped?"

"Why didn't you tell me that Bondy was the seller of the coat? What was the purpose of this charade?"

A nearby man stood very still to eavesdrop. "There is no charade," Carlotta said. "Josef sought to sell the coat. I acted as his agent."

"Why did you lead me to believe he might buy it, then?"

"I led you to believe nothing of the sort."

Other people had stopped their conversations to listen, now. In the sudden stillness, Frantisek became aware of the music—Mozart's Piano Sonata in F Major—in the background. "Why did you bring him here, if not to mislead me of his intentions?"

"He came because I asked him to, in order to help your business. Which I begin to regret."

Frantisek took her wine glass from her hand and put it aside. "The deal is off!" he shouted. "You will take it back. Take it—now!" He began to unbutton the coat to remove it from the mannequin. As his fingers fumbled, the brass button came off in his hand. Angrier still, he moved to the next button. Rather than slip through the buttonhole, the brass disk tore through the fabric around it.

People had put on their coats and were leaving. Carlotta stood watching him.

When Frantisek reached up to open the coat and pull the sleeves off the mannequin's arms, the lapel tore like wet tissue paper. When he tugged at a sleeve, it came off in his hands.

He fell back in dismay. As he and the remaining, startled guests stared, the coat began to slide into pieces, disintegrating before him. The facing of the lapel mottled like a time-lapse video of fruit molding. A second button fell to the floor and clittered across the hardwood. The sleeve in his hands fell into shreds that floated in the air like down. In minutes all that was left of the motorman's coat was a heap of fragments on the floor, and some bluish dust on Frantisek's numb fingertips.

The Closet

CARSON CAME out of the closet naked, holding his riding shorts in his right hand and carrying his bike shoes in his left. He dropped the shoes by the side of the bed, pulled on the shorts, got a bike shirt and socks from the dresser.

Over a breakfast of orange juice and toast he read the morning paper, checking out the sports and op-ed pages. No chance for healthcare reform, and good riddance. Yankees beat the Sox to move into first.

He went out to the garage, raised the door and wheeled his bike out around the Escalade. His bicycle was a Jamis Ventura Elite, superlight full carbon composite with Vittoria Zaffiro tires. He pulled on his gloves, settled his shades on the bridge of his nose, strapped on his helmet, mounted, and rode off down the street toward the greenway.

It was early enough that the greenway wasn't too crowded, and he built up some speed listening to the whir of the chain and the hum of the tires on the pavement. The wind whistled past his ears, carrying the sound of birdsong. He got a good rhythm going. As he approached the lake, however, the number of joggers and dog walkers and seniors and young mothers with strollers increased. Most of them oblivious, wandering all over the path, wrapped up in their precious brats, blissfully uncaring that they were sharing the public pavement with anyone.

He used his bell to alert them as he came up from behind. "Passing on your left!" he called out each time. Some of them started comically. Others jerked their dogs' leashes. Some turned their heads to look before moving to the right. The worst were the joggers with iPods plugged into their ears who would not have heard him unless he threw a stick of dynamite as he came up from behind. He sometimes wished for a stick of dynamite.

Near the end of the ride, he was moving along swiftly, his mind on work (he could see already he was going to be late), coming up on a woman with a stroller in the middle of the path. He shifted to the left to go by, but just as he approached he saw the woman had the toddler out of the stroller. She let the kid go and it staggered directly into his path.

"I'm passing!" he shouted. The woman jerked the kid's arm and fell over. Carson sped by. The baby started screaming. In his mirror he watched the woman clutch the bawling kid to her breast. He powered on up the last hill and past that to the street and his condo.

Because of the bike ride he was an hour late getting to the office. But it was Friday, and his boss was a wuss, always begging Carson to go full-time, and Carson didn't give a fuck. He wrote the best copy in the department, always finished his product on time. The clients, whom he alternately charmed or bullied, either loved or were afraid of him. So what if he was only there three days a week? They never complained.

He was writing a TV ad for an erectile dysfunction drug. His angle was different—instead of images of fit, blue-jeans-wearing men in their fifties with good hair, he went for a schlub guy thirty pounds overweight wearing a Giants jersey in a sports bar. On the big screen TV the Giants, losing big to the Eagles, line up for a field goal and miss, wide right. While the rest of the fans in the bar piss and moan, his wife, equally overweight, wearing a matching jersey, tosses off a shot and leans across the table to whisper in Mr. Schlub's ear. They both get up and head for the Ladies. Voice-over: "You never know when that special moment will come."

Halfway through the day he got a call from Clarice. Where was the last alimony check, she wanted to know. The school year started in another week and Ashton needed new clothes.

"You'll get your check," he said.

"I need the money now, not next month."

"I know what you need, and it's not money. And it's not something anybody else can give you."

"Carson, if you don't—"

"I can't talk to you." He hung up.

His stomach churned throughout the afternoon. Clarice, pouring poison into Ashton's ear, always made him feel that way, a complex stew of anxiety, resentment, and rage.

When he went into the break room for coffee, one of the new account girls was there whacking a jar of pickles against the counter. "Can you open this for me?" she asked. Carson had very strong hands; he took the jar and broke the seal on the lid easily.

"Thanks," she said.

"Don't mention it." She had a big nose with a bend in it, but she was still cute.

He felt better the rest of the afternoon. The last half hour of the work day he spent checking his email and watching the clock. As soon as it was five he hit the elevators down to the lot and headed for happy hour at The Hound and Hare.

He had two manhattans and scanned the bar room. The din of people shouting over the loud music pounded into his head. He had a little buzz on and the beginnings of a headache. There was a brunette with large brown eyes and too much eye makeup seated at a table with a dishwater blonde. The blonde got up and went to talk to some guy in a pink polo shirt. Carson carried his drink over to the table.

"I'm Carson," he said.

The brunette had watched him approach, and apparently he passed muster. "Linda."

"I'd like to kiss you, Linda. Would that be okay?"

"Piss off, Carson."

They ended up in the back seat of his Escalade in the corner of the parking deck, beside a concrete pillar with a big purple "3" stenciled on it. The light was dim. They struggled with her panty hose. Her breath smelled of cigarettes, but her breasts were large with dark brown areolas. Afterward she rolled off him and said, "That was good."

"Yeah, it was," Carson said.

"Do you come to the bar often?"

"Pretty often."

She had her purse open and was brushing her hair. "Maybe I'll see you again."

"If you recognize me."

She looked at him funny, and decided to laugh. He walked her to her car, and after she drove away stood at the edge of the deck, looking out over the lights of the city. The sound of traffic, smell of exhaust. Red tail lights on the interstate that swerved through the heart of town. He realized he was angry, that he was always angry. He had been cheated, and he did not understand how or why. Beside his black wing tip was a white pebble. He picked it up and dropped it over the side of the deck, watching as it fell three stories and bounced on the sidewalk. Look out below!

He checked his Rolex. It was 10:23.

He went back to his car and drove home, his stomach grinding against his backbone. From the refrigerator he took a slice of honey baked ham and ate it with a hard roll, standing up at the kitchen counter.

After brushing his teeth, he stripped off his clothes and threw them into the basket just inside the closet door. He stood naked in front of the full length mirror on the door and examined himself. He looked okay. He looked pretty decent for a man of his age.

Still, he was sick of it. He reached up under his chin, split the skin over his Adam's apple, drew open the seam straight down his chest and belly, parting the flesh. Shrugged shoulders out from under muscles, grabbed the thick black hair and pulled the face, grinning grotesquely as it stretched and distorted, up over the smooth head beneath it, and stepped out of the body. The balls had turned inside out; it took a good shake of the male envelope until its genitals flopped and hung straight. Stepping into the closet, Carson hung this body next to the other, the one with the breasts and flawless skin and long, pale blonde hair.

Turn out the light and get into bed.

Some Like It Cold

HER HEROES were Abraham Lincoln and Albert Einstein. Lincoln was out of the question, but with a little work I could look Einsteinesque. I grew a dark mustache, adopted wild graying hair. From wardrobe I requisitioned a pair of wool slacks, a white cotton shirt, a gabardine jacket with narrow lapels. The shoes were my own, my prized possession—genuine leather, Australian copies of mid-twentieth-century brogues, well broken in. The prep-room mirror reflected back a handsomer, taller, younger relative of old Albert, a cross between Einstein and her psychiatrist Dr. Greenson.

The moment-universes surrounding the evening of Saturday, August 4th were so thoroughly burned—tourists, biographers, conspiracy hunters, masturbators—that there was no sense arriving then. Besides, I wanted to get a taste of the old L.A., before the quake. So I selected the Friday evening 18:00 PDT moment-universe.

I materialized in a stall in the men's room at the Santa Monica Municipal Airport. Some aim for deserted places; I like airports, train stations, bus terminals. Lots of strangers if you've missed some detail of costume. Public transport easily available. Crowds to lose oneself in. The portable unit, disguised as an overnight bag, never looks out of place. I stopped in a shop and bought a couple of packs of Luckies. At the Hertz counter I rented a navy blue Plymouth with push-button transmission, threw my canvas camera bag and overnight case into the back and, checking the map, puzzled out the motel address on Wilshire Boulevard that Research had found for me.

The hotel was pink stucco and a red-tile roof, a courtyard pool where a teenaged boy in white T-shirt and D.A. haircut leaned on a cleaning net and flirted with a couple of fifteen-year-old girls. I sat in the shadowed doorway of my room, smoked a Lucky and watched until a big woman in a caftan came out and yelled at the boy to get back to work. The girls giggled.

The early evening I spent driving around. In Santa Monica I saw the pre-tsunami pier, the one she would tell Greenson she was going to visit Saturday night, before she changed her mind and stayed home. I ate at the Dancers; a slab of prime rib, a baked potato the size of a football, a bottle of zinfandel. Afterward I drove my Plymouth along the Miracle Mile. I rolled down the windows and let the warm air wash over me, inspecting the strip joints, theaters, bars and hookers. A number of the women, looking like her in cotton-candy hair and tight dresses, gave me the eye as I cruised by.

I pulled into the lot beside a club called the Third Degree. Over the door a blue neon martini glass swamped a green neon olive in gold neon gin. Inside I ordered a scotch and listened to a trio play jazz. A thin white guy with a goatee strangled his saxophone: somewhere in there might be a melody. These cutting-edge late moderns thought they had the future augured. The future would be cool and atonal, they thought. No squares allowed. They didn't understand that the future, like the present, would be dominated by saps, and the big rush of 2043 would be barbershop quartets.

I sipped scotch. A brutal high, alcohol, like putting your head in a vise. I liked it. I smoked a couple more Luckies, layering a nicotine buzz over the alcohol. I watched couples in the dim corners of booths talk about their pasts and their futures, all those words prelude to going to bed. Back in Brentwood she was spending another sleepless night harassed by calls telling her to leave Bobby Kennedy alone.

A woman with dark Jackie hair, black gloves and a very low-cut dress sat down on the stool next to me. The song expired and there was a smattering of applause. "I hate this modern crap, don't you?" the woman said.

"It's emblematic of the times," I said.

She gave me a look, decided to laugh. "You can have the times."

"I've seen worse," I said.

"You're not American, are you? The accent."

"I was born in Germany."

"Ah. So you've seen bad times?"

I sipped my scotch. "You could say so." Her eyelids were heavy with shadow, eyelashes a centimeter long. Pale pink lipstick made her thin lips look cool; I wondered if they really were. "Let me buy you a drink."

"Thanks." She watched me fumble with the queer, nineteenth-century-style currency. Pyramids with eyes on them, redeemable in silver on demand. I bought her a gin and tonic. "My name's Carol," she told me.

"I am Detlev."

"Detleff? Funny name."

"Not so common, even in Germany."

"So Detleff, what brings you to L.A? You come over the Berlin Wall?"

"I'm here to see a movie star."

She snorted. "Won't find any in here."

"I think you could be a movie star, Carol."

"You're not going to believe this, Detleff, but I've heard that line before."

We flirted through three drinks. She told me she was lonely, I told her I was a stranger. We fell toward a typical liaison of the Penicillin Era: we learned enough about each other (who knew how much of it true?) not to let what we didn't know come between us and what we wanted. Her image of me was compounded of her own fantasies. I didn't have so many illusions. Or maybe mine were larger still, since I knew next to nothing about these people other than what I'd gleaned from images projected on various screens. Images were my job.

I studied the cleavage displayed by Carol's dress, she leaned against my shoulder, and from this we generated a lust we imagined would make up for our losses and leave us blissfully complete in the same place. We would clutch each other's bodies until we were spent, lie holding each other, our souls commingled, the first moment of a perfect marriage that would extend forward from this night in an endless string of equally fulfilling nights. Then we'd part in the morning and never see each other again.

That was the dream. I followed her back to her apartment and we did our best to produce it. Afterward I lay awake thinking of Gabrielle, just after we'd married, sunbathing on the screened beach at Nice. I'd watched her, as had the men who passed by. How much did she want us to look at her? Was there any difference, in her mind, between my regard and theirs?

Just before dawn I left Carol asleep, made my way back to the pink hotel and got some sleep of my own.

Saturday I spent touring pre-quake L.A. I indulged vices I could not indulge in 2043. I smoked many cigarettes. I walked outside in direct sunlight. I bought a copy of the Wilhelm edition of the *I Ching,* printed on real paper. At mid-afternoon I stepped into a diner and ordered a bacon cheeseburger, rare, with lettuce and tomato and a side of fries. My mouth watered as the waitress set it in front of me, but after two bites a wave of nausea overcame me. Hands sticky with blood and mayonnaise, I watched the grease congeal in the corner of the plate.

So far, so good. I was a fan of the dirty pleasures of the twentieth century. Things were so much more complicated then. People walked the streets under the shadow of the bomb. At some almost biological level they knew that they might be vaporized at any second. Their blood vibrated with angst. Even the blond ones. I imagined my ancestors half a world away, in a country they expected momentarily to turn into a radioactive battleground, carrying their burden of guilt through the Englischer Garten. Sober Adenauer, struggling to stitch together half a nation. None of them fat, bored, or decadent.

And Marilyn, the world over, was their goddess. That improbable female body, that infantile voice, that oblivious demeanor.

Architecturally, 1962 Los Angeles was a disappointment. There was the appropriate amount of kitsch, hot dog stands shaped like hot dogs and chiropractors' offices like flying saucers, but the really big skyscrapers that would come down in the quake hadn't been built yet. Maybe some of them wouldn't be built in this timeline anymore, thanks to me. By now my presence had already set this history off down another path from the one of my home. Anything I did toppled dominoes. Perhaps Carol's life would be ruined by the memory of our night of perfect love. Perhaps the cigarettes I bought saved crucial lives. Perhaps the breeze of my Plymouth's passing brought rain to Belgrade, drought to India. For better or worse, who could say?

I killed time into the early evening. By now she was going through the two-hour session with Greenson, trying to shore up her personality against that night's depression.

At nine I took my camera bag and the portable unit and got into the rental car. It was still too early, but I was so keyed up I couldn't sit still. I drove up the Pacific Coast Highway, walked along the beach at Malibu, then turned around and headed back. Sunset Boulevard twisted through the hills. The lights of the houses flickered between trees. In Brentwood I had some trouble finding Carmelina, drove past, then doubled back. Marilyn's house was on Fifth Helena, a short street off Carmelina ending in a cul-de-sac. I parked at the end, slung my bags over my shoulder and walked back.

A brick and stucco wall shielded the house from the street. I circled around through the neighbor's yard, pushed through the bougainvillea and approached from the back. It was a modest hacienda-style ranch, a couple of bedrooms, tile roof. The patio lights were off and the water in the pool lay smooth as dark glass. Lights shone from the end bedroom.

First problem would be to get rid of Eunice Murray, her housekeeper. If what had happened in our history was true in this one, Murray had gone to sleep at mid-evening. I stepped quietly through the back door, found her in her bedroom and shot a sedative into her neck, holding my hand across her mouth against her struggling until she was out.

A long phone cord snaked down the hall from the living room and under the other bedroom door. The door was locked. Outside, I pushed through the shrubs, mucking up my shoes in the soft soil, reached in through the bars over the opened window and pushed aside the blackout curtains. Marilyn sprawled face-down across the bed, right arm dangling off the side, receiver clutched in her hand. I found the unbarred casement window on the adjacent side of the house, broke it open, then climbed inside. Her breathing was deep and irregular. Her skin was clammy. Only the faintest pulse at her neck.

I got my bag, rolled her onto her back, pried back her eyelid and shone a light into her eye. Her pupil barely contracted. I had come late on purpose, but this was not good.

I gave her a shot of apomorphine, lifted her off the bed and shouldered her toward the bathroom. She was surprisingly light—gaunt, even. I could feel her ribs. In the bathroom, full of plaster and junk from the remodelers, I held her over the toilet until she vomited. No food, but some undigested capsules. That would have been a good sign, except she habitually pierced them with a pin so they'd work faster. There was no way of telling how much Nembutal she had in her bloodstream.

I dug my thumb into the crook of her elbow, forcing the tendon. "Wake up, Norma Jeane," I said. "Time to wake up." No reaction.

I took her back to the bed and got the blood filter out of my camera bag. The studio'd had me practicing on indigents hired from the state. I wiped a pharmacy's worth of pill bottles from the flimsy table next to the bed and set up the machine. The shunt slipped easily into the vein in her arm, and I fiddled with the flow until the readout went green. What with one thing and another I had a busy half hour before she was resting in bed, bundled up, feet elevated, asleep but breathing normally, God in his heaven and her blood circulating merrily through the filter like money through my bank account.

I went outside and smoked a cigarette. The stars were out and a breeze had kicked up. On the tile threshold outside the front door words were emblazoned: CURSUM PERFICIO. *I am finishing my journey.* I looked in on the sleeping Mrs. Murray. I went back and sat in the bedroom. The place was a mess. Forests of pill bottles covered every horizontal surface. A stack of Sinatra records sat on the record player. On top: "No One Cares." A loose-leaf binder lay face down on the floor. I picked it up. It was a script for *Something's Got to Give.*

I read through the script. It wasn't very good. About two a.m. she moaned and started to move. I slapped a clarifier patch onto her arm. It wouldn't push the pentobarbital out of her system any faster, but when it began to take hold it would make her feel better.

About three the blood filter beeped. I removed the shunt, sat her up, made her drink a liter of electrolyte. It took her a while to get it all down. She looked at me through fogged eyes. She smelled sour.

"What happened?" she mumbled.

"You took too many pills. You're going to be all right."

I helped her into a robe, then walked her down the hallway and around the living room until she began to take some of the weight herself. At one end of the room hung a couple of lurid Mexican Day of the Dead masks, at the other a framed portrait of Lincoln. When I got tired of facing down the leering ghouls and honest Abe, I took her outside and we marched around the pool. The breeze wrote cat's paws on the surface of the water. After a while she began to come around. She tried to pull away but was weak as a baby. "Let me go," she said.

"You want to stop walking?"

"I want to sleep."

"Keep walking." We circled the pool for another quarter-hour. In the distance I heard sparse traffic on Sunset; nearer the breeze rustled the fan palms. I was sweaty, she was cold.

"Please," she whined. "Let's stop."

I let her down onto a patio chair, went inside, found some coffee and set a pot brewing. I brought out a blanket, wrapped her in it, poked her to keep her awake. Eventually she sat there sipping coffee, holding the cup in both hands to warm them, hair down in her eyes and eyelashes gummed together. She looked exhausted.

"How are you?" I asked.

"Alive. Bad luck." She started to cry. "Cruel, all of them, all those bastards. Oh, Jesus..."

I let her cry for a while. I gave her a handkerchief and she dried her eyes, blew her nose. The most desirable woman in the world. "Who are you?" she asked.

"My name is Detlev Gruber. Call me Det."

"What are you doing here? Where's Mrs. Murray?"

"You don't remember? You sent her home."

She took a sip of coffee, watching me over the rim of the cup.

"I'm here to help you, Marilyn. To rescue you."

"Rescue me?"

"I know how hard things are, how lonely you've been. I knew that you would try to kill yourself."

"I was just trying to get some sleep."

"Do you really think that's all there is to it?"

"Listen, mister, I don't know who you are but I don't need your help and if you don't get out of here pretty soon I'm going to call the police." At the end her voice trailed off pitifully. "I'm sorry," she said.

"Don't be sorry. I'm here to save you from all this."

Hands shaking, she put down the cup. I had never seen a face more vulnerable. She tried to hide it, but her expression was full of need. I felt an urge to protect her that, despite the fact she was a wreck, was pure sex. "I'm cold," she said. "Can we go inside?"

We went inside. We sat in the living room, she on the sofa and me in an uncomfortable Spanish chair, and I told her things about her life that nobody should have known but her. The abortions. The suicide attempts. The Kennedy affairs. More than that, the fear of loneliness, the fear of insanity, the fear of aging. I found myself warming to the role of rescuer. I really did want to help her. She was not able to keep up her hostility in the face of the knowledge that I was telling her the simple truth. Arthur Miller had written how grateful she was every time he'd saved her life, and it looked like that reaction was coming through for me now. She'd always liked being rescued, and the men who rescued her.

The clarifier might have had something to do with it, too. Finally she protested, "How do you know all this?"

"This is going to be the hardest part, Marilyn. I know because I'm from the future. If I had not shown up here, you would have died tonight. It's recorded history."

She laughed. "From the future?"

"Absolutely."

"Right."

"I'm not lying to you, Marilyn. If I didn't care, would you be alive now?"

She pulled the blanket tighter around her. "What does the future want with me?"

"You're the most famous actress of your era. Your death would be a great tragedy, and we want to prevent that."

"What good does this do me? I'm still stuck in the same shit."

"You don't have to be." She tried to look skeptical, but hope was written in every tremor of her body. It was frightening. "I want you to come with me back to the future, Marilyn."

She stared at me. "You must be crazy. I wouldn't know anybody. No friends, no family."

"You have no family. Your mother is in an institution. And where were your friends tonight?"

She put her hand to her head, rubbed her forehead, a gesture so full of intelligence that I had a sudden sense of her as a real person, a grown woman in a lot of trouble. "You don't want to mess with me," she said. "I'm not worth it. I'm nothing but trouble."

"I can cure your trouble. In the future we have ways. No one here really cares for you, Marilyn, no one truly understands you. That dark pit of despair that opens up inside you—we can fill it. We can heal the wounds you've had since you were a little girl, make up for all the neglect you've suffered. We can keep you young forever. We have these powers. It's my job to correct the mistakes of the past, for special people. You're one of them. I have a team of caregivers waiting, a home, emotional support, understanding."

"Yeah. Another institution. I can't take it."

I came over, sat beside her, lowered my voice, looked her in the eyes. Time for the closer. "You know that poem—that Yeats poem?"

"What poem?"

"'Never Give All the Heart.'" Research had made me memorize it. It was one of her favorites.

> "Never give all the heart, for love
> Will hardly seem worth thinking of
> To passionate women if it seem
> Certain, and they never dream
> That it fades out from kiss to kiss;
> For everything that's lovely is
> But a brief, dreamy, kind delight…"

She stopped me. "What about it?" Her voice was edgy.

"Just that life doesn't have to be like the poem, brief. You don't have to suffer. You don't have to give all the heart, and lose."

She sat there, wound in the blanket. Clearly I had touched something in her.

"Think about it," I said. I went outside and smoked another Lucky. When I'd started working for DAA I'd considered this a glamour job. Exotic times, famous people. And I was good at it. A quick study, smart, adaptable. Sincere. I was so good that Gabrielle came to hate me, and left.

After a considerable while Marilyn came outside, the blanket over her head and shoulders like an Indian.

"Well, kemosabe?" I asked.

Despite herself, she smiled. Although the light was dim, the crow's-feet at the corners of her eyes were visible. "If I don't like it, will you bring me back?"

"You'll like it. But if you don't I promise I'll bring you back."

"Okay. What do I have to do?"

"Just pack a few things to take with you—the most important ones."

I waited while she threw some clothes into a suitcase. She took the Lincoln portrait off the wall and put it in on top. I bagged the blood filter and set up the portable unit in the living room.

As I knelt to program it she exclaimed, "Maf!"

"What?"

"My dog!" She looked crushed, as if she were about to collapse. "Who'll take care of Maf?"

"Mrs. Murray will."

"She hates him! I can't trust her." She was disintegrating. "I can't go. This isn't a good idea."

"Where is Maf? We'll take him."

We went out to the guest house. The place stank. The dog, sleeping on an old fur coat, launched himself at me, yapping, as soon as we opened the door. It was one of those inbred over-groomed toy poodles that you want to drop-kick into the next universe. She picked him up, cooed over him, made me get a bag of dog food and his water dish. I gritted my teeth.

In the living room I moved the chair aside and made her stand in the center of the room while I laid the cable in a circle around us to outline the field. She was nervous. I held her hand, she held the dog. "Here we go, Marilyn."

I touched the switch on the case. Marilyn's living room receded from us in all directions, we fell like pebbles into a dark well, and from infinitely far away the transit stage at DAA rushed forward to surround us. The dog growled. Marilyn swayed, put a hand to her head. I held her arm.

From the control booth Scoville and a nurse came down to us. The nurse took Marilyn's other side. "Marilyn, this is a nurse who's going to help you get some rest. And this is Derek Scoville, who's running this operation."

We got her into the suite and the doctors shot her full of metabolic cleansers. I promised her I'd take care of Maf, then pawned the dog off on the staff. I held her hand, smiled reassuringly, sat with her until she went to sleep. Lying there she looked calm, confident. She liked being cared for. Now she had a whole new world waiting to take care of her. She thought.

It was all up to me.

I went to the prep room, showered and switched to street clothes: an onyx Singapore silk shirt, cotton baggies, spex. The weather report said it was a bad UV day: I selected a broad-brimmed hat. I was inspecting my shoes, muddied by the muck from Marilyn's garden, when a summons from Scoville showed in the corner of my spex: meet them in the conference room. Levine and Sally House were there, and the doctor, and Jason Cryer from publicity.

"So, what do you think?" Levine asked me.

"She's in pretty rough shape. Physically she can probably take it, but emotionally she's a wreck."

"Tomorrow we'll inject her with nanorepair devices," the doctor said. "She's probably had some degree of renal damage."

"Christ, have you seen her scars?" Levine said. "How many operations has she had? Did they just take a cleaver to them back then?"

"They took a cleaver first, then an airbrush," Sally said.

"We'll fix the scars," said Cryer. Legend had it that the most dangerous place in Hollywood was between Cryer and a news camera. "And Detlev here will be her protector, right, Det? After all, you saved her life. You're her friend. Her dad. Her lover, if it comes to that."

"Right," I said. I thought about Marilyn, asleep at last. What expectations did she have?

Scoville spoke for the first time. "I want us into production within three weeks. We've got eighty million already invested in this. Sally, you can crank publicity up to full gain. We're going to succeed where all the others have failed. We're going to put the first viable Marilyn on the wire. She may be a wreck, but she wants to be here. Not like Paramount's version."

"That's where we're smart," Cryer said. "We take into account the psychological factors."

I couldn't take much more. After the meeting I rode down to the lobby and checked out of the building. As I approached the front doors I saw a crowd of people had gathered outside in the bright sunlight. Faces slick with factor 400 sunscreen, they shouted and carried picket signs, "END TIME EXPLOITATION," "INFORMATION, NOT PEOPLE," "HANDS OFF THE PAST."

Not one gram of evidence existed that a change in a past moment-universe had ever affected our own time. They were as separate as two sides of a coin. Of course it was true that once you burned a particular universe you could never go back. But with an eternity of moment-universes to exploit, who cared?

The chronological protection fanatics would be better off taking care of the historicals who were coming to litter up the present, the ones who couldn't adjust, or outlasted their momentary celebrity, or turned out not to be as interesting to the present as their sponsors had imagined. A lot of money had been squandered on bad risks. Who really wanted to listen to new compositions by Gershwin? How was Shakespeare even going to understand the twenty-first century, let alone write VR scripts that anybody would want to experience?

I snuck out the side door and caught the metro down at the corner. Rode the train through Hollywood to my arcology. In the newsstand I uploaded the latest trades into my spex, then stopped outside the men's room to get my shoes polished. While the valet worked I smoked the last of my Luckies and checked the news. Jesus, still hotter than a pistol, was the lead on *Variety*. He smiled, new teeth, clean-shaven, homely little Jew, but even through the holo he projected a lethal charisma. That one was making Universal rich. Who would have thought that a religious mystic with an Aramaic accent would become such a talkshow shark, his virtual image the number one teleromantics' dream date? "Jesus' *Laying on of Hands* is the most spiritual experience I've ever had over fiber optic VR," gushed worldwide recording megastar Daphne Overdone.

On *Hollywood Grapevine*, gossip maven Hedley O'Connor reported Elisenbrunnen GMBH, which owned DAA, was unhappy with third-quarter earnings. If Scoville went down, the new boss would pull the plug on all his projects. My contractual responsibilities would then, as they say, be at an end.

"What a mess you made of these shoes, Herr Gruber," the valet muttered in German. I switched off my spex and watched him finish. The arco hired a lot of indigents. It was cheap, and good PR, but the valet was my personal reclamation project. His unruly head of hair danced as he buffed my shoes to a high luster. He looked up at me. "How is that?"

"Looks fine." I fished out a twenty-dollar piece. He watched me with his watery, sad, intelligent eyes. His brown hair was going gray.

"I see you got a mustache, like mine," he said.

"Only for work. For a while I need to look like you, Albert."

I gave him the twenty and went up to my apartment.

The Miracle
of Ivar Avenue

INSIDE THE coat pocket of the dead man, Corcoran found a lenspiece. "Looks like John Doe was a photographer," the pathologist said, gliding his rubber-gloved thumb over the lens. He handed it to Kinlaw.

Kinlaw walked over to the morgue's only window, more to get away from the smell of the autopsy table than to examine the lens. He looked through the lens at the parking lot. The device produced a rectangular frame around a man getting into a 1947 Packard. "This isn't from a camera," Kinlaw said. "It's a cinematographer's monocle."

"A what?'"

"A movie director uses it to frame a scene."

"You think our friend had something to do with the movies?"

Kinlaw thought about it. That morning a couple of sixth graders playing hooky had found the body on Cabrillo Beach. A man about fifty, big, over two hundred pounds, mustache, thick brown hair going gray. Wearing a beat-up tan double-breasted suit, silk shirt, cordovan shoes. Carrying no identification.

Corcoran hummed "Don't Get Around Much Anymore" while he examined the dead man's fingers. "Heavy smoker," he said. He poked in the corpse's nostrils, then opened the man's mouth and shone a light down his throat. "This doesn't look much like a drowning."

Kinlaw turned around. "Why not?"

"A drowning man goes through spasms, clutches at anything within his grasp; if nothing's there he'll usually have marks on his palms from his fingernails. Plus there's no foam in his trachea or nasal cavities."

"Don't you have to check for water in the lungs?"

"I'll cut him open, but that's not definitive anyway. Lots of drowning men don't get water in their lungs. It's the spasms, foam from mucus, and vomiting does them in."

"You're saying this guy was murdered?"

"I'm saying he didn't drown. And he wasn't in the water more than twelve hours."

"Can you get some prints?"

Corcoran looked at the man's hand again. "No problem."

Kinlaw slipped the monocle into his pocket. "Call me when you figure out the cause of death."

Corcoran began unbuttoning the dead man's shirt. "You know, he looks like that director, Sturges."

"Who?"

"Preston Sturges. He was pretty hot stuff a few years back. There was a big article in *Life*. Whoa. Got a major surgical scar here."

Kinlaw looked over Corcoran's shoulder. A long scar ran right to center across the dead man's abdomen. "Gunshot wound?"

Corcoran made a note on his clipboard. "Looks like appendectomy. Probably peritonitis, too. A long time ago—ten, twenty years."

Kinlaw took another look at the dead man. "What makes you think this is Preston Sturges?"

"I'm a fan. Plus, this dame I know pointed him out to me at the fights one Friday night during the war. Didn't you ever see *The Miracle of Morgan's Creek?*"

"We didn't get many movies in the Pacific." He took another look at the dead man's face.

When Corcoran hauled out his chest saw, Kinlaw spared his stomach and returned to the detectives' staff room. He checked missing-persons reports, occasionally stopping to roll the cameraman's monocle back and forth on his desk blotter. There was a sailor two weeks missing from the Long Beach

Naval Shipyard. A Mrs. Potter from Santa Monica had reported her husband missing the previous Thursday.

The swivel chair creaked as he leaned back, steepled his fingers and stared at the wall calendar from Free State Buick pinned up next to his desk. The weekend had brought a new month. Familiar April was a blonde in ski pants standing in front of a lodge in the snowy Sierras. He tore off the page: May's blonde wore white shorts and was climbing a ladder in an orange grove. He tried to remember what he had done over the weekend but it all seemed to dissolve into a series of moments connected only by the level of scotch in the glass by his reading chair. He found a pencil in his center drawer and drew a careful X through Sunday, May 1. Happy May Day. After the revolution they would do away with pinup calendars and anonymous dead men. Weekends would mean something and lives would have purpose.

An hour later the report came from Corcoran: there was no water in the man's lungs. Probable cause of death: carbon monoxide poisoning. But bruises on his ankles suggested he'd had weights tied to them.

There was no answer at Mrs. Potter's home. Kinlaw dug out the L.A. phone book. *Sturges, Preston* was listed at 1917 Ivar Avenue. Probably where Ivar meandered into the Hollywood hills. A nice neighborhood, but nothing compared to Beverly Hills. Kinlaw dialed the number. A man answered the phone. "Yes?"

"I'd like to speak to Mr. Preston Sturges," Kinlaw said.

"May I ask who is calling, please?" The man had the trace of an accent; Kinlaw couldn't place it.

"This is Detective Lemoyne Kinlaw from the Los Angeles Police Department."

"Just a minute."

There was a long wait. Kinlaw watched the smoke curling up from Sapienza's cigarette in the tray on the adjoining desk. An inch of ash clung to the end. He was about to give up when another man's voice came onto the line.

"Detective Kinlaw. How may I help you?" The voice was a light baritone with some sort of high class accent.

"You're Preston Sturges?"

"Last time I checked the mirror, I was."

"Mr. Sturges, the body of a man answering your description was found this morning washed up on the beach at San Pedro."

There was a long pause. "How grotesque."

"Yes, sir. I'm calling to see whether you are all right."

"As you can hear, I'm perfectly fine."

"Right," Kinlaw said. "Do you by any chance have a boat moored down in San Pedro?"

"I have a sailboat harbored in a marina there. But I didn't wash up on any beach last night, did I?"

"Yes, sir. Assuming you're Preston Sturges."

The man paused again. Kinlaw got ready for the explosion. Instead, Sturges said calmly, "I'm not going to be able to convince you who I am over the phone, right?"

"No, you're not."

"I'll tell you what. Come by the Players around eight tonight. You can put your finger through the wounds in my hands and feet. You'll find out I'm very much alive."

"I'll be there."

As soon as he hung up Kinlaw decided he must have been a lunatic to listen to Corcoran and his dames. He was just going to waste a day's pay on pricey drinks in a restaurant he couldn't afford. Then again, though Hollywood people kept funny hours, as he well knew from his marriage to Emily, what was a big time director doing home in the middle of the day?

He spent the rest of the afternoon following up on missing persons. The sailor from Long Beach, it turned out, had no ring finger on his left hand. He finally got through to Mrs. Potter and discovered that Mr. Potter had turned up Sunday night after a drunken weekend in Palm Springs. He talked to Sapienza about recent mob activity and asked a snitch named Bunny Witcover to keep his ears open.

At four-thirty, Kinlaw called the morgue. "Corcoran, do you remember when you saw that article? The one about the director?"

"I don't know. It was an old issue, at the dentist's office."

"Great." Kinlaw checked out of the office and headed down to the public library.

It was a Monday and the place was not busy. The mural that surrounded the rotunda, jam-packed with padres, Indians, Indian babies, gold miners, sheep, a mule, dancing senoritas, conquistadors, ships and flags, was busier than the room itself.

A librarian showed him to an index: the January 7, 1946 issue of *Life* listed a feature on Preston Sturges beginning on page 85. Kinlaw rummaged through the heaps of old magazines and finally tracked it down. He flipped to page 85 and sat there, hand resting on the large photograph. The man in the photograph, reclining on a sound stage, wearing a rumpled tan suit, was a dead ringer for the man lying on Corcoran's slab in the morgue.

KINLAW'S APARTMENT STOOD on West Marathon at North Manhattan Place. The building, a four-story reinforced concrete box, had been considered a futuristic landmark when it was constructed in 1927, but its earnest European grimness, the regularity and density of the kid's-block structure, made it seem more like a penitentiary than a work of art. Kinlaw pulled the mail out of his box: an electric bill, a flyer from the PBA, and a letter from Emily. He unlocked the door to his apartment and, standing in the entry, tore open the envelope.

It was just a note, conversational, guarded. Her brother was out of the army. She was working for Metro on the makeup for a new Dana Andrews movie. And oh, by the way, did he know what happened to the photo album with all the pictures of Lucy? She didn't have a single one.

Kinlaw dropped the note on the coffee table, took off his jacket and got the watering can, sprayer and plant food. First he sprayed the hanging fern in front of the kitchen window, then moved through the plants in the living room: the African violets, ficus and four varieties of coleus. Emily had never cared for plants, but he could tell she liked it that he did. It reassured her, told her something about his character that was not evident from looking at him. On the balcony he fed the big rhododendron and the planter full of day lilies. Then he put the sprayer back under the kitchen sink, poured himself a drink, and sat in the living room. He watched the late afternoon sun throw triangular shadows against the wall.

The *Life* article had painted Sturges as an eccentric genius, a man whose life had been a series of lucky accidents. His mother, a Europe-traipsing culture vulture, had been Isadora Duncan's best friend, his stepfather a prominent Chicago businessman. After their divorce Sturges' mother had dragged her son from opera in Bayreuth to dance recital in Vienna to private school in Paris. He came back to the U.S. and spent the twenties trying to make a go of it in her cosmetics business. In 1928 he almost died from a burst appendix; while recovering he wrote his first play; his *Strictly Dishonorable* was a smash Broadway hit in 1929. By the early thirties he had squandered the play's earnings and come to Hollywood, where he became Paramount's top screenwriter, and then the first writer-director of sound pictures. In four years he made eight movies, several of them big hits, before he quit to start a new film company with millionaire Howard Hughes. Besides writing and directing, Sturges owned an engineering company that manufactured diesel engines, and the Players, one of the most famous restaurants in the city.

Kinlaw noted the ruptured appendix, but there was little to set off his instincts except a passing reference to Sturges being "one of the most controversial figures in Hollywood." And the closing line of the article: "As for himself, he contemplates death constantly and finds it a soothing subject."

He fell asleep in his chair, woke up with his heart racing and his neck sweaty. It was seven o'clock. He washed and shaved, then put on a clean shirt.

The Players was an eccentric three-story building on the side of a hill at 8225 Sunset Boulevard, across Marmont Lane from the neo-gothic Chateau Marmont hotel. Above the ground level entrance a big neon sign spelled out "The Players" in easy script. At the bottom level drive-in girls in green caps and jumpers waited on you in your car. Kinlaw had never been upstairs in the formal rooms. It was growing dark when he turned off Sunset onto Marmont and pulled his Hudson up the hill to the terrace-level lot. An attendant in a white coat with his name stitched in green on the pocket took the car.

Kinlaw loitered outside and finished his cigarette while he admired the lights of the houses spread across the hillside above the restaurant. Kinlaw would never live in a house like those. There was a wall between some people and some ways of life. The twenty-four-year-old leftie he had been in 1938 would have called it money that kept him from affording such a home, and class that kept the people up there from wanting somebody like him for a neighbor, and principle that kept him from wanting to live there. But the thirty-five-year-old cop he was now knew it was something other than class, or money, or principle. It was something inside you. Maybe it was character. Maybe it was luck.

Kinlaw laughed. You ought to be able to tell the difference between luck and character, for pity's sake. He ground out the butt in the lot and went inside.

At the dimly lit bar on the second floor he ordered a gin and tonic and inspected the room. The place was mostly empty. At one of the tables Kinlaw watched a man and a woman whisper at each other as they peered around the room, hoping, no doubt, to catch a glimpse of Van Johnson or Lisabeth Scott. The man wore a white shirt with big collar and a white Panama hat with a pink hat band, the woman a yellow print dress. On the table they held two prudent drinks neatly in the center of prudent cocktail napkins, beside them a map of Beverly Hills folded open with bright red stars to indicate the homes of the famous. A couple of spaces down the bar a man was trying to pick up a blonde doing her best Lana Turner. She was mostly ignoring him but the man didn't seem to mind.

"So what do you think will happen in the next ten years?" he asked her.

"I expect I'll get some better parts. Eventually I want at least second leads."

"And you'll deserve them. But what if the Communists invade?"

"Communists schmomunists. That's the bunk."

"You're very prescient. The state department should hire you."

This was some of the more original pickup talk Kinlaw had ever heard. The man was a handsome fellow with an honest face, but his light brown hair and sideburns were too long. Maybe he was an actor working on some historical pic.

"You know, I think we should discuss the future in more detail. What do you say?"

"I say you should go away. I don't mean to be rude."

"Let me write this down for you, so if you change your mind." The man took a coaster and wrote something on it. He pushed the coaster toward her with his index finger.

Good luck, buddy. Kinlaw scanned the room. Most of the clientele seemed to be tourists. At one end of the room, on the bandstand, a jazz quintet was playing a smoky version of "Stardust." When the bartender came back to ask about a refill, Kinlaw asked him if Sturges was in.

"Not yet. He usually shows up around nine or after."

"Will you point him out to me when he gets here?"

The bartender looked suspicious. "Who are you?"

"Does it matter?"

"You look like you might be from a collection agency."

"I thought this place was a hangout for movie stars."

"You're four years late, pal. Now it's a hangout for bill collectors."

"I'm not after money."

"That's good. Because just between you and me, I don't think Mr. Sturges has much."

"I thought he was one of the richest men in Hollywood."

"Was, past tense."

Kinlaw slid a five dollar bill across the bar. "Do you know what he was doing yesterday afternoon?"

The bartender took the five note, folded it twice and stuck it into the breast pocket of his shirt. "Most of the afternoon he was sitting at that table over there looking for answers in the bottom of a glass of Black Label scotch."

"You're a mighty talkative employee."

"Manager's got us reusing the coasters to try to save a buck." He straightened a glass of swizzle sticks. "I earned the privilege of talking. Mr. Sturges is into me for three hundred in back pay."

Down the end of the bar the blonde left. The man with the sideburns waved at the bartender, who went down to refill his drink.

Kinlaw decided he could afford a second gin. Midway through the third the bartender nodded toward a table on the mezzanine; there was Sturges, looking a lot healthier than that morning's dead man. He saw the bartender gesture and waved Kinlaw over to his table. Sturges stood as Kinlaw approached. He had thick, unkempt brown hair with a gray streak in the front, a square face, jug ears and narrow eyes that would have given him a nasty look were it not for his quirky smile. A big, soft body. His resemblance to the dead man was uncanny. Next to him sat a dark-haired, attractive woman in her late thirties, in a blue silk dress.

"Detective Kinlaw. This is my wife, Louise."

"How do you do."

As Kinlaw was sitting down, the waiter appeared and slid a fresh drink onto the table in front of him.

"You've eaten?" Sturges asked.

"No."

"Robert, a menu for Mr. Kinlaw."

"Mr. Sturges, I'm not sure we need to spend much time on this. Clearly, unless you have a twin, the identification we had was mistaken."

"That's all right. There are more than a few people in Hollywood who will be disappointed it wasn't me."

Louise Sturges watched her husband warily, as if she weren't too sure what he was going to say next, and wanted pretty hard to figure it out.

"When were you last on your boat?"

"Yesterday. On Saturday I went out to Catalina on the *Island Belle* with my friends, Dr. Bertrand Woolford and his wife. We stayed at anchor in a cove there over Saturday night, then sailed back Sunday. We must have got back around one PM. I was back at home by three."

"You were with them, Mrs. Sturges?"

Louise looked from her husband to Kinlaw. "No."

"But you remember Mr. Sturges getting back when he says?"

"No. That is, I wasn't at home when he got there. I—"

"Louise and I haven't been living together for some time," Sturges said.

Kinlaw waited. Louise looked down at her hands. Sturges laughed.

"Come on, Louise, there's nothing for you to be ashamed of. I'm the one who was acting like a fool. Detective Kinlaw, we've been separated for more than a year. The divorce was final last November."

"One of those friendly Hollywood divorces."

"I wouldn't say that. But when I called her this morning, Louise was gracious enough to meet with me." He put his hand on his wife's. "I'm hoping she will give me the chance to prove to her I know what a huge mistake I made."

"Did anyone see you after you returned Sunday afternoon?"

"As I recall, I came by the restaurant and was here for some time. You can talk to Dominique, the bartender."

Eventually the dinner came and they ate. Or Kinlaw and Louise ate; Sturges regaled them with stories about how his mother had given Isadora the scarf that killed her, about his marriage to the heiress Eleanor Post Hutton, about an argument he'd seen between Sam Goldwyn and a Hungarian choreographer, in which he played both parts and put on elaborate accents.

Kinlaw couldn't help but like him. He had a sense of absurdity, and if he had a high opinion of his own genius, he seemed to be able to back it up. Louise watched Sturges affectionately, as if he were her son as much as her ex-husband. In the middle of one of his stories he stopped to glance at her for her reaction, then reached impulsively over to squeeze her hand, after which he launched off into another tale, about the time, at a pool, he boasted he was going to "dive into the water like an arrow," and his secretary said, "Yes, a Pierce-Arrow."

After a while Sturges wound down, and he and Louise left. At the cloakroom Sturges offered to help her on with her jacket, and Kinlaw noticed a moment's skepticism cross Louise's face before she let him. Kinlaw went back over to talk with the bartender.

"I've got a couple more questions."

The bartender shrugged. "Getting late."

"This place won't close for hours."

"It's time for me to go home."

Kinlaw showed him his badge. "Do I have to get official, Dominique?"

Dominique got serious. "Robert heard you talking to Sturges. Why didn't you let on you were a cop? What's this about?"

"Nothing you have to worry about, if you answer my questions." Kinlaw asked him about Sturges' actions the day before.

"I can't tell you about the morning, but the rest is pretty much like he says," Dominique told him. "He came by here about six. He was already drinking, and looked terrible. 'Look at this,' he says to me, waving the L.A. *Times* in my face. They'd panned his new movie. 'The studio dumps me and they still hang this millstone around my neck.' He sat there, ordered dinner but didn't eat anything. Tossing back one scotch after another. His girlfriend must have heard something, she came in and tried to talk to him, but he wouldn't talk."

"His girlfriend?"

"Frances Ramsden, the model. They've been together since he broke with Louise. He just sat there like a stone, and eventually she left. Later, when business began to pick up, he got in his car and drove away. I remember thinking, I hope he doesn't get in a wreck. He was three sheets to the wind, and already had some accidents."

"What time was that?"

"About seven-thirty, eight. I thought that was the last I'd see of him, but then he came back later."

"What time?"

"After midnight. Look, can you tell me what this is about?"

Kinlaw watched him. "Somebody's dead."

"Dead?" Dominique raised an eyebrow.

"I think Sturges might know something. Anything you remember about when he came back? How was he acting?"

"Funny. He comes in and I almost don't recognize him. The place was clearing out then. Instead of the suit he'd had on earlier he was wearing slacks and a sweatshirt, deck shoes. He was completely sober. His eyes were clear, his hands didn't shake—he looked like a new man. They sat there and talked all night."

"They?"

"Mr. Sturges and this other guy he came in with. Good looking, light hair. He had a kind of accent—German, maybe? I figure he must be some Hollywood expatriate—they all used to hang out here—this was little Europe. Mr. Sturges would talk French with them. He loved to show off."

"Had you seen this man before?"

"Never. But Mr. Sturges seemed completely familiar with him. Here's the funny thing—he kept looking around as if he'd never seen the place."

"You just said he'd never been here before."

"Not the German. It was Sturges looked as if he hadn't seen The Players. 'Dominique,' he said to me, 'How have you been?' 'I've been fine,' I said.

"They sat up at Mr. Sturges' table there and talked all night. Sturges was full of energy. The bad review might as well have happened to somebody else. The German guy didn't say much, but he was drinking as hard as Mr. Sturges was earlier. It was like they'd changed places. Mr. Sturges stood him to an ocean of scotch. When we closed up they were still here."

"Have you seen this man since then?"

The bartender looked down the bar. "Didn't you see him? He was right here when you came in, trying to pick up some blonde."

"The guy with the funny haircut?"

"That's the one. Mr. Sturges said to let him run a tab. He must've left. Wonder if he made her."

IT WAS A woozy drive home with nothing to show for the evening except the prospect of a Tuesday morning hangover. He might as well do the thing right: back in the apartment Kinlaw got out the bottle of scotch, poured a glass, and sat in the dark listening to a couple of blues records. Scotch after gin, a deadly combination. After a while he gave up and went to bed. He was almost asleep when the phone rang.

"Hello?"

"Lee? This is Emily."

Her voice was brittle. "Hello," he said. "It's late." He remembered the nights near the end when he'd find her sitting in the kitchen after midnight with the lights out, the tip of her cigarette trembling in the dark.

"Did you get my letter?"

"What letter?"

"Lee, I've been looking for the photo album with the pictures of Lucy," she said. "I can't find it anywhere. Then I realized you must have taken it when you moved out."

"Don't blame me if you can't find it, Emily."

"You know, I used to be impressed by your decency."

"We both figured out I wasn't as strong as you thought I was, didn't we? Let's not stir all that up again."

"I'm not stirring up anything. I just want the photographs."

"All I've got is a wallet photo. I'm lucky I've got a wallet."

Instead of getting mad, Emily said, quietly, "Don't insult me, Lee." Her voice was tired.

"I'm sorry," he said. "I'll look around. I don't have them, though."

"I guess they're lost, then. I'm sorry I woke you." She'd lost the edge of hysteria; she sounded like the girl he'd first met at a Los Angeles Angels game in 1936. It stirred emotions he'd thought were dead, but before he could think what to say she hung up.

It took him another hour to get to sleep.

In the morning he showered, shaved, grabbed some ham and eggs at the Indian Head Diner and headed in to Homicide. The fingerprint report was on his desk. If the dead guy was a mob button man, his prints showed up nowhere in any of their files. Kinlaw spent some time reviewing other missing persons reports. He kept thinking of the look on Louise Sturges' face when her husband held her coat for her. For a moment she looked as if she wasn't sure this was the same man she'd divorced. He wondered why Emily hadn't gotten mad when he'd insulted her over the phone. At one time it would have triggered an hour's argument, rife with accusations. Did people change that much?

He looked up Louise Sturges' number, but when he called he got the housekeeper. Mrs. Sturges wasn't home. Where was she? At the Ivar Avenue house.

So he'd taken her home with him. Sturges must be trying to make up with her in a hurry. Kinlaw called the Ivar number, and Louise answered.

"Mrs. Sturges? This is Lemoyne Kinlaw from the L.A.P.D. I wondered if we might talk."

"Yes?"

"I hoped we might speak in person."

"What's this about?"

"I want to follow up on some things from last night."

She paused. "Preston's gone off to talk to his business manager. Can you come over right now? It's 1917 Ivar."

"I'll be there in a half an hour."

Kinlaw drove out to quiet Ivar Avenue and into the curving drive before 1917. The white-shingled house sat on the side of a hill, looking modest by Hollywood standards. Kinlaw rang the bell and the door was answered by a Filipino houseboy.

Once inside Kinlaw saw that the modesty of the front was deceptive. The houseboy led him to a large room at the back that must have been sixty by thirty feet.

The walls were green and white, the floor dark hardwood. At one end of the room stood a massive pool table and brick inglenook fireplace. At the other end, a step up, surrounded by an iron balustrade, ran a bar upholstered in green leather, complete with a copper topped nightclub table and stools. Shelves crowded with scripts, folders and hundreds of books lined one long wall, and opposite them an expanse of French doors opened onto a kidney-shaped pool surrounded by hibiscus and fruit blossoms, Canary Island pines and ancient firs.

Louise Sturges, seated on a bench covered in pink velveteen, was talking to a towheaded boy of eight or nine. When Kinlaw entered she stood. "Mr. Kinlaw, this is our son, Mon. Mon, why don't you go outside for a while."

The boy raced out through the French doors. Louise wore a plum-colored cotton dress and black flats that did not hide her height. Her thick hair was brushed back over her ears. Poised as a Vogue model, she offered Kinlaw a seat. "Do you have children, Mr. Kinlaw?"

"A daughter."

"Preston very much wanted children, but Mon is the only one we are likely to have. At first I was sad, but after things started to go sour between us I was glad that we didn't have more."

"How sour were things?"

Louise smoothed her skirt. "Sour. Have you found out who that drowned man is?"

"No. I couldn't help but get the impression last night that you were surprised at your husband's behavior."

"He's frequently surprised me."

"Has he been acting strangely?"

"Well, when Preston called me yesterday I was pretty surprised. We haven't had much contact since before our separation. At the end we got so we'd communicate by leaving notes on the banister."

"But that changed?"

She watched him for a moment before answering. "When we met, Preston and I fell very much in love. He swept me off my feet. He was so intent on winning me, so funny. I couldn't imagine a more loving husband. Certainly he was an egotist, and totally involved in his work, but he was also such a charming and attentive man."

"What happened?"

"Well, he started directing, and that consumed all his energies. He would work into the evening at the studio, then spend the night at the Players. At first he wanted me totally involved in his career. He kept me by his side at the sound stage as the film was shot. Some of the crew came to resent me, but Preston didn't care. Eventually I complained, and Preston agreed that I didn't need to be there.

"Maybe that was a mistake. The less I was involved, the less he thought of me. After Mon was born he didn't have much time for us. He stopped seeing me as his wife and more as the mother of his son, then as his housekeeper and cook.

"Some time in there he started having affairs. After a while I couldn't put up with it any more, so I moved out. When I filed for divorce, he seemed relieved."

Kinlaw worried the brim of his hat. He wondered what Sturges' version of the story would be.

"That's the way things were for the last two years," Louise continued. "Then he called me Sunday night. He has to see me, he needs to talk. I thought, he's in trouble; that's the only time he needs me. Back when his deal with Hughes fell through, he showed up at my apartment and slept on my bed, beside me, like a little boy needing comfort. I thought this would just be more of the same. So I met with him Monday morning. He was contrite. He looked more like the man I'd married than he'd seemed for years. He begged me to give him another chance. He realized his mistakes, he said. He's selling the restaurant. He wants to be a father to our son."

"You looked at him last night as if you doubted his sincerity."

"I don't know what to think. It's what I wanted for years, but—he seems so different. He's stopped drinking. He's stopped smoking."

"This may seem like a bizarre suggestion, Mrs. Sturges, but is there any chance this man might not be your husband?"

Louise laughed. "Oh, no—it's Preston all right. No one else has that ego."

Kinlaw laid his hat on the end table. "Okay. Would you mind if I took a look at your garage?"

"The garage? Why?"

"Humor me."

She led him through the kitchen to the attached garage. Inside, a red Austin convertible sat on a wooden disk set into the concrete floor.

"What's this?"

"That's a turntable," Louise said. "Instead of backing up, you can flip this switch and rotate the car so that it's pointing out. Preston loves gadgets. I think this one's the reason he bought this house."

Kinlaw inspected the garage door. It had a rubber flap along the bottom, and would be quite airtight. There was a dark patch on the interior of the door where the car's exhaust would blow, as if the car had been running for some time with the door closed.

They went back into the house. In the back yard the boy, laughing, chased a border collie around the pool. Lucy had wanted a dog. "Let me ask you one more question, and then I'll go. Does your husband have any distinguishing marks on his body?"

"He has a large scar on his abdomen. He had a ruptured appendix when he was a young man. It almost killed him."

"Does the man who's claiming to be your husband have such a scar?"

Louise hesitated, then said, "I wouldn't know."

"If you should find that he doesn't, could you let me know?"

"I'll consider it."

"One last thing. Do you have any object he's held recently—a cup or glass?"

She pointed to the bar. "He had a club soda last night. I think that was the glass."

Kinlaw got out his handkerchief and wrapped the glass in it, put it into his pocket. "We'll see what we will see. I doubt that anything will come of it, Mrs. Sturges. It's probably that he's just come to his senses. Some husbands do that."

"You don't know Preston. He's never been the sensible type."

BACK AT THE office he sent the glass to the lab for prints. A note on his desk told him that while he had been out he'd received a call from someone named Nathan Lautermilk at Paramount.

He placed a call to Lautermilk. After running the gauntlet of the switchboard and Lautermilk's secretary, Kinlaw got him. "Mr. Lautermilk, this is Lee Kinlaw of the L.A.P.D. What can I do for you?"

"Thank you for returning my call, detective. A rumor going around here has it you're investigating the death of Preston Sturges. There's been nothing in the papers about him dying."

"Then he must not be dead."

Lautermilk had no answer. Kinlaw let the silence stretch until it became uncomfortable.

"I don't want to pry into police business, detective, but if Preston was murdered, some folks around here might wonder if they were suspects."

"Including you, Mr. Lautermilk?"

"If I thought you might suspect me, I wouldn't draw attention to myself by calling. I'm an old friend of Preston's. I was assistant to Buddy DeSylva before Preston quit the studio."

"I'll tell you what, Mr. Lautermilk. Suppose I come out there and we have a talk."

Lautermilk tried to put him off, but Kinlaw persisted until he agreed to meet him.

An hour later Kinlaw pulled up to the famous Paramount arch, like the entrance to a Moorish palace. Through the curlicues of the iron gate the sun-washed soundstages glowed like pastel munitions warehouses. The guard had his name and told him where to park.

Lautermilk met him in the long low white building that housed the writers. He had an office on the ground floor, with a view across the lot to the sound stages but close enough so he could keep any recalcitrant writers in line.

Lautermilk seemed to like writers, though, a rare trait among studio executives. He was a short, bald, popeyed man with a Chicago accent and an explosive laugh. He made Kinlaw sit down and offered him a cigarette from a brass box on his desk. Kinlaw took one, and Lautermilk lit it with a lighter fashioned into the shape of a lion's head. The jaws popped open and a flame sprang out of the lion's tongue. "Louie B. Mayer gave it to me," Lautermilk said. "Only thing I ever got from him he didn't take back later." He laughed.

"I'm curious. Can you arrange a screening of one of Preston Sturges's movies?"

"I suppose so." Lautermilk picked up his phone. "Judy, see if you can track down a print of *Miracle of Morgan's Creek* and get it set up to show in one of the screening rooms. Call me when it's ready."

Kinlaw examined the lion lighter. "Did Sturges ever give you anything?"

"Gave me several pains in the neck. Gave the studio a couple of hit movies. On the whole I'd say we got the better of the deal."

"So why is he gone?"

"Buddy DeSylva didn't think he was worth the aggravation. Look what's happened since Sturges left. Give him his head, he goes too far."

"But he makes good movies."

"Granted. But he made some flops, too. And he offended too many people along the way. Didn't give you much credit for having any sense, corrected your grammar, made fun of people's accents and read H.L. Mencken to the cast over lunch. And if you crossed him he would make you remember it later."

"How?"

"Lots of ways. On *The Palm Beach Story* he got irritated with Claudette Colbert quitting right at five every day. Preston liked to work till eight or nine if it was going well, but Colbert was in her late thirties and insisted she was done at five. So he accommodated himself to her. But one morning, in front of all the cast and crew, Preston told her, 'You know, we've got to take your close-ups as early as possible. You look great in the morning, but by five o'clock you're beginning to sag.'"

"So you were glad to see him go."

"I hated to see it, actually. I liked him. He can be the most charming man in Hollywood. But I'd be lying if I didn't tell you that the studios are full of people just waiting to see him slip. Once you start to slip, even the waitresses in the commissary will cut you."

"Maybe there's some who'd like to help him along."

"By the looks of the reactions to his last couple of pictures, they won't need to. *Unfaithfully Yours* might have made money if it hadn't been for the Carole Landis mess. Hard to sell a comedy about a guy killing his wife when the star's girlfriend just committed suicide. But *Beautiful Blonde* is a cast iron bomb. Daryl Zanuck must be tearing his hair out. A lot of people are taking some quiet satisfaction tonight, though they'll cry crocodile tears in public."

"Maybe they won't have to fake it. We found a body washed up on the beach in San Pedro answers to Sturges' description."

Lautermilk did not seem surprised. "No kidding."

"That's why I came out here. I wondered why you'd be calling the L.A.P.D. about some ex-director."

"I heard some talk in the commissary, one of the art directors who has a boat down in San Pedro heard some story. Preston was my friend. There have been rumors that's he's been depressed. Anyone who's seen him in the last six months knows he's been having a hard time. It would be big news around here if he died."

"Well, you can calm down. He's alive and well. I just talked to him last night, in person, at his restaurant."

"I'm glad to hear it."

"So what do you make of this body we found?"

"Maybe you identified it wrong."

"Anybody ever suspect that Sturges had a twin?"

"A thing like that would have come out. He's always talking about his family."

Kinlaw put the cinematographer's monocle on Lautermilk's desk. "We found this in his pocket."

Lautermilk picked it up, examined it, put it down again. "Lots of these toys in Hollywood."

The intercom buzzed and the secretary reported that they could see the film in screening room D at any time. Lautermilk walked with Kinlaw over to another building, up a flight of stairs to a row of screening rooms. They entered a small room with about twenty theater-style seats, several of which had phones on tables next to them. "Have a seat," Lautermilk said. "Would you like a drink?"

Kinlaw was thirsty. "No, thanks."

Lautermilk used the phone next to his seat to call back to the projection booth. "Let her rip, Arthur."

"If you don't mind," he said to Kinlaw, "I'll leave after the first few minutes."

The room went dark. "One more thing, then," Kinlaw said. "All these people you say would like to see Sturges fail. Any of them like to see him dead?"

"I can't tell you what's in people's heads." Lautermilk settled back and lit a cigarette. The movie began to roll.

The Miracle of Morgan's Creek was a frenetic comedy. By twenty minutes in Kinlaw realized the real miracle was that they had gotten it past the Hays Office. A girl gets drunk at a going-away party for soldiers, marries one, gets pregnant, doesn't remember the name of the father. All in one night. She sets her sights on marrying Norval Jones, a local yokel, but the yokel turns out to be so sincere she can't bring herself to do it. Norval tries to get the girl out of trouble. Everything they do only makes the situation worse. Rejection, disgrace, indictment, even suicide are all distinct possibilities. But at the last possible moment a miracle occurs to turn humiliation into triumph.

Kinlaw laughed despite himself, but after the lights came up the movie's sober undertone began to work on him. It looked like a rube comedy but it wasn't. The story mocked the notion of the rosy ending while allowing people who wanted one to have it. It implied a maker who was both a cruel cynic and a dizzy optimist. In Sturges' absurd universe anything could happen at any time, and what people did or said didn't matter at all. Life was a cruel joke with a happy ending.

Blinking in the sunlight, he found his car, rolled down the windows to let out the heat, and drove back to Homicide. When he got back the results of the fingerprint test were on his desk. From the tumbler they had made a good right thumb, index and middle finger. The prints matched the right hand of the dead man exactly.

ALL THAT AFTERNOON Kinlaw burned gas and shoe leather looking for Sturges. Louise had gone back to her apartment in the afternoon; she said she hadn't seen him since he'd left the Ivar Avenue house in the morning. He was not with Frances Ramsden or the Woolfords, nobody had run into him at Fox, the restaurant manager claimed he'd not been in, and a long drive down to the San Pedro marina was fruitless: Sturges' boat rocked empty in its slip and the man in the office claimed he hadn't seen the director since Sunday.

It was early evening and Kinlaw was driving back to Central Homicide when he passed the MGM lot where Emily was working. He wondered if she was still fretting over the photo album. In some ways his problems were simpler than hers; all he had to do was catch the identical twin of a man who didn't have a twin. It had to be a better distraction than Emily's job.

He remembered how, a week after he'd moved out, he'd found himself drunk one Friday night, coming back to the house to sit on the backyard swing and watch the darkened window to their bedroom, wondering whether she was sleeping any better than he. Fed up with her inability to cope, he'd known he didn't want to go inside and take up the pain again, but he could not bring himself to go away either. So he sat on the swing he had hung for Lucy and waited for something to release him. The galvanized chain links were still unrusted; they would last a long time.

A man watching a house, waiting for absolution. The memory sparked a hunch, and he turned around and drove to his apartment. He found the red Austin parked down the block. As he climbed the steps to his floor a shadow pulled back into the corner of the stairwell. Kinlaw drew his gun. "Come on out."

Sturges stepped out of the shadows.

"How long have you been waiting there?"

"Quite a while. You have a very boring apartment building. I like the bougainvillea, though."

Kinlaw waved Sturges ahead of him down the hall. "I bet you're an expert on bougainvillea."

"Yes. Some of the studio executives I've had to work with boast IQs that rival that of the bougainvillea. The common bougainvillea, that is."

Kinlaw holstered the gun, unlocked his apartment door and gestured for Sturges to enter. "Do you have any opinion of the IQ of police detectives?"

"I know little about them."

Sturges stood stiffly in the middle of Kinlaw's living room. He looked at the print on the wall. He walked over to Kinlaw's record player and leafed through the albums.

Kinlaw got the bottle of scotch from the kitchen. Sturges put on Ellington's "Perfume Suite."

"How about a drink?" Kinlaw asked.

"I'd love one. But I can't."

Kinlaw blew the dust out of a tumbler and poured three fingers. "Right. Your wife says you're turning over a new leaf."

"I'm working on the whole forest."

Kinlaw sat down. Sturges kept standing, shifting from foot to foot. "I've been looking for you all afternoon," Kinlaw said.

"I've been driving around."

"Your wife is worried about you. After what she told me about your marriage, I can't figure why."

"Have you ever been married, Detective Kinlaw?"

"Divorced."

"Children?"

"No children."

"I have a son. I've neglected him. But I intend to do better. He's nine. It's not too late, is it? I never saw my own father much past the age of eight. But whenever I needed him he was always there, and I loved him deeply. Don't you think Mon can feel that way about me?"

"I don't know. Seems to me he can't feel that way about a stranger."

Sturges looked at the bottle of scotch. "I could use a drink."

"I saw one of your movies this afternoon. Nathan Lautermilk set it up. *The Miracle of Morgan's Creek*."

"Yes. Everybody seems to like that one. Why I didn't win the Oscar for original screenplay is beyond me."

"Lautermilk said he was worried about you. Rumors are going around that you're dead. Did you ask him to call me?"

"Why would I do that?"

"To find out whether I thought you had anything to do with this dead man."

"Oh, I'm sure Nathan told you all about how he loves me. But where was he when I was fighting Buddy DeSylva every day? *Miracle* made more money than any other Paramount picture that year, after Buddy questioned my every decision making it." He was pacing the room now, his voice rising.

"I thought it was pretty funny."

"Funny? Tell me you didn't laugh until it hurt. No one's got such a performance out of Betty Hutton before or since. But I guess I can't expect a cop to see that."

"At Paramount they're not so impressed with your work since you left."

Sturges stopped pacing. He cradled a blossom from one of Kinlaw's spaths in his palm. "Neither am I, frankly. I've made a lot of bad decisions. I should have sold the Players two years ago. I hope to God I don't croak before I can get on my feet again."

Kinlaw remembered the line from the *Life* profile. He quoted it back at Sturges: "As for himself, he contemplates death constantly and finds it a soothing subject."

Sturges looked at him. He laughed. "What an ass I can be! Only a man who doesn't know what he's talking about could say such a stupid thing."

Could an impostor pick up a cue like that? The Ellington record reached the end of the first side. Kinlaw got up and flipped it over, to "Strange Feeling." A baritone sang the eerie lyric. "I forgot to tell you in the restaurant," Kinlaw said. "That dead man had a nice scar on his belly. Do you have a scar?"

"Yes. I do." When Kinlaw didn't say anything Sturges added, "You want me to show it to you?"

"Yes."

Sturges pulled out his shirt, tugged down his belt and showed Kinlaw his belly. A long scar ran across it from right to center. Kinlaw didn't say anything, and Sturges tucked the shirt in.

"You know we got some fingerprints off that dead man. And a set of yours, too."

Sturges poured himself a scotch, drank it off. He coughed. "I guess police detectives have pretty high IQs after all," he said quietly.

"Not so high that I can figure out what's going on. Why don't you tell me?"

"I'm Preston Sturges."

"So, apparently, was that fellow who washed up on the beach at San Pedro."

"I don't see how that can be possible."

"Neither do I. You want to tell me?"

"I can't."

"Who's the German you've been hanging around with?"

"I don't know any Germans."

Kinlaw sighed. "Okay. So why not just tell me what you're doing here."

Sturges started pacing again. "I want to ask you to let it go. There are some things—some things in life just won't bear too much looking into."

"To a cop, that's not news. But it's not a good enough answer."

"It's the only answer I can give you."

"Then we'll just have to take it up with the district attorney."

"You have no way to connect me up with this dead man."

"Not yet. But you've been acting strangely. And you admit yourself you were on your boat at San Pedro this weekend."

"Detective Kinlaw, I'm asking you. Please let this go. I swear to you I had nothing to do with the death of that man."

"You don't sound entirely convinced yourself."

"He killed himself. Believe me, I'm not indifferent to his pain. He was at the end of his rope. He had what he thought were good reasons, but they were just cowardice and despair."

"You know a lot about him."

"I know all there is to know. I also know that I didn't kill him."

"I'm afraid that's not good enough."

Sturges stopped pacing and faced him. The record had reached the end and the needle was ticking repetitively over the center groove. When Kinlaw got out of his chair to change it, Sturges hit him on the head with the bottle of scotch.

KINLAW CAME AROUND bleeding from a cut behind his ear. It couldn't have been more than a few minutes. He pressed a wet dish towel against it until the bleeding stopped, found his hat and headed downstairs. The air hung hot as the vestibule of hell. Out in the street he climbed into his Hudson and set off up Western Avenue.

The mess with Sturges was a demonstration of what happened when you let yourself think you knew a man's character. Kinlaw had let himself like Sturges, forgetting that mild-mannered wives tested the carving knife out on their husbands and stone-cold killers wept when their cats got worms.

An orange moon in its first quarter hung in the west as Kinlaw followed Sunset toward the Strip. When he reached the Players he parked in the upper lot. Down the end of one row was a red Austin; the hood was still warm. Head still throbbing, he went in to the bar. Dominique was pouring brandy into a couple of glasses; he looked up and saw Kinlaw.

"What's your poison?"

"I'm looking for Sturges."

"Haven't seen him."

"Don't give me that. His car's in the lot."

Dominique set the brandies on a small tray and a waitress took them away. "If he came in, I didn't spot him. If I had, I would have had a thing or two to tell him. Rumor has it he's selling this place."

"Where's his office?"

The bartender pointed to a door, and Kinlaw checked it out. The room was empty; a stack of bills sat on the desk blotter. The one on the top was the third notice from a poultry dealer, for $442.16. PLEASE REMIT IMMEDIATELY was stamped in red across the top. Kinlaw poked around for a few minutes, then went back to the bar. "Have you seen anything of that German since we talked yesterday?"

"No."

Kinlaw remembered something. He went down to where the foreigner and the blonde had been sitting. A stack of cardboard coasters sat next to a glass of swizzle sticks. Kinlaw riffled through the coasters: on the edge of one was written, *Suite 62.*

He went out to the lot and crossed Marmont to the Chateau Marmont. The elegant concrete monstrosity was dramatically floodlit. Up at the top floors, the building was broken into steep roofs with elaborate chimneys and dormers surrounding a pointed central tower. Around it wide terraces with traceried balustrades and striped awnings marked the luxury suites. Kinlaw entered the hotel through a gothic arcade with ribbed vaulting, brick paving and a fountain at the end.

"Six," he told the elevator operator, a wizened man who stared straight ahead as if somewhere inside he was counting off the minutes until the end of his life.

Kinlaw listened at the door to Suite 62. Two men's voices, muffled to the point he could not make out any words. The door was locked.

Back in the tower, opposite the elevator, a tall window looked out over the hotel courtyard. Kinlaw leaned out: the ledge was at least a foot and a half wide. Ten feet to his right were the balustrade and awning of the sixth-floor terrace. He eased himself through the narrow window and carefully down the ledge; though there was a breeze up at this height, he felt his brow slick with sweat. His nose an inch from the masonry, he could hear the traffic on the boulevard below.

He reached the terrace, threw his leg over the rail. The French doors were open and through them he could hear the voices more clearly. One of them was Sturges and the other was the man who'd answered the phone that first afternoon at the Ivar house.

"You've got to help me out of this."

"Got to? Not in my vocabulary, Preston."

"This police detective is measuring me for a noose."

"Only one way out then. I'll fire up my magic suitcase and take us back."

"No."

"Then don't lose it. There's nothing he can do to prove that you aren't you."

"We should never have dumped that body in the water."

"What do I know about disposing of bodies? I'm a talent scout, not an executive producer."

"That's easy for you to say. You won't be here to deal with the consequences."

"If you insist, I'm willing to try an unburned moment-universe. Next time we can bury the body in your basement. But really, I don't want to go through all this rumpus again. My advice is to tough it out."

"And once you leave and I'm in the soup, it will never matter to you."

"Preston, you are lucky I brought you back in the first place. It cost every dollar you made to get the studio to let us command the device. There are no guarantees. Use the creative imagination you're always talking about."

Sturges seemed to sober. "All right. But Kinlaw is looking for you, too. Maybe you ought to leave as soon as you can."

The other man laughed. "And cut short my holiday? That doesn't seem fair."

Sturges sat down. "I'm going to miss you. If it weren't for you I'd be the dead man right now."

"I don't mean to upset you, but in some real sense you are."

"Very funny. I should write a script based on all this."

"The Miracle of Ivar Avenue? Too fantastic, even for you."

"And I don't even know how the story comes out. Back here I'm still up to my ears in debt, and nobody in Hollywood would trust me to direct a wedding rehearsal."

"You are resourceful. You'll figure it out. You've seen the future."

"Which is why I'm back in the past."

"Meanwhile, I have a date tonight. A young woman, they tell me, who bears a striking resemblance to Veronica Lake. Since you couldn't get me to meet the real thing."

"Believe me," Sturges said. "The real thing is nothing but trouble."

"You know how much I enjoy a little trouble."

"Sure. Trouble is fun when you've got the perfect escape hatch. Which I don't have."

While they continued talking, Kinlaw sidled past the wrought iron furniture to the next set of French doors, off the suite's bedroom. He slipped inside. The bedclothes were rumpled and the place smelled of whiskey. A bottle of Paul Jones and a couple of glasses stood on the bedside table along with a glass ash tray filled with butts; one of the glasses was smeared with lipstick. Some of the butts were hand-rolled reefer. On the dresser Kinlaw found a handful of change, a couple of twenties, a hotel key, a list of names:

Jeanne d'Arc		Carole Lombard	X	
Claire Bloom		Germaine Greer	X	
Anne Boleyn	X	Vanessa Redgrave		
Eva Braun	X	Alice Roosevelt	X	
Louise Brooks	X	Christina Rossetti		
Charlotte Buff	X	Anne Rutledge		
Marie Duplessis		George Sand	X	
Veronica Lake				

Brooks had been a hot number when Kinlaw was a kid, everybody knew Hitler's pal Eva, and Alice Roosevelt was old Teddy's aging socialite daughter. But who was Vanessa Redgrave? And how had someone named George gotten himself into this company?

At the foot of the bed lay an open suitcase full of clothes; Kinlaw rifled through it but found nothing that looked magic. Beside the dresser was a companion piece, a much smaller case in matching brown leather. He lifted it. It was much heavier than he'd anticipated. When he shook it there was no hint of anything moving inside. It felt more like a portable radio than a piece of luggage.

He carried it out to the terrace and, while Sturges and the stranger talked, knelt and snapped open the latches. The bottom half held a dull gray metal panel with switches, what looked something like a typewriter keyboard, and a small flat glass screen. In the corner of the screen glowed green figures: 23:27:46 PDT 3 May 1949. The numbers pulsed and advanced as he watched...47...48...49... Some of the typewriter keys had letters, others numbers, and the top row was Greek letters. Folded into the top of the case was a long finger-thick cable, matte gray, made out of some braided material that wasn't metal and wasn't fabric.

"You have never seen anything like it, right?"

It was the stranger. He stood in the door from the living room.

Kinlaw snapped the case shut, picked it up and backed a step away. He reached into his jacket and pulled out his pistol.

The man swayed a little. "You're the detective," he said.

"I am. Where's Sturges?"

"He left. You don't need the gun."

"I'll figure that out myself. Who are you?"

"Detlev Gruber." He held out his hand. "Pleased to meet you."

Kinlaw backed another step.

"What's the matter? Don't tell me this is not the appropriate social gesture for the mid-twentieth. I know better."

On impulse, Kinlaw held the case out over the edge of the terrace, six stories above the courtyard.

"So!" Gruber said. "What is it you say? The plot thickens?"

"Suppose you tell me what's going on here? And you better make it quick; this thing is heavier than it looks."

"All right. Just put down the case. Then I'll tell you everything you want to know."

Kinlaw rested his hip against the balustrade, letting the machine hang from his hand over the edge. He kept his gun trained on Gruber. "What is this thing?"

"You want the truth, or a story you'll believe?"

"Pick one and see if I can tell the difference."

"It's a transmogrifier. A device that can change anyone into anyone else. I can change General MacArthur into President Truman, Shirley Temple into Marilyn Monroe."

"Who's Marilyn Monroe?"

"You will eventually find out."

"So you changed somebody into Preston Sturges?"

Gruber smiled. "Don't be so gullible. That's impossible. That case isn't a transmogrifier, it's a time machine."

"And I bet it will ring when it hits the pavement."

"Not a clock. A machine that lets you travel from the future into the past, and back again."

"This is the truth, or the story?"

"I'm from about a hundred years from now. 2043, to be precise."

"And who was the dead man in San Pedro? Buck Rogers?"

"It was Preston Sturges."

"And the man who was just here pretending to be him?"

"He was not pretending. He's Preston Sturges, too."

"You know, I'm losing my grip on this thing."

"I am chagrined. Once again, the truth fails to convince."

"I think the transmogrifier made more sense."

"Nevertheless. I'm a talent scout. I work for the future equivalent of a film studio, a big company that makes entertainment. In the future, Hollywood is still the heart of the industry."

"That's a nice touch."

"We have time machines in which we go back into the past. The studios hire people like me to recruit those from the past we think might appeal to our audience. I come back and persuade historicals to come to the future.

"Preston was one of my more successful finds. Sometimes the actor or director or writer can't make the transition, but Preston seems to have an intuitive grasp of the future. Cynicism combined with repression. In two years he was the hit of the interactive fiber optic lines. But apparently it didn't agree with him. The future was too easy, he said, he wanted to go back to a time where he was an exception, not the rule. So he took all the money he made and paid the studio to send him back for another chance at his old life."

"How can you bring him back if he's dead?"

"Very good! You can spot a contradiction. What I've told you so far isn't exactly true. This isn't the same world I took him from. I recruited him from another version of history. I showed up in his garage just as he was about to turn on the ignition and gas himself. In your version, nobody stopped him. So see, I bring back my live Sturges to the home of your dying one. We arrive a half hour after your Sturges is defunct. You should have seen us trying to get the body out of the car and onto the boat. What a comedy of errors. This stray dog comes barking down the pier. Preston was already a madman, carrying around his own still-warm corpse. The dog sniffs his crotch, Preston drops his end of the body. Pure slapstick.

"So we manhandle the ex-Sturges onto the boat and sail out past the breakwall. Dump the body overboard with window counterweights tied to its ankles, come back and my Sturges takes his place, a few years older and a lot wiser. He's had the benefit of some modern medicine; he's kicked the booze and cigarettes and now he's ready to step back into the place that he escaped earlier and try to straighten things out. He's got a second chance."

"You're right. That's a pretty good story."

"You like it?"

"But if you've done your job, why are you still here?"

"How about this: I'm actually a scholar, and I'm taking the opportunity to study your culture. My dissertation is on the effects of your Second World War on Hotel Tipping Habits. I can give you a lot of tips. How would you like to know who wins the Rose Bowl next year?"

"How'd you like to be trapped in 1949?"

Gruber sat down on one of the wrought iron chairs. "I probably would come to regret it. But you'd be amazed at the things you have here that you can't hardly get in 2043. T-bone steak. Cigarettes with real nicotine. Sex with guilt."

"I still don't understand how you can steal somebody out of your own past and not have it affect your present."

"It's not my past, it's yours. Every moment in time gives rise to a completely separate history. They're like branches splitting off from the same tree trunk. If I come out to lop a twig off your branch, it doesn't affect the branch I come from."

"You're not changing the future?"

"I'm changing *your* future. In my past, as a result of personal and professional failures, Preston Sturges committed suicide by carbon monoxide poisoning on the evening of May 1, 1949. But now there are two other versions. In one Sturges disappeared on the afternoon of May 1, never to be seen again. In yours, Sturges committed suicide that evening, but then I and the Sturges from that other universe showed up, dropped his body in the ocean off San Pedro, and set up this new Sturges in his place—if you go along."

"Why should I?'

"For the game! It's interesting, isn't it? What will he do? How will it work out?"

"Will you come back to check on him?"

"I already have. I saved him from his suicide, showed him what a difference he's made to this town, and now he's going to have a wonderful life. All his friends are going to get together and give him enough money to pay his debts and start over again."

"I saw that movie. Jimmy Stewart, Donna Reed."

Gruber slapped his knee. "And they wonder why I delight in the twenti-eth century. You're right, detective. I lied again. I have no idea how it will work out. Once I visit a time stream, I can't come back to the same one again. It's burned. A quantum effect; 137.04 Moment Universes are packed into every second. The probability of hitting the same M-U twice is vanishingly small."

"Look, I don't know how much of this is malarkey, but I know some-body's been murdered."

"No, no, there is no murder. The man I brought back really is Preston Sturges, with all the memories and experiences of the man who killed him-self. He's exactly the man Louise Sturges married, who made all those films, who fathered his son and screwed up his life. But he's had the advantage of a couple of years in the 21st century, and he's determined not to make the same mistakes again. For the sake of his son and family and all the others who've come to care about him, why not give him that chance?"

"If I drop this box, you're stuck here. You don't seem too worried."

"Well, I wouldn't be in this profession if I didn't like risk. What is life but risk? We've got a nice transaction going here, who knows how it will play out? Who knows whether Preston will straighten out his life or dismantle it?"

"In my experience, if a man is a foul ball, he's a foul ball. Doesn't matter how many chances you give him. His character tells."

"That's the other way to look at it. 'The fault, dear Brutus, is not in our stars, but in ourselves...' But I'm skeptical. That's why I like Preston. He talks as if he believes that character tells, but down deep he knows it's all out of control. You could turn my time machine into futuristic scrap, or you could give it to me and let me go back. Up to you. Or the random collision of atoms in your brain. You don't seem to me like an arbitrary man, Detective Kinlaw, but even if you are, basically I don't give a fuck."

Gruber sat back as calm as a gambler playing with house money. Kinlaw was tempted to drop the machine just to see how he would react. The whole story was too fantastic.

But there was no way around those identical fingerprints. And if it were true—if a man could be saved and given a second chance—then Kinlaw was holding a miracle in his hand, with no better plan than to dash it to pieces on the courtyard below.

His mouth was dry. "Tell you what," he said. "I'll let you have your magic box back, but you have to do something for me first."

"I aim to please, detective. What is it?"

"I had a daughter. She died of polio three years ago. If this thing really is a time machine, I want you to take me back so I can get her before she dies."

"Can't do it."

"What do you mean you can't? You saved Sturges."

"Not in this universe. His body ended up on the beach, remember? Your daughter gets polio and dies in all the branches."

"Unless we get her before she gets sick."

"Yes. But then the version of you in that other M-U has a kidnapped daughter who disappears and is never heard from again. Do you want to do that to a man who is essentially yourself? How is that any better than having her die?"

"At least I'd have her."

"Plus, we can never come back to this M-U. After we leave, it's burned. I'd have to take you to still a third branch, where you'd have to replace yet another version of yourself if you want to take up your life again. Only, since he won't be conveniently dead, you'll have to dispose of him."

"Dispose of him?"

"Yes."

Kinlaw's shoulder ached. His head was spinning trying to keep up with all these possibilities. He pulled the case in and set it down on the terrace. He holstered his .38 and rubbed his shoulder. "Show me how it works, first. Send a piece of furniture into the future."

Gruber watched him meditatively, then stepped forward and picked up the device. He went back into the living room, pushed aside the sofa, opened the case and set it in the center of the room. He unpacked the woven cable from the top and ran it in a circle of about ten feet in diameter around an armchair, ends plugged into the base of the machine. He stepped outside the circle, crouched and began typing a series of characters into the keyboard.

Kinlaw went into the bedroom, got the bottle of scotch and a glass from the bathroom and poured himself a drink. When he got back Gruber was finishing up with the keyboard. "How much of all this gas you gave me is true?"

Gruber straightened. His face was open as a child's. He smiled. "Some. A lot. Not all." He touched a switch on the case and stepped over the cable into the circle. He sat in the armchair.

The center of the room, in a sphere centered on Gruber and limited by the cable, grew brighter and brighter. Then the space inside suddenly collapsed, as if everything in it was shrinking from all directions toward the center. Gruber went from a man sitting in front of Kinlaw to a doll, to a speck, to nothing. The light grew very intense, then vanished.

When Kinlaw's eyes adjusted the room was empty.

WEDNESDAY MORNING KINLAW was sitting at his desk trying to figure out what to do with the case folder when his phone rang. It was Preston Sturges.

"I haven't slept all night," Sturges said. "I expected to wake up in jail. Why haven't you arrested me yet?"

"I still could. You assaulted a police officer."

"If that were the worst of it I'd be there in ten minutes. Last night you were talking about murder."

"Since then I had a conversation with a friend of yours at the Marmont."

"You—what did he tell you?" Sturges sounded rattled.

"Enough for me to think this case will end up unsolved."

Sturges was silent for a moment. "Thank you, Detective."

"Why? Because a miracle happened? You just get back to making movies."

"I have an interview with Larry Weingarten at MGM this afternoon. They want me to write a script for Clark Gable. I'm going to write them the best script they ever saw."

"Good. Sell the restaurant."

"You too? If I have to, I will."

After he hung up, Kinlaw rolled the cinematographer's monocle across his desk top. He thought of the body down in the morgue cooler, bound for an anonymous grave. If Gruber was telling the truth, the determined man he'd just spoken with was the same man who had killed himself in the garage on Ivar Avenue. Today he was eager to go forward; Kinlaw wondered how long that would last. He could easily fall back into his old ways, alienate whatever friends he had left. Or a stroke of bad luck like the Carole Landis suicide could sink him.

But it had to be something Sturges knew already. His movies were full of it. That absurd universe, the characters' futile attempts to control it. At the end of *Morgan's Creek* the bemused Norval is hauled out of jail, thrust into a national guard officer's uniform, and rushed to the hospital to meet his wife and children for the first time—a wife he isn't married to, children that aren't even his. He deliriously protests this miracle, a product of the hypocrisy of the town that a day earlier wanted to lock him up and throw away the key.

Then again, Norval had never given up hope, had done his best throughout to make things come out right. His character was stronger than anyone had ever given him credit for.

Kinlaw remembered the first time he'd seen his daughter, when they called him into the room after Emily had given birth. She was so tiny, swaddled tightly in a blanket: her little face, eyes clamped shut, the tiniest of eyelashes, mouth set in a soft line. How tentatively he had held her. How he'd grinned like an idiot at the doctor, at the nurse, at Emily. Emily, exhausted, face pale, had smiled back. None of them had realized they were as much at the mercy of fate as Sturges' manic grotesques.

He looked up at the calendar, got the pencil out and crossed off Monday and Tuesday. He got the telephone and dialed Emily's number. She answered the phone, voice clouded with sleep. "Hello?"

"Emily," he said. "I have the photo album. I've had it all along. I keep it on a shelf in the closet, take it out and look at the pictures and cry. I don't know what to do with it. Come help me—please."

Spirit Level

IN THE middle of the night, when he got up to use the bathroom, Michael encountered the ghost of his ex-wife.

He was sleeping in the house he had grown up in, on an inflatable mattress in the bedroom that had been his until he had gone away to college almost forty years ago. His sister Ellen had been living there, but she moved to Cincinnati to take a new job and the house had been on the market ever since. She asked Michael to keep an eye on it. She didn't expect him to move in, but Michael told her that, since Dad had built the house with his own hands, he wanted to spend a little time there before it passed out of the family forever. That was his story, anyway.

He'd had to get up to go to the bathroom with increasing frequency in recent years. Just one more of the pleasures of aging. He was shuffling down the dim hallway, the hardwood floor cool under his bare feet. He came to the bend just before the bathroom and there was Lauren, standing not six feet away. He stumbled back.

"Why did you leave me?" Lauren asked. The tone of her voice was one that Michael knew well: calm, but with a sea of turbulence beneath its surface. He had done something wrong. He knew he had; she didn't have to remind him. That had been his life in the last years of the marriage: a shuttle between the poles of resentment and guilt, with an occasional side trip into frustrated desire.

Lauren stood very still, looking at him, as real as a fist. She wore a light blue sweater with parallel black lines across her chest. Her hair was long, as in the first decade of their marriage. A pale beautiful oval ghostly face.

Maybe ten seconds passed. Finally, he managed some hoarse words. "Why are you here?"

"We spent twenty-eight years together," she said.

He felt his pulse in his throat. "What do you want from me?"

"I want the truth." She turned and walked into the living room. When he followed her, the room was empty.

He touched his hand to his head. He took a deep breath. Yes, he was awake. He went to the bathroom, relieved himself, then returned to the bedroom.

He told himself it was some vivid fantasy, but lying on the air mattress, hearing the furnace turn on and then off, he felt a bone-deep uneasiness. Lauren was not dead. She was alive and living in the house they had lived in for the last twenty years.

FOR THE FIRST six months after moving out, he'd taken a month-to-month lease on an upscale two-bedroom apartment. But the haggling over the separation agreement went on for a long time, and while it did, he was paying his own rent as well as covering the mortgage and utilities on the house. His savings account bled like a combat victim and by the time the papers were signed, he was in the red. At the software company, he was a contract worker and he worried that when his contract ran out they would let him go. So when Ellen moved out of their parents' house he was happy to ditch his apartment, put most of his furniture in storage, and live there as long as he could.

Michael's eerie feeling would not go away. He fished through the pocket of the jeans draped over his opened suitcase and got out his cell phone. He called Lauren's landline—eight months ago it had been his own number. It was three-thirty in the morning.

The phone rang five, six, seven times. After the ninth ring, he was about to give up when somebody answered.

"Hello?" It was Lauren. She sounded worried.

Now that he heard her voice, the absurdity of his call came down on him. He considered hanging up.

"Who is this?" she asked.

"It's me," he said. "Michael."

He heard her exhale. "What do you want?" No shouting, no hanging up. She was always civilized, but he heard the undertone of anger: more of his foolishness. He couldn't disagree with her.

"Are you all right?" he asked.

"For pity's sake, Michael. It's three a.m."

"I—I had a dream about you."

She laughed a curt laugh. "I have nightmares about you." She hung up.

He listened to the silent phone. "That went well," he told it.

AS MICHAEL DROVE to work through the freezing December morning, the radio began playing "Brand New Cadillac" by the Clash. He hadn't heard the song in years. He cranked up the volume as he waited at the Linden Boulevard intersection, shouting the words along with Joe Strummer.

When the light went green and he started into the intersection, he caught a flash of movement out of the corner of his eye.

He hit the brakes, his tires squealed, and the black Suburban ran the red light, missing his front bumper by inches. The driver, a woman, sped by, pretty as you please, and was gone.

Michael's heart slammed against his rib cage. The guy behind him leaned on his horn. Michael flipped the bird at him, got a grip on himself, and started again, trembling with adrenaline. If the woman had T-boned him, he would have been a dead man. "She ain't never coming back," Strummer moaned. Shaken, he drove the last few blocks to the office.

He was on a three-person team writing documentation for the operating system upgrade. The upgrade was three months late. The software engineers kept sending over revisions, and the perpetually revised copy Michael produced became a muddle. He was the oldest guy there, paid more than the others, but he worked in a cube for a boss who was fifteen years his junior.

"We need the documentation by the first," Franklin told him. Michael looked down on the younger man's thinning hair.

"When have I ever missed a deadline?"

"You don't miss deadlines, but your copy is neither precise nor graceful. For the salary you are drawing, we expect superior work."

Franklin was the kind of writer who put apostrophes in plural nouns. Michael bit his tongue and told him that he would do his best.

He preferred to work alone; it took twice as much time to do the writing collaboratively, and half of that extra time was spent correcting mistakes his team put into the copy that Michael only had to take out again.

Donna Cameron from marketing came by at 11:45. "Do you want to go to lunch?" she asked.

Michael and Donna had been dating off and on. "Sure," he said.

They drove from the office park to a strip mall, went into a deli, and ordered sandwiches. They took a table by the window. In the parking lot, women in winter coats and jeans wheeled carts laden with groceries. Dirty snow was piled at the foot of the light poles.

Michael took off his scarf. They talked about work for a while, made a tentative plan to go out to a movie that weekend. Donna told him a story about her mother. Michael didn't want to think about mothers. His mind went to the apparition he had seen the night before.

"Do you believe in ghosts?" he asked.

"Never seen one," she said. "Have you?"

"I think maybe I saw one last night."

"Really?"

"Except it wasn't a ghost. It was somebody who isn't dead. My ex." He told her the story.

Donna seemed excited by the prospect. "Maybe it was a doppelgänger. A double."

"If it were a doppelgänger, wouldn't it be me, not Lauren?"

"Be glad it wasn't you. A doppelgänger is supposed to be a sign that you're going to die soon."

"Seriously?"

"Some scientists have done experiments where, using electrical stimulation of the brain, they produced the feeling in a subject that there was another person in the room, their double. You didn't have your iPhone plugged into a socket near your head, did you?"

"How do you know all this stuff?"

"I majored in psychology. See how it got me this great job?"

Donna's playfulness was exhausting him. "Anyway, it freaked me out—what I saw." He decided he wouldn't go into his feelings of guilt. He didn't want to make her think he was some basket case.

"Or you could be the ghost," Donna said. "Like in that Nicole Kidman movie where she lives in the haunted house with her kids, but in the end it's them who are the ghosts, and the people they think are the ghosts are the living ones."

Michael tried to laugh. She saw he wasn't getting the joke. "Sorry. I didn't mean to make fun of your situation."

"It's okay."

"I don't think you're dead, Michael." She gave a shy smile and, beneath the table, bumped his leg with her knee.

"I don't think I'm dead, either. Dead men don't worry about paying the bills."

"I'll get lunch," said Donna.

THE TRUTH? THE truth was, Michael and Lauren had spent twenty-eight years together, and he had been unhappy for the last decade.

He'd told himself that everybody was unhappy; only fools or adolescents expected happiness. Michael and Lauren did their jobs, took care of their teenaged son Trevor, watched TV at night. They'd been seeing a counselor and had come to a way of living that suited Lauren; it did not satisfy him, but it left him with not enough to complain about. Lauren was not mean, nor was she crazy. In her late forties, she was an attractive woman who seemed to tolerate more than care for him. She had no interest in sleeping with him. Again, what did he expect? Sex was for young people, and short of reincarnation, he would never see the green side of fifty again.

They had to meet at the bank next week to get their signatures notarized on yet another document. He seldom saw Lauren anymore; their communication was mostly by email, and only about practical matters, mostly to do with Trevor. He knew how angry Lauren felt. Though he had not cheated on her, he had betrayed her by leaving.

What Michael felt for Lauren was complicated. Mostly he felt unmoored, as if all those years crowding his memory were inaccessible to him. He did not think that the whole marriage was a mistake. Too many good things, most notably Trevor, had come of it. He and Lauren had been good to each other for more than twenty years; why couldn't she join him in sadness over their loss instead of anger? But of course, to ask that of her wasn't reasonable, and if he was anything, he was a reasonable man. That must have been what shocked her the most—that after so many years of never doing anything crazy, he had suddenly left, without a plan; a month before, he had been reconciled to his situation, and then he was out the door.

So her ghost was there to demand an explanation. Could he tell all this to her? It would take an hour. He imagined standing there with a ghost for an hour going step by step through this tired litany. That was his kind of ghost story. A bunch of sketchy rationalizations. A pile of words. No blood, no passion. Maybe he could write it all out, break down the process of their coming apart, with diagrams, and hand it to her.

ON THE WAY home from work, he stopped by the liquor store and bought a bottle of brandy, a bottle of bourbon, and a bottle of gin. At the grocery he picked up a bag of limes and a six-pack of tonic. He had his sister's refrigerator and a paring knife and two glasses. What more did a man need?

In his head, he made a list of the things he had in the house. An iPhone, two suitcases, a box of kitchenware, a travel kit of shaving cream, razor, shampoo, toothbrush, etc., one table, one table lamp, one chair, one quilt that smelled of mildew, dress shoes, three pairs of sneakers, a pair of boots, a winter coat, a leather jacket, two sports coats, three ties, a box of socks and underwear, his laptop, some notebooks, a drawer full of office supplies dumped into a box, a plastic bag of T-shirts and summer clothes.

He had two books with him: the *Tao Te Ching* and *Moby-Dick*. He had been trying to read *Moby-Dick*, telling himself that since he had the time, now was the chance to finally get through it and prove to himself that his brain had not ossified. He was fifty pages in, but it was tough going.

He picked up the *Tao* and opened it at random.

> Know the raw silk,
> Hold the uncut wood.
> Need little,
> Want less.
> Forget the rules.
> Be untroubled.

Need little—he could do that. He had lost some few things in the divorce that he missed, but many more that he did not.

Want less—that was not so easy. The reason he had left was that he wanted more. He wanted all sorts of things. He wanted someone who wanted to touch him, who wanted him to touch her, who did not flinch or avoid him, who did not act as if sex were something that no longer applied to them. Love that didn't include sex did not feel like love to him. He figured Lao Tzu would not have much sympathy for that.

Forget the rules? He had always followed the rules. He stayed with Lauren for so long because he believed in rules. He still had them. Don't cry in public. That was a rule.

Be untroubled. Right.

He needed a drink. But if he was going to cut up limes, he didn't want to scar the countertop and damage his sister's chances of selling the place. He needed a cutting board.

There had to be some scrap wood around somewhere. He put down the knife and went out into the garage.

The garage had been their father's workshop. It was a large two-car garage, but it had been so full of Dad's junk that they couldn't park a car in it. A table saw, a router, a band saw, gray metal toolboxes, an unopened case of 10W-40 motor oil, old transformers, bottles of solvent, several shelves of old paint cans with the colors dripped down over the labels, shop rags, C-clamps, a pipe clamp, jelly jars full of metal screws, wood screws, and nails of various sizes, spools of electrical wire, a box of wire nuts, switch boxes and light fixtures, a welding helmet, the snowblower, three dented aluminum trash barrels, half a case of Genesee cream ale from forty years ago. Michael and his sister had spent a month cleaning out the garage, throwing away piles of junk.

Before then, it would have been the easiest thing in the world to find a board there on which to cut his limes. But now the place stood bare under the naked sixty watt bulbs. It was cold; he could see his breath. Michael pulled open cabinet drawers, empty now. When he pulled the one at the end of the bench, he heard something fall behind, inside the cabinet. He opened the door under the drawer, and in the darkness at the back found a spirit level.

He pulled it out and stood up—his knees creaked as he did. It was an old one, three feet long, inches marked out along one side of its frame. There were three bubbles, one at each end for vertical and 45-degree angles, and one in the middle to measure horizontals. He ran a thumb over the glass covering the middle one. The telltale bubble in its little yellow tube. Michael remembered his father using the level many times, holding it up against a doorframe to make sure it was plumb, testing the pitch of the new concrete walkway.

Michael's father had never heard of the *Tao Te Ching*, but knew about uncut wood. That was his job, cutting wood: He was a carpenter. Michael had seen him cut wood on his table saw, with a keyhole saw, with a plane, a drill press, a miter box. It all came back, vividly. The rhythm of the handsaw, the whine of the table saw. The scent of sawdust.

Behind him, someone sneezed explosively. Electricity ran down Michael's spine. He knew that sneeze. He gripped the level and turned.

There stood his father, leaning against the pegboard wall beside the door. His arms were crossed over his chest. He wore dark green work pants and a green shirt with flap pockets. Protruding from the left breast pocket was a flat carpenter's pencil.

He was not the old man he had been before his death; hair mussed, he looked forty-five or fifty, younger than Michael was today. He stared at Michael, blinked, and sneezed again.

"Gesundheit," Michael said.

"You should leave that thing alone," his father said, gesturing at the level. "You don't know the first thing about using it."

"What do you care?" Michael said. "You're dead."

"I care about things being done right."

That was true—if you allowed that done right usually meant done the way his father wanted it.

"Just find some wood, go slice your limes, and get yourself drunk. There's a square of varnished cherry under the sink. Use that."

"How do you know what I want?"

"I could always see through you, Michael. I made you like I made this house."

Michael realized how crazy it was for him to stand there arguing with a hallucination. He swung the level backhanded at the ghost, whipping it at its head. His father's hand flashed up and caught the level in mid-swing. The shock of it ran up Michael's arm, no match for the shock his heart felt that the man in front of him was a material being.

His father wrenched the level out of his hand and thrust it into Michael's belly. It hit him just under the rib cage then scraped down his gut, knocking the wind out of him. Michael fell onto his ass, gasping. He heard the level clatter to the concrete floor.

When he lifted his eyes, his father was gone. Michael gingerly pulled up his shirt and found a bloody scrape from his ribs down toward his navel.

In a neighborhood of blue-collar workers where corporal punishment was common, Michael's father had seldom hit him. The bad blood between them was more insidious than that. As a boy, Michael had worshipped the way his father could do anything. He wanted to learn and, to be fair, his father wanted to teach him. Michael's dad was a terrible teacher. He could not stand to see a job done badly, so at some point as Michael stumbled along trying to learn how to dovetail a joint, his father's guidance would turn to criticism—impatient, even angry—and he would step in to take over.

Michael ended up feeling incompetent. His father was a harsh judge, always ready to criticize. Michael came to hate him; it wasn't until he was an adult that he understood he wasn't a bad carpenter at all, and might have made a good one.

He got to his knees, picked up the level, and went back into the house. In the kitchen, under the sink, he found a foot-square scrap of cherry. Hold the uncut wood. He sliced a lime on it and made himself a gin and tonic.

IN THE MORNING, the scrape was scabbed over and there was a bruise on his belly. It hurt. He checked the medicine cabinet to see if there was any Tylenol.

There wasn't. But solitary as a sentinel stood a prescription bottle for oxycodone with his father's name on it: TAKE 1-2 TABLETS BY MOUTH EVERY 4-6 HOURS AS NEEDED FOR ARTHRITIS PAIN. USE ONLY UNDER DOCTOR'S SUPERVISION.

There were a couple dozen pills still in it. He put it warily back onto the shelf and closed the cabinet.

He decided to work from home. He didn't have to go into the office every day; he could communicate with the team members online—though it was risky to stay home, with no reason to shave or dress. Work was a routine whose structure kept him from following his self-obsession into a pit. It would distract him from the inexplicable bruise on his belly.

In the afternoon, he braved the freezing weather to go to Wegmans. He pushed his cart through the aisles while "Baby, It's Cold Outside" played from the ceiling.

On the way home, he drove past a lot near a gas station where some guys were selling Christmas trees. On impulse, he pulled in and bought a small tree and a stand. When he got back to the house, he stood it up in the corner of the empty living room where the family had always put the tree when he was a boy. Without ornaments, it looked forlorn, but he liked the smell.

Michael began to prowl through the house. He felt that he was not alone. No one had offered to buy it; his sister said it was because of the lousy local economy but Michael wondered if maybe the house did not want to be sold. It was exactly as old as Michael. His father had begun building it when his wife announced that she was pregnant, and the three of them had moved into the uncompleted home when Michael was seven months old.

All the years of Michael's boyhood, his father, after working all day for whatever contractor had hired him, would come home and work on the house. Some things never got done. Michael still had the door to the laundry room cabinet, which had sat in the closet but had never been hung.

Everywhere now he saw things that brought back memories. On the doorframe to the basement was a series of pencil marks, starting low and getting higher, with faint dates marked beside them, recording his growth from thirty-three inches to six feet one. In the shoe closet (how many houses had a shoe closet?), on the inside of the door were crayon drawings of controls and a viewscreen he'd made when he had crawled inside as a boy and pretended it was a spaceship. The counters in the kitchen reminded him of how, when he was growing up, they were covered with green Formica. He remembered the ludicrous blue tux he'd worn to his high school prom. He remembered fighting with his sister, locking her out of the bathroom. The smell of mothballs in the attic.

He measured things with the level. The window sills. The doorframes. Horizontal things remained horizontal, vertical things were vertical. His father had been good at that. As he held the level against the closet doorframe, Michael remembered his father cutting the molding on his table saw. He had made Michael, eight or nine years old, help him by holding up the long strips of wood as they came off the table so they would not bend. His father would feed the wood into the saw, his hand coming so close to the whirling blade that Michael was terrified he would lose a finger. The saw whirred when not cutting and whined loudly as the wood was fed through. Sawdust shot down under the table; there were piles of it on the floor.

Forty-five years later, Michael pressed the level against the wood that he had held as it came out of the saw. The bubble sat precisely between the two lines. All that time, and it was still true.

DURING MOST OF the winter, the city lay under a blanket of clouds. The only time the direct sun broke out was in the half hour before it slid below the horizon. This golden light was streaming in the west windows when Donna called him. "Hello, Michael?"

"Hello. How are you?" He hadn't seen her in four days. During that time, he had picked up his phone at least twice to call her, then put it back down again.

"Listen, can you help me out? My car won't start—I think the battery is dead. Can you come give me a jump?"

"I'll jump you any time you please."

She didn't laugh. "I'm parked across from the Bed, Bath and Beyond at the Rockwell Center. I'll come out when you get here."

When he drove up, he found her Honda sitting with cars parked on both sides of it. She came out of the store in her black pea coat with a purple scarf and matching knit hat. Her dark hair curled from under the hat. She looked lethally cute.

There was some confusion over who should try to start the car. She assured him that the battery was dead; why did he need to try it himself? Did he think she was incompetent? It wasn't that at all, he said. She finally surrendered the keys and he tried it. The ignition clicked and nothing happened. He got out of the car.

"You're adorable," she said, "in a slightly infuriating way."

"I don't know if I can get close enough for the cables to reach," he told her. "What side of the engine is your battery on?"

"If the cables won't reach, what does it matter?"

Michael popped the hood. While they were trying to figure out what to do, the owner of one of the adjacent cars came by, got in, and drove away. Michael pulled into the vacant slot, unspooled his jumper cables, and attached them. The engine started on the second try.

"There's an auto parts store on Saratoga Street," she said. "Follow me there."

After Donna bought a new battery and had it installed, they went for a drink. A few people sat in the bar; some Marvel superhero movie blared on the TV. They talked for a while, a little awkwardly. He did not want to tell her about the latest ghost, so instead he talked about how he had read comics aloud to Trevor before bedtime when he was little. Donna listened patiently, but he knew he was boring her.

He couldn't do anything right. He'd been too officious about the battery. But he had helped her. He could give a good simulation of a grown-up.

She updated him on the politics of the marketing department. He asked her about her own divorce. They talked about their marriages, and he supposed the things he said were sincere, but he did not reveal any secrets. By the time they left the bar it was full night. They walked down the block to a Middle Eastern deli and ate hummus and spicy tuna salad.

"Do you want to come by my place?" she asked.

"Yes," he said.

As soon as they were inside the door they were kissing, pawing at each other's coats, swaying as they tried to pull off their boots. They stumbled over her cat as they moved toward the bedroom. He pushed her down onto the bed and slid off her jeans.

Donna's ankles were very slender, but her calves were strong. He loved the long muscles along the tops of her thighs, the creamy smooth skin on their insides. Donna had a slender waist, and that was a huge turn-on, too. Strong shoulders, round cheeks, full lips. She would thrust her tongue into his mouth, bite his shoulder, lick his nipples. He liked the way she smelled. There was nothing about Donna's body he didn't like. There was nothing he didn't like about the way she made love.

Of course, he couldn't leave it at that. He enjoyed sex with her so much he worried he'd confuse it with love. He liked the way she talked, her obsessions so different from his, her political passion and sense of humor. But what did that amount to? Maybe despite being in his fifties he was just another adolescent asshole who didn't know anything more about love than some horny teenager. Often when he thought about Donna, he felt like a horny teenager.

He could second-guess himself like this for hours. Before encountering Lauren's ghost, he had kept himself up at night doing so.

Afterward, as they lay in the light of her candle, Donna asked, "What's this bruise?" She ran her finger over his belly.

"A ghost did it."

She looked him in the eyes. "You are an odd person, Michael."

"Yes. But I'm good at spelling."

In the middle of the night he lay awake beside her, unable to sleep, wondering what was going on back at the house. He slipped out of the bed, found his underwear, pants, and shirt. He could not find his socks, so he put on his shoes without them. He leaned over and kissed her on the cheek. She stirred. "Going home?" she asked.

"I can't sleep."

"Call me tomorrow, okay?"

"I will."

"Thanks for helping me."

"Thanks for accepting it." He went out into the winter night.

When he got home, the house was completely dark. He had not expected to be out all night, and had left no lights on. He unlocked the front door and stepped in, listening. It was warm inside. He took off his hat and scarf, unbuttoned his heavy coat. All he could hear was the ticking of the furnace and the faint creak of his step on the hardwood. A wedge of moonlight through the picture window illuminated his forlorn Christmas tree.

In the middle of the floor lay the spirit level. He had not left it there.

He picked it up; it was as solid as his memories. He felt his heart thudding in his ears. "Lauren?" he called. "Dad?" His voice sounded thin in the empty house.

He stepped tentatively into the hall and turned on the light. His bedroom door was half-closed, the room beyond pitch black. He reached a hand out and slowly pushed door all the way open. Light was cast on the mattress, his suitcase, a discarded shirt. He entered and dropped his coat on the chair, then, hearing some faint sound behind him, turned.

Trevor stood in the doorway. He wore the old yellow College of Wooster T-shirt he'd inherited from Michael: C.O.W., said the letters stenciled across his chest. His eyes were shadowed.

"I smell her on you," Trevor said. "You stink of her." He turned and ran away. Michael followed. In the kitchen, Trevor dashed through the doorway to the basement. "Trevor, wait," he said, angry now.

In the gloom at the bottom of the stairs, Michael caught a glimpse of Trevor's foot disappearing. He rushed down, tripped on something, bounced off the wall, fell to his knees, tumbled. His head hit the basement floor.

WHEN HE WOKE, his skull was throbbing. It was still dark. He got shakily to his feet and made his way up the stairs. He moved in a fog. His wrist ached where he had tried to break his fall. In the fluorescent light of the bathroom, his face was haggard. He wet a towel and held it to a cut on his forehead. He might have easily broken his neck. He'd lost consciousness for a moment and probably had a concussion. He ought to go to the emergency room.

He opened the medicine cabinet and took two of his father's oxycodone.

He returned to the stairs, flicked on the lights, and went down to the basement. He had tripped over a pair of old sneakers. He picked them up—they were a pair that Trevor had worn when he was eight or nine, purple with an image of the Incredible Hulk on the uppers. He inspected the cellar, behind the furnace, the storage room. No trace of anything.

He came back upstairs. He did smell of sex. He stripped and took a shower, then lay down on the mattress and in a few minutes was asleep.

THE NEXT MORNING, he had to go into the office, where Bobby Keiling asked, "What the hell happend to you?"

"I feel down the stairs."

"Were you drunk?"

"I wish."

He called Donna's extension in marketing. Her phone rang for a while before she picked up.

"Michael, hi," she said. She sounded harried.

"I need to speak with you."

"Not a great time." Her voice softened. "Last night was lovely."

"Some things are happening to me. I need to talk with you about it."

"I wish I could talk now, but I can't."

"Can we meet after work?"

"Not tonight. I'm swamped."

"I need to talk with you."

"You shouldn't call me in the office."

"You asked me to call you."

Donna's voice gained an edge. "You get a gold star. But you know Whitworth doesn't approve of interoffice relationships, and he's standing in his doorway right now looking at me."

"Sorry." Silence stretched. After a moment, he said, "Last night was good."

"Michael, I can't talk now. Thanks for helping me with my car. We'll talk later." She hung up.

THE GHOSTS MADE no sense. Ghosts were supposed to be remnants of dead people. His father had been dead for ten years, which fit the profile, but Lauren and Trevor were alive.

Ghosts were tied to a particular place. But Lauren and Trevor had no history with this house. They should haunt the house that Lauren and Michael had been haunting for the last ten years.

Ghosts were about the past. They had grievances. But he supposed the living had grievances as much as the dead.

He could see Lauren's grievances all too easily. And Trevor blamed Michael for wrecking their family. Michael's father?—by the age of twelve, Michael's hostility toward him was set in concrete. He had never understood his father enough to forgive him.

As for Lauren and Trevor not being dead, maybe he was taking that too literally. Some things inside you could die while you remained alive. What happened to those things? If the universe were sensitive to human desire, and it took those longings into itself in some way, what would those lost, frustrated selves become?

Maybe that's what ghosts were: an external manifestation of inner deficits, taken supernatural form to torment you. To make you trip on the basement stairs and almost kill yourself.

This was silly. These ghosts weren't real; they were projections of Michael's guilt. But how does a projection of your guilt snatch a level out of the air and stab you with it?

WEDNESDAY NIGHT AFTER work, instead of returning to the house, he drove across the city to the Sylvan Springs Care Center.

The lights of the building glistened off the parking lot's wet asphalt; the snow piled at the end of the lot still bore the mark of the plow. He wrapped his scarf around his neck and crossed to the lobby. A blast of warm air engulfed him as he came through the sliding doors.

Tinsel rope hanging from the ceiling swagged its way around the room, and softly over the speakers came Burl Ives singing "Have a Holly Jolly Christmas." On the counter beside the young woman doing desk duty lay a headband with plush antlers. Her name tag read "Marielle." He didn't remember her from his previous visits.

Michael signed in.

"Who are you here to see?" the woman asked.

"My mother, Gina DiFranco. She's in room 210."

"No, she's in 229."

"It's 210," Michael said with irritation.

"As long as I've worked here, Mrs. DiFranco's been in 229."

"She was in 210 the last..." Michael's voice trailed off. "Never mind." He headed for the wing housing the functionally and cognitively impaired.

It was not quite supper time. Supper was a good time to visit because the old people got some attention then as they were prepared to be fed. As a result of the stroke that had put her here, not to say her blindness, his mother had trouble feeding herself. Michael sometimes helped her to eat. He fed her with a small spoon, the way she had fed him when he was a baby.

He found her sitting in a wheelchair in the lounge next to another woman in a wheelchair. The TV was tuned to Turner Classic Movies.

He sat down beside her. When they'd first put her into the home, Michael and Ellen had come to see her often. Michael had tried to imagine some way to take her out of the home, but she was half-paralyzed from the stroke, blind, and needed constant care. There was nothing he could do, and as things soured between him and Lauren, he visited his mother less and less.

It was too depressing to see her. In her first days at Sylvan Springs, she had confabulated. Once, when he put her on the phone so Trevor could wish her a happy birthday, she had spun a tale about how she was out at Sears, Christmas shopping, on her way to get coffee next door at the Sweet Shoppe. Her voice was animated, and Michael could tell that, in her mind, she was really out shopping, and happy. But that was years ago.

Now she slumped in the chair with her good arm on the armrest, leaning her head on her hand. Her eyes were closed. Her hair had thinned to the point where he could see her scalp. She had lost so much weight, her skin hung on her bones.

"Mom, it's me, Michael."

She didn't reply, or even move.

Michael drew a chair close to her and sat. He touched the warm, useless hand that lay in her lap. He murmured something to her about his work, knowing that she didn't understand a word of what he was saying. He felt the birdlike bones of her wrist. The other wheelchair-bound woman was watching some movie with Doris Day, but Michael's mother might as well have been in a coma.

Down the hall came Marielle and a woman in a blue jacket with the Sylvan Springs logo on the breast pocket, looking like a hotel concierge. Her badge said "Lashonda Wilkins." Michael had met her before, but she didn't seem to recognize him.

"Sir, may we speak with you?"

"I don't want to speak with you," he replied. Marielle must have decided there was something suspicious about him and run to her boss.

"We'll need you to give us some ID," Wilkins said.

"ID? What?" Michael's voice rose. "What, am I going to kidnap her?"

"Sir, I think you need to calm down."

"I'm not going to fucking calm down. I'm her son, Michael DiFranco. Look at this place. You warehouse these people. It's like a kennel in here, with a TV."

A woman in scrubs who was wheeling another resident toward the dining room stopped.

"Sir, you need to lower your voice," Wilkins said.

Marielle had out her cell phone and was videoing him.

He felt a surge of pure rage. He tried to get a grip.

Wilkins said, "When was the last time you visited your mother, Mr. DiFranco?"

He had to breathe. He forced himself to breathe. "I'm sorry," he said to Marielle. "I'm sorry," he said to Wilkins. "I haven't been here in a long time."

"Apparently, you have not."

He swallowed his anger. "Please, can I sit with her now, for a little?"

Wilkins' lips were set in a firm line. "Okay," she said.

"He needs to control himself," Marielle said to Wilkins as they entered the dining room. Michael turned to his mother.

She had not paid attention to any of it. She still sat with her head propped on her hand, her eyes closed. An orderly come out with a tray with covered dishes for the woman in the other wheelchair. "I guess she's sleeping," Michael said to him.

The orderly looked at him. "Who?"

"My mother."

"She's not sleeping. She's just sad."

"Isn't it time for her to eat?" he asked.

"We'll try. She doesn't eat."

Michael closed his own eyes. He sat beside his mother again. What was he going to say to her? Aren't you hungry, Mom? Is there anything I can do?

ON FRIDAY, TO keep from thinking about his mother, he drank gin and tonics and read *Moby-Dick*. He got so thoroughly plowed that the words slid by him on the page and when he stood up to go to the bathroom, the room tilted. Whoa. Heavy seas, Ishmael.

He read Father Mapple's sermon. "And if we obey God, we must disobey ourselves; and it is in this disobeying ourselves, wherein the hardness of obeying God consists."

Michael had left Lauren in order to be true to himself. Father Mapple would not be impressed. Being "true to yourself" was a modern, wimpy kind of truth, not the hard truth of Mapple's sermon. Being true to yourself when it was in contradiction to your duty was the worst kind of sin. Jonah had sought to evade his duty to God by running away. Michael had sought to evade his duty to Lauren by running away. No wonder he felt so lost.

There was a carpenter in *Moby-Dick*. He was a mysterious character, Melville's carpenter. He knew how to fix everything aboard the ship, from a broken oar to a broken jaw, but he was indifferent to it all. He just did his work. Ishmael said he had "a certain impersonal stolidity...an all-ramifying heartlessness." Like a Zen master, Michael thought—or an idiot. "In his numerous trades, he did not seem to work so much by reason...but merely by a kind of deaf and dumb, spontaneous literal process...his brain, if he had ever had one, must have early oozed along into the muscles of his fingers."

Michael's dad had been like that, in some ways. The Pequod's carpenter was like a Swiss Army knife: He could serve any purpose without having a purpose of his own. What evidence was there that the carpenter even had a soul?

Nobody had a soul, Michael knew. All you had was the face you prepared to show to other people. Your character was a performance, a persona you put on; by the time you were a teenager, under the pressure of other people's expectations, you worked out who you were supposed to be. You lived your invented self to the point where you imagined that was who you were. Everybody thought they knew you—you thought you knew yourself. Until something happened, like Michael walking out on Lauren, to reveal that there was nothing inside you but a few desires and an echo chamber.

So what did it mean to be true to yourself when your self was a construct papering over a void?

SATURDAY, MICHAEL WOKE with a lethal hangover. He shuffled into the bathroom, popped open the bottle of oxycodone, and took two, sucking tap water from his cupped hand to wash them down. He slipped the bottle into his pocket and splashed water into his face. His eyes looked old. He could see remnants of the forty-year-old in his face, still, but he could see the coming seventy-year-old better.

His mother was killing herself by refusing to eat. Her life in the home where Michael and his sister had put her was that bleak. He could not keep it out of his head.

He called Ellen and got her voicemail. He didn't leave a message. He called Donna.

"Hello," she said.

"Donna, this is Michael. Can we talk?"

A pause. "I'm out of the house. Can you meet me at Café Canem at 11:00?"
He looked at his watch. It was 10:15. "Yes."

"Okay."

He showered and shaved and drove over to the coffee shop. Donna was not there yet. His stomach was queasy. He ordered a latte, then sat at one of the tiny tables watching the Christmas shoppers come and go, gloves poking from the pockets of their unbuttoned coats.

Donna came in, said hello, and got a coffee of her own. She wore the same purple scarf and hat from the night they had slept together.

"I'm sorry if I hurt your feelings on that office call," she said.

"It's not a problem," he said.

She was a little distant; he did not get the sense she didn't want to be there, but he did not get the sense that she did. He told her about his visit to his mother. Donna sat motionless as he explained his distress. Michael became increasingly self-conscious, acutely aware of his own voice.

In the silence that came when he finished, the sound of the milk steamer hissed through the shop. At the table behind him, two guys were arguing about the Patriots.

"I'm sorry," Donna finally said. "That sounds awful."

"The awful part is that I put her there, and—"

"You know that's absurd," Donna said. "The stroke put her there. She needs twenty-four-hour care; even when you were married, you couldn't do that."

"I abandoned her. I never thought of her."

Donna sighed. "I think you need to ask yourself a few questions, Michael. Is this about your mother or is it about you? If you can't stop beating yourself about the head and shoulders, you shouldn't expect someone else to stop you. You certainly shouldn't expect them to give you sympathy for something you're doing to yourself. Your mother's situation is tragic, but it's what happens. If you wanted to visit her more, you would, though I doubt it would make much difference."

"That's cold."

"I don't mean to be cold. You know I like you. You're not a bad guy. But I can't solve your problems for you. I'm sorry about your mother. At least you can be with her at the end, if you want to be."

He looked her in the eyes; she took a sip of coffee.

"I don't think we ought to keep seeing each other," Donna said.

HE CARRIED THE pills around with him all the time now. Occasionally, he would reach into his pocket and touch the bottle, but he hadn't taken any lately. He still had seventeen left.

Despite Donna's scolding, he did not go to see his mother. Instead he met with a real estate agent to try to kickstart the sale of the house. It would cost him a commission, but the sooner he got it sold, the sooner he could move out, split the money with Ellen, and try to begin his life again. He would find some other work. Maybe he would move south, somewhere where the sun was not a mythological belief from November till April.

Michael avoided seeing Donna by working from home, only going in when he had to meet with the other team members. He glimpsed her once in the parking lot but could not tell if she had seen him. He didn't know why the end of their affair should bother him so much. Sometimes after he woke in the middle of the night he thought about her.

As for the ghosts, he had not seen any since his fall down the stairs. The bruise on his belly had healed to the point where only a slight discoloration remained. If Lauren's ghost still wanted the truth, it was waiting. If Trevor's wanted to blame him, it bided its time. Maybe Michael's father would club him to death with the spirit level while he slept.

Two weeks passed. Christmas came and went. He was at home trying to read *Moby-Dick* when he got the call from Lauren.

"Michael?"

"What is it?"

She hesitated. "The rest home just called me. They thought this was still your number." Another hesitation. "Your mother died."

It was not a surprise, but he felt it like a blow. He closed his eyes. "When did it happen?"

"Just an hour ago. They didn't say much. You should call the manager—Ms. Wilkins."

Now it was Michael's turn to fumble for words. "Thank you," he said. "I'll talk to her."

"I'm sorry, Michael. She was a good woman."

"She was."

"If there's anything I can do—"

"I'll let you know about the funeral," Michael said, and hung up.

HE KEPT IT together through the funeral. First he called Ellen in Ohio, then the funeral home and church that had done the services for his father. They already had a plot reserved next to his father in a local cemetery. He and Ellen selected a coffin and split the cost. Everything went smoothly. The day of the burial, the temperature hit almost fifty. Lauren and Trevor were there; Trevor looked restive, and when Michael exchanged a few words with Lauren, she told him Trevor had not wanted to come. But he behaved well, and as people were getting into cars to leave the cemetery, he came up to Michael and hugged him. He seemed two inches taller than a year ago.

"I have a couple of Christmas presents for you," Michael said. "A 1971 copy of *The Incredible Hulk*, for one. Script by Harlan Ellison."

Trevor looked embarrassed. "Okay."

"I'll drop it by sometime."

"Okay," said Trevor. "My mother's waiting."

"You better go, then."

Michael watched his son cross the brown grass to the car where Lauren waited. It wasn't just the divorce that separated him from his son. Trevor wasn't a kid anymore. The distance between them would only grow as the years went by.

Two days later, Lashonda Wilkins called him about his mother's effects, the few personal possessions she'd had in her room at the facility. He arranged to meet her Thursday night. At the office that day there was a panic about the documentation due on Friday, and Michael had to stay late doing last-minute revisions. It was seven when he got out of the building; by the time he'd had supper at a noisy Mexican restaurant full of couples on dates, it was eight-thirty. He did not reach Sylvan Springs until after nine.

At the desk was Marielle; she expressed sympathy for his loss. Ms. Wilkins came out and did likewise. Michael was acutely aware that he had not been there since that night weeks ago; he imagined their condolences veiled contempt.

"We have a box of your mother's things ready for you," Ms. Wilkins said. "If you'll come around the back of the building, I'll meet you at the doors to the storage room."

Michael left the building and walked around to the rear.

Ms. Wilkins stood in the open doorway under a harsh area light; next to her, a bundle lay on top of a cardboard box. Michael recognized the bundle as a crocheted afghan his mother had made fifty years ago.

He felt he had to say something. "Thank you for taking care of her," he said. It was a stupid thing to say and he knew it the minute the words left his lips.

"We're just a kennel with TV," Wilkins said. She watched him. Michael wanted to snap back at her, but had nothing. If the place was as bad as he'd claimed, whose fault was it that his mother had spent the last years of her life there?

Wilkins fished a pack of cigarettes and a lighter out of her jacket pocket. She lit a cigarette, inhaled deeply, blew the smoke into the cold night.

"I don't know whether you have any reason to feel bad," she said. "Maybe you do, maybe you don't. From the little I've seen, you're no worse than the relatives of other people here. Some do better than you, some might as well not exist."

That sounded like about as much consideration as Michael deserved. "You don't have an easy job," he said.

"I've had worse. I guess I do see some things that other people don't think about."

"Thank you, anyway."

"You're welcome."

Michael picked up the afghan. It smelled like his mother—musty, a little sour, mixed with baby powder. "You can pitch the box," he said.

"You'll need to do that yourself. Good night."

She stepped back into the building and the door swung shut, the latch clicking with finality.

He peeked into the box—some slippers, a sweater, a bedside clock. Nothing worth keeping except maybe a framed family photo from ten years ago. Ellen and her husband and kids were there, and Michael and Lauren with seven-year-old Trevor, all smiling, surrounding a beaming Gina DiFranco. Michael thought about keeping it, but he didn't want to see himself or Lauren any more than he wanted to look at his mother. He dropped the photo back into the box and threw the box into the Dumpster at the end of the lot. He put the afghan onto the passenger's seat of his car, closed the door, and stood there. His breath fogged the air, reflecting the glare of the lights in the lot. It was well after visiting hours and the only cars left belonged to the staff. He shoved his hands into his pockets. There was the bottle of pills.

Michael took the bottle out and got into the car. He opened it and spilled the tabs into his palm. A little heap of yellow ovals. He took a deep breath. He smelled the odor of his mother from the afghan.

He couldn't blame Wilkins for making him feel bad. He couldn't blame the ghosts, even. He couldn't blame anybody, and he realized that the sadness overwhelming him was not a result of things he had done or failed to do. It was the result of the simple passage of time. Things changed. When you were young, you thought the past could be recovered, or if not, corrected by the future. When you were old, the silent, inexorable slide of now into then, and its associated accumulation of losses, small and large, crushed any future. You might throw yourself against the bars of your cage, but it got harder and harder to ignore time passing.

The only thing that stopped it was death. In *Moby-Dick*, Ishmael talked about "A speechlessly quick chaotic bundling of a man into Eternity." That could happen at any time. An SUV runs a red light. You trip on the stairs. You overdose on prescription medicine.

MICHAEL PULLED INTO the driveway, so tired that it was all he could do to open the door of the car and get out. His head felt fuzzy, and he had trouble drawing air into his lungs. He fumbled with the house key on the doorstep, dropped it, picked it up, and finally got the door open.

The furnace was running and hot air flowed from the registers. The living room was dark, but it was not empty. There was a rug, furniture. It all looked familiar.

Light came from the kitchen. Wondering, Michael entered it, and found his mother sitting at the yellow Formica table so familiar from his childhood. The kitchen was as it had been: the toaster and the canisters of flour and sugar on the counter, the avocado-green gas stove with a pot simmering on one of the burners, filling the air with the smell of homemade spaghetti sauce. The wooden plaque on the wall above the table that said God Bless Our Home.

And his mother. She was not the dying woman she had been at Sylvan Springs. She was a housewife, in her mid-thirties. Her thick, dark hair hung over her shoulders, held back with a couple of bobby pins. She wore a blue housedress with tiny flowers on it. She gazed at Michael. There were tears in her eyes.

"Michael." She wiped the back of her wrist against the corner of her eye, lurched out of the chair and stirred the spaghetti sauce. "You're late," she said over her shoulder. "Are you hungry? Have something to eat."

"I'm not hungry, Mom."

"You have to eat."

"I feel dizzy." He sat in one of the kitchen chairs.

She came to him and laid her palm against his forehead. "You don't have a fever. Maybe you're coming down with something." She made him take off his coat. "Come on, lie down for a while. Your father will be home soon. Maybe then you'll feel like eating."

Michael let her take him to his room. There were the comic books stacked on the shelf beside his bed, his baseball glove and bat leaning in the corner, the poster of Linda Ronstadt on the wall. His mother pulled back the crocheted afghan on top of the bedspread and laid him down, then pulled off his shoes.

She got him a glass of water, and he drank some. He had not realized how thirsty he was. "Are you still dizzy?" she asked.

"I feel sleepy."

"Rest. I'll come and get you later." She stepped away from the bed. "I'll leave the door cracked open. Call me if you need me."

She paused. "I'm so glad you're home, Michael," she said. "I wish you could stay here forever."

Michael lay in the darkness, warming to the overheated house, breathing slowly. Eyes open, head resting on the pillow, he could see across the bedroom where his father had left off nailing the closet molding to the doorframe. Always in the middle of some job. Michael wondered if he would ever be done. There lay his father's hammer, the nail set, the box of finishing nails, and, beside them, his spirit level.

Stories for Men

ONE

ERNO COULDN'T get to the club until an hour after it opened, so of course the place was crowded and he got stuck in the back behind three queens whose loud, aimless conversation made him edgy.

He was never less than edgy anyway, Erno—a seventeen-year-old biotech apprentice known for the clumsy, earnest intensity with which he propositioned almost every girl he met.

It was more people than Erno had ever seen in the Oxygen Warehouse. Even though Tyler Durden had not yet taken the stage, every table was filled, and people stood three deep at the bar. Rosamund, the owner, bustled back and forth providing drinks, her face glistening with sweat. The crush of people only irritated Erno. He had been one of the first to catch on to Durden, and the roomful of others, some of whom had probably come on his own recommendation, struck him as usurpers.

Erno forced his way to the bar and bought a tincture. Tyrus and Sid, friends of his, nodded at him from across the room. Erno sipped the cool, licorice-flavored drink and eavesdropped, and gradually his thoughts took on an architectural, intricate intellectuality.

A friend of his mother sat with a couple of sons who anticipated for her what she was going to see. "He's not just a comedian, he's a philosopher," said the skinny one. His foot, crossed over his knee, bounced in rhythm to the jazz playing in the background. Erno recognized him from a party he'd attended a few months back.

"We have philosophers," the matron said. "We even have comedians."

"Not like Tyler Durden," said the other boy.

"Tyler Durden—who gave him that name?"

"I think it's historical," the first boy said.

"Not any history I ever heard," the woman said. "Who's his mother?"

Erno noticed that there were more women in the room than there had been at any performance he had seen. Already the matrons were homing in. You could not escape their sisterly curiosity, their motherly tyranny. He realized that his shoulders were cramped; he rolled his head to try to loosen the spring-tight muscles.

The Oxygen Warehouse was located in what had been a shop in the commercial district of the northwest lava tube. It was a free-enterprise zone, and no one had objected to the addition of a tinctures bar, though some eyebrows had been raised when it was discovered that one of the tinctures sold was alcohol. The stage was merely a raised platform in one corner. Around the room were small tables with chairs. The bar spanned one end, and the other featured a false window that showed a nighttime cityscape of Old New York.

Rosamund Demisdaughter, who'd started the club, at first booked local jazz musicians. Her idea was to present as close to a retro Earth atmosphere as could be managed on the far side of the moon, where few of the inhabitants had ever even seen the Earth. Her clientele consisted of a few immigrants and a larger group of rebellious young cousins who were looking for an avant-garde. Erno knew his mother would not approve his going to the Warehouse, so he was there immediately.

He pulled his pack of fireless cigarettes from the inside pocket of his black twentieth-century suit, shook out a fag, inhaled it into life and imagined himself living back on Earth a hundred years ago. Exhaling a plume of cool, rancid smoke, he caught a glimpse of his razor haircut in the mirror behind the bar, then adjusted the knot of his narrow tie.

After some minutes the door beside the bar opened and Tyler Durden came out. He leaned over and exchanged a few words with Rosamund. Some of the men whistled and cheered. Rosamund flipped a brandy snifter high into the air, where it caught the ceiling lights as it spun in the low G, then slowly fell back to her hand. Having attracted the attention of the audience, she hopped over the bar and onto the small stage.

"Don't you people have anything better to do?" she shouted.

A chorus of rude remarks.

"Welcome to The Oxygen Warehouse," she said. "I want to say, before I bring him out, that I take no responsibility for the opinions expressed by Tyler Durden. He's not my boy."

Durden stepped onto the stage. The audience was quiet, a little nervous. He ran his hand over his shaved head, gave a boyish grin. He was a big man, in his thirties, wearing the blue coveralls of an environmental technician. Around his waist he wore a belt with tools hanging from it, as if he'd just come off shift.

"'Make love, not war!'" Durden said. "Remember that one? You got that from your mother, in the school? I never liked that one. 'Make love, not war,' they'll tell you. I hate that. I want to make love *and* war. I don't want my dick just to be a dick. I want it to stand for something!"

A heckler from the audience shouted, "Can't it stand on its own?"

Durden grinned. "Let's ask it." He addressed his crotch. "Hey, son!" He called down. "Don't you like screwing?"

Durden looked up at the ceiling, his face went simple, and he became his dick talking back to him. "Hiya dad!" he squeaked. "Sure, I like screwing!"

Durden winked at a couple of guys in makeup and lace in the front row, then looked down again: "Boys or girls?"

His dick: "What day of the week is it?"

"Thursday."

"Doesn't matter, then. Thursday's guest mammal day."

"Outstanding, son."

"I'm a Good Partner."

The queers laughed. Erno did, too.

"You want I should show you?"

"Not now, son," Tyler told his dick. "You keep quiet for a minute, and let me explain to the people, okay?"

"Sure. I'm here whenever you need me."

"I'm aware of that." Durden addressed the audience again. "Remember what Mama says, folks: *Keep your son close; let your semen go.*" He recited the slogan with exaggerated rhythm, wagging his finger at them, sober as a scolding grandmother. The audience loved it. Some of them chanted along with the catchphrase.

Durden was warming up. "But is screwing all there is to a dick? I say no!

"A dick is a sign of power. It's a tower of strength. It's the tree of life. It's a weapon. It's an incisive tool of logic. It's the seeker of truth.

"Mama says that being male is nothing more than a performance. You know what I say to that? Perform this, baby!" He grabbed his imaginary cock with both of his hands, made a stupid face.

Cheers.

"But of course, *they* can't perform this! I don't care how you plank the genes, Mama don't have the *machinery*. Not only that, she don't have the *programming*. But Mama wants to program *us* with *her* half-baked scheme of what women want a man to be. This whole place is about fucking up our *hardware* with their *software*."

He was laughing himself, now. Beads of sweat stood out on his scalp in the bright light.

"Mama says, 'Don't confuse your penis with a phallus.'" He assumed a female sway of his hips, lifted his chin and narrowed his eyes: just like that, he was an archetypal matron, his voice transmuted into a fruity contralto. "'Yes, you boys do have those nice little dicks, but we're living in a *post-phallic* society. A penis is merely a biological appendage.'"

Now he was her son, responding: "'Like a foot, Mom?'"

Mama: "'Yes, son. Exactly like a foot.'"

Quick as a spark, back to his own voice: "How many of you in the audience here have named your foot?"

Laughter, a show of hands.

"But Mama says the penis is designed solely for the propagation of the species. Sex gives pleasure in order to encourage procreation. A phallus, on the other hand—whichever hand you like—I prefer the left—"

More laughter.

"—a phallus is an idea, a cultural creation of the dead patriarchy, a symbolic sheath applied over the penis to give it meanings that have nothing to do with biology..."

Durden seized his invisible dick again. "Apply my symbolic sheath, baby...oohhh, yes, I like it..."

Erno had heard Tyler talk about his symbolic sheath before. Though there were variations, he watched the audience instead. Did they get it? Most of the men seemed to be engaged and laughing. A drunk in the first row leaned forward, hands on his knees, howling at Tyler's every word.

Queers leaned their heads together and smirked. Faces gleamed in the close air. But a lot of the men's laughter was nervous, and some did not laugh at all.

A few of the women, mostly the younger ones, were laughing. Some of them seemed mildly amused. Puzzled. Some looked bored. Others sat stonily with expressions that could only indicate anger.

Erno did not know how he felt about the women who were laughing. He felt hostility toward those who looked bored: why did you come here, he wanted to ask them. Who do you think you are? He preferred those who looked angry. That was what he wanted from them.

Then he noticed those who looked calm, interested, alert yet unamused. These women scared him.

In the back of the room stood some green-uniformed constables, male and female, carrying batons, red lights gleaming in the corner of their mirror spex, recording. Looking around the room, Erno located at least a half dozen of them. One, he saw with a start, was his mother.

He ducked behind a tall man beside him. She might not have seen him yet, but she would see him sooner or later. For a moment he considered confronting her, but then he sidled behind a row of watchers toward the back rooms. Another constable, her slender lunar physique distorted by the bulging muscles of a genetically engineered testosterone girl, stood beside the doorway. She did not look at Erno: she was watching Tyler, who was back to conversing with his dick.

"I'm tired of being confined," Tyler's dick was saying.

"You feel constricted?" Tyler asked.

He looked up in dumb appeal. "I'm stuck in your pants all day!"

Looking down: "I can let you out, but first tell me, are you a penis or a phallus?"

"That's a distinction without a difference."

"*Au contraire*, little man! You haven't been listening."

"I'm not noted for my listening ability."

"Sounds like you're a phallus to me," Tyler told his dick. "We have lots of room for penises, but Mama don't allow no phalluses 'round here."

"Let my people go!"

"Nice try, but wrong century. Look, son. It's risky when you come out. You could get damaged. The phallic liberation movement is in its infancy."

"I thought you Cousins were *all about* freedom."

"In theory. In practice, free phalluses are dangerous."

"Who says?"

"Well, Debra does, and so does Mary, and Sue, and Jamina most every time I see her, and there was this lecture in We-Explain-You-Listen class last week, and Ramona says so, too, and of course most emphatically Baba, and then there's that bitch Nora..."

Erno spotted his mother moving toward his side of the room. He slipped past the constable into the hall. There was the restroom, and a couple of other doors. A gale of laughter washed in from the club behind him at the climax of Tyler's story; cursing his mother, Erno went into the restroom.

No one was there. He could still hear the laughter, but not the cause of it. His mother's presence had cut him out of the community of male watchers as neatly as if she had used a baton. Erno felt murderously angry. He switched on a urinal and took a piss.

Over the urinal, a window played a scene in Central Park, on Earth, of a hundred years ago. A night scene of a pathway beneath some trees as large as the largest in Sobieski Park. A line of electric lights on poles threw pools of light along the path, and through the pools of light strolled a man and a woman. They were talking, but Erno could not hear what they were saying.

The woman wore a dress cinched tight at the waist, whose skirt flared out stiffly, ending halfway down her calves. The top of her dress had a low neckline that showed off her breasts. The man wore a dark suit like Erno's. They were completely differentiated by their dress, as if they were from different cultures, even species. Erno wondered where Rosamund had gotten the image.

As Erno watched, the man nudged the woman to the side of the path, beneath one of the trees. He slid his hands around her waist and pressed his body against hers. She yielded softly to his embrace. Erno could not see their faces in the shadows, but they were inches apart. He felt his dick getting hard in his hand.

He stepped back from the urinal, turned it off, and closed his pants.

As the hum of the recycler died, the restroom door swung open and a woman came in. She glanced at Erno and headed for one of the toilets. Erno went over to the counter and stuck his hands into the cleaner. The woman's presence sparked his anger.

Without turning to face her, but watching in the mirror, he said, "Why are you here tonight?"

The woman looked up (she had been studying her fingernails) and her eyes locked on his. She was younger than his mother and had a pretty, heart-shaped face. "I was curious. People are talking about him."

"Do you think men want you here?"

"I don't know what the men want."

"Yes. That's the point, isn't it? Are you learning anything?"

"Perhaps." The woman looked back at her hands. "Aren't you Pamela Megsdaughter's son?"

"So she tells me." Erno pulled his tingling hands out of the cleaner.

The woman used the bidet, and dried herself. She had a great ass. "Did she bring you or did you bring her?" she asked.

"We brought ourselves," Erno said. He left the restroom. He looked out into the club again, listening to the noise. The crowd was rowdier, and more raucous. The men's shouts of encouragement were like barks, their laughter edged with anger. His mother was still there. He did not want to see her, or to have her see him.

He went back past the restroom to the end of the hallway. The hall made a right angle into a dead end, but when Erno stepped into the bend he saw, behind a stack of plastic crates, an old door. He wedged the crates to one side and opened the door enough to slip through.

The door opened into a dark, dimly lit space. His steps echoed. As his eyes adjusted to the dim light he saw it was a very large room hewn out of the rock, empty except for some racks that must have held liquid-oxygen cylinders back in the early days of the colony, when this place had been an actual oxygen warehouse. The light came from ancient bioluminescent units on the walls. The club must have been set up in this space years before.

The tincture still lent Erno an edge of aggression, and he called out: "I'm Erno, King of the Moon!"

"—ooo—ooo—ooon!" the echoes came back, fading to stillness. He kicked an empty cylinder, which rolled forlornly a few meters before it stopped. He wandered around the chill vastness. At the far wall, one of the darker shadows turned out to be an alcove in the stone. Set in the back, barely visible in the dim light, was an ancient pressure door.

Erno decided not to mess with it—it could open onto vacuum. He went back to the club door and slid into the hallway.

Around the corner, two men were just coming out of the restroom, and Erno followed them as if he were just returning as well. The club was more crowded than ever. Every open space was filled with standing men, and others sat cross-legged up front. His mother and another constable had moved to the edge of the stage.

"—the problem with getting laid all the time is, you can't think!" Tyler was saying. "I mean, there's only so much blood in the human body. That's why those old Catholics back on Earth put the lock on the Pope's dick. He had an empire to run: the more time he spent taking care of John Thomas the less he spent thinking up ways of getting money out of peasants. The secret of our moms is that, if they keep that blood flowing below the belt, it ain't never gonna flow back above the shirt collar. Keeps the frequency of radical male ideas down!"

Tyler leaned over toward the drunk in the first row. "You know what I'm talking about, soldier?"

"You bet," the man said. He tried to stand, wobbled, sat down, tried to stand again.

"Where do you work?"

"Lunox." The man found his balance. "You're *right*, you—"

Tyler patted him on the shoulder. "An oxygen boy. You know what I mean, you're out there on the processing line, and you're thinking about how maybe if you were to add a little more graphite to the reduction chamber you could increase efficiency by 15 percent, and just then Mary Ellen Swivelhips walks by in her skintight and—bam!" Tyler made the face of a man who'd been poleaxed. "Uh—what was I thinking of?"

The audience howled.

"Forty I.Q. points down the oubliette. And nothing, NOTHING's gonna change until we get a handle on this! Am I right, brothers?"

More howls, spiked with anger.

Tyler was sweating, laughing, trembling as if charged with electricity. "Keep your son close! *Penis, no! Phallus, si!*"

Cheers now. Men stood and raised their fists. The drunk saw Erno's mother at the edge of the stage and took a step toward her. He said something, and while she and her partner stood irresolute, he put his big hand on her chest and shoved her away.

The other constable discharged his baton against the man. The drunk's arms flew back, striking a bystander, and two other men surged forward and knocked down the constable. Erno's mother raised her own baton. More constables pushed toward the stage, using their batons, and other men rose to stop them. A table was upended, shouts echoed, the room was hot as hell and turning into a riot, the first riot in the Society of Cousins in fifty years.

As the crowd surged toward the exits or toward the constables, Erno ducked back to the hallway. He hesitated, and then Tyler Durden came stumbling out of the melee. He took a quick look at Erno. "What now, kid?"

"Come with me," Erno said. He grabbed Tyler's arm and pulled him around the bend in the end of the hall, past the crates to the warehouse door. He slammed the door behind them and propped an empty oxygen cylinder against it. "We can hide here until the thing dies down."

"Who are you?"

"My name is Erno."

"Well, Erno, are we sure we want to hide? Out there is more interesting."

Erno decided not to tell Tyler that one of the constables was his mother. "Are you serious?"

"I'm always serious." Durden wandered back from the door into the gloom of the cavern. He kicked a piece of rubble, which soared across the warehouse and skidded up against the wall thirty meters away. "This place must have been here since the beginning. I'm surprised they're wasting the space. Probably full of toxics."

"You think so?" Erno said.

"Who knows?" Durden went toward the back of the warehouse, and Erno followed. It was cold, and their breath steamed the air. "Who would have figured the lights would still be growing?" Durden said.

"A well-established colony can last for fifty years or more," Erno said. "As long as there's enough moisture in the air. They break down the rock."

"You know all about it."

"I work in biotech," Erno said. "I'm a gene hacker."

Durden said nothing, and Erno felt the awkwardness of his boast.

They reached the far wall. Durden found the pressure door set into the dark alcove. He pulled a flashlight from his belt. The triangular yellow warning signs around the door were faded. He felt around the door seam.

"We probably ought to leave that alone," Erno said.

Durden handed Erno the flashlight, took a pry bar from his belt, and shoved it into the edge of the door. The door resisted, then with a grating squeak jerked open a couple of centimeters. Erno jumped at the sound.

"Help me out here, Erno," Durden said.

Erno got his fingers around the door's edge, and the two of them braced themselves. Durden put his feet up on the wall and used his legs and back to get leverage. When the door suddenly shot open Erno fell back and whacked his head. Durden lost his grip, shot sideways out of the alcove, bounced once, and skidded across the dusty floor. While Erno shook his head to clear his vision, Durden sat spread-legged, laughing. "Bingo!" he said. He bounced up. "You okay, Erno?"

Erno felt the back of his skull. He wasn't bleeding. "I'm fine," he said.

"Let's see what we've got, then."

Beyond the door a dark corridor cut through the basalt. Durden stepped into the path marked by his light. Erno wanted to go back to the club—by now things must have died down—but instead he followed.

Shortly past the door the corridor turned into a cramped lava tube. Early settlers had leveled the floor of the erratic tube formed by the draining away of cooling lava several billion years ago. Between walls that had been erected to form rooms ran a path of red volcanic gravel much like tailings from the oxygen factory. Foamy irregular pebbles kicked up by their shoes rattled off the walls. Dead light fixtures broke the ceiling at intervals. Tyler stopped to shine his light into a couple of the doorways, and at the third he went inside.

"This must be from the start of the colony," Erno said. "I wonder why it's been abandoned."

"Kind of claustrophobic." Durden shone the light around the small room.

The light fell on a small rectangular object in the corner. From his belt Durden pulled another tool, which he extended into a probe.

"Do you always carry this equipment?" Erno asked.

"Be prepared," Durden said. He set down the light and crouched over the object. It looked like a small box, a few centimeters thick. "You ever hear of the Boy Scouts, Erno?"

"Some early lunar colony?"

"Nope. Sort of like the Men's House, only different." Durden forced the probe under an edge, and one side lifted as if to come off. "Well, well!"

He put down the probe, picked up the object. He held it end-on, put his thumbs against the long side, and opened it. It divided neatly into flat sheets attached at the other long side.

"What is it?" Erno asked.

"It's a book."

"Is it still working?"

"This is an unpowered book. The words are printed right on these leaves. They're made of paper."

Erno had seen such old-fashioned books in vids. "It must be very old. What is it?"

Durden carefully turned the pages. "It's a book of stories." Durden stood up and handed the book to Erno. "Here. You keep it. Let me know what it's about."

Erno tried to make out the writing, but without Tyler's flashlight it was too dim.

Durden folded up his probe and hung it on his belt. He ran his hand over his head, smearing a line of dust over his scalp. "Are you cold? I suppose we ought to find our way out of here." Immediately he headed out of the room and back down the corridor.

Erno felt he was getting left behind in more ways than one. Clutching the book, he followed after Durden and his bobbing light. Rather than heading back to the Oxygen Warehouse, the comedian continued down the lava tube.

Eventually the tube ended in another old pressure door. When Durden touched the key panel at its side, amazingly, it lit.

"What do you think?" Durden said.

"We should go back," Erno said. "We can't know whether the lock door on the other side is still airtight. The fail-safes could be broken. We could open the door onto vacuum." He held the book under his armpit and blew on his cold hands.

"How old are you, Erno?"

"Seventeen."

"Seventeen?" Durden's eyes glinted in shadowed eye sockets. "Seventeen is no age to be cautious."

Erno couldn't help but grin. "You're right. Let's open it."

"My man, Erno!" Durden slapped him on the shoulder. He keyed the door open. They heard the whine of a long-unused electric motor. Erno could feel his heart beat, the blood running swiftly in his veins. At first nothing happened, then the door began to slide open. There was a chuff of air escaping from the lava tube, and dust kicked up. But the wind stopped as soon as it started, and the door opened completely on the old airlock, filled floor to ceiling with crates and bundles of fiberglass building struts.

It took them half an hour to shift boxes and burrow their way through the airlock, to emerge at the other end into another warehouse, this one still in use. They crept by racks of construction materials until they reached the entrance, and sneaked out into the colony corridor beyond.

They were at the far end of North Six, the giant lava tube that served the industrial wing of the colony. The few workers they encountered on the late shift might have noticed Erno's suit, but said nothing.

Erno and Tyler made their way back home. Tyler cracked jokes about the constables until they emerged into the vast open space of the domed crater that formed the center of the colony. Above, on the huge dome, was projected a night starfield. In the distance, down the rimwall slopes covered with junipers, across the crater floor, lights glinted among the trees in Sobieski Park. Erno took a huge breath of air, fragrant with piñon.

"The world our ancestors gave us," Tyler said, waving his arm as if offering it to Erno.

As Tyler turned to leave, Erno called out impulsively, "That was an adventure!"

"The first of many, Erno," Tyler said, and jogged away.

CELIBACY DAY

On Celibacy Day, everyone gets a day off from sex.

Some protest this practice, but they are relatively few. Most men take it as an opportunity to retreat to the informal Men's Houses that, though they have no statutory sanction, sprang up in the first generation of settlers.

In the Men's House, men and boys talk about what it is to be a man, a lover of other men and women, a father in a world where fatherhood is no more than a biological concept. They complain about their lot. They tell vile jokes and sing songs. They wrestle. They gossip. Heteros and queers and everyone in between compare speculations on what they think women really want, and whether it matters. They try to figure out what a true man is.

As a boy Erno would go to the Men's House with his mother's current partner or one of the other men involved in the household. Some of the men taught him things. He learned about masturbation, and cross-checks, and Micro Language Theory.

But no matter how welcoming the men were supposed to be to each other—and they talked about brotherhood all the time—there was always that little edge when you met another boy there, or that necessary wariness when you talked to an adult. Men came to the Men's House to spend time together and remind themselves of certain congruencies, but only a crazy person would want to live solely in the company of men.

TWO

THE FOUNDERS OF the Society of Cousins had a vision of women as independent agents, freethinkers forming alliances with other women to create a social bond so strong that men could not overwhelm them. Solidarity, sisterhood, motherhood. But Erno's mother was not like those women. Those women existed only in history vids, sitting in meeting circles, laughing, making plans, sure of themselves and complete.

Erno's mother was a cop. She had a cop's squinty eyes and a cop's suspicion of anyone who stepped outside of the norm. She had a cop's lack of imagination, except as she could imagine what people would do wrong.

Erno and his mother and his sister Celeste and his Aunt Sophie and his cousins Lena and Aphra, and various men, some of whom may have been fathers, some of them Good Partners, and others just men, lived in an apartment in Sanger, on the third level of the northeast quadrant, a small place looking down on the farms that filled the floor of the crater they called Fowler, though the real Fowler was a much larger crater five kilometers distant.

Erno had his own room. He thought nothing of the fact that the girls had to share a room, and would be forced to move out when they turned fourteen. *Keep your son close; let your daughter go*, went the aphorism Tyler had mocked. Erno's mother was not about to challenge any aphorisms. Erno remembered her expression as she had stepped forward to arrest the drunk: sad that this man had forced her to this, and determined to do it. She was comfortable in the world; she saw no need for alternatives. Her cronies came by the apartment and shared coffee and gossip, and they were just like all the other mothers and sisters and aunts. None of them were extraordinary.

Not that any of the men Erno knew were extraordinary, either. Except Tyler Durden. And now Erno knew Durden, and they had spent a night breaking rules and getting away with it.

Celeste and Aphra were dishing up oatmeal when Erno returned to the apartment that morning. "Where were you?" his mother asked. She looked up from the table, more curious than upset, and Erno noticed a bruise on her temple.

"What happened to your forehead?" Erno asked.

His mother touched a hand to her forehead, as if she had forgotten it. She waved the hand in dismissal.

"There was trouble at a club in the enterprise district," Aunt Sophie said. "The constables had to step in, and your mother was assaulted."

"It was a riot!" Lena said eagerly. "There's going to be a big meeting about it in the park today." Lena was a month from turning fourteen, and looking forward to voting.

Erno sat down at the table. As he did so he felt the book, which he had tucked into his belt at the small of his back beneath his now rumpled suit jacket. He leaned forward, pulled a bowl of oatmeal toward him, and took up a spoon. Looking down into the bowl to avoid anyone's eyes, he idly asked, "What's the meeting for?"

"One of the rioters was knocked into a coma," Lena said. "The social order committee wants this comedian Tyler Durden to be made invisible."

Erno concentrated on his spoon. "Why?"

"You know about him?" his mother asked.

Before he had to think of an answer, Nick Farahsson, his mother's partner, shambled into the kitchen. "Lord, Pam, don't you pay attention? Erno's one of his biggest fans."

His mother turned on Erno. "Is that so?"

Erno looked up from his bowl and met her eyes. She looked hurt. "I've heard of him."

"Heard of him?" Nick said. "Erno, I bet you were there last night."

"I bet *you* weren't there," Erno said.

Nick stretched. "I don't need to hear him. I have no complaints." He came up behind Erno's mother, nuzzled the nape of her neck, and cupped her breast in his hand.

She turned her face up and kissed him on the cheek. "I should hope not."

Lena made a face. "Heteros. I can't wait until I get out of here." She had recently declared herself gay and was quite judgmental about it.

"You'd better get to your practicum, Lena," Aunt Sophie said. "Let your aunt take care of her own sex life."

"This guy Durden is setting himself up for a major fall," said Nick. "Smells like a case of abnormal development. Who's his mother?"

Erno couldn't keep quiet. "He doesn't have a mother. He doesn't need one."

"Parthenogenesis," Aunt Sophie said. "I didn't think it had been perfected yet."

"If they ever do, what happens to me?" Nick said.

"You have your uses." Erno's mother nudged his hip.

"You two can go back to your room," Aunt Sophie said. "We'll take care of things for you."

"No need." Nick grabbed a bowl of oatmeal and sat down. "Thank you, sweetheart," he said to Aphra. "I can't see what this guy's problem is."

"Doesn't it bother you that you can't vote?" Erno said. "What's fair about that?"

"I don't want to vote," Nick said.

"You're a complete drone."

His mother frowned at him. Erno pushed his bowl away and left for his room.

"You're the one with special tutoring!" Lena called. "The nice clothes. What work do you do?"

"Shut up," Erno said softly, but his ears burned.

He had nothing to do until his 1100 biotech tutorial, and he didn't even have to go if he didn't want to. Lena was right about that, anyway. He threw the book on his bed, undressed, and switched on his screen. On the front page was a report of solar activity approaching its eleven-year peak, with radiation warnings issued for all surface activity. Erno called up the calendar. There it was: a discussion on Tyler Durden was scheduled in the amphitheater at 1600. Linked was a vid of the riot and a forum for open citizen comment. A cousin named Tashi Yokiosson had been clubbed in the fight and was in a coma, undergoing nanorepair.

Erno didn't know him, but that didn't prevent his anger. He considered calling up Tyrus or Sid, finding out what had happened to them, and telling them about his adventure with Tyler. But that would spoil the secret, and it might get around to his mother. Yet he couldn't let his night with Tyler go uncelebrated. He opened his journal, and wrote a poem:

Going outside the crater
finding the lost tunnels
of freedom
and male strength.
Searching with your brother
shoulder to shoulder
like men.

Getting below the surface
of a stifling society
sounding your XY shout.
Flashing your colors
like an ancient Spartan bird
proud, erect, never to be softened
by the silent embrace of woman

No females aloud.

Not bad. It had some of the raw honesty of the Beats. He would read it at the next meeting of the Poets' Club. He saved it with the four hundred other poems he had written in the last year: Erno prided himself on being the most prolific poet in his class. He had already won four Laurel Awards, one for best Lyric, one for best Sonnet, and two for best Villanelle—plus a Snappie for best limerick of 2097. He was sure to make Bard at an earlier age than anyone since Patrick Maurasson.

Erno switched off the screen, lay on his bed, and remembered the book. He dug it out from under his discarded clothes. It had a blue cover, faded to purple near the binding, made of some sort of fabric. Embossed on the front was a torch encircled by a laurel wreath. He opened the book to its title page: *Stories for Men*, "An Anthology by Charles Grayson." Published in August 1936, in the United States of America.

As a fan of Earth culture, Erno knew that most Earth societies used the patronymic, so that Gray, Grayson's naming parent, would be a man, not a woman.

Stories for men. The authors on the contents page were all men— except perhaps for odd names like "Dashiell." Despite Erno's interest in twentieth-century popular art, his knowledge was spotty and only a couple were familiar. William Faulkner he knew was considered a major Earth writer, and he had seen the name Hemingway before, though he had associated it only with a style of furniture. But even assuming the stories were all written by men, the title said the book was stories *for* men, not stories *by* men.

How did a story for a man differ from a story for a woman? Erno had never considered the idea before. He had heard storytellers in the park, and read books in school—Murasaki, Chopin, Cather, Ellison, Morrison, Ferenc, Sabinsdaughter. As a child, he had loved the Alice books, and *Flatland*, and Maria Hidalgo's kids' stories, and Seuss. None seemed particularly male or female.

He supposed the Cousins did have their own stories for men. Nick loved interactive serials, tortured romantic tales of interpersonal angst set in the patriarchal world, where men struggled against injustice until they found the right woman and were taken care of. Erno stuck to poetry. His favorite novel was Tawanda Tamikasdaughter's *The Dark Blood*—the story of a misunderstood young Cousin's struggles against his overbearing mother, climaxed when his father miraculously reveals himself and brings the mother to heel. At the Men's House, he had also seen his share of porn—thrillers set on Earth where men forced women to do whatever the men wanted, and like it.

But this book did not look like porn. A note at the beginning promised the book contained material to "interest, or alarm, or amuse, or instruct, or—and possibly most important of all—entertain you." Erno wondered that Tyler had found this particular 160-year-old book in the lava tube. It seemed too unlikely to be coincidence.

What sort of things would entertain an Earthman of 1936? Erno turned to the first story, "The Ambassador of Poker" by "Achmed Abdullah."

But the archaic text was frustratingly passive—nothing more than black type physically impressed on the pages, without links or explanations. After a paragraph or so rife with obscure cultural references—"cordovan brogues," "knickerbockers," "County Sligo," "a four-in-hand"—Erno's night without sleep caught up with him, and he dozed off.

HEROES

Why does a man remain in the Society of Cousins, when he would have much more authority outside of it, in one of the other lunar colonies, or on Earth?

For one thing, the sex is great.

Men are valued for their sexuality, praised for their potency, competed for by women. From before puberty, a boy is schooled by both men and women in how to give pleasure. A man who can give such pleasure has high status. He is recognized and respected throughout the colony. He is welcome in any bed. He is admired and envied by other men.

THREE

ERNO WOKE SUDDENLY, sweaty and disoriented, trailing the wisps of a dream that faded before he could call it back. He looked at his clock: 1530. He was going to miss the meeting.

He washed his face, applied personal hygiene bacteria, threw on his embroidered jumpsuit, and rushed out of the apartment.

The amphitheater in Sobieski Park was filling as Erno arrived. Five or six hundred people were already there; other Cousins would be watching on the link. The dome presented a clear blue sky, and the ring of heliotropes around its zenith flooded the air with sunlight. A slight breeze rustled the old oaks, hovering over the semicircular ranks of seats like aged grandmothers. People came in twos and threes, adults and children, along the paths that led down from the colony perimeter road through the farmlands to the park. Others emerged from the doors at the base of the central spire that supported the dome. Erno found a seat in the top row, far from the stage, off to one side where the seats gave way to grass.

Chairing the meeting was Debra Debrasdaughter. Debrasdaughter was a tiny sixty-year-old woman who, though she had held public office infrequently and never for long, was one of the most respected Cousins. She had been Erno's teacher when he was six, and he remembered how she'd sat with him and worked through his feud with Bill Grettasson. She taught him how to play forward on the soccer team. On the soccer field she had been fast and sudden as a bug. She had a warm laugh and sharp brown eyes.

Down on the stage, Debrasdaughter was hugging the secretary. Then the sound person hugged Debrasdaughter. They both hugged the secretary again. A troubled-looking old man sat down in the front row, and all three of them got down off the platform and hugged him. He brushed his hand along Debrasdaughter's thigh, but it was plain that his heart wasn't in it. She kissed his cheek and went back up on the stage.

A flyer wearing red wings swooped over the amphitheater and soared back up again, slowly beating the air. Another pair of flyers raced around the crater's perimeter, silhouetted against the clusters of apartments built into its walls. A thousand meters above his head, Erno could spy a couple of others on the edge of the launch platform at the top of the spire. As he watched, squinting against the sunlight, one of the tiny figures spread its wings and pushed off, diving down, at first ever so slowly, gaining speed, then, with a flip of wings, soaring out level. Erno could feel it in his own shoulders, the stress that maneuver put on your arms. He didn't like flying. Even in lunar gravity, the chances of a fall were too big.

The amplified voice of Debrasdaughter drew him back to the amphitheater. "Thank you, Cousins, for coming," she said. "Please come to order."

Erno saw that Tyler Durden had taken a seat off to one side of the stage. He wore flaming red coveralls, like a shout.

"A motion has been made to impose a decree of invisibility against Thomas Marysson, otherwise known as Tyler Durden, for a period of one year. We are met here for the first of two discussions over this matter, prior to holding a colony-wide vote."

Short of banishment, invisibility was the colony's maximum social sanction. Should the motion carry, Tyler would be formally ostracized. Tagged by an AI, continuously monitored, he would not be acknowledged by other Cousins. Should he attempt to harm anyone, the AI would trigger receptors in his brain stem to put him to sleep.

"This motion was prompted by the disturbances that have ensued as a result of public performances of Thomas Marysson. The floor is now open for discussion."

A very tall woman who had been waiting anxiously stood, and as if by prearrangement, Debrasdaughter recognized her. The hovering mikes picked up her high voice. "I am Yokio Kumiosdaughter. My son is in the hospital as a result of this shameful episode. He is a good boy. He is the kind of boy we all want, and I don't understand how he came to be in that place. I pray that he recovers and lives to become the good man I know he can be.

"We must not let this happen to anyone else's son. At the very least, invisibility will give Thomas Marysson the opportunity to reflect on his actions before he provokes another such tragedy."

Another woman rose. Erno saw it was Rosamund Demisdaughter.

"With due respect to Cousin Kumiosdaughter, I don't believe the riot in my club was Tyler's fault. Her son brought this on himself. Tyler is not responsible for the actions of the patrons. Since when do we punish people for the misbehavior of others?

"The real mistake was sending constables," Rosamund continued. "Whether or not the grievances Tyler gives vent to are real or only perceived, we must allow any Cousins to speak their mind. The founders understood that men and women are different. By sending armed officers into that club, we threatened the right of those men who came to see Tyler Durden to be different."

"It was stupid strategy!" someone interrupted. "They could have arrested Durden easily after the show."

"Arrested him? On what grounds?" another woman asked.

Rosamund continued. "Adil Al-Hafez said it when he helped Nora Sobieski raise the money for this colony: 'The Cousins are a new start for men as much as women. We do not seek to change men, but to offer them the opportunity to be other than they have been.'"

A man Erno recognized from the biotech facility took the floor. "It's all very well to quote the founders back at us, but they were realists, too. Men *are* different. Personalized male power has made the history of Earth one long tale of slaughter, oppression, rape, and war. Sobieski and Al-Hafez and the rest knew that, too: the California massacre sent them here. Durden's incitements will inevitably cause trouble. This kid wouldn't have gotten hurt without him. We can't stand by while the seeds of institutionalized male aggression are planted."

"This is a free-speech issue!" a young woman shouted.

"It's not about speech," the man countered. "It's about violence."

Debrasdaughter called for order. The man looked sheepish and sat down. A middle-aged woman with a worried expression stood. "What about organizing a new round of games? Let them work it out on the rink, the flying drome, the playing field."

"We have games of every description," another woman responded. "You think we can make Durden join the hockey team?"

The old man in the front row croaked out, "Did you see that game last week against Aristarchus? They could use a little more organized male aggression." That drew a chorus of laughter from the crowd.

When the noise died down, an elderly woman took the floor. "I have been a Cousin for seventy years," she said. "I've seen troublemakers. There will always be troublemakers. But what's happened to the Good Partners? I remember the North tube blowout of '62. Sixty people died. Life here was brutal and dangerous. But men and women worked together shoulder to shoulder; we shared each other's joys and sorrows. We were good bedmates then. Where is that spirit now?"

Erno had heard such tiresome sermonettes about the old days a hundred times. The discussion turned into a cacophony of voices.

"What are we going to do?" said another woman. "Deprive men of the right to speak?"

"Men are already deprived of the vote! How many voters are men?"

"By living on the colony stipend, men *choose* not to vote. Nobody is stopping you from going to work."

"We work already! How much basic science do men do? Look at the work Laurasson did on free energy. And most of the artists are men."

"They have the time to devote to science and art *because of* the material support of the community. They have the luxury of intellectual pursuit."

"And all decisions about what to do with their work are made by women."

"The decisions, which will affect the lives of everyone in the society, are made not by women, but by voters."

"And most voters are women."

"Full circle!" someone shouted. "Reload program and repeat."

A smattering of laughter greeted the sarcasm. Debrasdaughter smiled. "These are general issues, and to a certain degree I am content to let them be aired. But do they bear directly on the motion? What, if anything, are we to do about Thomas Marysson?"

She looked over at Tyler, who looked back at her coolly, his legs crossed.

A woman in a constable's uniform rose. "The problem with Thomas Marysson is that he claims the privileges of artistic expression, but he's not really an artist. He's a provocateur."

"Most of the artists in history have been provocateurs," shot back a small, dark man.

"He makes me laugh," said another.

"He's smart. Instead of competing with other men, he wants to organize them. He encourages them to band together."

The back-and-forth rambled on. Despite Debrasdaughter's attempt to keep order, the discussion ran into irrelevant byways, circular arguments, vague calls for comity, and general statements of male and female grievance. Erno had debated all this stuff a million times with the guys at the gym. It annoyed him that Debrasdaughter did not force the speakers to stay on point. But that was typical of a Cousins' meeting—they would talk endlessly, letting every nitwit have their say, before actually getting around to deciding anything.

A young woman stood to speak; it was Alicia Keikosdaughter. Alicia and he had shared a tutorial in math, and she had been the second girl he had ever had sex with.

"Of course Durden wants to be seen as an artist," Alicia said. "There's no mystique about the guy who works next to you in the factory. Who wants to sleep with him? The truth—"

"I will!" a good-looking woman interrupted Alicia.

The assembly laughed.

"The truth—" Alicia tried to continue.

The woman ignored her. She stood, her hand on the head of the little girl at her side, and addressed Tyler Durden directly. "I think you need to get laid!" She turned to the others. "Send him around to me! I'll take care of any revolutionary impulses he might have." More laughter.

Erno could see Alicia's shoulders slump, and she sat down. It was a typical case of a matron ignoring a young woman. He got up, moved down the aisle, and slid into a spot next to her.

Alicia turned to him. "Erno. Hello."

"It's not your fault they won't listen," he said. Alicia was wearing a tight satin shirt and Erno could not help but notice her breasts.

She kissed him on the cheek. She turned to the meeting, then back to him. "What do you think they're going to do?"

"They're going to ostracize him, I'll bet."

"I saw him on link. Have you seen him?"

"I was there last night."

Alicia leaned closer. "Really?" she said. Her breath was fragrant, and her lips full. There was a tactile quality to Alicia that Erno found deeply sexy—when she talked to you she would touch your shoulder or bump her knee against yours, as if to reassure herself that you were really there. "Did you get in the fight?"

A woman on the other side of Alicia leaned over. "If you two aren't going to pay attention, at least be quiet so the rest of us can."

Erno started to say something, but Alicia put her hand on his arm. "Let's go for a walk."

Erno was torn. Boring or not, he didn't want to miss the meeting, but it was hard to ignore Alicia. She was a year younger than Erno yet was already on her own, living with Sharon Yasminsdaughter while studying environmental social work. One time Erno had heard her argue with Sharon whether it was true that women on Earth could not use elevators because if they did they would inevitably be raped.

They left the amphitheater and walked through the park. Erno told Alicia his version of the riot at the club, leaving out his exploring the deserted lava tube with Tyler.

"Even if they don't make him invisible," Alicia said, "you know that somebody is going to make sure he gets the message."

"He hasn't hurt anyone. Why aren't we having a meeting about the constable who clubbed Yokiosson?"

"The constable was attacked. A lot of cousins feel threatened. I'm not even sure how I feel."

"The Unwritten Law," Erno muttered.

"The what?"

"Tyler does a bit about it. It was an Earth custom, in most of the patriar-chies. The 'unwritten law' said that, if a wife had sex with anyone other than her husband, the husband had the right to kill her and her lover, and no court would hold him guilty."

"That's because men had all the power."

"But you just said somebody would send Tyler a message. Up here, if a man abuses a woman, even threatens to, then the abused woman's friends take revenge. When was the last time anyone did anything about that?"

"I get it, Erno. That must seem unfair."

"Men don't abuse women here."

"Maybe that's why."

"It doesn't make it right."

"You're right, Erno. It doesn't. I'm on your side."

Erno sat down on the ledge of the pool surrounding the fountains. The fountains were the pride of the colony: in a conspicuous show of water con-sumption the pools surrounded the central spire and wandered beneath the park's trees. Genetically altered carp swam in their green depths, and the air was more humid here than anywhere else under the dome.

Alicia sat next to him. "Remind me why we broke up," Erno said.

"Things got complicated." She had said the same thing the night she told him they shouldn't sleep together anymore. He still didn't know what that meant, and he suspected she said it only to keep from saying something that might wound him deeply. Much as he wanted to insist that he would prefer her honesty, he wasn't sure he could stand it.

"I'm going crazy at home," he told Alicia. "Mother treats me like a child. Lena is starting to act like she's better than me. I do real work at Biotech, but that doesn't matter."

"You'll be in university soon. You're a premium gene hacker."

"Who says?" Erno asked.

"People."

"Yeah, right. And if I am, I still live at home. I'm going to end up just like Nick," he said, "the pet male in a household full of females."

"Maybe something will come of this. Things can change."

"If only," Erno said morosely. But he was surprised and gratified to have Alicia's encouragement. Maybe she cared for him after all. "There's one thing, Alicia... I could move in with you."

Alicia raised an eyebrow. He pressed on. "Like you say, I'll be studying at the university next session..."

She put her hand on his leg. "There's not much space, with Sharon and me. We couldn't give you your own room."

"I'm not afraid of sharing a bed. I can alternate between you."

"You're so manly, Erno!" she teased.

"I aim to please," he said, and struck a pose. Inside he cringed. It was a stupid thing to say, so much a boy trying to talk big.

Alicia did a generous thing—she laughed. There was affection and understanding in it. It made him feel they were part of some club together.

Erno hadn't realized how afraid he was that she would mock him. Neither said anything for a moment. A finch landed on the branch above them, turned its head sideways, and inspected them. "You know, you could be just like Tyler Durden, Erno."

Erno started—what did she mean by that? He looked her in the face. Alicia's eyes were green, flecked with gold. He hadn't looked into her eyes since they had been lovers.

She kissed him. Then she touched his lips with her finger. "Don't say anything. I'll talk to Sharon."

He put his arm around her. She melted into him.

In the distance the sounds of the debate were broken by a burst of laughter. "Let's go back," she said.

"All right," he said reluctantly.

They walked back to the amphitheater and found seats in the top row, beside two women in their twenties who joked with each other.

"This guy is no Derek Silviasson," one of them said.

"If he could fuck like Derek, now *that* would be comedy," said her blond partner.

Debrasdaughter was calling for order.

"We cannot compel any cousin to indulge in sex against his will. If he chooses to be celibate, and encourages his followers to be celibate, we can't prevent that without undermining the very freedoms we came here to establish."

Nick Farahsson, his face red and his voice contorted, shouted out, "You just said the key word—followers! We don't need followers here. Followers have ceded their autonomy to a hierarchy. Followers are the tool of phallocracy. Followers started the riot." Erno saw his mother, sitting next to Nick, try to calm him.

Another man spoke. "What a joke! We're all a bunch of followers! Cousins follow customs as slavishly as any Earth patriarch."

"What I don't understand," someone called out directly to Tyler, "is, if you hate it here so much, why don't you just leave? Don't let the airlock door clip your ass on the way out."

"This is my home, too," Tyler said.

He stood and turned to Debrasdaughter. "If you don't mind, I would like to speak."

"We'd be pleased to hear what you have to say," Debrasdaughter said. The trace of a smile on her pale face made her look girlish despite her gray hair. "Speaking for myself, I've been waiting."

Tyler ran his hand over his shaved scalp, came to the front of the platform. He looked out at his fellow citizens, and smiled. "I think you've outlined all the positions pretty clearly. I note that Tashi Yokiosson didn't say anything, but maybe he'll get back to us later. It's been a revealing discussion, and now I'd just like to ask you to help me out with a demonstration. Will you do this little thing for me?

"I'd like you all to put your hand over your eyes. Like this—" He covered his own eyes with his palm, peeked out. Most of the assembly did as he asked. "All of you got your eyes covered? Good!

"Because, sweethearts, this is the closest I am going to get to invisibility."

Tyler threw his arms wide, and laughed.

"Make me invisible? You can't see me now! You don't recognize a man whose word is steel, whose reality is not dependent on rules. Men have fought and bled and died for you. Men have put their lives on the line for every microscopic step forward our pitiful species has made. Nothing's more visible than the sacrifices men have made for the good of their wives and daughters. Yes, women died, too—*real* women, women not threatened by the existence of masculinity.

"You see that tower?" Tyler pointed to the thousand-meter spire looming over their heads. "I can climb that tower! I can fuck every real woman in this amphitheater. I eat a lot of food, drink a lot of alcohol, and take a lot of drugs. I'm *bigger* than you are. I sweat more. I howl like a dog. I make noise. You think anyone can make more noise than me?

"One way or another, Mama, I'm going to keep you awake all night! And *you* think you're the female that can stop me?

"My Uncle Dick told me when I was a boy, son, don't take it out unless you intend to use it! Well, it's out and it's in use! Rim ram god damn, sonafabitch fuck! It is to laugh. This whole discussion's been a waste of oxygen. I'm real, I'm here, get used to it.

"Invisible? Just *try* not to see me."

Then Tyler crouched and leapt three meters into the air, tucked, did a roll. Coming down, he landed on his hands and did a handspring. The second his feet touched the platform, he shot off the side and ran, taking long, loping strides out of the park and through the beanfields.

A confused murmur rippled through the assembly, broken by a few angry calls. Many puzzled glances. Some people stood.

Debrasdaughter called for order. "I'll ask the assembly to calm down," she said.

Gradually, quiet came.

"I'm sure we are all stimulated by that very original statement. I don't think we are going to get any farther today, and I note that it is coming on time for the swing-shifters to leave, so unless there are serious objections I would like to call this meeting to a close.

"The laws call for a second open meeting a week from today, followed by a polling period of three days, at the end of which the will of the colony will be made public and enacted. Do I hear any further discussion?"

There was none.

"Then I hereby adjourn this meeting. We will meet again one week from today at 1600 hours. Anyone who wishes to post a statement in regard to this matter may do so at the colony site, where a room will be open continuously for debate. Thank you for your participation."

People began to break up, talking. The two women beside Erno, joking, left the theater.

Alicia stood. "Was that one of his routines?"

Tyler's speech had stirred something in Erno that made him want to shout. He was grinning from ear to ear. "It is to laugh," he murmured.

Alicia grabbed Erno's wrist. She pulled a pen from her pocket, turned his hand so the palm lay open, and on it wrote "Gilman 334."

"Before you do anything stupid, Erno," she said, "call me."

"Define stupid," he said.

But Alicia had turned away. He felt the tingle of the writing on his hand as he watched her go.

WORK

Men are encouraged to apply for an exemption from the mita: the compulsory weekly labor that each cousin devotes to the support of the colony. The cost of this exemption is forfeiture of the right to vote. As artists, writers, artisans, athletes, performers, and especially as scientists, men have an easier path than women. Their interests are supported to the limits of the Cousins' resources. But this is not accorded the designation of work, and all practical decisions as to what to do with any creations of their art or discoveries they might make are left to voters, who are overwhelmingly women.

Men who choose such careers are praised as public-spirited volunteers, sacrificing for the sake of the community. At the same time, they live a life of relative ease, pursuing their interests. They compete with each other for the attentions of women. They may exert influence, but have no legal responsibilities, and no other responsibilities except as they choose them. They live like sultans, but without power. Or like gigolos. Peacocks, and studs.

And those who choose to do work? Work—ah, work is different. Work is mundane labor directed toward support of the colony. Male workers earn no honors, accumulate no status. And because men are always outnumbered by women on such jobs, they have little chance of advancement to a position of authority. They just can't get the votes.

"TWENTY-FIVE BUCKS"

Erno began to puzzle out some of the *Stories for Men*. One was about a "prize-fighter"—a man who fought another man with his fists for money. This aging fighter agrees with a promoter to fight a younger, stronger man for "twenty-five bucks," which from context Erno gathered was a small sum of money. The boxer spends his time in the ring avoiding getting beaten up. During a pause between the "rounds" of the fight, the promoter comes to him and complains that he is not fighting hard enough, and swears he will not pay the boxer if he "takes a dive." So in the next round the boxer truly engages in the brutal battle, and within a minute gets beaten unconscious.

But because this happens immediately after the promoter spoke to him, in the sight of the audience, the audience assumes the boxer was *told* by the promoter to take a dive. They protest. Rather than defend the boxer, the promoter denies him the twenty-five bucks anyway.

The boxer, unconscious while the promoter and audience argue, dies of a brain hemorrhage.

The story infuriated Erno. It felt so *wrong*. Why did the boxer take on the fight? Why did he allow himself to be beaten so badly? Why did the promoter betray the boxer? What was the point of the boxer's dying in the end? Why did the writer—someone named James T. Farrell—invent this grim tale?

FOUR

A WEEK AFTER the meeting, when Erno logged onto school, he found a message for him from "Ethan Edwards." It read:

> I saw you with that girl. Cute. But no sex, Erno.
> I'm counting on men like you.

Erno sent a reply: "You promised me another adventure. When?"

Then he did biochemistry ("Delineate the steps in the synthesis of human growth hormone") and read Gender & Art for three hours until he had to get to his practicum at Biotech.

In order to reduce the risk of stray bugs getting loose in the colony, the biotech factories were located in a bunker separate from the main crater. Workers had to don pressure suits and ride a bus for a couple of kilometers across the lunar surface. A crowd of other biotech workers already filled the locker room at the north airlock when Erno arrived.

"Tyrus told me you're fucking Alicia Keikosdaughter, Erno," said Paul Gwynethsson, whose locker was next to Erno's. "He was out flying. He saw you in the park."

"So? Who are you fucking?" Erno asked. He pulled on his skintight. The fabric, webbed with thermoregulators, sealed itself, the suit's environment system powered up, and Erno locked down his helmet. The helmet's heads-up display was green. He and Paul went to the airlock, passed their IDs through the reader, and entered with the others. The exit sign posted the solar storm warning. Paul teased Erno about Alicia as the air was cycled through the lock and they walked out through the radiation maze to the surface.

They got on the bus that had dropped off the previous biotech shift. The bus bumped away in slow motion down the graded road. It was late in the lunar afternoon, probably only a day or so of light before the two-week night. If a storm should be detected and the alert sounded, they would have maybe twenty minutes to find shelter before the radiation flux hit the exposed surface. But the ride to the lab went uneventfully.

A man right off the cable train from Tsander was doing a practicum in the lab. His name was Cluny. Like so many Earthmen, he was short and impressively muscled, and spoke slowly, with an odd accent. Cluny was not yet a citizen and had not taken a Cousins name. He was still going through training before qualifying to apply for exemption from the *mita*.

Erno interrupted Cluny as he carried several racks of microenvironment bulbs to the sterilizer. He asked Cluny what he thought of Tyler Durden.

Cluny was closemouthed; perhaps he thought Erno was testing him: "I think if he doesn't like it up here, I can show him lots of places on Earth happy to take him."

Erno let him get on with his work. Cluny was going to have a hard time over the next six months. The culture shock would be nothing next to the genetic manipulation he would have to undergo to adjust him for low-G. The life expectancy of an unmodified human on the moon was forty-eight. No exercise regimen or drugs could prevent the cardiovascular atrophy and loss of bone mass that humans evolved for Earth would suffer.

But the retroviruses could alter the human genome to produce solid fibrolaminar bones in one-sixth G, prevent plaque buildup in arteries, ensure pulmonary health, and prevent a dozen other fatal low-G syndromes.

At the same time, licensing biotech discoveries was the colony's major source of foreign exchange, so research was under tight security. Erno pressed his thumb against the gene scanner. He had to go through three levels of clearances to access the experiment he had been working on. Alicia was right—Erno was getting strokes for his rapid learning in gene techniques, and already had a rep. Even better, he liked it. He could spend hours brainstorming synergistic combinations of alterations in mice, adapting Earth genotypes for exploitation.

Right now he was assigned to the ecological design section under Lemmy Odillesson, the premier agricultural genobotanist. Lemmy was working on giant plane trees. He had a vision of underground bioengineered forests, entire ecosystems introduced to newly opened lava tubes that would transform dead, airless immensities into habitable biospheres. He wanted to live in a city of underground lunar tree houses.

Too soon Erno's six-hour shift was over. He suited up, climbed to the surface, and took the bus back to the north airlock. As the shift got off, a figure came up to Erno from the shadows of the radiation maze.

It was a big man in a tiger-striped skintight, his faceplate opaqued. Erno shied away from him, but the man held his hands, palms up, in front of him to indicate no threat. He came closer, leaned forward. Erno flinched. The man took Erno's shoulder, gently, and pulled him forward until the black faceplate of his helmet kissed Erno's own.

"Howdy, Erno." Tyler Durden's voice, carried by conduction from a face he could not see, echoed like Erno's own thought.

Erno tried to regain his cool. "Mr. Durden, I presume."

"Switch your suit to Channel Six," Tyler said. "Encrypted." He pulled away and touched the pad on his arm, and pointed to Erno's. When Erno did the same, his radio found Tyler's wavelength, and he heard Tyler's voice in his ear.

"I thought I might catch you out here."

The other workers had all passed by; they were alone. "What are you doing here?"

"You want adventure? We got adventure."

"What adventure?"

"Come along with me."

Instead of heading in through the maze, Tyler led Erno back out to the surface. The fan of concrete was deserted, the shuttle bus already gone back to the lab and factories. From around a corner, Tyler hauled out a backpack, settled it over his shoulders, and struck off east, along the graded road that encircled Fowler. The mountainous rim rose to their right, topped by the beginnings of the dome; to their left was the rubble of the broken highlands. Tyler moved along at a quick pace, taking long strides in the low G with a minimum of effort.

After a while Tyler asked him, "So, how about the book? Have you read it?"

"Some. It's a collection of stories, all about men."

"Learning anything?"

"They seem so primitive. I guess it was a different world back then."

"What's so different?"

Erno told him the story about the prize-fighter. "Did they really do that?"

"Yes. Men have always engaged in combat."

"For money?"

"The money is just an excuse. They do it anyway."

"But why did the writer tell that story? What's the point?"

"It's about elemental manhood. The fighters were men. The promoter was not."

"Because he didn't pay the boxer?"

"Because he knew the boxer had fought his heart out, but he pretended that the boxer was a coward in order to keep the audience from getting mad at him. The promoter preserved his own credibility by trashing the boxer's. The author wants you to be like the boxer, not the promoter."

"But the boxer dies—for twenty-five bucks."

"He died a man. Nobody can take that away from him."

"But nobody knows that. In fact, they all think he died a coward."

"The promoter knows he wasn't. The other fighter knows, probably. And thanks to the story, now you know, too."

Erno still had trouble grasping exactly the metaphor Tyler intended when he used the term "man." It had nothing to do with genetics. But before he could quiz Tyler, the older man stopped. By this time they had circled a quarter of the colony and were in the shadow of the crater wall. Tyler switched on his helmet light and Erno did likewise. Erno's thermoregulator pumped heat along the microfibers buried in his suit's skin, compensating for the sudden shift from the brutal heat of lunar sunlight to the brutal cold of lunar shadow.

"Here we are," Tyler said, looking up the crater wall. "See that path?"

It wasn't much of a path, just a jumble of rocks leading up the side of the crater, but once they reached it Erno could see that, by following patches of luminescent paint on boulders, you could climb the rim mountain to the top. "Where are we going?" Erno asked.

"To the top of the world," Tyler said. "From up there I'll show you the empire I'll give you if you follow me."

"You're kidding."

Tyler said nothing.

It was a hard climb to the crater's lip, where a concrete rim formed the foundation of the dome. From here, the dome looked like an unnaturally swollen stretch of *mare*, absurdly regular, covered in lunar regolith. Once the dome had been constructed over the crater, about six meters of lunar soil had been spread evenly over its surface to provide a radiation shield for the interior. Concentric rings every ten meters kept the soil from sliding down the pitch of the dome. It was easier climbing here, but surreal. The horizon of the dome moved ahead of them as they progressed, and it was hard to judge distances.

"There's a solar storm warning," Erno said. "Aren't you worried?"

"We're not going to be out long."

"I was at the meeting," Erno said.

"I saw you," Tyler said. "Cute girl, the dark-skinned one. Watch out. You know what they used to say on Earth?"

"What?"

"If women didn't have control of all the pussy, they'd have bounties on their heads."

Erno laughed. "How can you say that? They're our sisters, our mothers."

"And they still have control of all the pussy."

They climbed the outside of the dome.

"What are you going to do to keep from being made invisible?" Erno asked.

"What makes you think they're going to try?"

"I don't think your speech changed anybody's mind."

"So? No matter what they teach you, my visibility is not socially constructed. That's the lesson for today."

"What are we doing out here?"

"We're going to demonstrate this fact."

Ahead of them a structure hove into sight. At the apex of the dome, just above the central spire, stood a maintenance airlock. Normally, this would be the way workers would exit to inspect or repair the dome's exterior—not the way Erno and Tyler had come. This was not a public airlock, and the entrance code would be encrypted.

Tyler led them up to the door. From his belt pouch he took a key card and stuck it into the reader. Erno could hear him humming a song over his earphones. After a moment, the door slid open.

"In we go, Erno," Tyler said.

They entered the airlock and waited for the air to recycle. "This could get us into trouble," Erno said.

"Yes, it could."

"If you can break into the airlock you can sabotage it. An airlock breach could kill hundreds of people."

"You're absolutely right, Erno. That's why only completely responsible people like us should break into airlocks."

The interior door opened into a small chamber facing an elevator. Tyler put down his backpack, cracked the seal on his helmet, and began stripping off his garish suit. Underneath he wore only briefs. Rust-colored pubic hair curled from around the edges of the briefs. Tyler's skin was pale, the muscles in his arms and chest well developed, but his belly soft. His skin was criss-crossed with a web of pink lines where the thermoregulator system of the suit had marked him.

Feeling self-conscious, Erno took off his own suit. They were the same height, but Tyler outweighed him by twenty kilos. "What's in the backpack?" Erno asked.

"Rappelling equipment." Tyler gathered up his suit and the pack and, ignoring the elevator, opened the door beside it to a stairwell. "Leave your suit here," he said, ditching his own in a corner.

The stairwell was steep and the cold air tasted stale; it raised goose bumps on Erno's skin. Clutching the pack to his chest, Tyler hopped down the stairs to the next level. The wall beside them was sprayed with gray insulation. The light from bioluminescents turned their skin greenish yellow.

Instead of continuing down the well all the way to the top of the spire, Tyler stopped at a door on the side of the stairwell. He punched in a code. The door opened into a vast darkness, the space between the exterior and interior shells of the dome. Tyler shone his light inside: Three meters high, broken by reinforcing struts, the cavity stretched out from them into the darkness, curving slightly as it fell away. Tyler closed the door behind them and, in the light of his flash, pulled a notebook from the pack and called up a map. He studied it for a minute, and then led Erno into the darkness.

To the right about ten meters, an impenetrable wall was one of the great cermet ribs of the dome that stretched like the frame of an umbrella from the central spire to the distant crater rim.

Before long Tyler stopped, shining his light on the floor. "Here it is."

"What?"

"Maintenance port. Periodically they have to inspect the interior of the dome, repair the fiberoptics." Tyler squatted down and began to open the lock.

"What are you going to do?"

"We're going to hang from the roof like little spiders, Erno, and leave a gift for our cousins."

The port opened and Erno got a glimpse of the space that yawned below. A thousand meters below them the semicircular ranks of seats of the Sobieski Park amphitheater glowed ghostly white in the lights of the artificial night. Tyler drew ropes and carabiners from his pack, and from the bottom, an oblong device, perhaps fifty centimeters square, wrapped in fiber-optic cloth that glinted in the light of the flashlight. At one end was a timer. The object gave off an aura of threat that was both frightening and instantly attractive.

"What is that thing? Is it a bomb?"

"A bomb, Erno? Are you crazy?" Tyler snapped one of the lines around a reinforcing strut. He donned a harness and handed an identical one to Erno. "Put this on."

"I'm afraid of heights."

"Don't be silly. This is safe as a kiss. Safer, maybe."

"What are we trying to accomplish?"

"That's something of a metaphysical question."

"That thing doesn't look metaphysical to me."

"Nonetheless, it is. Call it the Philosopher's Stone. We're going to attach it to the inside of the dome."

"I'm not going to blow any hole in the dome."

"Erno, I couldn't blow a hole in the dome without killing myself. I guarantee you that, as a result of what we do here, I will suffer whatever consequences anyone else suffers. More than anyone else, even. Do I look suicidal to you, Erno?"

"To tell the truth, I don't know. You sure do some risky things. Why don't you tell me what you intend?"

"This is a test. I want to see whether you trust me."

"You don't trust *me* enough to tell me anything."

"Trust isn't about being persuaded. Trust is when you do something because your brother asks you to. I didn't have to ask you along on this adventure, Erno. I trusted you." Tyler crouched there, calmly watching Erno. "So, do you have the balls for this?"

The moment stretched. Erno pulled on the climbing harness.

Tyler ran the ropes through the harness, gave him a pair of gloves, and showed Erno how to brake the rope behind his back. Then, with the maybe-bomb Philosopher's Stone slung over his shoulder, Tyler dropped through the port. Feeling like he was about to take a step he could never take back, Erno edged out after him.

Tyler helped him let out three or four meters of rope. Erno's weight made the rope twist, and the world began to spin. They were so close to the dome's inner surface that the "stars" shining there were huge fuzzy patches of light in the braided fiberglass surface. The farmlands of the crater floor were swathed in shadow, but around the crater's rim, oddly twisted from this god's-eye perspective, the lights of apartment districts cast fans of illumination on the hanging gardens and switchbacked perimeter road. Erno could make out a few microscopic figures down there. Not far from Tyler and him, the top of the central spire obscured their view to the west. The flying stage, thirty meters down from where the spire met the roof, was closed for the night, but an owl nesting underneath flew out at their appearance and circled below them.

Tyler began to swing himself back and forth at the end of his line, gradually picking up amplitude until, at the apex of one of his swings, he latched himself onto the dome's inner surface. "C'mon, Erno! Time's wasting!"

Erno steeled himself to copy Tyler's performance. It took effort to get himself swinging, and once he did the arcs were ponderous and slow. He had trouble orienting himself so that one end of his oscillation left him close to Tyler. At the top of every swing gravity disappeared and his stomach lurched. Finally, after what seemed an eternity of trying, Erno swung close enough for Tyler to reach out and snag his leg.

He pulled Erno up beside him and attached Erno's belt line to a ringbolt in the dome's surface. Erno's heart beat fast.

"Now you know you're alive," Tyler said.

"If anyone catches us up here, our asses are fried."

"Our asses are everywhere and always fried. That's the human condition. Let's work."

While Tyler pulled the device out of the bag he had Erno spread glue onto the dome's surface. When the glue was set, the two of them pressed the Philosopher's Stone into it until it was firmly fixed. Because of its reflective surface it would be invisible from the crater floor. "Now, what time did Debra Debrasdaughter say that meeting was tomorrow?"

"1600," Erno said. "You knew that."

Tyler flipped open the lid over the Stone's timer and punched some keys. "Yes, I did."

"And you didn't need my help to do this. Why did you make me come?"

The timer beeped; the digital readout began counting down. Tyler flipped the lid closed. "To give you the opportunity to betray me. And if you want to, you still have" —he looked at his wristward— "fourteen hours and thirteen minutes."

MALE DOMINANCE BEHAVIOR

Erno had begun building his store of resentment when he was twelve, in Eva Evasdaughter's molecular biotechnology class. Eva Evasdaughter came from an illustrious family: her mother had been the longest serving member of the colony council. Her grandmother, Eva Kabatsumi, jailed with Nora Sobieski in California, had originated the matronymic system.

It took Erno a while to figure out that her ancestry didn't make Evasdaughter a good teacher. He was the brightest boy in the class. He believed in the Cousins, respected authority, and worshipped women like his mother and Evasdaughter.

Evasdaughter was a tall woman who wore tight short-sleeved tunics that emphasized her small breasts. Erno had begun to notice such things; sex play was everyone's interest that semester, and he had recently had several erotic fondling sessions with girls in the class.

One day they were studying protein engineering. Erno loved it. He liked how you could make a gene jump through hoops if you were clever enough. He got ahead in the reading. That day he asked Evasdaughter about directed protein mutagenesis, a topic they were not due to study until next semester.

"Can you make macro-modifications in proteins—I mean replace entire sequences to get new enzymes?" He was genuinely curious, but at some level he also was seeking Evasdaughter's approval of his doing extra work.

She turned on him coolly. "Are you talking about using site-directed mutagenesis, or chemical synthesis of oligonucleotides?"

He had never heard of site-directed mutagenesis. "I mean using oligonucleotides to change the genes."

"I can't answer unless I know if we're talking about site-directed or synthesized oligonucleotides. Which is it?"

Erno felt his face color. The other students were watching him. "I—I don't know."

"Yes, you don't," Evasdaughter said cheerfully. And instead of explaining, she turned back to the lesson.

Erno didn't remember anything that happened the rest of that day, except for looking at his shoes. Why had she treated him like that? She made him feel stupid. Yes, she knew more biotech than he did, but she was the teacher! Of course she knew more! Did that mean she had to put him down?

When he complained to his mother, she only said that he needed to listen to the teacher.

Only slowly did he realize that Evasdaughter had exhibited what he had always been taught was male dominance behavior. He had presented a challenge to her superiority, and she had smashed him flat. After he was smashed, she could afford to treat him kindly. But she would teach him only after he admitted that he was her inferior.

Now that his eyes were opened, he saw this behavior everywhere. Every day Cousins asserted their superiority in order to hurt others. He had been lied to, and his elders were hypocrites.

Yet when he tried to show his superiority, he was told to behave himself. Superior/inferior is wrong, they said. Difference is all.

FIVE

ONE THING TYLER had said was undoubtedly true: this was a test. How devoted was Erno to the Society of Cousins? How good a judge was he of Tyler's character? How eager was he to see his mother and the rest of his world made uncomfortable, and how large a discomfort did he think was justified? Just how angry was Erno?

After Erno got back to his room, he lay awake, unable to sleep. He ran every moment of his night with Tyler over in his mind, parsed every sentence, and examined every ambiguous word. Tyler had never denied that the Philosopher's Stone was a bomb. Erno looked up the term in the dictionary: a philosopher's stone was "an imaginary substance sought by alchemists in the belief that it would change base metals into gold or silver."

He did not think the change that Tyler's stone would bring had anything to do with gold or silver.

He looked at his palm, long since washed clean, where Alicia had written her number. She'd asked him to call her before he did anything stupid.

At 1545 the next day Erno was seated in the amphitheater among the crowds of cousins. More people were here than had come the previous week, and the buzz of their conversation, broken by occasional laughter, filled the air. He squinted up at the dome to try to figure out just where they had placed the stone. The dome had automatic safety devices to seal any minor air leak. But it couldn't survive a hole blasted in it. Against the artificial blue sky Erno watched a couple of flyers circling like hawks.

1552. Tyler arrived, trailing a gaggle of followers, mostly young men trying to look insolent. He'd showed up—what did that mean? Erno noted that this time, Tyler wore black. He seemed as calm as he had before, and he chatted easily with the others, then left them to take a seat on the stage.

At 1559 Debra Debrasdaughter took her place. Erno looked at his watch. 1600.

Nothing happened.

Was that the test? To see whether Erno would panic and fall for a ruse? He tried to catch Tyler's eye, but got nothing.

Debrasdaughter rapped for order. The ranks of cousins began to quiet, to sit up straighter. Near silence had fallen, and Debrasdaughter began to speak.

"Our second meeting to discuss—"

A flash of light seared the air high above them, followed a second later by a concussion. Shouts, a few screams.

Erno looked up. A cloud of black smoke shot rapidly from a point against the blue. One flyer tumbled, trying to regain his balance; the other had dived a hundred meters seeking a landing place. People pointed and shouted. The blue sky flickered twice, went to white as the imaging system struggled, then recovered.

People boiled out of the amphitheater, headed for pressurized shelter. Erno could not see if the dome had been breached. The smoke, instead of dissipating, spread out in an arc, then flattened up against the dome. It formed tendrils, shapes. He stood there, frozen. It was not smoke at all, he realized, but smart paint.

The nanodevices spread the black paint onto the interior of the dome. The paint crawled and shaped itself, forming letters. The letters, like a message from God, made a huge sign on the inside of the clear blue sky:

"BANG! YOU'RE DEAD!"

"YOU'RE DEAD!"

One of the other *Stories for Men* was about Harry Rodney and Little Bert, two petty criminals on an ocean liner that has struck an iceberg and is sinking, with not enough lifeboats for all the passengers. The patriarchal custom was that women and children had precedence for spaces in the boats. Harry gives up his space in a boat in favor of some girl. Bert strips a coat and scarf from an injured woman, steals her jewelry, abandons her belowdecks, and uses her clothes to sneak into a lifeboat.

As it happens, both men survive. But Harry is so disgusted by Bert's crime that he persuades him to run away and pretend he is dead. For years, whenever Bert contacts Harry, Harry tells him to stay away or else the police might discover him. Bert never returns home for fear of being found out.

SIX

IN THE PANIC and confusion, Tyler Durden disappeared. On his seat at the meeting lay a note: "I did it."

As a first step in responding to the threat to the colony, the Board of Matrons immediately called the question of ostracism, and by evening the population had voted: Tyler Durden was declared invisible.

As if that mattered. He could not be found.

SEVEN

IT TOOK SEVERAL days for the writing to be erased from the dome.

A manhunt did not turn up Tyler. Nerves were on edge. Rumors arose, circulated, were denied. Tyler Durden was still in the colony, in disguise. A cabal of followers was hiding him. No, he and his confederates had a secret outpost ten kilometers north of the colony. Durden was in the employ of the government of California. He had stockpiled weapons and was planning an attack. He had an atomic bomb.

At the gym entrance, AIs checked DNA prints, and Erno was conscious, as never before, of the cameras in every room. He wondered if any monitors had picked up his excursion with Tyler. Every moment he expected a summons on his wristward to come to the colony offices.

When Erno entered the workout room, he found Tyrus and a number of others wearing white T-shirts that said, **"BANG! YOU'RE DEAD!"**

Erno took the unoccupied rowing machine next to Ty. Ty was talking to Sid on the other side of him.

A woman came across the room to use the machines. She was tightly muscled, and her dark hair was pulled back from her sweaty neck. As she approached, the young men went silent and turned to look at her. She hesitated. Erno saw something on her face he had rarely seen on a woman's face before: fear. The woman turned and left the gym.

None of the boys said anything. If the others had recognized what had just happened, they did not let it show.

Erno pulled on his machine. He felt the muscles in his legs knot. "Cool shirt," he said.

"Tyrus wants to be invisible, too," said Sid. Sid wasn't wearing one of the shirts.

"Eventually someone will check the vids of Tyler's performances, and see me there," said Ty between strokes. "I'm not ashamed to be Tyler's fan." At thirteen, Erno and Ty had been fumbling lovers, testing out their sexuality. Now Ty was a blunt overmuscled guy who laughed like a hyena. He didn't laugh now.

"It was a rush to judgment," one of the other boys said. "Tyler didn't harm a single Cousin. It was free expression."

"He could just as easily have blown a hole in the dome," said Erno. "Do they need any more justification for force?"

Ty stopped rowing and turned toward Erno. Where he had sweated through the fabric, the "Bang!" on his shirt had turned blood red. "Maybe it will come to force. We do as much work, and we're second-class citizens." He started rowing again, pulled furiously at the machine, fifty reps a minute, drawing quick breaths.

"That Durden has a pair, doesn't he?" Sid said. Sid was a popular studboy. His thick chestnut hair dipped below one eye. "You should have seen the look on Rebecca's face when that explosion went off."

"I hear, if they catch him, the council's not going to stop at invisibility," Erno said. "They'll kick him out."

"Invisibility won't slow Tyler down," Ty said. "Would you obey the decree?" he asked Sid.

"Me? I'm too beautiful to let myself get booted. If Tyler Durden likes masculinists so much, let him go to one of the other colonies, or to Earth. I'm getting laid too often."

Erno's gut tightened. "They will kick him out. My mother would vote for it in a second."

"Let 'em try," Ty grunted, still rowing.

"Is that why you're working out so much lately, Ty?" Sid said. "Planning to move to Earth?"

"No. I'm just planning to bust your ass."

"I suspect it's not busting you want to do to my ass."

"Yeah. Your ass has better uses."

"My mother says Tyler's broken the social contract," Erno said.

"Does your mother—" Ty said, still rowing, "—keep your balls under her pillow?"

Sid laughed.

Erno wanted to grab Ty and tell him, *I helped him do it!* But he said nothing. He pulled on the machine. His face burned.

After a minute Erno picked up his towel and went to the weight machine. No one paid him any attention. Twenty minutes later he hit the sauna. Sweating in the heat, sullen, resentful. He had *been* there, had taken a bigger risk than any of these fan-boys.

Coming out of the sauna he saw Sid heading for the sex rooms, where any woman who was interested could find a male partner who was willing. Erno considered posting himself to one of the rooms. But he wasn't a stud; he was just an anonymous minor male. He had no following. It would be humiliating to sit there waiting for someone, or worse, to be selected by some old bag.

A day later Erno got himself one of the T-shirts. Wearing it didn't make him feel any better.

It came to him that maybe this was the test Tyler intended: not whether Erno would tell about the Philosopher's Stone before it happened, but whether he would admit he'd helped set it after he saw the uproar it caused in the colony.

If that was the test, Erno was failing. He thought about calling Tyler, but the constables were sure to be monitoring that number. A new rumor had it Tyler had been captured and was being held in protective custody—threats had been made against his life—until the Board of Matrons could decide when and how to impose the invisibility. Erno imagined Tyler in some bare white room, his brain injected with nanoprobes, his neck fitted with a collar.

At Biotech, Erno became aware of something he had never noticed before: how the women assumed first pick of the desserts in the cafeteria. Then, later, when he walked past their table, four women burst into laughter. He turned and stared at them, but they never glanced at him.

Another day he was talking with a group of engineers on break: three women, another man, and Erno. Hana from materials told a joke: "What do you have when you have two little balls in your hand?"

The other women grinned. Erno watched the other man. He stood as if on a trapdoor, a tentative smile on his face. The man was getting ready to laugh, because that was what you did when people told jokes, whether or not they were funny. It was part of the social contract—somebody went into joke-telling mode, and you went into joke-listening mode.

"A man's undivided attention," Hana said.

The women laughed. The man grinned.

"How can you tell when a man is aroused?" Pearl said. "He's breathing."

"That isn't funny," Erno said.

"Really? I think it is," Hana said.

"It's objectification. Men are just like women. They have emotions, too."

"Cool off, Erno," said Pearl. "This isn't gender-equity class."

"There is no gender equity here."

"Someone get Erno a T-shirt."

"Erno wants to be invisible."

"We're already invisible!" Erno said, and stalked off. He left the lab, put on his exosuit, and took the next bus back to the dome. He quit going to his practicum: he would not let himself be used anymore. He was damned if he would go back there again.

A meeting to discuss what to do about the missing comedian was disrupted by a group of young men marching and chanting outside the meeting room. Constables were stationed in public places, carrying batons. In online discussion rooms, people openly advocated closing the Men's Houses for fear conspiracies were being hatched in them.

And Erno received another message. This one was from "Harry Callahan."

> Are you watching, Erno? If you think our gender situation
> is GROSS, you can change it. Check exposition.

CRIMES OF VIOLENCE

The incidence of crimes of violence among the Cousins is vanishingly small. Colony archives record eight murders in sixty years. Five of them were man against man, two man against woman, and one woman against woman.

This does not count vigilante acts of women against men, but despite the lack of official statistics, such incidents, too, are rare.

EIGHT

"IT'S NO TRICK to be celibate when you don't like sex."

"That's the point," Erno insisted. "He does like sex. He likes sex fine. But he's making a sacrifice in order to establish his point: He's not going to be a prisoner of his dick."

Erno was sitting out on the ledge of the terrace in front of their apartment, chucking pebbles at the recycling bin at the corner and arguing with his cousin Lena. He had been arguing with a lot of people lately, and not getting anywhere. Every morning he still left as if he were going to Biotech, but instead he hung out in the park or gym. It would take some time for his mother to realize he had dropped out.

Lena launched into a tirade, and Erno was suddenly very tired of it all. Before she could gain any momentum, he threw a last pebble that whanged off the bin, got up and, without a word, retreated into the apartment. He could hear Lena's squawk behind him.

He went to his room and opened a screen on his wall. The latest news was that Tashi Yokiosson had regained consciousness, but that he had suffered neurological damage that might take a year or more to repair. Debate on the situation raged on the net. Erno opened his documents locker and fiddled with a melancholy sonnet he was working on, but he wasn't in the mood.

He switched back to Tyler's cryptic message. *You can change it. Check exposition.* It had something to do with Biotech, Erno was pretty sure. He had tried the public databases, but had not come up with anything. There were databases accessible only through the biotech labs, but he would have to return to his practicum to view them, and that would mean he would have to explain his absence. He wasn't ready for that yet.

On impulse, Erno looked up Tyler in the colony's genome database. What was the name Debrasdaughter had called him?—Marysson, Thomas Marysson. He found Tyler's genome. Nothing about it stood out.

Debaters had linked Tyler's biography to the genome. Marysson had been born thirty-six years ago. His mother was a second-generation Cousin; his grandmother had arrived with the third colonization contingent, in 2048. He had received a general education, neither excelling nor failing anything. His mother had died when he was twenty. He had moved out into the dorms, had worked uneventfully in construction and repair for fourteen years, showing no sign of rebelliousness before reinventing himself as Tyler Durden, the comedian.

Until two years ago, absolutely nothing had distinguished him from any of a thousand male Cousins.

Bored, Erno looked up his own genome.

There he lay in rows of base pairs, neat as a tile floor. Over at Biotech, some insisted that everything you were was fixed in those sequences in black-and-white. Erno didn't buy it. Where was the gene for desire there, or hope, or despair, or frustration? Where was the gene that said he would sit in front of a computer screen at the age of seventeen, boiling with rage?

He called up his mother's genome. There were her sequences. Some were the same as his. Of course there was no information about his father. To prevent dire social consequences, his father must remain a blank spot in his history, as far as the Society of Cousins was concerned. Maybe some families kept track of such things, but nowhere in the databases were fathers and children linked.

Of course they couldn't stop him from finding out. He knew others who had done it. His father's genome was somewhere in the database, for medical purposes. If he removed from his own those sequences that belonged to his mother, then what was left—at least the sequences she had not altered when she had planned him—belonged to his father. He could cross-check those against the genomes of all the colony's men.

From his chart, he stripped those genes that matched his mother's. Using what remained, he prepared a search engine to sort through the colony's males.

The result was a list of six names. Three were brothers: Stuart, Simon, and Josef Bettesson. He checked the available public information on them. They were all in their nineties, forty years older than Erno's mother. Of the remaining men, two were of about her age: Sidney Orindasson and Micah Avasson. Of those two, Micah Avasson had the higher correlation with Erno's genome.

He read the public records for Micah Avasson. Born in 2042, he would be fifty-six years old. A physical address: men's dormitory, East Five lava tube. He keyed it into his notebook.

Without knocking, his mother came into the room. Though he had no reason to be ashamed of his search, Erno shoved the notebook into his pocket.

She did not notice. "Erno, we need to talk."

"By talk do you mean interrogate, or lecture?"

His mother's face stiffened. For the first time he noticed the crow's feet at the corners of her eyes. She moved around his room, picking up his clothes, sorting, putting them away. "You should keep your room tidier. Your room is a reflection of your mind."

"Please, mother."

She held one of his shirts to her nose, sniffed, and made a face. "Did I ever tell you about the time I got arrested? I was thirteen, and Derek Silviasson and I were screwing backstage in the middle of a performance of *A Doll's House*. We got a little carried away. When Nora opened the door to leave at the end of the second act, she tripped over Derek and me in our second act."

"They arrested you? Why?"

"The head of the Board was a prude. It wouldn't have mattered so much but *A Doll's House* was her favorite play."

"You and Derek Silviasson were lovers?"

She sat down on his bed, a meter from him, and leaned forward. "After the paint bombing, Erno, they went back to examine the recordings from the spex of the officers at the Oxygen Warehouse riot. Who do you suppose, to my surprise, they found there?"

Erno swiveled in his chair to avoid her eyes. "Nick already told you I went there."

"But *you* didn't. Not only were you there, but at one point you were together with Durden."

"What was I doing?"

"Don't be difficult. I'm trying to protect you, Erno. The only reason I know about this is that Harald Gundasson let me know on the sly. Another report says Durden met you outside the North airlock one day. You're likely to be called in for questioning. I want to know what's going on. Are you involved in some conspiracy?"

His mother looked so forlorn he found it hard to be hostile. "As far as I know there is no conspiracy."

"Did you have something to do with the paint bomb?"

"No. Of course not."

"I found out you haven't been to your practicum. What have you been doing?"

"I've been going to the gym."

"Are you planning a trip to Earth?"

"Don't be stupid, mother."

"Honestly, Erno, I can't guess what you are thinking. You're acting like a spy."

"Maybe I am a spy."

His mother laughed.

"Don't laugh at me!"

"I'm not laughing because you're funny. I'm laughing because I'm scared! This is an ugly business, Erno."

"Stop it, Mother. Please."

She stared at him. He tried not to look away. "I want you to listen. Tyler Durden is a destroyer. I've been to Aristarchus, to Tycho. I've seen the patriarchy. Do you want that here?"

"How would I know? I've never been there!" His eyes fell on the copy of *Stories for Men*. "Don't tell me stories about rape and carnage," he said, looking at the book's cover. "I've heard them all before. You crammed them down my throat with my baby food."

"They're true. Do you deny them?"

Erno clenched his jaw, tried to think. Did she have to browbeat him? "I don't know!"

"It's not just carnage. It's waste and insanity. You want to know what they're like—one time I had a talk with this security man at Shackleton. They were mining lunar ice for reaction mass in the shuttles.

"I put it to him that using lunar ice for rocket fuel was criminally wasteful. Water is the most precious commodity on the moon, and here they are blowing it into space.

"He told me it was cheaper to use lunar ice than haul water from Earth. My argument wasn't with him, he said, it was with the laws of the marketplace. Like most of them, he condescended to me, as if I were a child. He thought that invoking the free market settled the issue, as if to go against the market were to go against the laws of nature. The goal of conquering space justified the expenditure, he said—they'd get more water somewhere else when they used up the lunar ice."

"He's got an argument."

"The market as a law of nature? 'Conquering space?' How do you conquer space? That's not a goal, it's a disease."

"What does this have to do with Tyler Durden?"

"Durden is bringing the disease here!"

"He's fighting oppression! Men have no power here; they are stifled and ignored. There are no real male Cousins."

"There are plenty of male Cousins. There are lots of role models. Think of Adil Al-Hafaz, of Peter Sarahsson—of Nick, for pity's sake!"

"Nick? Nick?" Erno laughed. He stood. "You might as well leave now, officer."

His mother looked hurt. "Officer?"

"That's why you're here, isn't it?"

"Erno, I know you don't like me. I'm dull and conventional. But being unconventional, by itself, isn't a virtue. I'm your mother."

"And you're a cop."

That stopped her for a moment. She took a deep breath. "I dearly love you, Erno, but if you think—"

That tone of voice. He'd heard it all his life: all the personal anecdotes are over, now. We're done with persuasion, and it's time for you to do what I say.

"You dearly love nothing!" Erno shouted. "All you want is to control me!"

She started to get up. "I've given you every chance—"

Erno threw *Stories for Men* at her. His mother flinched, and the book struck her in the chest and fell slowly to the floor. She looked more startled than hurt, watching the book fall, tumbling, leaves open; she looked as if she were trying to understand what it was—but when she faced him again, her eyes clouded. Trembling, livid, she stood, and started to speak. Before she could say a word Erno ran from the room.

PROPERTY

A man on his own is completely isolated. Other men might be his friends or lovers, but if he has a legal connection to anyone, it is to his mother.

Beyond a certain point, property among the Cousins is the possession of the community. Private property passes down from woman to woman, but only outside of the second degree of blood relation. A woman never inherits from her biological mother. A woman chooses her friends and mates, and in the event of her death, her property goes to them. If a woman dies without naming an heir, her property goes to the community.

A man's property is typically confined to personal possessions. Of course, in most families he is petted, and has access to more resources than any female, but the possessions are gotten for him by his mother or his mate, and they belong to her. What property he might hold beyond that belongs to his mother. If he has no mother, then it belongs to his oldest sister. If he has no sister, then it goes to the community.

A man who forsakes his family has nowhere to go.

NINE

THE GREAT JAZZMEN were all persecuted minorities. Black men like Armstrong, Ellington, Coltrane, Parker. And the comedians were all Jews or black men. Leaving his mother's apartment, Erno saw himself the latest in history's long story of abused fighters for expressive freedom.

Erno stalked around the perimeter road, head down. To his left, beyond the parapet, the crater's inner slope, planted with groundsel, wildflowers, and hardy low-G modifications of desert scrub, fell away down to the agricultural fields, the park, and two kilometers distant, clear through the low-moisture air, the aspen-forested opposite slopes. To his right rose the ranks of apartments, refectories, dorms, public buildings and labs, clusters of oblong boxes growing higgledy-piggledy, planted with vines and hanging gardens, divided by ramps and stairs and walkways, a high-tech cliff city in pastel concrete glittering with ilemenite crystals. A small green lizard scuttled across the pebbled composite of the roadway and disappeared among some ground cover.

Erno ignored the people on their way to work and back, talking or playing. He felt like smashing something. But smashing things was not appropriate Cousins behavior.

In the southwest quad he turned up a ramp into a residential district. These were newer structures, products of the last decade's planned expansion of living quarters, occupied for the most part by new families.

He moved upward by steady leaps, feeling the tension in his legs, enjoying the burn it generated.

Near the top of the rimwall he found Gilman 334. He pressed the door button. The screen remained blank, but after a moment Alicia's voice came from the speaker. "Erno. Come on in."

The door opened and he entered the apartment. It consisted mostly of an open lounge, furnished in woven furniture, with a couple of small rooms adjoining. Six young women were sitting around inhaling mood enhancers, listening to music. The music was Monk, "Brilliant Corners." Erno had given it to Alicia; she would never have encountered twentieth-century jazz otherwise.

There was something wrong with Monk in this context. These girls ought to be listening to some lunar music—one of the airy mixed choral groups, or Shari Cloudsdaughter's "Sunlight or Rock." In this circle of females, the tossed-off lines of Sonny Rollins' sax, the splayed rhythms of Monk's piano, seemed as if they were being stolen. Or worse still, studied—by a crew of aliens for whom they could not mean what they meant to Erno.

"Hello," Erno said. "Am I crashing your party?"

"You're not crashing." Alicia took him by the arm. "This is Erno," she said to the others. "Some of you know him."

Sharon was there, one of the hottest women in Alicia's cohort at school— he had heard Sid talk about her. He recognized Betty Sarahsdaughter, Liz Bethsdaughter, both of them, like Alicia, studying social work, both of whom had turned him down at one time or another. Erno liked women as individuals, but in a group, their intimate laughter, gossip, and private jokes—as completely innocent as they might be— made him feel like he knew nothing about them. He drew Alicia aside. "Can we talk—in private?"

"Sure." She took Erno to one of the bedrooms. She sat on the bed, gestured to a chair. "What's the matter?"

"I had a fight with my mother."

"That's what mothers are for, as far as I can tell."

"And the constables are going to call me in for questioning. They think I may be involved in some conspiracy with Tyler Durden."

"Do you know where he is?"

Erno's defenses came up. "Do you care?"

"I don't want to know where he is. If you know, keep it to yourself. I'm *not* your mother."

"I could be in trouble."

"A lot of us will stand behind you on this, Erno. Sharon and I would." She reached out to touch his arm. "I'll go down to the center with you."

Erno moved to the bed beside her. He slid his hand to her waist, closed his eyes, and rubbed his cheek against her hair. To his surprise, he felt her hand between his shoulder blades. He kissed her, and she leaned back. He looked into her face: her green eyes, troubled, searched his. Her bottom lip was full. He kissed her again, slid his hand to her breast, and felt the nipple taut beneath her shirt.

Leave aside the clumsiness—struggling out of their clothes, the distraction of "Straight, No Chaser" from the other room, Erno's momentary thought of the women out there wondering what was going on in here—and it was the easiest thing in the world. He slid into Alicia as if he were coming home. Though his head swirled with desire, he tried to hold himself back, to give her what she wanted. He kissed her all over. She giggled and teased him and twisted her fingers in his hair to pull him down to her, biting his lip. For fifteen or twenty minutes, the Society of Cousins disappeared.

Erno watched her face, watched her closed eyes and parted lips, as she concentrated on her pleasure. It gave him a feeling of power. Her skin flushed, she gasped, shuddered, and he came.

He rested his head upon her breast, eyes closed, breathing deeply, tasting the salt of her sweat. Her chest rose and fell, and he could hear her heart beating fast, then slower. He held her tight. Neither said anything for a long time.

After a while he asked her, quietly, "Can I stay here?"

Alicia stroked his shoulder, slid out from beneath him, and began to pull on her shirt. "I'll talk to Sharon."

Sharon. Erno wondered how many of the other women in the next room Alicia was sleeping with. Alicia was a part of that whole scene, young men and women playing complex mating games that Erno was no good at. He had no idea what "talking to Sharon" might involve. But Alicia acted as if the thought of him moving in was a complete surprise.

"Don't pull a muscle or anything stretching to grasp the concept," Erno said softly.

Alicia reacted immediately. "Erno, we've never exchanged two words about partnering. What do you expect me to say?"

"We did talk about it—in the park. You said you would talk to Sharon then. Why didn't you?"

"Please, Erno." She drew up her pants and the fabric seamed itself closed over her lovely, long legs. "When you're quiet, you're so sweet."

Sweet. Erno felt vulnerable, lying there naked with the semen drying on his belly. He reached for his clothes. "That's right," he muttered, "I forgot. Sex is the social glue. Fuck him so he doesn't cause any trouble."

"Everything isn't about your penis, Erno. Durden is turning you into some self-destructive *boy*. Grow up."

"Grow up?" Erno tugged on his pants. "You don't want me grown up. You want the sweet boy, forever. I've figured it out now—you're never even there with me, except maybe your body. At least I think it was you."

Alicia stared at him. Erno recognized that complete exasperation: he had seen it on his mother. From the next room drifted the sound of "Blue Monk," and women laughing.

"Sharon was right," Alicia said, shaking her head. And she chuckled, a little rueful gasp, as if to say, *I can't believe I'm talking with this guy.*

Erno took a step forward and slapped her face. "You bitch," he breathed. "You fucking bitch."

Alicia fell back, her eyes wide with shock. Erno's head spun. He fled the room, ran through the party and out of the apartment.

It was full night now, the dome sprinkled with stars. He stalked down the switchback ramps toward the perimeter road, through the light thrown by successive lampposts, in a straight-legged gait that kicked him off the pavement with every stride. He hoped that anyone who saw him would see his fury and think him dangerous. Down on the road he stood at the parapet, breathing through his mouth and listening to the hum of insects in the fields below.

In the lamplight far to his left, a person in a green uniform appeared. On impulse Erno hopped over the parapet to the slope. Rather than wait for the constable to pass, he bounced off down toward the crater's floor, skidding where it was steep, his shoes kicking up dust. He picked up speed, making headlong four- or five-meter leaps, risking a fall every time his feet touched.

It was too fast. Thirty meters above the floor he stumbled and went flying face forward. He came down sideways, rolled, and slammed his head as he flipped and skidded to a halt. He lay trying to catch his breath. He felt for broken limbs. His shirt was torn and his shoulder ached. He pulled himself up and went down the last few meters to the crater floor, then limped through the fields for Sobieski Park.

In a few minutes he was there, out of breath and sweating. At the fountain he splashed water on his face. He felt his shoulder gingerly, then made his way to the amphitheater. At first he thought the theater was deserted, but then he saw, down on the stage, a couple of women necking, oblivious of him.

He stood in the row where he had spotted Alicia some weeks before. He had hit her. He couldn't believe he had hit her.

TEN

ERNO SLEPT IN the park and in the morning headed for his biotech shift as if he had never stopped going. No one at the airlock questioned him. Apparently, even though his mind was chaos, he looked perfectly normal. The radiation warning had been renewed; solar monitors reported conditions ripe for a coronal mass ejection. Cousins obliged to go out on the surface were being advised to keep within range of a radiation shelter.

When Erno arrived at the bunker he went to Lemmy Odilleson's lab. Lemmy had not arrived yet. He sat down at his workstation, signed onto the system, pressed his thumb against the gene scanner and accessed the database.

He tried the general index. There was no file named "exposition." Following Tyler's reference to "gross," he looked for any references to the number 144. Nothing. Nothing on the gross structures of nucleotides, either. He tried coming at it from the virus index. Dozens of viruses had been engineered by the Cousins to deal with problems from soil microbes to cellular breakdowns caused by exposure to surface radiation. There was no virus called "exposition."

While he sat there Lemmy showed up. He said nothing of Erno's sudden appearance after his extended absence. "We're making progress on integrating the morphological growth genes into the prototypes," he said excitedly. "The sequences for extracting silicon from the soil are falling into place."

"That's good," Erno said. He busied himself cleaning up the chaos Lemmy typically left in his notes. After a while, he asked casually, "Lemmy, have you ever heard about a virus called 'exposition'?"

"X-position?" Lemmy said vaguely, not looking up from a rack of test bulbs. "Those prefixes go with female sex-linked factors. The Y-position are the male."

"Oh, right."

As soon as Erno was sure Lemmy was caught up in his lab work, he turned back to the archives. First he went to Gendersites, a database he knew mostly for its concentration of anticancer modifications. X-position led him to an encyclopedia of information on the X chromosome. Erno called up a number of files, but he saw no point in digging through gene libraries at random. He located a file of experiments on female-linked syndromes from osteoporosis to postmenopausal cardiac conditions.

On a whim, he did a search on "gross."

Up popped a file labeled Nucleotide Repeats. When Erno opened the file, the heading read:

<blockquote>
Get
Rid
Of
Slimy
girlS
</blockquote>

The sounds of the lab around him faded as he read the paper.

It described a method for increasing the number of unstable trinucleotide repeats on the X chromosome. All humans had repeat sequences, the presence of which were associated with various diseases: spinal and bulbar muscular atrophy, fragile X mental deficiencies, myotonic dystrophy, Huntington disease, spinocerebrellar ataxia, dentatorubralpallidoluysian atrophy, and Machado-Joseph disease. All well understood neurological disorders.

In normal DNA, the repeats were below the level of expression of disease. Standard tests of the zygote assured this. The GROSS paper told how to construct two viruses: the first would plant a time bomb in the egg. At a particular stage of embryonic development the repetition of trinucleotides would explode. The second virus would plant compensating sequences on the Y chromosome.

Creating the viruses would be a tricky but not impossible problem in plasmid engineering. Their effect, however, would be devastating. In males the Y chromosome would suppress the X-linked diseases, but in females the trinucleotide syndromes would be expressed. When the repeats kicked in, the child would develop any one of a host of debilitating or fatal neurological disorders.

Of course once the disorder was recognized, other gene engineers would go to work curing it, or at least identifying possessors prenatally. The GROSS virus would not destroy the human race—but it could burden a generation of females with disease and early death.

Tyler had led Erno to this monstrosity. What was he supposed to do with it?

Nonetheless, Erno downloaded the file into his notebook. He had just finished when Cluny came into the lab.

"Hello, Professor Odillesson," Cluny said to Lemmy. He saw Erno and did a double take. Erno stared back at him.

"I'm not a professor, Michael," Lemmy said.

Cluny pointed at Erno. "You know the constables are looking for him?"

"They are? Why?"

Erno got up. "Don't bother explaining. I'll go."

Cluny moved to stop him. "Wait a minute."

Erno put his hand on Cluny's shoulder to push him aside. Cluny grabbed Erno's arm.

"What's going on?" Lemmy asked.

Erno tried to free himself from Cluny, but the Earthman's grip was firm. Cluny pulled him, and pain shot through the shoulder Erno had hurt in yesterday's spill. Erno hit Cluny in the face.

Cluny's head jerked back, but he didn't let go. His jaw clenched and his expression hardened into animal determination. He wrestled with Erno; they lost their balance, and in slow motion stumbled against a lab bench. Lemmy shouted and two women ran in from the next lab. Before Erno knew it he was pinned against the floor.

"DEAD MAN"

Many of the stories for men were about murder. The old Earth writers seemed fascinated by murder, and wrote about it from a dozen perspectives.

In one of the stories, a railroad detective whose job it is to throw illegal riders off cargo trains finds a destitute man—a "hobo"—hiding on the train. While being brutally beaten by the detective, the hobo strikes back and unintentionally kills him.

The punishment for such a killing, even an accidental one, is death. Terrified, knowing that he has to hide his guilt, the hobo hurries back to the city. He pretends he never left the "flophouse" where he spent the previous night. He disposes of his clothes, dirty with coal dust from the train.

Then he reads a newspaper report. The detective's body has been found, but the investigators assume that he fell off the train and was killed by accident, and are not seeking anyone. The hobo is completely free from suspicion. His immediate reaction is to go to the nearest police station and confess.

ELEVEN

ERNO WAITED IN a small white room at the constabulary headquarters. As a child Erno had come here many times with his mother, but now everything seemed different. He was subject to the force of the state. That fucking cow Cluny. The constables had taken his notebook. Was that pro forma, or would they search it until they found the GROSS file?

He wondered what Alicia had done after he'd left the day before. What had she told her friends?

The door opened and two women came in. One of them was tall and good-looking. The other was small, with a narrow face and close-cropped blond hair. She looked to be a little younger than his mother. She sat down across from him; the tall woman remained standing.

"This can be simple, Erno, if you let it," the small woman said. She had an odd drawl that, combined with her short stature, made Erno wonder if she was from Earth. "Tell us where Tyler Durden is. And about the conspiracy."

Erno folded his arms across his chest. "I don't know where he is. There is no conspiracy."

"Do we have to show you images of you and him together during the Oxygen Warehouse riot?"

"I never saw him before that, or since. We were just hiding in the back room."

"You had nothing to do with the smartpaint explosion?"

"No."

The tall woman, who still had not spoken, looked worried. The blond interrogator leaned forward, resting her forearms on the table. "Your DNA was found at the access portal where the device was set."

Erno squirmed. He imagined a sequence of unstable nucleotide triplets multiplying in the woman's cells. "He asked me to help him. I had no idea what it was."

"No idea. So it could have been a bomb big enough to blow a hole in the dome. Yet you told no one about it."

"I knew he wasn't going to kill anyone. I could tell."

The interrogator leaned back. "I hope you will excuse the rest of us if we question your judgment."

"Believe me, I would never do anything to hurt a Cousin. Ask my mother."

The tall woman finally spoke. "We have. She does say that. But you have to help us out, Erno. I'm sure you can understand how upset all this has made the polity."

"Forget it, Kim," the other said. "Erno here's not going to betray his lover."

"Tyler's not my lover," Erno said.

The blond interrogator smirked. "Right."

The tall one said, "There's nothing wrong with you being lovers, Erno."

"They why did this one bring it up?"

"No special reason," said the blonde. "I'm just saying you wouldn't betray him."

"Well, we're not lovers."

"Too bad," the blonde muttered.

"You need to help us, Erno," the tall one said. "Otherwise, even if we let you go, you're going to be at risk of violence from other Cousins."

"Only if you tell everyone about me."

"So we should just let you go, and not inconvenience you by telling others the truth about you," said the blonde.

"What truth? You don't know me."

She came out of her chair, leaning forward on her clenched fists. Her face was flushed. "Don't know you? I know all about you."

"Mona, calm down," the other woman said.

"Calm down? Earth history is full of this! Men sublimate their sexual attraction in claims of brotherhood—with the accompanying military fetishism, penis comparing, suicidal conquer-or-die movements. Durden is heading for one of those classic orgasmic armageddons: Masada, Hitler in the bunker, David Koresh, 9/11, the California massacre."

The tall one grabbed her shoulder and tried to pull her back. "Mona."

Mona threw off the restraining hand, and pushed her face up close to Erno's. "If we let this little shit go, I guarantee you he'll be involved in some transcendent destructive act—suicidally brave, suicidally cowardly—aimed at all of us. The signs are all over him." Spittle flew in Erno's face.

"You're crazy," Erno said. "If I wanted to fuck him, I would just fuck him."

The tall one tried again. "Come away, officer."

Mona grabbed Erno by the neck. "Where is he!"

"Come away, now!" The tall cop yanked the small woman away, and she fell back. She glared at Erno. The other, tugging her by the arm, pulled her out of the room.

Erno tried to catch his breath. He wiped his sleeve across his sweating face. He sat there alone for a long time, touching the raw skin where she had gripped his neck. Then the door opened and his mother came in.

"Mom!"

She carried some things in her hands, put them on the table. It was the contents of his pockets, including his notebook. "Get up."

"What's going on?"

"Just shut up and come with me. We're letting you go."

Erno stumbled from the chair. "That officer is crazy."

"I'm not sure she isn't right. It's up to you to prove she isn't."

She hustled him out of the office and into the hall. In seconds Erno found himself, dizzy, in the plaza outside the headquarters. "You are not out of trouble. Go home, and stay there," his mother said, and hurried back inside.

Passersby in North Six watched him as he straightened his clothes. He sat on the bench beneath the acacia trees at the lava tube's center. He caught his breath.

Erno wondered if the cop would follow through with her threat to tell about his helping with the explosion. He felt newly vulnerable. But it was not just vulnerability he felt. He had never seen a woman lose it as clearly as the interrogator had. He had gotten to her in a way he had never gotten to a matron in his life. She was actually *scared* of him!

Now what? He put his hand in his pocket, and felt the notebook.

He pulled it out. He switched it on. The GROSS file was still there, and so was the address he'd written earlier.

A DREAM

Erno was ten when his youngest sister Celeste was born. After the birth, his mother fell into a severe depression. She snapped at Erno, fought with Aunt Sophie, and complained about one of the husbands until he moved out. Erno's way of coping was to disappear; his cousin Aphra coped by misbehaving.

One day Erno came back from school to find a fire in the middle of the kitchen floor, a flurry of safetybots stifling it with foam, his mother screaming, and Aphra— who had apparently started the fire—shouting back at her. Skidding on the foam, Erno stepped between the two of them, put his hands on Aphra's chest, and made her go to her room.

The whole time, his mother never stopped shouting. Erno was angrier at her than at Aphra. She was supposed to be the responsible one. When he returned from quieting Aphra, his mother ran off to her room and slammed the door. Erno cleaned the kitchen and waited for Aunt Sophie to come home.

The night of the fire he had a dream. He was alone in the kitchen, and then a man was there. The man drew him aside. Erno was unable to make out his face. "I am your father," the man said. "Let me show you something." He made Erno sit down and called up an image on the table. It was Erno's mother as a little girl. She sat, cross-legged, hunched over some blocks, her face screwed up in troubled introspection. "That's her second phase of work expression," Erno's father said.

With a shock, Erno recognized the expression on the little girl's face as one he had seen his mother make as she concentrated.

"She hates this photo," Erno's father said, as if to persuade Erno not to judge her: she still contained that innocence, that desire to struggle against a problem she could not solve. But Erno was mad. As he resisted, the father pressed on, and began to lose it too. He ended up screaming at Erno, "You can't take it? I'll make you see! I'll make you see!"

Erno put his hands over his ears. The faceless man's voice was twisted with rage. Eventually he stopped shouting. "There you go, there you go," he said quietly, stroking Erno's hair. "You're just the same."

TWELVE

ON HIS WAY to the East Five tube, Erno considered the officer's rant. Maybe Tyler did want to sleep with him. So what? The officer was some kind of homophobe and ought to be relieved. Raving about violence while locking him up in a room. And then trying to choke him. Yes, he had the GROSS file in his pocket, yes, he had hit Alicia—but he was no terrorist. The accusation was just a way for the cop to ignore men's legitimate grievances.

But they must not have checked the file, or understood it if they did. If they knew about GROSS, he would never have been freed.

Early in the colony's life, the East Five lava tube had been its major agricultural center. The yeast vats now produced only animal fodder, but the hydroponics rack farms still functioned, mostly for luxury items. The rote work of tending the racks fell to cousins who did not express ambition to do anything more challenging. They lived in the tube warrens on the colony's Minimum Living Standard.

A stylized painting of a centaur graced the entrance of the East Five men's warren. Since the artist had not likely ever studied a real horse, the stance of the creature looked deeply suspect to Erno. At the lobby interface Erno called up the AI attendant. The AI came onscreen as a dark brown woman wearing a glittery green shirt.

"I'm looking for Micah Avasson," Erno asked it.

"Who is calling?"

"Erno Pamelasson."

"He's on shift right now."

"Can I speak with him?"

"Knock yourself out." The avatar pointed offscreen toward a dimly lit passageway across the room. She appeared on the wall near the doorway, and called out to Erno, "Over here. Follow this corridor, third exit left to the Ag tube."

Outside of the lobby, the corridors and rooms here had the brutal utilitarian quality that marked the early colony, when survival had been the first concern and the idea of humane design had been to put a mirror at the end of a room to try to convince the eye that you weren't living in a cramped burrow some meters below the surface of a dead world. An environmental social worker would shudder.

The third exit on the left was covered with a clear permeable barrier. From the time he was a boy Erno had disliked passing through these permeable barriers; he hated the feel of the electrostatics brushing his face. He took a mask from the dispenser, fitted it over his nose and mouth, closed his eyes and passed through into the Ag tube. Above, layers of gray mastic sealed the tube roof; below, a concrete floor supported long rows of racks under light transmitted fiberoptically from the heliostats. A number of workers wearing coveralls and oxygen masks moved up and down the rows tending the racks. The high-CO_2 air was laden with humidity, and even through the mask smelled of phosphates.

Erno approached a man bent over a drawer of seedlings he had pulled out of a rack. The man held a meter from which wires dangled to a tube immersed in the hydroponics fluid. "Excuse me," Erno said. "I'm looking for Micah Avasson."

The man lifted his head, inspected Erno, then without speaking turned. "Micah!" He called down the row.

A tall man a little farther down the aisle looked up and peered at them. He had a full head of dark hair, a birdlike way of holding his shoulders. After a moment he said, "I'm Micah Avasson."

Erno walked down toward him. Erno was nonplussed—the man had pushed up his mask from his mouth and was smoking a cigarette, using real fire. No, not a cigarette—a joint.

"You can smoke in here? What about the fire regulations?"

"We in the depths are not held to as high a standard as you." Micah said this absolutely deadpan, as if there were not a hint of a joke. "Not enough O$_2$ to make a decent fire anyway. It takes practice just to get a good buzz off this thing in here without passing out."

Joint dangling from his lower lip, the man turned back to the rack. He wore yellow rubber gloves, and was pinching the buds off the tray of squat green leafy plants. Erno recognized them as a modified broadleaf sensimilla.

"You're using the colony facilities to grow pot."

"This is my personal crop. We each get a personal rack. Sparks initiative." Micah kept pinching buds. "Want to try some?"

Erno gathered himself. "My name is Erno Pamelasson. I came to see you because—"

"You're my son," Micah said, not looking at him.

Erno stared, at a loss for words. Up close the lines at the corners of the man's eyes were distinct, and there was a bit of sag to his chin. But the shape of Micah's face reminded Erno of his own reflection in the mirror.

"What did you want to see me about?" Micah pushed the rack drawer closed and looked at Erno. When Erno stood there dumb, he wheeled the stainless-steel cart beside him down to the next rack. He took a plastic bin from the cart, crouched, pulled open the bottom drawer of the rack, and began harvesting cherry tomatoes.

Finally, words came to Erno. "Why haven't I ever seen you before?"

"Lots of boys never meet their fathers."

"I'm not talking about other fathers. Why aren't you and my mother together?"

"You assume we were together. How do you know that we didn't meet in the sauna some night, one time only?"

"Is that how it was?"

Micah lifted a partially yellow tomato on his fingertips, then left it on the vine to ripen. He smiled. "No. Your mother and I were in love. We lived together for twenty-two months. And two days."

"So why did you split?"

"That I don't remember so well. We must have had our reasons. Everybody has reasons."

Erno touched his shoulder. "Don't give me that."

Micah stood, overbalancing a little. Erno caught his arm to steady him. "Thanks," Micah said. "The knees aren't what they used to be." He took a long drag on the joint, exhaled at the roof far overhead. "All right, then. The reason we broke up is that your mother is a cast-iron bitch. And I am a cast-iron bastard. The details of our breakup all derive from those simple facts, and I don't recall them. I do recall that we had good fun making you, though. I remember that well."

"I bet."

"You were a good baby, as babies go. Didn't cry too much. You had a sunny disposition." He took a final toke on the joint, and then dropped the butt into the bin of tomatoes. "Doesn't seem to have lasted."

"Were you there when I was born?"

"So we're going to have this conversation." Micah exhaled the last cloud of smoke, slipped his mask down, and finally fixed his watery brown eyes on Erno. "I was there. I was there until you were maybe six or seven months. Then I left."

"Did she make you leave?"

"Not really." His voice was muffled now. "She was taken with me at first because of the glamor—I was an acrobat, the *Cirque Jacinthe*? But her sister was in the marriage, and her friends. She had her mentor, her support group. I was just the father. It was okay while it was fun, and maybe I thought it was something more when we first got together, but after a while it wasn't fun anymore."

"You just didn't want the responsibility!"

"Erno, to tell you the truth, that didn't have much to do with it. I liked holding you on my lap and rubbing you with my beard. You would giggle. I would toss you up into the air and catch you. You liked that. Drove your mother crazy—you're going to hurt him, she kept saying."

Erno had a sudden memory of being thrown high, floating, tumbling. Laughing.

"So why did you leave?"

"Pam and I just didn't get along. I met another woman, that got hot, and Pam didn't seem to need me around anymore. I had filled my purpose."

Emotion worked in Erno. He shifted from foot to foot. "I don't understand men like you. They've stuck you down here in a dorm! You're old, and you've got nothing."

"I've got everything I need. I have friends."

"Women shit on you, and you don't care."

"There are women just like me. We have what we want. I work. I read. I grow my plants. I have no desire to change the world. The world works for me.

"The genius of the founders, Erno"—Micah opened another drawer and started on the next rack of tomatoes—"was that they minimized the contact of males and females. They made it purely voluntary. Do you realize how many centuries men and women tore themselves to pieces through forced intimacy? In every marriage, the decades of lying that paid for every week of pleasure? That the vast majority of men and women, when they spoke honestly, regretted the day they had ever married?"

"We have no power!"

Micah made a disgusted noise. "Nobody has any power. On Earth, for every privilege, men had six obligations. I'm sorry you feel that something has been taken from you. If you feel that way, I suggest you work on building your own relationships. Get married, for pity's sake. Nothing is stopping you."

Erno grabbed Micah's wrist. "Look at me!"

Micah looked. "Yes?"

"You knew I was your son. Doesn't that mean you've been paying attention to me?"

"From a distance. I wish you well, you understand."

"You know I was responsible for the explosion at the meeting! The constables arrested me!"

"No. Really? That sounds like trouble, Erno."

"Don't you want to ask me anything?"

"Give me your number. If I think of something, I'll call. Assuming you're not banished by then."

Erno turned away. He stalked down the row of hydroponics.

"Come by again, Erno!" Micah called after him. "Anytime. I mean it. Do you like music?"

The next man down was watching Erno now. He passed through the door out of the Ag tube, tore off the mask, and threw it down.

Some of the permeable barrier must have brushed Erno's face when he passed through, because as he left East Five he found he couldn't keep his eyes from tearing up.

"THE GRANDSTAND COMPLEX"

Two motorcycle racers have been rivals for a long time. The one telling the story has been beating the other, whose name is Tony Lukatovich, in every race. Tony takes increasing risks to win the crowd's approval, without success. Finally he makes a bet with the narrator: whoever wins the next race, the loser will kill himself.

The narrator thinks Tony is crazy. He doesn't want to bet. But when Tony threatens to tell the public he is a coward, he agrees.

In the next race, Tony and another rider are ahead of the narrator until the last turn, where Tony's bike bumps the leader's and they both crash. The narrator wins, but Tony is killed in the crash.

Then the narrator finds out that, *before the race*, Tony told a newspaper reporter that the narrator had decided to retire after the next fatal crash. Did Tony deliberately get himself killed in order to make him retire?

Yet, despite the news report, the winner doesn't have to retire. He can say he changed his mind. Tony hasn't won anything, has he? If so, what?

THIRTEEN

ERNO HAD NOT left the apartment in days. In the aftermath of his police interview, his mother had hovered over him like a bad mood, and it was all he could do to avoid her reproachful stare. Aunt Sophie and Lena and even Aphra acted like he had some terminal disease that might be catching. They intended to heap him with shame until he was crushed. He holed up in his room listening to an ancient recording, "Black and Blue," by Louis Armstrong. The long-dead jazzman growled, "What did I do, to feel so black and blue?"

A real man would get back at them. Tyler would. And they would know that they were being gotten, and they would be gotten in the heart of their assumption of superiority. Something that would show women permanently that men were not to be disregarded.

Erno opened his notebook and tried writing a poem.

> *When you hit someone*
> *It changes their face.*
>
> *Your mother looks shocked and old.*
> *Alicia looks younger.*
> *Men named Cluny get even stupider than they are.*
>
> *It hurts your fist.*
> *It hurts your shoulder.*
>
> *The biggest surprise: you can do it.*
> *Your fist waits there at the end of your arm*
> *At any and every moment*
> *Whether you are aware of it or not.*

Once you know this
The world changes.

He stared at the lines for some minutes, then erased them. In their place he tried writing a joke.

Q: How many matrons does it take to screw in a lightbulb?
A: Lightbulbs don't care to be screwed by matrons.

He turned off his screen and lay on his bed, his hands behind his head, and stared at the ceiling. He could engineer the GROSS virus. He would not even need access to the biotech facilities; he knew where he could obtain almost everything required from warehouses within the colony. But he would need a place secret enough that nobody would find him out.

Suddenly he knew the place. And with it, he knew where Tyler was hiding.

The northwest lava tube was fairly busy when Erno arrived at 2300. Swing-shift Cousins wandered into the open clubs, and the free-enterprise shops were doing their heaviest business. The door to the Oxygen Warehouse was dark, and a public notice was posted on it. The door was locked, and Erno did not want to draw attention by trying to force it.

So he returned to the construction materials warehouse in North Six. Little traffic here, and Erno was able to slip inside without notice. He kept behind the farthest aisle until he reached the back wall and the deserted airlock that was being used for storage. It took him some minutes to move the building struts and slide through to the other end. The door opened and he was in the deserted lava tube.

It was completely dark. He used his flashlight to retrace their steps from weeks ago.

Before long, Erno heard a faint noise ahead. He extinguished the flash and saw, beyond several bends in the distance, a faint light. He crept along until he reached a section where light fell from a series of open doorways. He slid next to the first and listened.

The voices from inside stopped. After a moment one of them called, "Come in."

Nervous, Erno stepped into the light from the open door. He squinted and saw Tyler and a couple of other men in a room cluttered with tables, cases of dried food, oxygen packs, scattered clothes, blankets, exosuits. On the table were book readers, half-filled juice bulbs, constables' batons.

One of the younger men came up to Erno and slapped him on the back. "Erno. My man!" It was Sid.

The others watched Erno speculatively. Tyler leaned back against the table. He wore a surface skintight; beside him lay his utility belt. His hair had grown out into a centimeter of red bristle. He grinned. "I assume you've brought the goods, Erno."

Erno pulled his notebook from his pocket. "Yes."

Tyler took the notebook and, without moving his eyes from Erno's, put it on the table. "You can do this, right?"

"Erno's a wizard," Sid said. "He can do it in his sleep."

The other young men just watched Erno. They cared what he was going to say.

"I can do it."

Tyler scratched the corner of his nose with his index finger. "Will you?"

"I don't know."

"Why don't you know? Is this a hard decision?"

"Of course it is. A lot of children will die. Nothing will ever be the same."

"We're under the impression that's the point, Erno. Come with me," Tyler said, getting off the table. "We need to talk."

Tyler directed the others to go back to work and took Erno into another room. This one had a cot, a pile of clothes, and bulbs of alcohol lying around. On a wall screen was a schematic of the colony's substructure.

Tyler pushed a pile of clothes off a chair. "Sit down."

Erno sat. "You knew about this place before we came here the night of the riot."

Tyler said nothing.

"They asked me if there was a conspiracy," Erno continued. "I told them no. Is there?"

"Sure there is. You're part of it."

"I'm not part of anything."

"That's the trouble with men among the Cousins, Erno. We're not part of anything. If a man isn't part of something, then he's of no use to anybody."

"Help me out, Tyler. I don't get it."

"They say that men can't live only with other men. I don't believe that. Did you ever study the warrior culture?"

"No."

"Men banding together—for duty, honor, clan. That's what the warrior lived by throughout history. It was the definition of manhood.

"The matrons say men are extreme, that they'll do anything. They're right. A man will run into a collapsing building to rescue a complete stranger. That's why, for most of human history, the warrior was necessary for the survival of the clan—later the nation.

"But the twentieth century drained all the meaning out of it. First the great industrial nations exploited the warrior ethic, destroying the best of their sons for money, for material gain, for political ideology. Then the feminist movement, which did not understand the warrior, and feared and ridiculed him, grew. They even persuaded some men to reject masculinity.

"All this eventually erased the purpose from what was left of the warrior culture. Now, if the warrior ethic can exist at all, it must be personal. 'Duty, honor, self.'"

"Self?"

"Self. In some way it was always like that. Sacrifice for others is not about the others, it's the ultimate assertion of self. It's the self, after all, that decides to place value in the other. What's important is the *self* and the *sacrifice*, not the cause for which you sacrifice. In the final analysis, all sacrifices are in service of the self. The pure male assertion."

"You're not talking about running into a collapsing building, Tyler."

Tyler laughed. "Don't you get it yet, Erno? We're living in a collapsing building!"

"If we produce this virus, people are going to die."

"Living as a male among the Cousins is death. They destroy certain things, things that are good—only this society defines them as bad. Fatherhood. Protection of the weak by the strong. There's no *force* here, Erno. There's no *growth*. The Cousins are an evolutionary dead end. In time of peace it may look fine and dandy, but in time of war, it would be wiped out in a moment."

Erno didn't know what to say.

"This isn't some scheme for power, Erno. You think I'm in this out of some abstract theory? This is life's blood. This—"

Sid ran in from the hall. "Tyler," he said. "The warehouse door has cycled again!"

Tyler was up instantly. He grabbed Erno by the shirt. "Who did you tell?"

"Tell? No one!"

"Get the others!" Tyler told Sid. But as soon as Sid left the room an explosion rocked the hall, and the lights went out. Tyler still had hold of Erno's shirt, and dragged him to the floor. The air was full of stinging fumes.

Tyler whispered, "If you want to live, follow me."

They crawled away from the hall door, toward the back of the room. In the light of the wall screen, Tyler upended the cot and yanked open a meter-square door set into the wall. When Erno hesitated, Tyler dragged him into the dark tunnel beyond.

They crawled on hands and knees for a long time. Erno's eyes teared from the gas, and he coughed until he vomited. Tyler pulled him along in the blackness until they reached a chamber, dimly lit in red, where they could stand. On the other side of the chamber was a pressure door.

"Put this on," Tyler said, shoving a surface suit into Erno's arms. "Quickly!"

Erno struggled to pull on the skintight, still gasping for breath. "I swear I had nothing to do with this," he said.

"I know," Tyler said. He sealed up his own suit and locked down his tiger-striped helmet.

"Brace yourself. This isn't an airlock," Tyler said, and hit the control on the exterior door.

The moment the door showed a gap, the air blew out of the chamber, almost knocking Erno off his feet. When it opened wide enough, they staggered through into a crevasse. The moisture in the escaping air froze and fell as frost in the vacuum around them. Erno wondered if their pursuers would be able to seal the tube or get back behind a pressure door before they passed out.

Tyler and Erno emerged from the crevasse into a sloping pit, half of which was lit by the glare of hard sunlight. They scrambled up the slope through six centimeters of dust and reached the surface.

"Now what?" Erno said.

Tyler shook his head and put his hand against Erno's faceplate. He leaned over and touched his helmet to Erno's. "Private six, encrypted."

Erno switched his suit radio.

"They won't be out after us for some time," Tyler said. "Since we left that Judas book of yours behind, they may not even know where we are."

"Judas book?"

"Your notebook—you must have had it with you when the constables questioned you."

"Yes. But they didn't know what the download meant or they wouldn't have returned it to me."

"Returned it to you? Dumbass. They put a tracer in it."

Erno could see Tyler's dark eyes dimly through the faceplate, inches from his own, yet separated by more than glass and vacuum. "I'm sorry."

"Forget it."

"When we go back, we'll be arrested. We might be banished."

"We're not going back just yet. Follow me."

"Where can we go?"

"There's a construction shack at an abandoned ilemenite mine south of here. It's a bit of a hike—two to three hours—but what else are we going to do on such a fine morning?"

Tyler turned and hopped off across the surface. Erno stood dumbly for a moment, then followed.

They headed south along the western side of the crater. The ground was much rockier, full of huge boulders and pits where ancient lava tubes had collapsed millennia ago. The suit Erno wore was too tight, and pinched him in the armpits and crotch. His thermoregulators struggled against the open sunlight, and he felt his body inside the skintight slick with sweat. The bind in his crotch became a stabbing pain with every stride.

Around to the south side of Fowler, they struck off to the south. Tyler followed a line of boot prints and tractor treads in the dust. The land rose to Adil's Ridge after a couple of kilometers, from which Erno looked back and saw, for the first time, all of the domed crater where he had spent his entire life.

"Is this construction shack habitable?" he asked.

"I've got it outfitted."

"What are we going to do? We can't stay out here forever."

"We won't. They'll calm down. You forget that we haven't done anything but spray a prank message on the dome. I'm a comedian. What do they expect from a comedian?"

Erno did not remind Tyler of the possible decompression injuries their escape might have caused. He tucked his head down and focused on keeping up with the big man's steady pace. He drew deep breaths. They skipped along without speaking for an hour or more. Off to their left, Erno noticed a line of distant pylons, with threads of cable strung between them. It was the cable train route from Fowler to Tsander several hundred kilometers south.

Tyler began to speak. "I'm working on some new material. For my comeback performance. It's about the difference between love and sex."

"Okay. So what's the difference?"

"Sex is like a fresh steak. It smells great, you salivate, you consume it in a couple of minutes, you're satisfied, you feel great, and you fall asleep."

"And love?"

"Love is completely different. Love is like flash-frozen food—it lasts forever. Cold as liquid hydrogen. You take it out when you need it, warm it up. You persuade yourself it's just as good as sex. People who promote love say it's even better, but that's a lie constructed out of necessity. The only thing it's better than is starving to death."

"I think the routine needs a little work," Erno said. After a moment he added, "There's a story in *Stories for Men* about love."

"I'd think the stories for men would be about sex."

"No. There's no sex in any of them. There's hardly any women at all. Most of them are about men competing with other men. But there's one about a rich man who bets a poor young man that hunger is stronger than love. He locks the poor man and his lover in separate rooms with a window between them, for seven days, without food. At the end of the seven days they're starving. Then he puts them together in a room with a single piece of bread."

"Who eats it?"

"The man grabs it, and is at the point of eating it when he looks over at the woman, almost unconscious from hunger. He gives it to her. She refuses it, says he should have it because he's more hungry than she is. So they win the bet."

Tyler laughed. "If it had been a steak, they would have lost." They continued hiking for a while. "That story isn't about love. It's about the poor man beating the rich man."

Erno considered it. "Maybe."

"So what have you learned from that book? Anything?"

"Well, there's a lot of killing—it's like the writers are obsessed with killing. The characters kill for fun, or sport, or money, or freedom, or to get respect. Or women."

"That's the way it was back then, Erno. Men—"

Tyler's voice was blotted out by a tone blaring over their earphones. After fifteen seconds an AI voice came on:

"SATELLITES REPORT A MAJOR SOLAR CORONAL MASS EJECTION. PARTICLE FLUX WILL BEGIN TO RISE IN TWENTY MINUTES, REACHING LETHAL LEVELS WITHIN THIRTY. ALL PERSONS ON THE SURFACE SHOULD IMMEDIATELY SEEK SHELTER. REFRAIN FROM EXPOSURE UNTIL THE ALL CLEAR SOUNDS.

"REPEAT: A MAJOR SOLAR RADIATION EVENT HAS OCCURRED. ALL PERSONS SHOULD IMMEDIATELY TAKE SHELTER."

Both of them stopped. Erno scanned the sky, frantic. Of course there was no difference. The sun threw the same harsh glare it always threw. His heart thudded in his ears. He heard Tyler's deep breaths in his earphones.

"How insulated is this shack?" he asked Tyler. "Can it stand a solar storm?"

Tyler didn't answer for a moment. "I doubt it."

"How about the mine? Is there a radiation shelter? Or a tunnel?"

"It was a strip mine. Besides," Tyler said calmly, "we couldn't get there in twenty minutes."

They were more than an hour south of the colony.

Erno scanned the horizon, looking for some sign of shelter. A crevasse, a lava tube—maybe they'd run out of air, but at least they would not fry. He saw, again, the threads of the cable towers to the east.

"The cable line!" Erno said. "It has radiation shelters for the cable cars all along it."

"If we can reach one in time."

Erno checked his clock readout. 0237. Figure they had until 0300. He leapt off due east, toward the cable towers. Tyler followed.

The next fifteen minutes passed in a trance, a surreal slow-motion broken-field race through the dust and boulders toward the pylons to the east. Erno pushed himself to the edge of his strength, until a haze of spots rose before his eyes. He seemed to move with agonizing slowness.

They were 500 meters from the cable pylon. 300 meters. 100 meters. They were beneath it.

When they reached the pylon, Erno scanned in both directions for a shelter. The cable line was designed to dip underground for radiation protection periodically all along the length of its route. The distance between the tunnels was determined by the top speed of the cable car and the amount of advance warning the passengers were likely to get of a solar event. There was no way of telling how far they were from a shelter, or in which direction the closest lay.

"South," Tyler said. "The colony is the next shelter north, and it's too far for us to run, so our only shot should be south."

It was 0251. They ran south, their leaps no longer strong and low, but with a weary desperation to them now. Erno kept his eyes fixed on the horizon. The twin cables stretched above them like strands of spiderweb, silver in the sunlight, disappearing far ahead where the next T pylon stood like the finish line in a race.

The T grew, and suddenly they were on it. Beyond, in its next arc, the cable swooped down to the horizon. They kept running, and as they drew closer, Erno saw that a tunnel opened in the distance, and the cable ran into it. He gasped out a moan that was all the shout he could make.

They were almost there when Erno realized that Tyler had slowed, and was no longer keeping up. He willed himself to stop, awkwardly, almost pitching face first into the regolith. He looked back. Tyler had slowed to a stroll.

"What's wrong?" Erno gasped.

"Nothing," Tyler said. Though Erno could hear Tyler's ragged breath, there was no hurry in his voice.

"Come on!" Erno shouted.

Tyler stopped completely. "Women and children first."

Erno tried to catch his breath. His clock read 0304. "What?"

"You go ahead. Save your pathetic life."

"Are you crazy? Do you want to die?"

"Of course not. I want you to go in first."

"Why?"

"If you can't figure it out by now, I can't explain it, Erno. It's a story for a man."

Erno stood dumbstruck.

"Come out here into the sunshine with me," Tyler said. "It's nice out here."

Erno laughed. He took a step back toward Tyler. He took another. They stood side by side.

"That's my man Erno. Now, how long can you stay out here?"

The sun beat brightly down. The tunnel mouth gaped five meters in front of them. 0307. 0309. Each watched the other, neither budged.

"My life isn't pathetic," Erno said.

"Depends on how you look at it," Tyler replied.

"Don't you think yours is worth saving?"

"What makes you think this is a real radiation alert, Erno? The broadcast could be a trick to make us come back."

"There have been warnings posted for weeks."

"That only makes it a more plausible trick."

"That's no reason for us to risk our lives—on the chance it is."

"I don't think it's a trick, Erno. I'll go into that tunnel. After you."

Erno stared at the dark tunnel ahead. 0311. A single leap from safety. Even now lethal levels of radiation might be sluicing through their bodies. A bead of sweat stung his eye.

"So this is what it means to be a man?" Erno said softly, as much to himself as to Tyler.

"This is it," Tyler said. "And I'm a better man than you are."

Erno felt an adrenaline surge. "You're not better than me."

"We'll find out."

"You haven't accomplished anything."

"I don't need you to tell me what I've accomplished. Go ahead, Erno. Back to your cave."

0312. 0313. Erno could feel the radiation. It was shattering proteins and DNA throughout his body, rupturing cell walls, turning the miraculously ordered organic molecules of his brain into sludge. He thought about Alicia, the curve of her breast, the light in her eyes. Had she told her friends that he had hit her? And his mother. He saw the shock and surprise in her face when the book hit her. How angry he had been. He wanted to explain to her why he had thrown it. It shouldn't be that hard to explain.

He saw his shadow reaching out beside him, sharp and steady, two arms, two legs and a head, an ape somehow transported to the moon. No, not an ape—a man. What a miracle that human beings could keep themselves alive in this harsh place—not just keep alive, but make a home of it. All the intellect and planning and work that had gone to put him here, standing out under the brutal sun, letting it exterminate him.

He looked at Tyler, fixed as stone.

"This is insane," Erno said—then ran for the tunnel.

A second after he sheltered inside, Tyler was there beside him.

FOURTEEN

THEY FOUND THE radiation shelter midway through the tunnel, closed themselves inside, stripped off their suits, drank some water, breathed the cool air. They crowded in the tiny stone room together, smelling each other's sweat. Erno started to get sick: he had chills, he felt nausea. Tyler made him sip water, put his arm around Erno's shoulders.

Tyler said it was radiation poisoning, but Erno said it was not. He sat wordless in the corner the nine hours it took until the all-clear came. Then, ignoring Tyler, he suited up and headed back to the colony.

FIFTEEN

SO THAT IS the story of how Erno discovered that he was not a man. That, indeed, Tyler was right, there was no place for men in the Society of Cousins. And that he, Erno, despite his grievances and rage, was a Cousin.

The cost of this discovery was Erno's own banishment, and one thing more.

When Erno turned himself in at the constabulary headquarters, eager to tell them about GROSS and ready to help them find Tyler, he was surprised at their subdued reaction. They asked him no questions. They looked at him funny, eyes full of rage and something besides rage. Horror? Loathing? Pity? They put him in the same white room where he had sat before, and left him there alone. After a while the blond interrogator, Mona, came in and told him that three people had been injured when Tyler and Erno had blown the vacuum seal while escaping. One, who had insisted on crawling after them through the escape tunnel, had been caught in there and died: Erno's mother.

Erno and Tyler were given separate trials, and the colony voted: they were to be expelled. Tyler's banishment was permanent; Erno was free to apply for readmission in ten years.

The night before he left, Erno, accompanied by a constable, was allowed to visit his home. Knowing how completely inadequate it was, he apologized to his sister, his aunt, and his cousins. Aunt Sophie and Nick treated him with stiff rectitude. Celeste, who somehow did not feel the rage against him that he deserved, cried and embraced him. They let him pack a duffel with a number of items from his room.

After leaving, he asked the constable if he could stop a moment on the terrace outside the apartment before going back to jail. He took a last look at the vista of the domed crater from the place where he had lived every day of his life. He drew a deep breath and closed his eyes. His mother seemed everywhere around him. All he could see was her crawling, on hands and knees in the dark, desperately trying to save him from himself. How angry she must have been, and how afraid. What must she have thought, as the air flew away and she felt her coming death? Did she regret giving birth to him?

He opened his eyes. There on the terrace stood the recycler he had thrown pebbles at for years. He reached into his pack, pulled out *Stories for Men*, and stepped toward the bin.

Alicia came around a corner. "Hello, Erno," she said.

A step from the trash bin, Erno held the book awkwardly in his hand, trying to think of something to say. The constable watched them.

"I can't tell you how sorry I am," he told Alicia.

"I know you didn't mean this to happen," she said.

"It doesn't matter what I meant. It happened."

On impulse, he handed her the copy of *Stories for Men*. "I don't know what to do with this," he said. "Will you keep it for me?"

The next morning they put him on the cable train for Tsander. His exile had begun.

The Pure Product

I **ARRIVED IN** Kansas City at one o'clock on the afternoon of the thirteenth of August. A Tuesday. I was driving the beige 1983 Chevrolet Citation that I had stolen two days earlier in Pocatello, Idaho. The Kansas plates on the car I'd taken from a different car in a parking lot in Salt Lake City. Salt Lake City was founded by the Mormons, whose god tells them that in the future Jesus Christ will come again.

I drove through Kansas City with the windows open and the sun beating down through the windshield. The car had no air conditioning, and my shirt was stuck to my back from seven hours behind the wheel. Finally I found a hardware store, "Hector's" on Wornall. I pulled into the lot. The Citation's engine dieseled after I turned off the ignition; I pumped the accelerator once and it coughed and died. The heat was like syrup. The sun drove shadows deep into corners, left them flattened at the feet of the people on the sidewalk. It turned the plate glass of the store window into a dark negative of the positive print that was Wornall Road. August.

The man behind the counter in the hardware store I took to be Hector himself. He looked like Hector, slain in vengeance beneath the walls of paintbrushes—the kind of semi-friendly, publicly optimistic man who would tell you about his crazy wife and his ten-penny nails. I bought a gallon of kerosene and a plastic paint funnel, put them into the trunk of the Citation, then walked down the block to the Mark Twain Bank. Mark Twain died at the age of seventy-five with a heart full of bitter accusations against the Calvinist god and no hope for the future of humanity. Inside the bank I went to one of the desks, at which sat a Nice Young Lady. I asked about starting a business checking account. She gave me a form to fill out, then sent me to the office of Mr. Graves.

Mr. Graves wielded a formidable handshake. "What can I do for you, Mr....?"

"Tillotsen, Gerald Tillotsen," I said. Gerald Tillotsen, of Tacoma, Washington, died of diphtheria at the age of four weeks—on September 24, 1938.I have a copy of his birth certificate.

"I'm new to Kansas City. I'd like to open a business account here, and perhaps take out a loan. I trust this is a reputable bank? What's your exposure in Brazil?" I looked around the office as if Graves were hiding a woman behind the hat stand, then flashed him my most ingratiating smile.

Mr. Graves did his best. He tried smiling back, then decided to ignore my little joke. "We're very sound, Mr. Tillotsen."

I continued smiling.

"What kind of business do you own?"

"I'm in insurance. Mutual Assurance of Hartford. Our regional office is in Oklahoma City, and I'm setting up an agency here, at 103rd and State Line." Just off the interstate.

He examined the form. His absorption was too tempting.

"Maybe I can fix you up with a policy? You look like dead meat."

Graves' head snapped up, his mouth half-open. He closed it and watched me guardedly. The dullness of it all! How I tire. He was like some cow, like most of the rest of you in this silly age, unwilling to break the rules in order to take offense. "Did he really say that?" he was thinking. "Was that his idea of a joke? He looks normal enough." I did look normal, exactly like an insurance agent. I was the right kind of person, and I could do anything. If at times I grate, if at times I fall a little short of or go a little beyond convention, there is not one of you who can call me to account.

Graves was coming around. All business.

"Ah—yes, Mr. Tillotsen. If you'll wait a moment, I'm sure we can take care of this checking account. As for the loan—"

"Forget it."

That should have stopped him. He should have asked after my credentials, he should have done a dozen things. He looked at me, and I stared calmly back at him. And I knew that, looking into my honest blue eyes, he could not think of a thing.

"I'll just start the checking account with this money order," I said, reaching into my pocket. "That will be acceptable, won't it?"

"It will be fine," he said. He took the form and the order over to one of the secretaries while I sat at the desk. I lit a cigar and blew some smoke rings. I'd purchased the money order the day before in a post office in Denver. One hundred dollars. I didn't intend to use the account very long. Graves returned with my sample checks, shook hands earnestly, and wished me a good day. Have a *good* day, he said. I *will*, I said.

Outside, the heat was still stifling. I took off my sports coat. I was sweating so much I had to check my hair in the sideview mirror of my car. I walked down the street to a liquor store and bought a bottle of chardonnay and a bottle of Chivas Regal. I got some paper cups from a nearby grocery. One final errand, then I could relax for a few hours.

In the shopping center that I had told Graves would be the location for my nonexistent insurance office, I had noticed a sporting goods store. It was about three o'clock when I parked in the lot and ambled into the shop. I looked at various golf clubs: irons, woods, even one set with fiberglass shafts. Finally I selected a set of eight Spalding irons with matching woods, a large bag, and several boxes of Top Flites. The salesman, who had been occupied with another customer at the rear of the store, hustled up, his eyes full of commission money. I gave him little time to think. The total cost was $812.32. I paid with a check drawn on my new account, cordially thanked the man, and had him carry all the equipment out to the trunk of the car.

I drove to a park near the bank; Loose Park, they called it. I felt loose. Cut loose, drifting free, like one of the kites people were flying that had broken its string and was ascending into the sun. Beneath the trees it was still hot, though the sunlight was reduced to a shuffling of light and shadow on the brown grass. Kids ran, jumped, swung on playground equipment. I uncorked my bottle of wine, filled one of the paper cups, and sat down beneath a tree, enjoying the children, watching young men and women walking along the footpaths.

A girl approached. She didn't look any older than seventeen. Short, slender, with clean blond hair cut to her shoulders. Her shorts were very tight.

I watched her unabashedly; she saw me watching and left the path to come over to me. She stopped a few feet away, hands on her hips. "What are you looking at?" she asked.

"Your legs," I said. "Would you like some wine?"

"No thanks. My mother told me never to accept wine from strangers." She looked right through me.

"I take what I can get from strangers," I said. "Because I'm a stranger."

I guess she liked that. She sat down and we chatted for a while. There was something wrong about her imitation of a seventeen-year-old; I began to wonder whether hookers worked the park. She crossed her legs and her shorts got tighter. "Where are you from?" she asked.

"San Francisco. But I've just moved here to stay. I have a part interest in the sporting goods store at the Eastridge Plaza."

"You live near here?"

"On West Eighty-ninth." I had driven down Eighty-ninth on my way to the bank.

"I live on Eighty-ninth! We're neighbors."

It was exactly what one of my own might have said to test me. I took a drink of wine and changed the subject. "Would you like to visit San Francisco someday?"

She brushed her hair back behind one ear. She pursed her lips, showing off her fine cheekbones. "Have you got something going?" she asked, in queerly accented English.

"Excuse me?"

"I said, have you got something going," she repeated, still with the accent—the accent of my own time.

I took another sip. "A bottle of wine," I replied in good mid-western 1980s.

She wasn't having any of it. "No artwork, please. I don't like artwork."

I had to laugh: my life was devoted to artwork. I had not met anyone real in a long time. At the beginning I hadn't wanted to, and in the ensuing years I had given up expecting it. If there's anything more boring than you people it's us people. But that was an old attitude. When she came to me in K.C., I was lonely and she was something new.

"Okay," I said. "It's not much, but you can come for the ride. Do you want to?"

She smiled and said yes.

As we walked to my car, she brushed her hip against my leg. I switched the bottle to my left hand and put my arm around her shoulders in a fatherly way. We got into the front seat, beneath the trees on a street at the edge of the park. It was quiet. I reached over, grabbed her hair at the nape of her neck, and jerked her face toward me, covering her little mouth with mine. Surprise: she threw her arms around my neck and slid across the seat into my lap. We did not talk. I yanked at the shorts; she thrust her hand into my pants. St. Augustine said "Lord give me chastity, but not yet."

At the end she slipped off me, calmly buttoned her blouse, brushed her hair back from her forehead. "How about a push?" she asked. She had a nail file out and was filing her index fingernail to a point.

I shook my head and looked at her. She resembled my grandmother. I had never run into my grandmother, but she had a hellish reputation. "No thanks. What's your name?"

"Call me Ruth." She scratched the inside of her left elbow with her nail. She leaned back in her seat, sighed deeply. Her eyes became a very bright, very hard blue.

While she was aloft I got out, opened the trunk, emptied the rest of the chardonnay into the gutter, and used the funnel to fill the bottle with kerosene. I plugged it with a kerosene-soaked rag. Afternoon was sliding into evening as I started the car and cruised down one of the residential streets. The houses were like those of any city or town of that era of the Midwestern USA: white frame, forty or fifty years old, with large porches and small front yards. Dying elms hung over the street. Shadows stretched across the sidewalks. Ruth's nose wrinkled; she turned her face lazily toward me, saw the kerosene bottle, and smiled.

Ahead on the sidewalk I saw a man walking leisurely. He was middle-aged, probably just returning from work, enjoying the quiet pause dusk was bringing to the hot day. It might have been Hector; it might have been Graves. It might have been any one of you. I punched the cigarette lighter, readied the bottle in my right hand, steering with my leg as the car moved slowly forward.

"Let me help," Ruth said. She reached out and steadied the wheel with her slender fingertips. The lighter popped out. I touched it to the rag; it smoldered and caught. Greasy smoke stung my eyes. By now the man had noticed us. I hung my arm, holding the bottle, out the window. As we passed him, I flipped the bottle at the sidewalk like a newsboy tossing a rolled-up newspaper. The rag flamed brighter as it whipped through the air; the bottle landed at his feet and exploded, dousing him with burning kerosene. I floored the accelerator; the motor coughed, then roared, the tires and Ruth both squealing in delight. I could see the flaming man in the rearview mirror as we sped away.

ON THE GREAT American Plains, the summer nights are not silent. The fields sing the summer songs of insects—not individual sounds, but a high-pitched drone of locusts, crickets, cicadas, small chirping things for which I have no names. You drive along the superhighway and that sound blends with the sound of wind rushing through your opened windows, hiding the thrum of the automobile, conveying the impression of incredible velocity. Wheels vibrate, tires beat against the pavement, the steering wheel trembles, alive in your hands, droning insects alive in your ears. Reflecting posts at the roadside leap from the darkness with metronomic regularity, glowing amber in the headlights, only to vanish abruptly into the ready night when you pass. You lose track of how long you have been on the road, where you are going. The fields scream in your ears like a thousand lost, mechanical souls, and you press your foot to the accelerator, hurrying away.

When we left Kansas City that evening we were indeed hurrying. Our direction was in one sense precise: Interstate 70, more or less due east, through Missouri in a dream. They might remember me in Kansas City, at the same time wondering who and why. Mr. Graves scans the morning paper over his grapefruit: man burned by gasoline bomb. The clerk wonders why he ever accepted an unverified counter check, without a name or address printed on it, for eight hundred dollars. The check bounces. They discover it was a bottle of chardonnay. The story is pieced together. They would eventually figure out how—I wouldn't lie to myself about that (I never lie to myself)—but the why would always escape them. Organized crime, they would say. A plot that misfired.

Of course, they still might have caught me. The car became more of a liability the longer I held on to it. But Ruth, humming to herself, did not seem to care, and neither did I. You have to improvise these things; that's what gives them whatever interest they have.

Just shy of Columbia, Missouri, Ruth stopped humming and asked me, "Do you know why Helen Keller can't have any children?"

"No."

"Because she's dead."

I rolled up the window so I could hear her better. "That's pretty funny," I said.

"Yes. I overheard it in a restaurant." After a minute she asked, "Who's Helen Keller?"

"A dead woman." An insect splattered itself against the windshield. The lights of the oncoming cars glinted against the smear it left.

"She must be famous," said Ruth. "I like famous people. Have you met any famous people? Was that man you burned famous?"

"Probably not. I don't care about famous people anymore." The last time I had anything to do, even peripherally, with anyone famous was when I changed the direction of the tape over the lock in the Watergate Hotel so Frank Wills would notice it. Ruth did not look like the kind who would know about that. "I was there for the Kennedy assassination," I said, "but I had nothing to do with it."

"Who was Kennedy?"

That made me smile. "How long have you been here?" I pointed at her tiny purse. "That's all you've got with you?"

She slid across the bench seat of the crappy car and leaned her head against my shoulder. "I don't need anything else."

"No clothes?"

"I left them in Kansas City. We can get more."

"Sure," I said.

She opened the purse and took out a plastic Bayer aspirin case. From it she selected two blue-and-yellow caps. She shoved her palm up under my nose. "Serometh?"

"No thanks."

She put one of the caps back into the box and popped the other under her nose. She sighed and snuggled tighter against me. We had reached Columbia and I was hungry. When I pulled in at a McDonald's she ran across the lot into the shopping mall before I could stop her. I was a little nervous about the car and sat watching it as I ate (Big Mac, small Dr. Pepper). She did not come back. I crossed the lot to the mall, found a drugstore, and bought some cigars. When I strolled back to the car she was waiting for me, hopping from one foot to another and tugging at the door handle. Serometh makes you impatient. She was wearing a pair of shiny black pants, pink-and-white-checked sneakers, and a hot pink blouse.

"'s go!" she hissed.

I moved even slower. She looked like she was about to wet herself, biting her soft lower lip with a line of perfect white teeth. I dawdled over my keys. A security guard and a young man in a shirt and tie hurried out of the mall entrance and scanned the lot. "Nice outfit," I said. "Must have cost you something."

She looked over her shoulder, saw the security guard, who saw her. "Hey!" he called, running toward us. I slid into the car, opened the passenger door. Ruth had snapped open her purse and pulled out a small gun. I grabbed her arm and yanked her into the car; she squawked and her shot went wide. The guard fell down anyway, scared shitless. For the second time that day I tested the Citation's acceleration; Ruth's door slammed shut and we were gone.

"You scut!" she said as we hit the entrance ramp of the interstate. "You're a scut-pumping Conservative. You made me miss." But she was smiling, running her hand up the inside of my thigh. She hadn't ever had so much fun in the twentieth century.

For some reason I was shaking. "Give me one of those seromeths," I said.

AROUND MIDNIGHT WE stopped in St. Louis at a Holiday Inn. We registered as Mr. and Mrs. Gerald Bruno (an old acquaintance) and paid in advance. No one remarked on the apparent difference in our ages. So discreet. I bought a copy of the *Post-Dispatch,* and we went to the room. Ruth flopped down on the bed, looking bored, but thanks to her gunplay I had a few more things to take care of. I poured myself a glass of Chivas, went into the bathroom, removed the toupee and flushed it down the toilet, showered, put a new blade in my old safety razor, and shaved the rest of the hair from my head. The Lex Luthor look. I cut my scalp. That got me laughing, and I could not stop. Ruth peeked through the doorway to find me dabbing the crown of my head with a bloody Kleenex.

"You're a wreck," she said.

I almost fell off the toilet laughing. She was absolutely right. Between giggles I managed to say, "You must not stay anywhere too long, if you're as careless as you were tonight."

She shrugged. "I bet I've been at it longer than you." She stripped and got into the shower. I climbed into bed.

The room enfolded me in its gold-carpet green-bedspread mediocrity. Sometimes it's hard to remember that things were ever different. In 1596 I rode to court with Essex; I slept in a chamber of supreme garishness (gilt escutcheons in the corners of the ceiling, pink cupids romping on the walls), in a bed warmed by any of the trollops of the city I might want. And there in the Holiday Inn I sat with my drink, in my pastel blue pajama bottoms, reading a late-twentieth-century newspaper, smoking a cigar. An earthquake in Peru estimated to have killed eight thousand in Lima alone. Nope. A steel worker in Gary, Indiana, discovered to be the murderer of six prepubescent children, bodies found buried in his basement. Perhaps. The president refuses to enforce the ruling of his Supreme Court because it "subverts the will of the American people." Probably not.

We are everywhere. But not everywhere.

Ruth came out of the bathroom, saw me, did a double take. "You look— perfect!" she said. She slid in the bed beside me, naked, and sniffed at my glass of Chivas. Her lip curled. She looked over my shoulder at the paper. "You can understand that stuff?"

"Don't kid me. Reading is a survival skill. You couldn't last here without it."

"Wrong."

I drained the scotch. Took a puff on the cigar. Dropped the paper to the floor beside the bed. I looked her over. Even relaxed, the muscles in her arms and along the tops of her thighs were well-defined.

"You even smell like one of them," she said.

"How did you get the clothes past their store security? They have those beeper tags clipped to them."

"Easy. I tried on the shoes and walked out when they weren't looking. In the second store I took the pants into a dressing room, cut the alarm tag out of the waistband, and put them on. I held the alarm tag that was clipped to the blouse in my armpit and walked out of that store, too. I put the blouse on in the mall women's room."

"If you can't read, how did you know which was the women's room?"

"There's a picture on the door.".

I felt tired and old. Ruth moved close. She rubbed her foot up my leg, drawing the pajama leg up with it. Her thigh slid across my groin. I started to get hard. "Cut it out," I said. She licked my nipple.

I could not stand it. I got off the bed. "I don't like you."

She looked at me with true innocence. "I don't like you, either."

Although he was repulsed by the human body, Jonathan Swift was passionately in love with a woman named Esther Johnson. "What you did at the mall was stupid," I said. "You would have killed that guard."

"Which would have made us even for the day."

"Kansas City was different."

"We should ask the cops there what they think."

"You don't understand. That had some grace to it. But what you did was inelegant. It was not gratuitous. You stole those clothes for yourself, and I hate that." I was shaking.

"Who made all these rules?"

"I did."

She looked at me with amazement. "You're not just a Conservative. You've gone native!"

I wanted her so much I ached. "No I haven't," I said, but even to me my voice sounded frightened.

Ruth got out of the bed. She glided over, reached one hand around to the small of my back, pulled herself close. She looked up at me with a face that held nothing but avidity. "You can do whatever you want," she whispered. With a feeling that I was losing everything, I kissed her.

You don't need to know what happened then.

I woke when she displaced herself: there was a sound like the sweep of an arm across fabric, a stirring of air to fill the place where she had been. I looked around the still brightly lit room. It was not yet morning. The chain was across the door; her clothes lay on the dresser. She had left the aspirin box beside my bottle of scotch.

She was gone. Good, I thought, now I can go on. But I found that I couldn't sleep, could not keep from thinking. Ruth must be very good at that, or perhaps her thought is a different kind of thought from mine. I got out of the bed, resolved to try again but still fearing the inevitable. I filled the tub with hot water. I got in, breathing heavily. I took the blade from my razor. Holding my arm just beneath the surface of the water, hesitating only a moment, I cut deeply one, two, three times along the veins in my left wrist. The shock was still there, as great as ever. With blood streaming from me I cut the right wrist. Quickly, smoothly. My heart beat fast and light, the blood flowed frighteningly; already the water was stained. I felt faint—yes—it was going to work this time, yes. My vision began to fade—but in the last moments before consciousness fell away I saw, with sick despair, the futile wounds closing themselves once again, as they had so many times before. For in the future the practice of medicine may progress to the point where men need have little fear of death.

THE DAWN'S ROSY fingers found me still unconscious. I came to myself about eleven, my head throbbing, so weak I could hardly rise from the cold bloody water. There were no scars. I stumbled into the other room and washed down one of Ruth's mega-amphetamines with two fingers of scotch. I felt better immediately. It's funny how that works sometimes, isn't it? The maid knocked as I was cleaning the bathroom. I shouted for her to come back later, finished as quickly as possible, and left the hotel immediately. At an IHOP I ate Shredded Wheat with milk and strawberries for breakfast. I was full of ideas. A phone book gave me the location of a likely country club.

The Oak Hill Country Club of Florissant, Missouri, is not a spectacularly wealthy institution, or at least it does not give that impression. I'll bet you that the membership is not as purely white as the stucco clubhouse. That was all right with me. I parked the Citation in the mostly empty parking lot, hauled my new equipment from the trunk, and set off for the locker room, trying hard to look like a dentist. I successfully ran the gauntlet of the pro shop, where the proprietor was telling a bored caddy why the Cardinals would fade in the stretch. I could hear running water from the showers as I shuffled into the locker room and slung the bag into a corner. Someone was singing the "Ode to Joy," abominably.

I began to rifle through the lockers, hoping to find an open one with someone's clothes in it. I would take the keys from my benefactor's pocket and proceed along my merry way. Ruth would have accused me of self-interest; there was a moment in which I accused myself. Such hesitation is the seed of failure: as I paused before a locker containing a likely set of clothes, another golfer entered the room along with the locker-room attendant. I immediately began undressing, lowering my head so that the locker door hid my face. The golfer was soon gone, but the attendant sat down and began to leaf through a worn copy of *Penthouse*. I could come up with no better plan than to strip and enter the showers. Amphetamine daze. Perhaps the kid would develop a hard-on and go to the john to take care of it.

There was only one other man in the shower, the symphonic soloist, a somewhat portly gentleman who mercifully shut up as soon as I entered. He worked hard at ignoring me. I ignored him in return: *alle Menschen werden Brüder.* I waited a long five minutes after he left; two more men came into the showers, and I walked out with what composure I could muster. The locker-room boy was stacking towels on a table. I fished a five from my jacket in the locker and walked up behind him. Casually I took a towel.

"Son, get me a pack of Marlboros, will you?"

He took the money and left.

In the second locker I found a pair of pants that contained the keys to some sort of Audi. I was not choosy. Dressed in record time, I left the new clubs beside the rifled locker. My note read, "The pure products of America go crazy." There were three eligible cars in the lot, two 4000s and a Fox. The key would not open the door of the Fox. I was jumpy, but almost home free, coming around the front of a big Chrysler...

"Hey!"

My knee gave way and I ran into the fender of the car. The keys slipped out of my hand and skittered across the hood to the ground, jingling. Grimacing, I hopped toward them, plucked them up, glancing over my shoulder at my pursuer as I stooped. It was the locker-room attendant.

"Your cigarettes." He looked at me the way a sixteen-year-old looks at his father; that is, with bored skepticism. All our gods in the end become pitiful. It was time for me to be abruptly courteous. As it was, he would remember me too well.

"Thanks," I said. I limped over, put the pack into my shirt pocket. He started to go, but I couldn't help myself. "What about my change?"

Oh, such an insolent silence! I wonder what you told them when they asked you about me, boy. He handed over the money. I tipped him a quarter, gave him a piece of Mr. Graves' professional smile. He studied me. I turned and inserted the key into the lock of the Audi. A fifty-percent chance. Had I been the praying kind I might have prayed to one of those pitiful gods. The key turned without resistance; the door opened. The kid slouched back toward the clubhouse, pissed at me and his lackey's job. Or perhaps he found it in his heart to smile. Laughter—the Best Medicine.

A bit of a racing shift, then back to Interstate 70. My hip twinged all the way across Illinois.

I HAD ORIGINALLY intended to work my way east to Buffalo, New York, but after the Oak Hill business I wanted to cut it short. If I stayed on the interstate I was sure to get caught; I had been lucky to get as far as I had. Just outside of Indianapolis I turned onto Route 37 north to Fort Wayne and Detroit.

I was not, however, entirely cowed. Twenty-five years in one era had given me the right instincts, and with the coming of the evening and my friendly insects to sing me along, the boredom of the road became a new recklessness. Hadn't I already been seen by too many people in those twenty-five years? Thousands had looked into my honest face—and where were they? Ruth had reminded me that I was not stuck here. I would soon make an end to this latest adventure one way or another, and once I had done so, there would be no reason in God's green earth to suspect me.

And so: north of Fort Wayne, on Highway 6 east, a deserted country road (what was he doing there?), I pulled over to pick up a young hitchhiker. He wore a battered black leather jacket. His hair was short on the sides, stuck up in spikes on top, hung over his collar in back; one side was carrot-orange, the other brown with a white streak. His sign, pinned to a knapsack, said "?" He threw the pack into the back seat and climbed into the front.

"Thanks for picking me up." He did not sound like he meant it. "Where you going?"

"Flint. How about you?"

"Flint's as good as anywhere."

"Suit yourself." We got up to speed. I was completely calm. "You should fasten your seat belt," I said.

"Why?"

The surly type. "It's not just a good idea. It's the law."

He ignored me. He pulled a crossword puzzle book and a pencil from his jacket pocket. "How about turning on the light."

I flicked on the dome light for him. "I like to see a young man improve himself," I said.

His look was an almost audible sigh. "What's a five-letter word for 'the lowest point'?"

"Nadir," I replied.

"That fits. How about 'widespread'; four letters."

"Rife."

"You're pretty good." He stared at the crossword for a minute, then rolled down his window and threw the book, and the pencil, out of the car. He rolled up the window and stared at his reflection in it. I couldn't let him get off that easily. I turned off the interior light, and the darkness leapt inside.

"What's your name, son? What are you so mad about?"

"Milo. Look, are you queer? If you are, it doesn't matter to me but it will cost you...if you want to do anything about it."

I smiled and adjusted the rearview mirror so I could watch him—and he could watch me. "No, I'm not queer. The name's Loki." I extended my right hand, keeping my eyes on the road.

He looked at the hand. "Loki?"

As good a name as any. "Yes. Same as the Norse god."

He laughed. "Sure, Loki. Anything you like. Fuck you."

Such a musical voice. "Now there you go. Seems to me, Milo—if you don't mind my giving you my unsolicited opinion—that you have something of an attitude problem." I punched the cigarette lighter, reached back and pulled a cigar from my jacket on the back seat, in the process weaving the car all over Highway 6. I bit the end off the cigar and spat it out the window, stoked it up. My insects wailed. I cannot explain to you how good I felt.

"Take for instance this crossword puzzle book. Why did you throw it out the window?"

I could see Milo watching me in the mirror, wondering whether he should take me seriously. The headlights fanned out ahead of us, the white lines at the center of the road pulsing by like a rapid heartbeat. Take a chance, Milo. What have you got to lose?

"I was pissed," he said. "It's a waste of time. I don't care about stupid games."

"Exactly. It's just a game, a way to pass the time. Nobody ever really learns anything from a crossword puzzle. Corporation lawyers don't get their Porsches by building their word power with crosswords, right?"

"I don't care about Porsches."

"Neither do I, Milo. I drive an Audi."

Milo sighed.

"I know, Milo. That's not the point. The point is that it's all a game, crosswords or corporate law. Some people devote their lives to Jesus; some devote their lives to artwork. It all comes to pretty much the same thing. You get old. You die."

"Tell me something I don't already know."

"Why do you think I picked you up, Milo? I saw your question mark and it spoke to me. You probably think I'm some pervert out to take advantage of you. I have a funny name. I don't talk like your average middle-aged businessman. Forget about that." The old excitement was upon me; I was talking louder and louder, leaning on the accelerator. The car sped along. "I think you're as troubled by the materialism and cant of life in America as I am. Young people like you, with orange hair, are trying to find some values in a world that offers them nothing but crap for ideas. But too many of you are turning to extremes in response. Drugs, violence, religious fanaticism, hedonism. Some, like you I suspect, to suicide. Don't do it, Milo. Your life is too valuable." The speedometer touched eighty, eighty-five. Milo fumbled for his seat belt but couldn't find it.

I waved my hand, holding the cigar, at him. "What's the matter, Milo? Can't find the belt?" Ninety now. A pickup went by us going the other way, the wind of its passing beating at my head and shoulder. Ninety-five.

"Think, Milo! If you're upset with the present, with your parents and the schools, think about the future. What will the future be like if this breakdown of values continues in the next hundred years? Think of the impact of the new technologies! Gene splicing, gerontology, artificial intelligence, space exploration, biological weapons, nuclear proliferation! All accelerating this process! Think of the violent reactionary movements that could arise—are arising already, Milo, as we speak—from people's desire to find something to hold on to. Paint yourself a picture, *Milo,* of the kind of man or woman another hundred years of this process might produce!"

"What are you talking about?" He was terrified.

"I'm talking about the survival of values in America! Simply that." Cigar smoke swirled in front of the dashboard lights, and my voice had reached a shout. Milo was gripping the sides of his seat. The speedometer read 105. "And you, *Milo,* are at the heart of this process! If people continue to think the way you do, *Milo,* throwing their crossword puzzle books out the windows of their Audis all across America, the future will be full of absolutely valueless people! Right, MILO?" I leaned over, taking my eyes off the road, and blew smoke into his face, screaming, "ARE YOU LISTENING, MILO? MARK MY WORDS!"

"Y-yes."

"GOO, GOO, GA-GA-GAA!"

I put my foot all the way to the floor. The wind howled through the window, the gray highway flew beneath us,

"Mark my words, Milo," I whispered. He never heard me. "Twenty-five across. Eight letters. N-i-h-i-l—"

My pulse roared in my ears, there joining the drowned choir of the fields and the roar of the engine. Body slimy with sweat, fingers clenched through the cigar, fists clamped on the wheel, smoke stinging my eyes. I slammed on the brakes, downshifting immediately, sending the transmission into a painful whine as the car slewed and skidded off the pavement, clipping a reflecting marker and throwing Milo against the windshield. The car stopped with a jerk in the gravel at the side of the road, just shy of a sign announcing, WELCOME TO OHIO.

There were no other lights on the road, I shut off my own and sat behind the wheel, trembling, the night air cool on my skin. The insects wailed. The boy was slumped against the dashboard. There was a star fracture in the glass above his head, and warm blood came away on my fingers when I touched his hair. I got out of the car, circled around to the passenger's side, and dragged him from the seat into the field adjoining the road. He was surprisingly light. I left him there, in a field of Ohio soybeans on the evening of a summer's day.

THE CITY OF Detroit was founded by the French adventurer Antoine de la Mothe, sieur de Cadillac, a supporter of Comte de Pontchartrain, minister of state to the Sun King, Louis XIV. All of these men worshiped the Roman Catholic god, protected their political positions, and let the future go hang. Cadillac, after whom an American automobile was named, was seeking a favorable location to advance his own economic interests. He came ashore on July 24,1701, with fifty soldiers, an equal number of settlers, and about one hundred friendly Indians near the present site of the Veterans Memorial Building, within easy walking distance of the Greyhound Bus Terminal.

The car did not run well after the accident, developing a reluctance to go into fourth, but I didn't care. The encounter with Milo had gone exactly as such things should go, and was especially pleasing because it had been totally unplanned. A chance meeting—no order, one would guess—but exactly as if I had laid it all out beforehand. I came into Detroit late at night via Route 12, which eventually turned into Michigan Avenue. The air was hot and sticky. I remember driving past the Cadillac plant; multitudes of red, yellow, and green lights glinting off dull masonry and the smell of auto exhaust along the city streets. I found the sort of neighborhood I wanted not far from Tiger Stadium:

pawnshops, an all-night deli, laundromats, dimly lit bars with red Stroh's signs in the windows. Men on street corners walked casually from noplace to noplace.

I parked on a side street just around the corner from a 7-Eleven. I left the motor running. In the store I dawdled over a magazine rack until at last I heard the racing of an engine and saw the Audi flash by the window. I bought a copy of *Time* and caught a downtown bus at the corner. At the Greyhound station I purchased a ticket for the next bus to Toronto and sat reading my magazine until departure time.

We got onto the bus. Across the river we stopped at customs and got off again. "Name?" they asked me.

"Gerald Spotsworth."

"Place of birth?"

"Calgary." I gave them my credentials. The passport photo showed me with hair. They looked me over. They let me go.

I work in the library of the University of Toronto. I am well-read, a student of history, a solid Canadian citizen. There I lead a sedentary life. The subways are clean, the people are friendly, the restaurants are excellent. The sky is blue. The cat is on the mat.

We got back on the bus. There were few other passengers, and most of them were soon asleep; the only light in the darkened interior was that which shone above my head. I was very tired, but I did not want to sleep. Then I remembered that I had Ruth's pills in my jacket pocket. I smiled, thinking of the customs people. All that was left in the box were a couple of tiny pink tabs. I did not know what they were, but I broke one down the middle with my fingernail and took it anyway. It perked me up immediately. Everything I could see seemed sharply defined. The dark green plastic of the seats. The rubber mat in the aisle. My fingernails. All details were separate and distinct, all interdependent. I must have been focused on the threads in the weave of my pants leg for ten minutes when I was surprised by someone sitting down next to me. It was Ruth. "You're back!" I exclaimed.

"We're all back," she said. I looked around and it was true: on the opposite side of the aisle, two seats ahead, Milo sat watching me over his shoulder, a trickle of blood running down his forehead. One corner of his mouth pulled tighter in a rueful smile. Mr. Graves came back from the front and shook my hand. I saw the fat singer from the country club, still naked. The locker-room boy. A flickering light from the back of the bus: when I turned around there stood the burning man, his eye sockets two dark hollows behind the wavering flames. The shopping-mall guard. Hector from the hardware store. They all looked at me.

"What are you doing here?" I asked Ruth.

"We couldn't let you go on thinking like you do. You act like I'm some monster. I'm just a person."

"A rather nice-looking young lady," Graves added.

"People are monsters," I said.

"Like you, huh?" Ruth said. "But they can be saints, too."

That made me laugh. "Don't feed me platitudes. You can't even read."

"You make such a big deal out of reading. Yeah, well, times change. I get along fine, don't I?"

The mall guard broke in. "Actually, miss, the reason we caught on to you is that someone saw you walk into the men's room." He looked embarrassed.

"But you didn't catch me, did you?" Ruth snapped back. She turned to me. "You're afraid of change. No wonder you live back here."

"This is all in my imagination," I said. "It's because of your drugs."

"It is all in your imagination," the burning man repeated. His voice was a whisper. "What you see in the future is what you are able to see. You have no faith in God or your fellow man."

"He's right," said Ruth.

"Psychobabble."

"Speaking of babble," Milo said, "I figured out where you got that goo-goo-goo stuff. Talk—"

"Never mind that," Ruth broke in. "Here's the truth. The future is just a place. The people there are just people. They live differently. So what? People make what they want of the world. You can't escape human failings by running into the past." She rested her hand on my leg. "I'll tell you what you'll find when you get to Toronto," she said. "Another city full of human beings."

This was crazy. I knew it was crazy. I knew it was all unreal, but somehow I was getting more and more afraid. "So the future is just the present writ large," I said bitterly. "Bullshit."

"You tell her, pal," the locker-room boy said.

Hector, who had been listening quietly, broke in. "For a man from the future, you talk a lot like a native."

"You're the king of bullshit, man," Milo said. " 'Some people devote themselves to artwork'! Jesus!"

I felt dizzy. "Scut down, Milo. That means 'Fuck you too.'" I shook my head to try to make them go away. That was a mistake: the bus began to pitch like a sailboat. I grabbed for Ruth's arm but missed. "Who's driving this thing?" I asked, trying to get out of the seat.

"Don't worry," said Graves. "He knows what he's doing."

"He's brain-dead," Milo said.

"You couldn't do any better," said Ruth, pulling me back down.

"No one is driving," said the burning man.

"We'll crash!" I was so dizzy now that I could hardly keep from being sick. I closed my eyes and swallowed. That seemed to help. A long time passed; eventually I must have fallen asleep.

When I woke it was late morning and we were entering the city, cruising down Eglinton Avenue. The bus had a driver after all—a slender black man with neatly trimmed sideburns who wore his uniform hat at a rakish angle. A sign above the windshield said, YOUR DRIVER—SAFE, COURTEOUS, and below that, on the slide-in nameplate, WILBERT CAUL. I felt like I was coming out of a nightmare. I felt okay. I stretched some of the knots out of my back. A young soldier seated across the aisle from me looked my way; I smiled, and he returned it briefly.

"You were mumbling to yourself in your sleep last night," he said.

"Sorry. Sometimes I have bad dreams."

"I do too, sometimes." He had a round open face, an apologetic grin. He was twenty, maybe. Who knew where his dreams came from? We chatted until the bus reached the station; he shook my hand and said he was pleased to meet me. He called me "sir."

I was not due back at the library until Monday, so I walked over to Yonge Street. The stores were busy, the tourists were out in droves, the adult theaters were doing a brisk business. Policemen in sharply creased trousers, white gloves, sauntered along among the pedestrians. It was a bright, cloudless day, but the breeze coming up the street from the lake was cool. I stood on the sidewalk outside one of the strip joints and watched the video-taped come-on over the closed circuit. The Princess Laya. Sondra Nieve, the Human Operator. Technology replaces the traditional barker, but the bodies are more or less the same. The persistence of your faith in sex and machines is evidence of your capacity for hope.

Francis Bacon, in his masterwork *The New Atlantis,* foresaw the utopian world that would arise through the application of experimental science to social problems. Bacon, however, could not solve the problems of his own time and was eventually accused of accepting bribes, fined £40,000, and imprisoned in the Tower of London. He made no appeal to God, but instead applied himself to the development of the virtues of patience and acceptance. Eventually he was freed.

Soon after, on a freezing day in late March, we were driving near Highgate when I suggested to him that cold might delay the process of decay. He was excited by the idea. On impulse he stopped the carriage, purchased a hen, wrung its neck, and stuffed it with snow. He eagerly looked forward to the results of his experiment. Unfortunately, in haggling with the street vendor he had exposed himself thoroughly to the cold and was seized by a chill that rapidly led to pneumonia, of which he died on April 9, 1626.

There's no way to predict these things.

When the videotape started repeating itself I got bored, crossed the street, and lost myself in the crowd.

Gulliver At Home

NO, **ELIZA,** I did not wish your grandfather dead, though he swears that is what I said upon his return from his land of horses. What I said was that, given the neglect with which he has served us, and despite my Christian duties, even the best of wives might have wished him dead. The truth is, in the end, I love him.

"Seven months," he says, "were a sufficient time to correct every vice and folly to which Yahoos are subject, if their natures had been capable of the least disposition to virtue or wisdom."

There he sits every afternoon with the horses. He holds converse with them. Many a time have I stood outside that stable door and listened to him unburden his soul to a dumb beast. He tells them things he has never told me, except perhaps years ago during those hours in my father's garden. Yet when I close my eyes, his voice is just the same.

HIS LIPS WERE full, his voice low and assured. With it he conjured up a world larger, more alive than the stifling life of a hosier's youngest daughter.

"I had no knowledge of the deepest soul of man until I saw the evening light upon the Pyramids," he was saying. "The geometry of Euclid, the desire to transcend time. Riddles that have no answer. The Sphinx."

We sat in the garden of my father's house in Newgate Street. My father was away, on a trip to the continent purchasing fine holland, and Mother had retired to the sitting room to leave us some little privacy.

For three and a half years Lemuel had served as a surgeon on the merchantman *Swallow*. He painted for me an image of the Levant: the camels, the deserts, the dead salt sea, and the dry stones that Jesus Himself trod.

"Did you not long for England's green hills?" I asked him.

He smiled. Your grandfather was the comeliest man I had ever seen. The set of his jaw, his eyes. Long, thick hair, the chestnut brown of a young stallion. He seemed larger than any of my other suitors. "From my earliest days I have had a passion to see strange lands and people," he told me. "To know their customs and language. This world is indeed a fit habitation for gods. But it seems I am never as desirous for home as when I am far away from it, and from the gentle conversation of such as yourself."

My father was the most prudent of men. In place of a mind, he carried a purse. Lemuel was of another sort. As I sat there trying to grasp these wonders he took my hand and told me I had the grace of the Greek maidens, who wore no shoes and whose curls fell down round their shoulders in the bright sun. My eyes were the color, he said, of the Aegean sea. I blushed. I was frightened that my mother might hear, but I cannot tell you how my heart raced. His light brown eyes grew distant as he climbed the structures of his fancy, and it did not occur to me that I might have difficulty getting him to return from those imaginings to see me sitting beside him.

You are coming to be a woman, Eliza. But you cannot know what it was like to feel the force of his desire. He had a passion to embrace all the world and make it his. Part of that world he hoped to embrace, I saw as I sat beside him in that garden, was me.

"Mistress Mary Burton," he said, "help me to become a perfect man. Let me be your husband."

LITTLE LEMUEL, THE child of our middle age, is just nine. Of late he has ceased calling on his friends in town. I found him yesterday in the garden, playing with his lead soldiers. He had lined them up, in their bright red coats, outside a fort of sticks and pebbles. He stood inside the fort's walls, giving orders to his toys. "Get away, you miserable Yahoos! You can't come in this house! Don't vex me! Your smell is unredurable!"

THE THIRD OF five sons, Lemuel hailed from Nottinghamshire, where his father held a small estate. He had attended Emanuel College in Cambridge and was apprenticed to Mr. James Bates, the eminent London surgeon. Anticipating the advantage that would be mine in such a match, my father agreed on a dowry of 400 pounds.

Having got an education, it was up to Lemuel now to get a living as best he could. There was to be no help for us from his family; though they were prosperous they were not rich, and what estate they had went to Lemuel's eldest brother John.

My wedding dress? Foolish girl, what matters a wedding dress in this world?

My wedding dress was of Orient silk, silk brought to England on some ship on which Lemuel perhaps served. My mother labored over it for three months. It was not so fine as that of my older sister Nancy, but it was fine enough for me to turn Lemuel's head as I walked up the aisle of St. Stephen's church.

We took a small house in the Old Jury. We were quite happy. Mr. Bates recommended Lemuel to his patients, and for a space we did well. In those first years I bore three children. The middle one, Robert, we buried before his third month. But God smiling, my Betty, your mother, and your uncle John did survive and grow.

But after Mr. Bates died, Lemuel's practice began to fail. He refused to imitate the bad practice of other physicians, pampering hypochondriacs, promising secret cures for fatal disease. We moved to Wapping, where Lemuel hoped to improve our fortune by doctoring to sailors, but there was scant money in that, and his practice declined further. We discussed the matter for some time, and he chose to go to sea.

He departed from Bristol on May 4, 1699, on the *Antelope*, as ship's surgeon, bound for the south seas, under Master William Prichard.

The *Antelope* should have returned by the following spring. Instead it never came back. Much later, after repeated inquiries, I received report that the ship had never made its call at Sumatra. She was last seen when she landed to take on water at the Cape of Good Hope, and it was assumed that she had been lost somewhere in the Indian Ocean.

Dearest granddaughter, I hope you never have cause to feel the distress I felt then. But I did not have time to grieve, because we were in danger of being made paupers.

What money Lemuel had left us, in expectation of his rapid return, had gone. Our landlord, a goodly Christian man, Mr. Henry Potts of Wapping, was under great hardship himself, as his trade had slackened during the late wars with France and he was dependent on the rent from his holdings. Betty was nine and Johnny seven, neither able to help out. My father sent us what money he could, but owing to reverses of his own he could do little. As the date of Lemuel's expected return receded, Mr. Potts's wife and son were after Mr. Potts to put us out.

I took in sewing—thank God and my parents I was a master seamstress. We raised a few hens for meat and eggs. We ate many a meal of cabbage and potatoes. The neighbors helped. Mr. Potts forbore. But in the bitter February of 1702 he died, and his son, upon assuming his inheritance, threatened to put us into the street.

One April morning, at our darkest moment, some three years after he sailed on the *Antelope*, Lemuel returned.

THE COACH JOUNCED and rattled over the Kent high road. "You won't believe me when I tell you, these miniscule people, not six inches high, had a war over which end of the egg to break."

Lemuel had been telling these tales for two weeks without stop. He'd hired the coach using money we did not have. I was vexed with the effort to force him to confront our penury.

"We haven't seen an egg here in two years!" I said. "Last fall came a pip that killed half the chickens. They staggered about with their little heads pointed down, like drunkards searching for coins on the street. They looked so sad. When it came time to market we left without a farthing."

Lemuel carefully balanced the box he carried on his knees. He peeked inside, to assure himself for the hundreth time that the tiny cattle and sheep it held were all right. We were on our way to the country estate of the Earl of

Kent, who had summoned Lemuel when the rumors of the miniature creatures he'd brought back from Lilliput spread throughout the county. "Their empress almost had me beheaded. She didn't approve my method of dousing a fire that would have otherwise consumed her."

"In the midst of that, Betty almost died of the croup. I was up with her every night for a fortnight, cold compresses and bleeding."

"God knows I'd have given a hundred guineas for a cold compress when I burned with fever, a castaway on the shores of Lilliput."

"Once the novelty fades, cattle so tiny will be of no use. There's not a scrap of meat on them."

"True enough. I would eat thirty oxen at a meal." He sat silent, deep in thought. The coach lurched on. "I wonder if His Grace would lend me the money to take them on tour?"

"Lemuel, we owe Stephen Potts eleven pounds sixpence. To say nothing of the grocer. And if he is to have any chance at a profession, Johnny must be sent to school. We cannot even pay for his clothes."

"Lilliputian boys are dressed by men until four years of age, and then are obliged to dress themselves. They always go in the presence of a Professor, whereby they avoid those early impressions of vice and folly to which our children are subject. Would that you had done this for our John."

"Lemuel, we have no money! It was all I could do to keep him alive!"

He looked at me, and his brow furrowed. He tapped his fingers on the top of the cattle box. "I don't suppose I can blame her. It was a capital crime for any person whatsoever to make water within the precincts of the palace."

LAST NIGHT YOUR grandfather quarreled with your uncle John, who had just returned from the Temple. Johnny went out to the stables to speak with Lemuel concerning a suit for libel threatened by a nobleman who thinks himself the object of criticism in Lemuel's book. I followed.

Before Johnny could finish explaining the situation, Lemuel flew into a rage. "What use have I for lawyers? I had rather see them dropped to the deepest gulf of the sea."

In the violence of his gesture Lemuel nearly knocked over the lamp that stood on the wooden table. His long gray hair flew wildly as he stalked past the stall of the dappled mare he calls "Mistress Mary," to my everlasting dismay. I rushed forward to steady the lamp. Lemuel looked upon me with a gaze as blank as a brick.

"Father," Johnny said. "you may not care what this man does, but he is a cabinet minister, and a lawsuit could ruin us. It would be politic if you would publicly apologize for any slight your satire may have given."

Lemuel turned that pitiless gaze on our son. "I see you are no better than the other animals of this midden, and all my efforts to make something better of you are in vain. If you were capable of logic, I would ask you to explain to me how my report of events that occurred so many years ago, during another reign, and above five thousand leagues distant from this pathetic isle, might be applied to any of the Yahoos who today govern this herd. Yet in service of this idiocy you ask me to *say the thing that is not*. I had rather all your law books, and you immodest pleaders with them, were heaped into a bonfire in Smithfield for the entertainment of children."

I watched Johnny's face grow livid, but he mastered his rage and left the stable. Lemuel and I stood in silence. He would not look at me, and I thought for a moment he felt some regret at his intemperance. But he turned from me to calm the frightened horses. I put the lamp down on the table and ran back to the house.

JOHNNY WAS TEN when Lemuel returned from Lilliput. He was overjoyed to see his father again, and worshipped him as a hero. When others of the townschildren mocked Lemuel, calling him a madman, Johnny fought them.

The Lilliputian cattle and sheep, despite my misgivings, brought us some advantage. Following the example of the Earl of Kent, Sir Humphrey Glover, Lord Sidwich, and other prominent men commanded Lemuel to show these creatures. Johnny prated on about the tiny animals all day, and it was all I could do to keep him from sleeping with them beneath his bedclothes, which would have gone the worse for them, as he was a restless child and in tossing at night would surely have crushed the life out of them. He built a little stable in the corner of his room. At first we fed them with biscuit, ground as fine as we could, and spring water. Johnny took great pains to keep the rats away.

It was his idea to build a pasture on the bowling green, where the grass was fine enough that they might eat and prosper. Lemuel basked in Johnny's enthusiasm. He charmed the boy with the tale of how he had captured the entire fleet of Blefescu using thread and fish-hooks, and towed it back to Lilliput. Johnny said that he would be a sea captain when he grew up.

As if in a dream, our fortunes turned. Lemuel's Uncle John passed away, leaving him five hundred sterling and an estate in land near Epping that earned an income of about thirty pounds a year. Lemuel sold the Lilliputian cattle for 600 pounds. He bought our big house in Redriff. After years of hardship, after I had lost hope, he had returned to save us.

We had been better served by bankruptcy if that would have kept him beside me in our bed.

YOU WILL FIND, Eliza, that a husband needs his wife in that way, and it can be a pleasant pastime. But it is different for them. Love is like a fire they cannot control, overwhelming, easily quenched, then as often as not forgotten, even regretted. Whenever Lemuel returned from these voyages he wanted me, and I do not hesitate to say, I him. Our bed was another country to which he would return, and explore for its mysteries. He embraced me with a fury that sought to extinguish all our time apart, and the leagues between us, in the heat of that moment. Spent, he would rest his head on my bosom, and I would stroke his hair. He was like a boy again, quiet and kind. He would whisper to me, in a voice of desperation, how I should never let him leave again.

TWO MONTHS AFTER his return he was gone again. His wild heart, he said, would not let him rest.

This time he left us well set. Fifteen hundred pounds, the house in Redriff, the land in Epping. He took a long lease on the Black Bull public house in Fetter Lane, which brought a regular income.

We traveled with him to Liverpool, where in June of 1702 he took ship aboard the *Adventure*, Captain John Nicholas commanding, bound for Surat.

It was a dreary day at the downs, the kind of blustery weather Liverpool has occasion for even in summer, low leaden clouds driven before a strong wind, the harbor rolling in swells and the ends of furled sails flapping above us. With tears in my eyes, I embraced him; he would not let me go. When I did pull away I saw that he wept as well. "Fare thee well, good heart," he whispered to me. "Forgive me my wandering soul."

Seeing the kindness and love in his gaze, the difficulty with which he tore himself from my bosom, I would have forgiven him anything. It occurred to me just how powerful a passion burned within him, driving him outside the circle of our hearth. Little Johnny shook his hand, very manly. Betty leapt into his arms, and he pressed her to his cheek, then set her down. Then he took up his canvas bag, turned and went aboard.

IT IS NO easy matter being the wife of a man famous for his wild tales. The other day in town with Sarah to do the marketing, in the butcher's shop, I overheard Mrs. Boyle the butcher's wife insisting to a customer that the chicken was fresh. By its smell anyone past the age of two would know it was a week dead. But Mrs. Boyle insisted.

The shop was busy, and our neighbor Mr. Trent began to mock her, in a low voice, to some bystanders. He said, "Of course it is fresh. Mrs. Boyle insists it's fresh. It's as true as if Mr. Gulliver had said it."

All the people in the shop laughed. My face burned, and I left.

ONE JUNE MORNING in 1706, three long years after Lemuel was due to return, I was attending to the boiling of some sheets in the kitchen when a cry came from Sarah, our housemaid. "God save me! Help!"

I rushed to the front door, there to see an uncouth spectacle. Sarah was staring at a man who had entered on all fours, peering up, his head canted to the side, so that his long hair brushed the ground (he wore no periwig) as he spied up at us. It was a moment before I recognized him as my Lemuel. My heart leapt within my breast as I went from widow to wife in a single instant.

When he came to the house, for which he had been forced to enquire, Sarah had opened the door. Lemuel bent down to go in, for fear of striking his head. He had been living among giants and fancied himself sixty feet tall. Sarah had never met Mr. Gulliver, and thought him a madman. When I tried to embrace him, he stooped to my knees until I was forced to get down on my own to kiss him.

When Betty, your mother, who was then sixteen, ran in, holding some needlework, Lemuel tried to pick her up by her waist, in one hand, as if she had been a doll. He complained that the children and I had starved ourselves, so that we were wasted away to nothing. It was some weeks before he regained his sense of proper proportion.

I told him it was the last time he should ever go to sea.

It wasn't ten days before a Cornish captain, William Robinson, under whom Lemuel had served on a trip to the Levant some years before we were married, called upon us. That visit was purely a social one, or so he avowed, but within a month he was importuning Lemuel to join him as ship's surgeon on another trip to the East Indies.

That night, as we prepared for bed, I accosted him. "Lemuel, are you considering going with Robinson?"

"What matter if I did? I am the master of this house. You are well taken care of."

"Taken care of by servants, not my husband."

"He is offering twice the usual salary, a share of the profits, two mates and a surgeon under me. I shall be gone no more than a year, and you will see us well off, so that I might never have to go to sea again."

"You don't have to go to sea now. We have a comfortable life."

He removed his leather jerkin and began to unbutton his shirt. "And our children? Betty is nearly of marriageable age. What dowry can we offer her? Johnny must go to Cambridge, and have money to establish himself in some honorable profession. I want to do more for him than my father did for me."

"The children mourn your absences." I touched his arm. The muscles were taut as cords. "When you disappeared on the *Antelope*, we suffered more from the thought that you were dead than from the penury we lived in. Give them a father in their home and let the distant world go."

"You are thinking like a woman. The distant world comes into the home. It is a place of greed, vice and folly. I seek for some understanding I can give to cope with it."

"Lemuel, what is this desire for strange lands but a type of greed, this abandonment of your family but the height of folly? And your refusal to admit your true motives is the utmost dishonesty, to the woman who loves you, and whom you vowed to love."

Lemuel took up his coat, pulled on his shoes.

"Where are you going?"

"Out. I need to take some air. Perhaps I can determine my true motives for you."

He left.

A week later, on the 5th of August, 1706, he left England on the *Hope-Well*, bound for the Indies. I did not see him again for four years.

THE ONLY TIME I can coax him into the house is when he deigns to bathe. He is most fastidious, and insists that no one must remain on the same floor, let alone the same room, when he does.

I crept to the door last week and peeked in. He had finished, and dried himself, and now stood naked in front of the mirror, trembling. At first I thought he was cold, but the fire roared in the grate. Then he raised his hands from his sides, covered his eyes, and sobbed, and I understood that he recoiled in horror from his own image.

WHEN HE LEFT on the third voyage I was five-and-thirty years old. In the previous seven years he had spent a total of four months with me. I had no need to work, I was not an old woman, and my children had no father. When Lemuel did not return in the promised year, when that year stretched to two and the *Hope-Well* returned to Portsmouth without Lemuel aboard, I fell into despair. Captain Robinson came to the house in Redriff and told the tale. Stuck in the port of Tonquin awaiting the goods they were to ship back to England, Robinson hit on the plan of purchasing a sloop, giving command of it to Lemuel, and bidding him trade among the islands, returning in several months at which time, the *Hope-Well* being loaded, they might return. Lemuel set off on the sloop and was not heard from again. Robinson supposed that they might have been taken by the barbarous pirates of those Islands, in which case Lemuel had undoubtedly been slain, as Christian mercy is a virtue unknown in those heathen lands.

I cannot say that I was surprised. I was angry, and I wept.

Being the wealthiest widow in the town, and by no means an old woman, I did not lack for suitors. Sir Robert Davies himself called on me more than once. It was all I could do to keep from having my head turned. "Marry me," he said. "I will be a father to your daughter, an example to your son."

"Johnny is about to go off to school, and Betty soon to be married," I told him. "One wedding is enough to worry about right now." Thus I put him off.

In truth I did lose myself in preparing your mother's wedding; Betty was giddy with excitement, and your father, her betrothed, was about continually, helping put the house in order, traveling with Johnny to school. So it was I kept myself chaste.

The townspeople thought I was a fool. My mother commended me for my faithfulness, but I could tell she regretted the loss of a connection with Sir Robert. Betty and Johnny stood by me. I don't need another father, Johnny said, I have one.

My reasons? Wherever he went Sir Robert carried a silver-headed cane, with which he would gently tap his footman's shoulder as he instructed him. I was mistress of my own home. I had given my heart once, and still treasured a hope of Lemuel's return. There are a hundred reasons, child, and there are things I cannot explain.

Lemuel did return, and despite his ravings about a flying island and the curse of immortality, I felt that all my trouble had been justified. He seemed weary, but still my husband, the love of my youth come again. The joy of our meeting was great. Within three months he had got me with child.

Within five he had left again.

AND SO HE came back, five years later, from the longest of his absences. He was aged three-and-fifty, I one-and-forty. He saw his son Lemuel for the first time. His daughter, married and a mother herself; his son, grown and a solicitor. His wife, longing to hold him again.

No, I have not, Eliza. He shudders at my touch. He washes his hands. He accuses me of trying to seduce him.

"Are you ashamed of the touch that got you your sons and daughter?" I once asked him. "That got us poor Robert? That gave us young Lemuel, to be our comfort in our old age?

His face registered at first revulsion, and then, as he sat heavily in his chair, fatigue. "I can't regret our children if they be good, but I most certainly regret them if they be bad. There are Yahoos enough in the world."

WE HAD LONG given him up for dead. I had made my peace, and held in my memory the man who had kissed me in my father's garden.

At first I thought that he had caught some foreign disease. As thin as a fence post, he stood in the doorway, his face a mask of dismay. It was the fifth of December, 1715. Three o'clock in the afternoon. I ran to him, kissed him. He fell into a swoon that lasted most of an hour. With difficulty we carried him to his bed. When he awoke, I put my hand to his face: he pulled away as if his skin had been flayed.

And so we live by these rules: "Save for the sabbath, you may not eat in the same room with me. You may not presume to touch my bread. You may not drink out of the same cup, or use my spoon or plate. You may not take me by the hand. That I might bear the reek of this house, fresh horse droppings shall be brought into my chambers each morning, and kept there in a special container I have had fashioned for that purpose."

My father's house was not far from Newgate Prison. Outside, on the days of executions, straw was scattered on the street to muffle the wheels of passing wagons, in deference to the men being hanged inside. Here we scatter straw over the cobbled courtyard outside the stables because the noise of the wheels troubles him.

As a young man his heart was full of hope, but his heart has been beaten closed, not only by the sea and the storms and the mutinies and the pirates—but by some hard moral engine inside of him. He would rather be dead, I think, than to abide his flesh. Perhaps he soon will be. And I will go on living without him, as I have learned to do over these many years.

Might it have been different? I could say yes, but something I saw in his eyes that first afternoon in Newgate Street rises to stop me. He was a man who looked outward while the inward part of himself withered. He was drawn to the blank spaces on maps, outside the known world; we are too small to make a mark on his map. To Lemuel people are interesting only as we represent large things.

He asked me to make him a perfect man. In seeking perfection he has gulled himself, and the postscript is that he spends four hours every day attempting to communicate with a horse, while his children, his grandchildren, his wife wait in his well-appointed home, the home they have prepared for him and labored to keep together in his absence, maintaining a place for him at every holiday table, praying for him at every service, treasuring him up in their hearts and memories, his portrait on the wall, his merest jottings pressed close in the book of memory, his boots in the wardrobe, maps in the cabinet, glass on the sideboard.

At Christmas, when we can coax him to eat with us, I sit at the other end of twelve feet of polished mahogany table and look across at a stranger who is yet the man I love.

DURING OUR CONVERSATION in the garden thirty years ago, Lemuel told me a story. The Greeks, he told me, believed that once there existed a creature that was complete and whole unto itself, perfect and without flaw. But in the beginning of time the gods split this being into two halves, and that is how man and woman came into the world. Each of us knows that we are not complete, and so we seek desperately after each other, yearning to possess our missing halves, pressing our bodies together in hope of becoming that one happy creature again. But of course we cannot, and so in frustration we turn away from each other, tearing ourselves apart all of our lives.

HIS BOOK HAS been a great success. It is all they speak of in London. It has made us more money than his years of voyages.

He accuses us of enticing him into writing the wretched thing, and deems it a failure because it didn't immediately reform all of humanity. He told his story in the hope that it would magically turn the world into something perfect. I tell you mine, Eliza... I tell you mine because...bless me, I believe I've burned my hand on this kettle. Fetch me the lard.

That's better.

Soon you'll come of age to choose a husband, if your parents give you leave to choose. I don't doubt you tremble at the prospect. But remember: it is the only choice a woman is given to make in her life, save for the choice of clothes for her funeral.

And now, help me carry this soup up to him; help me to cover him, and make sure he is warm for the night.

Buddha Nostril Bird

AFTER WE killed the guard, Glaucon and I ran down the corridor away from the Well. Glaucon had been seriously aged in the fight. He limped and cursed, a piece of dying meat and he knew it. I brushed my hand along the wall looking for a door.

"We'll make it," I said.

"Sure," he said. He held his arm against his side.

We ran past a series of ontological windows: a forest fire, a sun in space, a factory fashioning children into flowers. I worried that the corridor might be a loop. For all I knew the sole purpose of such corridors was to confuse and recapture escapees. Or maybe they were just for fun. Relativists delight in such absurdities.

More windows: a snowstorm, a cloudy seascape, a corridor exactly like the one we were in, in which two men wearing yellow robes—prison kosodes exactly like ours—searched for a way out. Glaucon stopped. The hand of his double reached out to meet his. The face of mine glared at me angrily; a strong face, an intelligent one. "It's just a mirror," I said.

"Mirror?"

"A mirror," a voice said. Protagoras appeared ahead of us in the corridor. "Like sex, it reproduces human beings."

An old joke, and typical of Protagoras to quote it without attribution.

Glaucon raised his clock. In the face of Protagoras' infinite mutability it was less than useless: there was no way Glaucon would even get a shot off. My spirit sank as I watched the change come over him. Protagoras dripped fellowship. Glaucon liked him. Nobody but a maniac could dislike Protagoras.

It took all my will to block the endorphin assault, but Glaucon was never as strong as I. A lot of talk about brotherhood had passed between us, but if I'd had my freedom I would have crisped him on the spot. Instead I hid myself from Protagoras' blue eyes, as cold as chips of aquamarine in a mosaic.

"Where are you going?" Protagoras said.

"We were going—" Glaucon started.

"—nowhere," I said.

"A hard place to get to," said Protagoras.

Glaucon's head bobbed like a dog's.

"I know a short way," Protagoras said. "Come with me."

"Sure," said Glaucon.

I struggled to maintain control. If you had asked him, Protagoras would have denied controlling anyone: "The Superior Man rules by humility." Another sophistry.

We turned back down the corridor. If I stayed with them until we got to the center, there would be no way I could escape. Desperation forced me to test one of the windows. As we passed the ocean scene I pushed Glaucon into Protagoras and threw my shoulder against the glass.

The window shattered; I was falling. My kosode flapped like the melting wings of Icarus as sky and sea whirled around me, and I hit the water. My breath exploded from me. I flailed and tumbled. At last I found the surface. I sputtered and gasped, my right arm in agony; my ribs ached. I kicked off my slippers and leaned onto my back. The waves rolled me up and down. The sky was low and dark. At the top of each swell I could see to the storm-clouded horizon, flat as a psychotic's affect—but in the other direction was a beach.

I swam. The bad shoulder and the kosode made it hard, but at that moment I would not have traded places with Glaucon for all the enlightenment of the ancients.

WHEN THEY SENT me to the penal colony they told me, "Prisons ought to be places where people are lodged only temporarily, as guests are. They must not become dwelling places."

Their idea of temporary is not mine. Temporary doesn't mean long enough for your skin to crack like the dry lakebed outside your window, for the memory of your lover's touch to recede until it's only a torment in your dreams, as distant as the mountains that surround the colony. These distinctions are lost on Relativists, as are all distinctions. Which, I suppose, is why I was sent there.

They keep you alone, mostly. I didn't mind the isolation—it gave me time to understand exactly how many ways I had been betrayed. I spent hours thinking of Arete, etching her ideal features in my mind. I judged in precise retrospect how she'd been ripped away from me. I wondered if she still lived, and if I would ever see her again. Eventually, when memory had faded, I conquered the passage of time itself: I reconstructed her image from incorruptible ideas and planned the revenge I would take once I was free again, so that the past and the future became more real to me than the endless, featureless present. Such is the power of idea over reality. To the guards I must have looked properly meditative. Inside I burned.

Each day at dawn we would be awakened by the rapping of sticks on our iron bedsteads. In the first hour we drew water from the Well of Changes. In the second we were encouraged to drink (I refused). In the third we washed floors with the water. From the fourth through the seventh we performed every other function that was necessary to maintain the prison. In the eighth we were tortured. In the ninth we were fed. At night, exhausted, we slept.

The torture chamber is made of ribbed concrete. It is a cold room, without windows. In its center is a chair, and beside the chair a small table, and on the table the hood. The hood is black and appears to be made of ordinary fabric, but it is not. The first time I held it, despite the evidence of my eyes I thought it had slipped through my fingers. The hood is not a material object: you cannot feel it, and it has no texture, and although it absorbs all light it is neither warm nor cold.

Your inquisitor invites you to sit in the chair and slip the hood over your head. You do so. He speaks to you. The room disappears. Your body melts away and you are made into something else. You are an animal. You are one of the ancients. You are a stone, a drop of rain in a storm, a planet. You are in another time and place. This may sound intriguing, and the first twenty times it is. But it never ends. The sessions are indiscriminate. They are deliberately pointless. They continue to the verge of insanity.

I recall one of these sessions, in which I lived in an ancient city and worked a hopeless routine in a store called the "World of Values." The values we sold were merchandise. I married, had children, grew old, lost my health and spirit. I worked fifty years. Some days were happy, others sad; most were neither. The last thing I remembered was lying in a hospital, unable to see, dying, and hearing my wife talk with my son about what they should have for dinner. When I came out from under the hood Protagoras yanked me from the chair and recited this poem:

> Out from the nostrils of the Great Buddha
> Flew a pair of nesting swallows.

I could still hear my phantom wife's cracking voice. I was in no mood for riddles. "Tell me what it means, or shut up."

"Drink from the Well and I'll tell you."

I turned my back on him.

Protagoras had made a career out of tormenting me. I had known him for too many years. He put faith in nothing, was without honor, yet wielded power, casually. His intellect was available for any use. He wasted years on banalities. He would argue any side of a case, not because he sought advantage, but because he did not care about right or wrong. He was intolerably lucky. Irresponsible as a child. Inconstant as the wind. His opaque blue gaze could be as witless as a scientist's.

And he had been my first teacher. He had introduced me to Arete, offered me useless advice throughout our stormy relationship, given ambiguous testimony at my trial, and upon the verdict abandoned the university in order to come to the prison and become my inquisitor. The thought that I had once idolized him tormented me more than any session under the hood.

After my plunge through the window into the sea, I fought my way through the surf to the beach. For an unknown time I lay gasping on the wet sand. When I opened my eyes I saw a flock of gulls had waddled up to me. An arm's length away the lead gull, a great bull whose ragged feathers stood out from his neck in a ruff, watched me with beady black eye. Others, of various sizes and markings, stood in a wedge behind him. I raised my head; the gulls retreated a few steps, still holding formation. I understood immediately that they were ranked according to their stations in the flock. Thus does nature shadow forth fundamental truth: the rule of the strong over the weak, the relation of one to the many in hierarchical order.

Off to the side stood a single scrawny gull, quicker than the rest, but separate, aloof. I supposed him to be a gullish philosopher. I saluted him, my brother.

A sandpiper scuttled along the edge of the surf. Dipping a handful of seawater, I washed sand and fragments of shell from my cheek. Up the slope, sawgrass and sea oats held the dunes against the tides. The scene was familiar. With wonder and some disquiet I understood that the window had dumped me into the Great Water quite near the Imperial City.

I stumbled up the sand to the crest of the dunes. In the east, beneath piled thunderheads, lighting flashed over the dark water. To the west, against the sunset's glare, the sand and scrub turned into fields. I started inland. Night fell swiftly. From behind me came clouds, strong winds, then rain. I trudged on, singing into the downpour. The thunder sang back. Water streamed down the creases of my face, the wet kosode weighed on my chest and shoulders, the rough grass cut my feet. In the profound darkness I could continue only by memorizing the landscape revealed by flashes of lightning. Exhilarated, I hurried toward my lover. I shouted at the raindrops, any one of which might be one of my fellow prisoners under the hood. "I'm free!" I told them. I forded the swollen River of Indifference. I stumbled through Iron Tree Forest. Throughout the night I put one foot before the other, and some hours before dawn, in a melancholy drizzle, passed through the Heron's Gate into the city.

In the Processor's Quarter I found a doorway whose overhang kept out the worst of the rain. Above hung the illuminated sign of the Rat. In the corner of this doorway, under this sign, I slept.

I WAS AWAKENED by the arrival of the owner of the communications shop in whose doorway I had slept.

"I am looking for the old fox," I said. "Do you know where I can find him?"

"Who are you?"

"You may call me the little fox."

He pushed open the door. "Well, Mr. Fox, I can put you in touch with him instantly. Just step into one of our booths."

He must have known I had no money. "I don't want to communicate. I want to see him."

"Communication is much better," the shopowner said. He took a towel, a copper basin and an ornamental blade from the cupboard beneath his terminal. "No chance of physical violence. No distress other than psychological. Completely accurate reproduction. Sensory enhancement: olfactory, visual, auditory." He opened a cage set into the wall and seized a docile black rat by the scruff of the neck. "Recordability. Access to a network of supporting information services. For slight additional charge we offer intelligence augmentation and instant semiotic analysis. We make the short man tall. Physical presence has nothing to compare."

"I want to speak with him in private."

Not looking at me, he took the rat to the stone block. "We are bonded."

"I don't question your integrity."

"You have religious prejudices against communication? You are a Traveler?"

He would not rest until he forced me to admit I was penniless. I refrained from noting that, if he was such a devout communicator, he could easily have stayed home. Yet he had walked to his shop in person. Swallowing my rage, I said, "I have no money."

He sliced the rat's neck open. The animal made no sound.

After he had drained the blood and put the carcass into the display case, he washed his hands and turned to me. He seemed quite pleased with himself. He took a small object from a drawer. "He is to be found at the

University. This map will guide you through the maze." He slipped it into my hand.

For this act of gratuitous charity, I vowed that one day I would have revenge. I left.

The streets were crowded. Dusty gold light filtered down between the ranks of ancient buildings. Too short to use the moving Ways, I walked. Orange-robed messengers threaded their way through the crowd. Sweating drivers in loincloths pulled pedicabs; I imagined the perfumed lottery winners who reclined behind the opaqued glass of their passenger compartments. In the Medical Quarter, streetside surgeons hawked their services before racks of breasts and penises of prodigious size. As before, the names of the streets changed hourly to mark the progress of the sun across the sky.

All streets but one, and I held my breath when I came to it: the Way of Enlightenment, which ran between the Reform Temple and the Imperial Palace. As before, metamorphs entertained the faithful on the stage outside the Temple. One of them changed shape as I watched, from a dog-faced man wearing the leather skirt of an athlete to a tattooed CEO in powered suit. "Come drink from the Well of Changes!" he called ecstatically to passersby. "Be Reformed!"

The Well he spoke of is both literal and symbolic. The prison Well was its brother; the preachers of the Temple claim that all the Wells are one Well. Its water has the power to transform both body and mind. A scientist could tell you how it is done: viruses, brain chemistry, hypnosis, some insane combination of the three. But that is all a scientist could tell you. Unlike a scientist, I could tell you why its use is morally wrong. I could explain that some truths are eternal and ought to be held inviolate, and why a culture that accepts change indiscriminately is rotten at its heart. I could demonstrate, with inescapable logic, that reason is better than emotion. That spirit is greater than flesh. That Relativism is the road to hell.

Instead of relief at being home, I felt distress. The street's muddle upset me, but it was not simply that: the city was exactly as I had left it. The wet morning that dawned on me in the doorway might have been the morning after I was sent away. My absence had made no discernible difference. The tyranny of the Relativists that I and my friends had struggled against had not culminated in the universal misery we had predicted. Though everything changed minute to minute, it remained the same. The one thing that ought to remain constant, Truth, was to them as chimerical as the gene-changers of the Temple.

They might have done better, had they had teachers to tell them good from bad.

Looking down the boulevard, in the distance, at the heart of the city, I could see the walls of the palace. By midday I had reached it. Vendors of spiced cakes pushed their carts among the petitioners gathered beneath the great red lacquered doors. One, whose cakes each contained a free password, did a superior business. That the passwords were patent frauds was evident by the fact that the gatekeeper ignored those petitioners who tried using them. But that did not hurt sales. Most of the petitioners were halflings, and a dimwitted rabbit could best them in a deal.

I wept for my people, their ignorance and illogic. I discovered that I was clutching the map in my fist so tightly that the point of it had pierced my skin. I turned from the palace and walked away, and did not feel any relief until I saw the towers of the university rising above Scholars' Park. I remembered my first sight of them, a young boy down from the hills, the smell of cattle still about me, come to study under the great Protagoras. The meticulously kept park, the calm proportions of the buildings, spoke to the soul of that innocent boy: Here you'll be safe from blood and passion. Here you can lose yourself in the world of the mind.

The years had worn the polish off that dream, but I can't say that, seeing it now, once more a fugitive from a dangerous world, I did not feel some of the same joy. I thought of my mother, a loutish farmer who would whip me for reading; of my gentle father, brutalized by her, trying to keep the flame of truth alive in his boy.

On the quadrangle I approached a young woman wearing the topknot and scarlet robe of a humanist. Her head bounced to some inner rhythm, and as I imagined she was pursuing some notion of the Ideal, my heart went out to her. I was about to ask her what she studied when I saw the pin in her temple. She was listening to transtemporal music: her mind eaten by puerile improvisations played on signals picked up from the death agonies of the cosmos. Generations of researchers had devoted their lives to uncovering these secrets, only to have their efforts used by "artists" to erode people's connections with reality. I spat on the walk at her feet; she passed by, oblivious.

At the entrance to the Humanities maze I turned on the map and followed it into the gloom. Fifteen minutes later it guided me into the Department of Philosophy. It was the last place I expected to find the fox—the nest of our enemies, the place we had plotted against tirelessly. The secretary greeted me pleasantly.

"I'm looking for a man named Socrates," I said. "Some call him 'the old fox.'"

"Universe of Discourse 3," she said.

I walked down the hall, wishing I had Glaucon's clock. The door to the hall stood open. In the center of the cavelike room, in a massive support chair, sat Socrates. At last I had found a significant change: he was grossly obese. The ferretlike features I remembered were folded in fat. Only the acute eyes remained. I was profoundly shaken. As I approached, his eyes followed me.

"Socrates."

"Blume."

"What happened to you?"

Socrates lifted his dimpled hand, as if to wave away a triviality. "I won."

"You used to revile this place."

"I reviled its usurpers. Now I run it."

"You run it?"

"I'm the dean."

I should have known Socrates had turned against our cause, and perhaps at some level I had. If he had remained true he would have ended up in the cell next to mine. "You used to be a great teacher," I said.

"Right. Let me tell you what happens when a man starts claiming he's a great teacher. First he starts wearing a brocade robe. Then he puts lifts in his sandals. The next thing you know the department's got a nasty paternity suit on its hands."

His senile chuckle was like the bubbling of water in an opium pipe.

"How did you get to be dean?"

"I performed a service for the Emperor."

"You sold out!"

"Blume the dagger," he said. Some of the old anger shaded his voice. "So sharp. So rigid. You always were a prig."

"And you used to have principles."

"Ah, principles," he said. "I'll tell you what happened to my principles. You heard about Philomena the Bandit?"

"No. I've been somewhat out of touch."

Socrates ignored the jab. "It was after you left. Philomena invaded the system, established her camp on the moon, and made her living raiding the empire. The city was at her mercy. I saw my opportunity. I announced that I would reform her. My students outfitted a small ship, and Arete and I launched for the moon."

"Arete!"

"We landed in a lush valley near the camp. Arete negotiated an audience for me. I went, alone. I described to Philomena the advantages of politic behavior. The nature of truth. The costs of living in the world of shadows and the glory of moving into the world of light. How, if she should turn to Good, her story would be told for generations. Her fame would spread throughout the world and her honor outlast her lifetime by a thousand years.

"Philomena listened. When I was finished she drew a knife and asked me, 'How long is a thousand years?'

"Her men stood all around, waiting for me to slip. I began to speak, but before I could she pulled me close and set the blade against my throat.

"'A thousand years,' Philomena said, 'is shorter than the exposure of a neutrino passing through a world. How long is life?'"

"I was petrified. She smiled. 'Life,' she said, 'is shorter than this blade.'

"I begged for mercy. She threw me out. I ran to the ship, in fear for my life. Arete asked what happened: I said nothing. We set sail for home.

"We landed amid great tumult. I first thought it was riot but soon found it celebration. During our voyage back Philomena had left the moon. People assumed I had convinced her. The Emperor spoke. Our enemies in philosophy were shortened, and the Regents stretched me into Dean.

"Since then," Socrates said, "I have had trouble with principles."

"You're a coward," I said.

Despite the mask of suet, I could read the ruefulness in Socrates' eyes. "You don't know me," he said.

"What happened to Arete?"

"I have not seen her since."

"Where is she?"

"She's not here." He shifted his bulk, watching the screen that encircled the room. "Turn yourself in, Blume. If they catch you, it will only go harder."

"Where is she?"

"Even if you could get to her, she won't want to see you."

I seized his arm, twisted. "Where is Arete!"

Socrates inhaled sharply. "In the palace," he said.

"She's a prisoner?"

"She's the Empress."

THAT NIGHT I took a place among the halflings outside the palace gate. Men and women regrown from seed after their deaths, imprinted with stored files of their original personalities, all of them had lost resolution, for no identity file could encapsulate human complexity. Some could not speak, others displayed features too stiff to pass for human, and still others had no personalities at all. Their only chance for wholeness was to petition the Empress to perform a transfinite extrapolation from their core data. To be miraculously made complete.

An Athlete beside me showed me his endorsements. An Actress showed me her notices. A Banker showed me his lapels. They asked me my profession. "I am a philosopher," I said.

They laughed. "Prove it," the Actress said.

"In the well-ordered state," I told her, "there will be no place for you." To the athlete I said, "Yours is a good and noble profession." I turned to the Banker, "Your work is more problematical," I said. "Unlike the Actress, you fulfill a necessary function, but unlike the Athlete, by accumulating wealth you are likely to gain more power than is justified by your small wisdom."

This speech was beyond them: the Actress grumbled and went away. I left the two men and walked along below the battlements. Two bartizans framed the great doors, and archers strolled along the ramparts or leaned through the embrasures to spit on the petitioners. For this reason the halflings camped as far back from the walls as they might without blocking the street. The archers, as any educated man knew, were there for show: the gates were guarded only by a single gatekeeper, a monk who could open the door if bested in a battle of wits, but without whose acquiescence the door could not be budged.

He sat on his stool beside the gate, staring quietly ahead. Those who sought to speak with him could not tell whether they'd get a cuff on the ear or a friendly conversation. His flat, peasant's face was so devoid of intellect that it was some time before I recognized him as Protagoras.

His disguised presence could be one of his whims. It could be he was being punished for letting me escape; it could be that he waited for me. I felt an urge to flee. But I would not duplicate Socrates' cowardice. If Protagoras recognized me he did not show it, and I resolved to get in or get caught. I was not some halfwit, and I knew him. I approached. "I wish to see the Empress," I said.

"You must wait."

"I've been waiting for years."

"That doesn't matter."

"I have no more time."

He studied me. His manner changed. "What will you pay?"

"I'll pay you a story that will make you laugh until your head aches."

He smiled. I saw that he recognized me; my stomach lurched. "I know many such stories," he said.

"Not like mine."

"Yes. I can see you are a great breeder of headaches."

Desperation drove me forward. "Listen, then: once there was a warlord who discovered that someone had stolen his most precious possession, a jewel of power. He ordered his servants to scour the fortress for strangers. In the bailey they found a beggar heading for the gate. The lord's men seized him and carried him to the well. 'The warlord's great jewel is missing,' they said to him. They thrust the beggar's head beneath the water. He struggled. They pulled him up and asked, 'Where is the jewel?'

"'I don't know,' he said.

"They thrust him down again, longer this time. When they pulled him up he sputtered like an old engine. 'Where is the jewel?' they demanded. 'I don't know!' he replied.

"Furious at his insolence, fearful for their lives if they should rouse their lord's displeasure, the men pushed the beggar so far into the well that a bystander thought, 'He will surely drown.' The beggar kicked so hard it took three strong men to hold him. When at last they pulled him up he coughed and gasped, face purple, struggling to speak. They pounded him on the back. Finally he drew breath enough for words.

"'I think you should get another diver,' the beggar said. 'I can't see it anywhere down there.'"

Protagoras regarded me dispassionately. Then he slipped into a sly smile. "That's not funny," he said.

"What?"

"Maybe for us, but not for the beggar. Or the bystander. Or the servants. The warlord probably had them shortened."

"Don't play games. What do you really think?"

"I think of poor Glaucon. He misses you."

Then I saw that Protagoras only meant to torment me, as he had so many times before. He would answer my desperate need with feeble jokes until I wept or went mad. A fury more powerful than the sun itself swept over me, and I lost control. I knocked him from the stool and fell on him, kicking, biting. The other petitioners looked on in amazement. Shouts echoed from the ramparts. I didn't care. I'd forgotten everything but my rage; all I knew was that at last I had him in my hands. I scratched at his eyes, I beat his head against the pavements. Protagoras struggled to speak. I dragged him up and slammed his head against the doors. The tension went out of his muscles. Crosslegggged, as if preparing to meditate, he slid to the ground. Blood glistened in the torchlight on the lacquered doors.

"Now that's funny," he whispered, and died.

The weight of his body against the door pushed it ajar. It had been open all along.

NO ONE CAME to arrest me. Across the inner ward, at the edge of an ornamental garden, a person stood in the darkness beneath a plane tree. Most of
the lights of the palace were unlit, but radiance from the clerestory above
heightened the shadows. Hesitantly I drew closer, too unsteady after my sudden fit of violence to hide. In my confusion I could think to do no more than
approach the figure in the garden, who stood patiently as if in long expectation of me. From ten paces away I saw it was a woman dressed as a clown.
From five I saw it was Arete.

Her laughter, like shattering crystal, startled me. "Allan! How serious
you look."

My head was full of questions. She pressed her fingers against my lips,
silencing them. I embraced her. Red circles were painted on her cheeks, and
she wore a crepe beard, but her skin was still smooth, her eyes bright, her
perfume the same. She was not a day older.

The memory of dead Protagoras' slack mouth marred my triumph. She
ducked out of my arms, laughing again. "You can't have me unless you catch me!"

"Arete!"

She darted through the trees. I ran after her. My heart was not in it, and
I lost her until she paused beneath a tree, hands on knees, panting. "Come on!
I'm not so hard to catch."

The weight was lifted from my heart. I dodged after her. Beneath the
trees, through the hedge maze, among the night blooming jasmine and bou-
ganvillea, the silver moon tipping the edges of the leaves, I chased her. At last
she let herself be caught; we fell together into a damp bed of ivy. I rested my
head on her breast. The embroidery of her costume was rough against my
cheek.

She took my head in her hands and made me look her in the face. Her
teeth were pearly white, breath sweet as the scented blossoms around us.

We kissed, through the ridiculous beard (I could smell the spirit gum
she'd used to affix it), and the goal they had sought to instill in me at the
penal colony was attained: my years of imprisonment vanished into the
immediate moment as if they had never existed.

THAT KISS WAS the limit of our contact. I expected to spend the night with her; instead, she had a slave take me to a guest house for visiting dignitaries, where I was quartered with three minor landholders from the mountains. They were already asleep. After my day of confusion, rage, desire and fear, I lay there weary but hard awake, troubled by the sound of my own breathing. My thoughts were jumbled white noise. I had killed him. I had found her. Two of the fantasies of my imprisonment fulfilled in a single hour. Yet no peace. The murder of Protagoras would not long go unnoticed. I assumed Arete already knew but did not care. But if she was truly the Empress, why had he not been killed years before? Why had I rotted in prison under him?

I had no map for this maze, and eventually fell asleep.

In the morning the slave, Pismire, brought me a wig of human hair, a green kimono, a yellow silk sash, and solid leather sandals: the clothes of a prosperous nonentity. My roommates appeared to be barely lettered country bumpkins, little better than my mother, come to court seeking a judgment against a neighbor or a place for a younger child or protection from some bandit. One of them wore the colors of an inferior upland collegium; the others no colors at all.

I suspected at least one of them was Arete's spy; they might have thought me one as well. We looked enough alike to be brothers.

We ate in a dining room attended by machines. I spent the day studying the public rooms of the palace, hoping to get some information. At the tolling of sixth hour Pismire found me in the vivarium. He handed me a message under the Imperial seal, and left. I turned it on.

"You are invited to an important meeting," the message said.

"With whom?" I asked. "For what purpose?"

The message ignored me. "The meeting begins promptly at ninth hour. Prepare yourself." There followed directions to the site.

When I arrived the appointed room was empty. A long oak table, walls lined with racks of document spindles. At the far end French doors gave onto a balcony overlooking an ancient city of glass and metal buildings. I could hear the faint sounds of traffic below.

A side door opened and a woman in the blue suit of the Lawyer entered, followed by a clerk. The woman's glossy black hair was stranded with gray, but her face was smooth. She wore no makeup. She stood at the end of the table, back to the French doors, and set down a leather box. The clerk sat at her right hand. I realized that this forbidding figure was Arete. She had become as mutable as Protagoras.

"Be seated," she said. "We are here to take your deposition."

"Deposition?"

"Your statement on the matter at hand."

"What matter?"

"Your escape from the penal colony. Your murder of the gatekeeper, the honored philosopher Protagoras."

The injustice of this burned through my dismay. "Not murder. Self-defense. Or better still, euthanasia."

"Don't quibble with us. We are deprived of his presence."

"Grow a duplicate. Bring him back to life."

For reply she merely stared at me across the table. The air tasted stale, and I felt a bead of sweat run down my breast beneath my robe. "Is this some game?"

"You may well wish it a game."

"Arete!"

"I am not Arete. I am a Lawyer." She leaned toward me. "Why were you sent to prison?"

"You were with me! You know."

"We are taking your version of events for the record."

"You know as well as I that I was imprisoned for seeking the truth."

"Which truth?"

There was only one. "The one that people don't want to hear," I said.

"You had access to a truth people did not acknowledge?"

"They are blinded by custom and self-interest."

"You were not?"

"I had, though years of self-abnegation and study, risen above them. I had broken free of the chains of prejudice, climbed out of the cave of shadows that society lives in, and looked at the sun direct."

The clerk smirked as I made this speech. It was the first expression he'd shown.

"And you were blinded by it," Arete said.

"I saw the truth. But when I came back they said I was blind. They would not listen, so they put me away."

"The trial record says that you assisted in the corruption of youth."

"I was a teacher."

"The record says you refused to listen to your opponents."

"I refuse to listen to ignorance and illogic. I refuse to submit to fools, liars, and those who let passion overcome reason."

"You have never been fooled?"

"I was, but not now."

"You never lie?"

"If I do, I still know the difference between a lie and the truth."

"You never act out of passion?"

"Only when supported by reason."

"You never suspect your own motives?"

"I know my motives."

"How?"

"I examine myself. Honestly, critically. I apply reason."

"Spare me your colossal arrogance, your revolting self-pity. Eyewitnesses say you killed the gatekeeper in a fit of rage."

"I had reason. Do you presume to understand my motives better than I? Do you understand your own?"

"No. But that's because I am dishonest. And totally arbitrary." She opened the box and took out a clock. Without hesitation she pointed it at the clerk. His smugness punctured, he stumbled back, overturning his chair. She pressed the trigger. The weapon must have been set for maximum entropy: before my eyes the clerk aged ten, twenty, fifty years. He died and rotted. In less than a minute he was a heap of bones and gruel on the floor.

"You've been in prison so long you've invented a harmless version of me," Arete said. "I am capable of anything." She laid the clock on the table, turned and opened the doors to let in a fresh night breeze. Then she climbed onto the table and crawled toward me. I sat frozen.

"I am the Destroyer," she said, loosening her tie as she approached. Her eyes were fixed on mine. When she reached me she pushed me over backwards, falling atop me. "I am the force that drives the blood through your dying body, the nightmare that wakes you sweating in the middle of the night. I am the fiery cauldron within whose heat you are reduced to a vapor, extended from the visible into the invisible, dissipated on the winds of time, of fading memory, of inevitable human loss. In the face of me, you are incapable of articulate speech. About me you understand nothing."

She wound the tie around my neck, drew it tight. "Remember that," she said, strangling me.

I PASSED OUT on the floor of the interview room and awoke the next morning in a bed in a private chamber. Pismire was drawing the curtains on a view of an ocean beach: half asleep I watched the tiny figure of a man materialize in a spray of glass, in mid-air, and fall precipitously into the sea.

Pismire brought me a breakfast of fruit and spiced coffee. Touching the bruises on my neck, I watched the man resurface in the sea and swim ashore. He collapsed on the sand. A flock of gulls came to stand by his head. If I broke through this window, I could warn him. I could say: Socrates is fat. Watch out for the gatekeeper. Arete is alive, but she is changed.

But what could I tell him for certain? Had Arete turned Relativist, like Socrates? Was she free, or being made to play a part? Did she intend to prosecute me for the murder of Protagoras? But if so, why not simply return me to the penal colony?

I did not break through the window, and the man eventually moved up the beach toward the city.

That day servants followed me everywhere. Minor lords asked my opinions. Evidently I was a taller man than I had been the day before. I drew Pismire aside and asked him what rumors were current. He was a stocky fellow with a topknot of coarse black hair and shaved temples, silent, but when I pressed him he opened up readily enough. He said he knew for a fact that Protagoras had set himself up to be killed. He said the Emperor was dead and the Empress was the focus of a perpetual struggle. That many men had sought to make Arete theirs, but none had so far succeeded. That disaster would surely follow any man's success.

"Does she always change semblance from day to day?"

He said he had never noticed any changes.

In mid-afternoon, at precisely the same time I had yesterday received the summons to the deposition, a footman with the face of a frog handed me an invitation to dine with the Empress that evening.

Three female expediters prepared a scented bath for me; a fourth laid out a kimono of blue crepe embroidered with gold fishing nets. The mirror they held before me showed a man with wary eyes. At the tolling of ninth hour I was escorted to the banquet hall. The room was filled with notables in every finery. A large, low table stretched across the tessellated floor, surrounded by cushions. Before each place was an enamel bowl and in the center of the table was a large, three-legged brass cauldron. Arete, looking no more than twenty, stood talking to an extremely handsome man near the head of the table.

"I thank you for your courtesy," I told her.

The man watched me impassively. "No more than is your due," Arete replied. She wore a bright costume of synthetics with pleated shoulders and elbows. She looked like a toy. Her face was painted into a hard mask.

She introduced me to the man, whose name was Meno. I drew her away from him. "You frightened me last night," I said. "I thought you had forgotten me."

Only her soft brown eyes showed she wasn't a pleasure surrogate. "What makes you think I remember?"

"You could not forget and still be the one I love."

"That's probably true. I'm not sure I'm worth such devotion."

Meno watched us from a few paces away. I turned my back to him and leaned closer to her. "I can't believe you mean that," I said quickly. "I think you say such things because you have been imprisoned by liars and self-aggrandizers. But I am here for you now. I am an objective voice. Just give me a sign, and I will set you free."

Before she could answer, a bell sounded and the people took their places. Arete guided me to a place beside her. She sat, and we all followed suit.

335

The slaves stood ready to serve, waiting for Arete's command. She looked around the table. "We are met here to eat together," she said. "To dine on ambrosia, because there has been strife in the city, and ambition, and treachery. But now it is going to stop."

Meno now looked openly angry. Others were worried.

"You are the favored ones," said Arete. She turned to me. "And our friend here, the little fox, is the most favored of all. Destiny's author—our new and most trusted advisor."

Several people started to protest. I seized the opportunity given by their shock. "Am I indeed your advisor?"

"You may test it by deeds."

"You and you—" I beckoned to the guards. "Clear these people from the room."

The guests were in turmoil. Meno tried to speak to Arete, but I stepped between them. The guards came forward and forced the men and women to leave. After they were gone I had the guards and slaves leave as well. The doors closed and the hall was silent. I turned. Arete had watched it all calmly, sitting crosslegged at the head of the table.

"Now, Arete, you must listen to me. Your commands have been twisted throughout this city. You and I have an instinctive sympathy. You must let me determine who sees you. I will interpret your words. The world is not ready to understand without an interpreter; they need to be educated."

"And you are the teacher."

"I am suited to it by temperament and training."

She smiled meekly.

I told Arete that I was hungry. She rose and prepared a bowl of soup from the cauldron. I sat at the head of the table. She came and set the bowl before me, then kneeled and touched her forehead to the floor.

"Feed me," I said.

She took the bowl and a napkin. She blew on the ambrosia to cool it, lips pursed. Like a serving girl, she held the bowl to my lips. Arete fed me all of it, like mother to child, lover to lover. It tasted better than anything I had ever eaten. It warmed my belly and inflamed my desire. When the bowl was empty I pushed it away, knocking it from her hand. It clattered on the marble floor. I would be put off no longer. I took her right there, amid the cushions.

She was indeed the hardest of toys.

IT HAD TAKEN me three days from my entrance to the palace to become Arete's lover and voice. The Emperor over the Empress. On the first day of my reign I had the shopkeeper who had insulted me whipped the length of the Way of Enlightenment. On the second I ordered that only those certified in philosophy be qualified to vote. On the third I banished the poets.

Each evening Arete fed me ambrosia from a bowl. Each night we shared the Imperial bed. Each morning I awoke calmer, in more possession of myself. I moved more slowly. The hours of the day were drained of their urgency. Arete stopped changing. Her face settled with a quiet clarity into my mind, a clarity unlike the burning image I had treasured up during my years in the prison.

On the morning of the third day I awoke fresh and happy. Arete was not there. Pismire entered the room bearing a basin, a towel, a razor, a mirror. He washed and shaved me, then held the mirror before me. For the first time I saw the lines about my eyes and mouth were fading, and realized that I was being Reformed.

I looked at Pismire. I saw him clearly: eyes cold as aquamarines.

"It's time for you to come home, Blume," he said.

No anger, no protest arose in me. No remorse. No frustration. "I've been betrayed," I said. "Some virus, some drug, some notion you've put in my head."

Protagoras smiled. "The ambrosia. Brewed with water from the Well."

NOW I AM back in the prison. Escape is out of the question. Every step outward would be a step backward. It's all relative.

Instead I draw water from the Well of Changes. I drink. Protagoras says whatever changes happen to me will be a reflection of my own psyche. My new form is not determined by the water, but by me. How do I control it, I ask. You don't, he replies.

Glaucon has become a feral dog.

Protagoras and I go for long walks across the dry lake. He seldom speaks. I am not angry. Still, I fear a relapse. I am close to being nourished, but as yet I am not sure I am capable of it. I don't understand, as I never understood, where the penal colony is. I don't understand, as I never understood, how I can live without Arete.

Protagoras sympathizes. "Can't live with her, can't live without her," he says. "She's more than just a woman, Blume. You may experience her but you can't own her."

Right. When I complain about such gnomic replies Protagoras only puts me under the hood again. I think he carries some secret he wants me to guess, yet he gives no hints. I don't think that's fair.

After our most recent session, I told Protagoras my latest theory of the significance of the poem about the swallows. The poem, I said, was an emblem of the ultimate and absolute truth of the universe. All things are determined by the ideas behind them, I said. There are three orders of existence, the Material (represented by the physical statue of the Buddha), the Spiritual (represented by its form), and the highest, which transcends both the Physical and the Spiritual, the Ideal (represented by the flight of the birds). I begged Protagoras humbly to tell me whether my analysis was true.

Protagoras said, "You are indeed wise. But in order for me to reveal the answer to a question of such profound significance you must first bow down before the sacred Well."

At last I was to be enlightened. Eyes brimming with tears of hope, I turned to the Well and, with the utmost sincerity, bowed.

Then Protagoras kicked me in the ass.

Invaders

15 November 1532

THAT NIGHT no one slept. On the hills outside Cajamarca, the campfires of the Inca's army shone like so many stars in the sky. De Soto reported that Atahualpa had perhaps forty thousand troops under arms, but looking at the myriad lights spread across those hills, de Candia realized that estimate was, if anything, low.

Against them, Pizarro could throw one hundred foot soldiers, sixty horse, eight muskets, and four harquebuses. Pizarro, his brother Hernando, de Soto, and Benalcázar laid out plans for an ambush. They would invite the Inca to a parlay. De Candia and his artillery would be hidden in the building along one side of the square, the cavalry and infantry along the others. De Candia watched Pizarro prowl through the camp that night, checking the men's armor, joking with them, reminding them of the treasure they would have, and the women. The men laughed nervously and whetted their swords.

They might sharpen them until their hands fell off; when morning dawned, they would be slaughtered. De Candia breathed deeply of the thin air and turned from the wall.

Ruiz de Arce, an infantryman with a face like a clenched fist, hailed him as he passed. "Are those guns of yours ready for some work tomorrow?"

"We need prayers more than guns."

"I'm not afraid of these brownies," de Arce said.

"Then you're a half-wit."

"Soto says they have no swords."

The man was probably just trying to reassure himself, but de Candia couldn't abide it. "Will you shut your stinking fool's trap! They don't need swords! If they only spit all at once, we'll be drowned."

Pizarro overheard him. He stormed over, grabbed de Candia's arm, and shook him. "Have they ever seen a horse, Candia? Have they ever felt steel? When you fired the harquebus on the seashore, didn't the town chief pour beer down its barrel as if it were a thirsty god? Pull up your balls and show me you're a man!"

His face was inches away. "Mark me! Tomorrow, Saint James sits on your shoulder, and we win a victory that will cover us in glory for five hundred years."

2 December 2001

"DEE-FENSE! DEE-FENSE!" THE crowd screamed. During the two-minute warning, Norwood Delacroix limped over to the Redskins' special conditioning coach.

"My knee's about gone," said Delacroix, an outside linebacker with eyebrows that ran together and all the musculature that modern pharmacology could load onto his six-foot-five frame. "I need something."

"You need the power of prayer, my friend. Stoner's eating your lunch."

"Just do it."

The coach selected a popgun from his rack, pressed the muzzle against Delacroix's knee, and pulled the trigger. A flood of well-being rushed up Delacroix's leg. He flexed it tentatively. It felt better than the other one now. Delacroix jogged back onto the field.

"DEE-fense!" the fans roared. The overcast sky began to spit frozen rain. The ref blew the whistle, and the Bills broke huddle.

Delacroix looked across at Stoner, the Bills' tight end. The air throbbed with electricity. The quarterback called the signals; the ball was snapped; Stoner surged forward. As Delacroix backpedaled furiously, sudden sunlight flooded the field. His ears buzzed. Stoner jerked left and went right, twisting Delacroix around like a cork in a bottle. His knee popped. Stoner had two steps on him. TD for sure. Delacroix pulled his head down and charged after him.

But instead of continuing downfield, Stoner slowed. He looked straight up into the air. Delacroix hit him at the knees, and they both went down. He'd caught him! The crowd screamed louder, a scream edged with hysteria.

Then Delacroix realized the buzzing wasn't just in his ears. Elation fading, he lifted his head and looked toward the sidelines. The coaches and players were running for the tunnels. The crowd boiled toward the exits, shedding Thermoses and beer cups and radios. The sunlight was harshly bright. Delacroix looked up. A huge disk hovered no more than fifty feet above, pinning them in its spotlight. Stoner untangled himself from Delacroix, stumbled to his feet, and ran off the field.

Holy Jesus and the Virgin Mary on toast, Delacroix thought.

He scrambled toward the end zone. The stadium was emptying fast, except for the ones who were getting trampled. The throbbing in the air increased in volume, lowered in pitch, and the flying saucer settled onto the NFL logo on the forty-yard line. The sound stopped as abruptly as if it had been sucked into a sponge.

Out of the corner of his eye, Delacroix saw an NBC cameraman come up next to him, focusing on the ship. Its side divided, and a ramp extended itself to the ground. The cameraman fell back a few steps, but Delacroix held his ground. The inside glowed with the bluish light of a UV lamp.

A shape moved there. It lurched forward to the top of the ramp. A large manlike thing, it advanced with a rolling stagger, like a college freshman at a beer blast. It wore a body-tight red stretchsuit, a white circle on its chest with a lightning bolt through it, some sort of flexible mask over its face. Blond hair covered its head in a kind of brush cut, and two cup-shaped ears poked comically out of the sides of its head. The creature stepped off onto the field, nudging aside the football that lay there.

Delacroix, who had majored in public relations at Michigan State, went forward to greet it. This could be the beginning of an entirely new career. His knee felt great.

He extended his hand. "Welcome," he said. "I greet you in the name of humanity and the United States of America."

"Cocaine," the alien said. "We need cocaine."

Today

I SIT AT my desk writing a science fiction story, a tall, thin man wearing jeans, a white T-shirt with the abstract face of a man printed on it, white high-top basketball shoes, and gold-plated wire-rimmed glasses.

In the morning I drink coffee to get me up for the day, and at night I have a gin and tonic to help me relax.

16 November 1532

"WHAT ARE THEY waiting for, the shitting dogs!" the man next to de Arce said. "Are they trying to make us suffer?"

"Shut up, will you?" De Arce shifted his armor. Wedged into the stone building on the side of the square, sweating, they had been waiting since dawn, in silence for the most part except for the creak of leather, the uneasy jingle of cascabels on the horses' trappings. The men stank worse than the restless horses. Some had pissed themselves. A common foot soldier like de Arce was lucky to get a space near enough to the door to see out.

As noon came and went with still no sign of Atahualpa and his retinue, the mood of the men went from impatience to near panic. Then, late in the day, word came that the Indians again were moving toward the town.

An hour later, six thousand brilliantly costumed attendants entered the plaza. They were unarmed. Atahualpa, borne on a golden litter by eight men in cloaks of green feathers that glistened like emeralds in the sunset, rose above them. De Arce heard a slight rattling, looked down, and found that his hand, gripping the sword so tightly the knuckles stood out white, was shaking uncontrollably. He unknotted his fist from the hilt, rubbed the cramped fingers, and crossed himself.

"Quiet now, my brave ones," Pizarro said.

Father Valverde and Felipillo strode out to the center of the plaza, right through the sea of attendants. The priest had guts. He stopped before the litter of the Inca, short and steady as a fence post. "Greetings, my lord, in the name of Pope Clement VII, His Majesty the Emperor Charles V, and Our Lord and Savior Jesus Christ."

Atahualpa spoke and Felipillo translated: "Where is this new god?"

Valverde held up the crucifix. "Our God died on the cross many years ago and rose again to Heaven. He appointed the Pope as His viceroy on earth, and the Pope has commanded King Charles to subdue the peoples of the world and convert them to the true faith. The king sent us here to command your obedience and to teach you and your people in this faith."

"By what authority does this pope give away lands that aren't his?"

Valverde held up his Bible. "By the authority of the word of God."

The Inca took the Bible. When Valverde reached out to help him get the cover unclasped, Atahualpa cuffed his arm away. He opened the book and leafed through the pages. After a moment he threw it to the ground. "I hear no words," he said.

Valverde snatched up the book and stalked back toward Pizarro's hiding place. "What are you waiting for?" he shouted. "The saints and the Blessed Virgin, the bleeding wounds of Christ himself, cry vengeance! Attack, and I'll absolve you!"

Pizarro had already stridden into the plaza. He waved his kerchief. "Santiago, and at them!"

On the far side, the harquebuses exploded in an enfilade. The lines of Indians jerked like startled cats. Bells jingling, de Soto's and Hernando's cavalries burst from the lines of doorways on the adjoining side. De Arce clutched his sword and rushed out with the others from the third side. He felt the power of God in his arm. "Santiago!" he roared at the top of his lungs, and hacked halfway through the neck of his first Indian. Bright blood spurted. He put his boot to the brown man's shoulder and yanked free, lunged for the belly of another wearing a kilt of bright red and white checks. The man turned, and the sword caught between his ribs. The hilt was almost twisted from de Arce's grasp as the Indian went down. He pulled free, shrugged another man off his back, and daggered him in the side.

After the first flush of glory, it turned to filthy, hard work, an hour's wade through an ocean of butchery in the twilight, bodies heaped waist-high, boots skidding on the bloody stones. De Arce alone must have killed forty. Only after they'd slaughtered them all and captured the Sapa Inca did it end. A silence settled, broken only by the moans of dying Indians and distant shouts of the cavalry chasing the ones who had managed to break through the plaza wall to escape.

Saint James had indeed sat on their shoulders. Six thousand dead Indians, and not one Spaniard nicked. It was a pure demonstration of the power of prayer.

31 January 2002

IT WAS COLONEL Zipp's third session interrogating the alien. So far the thing had kept a consistent story, but not a credible one. The only consideration that kept Zipp from panic at the thought of how his career would suffer if this continued was the rumor that his fellow case officers weren't doing any better with any of the others. That, and the fact that the Krel possessed technology that would reestablish American superiority for another two hundred years. He took a drag on his cigarette, the first of his third pack of the day.

"Your name?" Zipp asked.

"You may call me Flash."

Zipp studied the red union suit, the lightning bolt. With the flat chest, the rounded shoulders, pointed upper lip, and pronounced underbite, the alien looked like a cross between Wally Cleaver and the Mock Turtle. "Is this some kind of joke?"

"What is a joke?"

"Never mind." Zipp consulted his notes. "Where are you from?"

"God has ceded us an empire extending over sixteen solar systems in the Orion arm of the galaxy, including the systems around the stars you know as Tau Ceti, Epsilon Eridani, Alpha Centauri, and the red dwarf Barnard's Star."

"God gave you an empire?"

"Yes. We were hoping He'd give us your world, but all He kept talking about was your cocaine."

The alien's translating device had to be malfunctioning. "You're telling me that God sent you for cocaine?"

"No. He just told us about it. We collect chemical compounds for their aesthetic interest. These alkaloids do not exist on our world. Like the music you humans value so highly, they combine familiar elements—carbon, hydrogen, nitrogen, oxygen—in pleasing new ways."

The colonel leaned back, exhaled a cloud of smoke. "You consider cocaine like—like a symphony?"

"Yes. Understand, Colonel, no material commodity alone could justify the difficulties of interstellar travel. We come here for aesthetic reasons."

"You seem to know what cocaine is already. Why don't you just synthesize it yourself?"

"If you valued a unique work of aboriginal art, would you be satisfied with a mass-produced duplicate manufactured in your hometown? Of course not. And we are prepared to pay you well, in a coin you can use."

"We don't need any coins. If you want cocaine, tell us how your ships work."

"That is one of the coins we had in mind. Our ships operate according to a principle of basic physics. Certain fundamental physical reactions are subject to the belief system of the beings promoting them. If I believe that X is true, then X is more probably true than if I did not believe so."

The colonel leaned forward again. "We know that already. We call it the 'observer effect.' Our great physicist Werner Heisenberg—"

"Yes. I'm afraid we carry this principle a little further than that."

"What do you mean?"

Flash smirked. "I mean that our ships move through interstellar space by the power of prayer."

13 May 1533

ATAHUALPA OFFERED TO fill a room twenty-two feet long and seventeen feet wide with gold up to a line as high as a man could reach, if the Spaniards would let him go. They were skeptical. How long would this take? Pizarro asked. Two months, Atahualpa said.

Pizarro allowed the word to be sent out, and over the next several months, bearers, chewing the coca leaf in order to negotiate the mountain roads under such burdens, brought in tons of gold artifacts. They brought plates and vessels, life-sized statues of women and men, gold lobsters and spiders and alpacas, intricately fashioned ears of maize, every kernel reproduced, with leaves of gold and tassels of spun silver.

Martin Bueno was one of the advance scouts sent with the Indians to Cuzco, the capital of the empire. They found it to be the legendary city of gold. The Incas, having no money, valued precious metals only as ornament. In Cuzco the very walls of the Sun Temple, Coricancha, were plated with gold. Adjoining the temple was a ritual garden where gold maize plants supported gold butterflies, gold bees pollinated gold flowers.

"Enough loot that you'll shit in a gold pot every day for the rest of your life," Bueno told his friend Diego Leguizano upon his return to Cajamarca.

They ripped the plating off the temple walls and had it carried to Cajamarca. There they melted it down into ingots.

The huge influx of gold into Europe was to cause an economic catastrophe. In Peru, at the height of the conquest, a pair of shoes cost $850, and a bottle of wine $1,700. When their old horseshoes wore out, iron being unavailable, the cavalry shod their horses with silver.

21 April 2003

IN THE EXECUTIVE washroom of Bellingham, Winston, and McNeese, Jason Prescott snorted a couple of lines and was ready for the afternoon. He returned to the brokerage to find the place in a whispering uproar. In his office sat one of the Krel. Prescott's secretary was about to piss himself. "It asked specifically for you," he said.

What would Attila the Hun do in this situation? Prescott thought. He went into the office. "Jason Prescott," he said. "What can I do for you, Mr....?"

The alien's bloodshot eyes surveyed him. "Flash. I wish to make an investment."

"Investments are our business." Rumors had flown around the New York Merc for a month that the Krel were interested in investing. They had earned vast sums selling information to various computer, environmental, and biotech firms. Several of the aliens had come to observe trading in the currencies pit last week, and only yesterday Jason had heard from a reliable source that they were considering opening an account with Merrill Lynch. "What brings you to our brokerage?"

"Not the brokerage. You. We heard that you are the most ruthless currencies trader in this city. We worship efficiency. You are efficient."

Right. Maybe there was a hallucinogen in the toot. "I'll call in some of our foreign-exchange experts. We can work up an investment plan for your consideration in a week."

"We already have an investment plan. We are, as you say in the markets, 'long' in dollars. We want you to sell dollars and buy francs for us."

"The franc is pretty strong right now. It's likely to hold for the next six months. We'd suggest—"

"We wish to buy fifty billion dollars' worth of francs."

Prescott stared. "That's not a very good investment." Flash said nothing. The silence grew uncomfortable. "I suppose if we stretch it out over a few months, and hit the exchanges in Hong Kong and London at the same time—"

"We want these francs bought in the next week. For the week after that, a second fifty billion dollars. Fifty billion a week until we tell you to stop."

Hallucinogens for sure. "That doesn't make any sense."

"We can take our business elsewhere."

Prescott thought about it. It would take every trick he knew—and he'd have to invent some new ones—to carry this off. The dollar was going to drop through the floor, while the franc would punch through the sell-stops of every trader on ten world markets. The exchanges would scream bloody murder. The repercussions would auger holes in every economy north of Antarctica. Governments would intervene. It would make the historic Hunt silver squeeze look like a game of Monopoly.

Besides, it made no sense. Not only was it criminally irresponsible, it was stupid. The Krel would squander every dime they'd earned.

Then he thought about the commission on $50 billion a week.

Prescott looked across at the alien. From the right point of view, Flash resembled a barrel-chested college undergraduate from Special Effects U. He felt an urge to giggle, a euphoric feeling of power. "When do we start?"

19 May 1533

IN THE FIELDS the *purics*, singing praise to Atahualpa, son of the sun, harvested the maize. At night they celebrated by getting drunk on *chicha*. It was, they said, the most festive month of the year.

Pedro Sancho did his drinking in the dark of the treasure room, in the smoke of the smelters' fire. For months he had been troubled by nightmares of the heaped bodies lying in the plaza. He tried to ignore the abuse of the Indian women, the brutality toward the men. He worked hard. As Pizarro's squire, it was his job to record daily the tally of Atahualpa's ransom. When he ran low on ink, he taught the *purics* to make it for him from soot and the juice of berries. They learned readily.

Atahualpa heard about the ink and one day came to him. "What are you doing with those marks?" he said, pointing to the scribe's tally book.

"I'm writing the list of gold objects to be melted down."

"What is this 'writing'?"

Sancho was nonplussed. Over the months of Atahualpa's captivity, Sancho had become impressed by the sophistication of the Incas. Yet they were also queerly backward. They had no money. It was not beyond belief that they should not know how to read and write.

"By means of these marks, I can record the words that people speak. That's writing. Later other men can look at these marks and see what was said. That's reading."

"Then this is a kind of quipu?" Atahualpa's servants had demonstrated for Sancho the quipu, a system of knotted strings by which the Incas kept tallies. "Show me how it works," Atahualpa said.

Sancho wrote on the page: *God have mercy on us.* He pointed. "This, my lord, is a representation of the word 'God.' "

Atahualpa looked skeptical. "Mark it here." He held out his hand, thumbnail extended.

Sancho wrote "God" on the Inca's thumbnail.

"Say nothing now." Atahualpa advanced to one of the guards, held out his thumbnail. "What does this mean?" he asked.

"God," the man replied.

Sancho could tell the Inca was impressed, but he barely showed it. That the Sapa Inca had maintained such dignity throughout his captivity tore at Sancho's heart.

"This writing is truly a magical accomplishment," Atahualpa told him. "You must teach my *amautas* this art."

Later, when the viceroy Estete, Father Valverde, and Pizarro came to chide him for the slow pace of the gold shipments, Atahualpa tested each of them separately. Estete and Valverde each said the word "God." Atahualpa held his thumbnail out to the conquistador.

Estete chuckled. For the first time in his experience, Sancho saw Pizarro flush. He turned away. "I don't waste my time on the games of children," Pizarro said.

Atahualpa stared at him. "But your common soldiers know this art."

"Well, I don't."

"Why not?"

"I was a swineherd. Swineherds don't need to read."

"You are not a swineherd now."

Pizarro glared at the Inca. "I don't need to read to have you put to death." He marched out of the room.

After the others had left, Sancho told Atahualpa, "You ought not to humiliate the governor in front of his men."

"He humiliates himself," Atahualpa said. "There is no skill in which a leader ought to let himself fall behind his followers."

Today

THE PART OF this story about the Incas is as historically accurate as I could make it, but this Krel business is science fiction. I even stole the name "Krel" from a 1950s SF flick. I've been addicted to SF for years. In the evening my wife and I wash the bad taste of the news out of our mouths by watching old movies on videotape.

A scientist, asked why he read SF, replied, "Because in science fiction the experiments always work." Things in SF stories resolve more neatly than in reality. Nothing is impossible. Spaceships move faster than light. Atomic weapons are neutralized. Disease is abolished. People travel in time. Why, Isaac Asimov even wrote a story once that ended with the reversal of entropy!

The descendants of the Incas, living in grinding poverty, find their most lucrative crop in coca, which they refine into cocaine and sell in vast quantities to North Americans.

23 August 2008

"CATALOG NUMBER 208," said John Bostock. "Georges Seurat, *Bathers*."

FRENCH GOVERNMENT FALLS, the morning *Times* had announced. JAPAN BANS U.S. IMPORTS. FOOD RIOTS IN MADRID. But Bostock had barely glanced at the newspaper over his coffee; he was buzzed on caffeine and adrenaline, and it was too late to stop the auction, the biggest day of his career. The lot list would make an art historian faint. *Guernica. The Potato Eaters. The Scream.* Miro, Rembrandt, Vermeer, Gauguin, Matisse, Constable, Magritte, Pollock, Mondrian. Six desperate governments had contributed to the sale. And rumor had it the Krel would be among the bidders.

The rumor proved true. In the front row, beside the solicitor Patrick McClannahan, sat one of the unlikely aliens, wearing red tights and a lightning-bolt insignia. The famous Flash. The creature leaned back lazily while McClannahan did the bidding with a discreetly raised forefinger.

Bidding on the Seurat started at ten million and went orbital. It soon became clear that the main bidders were Flash and the U.S. government. The American campaign against cultural imperialism was getting a lot of press, ironic since the Yanks could afford to challenge the Krel only because of the technology the Krel had lavished on them. The probability suppressor that prevented the detonation of atomic weapons. The autodidactic antivirus that cured most diseases. There was talk of an immortality drug. Of a time machine. So what if the European Community was in the sixth month of an economic crisis that threatened to dissolve the unifying efforts of the past twenty years? So what if Krel meddling destroyed humans' capacity to run the world? The Americans were making money, and the Krel were richer than Croesus.

The bidding reached $1.2 billion, at which point the American ambassador gave up. Bostock tapped his gavel. "Sold," he said in his most cultured voice, nodding toward the alien.

The crowd murmured. The American stood. "If you can't see what they're doing to us, then you don't deserve our help!"

For a minute Bostock thought the auction was going to turn into a riot. Then the new owner of the pointillist masterpiece stood, smiled. Ingenuous, clumsy. "We know that there has been considerable disquiet over our purchase of these historic works of art," Flash said. "Let me promise you, they will be displayed where all humans—not just those who can afford to visit the great museums—can see them."

The crowd's murmur turned into applause. Bostock put down his gavel and joined in. The American ambassador and his aides stalked out. Thank God, Bostock thought. The attendants brought out the next item.

"Catalog number 209," Bostock said. "Leonardo da Vinci, *Mona Lisa*."

26 July 1533

THE SOLDIERS, SEEING the heaps of gold grow, became anxious. They consumed stores of coca meant for the Inca messengers. They fought over women.

They grumbled over the airs of Atahualpa. "Who does he think he is? The governor treats him like a hidalgo."

Father Valverde cursed Pizarro's inaction. That morning, after matins, he spoke with Estete. "The governor has agreed to meet and decide what to do," Estete said.

"It's about time. What about Soto?" De Soto was against harming Atahualpa. He maintained that, since the Inca had paid the ransom, he should be set free, no matter what danger this would present. Pizarro had stalled. Last week he had sent de Soto away to check out rumors that the Tahuantinsuyans were massing for an attack to free the Sapa Inca.

Estete smiled. "Soto's not back yet."

They went to the building Pizarro had claimed as his and found the others already gathered. The Incas had no tables or proper chairs, so the Spaniards were forced to sit in a circle on mats as the Indians did. Pizarro, only a few years short of threescore, sat on a low stool of the sort that Atahualpa used when he held court. His left leg, whose old battle wound still pained him at times, was stretched out before him. His loose white shirt had been cleaned by some *puric's* wife. Valverde sat beside him. Gathered were Estete, Benalcázar, Almagro, de Candia, Riquelme, Pizarro's young cousin Pedro, the scribe Pedro Sancho, Valverde, and the governor himself.

As Valverde and Estete had agreed, the viceroy went first.

"The men are jumpy, governor," Estete said. "The longer we stay cooped up here, the longer we give these savages the chance to plot against us."

"We should wait until Soto returns," de Candia said, already looking guilty as a dog. "We've got nothing but rumors so far. I won't kill a man on a rumor."

Silence. Trust de Candia to speak aloud what they were all thinking but were not ready to say. The man had no political judgment—but maybe it was just as well to face it directly. Valverde seized the opportunity. "Atahualpa plots against us even as we speak," he told Pizarro. "As governor, you are responsible for our safety. Any court would convict him of treason and execute him."

"He's a king," de Candia said. Face flushed, he spat out a cud of leaves. "We don't have authority to try him. We should ship him back to Spain and let the emperor decide what to do."

"This is not a king," Valverde said. "It isn't even a man. It is a creature that worships demons, that weaves spells about halfwits like Candia. You saw him discard the Bible. Even after my months of teaching, after the extraordinary mercies we've shown him, he doesn't acknowledge the primacy of Christ! He cares only for his wives and his pagan gods. Yet he's satanically clever. Don't think we can let him go. If we do, the day will come when he'll have our hearts for dinner."

"We can take him with us to Cuzco," Benalcázar said. "We don't know the country. His presence would guarantee our safe conduct."

"We'll be traveling over rough terrain, carrying tons of gold, with not enough horses," Almagro said. "If we take him with us, we'll be ripe for ambush at every pass."

"They won't attack if we have him."

"He could escape. We can't trust the rebel Indians to stay loyal to us. If they turned to our side, they can just as easily turn back to his."

"And remember, he escaped before, during the civil war," Valverde said. "Huascar, his brother, lived to regret that. If Atahualpa didn't hesitate to murder his own brother, do you think he'll stop for us?"

"He's given us his word," Candia said.

"What good is the word of a pagan?"

Pizarro, silent until now, spoke. "He has no reason to think the word of a Christian much better."

Valverde felt his blood rise. Pizarro knew as well as any of them what was necessary. What was he waiting for? "He keeps a hundred wives! He betrayed his brother! He worships the sun!" The priest grabbed Pizarro's hand, held it up between them so they could both see the scar there, where Pizarro had gotten cut preventing one of his own men from killing Atahualpa. "He isn't worth an ounce of the blood you spilled to save him."

"He's proved worth twenty-four tons of gold." Pizarro's eyes were hard and calm.

"There is no alternative!" Valverde insisted. "He serves the Antichrist! God demands his death."

At last Pizarro seemed to have gotten what he wanted. He smiled. "Far be it from me to ignore the command of God," he said. "Since God forces us to it, let's discuss how He wants it done."

5 October 2009

"WHAT A LOVELY country Chile is from the air. You should be proud of it."

"I'm from Los Angeles," Leon Sepulveda said. "And as soon as we close this deal, I'm going back."

"The mountains are impressive."

"Nothing but earthquakes and slag. You can have Chile."

"Is it for sale?"

Sepulveda stared at the Krel. "I was just kidding."

They sat at midnight in the arbor, away from the main buildings of Iguassu Microelectronics of Santiago. The night was cold and the arbor was overgrown and the bench needed a paint job—but then, a lot of things had been getting neglected in the past couple of years. All the more reason to put yourself in a financial situation where you didn't have to worry. Though Sepulveda had to admit that, since the advent of the Krel, such positions were harder to come by, and less secure once you had them.

Flash's earnestness aroused a kind of horror in him. It had something to do with Sepulveda's suspicion that this thing next to him was as superior to him as he was to a guinea pig, plus the alien's aura of drunken adolescence, plus his own willingness, despite the feeling that the situation was out of control, to make a deal with it. He took another Valium and tried to calm down.

"What assurance do I have that this time-travel method will work?" he asked.

"It will work. If you don't like it in Chile, or back in Los Angeles, you can use it to go into the past."

Sepulveda swallowed. "Okay. You need to read and sign these papers."

"We don't read."

"You don't read Spanish? How about English?"

"We don't read at all. We used to, but we gave it up. Once you start reading, it gets out of control. You tell yourself you're just going to stick to nonfiction—but pretty soon you graduate to fiction. After that, you can't kick the habit. And then there's the oppression."

"Oppression?"

"Sure. I mean, I like a story as much as the next Krel, but any pharmacologist can show that arbitrary cultural, sexual, and economic assumptions determine every significant aspect of a story. Literature is a political tool used by ruling elites to ensure their hegemony. Anyone who denies that is a fish who can't see the water it swims in. Or the fascist who tells you, as he beats you, that those blows you feel are your own delusion."

"Right. Look, can we settle this? I've got things to do."

"This is, of course, the key to temporal translation. The past is another arbitrary construct. Language creates reality. Reality is smoke."

"Well, this time machine better not be smoke. We're going to find out the truth about the past. Then we'll change it."

"By all means. Find the truth." Flash turned to the last page of the contract, pricked his thumb, and marked a thumbprint on the signature line.

After they sealed the agreement, Sepulveda walked the alien back to the courtyard. A Krel flying pod with Vermeer's *The Letter* varnished onto its door sat at the focus of three spotlights. The painting was scorched almost into unrecognizability by atmospheric friction. The door peeled downward from the top, became a canvas-surfaced ramp.

"I saw some interesting lines inscribed on the coastal desert on the way here," Flash said. "A bird, a tree, a big spider. In the sunset, it looked beautiful. I didn't think you humans were capable of such art. Is it for sale?"

"I don't think so. That was done by some old Indians a long time ago. If you're really interested, though, I can look into it."

"Not necessary." Flash waggled his ears, wiped his feet on Mark Rothko's *Earth and Green,* and staggered into the pod.

26 July 1533

ATAHUALPA LOOKED OUT of the window of the stone room in which he was kept, across the plaza to where the priest Valverde stood outside his chapel after his morning prayers. Valverde's chapel had been the house of the virgins;

the women of the house had long since been raped by the Spanish soldiers, as the house had been by the Spanish god. Valverde spoke with Estete. They were getting ready to kill him, Atahualpa knew. He had known ever since the ransom had been paid.

He looked beyond the thatched roofs of the town to the crest of the mountains, where the sun was about to break in his tireless circuit of Tahuantinsuyu. The cold morning air raised dew on the metal of the chains that bound him hand and foot. The metal was queer, different from the bronze the *purics* worked or the gold and silver Atahualpa was used to wearing. If gold was the sweat of the sun, and silver the tears of the moon, what was this metal, dull and hard like the men who held him captive, yet strong, too—stronger, he had come to realize, than the Inca. It, like the men who brought it, was beyond his experience. It gave evidence that Tahuantinsuyu, the Four Quarters of the World, was not the entire world after all. Atahualpa had thought none but savages lived beyond their lands. He'd imagined no man readier to face ruthless necessity than himself. He had ordered the death of Huascar, his own brother. But he was learning that these men were capable of enormities against which the Inca civil war would seem a minor discomfort.

That evening they took him out of the building to the plaza. In the plaza's center, the soldiers had piled a great heap of wood on flagstones that were still stained with the blood of his six thousand slaughtered attendants. They bound him to a stake amid the heaped fagots, and Valverde appealed one last time for the Inca to renounce Satan and be baptized. Valverde promised that if Atahualpa would do so, he would earn God's mercy: they would strangle him rather than burn him to death.

The rough wood pressed against his spine. Atahualpa looked at the priest, and the men gathered around, and the women weeping beyond the circle of soldiers. The moon, his mother, rode high above. Firelight flickered on the breastplates of the Spaniards, and from the waiting torches drifted the smell of pitch. The men shifted nervously. Creak of leather, clink of metal. Men on horses shod with silver. Sweat shining on Valverde's forehead. Valverde stared at Atahualpa as if he desired something, but was prepared to destroy him without getting it if need be. The priest thought he was showing resolve, but Atahualpa saw that beneath Valverde's face he was a dead man. Pizarro stood aside, with the Spanish viceroy Estete and the scribe. Pizarro was an old man. He ought to be sitting quietly in some village, outside the violence of life, giving advice and teaching the children. What kind of world did he come from, that sent men into old age still charged with the lusts and bitterness of the young?

Pizarro, too, looked as if he wanted this to end.

Atahualpa knew that it would not end. This was only the beginning. These men would suffer for this moment as they had already suffered for it all their lives, seeking the pain blindly over oceans, jungles, deserts, probing it like a sore tooth until they'd found and grasped it in this plaza of Cajamarca, thinking they sought gold. They'd come all this way to create a moment that would reveal to them their own incurable disease. Now they had it. In a few minutes, they thought, it would at last be over, that once he was gone, they would be free—but Atahualpa knew it would be with them ever after, and with their children and grandchildren and the millions of their race in times to come, whether they knew of this hour in the plaza or not, because they were sick and would pass the sickness on with their breath and semen. They could not burn out the sickness so easily as they could burn the Son of the Sun to ash. This was a great tragedy, but it contained a huge jest. They were caught in a wheel of the sky and could not get out. They must destroy themselves.

"Have your way, priest," Atahualpa said. "Then strangle me, and bear my body to Cuzco, to be laid with my ancestors." He knew they would not do it, and so would add an additional curse to their faithlessness.

He had one final curse. He turned to Pizarro. "You will have responsibility for my children."

Pizarro looked at the pavement. They put up the torch and took Atahualpa from the pyre. Valverde poured water on his head and spoke words in the tongue of his god. Then they sat him upon a stool, bound him to another stake, set the loop of cord around his neck, slid the rod through the cord, and turned it. His women knelt at his side and wept. Valverde spoke more words. Atahualpa felt the cord, woven by the hands of some faithful *puric* of Cajamarca, tighten. The cord was well made. It cut his access to the night air; Atahualpa's lungs fought, he felt his body spasm, and then the plaza became cloudy and he heard the voice of the moon.

12 January 2011

ISRAEL LAMONT WAS holding big-time when a Krel monitor zipped over the alley. A minute later one of the aliens lurched around the corner and approached him. Lamont was ready.

"I need to achieve an altered state of consciousness," the alien said. It wore a red suit, a lightning bolt on its chest.

"I'm your man," Lamont said. "You just try this. Best stuff on the street." He held the vial out in the palm of his hand. "Go ahead, try it." The Krel took it.

"How much?"

"One million."

The Krel gave him a couple hundred thousand. "Down payment," it said. "How does one administer this?"

"What, you don't know? I thought you guys were hip."

"I have been working hard, and am unacquainted."

This was ripe. "You burn it," Lamont said.

The Krel started toward the trash-barrel fire. Before he could empty the vial into it, Lamont stopped him. "Wait up, homes! You use a pipe. Here, I'll show you."

Lamont pulled a pipe from his pocket, torched up, and inhaled. The Krel watched him. Brown eyes like a dog's. Goofy honkie face. The rush took him, and Lamont saw in the alien's face a peculiar need. The thing was hungry. Desperate.

"I may try?" The alien reached out. Its hand trembled.

Lamont handed over the pipe. Clumsily, the creature shook a block of crack into the bowl. Its beaklike upper lip, however, prevented it from getting its mouth tight against the stem. It fumbled with the pipe, from somewhere producing a book of matches. "Shit, I'll light it," Lamont said.

The Krel waited while Lamont held his Bic over the bowl. Nothing happened. "Inhale, man."

The creature inhaled. The blue flame played over the crack; smoke boiled through the bowl. The creature drew in steadily for what seemed to be minutes. Serious capacity. The crack burned totally through. Finally the Krel exhaled.

It looked at Lamont. Its eyes were bright.

"Good shit?" Lamont said.

"A remarkable stimulant effect."

"Right." Lamont looked over his shoulder toward the alley's entrance. It was getting dark. Yet he hesitated to ask for the rest of the money.

"Will you talk with me?" the Krel asked, swaying slightly.

Surprised, Lamont said, "Okay. Come with me."

Lamont led the Krel back to a deserted store that abutted the alley. They went inside and sat down on some crates against the wall.

"Something I been wondering about you," Lamont said. "You guys are coming to own the world. You fly across the planets, Mars and that shit. What you want with crack?"

"We seek to broaden our minds."

Lamont snorted. "Right. You might as well hit yourself in the head with a hammer."

"We seek escape," the alien said.

"I don't buy that, neither. What you got to escape from?"

The Krel looked at him. "Nothing."

They smoked another pipe. The Krel leaned back against the wall, arms at its sides like a limp doll. It started a queer coughing sound, chest spasming. Lamont thought it was choking and tried to slap it on the back. "Don't do that," it said. "I'm laughing."

"Laughing? What's so funny?"

"I lied to Colonel Zipp," it said. "We want cocaine for kicks."

Lamont relaxed a little. "I hear you now."

"We do everything for kicks."

"Makes for hard living."

"Better than maintaining consciousness continuously without inter-ruption."

"You said it."

"Human beings cannot stand too much reality," the Krel said. "We don't blame you. Human beings! Disgust, horror, shame. Nothing personal."

"No problem."

"Nonbeing penetrates that in which there is no space."

"Uh-huh."

The alien laughed again. "I lied to Sepulveda, too. Our time machines take people to the past they believe in. There is no other past. You can't change it."

"Who the fuck's Sepulveda?"

"Let's do some more," it said.

They smoked one more. "Good shit," it said. "Just what I wanted."

The Krel slid off the crate. Its head lolled. "Here is the rest of your payment," it whispered, and died.

Lamont's heart raced. He looked at the Krel's hand, lying open on the floor. In it was a full-sized ear of corn, fashioned of gold, with tassels of finely spun silver wire.

Today

IT'S NOT JUST physical laws that science fiction readers want to escape. Just as commonly, they want to escape human nature. In pursuit of this, SF offers comforting alternatives to the real world. For instance, if you start reading an SF story about some abused wimp, you can be pretty sure that by chapter two he's going to discover he has secret powers unavailable to those tormenting him, and by the end of the book, he's going to save the universe. SF is full of this sort of thing, from the power fantasy of the alienated child to the alternate history where Hitler is strangled in his cradle and the Library of Alexandria is saved from the torch.

Science fiction may in this way be considered as much an evasion of reality as any mind-distorting drug. I know that sounds a little harsh, but think about it. An alkaloid like cocaine or morphine invades the central nervous system. It reduces pain, produces euphoria, enhances our perceptions. Under its influence we imagine we have supernormal abilities. Limits dissolve. Soon, hardly aware of what's happened to us, we're addicted.

Science fiction has many of the same qualities. The typical reader comes to SF at a time of suffering. He seizes on it as a way to deal with his pain. It's bigger than his life. It's astounding. Amazing. Fantastic. Some grow out of it; many don't. Anyone who's been around SF for a while can cite examples of longtime readers as hooked and deluded as crack addicts.

Like any drug addict, the SF reader finds desperate justifications for his habit. SF teaches him science. SF helps him avoid "future shock." SF changes the world for the better. Right. So does cocaine.

Having been an SF user myself, however, I have to say that, living in a world of cruelty, immersed in a culture that grinds people into fish meal like some brutal machine, with histories of destruction stretching behind us back to the Pleistocene, I find it hard to sneer at the desire to escape. Even if escape is delusion.

18 October 1527

TIMU DROVE THE foot plow into the ground, leaned back to break the crust, drew out the pointed pole, and backed up a step to let his wife, Collyur, turn the earth with her hoe. To his left was his brother, Okya; and to his right, his cousin, Tupa; before them, their wives planting the seed. Most of the *purics* of Cajamarca were there, strung out in a line across the terrace, the men wielding the foot plows, and the women or children carrying the sacks of seed potatoes.

As he looked up past Collyur's shoulders to the edge of the terrace, he saw a strange man approach from the post road. The man stumbled into the next terrace up from them, climbed down steps to their level. He was plainly excited.

Collyur was waiting for Timu to break the next row; she looked up at him questioningly.

"Who is that?" Timu said, pointing past her at the man.

She stood up straight and looked over her shoulder. The other men had noticed, too, and stopped their work.

"A *chasqui* come from the next town," said Okya.

"A *chasqui* would go to the *curaca*," said Tupa.

"He's not dressed like a *chasqui*," Timu said.

The man came up to them. Instead of a cape, loincloth, and flowing *onka*, the man wore uncouth clothing: cylinders of fabric that bound his legs tightly, a white short-sleeved shirt that bore on its front the face of a man, and flexible white sandals that covered all his foot to the ankle. He shivered in the spring cold.

He was extraordinarily tall. His face, paler than a normal man's, was long, his nose too straight, mouth too small, and lips too thin. Upon his face he wore a device of gold wire that, hooking over his ears, held disks of crystal before his eyes. The man's hands were large, his limbs long and spiderlike. He moved suddenly, awkwardly.

Gasping for air, the stranger spoke rapidly the most abominable Quechua Timu had ever heard.

"Slow down," Timu said. "I don't understand."

"What year is this?" the man asked.

"What do you mean?"

"I mean, what is the year?"

"It is the thirty-fourth year of the reign of the Sapa Inca Huayna Capac."

The man spoke some foreign word. "Goddamn," he said in a language foreign to Timu, but which you or I would recognize as English. "I made it."

Timu went to the *curaca*, and the *curaca* told Timu to take the stranger in. The stranger told them that his name was "Chuan." But Timu's three-year-old daughter, Curi, reacting to the man's sudden gestures, unearthly thinness, and piping speech, laughed and called him "the Bird." So he was ever after to be known in that town.

There he lived a long and happy life, earned trust and respect, and brought great good fortune. He repaid them well for their kindness, alerting the people of Tahuantinsuyu to the coming of the invaders. When the first Spaniards landed on their shores a few years later, they were slaughtered to the last man, and everyone lived happily ever after.

The Lecturer

I HAD, OF course, heard about the Lecturer before I accepted the position at the university. Stories of him had reached the West Coast, but his was not the kind of notoriety that makes any deep impression. The university, though reasonably well-known, was not first-rate, and the Lecturer's existence was less remarked upon than the record of the school's football team. None of this mattered to me. I could scarcely care less about unique features of the campus; all I knew was that no one had worked harder than I had to earn a degree, and no one deserved a tenure-track position more. When I received the job offer I felt a triumph that did not lessen my bitterness. When I told my friends, they did not talk about the Lecturer, but about how severe the winters in the Northeast were.

The move exhausted both of us; Jane and I worked very hard trying to make something of the small house we were able to rent on an assistant professor's salary. Money was tight for some time, and Jane was unable to find work. Yet it seemed we were quite happy at first. We spent our evenings reading or listening to music, we took turns cooking, we took walks on the Saturdays of that Indian summer through the wooded lanes outside the town. When the possibility of a job at the university gallery fell through, Jane concentrated on her painting, ran off some flyers, and started teaching a class in oils out of our home.

Each morning I would rise early and walk up to the campus, which was only five blocks from our house. The department was located in a building on the far side of the quadrangle, and so I would have to walk past the Lecturer where he stood on the truncated Greek pillar at the top of the slope in front of the library. The first few times I strolled by self-consciously, trying to act as if I were accustomed to him; I kept my eyes on the buildings ahead and gripped the handle of my briefcase tighter. I did not listen to what he was saying. A few days later I was comfortable enough with the new surroundings to stop for some minutes. It was soon after classes had started and the campus bustled with students: a few sprawled on the grass of the quadrangle, and a nervous freshman here and there had also stopped to listen. Other students threw their Frisbees past him.

"The first notable feature of contemporary architecture is its concern with a greater and more profound reality than that encompassed by the psyche of one individual," he was saying. "The proper focus of architecture, the modernist tells us, is on the space outside the individual and the clash of impersonal forces within that outer space. There is no place in architecture for the kind of philosophy that sees reality as determined by individual perception."

He looked exactly like a stocky middle-aged man. His legs were short and strong, and he had the neck of a pit bulldog. He was not going to fat. His complexion was florid, his hair bright red, thinning on top, and a bushy mustache dominated his face. I was later told that during the sixties he had worn his hair long with a red bandanna tied around his head, and I came across an old yearbook photograph of him, taken in the 1890s, that showed him with full beard, neatly trimmed, and flowing academic robes. My first September at the university he wore a wool suit despite the high heat of the waning summer, and he was to wear that same suit through the year, adding a scarf and heavy overcoat as winter approached.

He spoke vigorously. Gestures of his right arm would punctuate his rhetoric; spreading his fingers, he would slice home a point with a sweep of his extended hand. His voice was strong, if rather high-pitched. His tone was dogmatic. There could be no doubt, it told us, that the things he said were the absolute truth.

Architecture is not one of my interests, and I soon moved on to my office. I'd been forced to listen to too much of such academic sausage-grinding in my graduate career. Now that I had moved on, I worked hard at teaching, rewriting my dissertation for publication, and being agreeable to all factions in my new department. Yet he bothered me, perhaps especially because he seemed to bother no one else. I could not keep myself from occasionally thinking about the man on the pedestal. The responses of my colleagues to my questions were not illuminating. Once at lunch I managed to turn the conversation around to the Lecturer.

"Why do they keep him around?" I asked.

"Nobody's keeping him," said Duthie, whose specialty was the Restoration. "He's free to do whatever he likes. You might as well ask why they keep the weather."

Judy Boisner, who wore bright scarves and a grin, said, "It's a tradition. Like the exam policy and the Chancellor's Oak."

I nodded at both of them. I was not skeptical.

"Nobody knows," old Dr. White said, not lifting his eyes from his corned beef on rye. "I wondered once. I was convinced there was a good reason. It doesn't matter."

"I see," I said.

Killworthy, sitting next to me, said nothing. Later, as we walked back to our offices, shoulders hunched and hands holding lapels closed against a cold breeze, he told me the real reason was political.

"The Lecturer has nothing to do with the university." His voice was bright with eagerness to initiate me. "It's all a matter of creating the proper impression on those whose decisions can really make a difference to the people who want to continue in positions of comfortable security—and influence—in this circus. Ask yourself: who stands to gain the most from such a creature as the Lecturer?"

I opened the door for him, and we shook ourselves in the warmth of the hallway. We retreated to our separate offices. I had no idea what Killworthy was talking about. I doubted that he did himself.

Our small house smelled of the oils with which Jane and her few students cluttered the spare bedroom. The artistic crowd—or more accurately, the crowd of artistic dilettantes—Jane was keeping company with did not appeal to me. I began to spend more time on campus reading, grading papers, sitting in my office staring out the window at the treetops, gazing absently down at the footpaths crisscrossing the quad.

In November I assigned the students in my composition class a paper on the Lecturer. A five-hundred-word description. Many of the male students wrote papers that began like this:

> Throughout history there has been many types of institutions of higher learning from the Middle Ages until now. Many of these presented the university professor as the originator of information it was useful for the students to have. Here at State is the home of the famous Lecturer that is renown not only for his superior brain and his intellectual lectures, but also the ability of anyone that touches his shoe before a date to have sexual "relations" that very night.

Few of the women mentioned shoes or sex. During conferences that week I made some inquiries and discovered that "rubbing the Lecturer" for luck was authentic campus folklore. For sure, Chuck Bennetti, a sophomore, told me.

The unspoken truth was that the Lecturer was unconscionably boring, and the students realized it, and the only notice they took of him—such as that surrounding the sex-charm stories—was the result of their boredom. Before homecoming, students from arch-rival Syracuse would paint the Lecturer orange, but it aroused little indignation on campus and it did not slow him down. His methods for dealing with hecklers were antiquated.

"According to Faraday's Law, the line integral of the electric field around a closed path is equal to the time rate of change of the flux of the magnetic field calculated over the open surface bounded by the path of integration..."

"Shut up, shut up! I don't want to hear it!" a young man walking across the quad would shout, while his companions burst into laughter.

The Lecturer would ignore him. "If the surface of integration is fixed in space..."

"You mean lost in space, airhead!" one of the others would shout.

The Lecturer then might actually look at them, and smile. Not a smile of superior knowledge, or tolerance, or contempt. Not a smile older than the university, than any university. "No applause," he might say then. "Just throw money."

"I'm in pain," the first student would say. "I'm laughing so hard, Grandpa."

"So stop laughing and listen, Bub. You might learn something. If the surface of integration is..."

"SHUT UP!"

He would stop. "Student here wants to speak. What do you want to tell us, student?"

"Fuck you."

"That's all?"

"Fuck you! Asshole! Fuck you!"

"Thanks very much," the Lecturer would say. "If the surface of integration is fixed..."

I saw one such encounter late in the semester, a day when I was preoccupied with late papers and my first committee assignment. It made me unaccountably melancholy. On impulse I walked up to his pedestal.

It was around six, dark already. The quad was virtually empty of students, and the regular staff had all gone home. No one paid any attention after the hecklers moved away. The Lecturer glanced down at me without pausing in his delineation of the ideals of Jeffersonian democracy. I reached out and touched his left shoe. The leather was dull from generations of furtive contacts; I wondered that it had not been worn away entirely. Perhaps these were not the same shoes that he had worn fifty years before. But to begin to consider the source of his clothing was to open the first Chinese box in an infinite series of boxes, with little assurance of an answer in the opening and less that one would ever be able to stop.

I had a slight smudge of dirt on my fingertips. Nothing more. Feeling foolish, I returned to my office and a stack of ungraded papers.

The first flakes of the winter storm that had been predicted for that evening—the first of the season—had begun falling outside my window when a knock caused me to look up from the paper on which I was working. Stacey Branham, a student in my Postwar American Fiction class, stood uncertainly in the doorway.

It was quite late for an office visit. "Yes, Stacey," I said. "What's up?"

She shifted from foot to foot. "Can I talk to you about my term paper?"

"Sure."

She came in, closing the door behind her. I put the papers aside. She sat on the edge of the chair beside my desk and told me she was having trouble coming up with things to say. I had never noticed this problem as she dealt deftly with the boys who talked to her before and after class: she was a tall, slender blonde with intelligent gray eyes. I had more than once watched her cross her legs in the first row of seats in the Walton Annex. Lecture Hall B.

It soon became clear that she had not come to talk about her term paper, and that she had not happened by in the early evening, when the humanities building was deserted, by accident. She put her purse on the floor beside her, drew her chair closer, and as she leaned forward to ask an earnest question about Flannery O'Connor, rested her finely manicured hand on my leg.

"Stacey," I said. "You're not really interested in Flannery O'Connor, are you?"

"Yes, I am. 'Everything That Rises Must Converge' is my favorite story."

"Well." I was very nervous. "It's a masterpiece of irony."

"That's what I'm having trouble with." She smiled; I drew a deep breath. She smelled of Chanel.

I wheeled my chair back suddenly. "Why don't you come back, then... when you've worked out your ideas more completely."

She looked puzzled, a little frightened. "I didn't mean to—"

"No problem. I'll see you in class Friday, right?"

She took her purse and left, drawing her wool coat tighter around her hips as she swirled out the door.

I sat there for some time, closed my eyes, breathed slowly. My mind was without thought. I looked down at my hands resting on the desk; they shook ever so slightly, and I realized that I was terrified. There was a smudge of dirt on the first two fingers of my right hand.

By the time I left the building, an inch of snow had accumulated. Instead of crossing the quad I went down the access road behind the building so that I could avoid him. It was one of those crisp, cold nights on which sound carries for great distances. I could faintly hear his voice despite the still-falling snow. My vision seemed exceptionally clear: I could see every swirling flake in the pools of light beneath the streetlights. I felt my warm breath on my face, the moisture freezing in my mustache; I saw the condensation in the air. My footsteps made no sound on the sidewalk.

Jane had already eaten, and I could hear her in the studio with one of her students, Marsha, when I reached home. I didn't go up to say hello; instead I fixed my own supper from the lukewarm Stroganoff on the stove and the day-old salad in the refrigerator. I watched part of one of the Shakespeare plays—*A Midsummer Night's Dream*—on PBS and went to bed before it was over. Marsha hadn't left yet. I got into bed and turned off the light, but could not get to sleep. Papers remained to be graded, Stacey Branham remained to be faced, the man remained speaking on the quadrangle as snow caught and melted in his hair. I could hear the low voices of Jane and Marsha but could not make out more than a few words of Jane's instructions on how to use the palette knife.

I got up and washed the dirt from my fingers.

When Jane came to bed I was still not asleep. The clock radio read 12:17.

"I'm sorry I woke you," she said quietly.

"That's okay. It's late."

"Marsha stayed to talk and have some wine."

I turned from her, adjusted my arm beneath my pillow. After a moment I felt her touch my back.

"What's the matter?" she asked.

"Nothing," I answered quickly, then said, more slowly, "I don't know."

"You want me to stop this class?"

I still did not turn to her. "No. It's important that you teach."

She moved close, slipped her arm under mine and held me. We lay silent for a while. Her breath was warm against my back. She moved her leg over my hip; I rolled onto my back and she slid on top of me.

We made love with an intensity we hadn't had in a very long time. Jane wanted, needed me: the shock of that burned each moment into my senses. I realized that I needed her as much, if not more, and wondered that we had been living together for the last three months—and before that, back in California—so unaware of each other that we might only have been sharing an office. These truths came to me without thought, showed themselves in a carnality that was frightening in directness and austerity. Jane rocked over me with her eyes closed, the lines at their corners drawn so tight she looked to be in pain. I ran my hands over her hips and waist; her skin was feverish. The muscles of my belly were tight, my back arched. I cried and held Jane to me as if to make up for years of indifference in those few moments, as if we were doing penance for a multitude of casual sins, as if I might never have her again. She touched my face. Afterward, Jane fell asleep as if she had been poisoned. I lay awake while my sweat slowly dried; I shivered in the cold bedroom, wondering what had happened. Where were we? How had we gotten here?

The Lecturer. Like the body of a drowned man surfacing in a lake days after the storm that drew him under, he rose to trouble my circling thoughts. He came to the center, and he did not go away.

He did not go away. I tried to concentrate on the sound of Jane's slow breathing, the ticking of the furnace, the soft flip as the clock counted out each minute, the wind outside. I could not keep him out. I slipped quietly out of bed, pulled on clothes, and left Jane asleep. Unable to find my gloves, I threw on my coat and headed up to the campus, hands jammed into my pockets. It was bitterly cold. I walked briskly, but my feet were soon freezing.

I could hear his voice before I could see him. He was speaking as strongly, gesturing as fervently, as he did when there were people up and around to hear him. Instead he faced an unbroken sweep of snow that ran two hundred yards, from the library, over footpaths, beneath lampposts and trees, to the administration building at the other end of the quadrangle. As I approached, he turned to me and I could make out what he was saying.

"Descartes' second objection to placing faith in the reality of sensory experience amounts to this: however good our empirical evidence may be for the proposition that, for instance, we see a man, another feeling being, in front of us, such evidence is never good enough that reason is forced to accept it. The creature we see might be a diabolically ingenious conjuring trick by the malignant demon. And this possibility of error will apply to any empirical proposition; to be true it must be certified in a way stronger than any amount of empirical evidence could ever provide."

I stopped directly in front of him, in a snowdrift halfway to my knees. I looked up at him; he looked down at me. He kept talking.

"I want to speak to you," I said.

"Descartes found his solution in mathematics—"

"Please listen to me," I said.

"I'm doing the talking; you listen. You might learn something. In mathematics, some propositions we know to be intuitively true—"

"What are you doing? How did you get here?"

He then smiled that vacant smile. He sighed, and his breath fogged the air. "Student here has something to say. Speak up, student."

"That campus legend about you. Does what happened to me mean that it's true?"

"Accept as true only what can clearly and distinctly be perceived as being so."

My face burned. "What's that supposed to mean?" I said angrily. "The words you say don't mean anything. Things happen anyway."

"Analyze any problem into its simplest possible elements." The snow had gathered so thickly on his head that the strong light from the lamps behind him gave him a glittering halo. He ought to have caught pneumonia.

"Damn you! Give me a straight answer!"

"I don't give answers. I give lectures."

He towered over me, so obtuse he might have been made of stone. Suddenly I could not stand it. I leapt forward and grabbed his leg with both of my hands. He was taken by surprise, I think; this had to have happened to him before, but perhaps he did not expect violence from someone asking the bitter questions that only a man who didn't have any answers—a faculty member—would ask.

I tugged furiously; I screamed at him, not knowing what or why I screamed. He slipped momentarily, regained his balance and beat me on the head and shoulders with his fists. My rage grew and gave me a blind strength. I braced my leg against the pedestal and jerked harder, and this time when he lost his footing he came tumbling down on top of me. We sprawled in the snow.

Once I had him off I lost my purpose. He struggled out of my grasp and got to his feet. He was breathing hard. He was just another man, like me; he might have been Duthie, he might have been Killworthy.

"Excuse me," he said, and climbed back onto the pedestal.

That was fifteen years ago. He's still out there. He's still talking.

Buffalo

—for my father

I N APRIL of 1934 H. G. Wells traveled to the United States, where he visited Washington, D.C. and met with President Franklin Delano Roosevelt.
Wells, 68 years old, hoped the New Deal might herald a revolutionary
change in the U.S. economy, a step forward in an "Open Conspiracy" of
rational thinkers that would culminate in a world socialist state. For thirty
years he'd subordinated every scrap of his artistic ambition to promoting
this vision. But by 1934 Wells' optimism, along with his energy for saving the
world, was waning.

While in Washington he asked to see something of the new social welfare
agencies, and Harold Ickes, Roosevelt's Interior Secretary, arranged for Wells
to visit a Civilian Conservation Corps camp at Fort Hunt, Virginia.

It happens that at that time my father was a CCC member at that camp.
From his boyhood he had been a reader of adventure stories; he was a big
fan of Edgar Rice Burroughs, and of H. G. Wells. This is the story of their
encounter, which never took place.

IN BUFFALO IT'S cold, but here the trees are in bloom, the mockingbirds sing
in the mornings, and the sweat the men work up clearing brush, planting
dogwoods and cutting trails is wafted away by warm breezes. Two hundred

of them live in the Fort Hunt barracks on the bluff above the Virginia side of the Potomac. They wear surplus army uniforms. In the morning, after a breakfast of grits, Sgt. Sauter musters them up in the parade yard, they climb onto trucks and are driven by forest service men out to wherever they're to work that day.

For several weeks Kessel's squad has been working along the river, pruning trees along the road from Mt. Vernon to Alexandria. The tall pines have shallow root systems, and spring rain has softened the earth to the point where wind is forever knocking trees across the road. While most of the men work on the ground, a couple are sent up to trim the tops of the pines adjoining the road, so if they do fall, they won't block it. Most of the men claim to be afraid of heights. Kessel isn't. A year or two ago back in Michigan he worked in a logging camp. It's hard work, but he is used to hard work. And at least he's out of Buffalo.

The truck rumbles and jounces out the river road that's going to be the George Washington Memorial Parkway in our time. The humid air is cool now, but it will be hot again today, in the 80s. A couple of the guys get into a debate about whether the feds will ever catch Dillinger. Some others talk women. They're planning to go into Washington on the weekend and check out the dance halls. Kessel likes to dance; he's a good dancer. The foxtrot, the Lindy Hop. When he gets drunk he likes to sing, and has a ready wit. He talks a lot more, kids the girls.

When they get to the site, the foreman sets most of the men to work clearing the roadside for a scenic overlook. Kessel straps on a climbing belt, takes an axe and climbs his first tree. The first twenty feet are limbless, then climbing gets trickier. He looks down only enough to estimate when he's gotten high enough. He sets himself, cleats biting into the shoulder of a lower limb, and chops away at the road side of the trunk. There's a trick to cutting the top so that it falls the right way. When he's got it ready to go he calls down to warn the men below. Then a few quick bites of the axe on the opposite side of the cut, a shove, a crack and the top starts to go. He braces his legs, ducks his head and grips the trunk. The treetop skids off and the bole of the pine waves ponderously back and forth, with Kessel swinging at its end like an ant on a metronome. After the pine stops swinging he shinnies down and climbs the next tree.

He's good at this work, efficient, careful. He's not a particularly strong man—slender, not burly—but even in his youth he shows the attention to detail that, as a boy, I remember seeing when he built our house.

The squad works through the morning, then breaks for lunch from the mess truck. The men are always complaining about the food, and how there isn't enough of it, but until recently a lot of them were living in Hoovervilles—shack cities—and eating nothing at all. As they're eating a couple of the guys rag Kessel for working too fast. "What do you expect from a Yankee?" one of the southern boys says.

"He ain't a Yankee. He's a Polack."

Kessel tries to ignore them.

"Whyn't you lay off him, Turkel?" says Cole, one of Kessel's buddies.

Turkel is a big blond guy from Chicago. Some say he joined the CCCs to duck an armed robbery rap. "He works too hard," Turkel says. "He makes us look bad."

"Don't have to work much to make you look bad, Lou," Cole says. The others laugh, and Kessel appreciates it. "Give Jack some credit. At least he had enough sense to come down out of Buffalo." More laughter.

"There's nothing wrong with Buffalo," Kessel says.

"Except fifty thousand out-of-work Polacks," Turkel says.

"I guess you got no out-of-work people in Chicago," Kessel says. "You just joined for the exercise."

"Except he's not getting any exercise, if he can help it!" Cole says.

The foreman comes by and tells them to get back to work. Kessel climbs another tree, stung by Turkel's charge. What kind of man complains if someone else works hard? It only shows how even decent guys have to put up with assholes dragging them down. But it's nothing new. He's seen it before, back in Buffalo.

Buffalo, New York, is the symbolic home of this story. In the years preceeding the First World War it grew into one of the great industrial metropolises of the United States. Located where Lake Erie flows into the Niagara river, strategically close to cheap electricity from Niagara Falls and cheap transportation by lakeboat from the Midwest, it was a center of steel, automobiles, chemicals, grain milling and brewing. Its major employers—Bethlehem

Steel, Ford, Pierce Arrow, Gold Medal Flour, the National Biscuit Company, Ralston Purina, Quaker Oats, National Aniline—drew thousands of immigrants like Kessel's family. Along Delaware Avenue stood the imperious and stylized mansions of the city's old money, ersatz-Renaissance homes designed by Stanford White, huge Protestant churches, and a Byzantine synagogue. The city boasted the first modern skyscraper, designed by Louis Sullivan in the 1890s. From its productive factories to its polyglot work force to its class system and its boosterism, Buffalo was a monument to modern industrial capitalism. It is the place Kessel has come from—almost an expression of his personality itself—and the place he, at times, fears he can never escape. A cold, grimy city dominated by church and family, blinkered and cramped, forever playing second fiddle to Chicago, New York and Boston. It offers the immigrant the opportunity to find steady work in some factory or mill, but, though Kessel could not have put it into these words, it also puts a lid on his opportunities. It stands for all disappointed expectations, human limitations, tawdry compromises, for the inevitable choice of the expedient over the beautiful, for an American economic system that turns all things into commodities and measures men by their bank accounts. It is the home of the industrial proletariat.

It's not unique. It could be Youngstown, Akron, Detroit. It's the place where my father, and I, grew up.

The afternoon turns hot and still; during a work break Kessel strips to the waist. About two o'clock a big black de Soto comes up the road and pulls off onto the shoulder. A couple of men in suits get out of the back, and one of them talks to the Forest Service foreman, who nods deferentially. The foreman calls over to the men.

"Boys, this here's Mr. Pike from the Interior Department. He's got a guest here to see how we work, a writer, Mr. H. G. Wells from England."

Most of the men couldn't care less, but the name strikes a spark in Kessel. He looks over at the little, pot-bellied man in the dark suit. The man is sweating; he brushes his mustache.

The foreman sends Kessel up to show them how they're topping the trees. He points out to the visitors where the others with rakes and shovels are leveling the ground for the overlook. Several other men are building a log rail fence from the treetops. From way above, Kessel can hear their voices between the thunks of his axe. H. G. Wells. He remembers reading *The War of the Worlds* in *Amazing Stories*. He's read *The Outline of History*, too. The stories, the history, are so large, it seems impossible that the man who wrote them could be standing not thirty feet below him. He tries to concentrate on the axe, the tree.

Time for this one to go. He calls down. The men below look up. Wells takes off his hat and shields his eyes with his hand. He's balding, and looks even smaller from up here. Strange that such big ideas could come from such a small man. It's kind of disappointing. Wells leans over to Pike and says something. The treetop falls away. The pine sways like a bucking bronco, and Kessel holds on for dear life.

He comes down with the intention of saying something to Wells, telling him how much he admires him, but when he gets down the sight of the two men in suits and his awareness of his own sweaty chest make him timid. He heads down to the next tree. After another ten minutes the men get back in the car, drive away. Kessel curses himself for the opportunity lost.

THAT EVENING AT the New Willard hotel, Wells dines with his old friends Clarence Darrow and Charles Russell. Darrow and Russell are in Washington to testify before a congressional committee on a report they have just submitted to the administration concerning the monopolistic effects of the National Recovery Act. The right wing is trying to eviscerate Roosevelt's program for large-scale industrial management, and the Darrow Report is playing right into their hands. Wells tries, with little success, to convince Darrow of the shortsightedness of his position.

"Roosevelt is willing to sacrifice the small man to the huge corporations," Darrow insists, his eyes bright.

"The small man? Your small man is a romantic fantasy," Wells says. "It's not the New Deal that's doing him in—it's the process of industrial progress. It's the twentieth century. You can't legislate yourself back into 1870."

"What about the individual?" Russell asks.

Wells snorts. "Walk out into the street. The individual is there on the street corner selling apples. The only thing that's going to save him is some co-ordinated effort, by intelligent, selfless men. Not your free market."

Darrow puffs on his cigar, exhales, smiles. "Don't get exasperated, H. G. We're not working for Standard Oil. But if I have to choose between the bureaucrat and the man pumping gas at the filling station, I'll take the pump jockey."

Wells sees he's got no chance against the American mythology of the common man. "Your pump jockey works for Standard Oil. And the last I checked, the free market hasn't expended much energy looking out for his interests."

"Have some more wine," Russell says.

Russell refills their glasses with the excellent bordeaux. It's been a first rate meal. Wells finds the debate stimulating even when he can't prevail; at one time that would have been enough, but as the years go on the need to prevail grows stronger in him. The times are out of joint, and when he looks around he sees desperation growing. A new world order is necessary—it's so clear that even a fool ought to see it—but if he can't even convince radicals like Darrow, what hope is there of gaining the acquiescence of the shareholders in the utility trusts?

The answer is that the changes will have to be made over their objections. As Roosevelt seems prepared to do. Wells's dinner with the President has heartened him in a way that this debate cannot negate.

Wells brings up an item he read in the *Washington Post*. A lecturer for the communist party—a young Negro—was barred from speaking at the University of Virginia. Wells's question is, was the man barred because he was a communist or because he was Negro?

"In Virginia," Darrow says sardonically, "either condition is fatal."

"But students point out the University has allowed communists to speak on campus before, and has allowed Negroes to perform music there."

"They can perform, but they can't speak," Russell says. "This isn't unusual. Go down to the Paradise Ballroom, not a mile from here. There's a Negro orchestra playing there, but no Negroes are allowed inside to listen."

"You should go to hear them anyway," Darrow says. "It's Duke Ellington. Have you heard of him?"

"I don't get on with the titled nobility," Wells quips.

"Oh, this Ellington's a noble fellow, all right, but I don't think you'll find him in the peerage," Russell says.

"He plays jazz, doesn't he?"

"Not like any jazz you've heard," Darrow says. "It's something new. You should find a place for it in one of your utopias."

All three of them are for helping the colored peoples. Darrow has defended Negroes accused of capital crimes. Wells, on his first visit to America almost thirty years ago, met with Booker T. Washington and came away impressed, although he still considers the peaceable co-existence of the white and colored races problematical.

"What are you working on now, Wells?" Russell asks. "What new improbability are you preparing to assault us with? Racial equality? Sexual liberation?"

"I'm writing a screen treatment based on *The Shape of Things to Come*," Wells says. He tells them about his screenplay, sketching out for them the future he has in his mind. An apocalyptic war, a war of unsurpassed brutality that will begin, in his film, in 1939. In this war, the creations of science will be put to the services of destruction in ways that will make the horrors of the Great War pale in comparison. Whole populations will be exterminated. But then, out of the ruins will arise the new world. The orgy of violence will purge the human race of the last vestiges of tribal thinking. Then will come the organization of the directionless and weak by the intelligent and purposeful. The new man. Cleaner, stronger, more rational. Wells can see it. He talks on, supplely, surely, late into the night. His mind is fertile with invention, still. He can see that Darrow and Russell, despite their Yankee individualism, are caught up by his vision. The future may be threatened, but it is not entirely closed.

FRIDAY NIGHT, BACK in the barracks at Fort Hunt, Kessel lies on his bunk reading a second-hand *Wonder Stories*. He's halfway through the tale of a scientist who invents a device that progresses him through 50,000 years of evolution in an hour, turning him into a big-brained telepathic monster. The evolved scientist is totally without emotions and wants to control the world. But his body's atrophied. Will the hero, a young engineer, be able to stop him?

At a plank table in the aisle a bunch of men are playing poker for cigarettes. They're talking about women and dogs. Cole throws in his hand and comes over to sit on the next bunk. "Still reading that stuff, Jack?"

"Don't knock it until you've tried it."

"Are you coming into D.C. with us tomorrow? Sgt. Sauter says we can catch a ride in on one of the trucks."

Kessel thinks about it. Cole probably wants to borrow some money. Two days after he gets his monthly pay he's broke. He's always looking for a good time. Kessel spends his leave more quietly; he usually walks into Alexandria—about six miles—and sees a movie or just walks around town. Still, he would like to see more of Washington. "Okay."

Cole looks at the sketchbook poking out from beneath Kessel's pillow. "Any more hot pictures?"

Immediately Kessel regrets trusting Cole. Yet there's not much he can say—the book is full of pictures of movie stars he's drawn. "I'm learning to draw. And at least I don't waste my time like the rest of you guys."

Cole looks serious. "You know, you're not any better than the rest of us," he says, not angrily. "You're just another Polack. Don't get so high-and-mighty."

"Just because I want to improve myself doesn't mean I'm high-and-mighty."

"Hey, Cole, are you in or out?" Turkel yells from the table.

"Dream on, Jack," Cole says, and returns to the game.

Kessel tries to go back to the story, but he isn't interested anymore. He can figure out that the hero is going to defeat the hyper-evolved scientist in the end. He folds his arms behind his head and stares at the knots in the rafters.

It's true, Kessel does spend a lot of time dreaming. But he has things he wants to do, and he's not going to waste his life drinking and whoring like the rest of them.

Kessel's always been different. Quieter, smarter. He was always going to do something better than the rest of them; he's well spoken, he likes to read. Even though he didn't finish high school he reads everything: *Amazing, Astounding, Wonder Stories*. He believes in the future. He doesn't want to end up trapped in some factory his whole life.

Kessel's parents immigrated from Poland in 1913. Their name was Kisiel, but his got Germanized in Catholic school. For ten years the family moved from one to another middle-sized industrial town, as Joe Kisiel bounced from job to job. Springfield. Utica. Syracuse. Rochester. Kessel remembers them loading up a wagon in the middle of the night with all their belongings in order to jump the rent on the run-down house in Syracuse. He remembers pulling a cart down to the Utica Club brewery, a nickel in his hand, to buy his father a pail of beer. They finally settled in the First Ward of Buffalo. The First Ward, at the foot of the Erie Canal, was an Irish neighborhood as far back as anybody could remember, and the Kisiels were the only Poles there. That's where he developed his chameleon ability to fit in, despite the fact he wanted nothing more than to get out. But he had to protect his mother, sister and little brothers from their father's drunken rages. When Joe Kisiel died in 1927 it was a relief, despite the fact that Jack ended up supporting the family.

For years Kessel has strained against the tug of that responsibility. He's sought the free and easy feeling of the road, of places different from where he grew up, romantic places where the sun shines and he can make something entirely American of himself.

Despite his ambitions, he's never accomplished much. He's been essentially a drifter, moving from job to job. Starting as a pinsetter in a bowling alley, he moved on to a flour mill. He would have stayed in the mill only he developed an allergy to the flour dust, so he became an electrician. He would have stayed an electrician except he had a fight with a boss and got blacklisted. He left Buffalo because of his father; he kept coming back because of his mother. When the Depression hit he tried to get a job in Detroit at the auto factories, but that was plain stupid in the face of the universal collapse, and he ended up working up in the peninsula as a farm hand, then as a logger. It was seasonal work, and when the season was over he was out of a job. In the winter of 1933, rather than freeze his ass off in northern Michigan, he joined the CCC. Now he sends twenty-five of his thirty dollars a month back to his mother and brothers back in Buffalo. And imagines the future.

When he thinks about it, there are two futures. The first one is the one from the magazines and books. Bright, slick, easy. We, looking back on it, can see it to be the fifteen-cent utopianism of Hugo Gernsback's *Popular*

Electrics that flourished in the midst of the Depression. A degradation of the marvelous inventions that made Wells his early reputation, minus the social theorizing that drove Wells's technological speculations. The common man's boosterism. There's money to be made telling people like Jack Kessel about the wonderful world of the future.

The second future is Kessel's own. That one's a lot harder to see. It contains work. A good job, doing something he likes, using his skills. Not working for another man, but making something that would be useful for others. Building something for the future. And a woman, a gentle woman, for his wife. Not some cheap dancehall queen.

So when Kessel saw H. G. Wells in person, that meant something to him. He's had his doubts. He's 29 years old, a decade older than most of the other CCC workers. If he's ever going to get anywhere, it's going to have to start happening soon. He has the feeling that something significant is going to happen. Wells is a man who sees the future. He moves in that bright world where things make sense. He represents something that Kessel wants.

But the last thing Kessel wants is to end up back in Buffalo.

He pulls the sketchbook he was to show me twenty years later from under his pillow. He turns past drawings of movie stars: Jean Harlow, Mae West, Carole Lombard—the beautiful, unreachable faces of his longing—and of natural scenes: rivers, forests, birds—to a blank page. The page is as empty as the future, waiting for him to write upon it. He lets his imagination soar. He envisions an eagle, gliding high above the mountains of the west that he has never seen, but that he knows he will visit someday. The eagle is America; it is his own dreams. He begins to draw.

KESSEL DID NOT know that Wells's life had not worked out as well as he planned. At that moment Wells is pining after the Russian emigre Moura Budberg, once Maxim Gorky's secretary, with whom Wells has been carrying on an off-and-on affair since 1920. His wife of thirty years, Amy Catherine "Jane" Wells, died in 1927. Since that time Wells has been adrift, alternating spells of furious pamphleteering with listless periods of suicidal depression.

Meanwhile, all London is gossiping about the recent attack published in *Time and Tide* by his vengeful ex-lover Odette Keun. Have his mistakes followed him across the Atlantic to undermine his purpose? Does Darrow think him a jumped-up cockney? A moment of doubt overwhelms him. In the end, the future depends as much on the open-mindedness of men like Darrow as it does on a reorganization of society. What good is a guild of samurai if no one arises to take the job?

Wells doesn't like the trend of these thoughts. If human nature lets him down, then his whole life has been a waste.

But he's seen the president. He's seen those workers on the road. Those men climbing the trees risk their lives without complaining, for minimal pay. It's easy to think of them as stupid or desperate or simply young, but it's also possible to give them credit for dedication to their work. They don't seem to be ridden by the desire to grub and clutch that capitalism demands; if you look at it properly that may be the explanation for their ending up wards of the state. And is Wells any better? If he hadn't got an education he would have ended up a miserable draper's assistant.

Wells is due to leave for New York on Sunday. Saturday night finds him sitting in his room, trying to write, after a solitary dinner in the New Willard. Another bottle of wine, or his age, has stirred something in Wells, and despite his rationalizations he finds himself near despair. Moura has rejected him. He needs the soft, supportive embrace of a lover, but instead he has this stuffy hotel room in a heat wave.

He remembers writing *The Time Machine*, he and Jane living in rented rooms in Sevenoaks with her ailing mother, worried about money, about whether the landlady would put them out. In the drawer of the dresser was a writ from the court that refused to grant him a divorce from his wife Isabel. He remembers a warm night, late in August—much like this one—sitting up late after Jane and her mother went to bed, writing at the round table before the open window, under the light of a paraffin lamp. One part of his mind was caught up in the rush of creation, burning, following the Time Traveller back to the sphinx, pursued by the Morlocks, only to discover that his machine is gone and he is trapped without escape from his desperate circumstance. At the same moment he could hear the landlady, out in the garden, fully aware that he could hear her, complaining to the neighbor about his and Jane's scandalous affair. On the one side, the petty conventions of a crabbed world; on the other, in his mind—the future, their peril and hope. Moths fluttering through the window beat themselves against the lampshade and fell onto the manuscript; he brushed them away unconsciously and continued, furiously, in a white heat. The Time Traveller, battered and hungry, returning from the future with a warning, and a flower.

He opens the hotel windows all the way but the curtains aren't stirred by a breath of air. Below, in the street, he hears the sound of traffic, and music. He decides to send a telegram to Moura, but after several false starts he finds he has nothing to say. Why has she refused to marry him? Maybe he is finally too old, and the magnetism of sex or power or intellect that has drawn women to him for forty years has finally all been squandered. The prospect of spending the last years remaining to him alone fills him with dread.

He turns on the radio, gets successive band shows: Morton Downey, Fats Waller. Jazz. Paging through the newspaper, he comes across an advertisement for the Ellington orchestra Darrow mentioned: it's at the ballroom just down the block. But the thought of a smoky room doesn't appeal to him. He considers the cinema. He has never been much for the "movies." Though he thinks them an unrivaled opportunity to educate, that promise has never been properly seized—something he hopes to do in *Things to Come*. The newspaper reveals an uninspiring selection: at the Earle, a musical, "20 Million Sweethearts"; at the Rialto, "The Black Cat," with Boris Karloff and Bela Lugosi; at the Palace, "Tarzan and His Mate." To these Americans he is the equivalent of this hack, Edgar Rice Burroughs. The books that I read as a child, that fired my father's imagination and my own, Wells considers his frivolous apprentice work. His serious writing is discounted. His ideas mean nothing.

Wells decides to try the Tarzan movie. He dresses for the sultry weather—Washington in spring is like high summer in London—and goes down to the lobby. He checks his street guide and takes the streetcar to the Palace Theater, where he buys an orchestra seat, for twenty-five cents, to see "Tarzan and His Mate."

It is a perfectly wretched movie, comprised wholly of romantic fantasy, melodrama and sexual innuendo. The dramatic leads perform with wooden idiocy surpassed only by the idiocy of the screenplay. Wells is attracted by the undeniable charms of the young heroine, Maureen O'Sullivan, but the film is devoid of intellectual content. Thinking of the audience at which such a farrago must be aimed depresses him. This is art as fodder. Yet the theater is filled, and the people are held in rapt attention. This only depresses Wells more. If these citizens are the future of America, then the future of America is dim.

An hour into the film the antics of a humanized chimpanzee, a scene of transcendent stupidity which nevertheless sends the audience into gales of laughter, drives Wells from the theater. It is still mid-evening. He wanders down the avenue of theaters, restaurants and clubs. On the sidewalk are beggars, ignored by the passersby. In an alley behind a hotel Wells spots a woman and child picking through the ashcans beside a restaurant kitchen.

Unexpectedly, he comes upon the marqee announcing "Duke Ellington and his Orchestra." From within the open doors of the ballroom wafts the sound of jazz. Impulsively, Wells buys a ticket and goes in.

KESSEL AND HIS cronies have spent the day walking around the mall, which the WPA is re-landscaping. They've seen the Lincoln Memorial, the Capitol, the Washington Monument, the Smithsonian, the White House. Kessel has his picture taken in front of a statue of a soldier—a photo I have sitting on my desk. I've studied it many times. He looks forthrightly into the camera, faintly smiling. His face is confident, unlined.

When night comes they hit the bars. Prohibition was lifted only last year and the novelty has not yet worn off. The younger men get plastered, but Kessel finds himself uninterested in getting drunk. A couple of them set their minds on women and head for the Gayety Burlesque; Cole, Kessel and Turkel end up in the Paradise Ballroom listening to Duke Ellington.

They have a couple of drinks, ask some girls to dance. Kessel dances with a short girl with a southern accent who refuses to look him in the eyes. After thanking her he returns to the others at the bar. He sips his beer. "Not so lucky, Jack?" Cole says.

"She doesn't like a tall man," Turkel says.

Kessel wonders why Turkel came along. Turkel is always complaining about "niggers," and his only comment on the Ellington band so far has been to complain about how a bunch of jigs can make a living playing jungle music while white men sleep in barracks and eat grits three times a day. Kessel's got nothing against the colored, and he likes the music, though it's not exactly the kind of jazz he's used to. It doesn't sound much like dixieland. It's darker, bigger, more dangerous. Ellington, resplendent in tie and tails, looks like he's enjoying himself up there at his piano, knocking out minimal solos while the orchestra plays cool and low.

Turning from them to look across the tables, Kessel sees a little man sitting alone beside the dance floor, watching the young couples sway in the music. To his astonishment he recognizes Wells. He's been given another chance. Hesitating only a moment, Kessel abandons his friends, goes over to the table and introduces himself.

"Excuse me, Mr. Wells. You might not remember me, but I was one of the men you saw yesterday in Virginia working along the road. The CCC?"

Wells looks up at a gangling young man wearing a khaki uniform, his olive tie neatly knotted and tucked between the second and third buttons of his shirt. His hair is slicked down, parted in the middle. Wells doesn't remember anything of him. "Yes?"

"I—I been reading your stories and books a lot of years. I admire your work."

Something in the man's earnestness affects Wells. "Please sit down," he says.

Kessel takes a seat. "Thank you." He pronounces "th" as "t" so that "thank" comes out "tank." He sits tentatively, as if the chair is mortgaged, and seems at a loss for words.

"What's your name?"

"John Kessel. My friends call me Jack."

The orchestra finishes a song and the dancers stop in their places, applauding. Up on the bandstand, Ellington leans into the microphone. "Mood Indigo," he says, and instantly they swing into it: the clarinet moans in low register, in unison with the muted trumpet and trombone, paced by the steady rhythm guitar, the brushed drums. The song's melancholy suits Wells's mood.

"Are you from Virginia?"

"My family lives in Buffalo. That's in New York."

"Ah—yes. Many years ago I visited Niagara Falls, and took the train through Buffalo." Wells remembers riding along a lakefront of factories spewing waste water into the lake, past heaps of coal, clouds of orange and black smoke from blast furnaces. In front of dingy terraced houses, ragged hedges struggled through the smoky air. The landscape of *laissez faire*. "I imagine the Depression has hit Buffalo severely."

"Yes sir."

"What work did you do there?"

Kessel feels nervous, but he opens up a little. "A lot of things. I used to be an electrician until I got blacklisted."

"Blacklisted?"

"I was working on this job where the super told me to set the wiring wrong. I argued with him but he just told me to do it his way. So I waited until he went away, then I sneaked into the construction shack and checked the blueprints. He didn't think I could read blueprints, but I could. I found out I was right and he was wrong. So I went back and did it right. The next day when he found out, he fired me. Then the so-and-so went and got me blacklisted."

Though he doesn't know how much credence to give to this story, Wells's sympathies are aroused. It's the kind of thing that must happen all the time. He recognizes in Kessel the immigrant stock that, when Wells visited the U.S. in 1906, made him skeptical about the future of America. He'd theorized that these Italians and Slavs, coming from lands with no democratic tradition, unable to speak English, would degrade the already corrupt political process. They could not be made into good citizens; they would not work well when they could work poorly, and given the way the economic deal was stacked against them would seldom rise high enough to do better.

But Kessel is clean, well-spoken despite his accent, and deferential. Wells realizes that this is one of the men who was topping trees along the river road.

Meanwhile, Kessel detects a sadness in Wells's manner. He had not imagined that Wells might be sad, and he feels sympathy for him. It occurs to him, to his own surprise, that he might be able to make *Wells* feel better. "So—what do you think of our country?" he asks.

"Good things seem to be happening here. I'm impressed with your President Roosevelt."

"Roosevelt's the best friend the working man ever had." Kessel pronounces the name "Roozvelt." "He's a man that—" he struggles for the words, "—that's not for the past. He's for the future."

It begins to dawn on Wells that Kessel is not an example of a class, or a sociological study, but a man like himself with an intellect, opinions, dreams. He thinks of his own youth, struggling to rise in a classbound society. He leans forward across the table. "You believe in the future? You think things can be different?"

"I think they have to be, Mr. Wells."

Wells sits back. "Good. So do I."

Kessel is stunned by this intimacy. It is more than he had hoped for, yet it leaves him with little to say. He wants to tell Wells about his dreams, and at the same time ask him a thousand questions. He wants to tell Wells everything he has seen in the world, and to hear Wells tell him the same. He casts about for something to say.

"I always liked your writing. I like to read scientifiction."

"Scientifiction?"

Kessel shifts his long legs. "You know—stories about the future. Monsters from outer space. The Martians. *The Time Machine.* You're the best scientifiction writer I ever read, next to Edgar Rice Burroughs." Kessel pronounces "Edgar," "Eedgar."

"Edgar Rice Burroughs?"

"Yes."

"You *like* Burroughs?"

Kessel hears the disapproval in Wells's voice. "Well—maybe not as much as, as *The Time Machine*," he stutters. "Burroughs never wrote about monsters as good as your Morlocks."

Wells is nonplussed. "Monsters."

"Yes." Kessel feels something's going wrong, but he sees no way out. "But he does put more romance in his stories. That princess—Dejah Thoris?"

All Wells can think of is Tarzan in his loincloth on the movie screen, and the moronic audience. After a lifetime of struggling, a hundred books written to change the world, in the service of men like this, is this all his work has come to? To be compared to the writer of pulp trash? To "Eedgar" Rice Burroughs? He laughs aloud.

At Wells's laugh, Kessel stops. He knows he's done something wrong, but he doesn't know what.

Wells's weariness has dropped down onto his shoulders again like an iron cloak. "Young man—go away," he says. "You don't know what you're saying. Go back to Buffalo."

Kessel's face burns. He stumbles from the table. The room is full of noise and laughter. He's run up against that wall again. He's just an ignorant Polack; it's his stupid accent, his clothes. He should have talked about something else—*The Outline of History*, politics. But what made him think he could talk like an equal with a man like Wells in the first place? Wells lives in a different world. The future is for men like him. Kessel feels himself the prey of fantasies. It's a bitter joke.

He clutches the bar, orders another beer. His reflection in the mirror behind the ranked bottles is small and ugly.

"Whatsa matter, Jack?" Turkel asks him. "Didn't he want to dance neither?"

AND THAT'S THE story, essentially, that never happened.

Not long after this, Kessel did go back to Buffalo. During the Second World War he worked as a crane operator in the 40-inch rolling mill of Bethlehem Steel. He met his wife, Angela Giorlandino, during the war, and they married in June 1945. After the war he quit the plant and became a carpenter. Their first child, a girl, died in infancy. Their second, a boy, was born in 1950. At that time Kessel began building the house that, like so many things in his life, he was never to entirely complete. He worked hard, had two more children. There were good years and bad ones. He held a lot of jobs. The recession of 1958 just about flattened him; our family had to go on welfare. Things got better, but they never got good. After the 1950s, the economy of Buffalo, like that of all U.S. industrial cities caught in the transition to a post-industrial age, declined steadily. Kessel never did work for himself, and as an old man was no more prosperous than he had been as a young one.

In the years preceding his death in 1946 Wells was to go on to further disillusionment. His efforts to create a sane world met with increasing frustration. He became bitter, enraged. Moura Budberg never agreed to marry him, and he lived alone. The war came, and it was, in some ways, even worse than he had predicted. He continued to propagandize for the socialist world state throughout, but with increasing irrelevance. The new leftists like Orwell considered him a dinosaur, fatally out of touch with the realities of world politics, a simpleminded technocrat with no understanding of the darkness of the human heart. Wells's last book, *Mind at the End of its Tether*, proposed that the human race faced an evolutionary crisis that would lead to its extinction unless humanity leapt to a higher state of consciousness; a leap about which Wells speculated with little hope or conviction.

Sitting there in the Washington ballroom in 1934, Wells might well have understood that for all his thinking and preaching about the future, the future had irrevocably passed him by.

BUT THE STORY isn't quite over yet. Back in the Washington ballroom Wells sits humiliated, a little guilty for sending Kessel away so harshly. Kessel, his back to the dance floor, stares humiliated into his glass of beer. Gradually, both of them are pulled back from dark thoughts of their own inadequacies by the sound of Ellington's orchestra.

Ellington stands in front of the big grand piano, behind him the band: three saxes, two clarinets, two trumpets, trombones, a drummer, guitarist, bass. "Creole Love Call," Ellington whispers into the microphone, then sits again at the piano. He waves his hand once, twice, and the clarinets slide into a low, wavering theme. The trumpet, muted, echoes it. The bass player and guitarist strum ahead at a deliberate pace, rhythmic, erotic, bluesy. Kessel and Wells, separate across the room, each unaware of the other, are alike drawn in. The trumpet growls eight bars of raucous solo. The clarinet follows, wailing. The music is full of pain and longing—but pain controlled, ordered, mastered. Longing unfulfilled, but not overpowering.

As I write this, it plays on my stereo. If anyone had a right to bitterness at thwarted dreams, a Black man in 1934 had that right. That such men could, in such conditions, make this music opens a world of possibilities.

Through the music speaks a truth about art that Wells does not understand, but that I hope to: that art doesn't have to deliver a message in order to say something important. That art isn't always a means to an end but sometimes an end in itself. That art may not be able to change the world, but it can still change the moment.

Through the music speaks a truth about life that Kessel, sixteen years before my birth, doesn't understand, but that I hope to: that life constrained is not life wasted. That despite unfulfilled dreams, peace is possible.

Listening, Wells feels that peace steal over his soul. Kessel feels it too.

And so they wait, poised, calm, before they move on into their respective futures, into our own present. Into the world of limitation and loss. Into Buffalo.

Clean

HER FATHER taught electrical engineering at the university and had a passion for vacuum tubes. When she was eight, he taught her how to repair old radios. They would sit on high stools in his basement workroom and inspect the blackened interiors of battered old Philcos and Stromburg-Carlsons.

"Lee De Forest held the patent on the regenerative circuit," her father told her, "but that was an act of piracy. It was actually invented by Edwin Armstrong. Tell me what kind of tube this is."

"It's a triode," she would say.

"Smart girl." Her father took apart the wiring and made her, with a soldering gun, put it back together. Back then his hair was dark, and had not receded. She liked the way the skin at the corners of his eyes wrinkled when he squinted at some wiring diagram.

"This is hard work," he said after a while. "How about a poem?"

Her father had memorized scores of odd poems and obsolete songs. She blew on the bead of solder at the end of the wire. The pungent, hot smell got up her nose. "Okay."

"Here's one of my favorites," her father said. "*The Cremation of Sam McGee.*"

> "There are strange things done in the midnight sun
> By the men who moil for gold.
> The arctic trails—"

"Moil?" she said, laughing. "What does that mean?"

"You don't know what moil means? What are they teaching you in that school?

"Arithmetic."

"Moil means 'to toil, to work very hard.' Like we're doing right now."

"So why don't they just say 'toil?' It sounds the same."

"It's poetry, dear. It doesn't have to make sense. Hand me that spool of solder."

She couldn't remember how many weekend afternoons they spent down there in his workshop. Many. Not enough. She would never forget them.

ON THE MANTEL over the fireplace that they only used during Christmas sat a framed photograph. It showed Jinny's mother and father and a little red-haired girl who was Jinny, standing on a beach, squinting into the sun. Her father had one arm around her mother, and his other hand resting on Jinny's head.

Jinny hated going home for the holidays. Christmas was difficult; they had never been a religious family, and the celebrations seemed to involve increasing amounts of gin and vermouth. Her mother had checked out of the marriage emotionally years ago, her father spent hours in his workshop, but with Jinny there they felt obliged to spend time in the same room, and each of them bounced comments meant for the other off Jinny. As much as Jinny enjoyed seeing her dad again, she did not enjoy being the backboard for their loveless marriage.

She was in her third year of the PhD program in Sociolinguistics at Harvard. The night before she had gone out with some old friends to a club in Santa Monica, and she awoke with a head muzzy with a scotch hangover. She went down to the kitchen to find her father at the breakfast table in his bathrobe, staring at a cup of coffee.

He looked up at her with a dazed expression on his face. "Who are you?" he asked.

Always a joke with her father. "I'm the ghost of Christmas past," she said.

Her father's face worked with strong emotion. Jinny got worried. Her mother came into the kitchen then. "Dan, what's the matter?"

Jinny's father turned to her mother, looking even more puzzled. "Who are you? What is this place?"

"This is our home. I'm your wife, Elizabeth."

"Elizabeth? You're so old! What happened to you?"

"I got old, Dan. We both got old. It took a while, but it happened."

Jinny hated the bitterness in her mother's voice. "Mom, can't you see something's wrong?"

Dan raised a hand to point at Jinny. "Who's that?"

"That's your daughter, Jinny," Elizabeth said.

"My daughter? I don't have a daughter."

They calmed him, made him lie down and called the doctor. The doctor said they should bring him to the hospital for some tests. They took him to the emergency room. By the time they had arrived he seemed normal, recognized them both, and was complaining that he wanted his breakfast. The doctor had called ahead and they admitted Dan to a private room, gave him a sedative, and he went to sleep. Once they had gotten him settled, Jinny turned on Elizabeth.

"What's going on?" Jinny asked her mother. "This doctor expected you to call. This isn't the first time, is it."

"Your father has Alzheimer's. You talk to him on the phone. You haven't noticed him forgetting things?"

Jinny had. But she had chalked it up to normal aging. "Why didn't you tell me?"

"You're the one who is supposed to be so close to him. I just live with him. I'm going to the ladies' room." She turned away and walked down the hall.

Jinny sat by the bedside watching her father sleep. His gnarled hands lay on the blanket. A burn scar ran across the back of his right. His eyelids fluttered and he took an occasional restless breath; he was dreaming. She wondered of what. She remembered how as a girl she had had a recurring nightmare about some witch living in the basement, so that whenever he asked her to go downstairs to fetch something from his workbench she turned on the stairway light and rushed down and up as fast as she could, not looking into the dark corners. She'd grab the shop manual or screwdriver he'd requested and dash up the stairs two at a time.

She put her hand out and brushed his thinning hair behind his ear. He needed a haircut.

She tried to understand why her mother was so cold. After a while she heard her voice in the corridor, talking to someone. She moved toward the door and listened.

"You can bring him in anytime after he's released," a woman's voice said. Jinny peeked out of the gap in the door and saw a woman in a nurse's smock, maybe in her thirties, attractive in a mousy way.

"I'm not sure he'll want to go through with it," Elizabeth said

"Have him talk with Phoebe Meredith," the woman said. "Phoebe will draw him out."

Jinny pushed the door open. "Hello," she said.

The woman smiled nervously, "Hello. You must be Jinny."

"Who are you?"

Elizabeth started to protest, but the woman placed a hand on her arm. "I'm Connie Gray. I work in the trauma center,"

"This isn't the trauma center."

The woman seemed determined not to take offence. "Just talking to your mother. We met before."

"Jinny, please be civil," Elizabeth said.

"It's okay," Connie said. "This is hard on everyone."

"Is that Jinny?" Her father called sleepily from inside the room. His voice made Jinny's heart leap. She went back into the room, closing the door on her mother and the nurse. Her father was trying to prop himself up; she helped him get the pillow situated. His belly protruded under the blanket; she had not realized how much weight he had gained in recent years. "Sit down," he said, breathing heavily. "We've got a problem to face."

She sat in the chair beside the bed. "How do you feel?"

"Like they hit me with a sledgehammer. I didn't need the drug."

Jinny didn't tell him how upset and irrational he had been. She studied his face. He looked tired, but still her father. His smile was grim.

"Did your mother tell you about the plan?"

"What plan?"

He looked away. "There's a treatment that might help me. They say, if it works, that it can arrest the Alzheimer's and prevent dementia."

"That would be wonderful."

"There's a cost."

"We can afford it. Mom and I will find a way."

He rubbed his stubbly cheeks with his thumb and fingers, then slid them down his throat. "Not that cost. In order to not end up forgetting everything, I would have to forget a lot."

"I don't understand. Isn't loss of memory the problem?"

"It's the problem and the solution. It's just a matter of how much, and I don't know how much. They can't tell me, they say. But the more I give up, the better my chances."

Jinny wondered if she should call the doctor. He wasn't making much sense.

"I don't want to be useless," he said. "To be a burden on your mother, and you. I won't have that."

"You wouldn't be a burden."

"And I won't be. I won't be, Jinny. That's the point."

ELIZABETH DROVE THEM home from the hospital, Dan fidgeting in the passenger's seat.

"Calm down, Dan,' she said.

"I should drive,"

"You don't have to drive all the time."

"I can still drive," he said.

Elizabeth looked at him out of the corner of her eye. If only he would say what he felt. Did he even realize how he was withholding it? "I know, Dan," she said. "You can still drive."

Jinny was following them in the other car. When they got home Dan insisted he was fine and went down to his workroom. Jinny went down with him. Elizabeth sat in an armchair in the living room to read one of the briefs she had brought back from her office.

Her eyes kept slipping over the words. She had a silly kid's song in her mind. *I went to the animal fair, the birds and the beasts were there...* Dan had sung that song to Jinny when she was a child. He'd had a head full of such songs. Long before Jinny had been born he had sung them to Elizabeth in bed, after sex. The sex had been good at the beginning, and Dan's childlike remoteness, those moments when he seemed to drop out of the human universe into some near-autistic world of abstract thought, had not bothered Elizabeth then.

He had never been warm or demonstrative. He was at his best with ideas and objects. She might have been put off if not for his vulnerability and her understanding that he did not choose the way he was. And there were those songs.

At the university, he was not beloved by students. He had strict rules and he stuck to them. With his colleagues he was just as bad, and had never advanced within the department. Elizabeth ran interference between Dan and the social world he negotiated so poorly. The animal fair.

She gave up on the pile of papers—a sheaf of uncontested divorces, pure boilerplate—and listened for sounds from the basement.

Elizabeth wished that Jinny had not been home to witness Dan's latest episode. She supposed she should have told Jinny about Dan's deterioration, but she had dreaded Jinny's reaction. Jinny assumed that Elizabeth was jealous of her closeness to Dan, but that was not true. Rather, Elizabeth resented the fact that Jinny saw only Dan's good side whereas she had to deal with his depressions, his temper, his increasing distance. For Jinny he had infinite amounts of time and attention. For Elizabeth he had nothing.

After a half hour Jinny came back upstairs and paced around the room like a nervous cat. She had grown more angular since she had gone away, and Elizabeth wondered how her life was going. Like her father, she seldom confided in Elizabeth.

Finally, Elizabeth spoke. "For pity's sake, Jinny, please stop pacing."

Jinny abruptly sat down on the sofa and waited until Elizabeth looked her in the eye.

"New Life Choices, mom? It sounds like some online dating service. How did you even hear about them?"

"That nurse, Connie Gray."

"Dad told me what you're planning."

"I'm not planning anything."

"How could you consider having him erase his memory? Do you want him to forget you were ever married? That he ever had a daughter?"

"You saw him this morning. Did he know he had a daughter then?"

"But that's an illness. This is deliberate! You want to take away his life?"

"His life is coming apart. You don't have to live with it. You call on the phone every couple of months, come flying in here like a princess once a year, and you think you know him? I know him. I've known him for thirty-five years. I sleep in the same bed with him. I cook his meals. I take care of him when he's sick. I wash his clothes. I make sure his socks match."

"That was your *choice*, you—"

Elizabeth felt tears coming to her eyes. "I watch him across the dinner table and I can see that he's not exactly sure what I just said. I go to find him when he calls because he's forgotten the way home. When he forgets the first time we met."

"Mother—"

"It's too hard, Jinny. I'd rather see him lose it all in one clean sweep than lose it bit by bit."

She seemed to have gotten Jinny's attention. "I don't want him to forget me," Jinny said.

"He's going to, regardless. There's nothing anyone can do about it. What did he tell you?"

"He said—he said what you're saying. That he'd rather forget everything all at once."

"And the erasure people say that if his memory is cleaned far back enough, he won't suffer from dementia. He won't feel afraid, or lost, or paranoid. Do you want to see him raving, strapped to a bed, or medicated just to keep him from hurting himself? And he's going to need caretakers. I can't do it alone."

"If he gets erased, you won't have to do it at all! You'll just move on. Like you've wanted to do for ten years."

Elizabeth looked at her daughter. She could recall looking into the mirror thirty years ago and seeing in her own reflection that same certitude.

"You may think that I don't care about him anymore, but you don't have the right to say that."

"You made a promise. You're supposed to catch him if he falls. You're his wife."

"And who will catch me? Are you going to catch me, Jinny? Your father won't. I'll be alone. I've been alone for fifteen years."

Jinny launched herself from the sofa, her voice rising. "My god, *you* thought this up. You want to get rid of him. This is going to happen, and I won't be able to stop you."

"That's not fair."

Jinny turned and stomped out of the room.

Elizabeth listened to the sound of her steps climbing the stairs to her old room. From the basement she heard nothing. She wondered if Dan had heard any of this, and if he did, why wasn't he there to explain, to take responsibility for his own actions?

Why wasn't he there to tell *Elizabeth* what he thought about erasing *her* from his memory?

THERE WAS NO such thing as a soul. There were only the brain and its structures: the cerebrum, the cerebellum, the limbic system, the brain stem. And the substructures: the frontal, parietal, occipital, and temporal lobes. The thalamus, hypothalamus, amygdala, and hippocampus. That was all: the soul was a bunch of neurons firing. Or not firing.

Reuben read souls for a living. He knew where love hid in the brain. Lust, fear, confusion, faith, embarrassment, guilt. He saw them on his screen. He mapped them, in preparation for wiping them out.

But today Reuben was having trouble concentrating. Last night he had failed to ask Maria Sousa Gonsalves to marry him.

He glanced at the monitor showing the interview room where Phoebe was talking to the prospective client, an older man with thinning red hair. The guy—the tag on the screen read "Daniel McClendon"—was, according to the file, sixty-one years old. The pressure and temperature sensors of the chair in which he sat revealed a calm man, not anxious the way most of their clients were. The physiognomic software reading his face also raised no red flags.

Last night Reuben had meant to ask her at the restaurant, but in the presence of the other diners he lost his nerve. What if she said no? But when they went back to her apartment and made love, Reuben realized he could never be with another woman. The glint of her brown eyes in the faint light. The smell of her sweat beneath the perfume. As vivid in his memory as if it had happened a second ago.

Reuben checked the brain scan. Normal activity in McClendon's audio and visual centers. Though Reuben had the volume on the speakers turned down, he could hear the man's voice as he answered Phoebe's questions. Phoebe was good at putting clients at ease. That was one of her gifts.

Phoebe handed McClendon the pad and said, "On this pad you are going to see a number of perception and recognition tests. For example, you might see a page of the letter 'O'; and among them one letter 'C.' As soon as you spot the C among the O's, touch the indicator to move to the next image."

"I did these tests already, at the neurologist's," McLendon protested.

"I know," Phoebe said. "Just humor me on this."

As McLendon moved through the tests, Reuben noted his response. The man took a minute and a half to pick out the N in the field of M's. A normal response was ten seconds.

Phoebe thanked him and took the pad from his lap. "Okay then," she said. "Let me ask a few questions. What did you have for breakfast today?"

"A bowl of oatmeal. With bananas. Black coffee."

"Who is the president of the United States?"

"Please. Don't remind me."

"Do I need to remind you?"

"No, you don't," McClendon said. "Next question."

"What is Ohm's Law?"

"I'm not an idiot," McClendon said. A surge of activity in the amygdala. Anger, irritation—fear?

"Of course you aren't," Phoebe said. "You are a grown man, and an electrical engineer. Can you tell me Ohm's Law?"

"The current through a conductor between two points is directly proportional to...to the proportional...to the *potential* difference...to the *voltage* across the two points...and inversely proportional to the resistance between them."

Phoebe looked at her notes. "Can you tell me about the time you won the Draper Prize?"

McClendon answered. Reuben's mind drifted. He wished he could bring Maria in and put her under the scanner. He could ask her questions, watch the activity in her brain, and know for sure how she felt. Then he could take out the ring and give it to her and then she would say yes. They would marry and be together as long as they lived.

"Tell me about the first time you met your wife," Phoebe said.

"It was thirty years ago. I don't remember the details."

"Do you remember where it happened?"

"Her boyfriend—her boyfriend was another student in the EE program with me at Michigan State. We met at a party, or a restaurant, something like that."

"What did she look like?"

"She looked...she looked beautiful."

Phoebe continued through her inventory of questions. At the end, she asked, "Are there things that you don't want to forget?"

"Do I have a choice?"

Choice, Reuben thought. Choice was a function of the frontal lobe, the site of reason and analysis. Of course that was layered over activity all the way down to the lizard brain.

"Mr. McClendon, what you have erased, and the amount, is your choice. In order to give yourself the best chance at recovery, you will have to make some tough decisions."

"I know."

Phoebe waited, letting silence stretch. Reuben observed the flare of firing neurons in McClendon's cortex. McClendon leaned forward, his hands clasped together, looking at the carpet instead of at Phoebe. "Ms. Meredith, I'm a man who could recite you the twelve major sections, with the subheads, of the *Electrical Engineering Handbook*. That's who I am. And now it's going."

"Yes. It's going."

"I don't like it. The more I'm willing to erase, the better my chance to beat the Alzheimer's?"

"That seems to be the case. This is a radical treatment. Treating Alzheimer's is not something we normally do."

McClendon sat silent.

"We can peel your memory back as far as you will accept. How do you feel about losing your memories of your wife, your daughter?"

The temporal lobe activity flared higher, and there was a spike—probably some sharp image brought to mind—in McClendon's visual memory.

"Jinny was a surprise," he said. "We didn't plan to have children." McClendon picked at the knee of his trousers. "I didn't want to be a father. But when she was born—" he paused. "She was like a little animal in the house. I was intrigued by her. I watched her change. I taught her things."

He looked up at her. "It was very interesting."

"What will you miss the most?"

In McClendon's mind: fireworks. Electrical impulses spilled across his brain. Broca's region, the temporal and occipital lobes, cerebrum, and deep down, in the hypothalamus, amygdala, hippocampus. Something big, something emotional.

McClendon leaned back in the chair. He said nothing.

Reuben recorded it all, but it was useless unless McClendon gave them some outside reference. McClendon crossed his legs, rubbed the palm of his hand back over the top of his skull, flattening his hair. It would help if Phoebe got some verbal correlative out of him.

"What are you thinking about?" she asked.

"How can I say what I'll miss the most? How can you say what's the most important thing in your life? It's—it's really none of your business."

Reuben snorted. It *was* their business. He would be responsible for navigating precisely these minute regions when the time came to clean his memories. Locate the mysteries. Wipe them out.

Reuben didn't need any mysteries. In his pocket his hand played with the case containing the engagement ring. He knew what he wanted. He would ask her tonight. He would not hesitate, he would ask, and Maria would say yes, and they would be together.

DAN MCCLENDON WAS willing to take an aggressive stance. Phoebe needed that.

Most of the people who came to New Life Choices were looking to get rid of some specific memory and go on with their lives. Some of them were frivolous. McClendon was different. He didn't need to forget anything for emotional reasons—he was dealing with a physiological condition. Alzheimer's was going to empty his mind like a jug with a dozen leaks, and in the process break him. He was here to empty himself prematurely, with the hope that it would leave him unbroken.

But the volume of memories he needed to clear in order to do that was without precedent. He would not, in some way, be the same man. It was unknown territory.

In the beginning, Phoebe had considered cleaning to be a great boon to their clients. Deeply scarred individuals walked out of the clinic with a new ability to face the world, no longer with some debilitating cloud hovering over their heads. But years of observing people—and helping them—use cleaning for trivial purposes had increased her doubts. What kind of world would exist when everyone, instead of dealing with their problems, simply had them expunged? Her boss Derek seemed blissfully unaware of any drawbacks; he wanted her to take on more clients, but Phoebe was determined not to make cleaning become cosmetic brain surgery for people who got dumped by their girlfriends.

She needed to get a look at the scans Reuben had made during the screening. McClendon had not been forthcoming about his emotional investment in various elements of his past. Phoebe needed to know where the power memories lay.

She was packing up her briefcase when a young woman pushed into the office. She had flaming red hair and a distraught expression on her face. "Yes?" Phoebe asked.

"I'm Jinny McClendon."

"Come in. Sit down."

Jinny sat in the chair opposite her desk.

"How may I help you?"

"Right. I'll get to the point. I want you not to erase my father. I don't think you understand the situation. My mother is behind this. She's wanted to leave Dad for years, but she couldn't without feeling like the villain. This way she gets him to forget her, stashes him in some institution and walks away with a clean conscience. And the house, and his investments, and everything else."

Jinny McClendon's face was pale, eyes red. Phoebe tried to assess how seriously to take this.

She could understand Jinny's reaction—she had seen variations on it dozens of times before—but that did not make it the best one for either her father or herself. If she talked to her father, he might just change his mind and call off the procedure. For the sake of her daughter's feelings he might sacrifice himself.

"Your father won't be in an institution. I've spoken with both of your parents, independently and together. Your mother said that she doesn't want the house. She wants your father to still live there, so he can have some familiar things around him."

"Familiar things? How will he even remember them?"

"Many of them he won't. Understand, it's not easy for him. Cleaning gives him at least a chance of remaining a functioning human being. Maybe even better than just functioning."

"But he'll be alone, abandoned! Who will take care of him?" Jinny stood up. "I can't take this anymore." She opened the office door, but Phoebe called her back. "Miss McClendon. Jinny."

She hesitated, came back, but did not sit down.

"He must choose what he is going to clean from his memory," Phoebe said. "Yes, he will be alone, but he will have most of his rational capacities intact. He's be able to make a new life."

"He has a life already!"

"You know him better than I. But in order to save himself, he will have to erase the things that he would find it most painful to forget. He's going to forget you, and your mother, and most of the other people he's come to know in the last thirty years."

"The only thing he keeps are the things that don't matter?"

"Or the oldest. Alzheimer's patients often can vividly recall things that happened forty or fifty years earlier, but not remember what they had for breakfast." Phoebe took a deep breath. Sometimes the best way to deal with reactions like this was to come at them sideways. "Could it be, Jinny, that the reason your father's erasing you bothers you so much is because of your own needs? That wouldn't be an unnatural thing—for a daughter to fear the loss of her father's affections so much that she forgot the cost to him if he didn't go through with this."

"What do you mean?"

"I mean that maybe it's what you want that's in your mind, not what your father wants."

Jinny's face colored. Quietly, she said, "You're saying I'm being selfish?"

"That's not the best way to put it."

Jinny sat silent for a moment. "So I'm selfish. But what about you? Why are you so interested in doing this? I've heard Mom say that you're excited about the chance to use your erasing process to attack Alzheimer's. There's big money in this."

"I'm not interested in making money."

Jinny snorted. "But if it works, your boss will make a lot of money. And you'll be famous. All because you cleared away half of a man's life. Aren't you just a little bothered by that?"

"Of course I'm bothered. It's not something I'd do easily. I've worried about cleaning. I don't think it's a panacea. Far from it, in fact. Too many people treat it as one."

"Because you advertise it that way."

"I don't write the ad copy. I deal with the clients. I get to know them, I worry about them, I understand their motives."

"What, you have no self-interest? You're getting paid!"

"Believe me, I could find other ways to make a living."

Jinny's eyes narrowed. "Your conscience is bothering you."

Phoebe didn't know what to say. She sat there.

"You *don't* think this is the right thing to do!" Jinny said. "You don't care about my father—you're trying to prove something."

Phoebe stood up. "I've got nothing to prove. You're the one who is putting her self-interest above her father's welfare."

"It's not about helping him, it's about helping you."

"Ms. McClendon, I think we've gotten as far as we are going to get. Your father signed the papers. Your mother had medical power of attorney. If you have issues, you need to take it up with them."

Jinny McClendon got up to leave. She stopped at the door and looked back at Phoebe. Phoebe tried not to shrink under her gaze. She was not sure if she succeeded.

THE ASSISTANT'S HANDS were warm as she touched his forehead and throat peeled the paper off adhesive sensor pads stuck them on his temples brow base of his neck right and left connected them to heavy wires that tugged on his skin laid him down on the bed he didn't like lying on his back it left him stiff but the drug calmed him close your eyes she said breathe deeply think about a pleasant place a place you feel safe and secure the basement the workbench the old radios blow the dust away how many years had this one sat in a barn pigeon shit on the cabinet but when he hooked it up the dial still glowed green it took a while no sound instantly you had to let it warm up the tubes giving off heat glowing in the dusky interior wooden bench top covered with black scars from the soldering iron and a voice came out of the speakers

her hands on his chest in his hair touching his face you have freckles all over your shoulders she said and he laughed and covered her mouth with his pressed her down onto the motel bed is this a freckle he said touching her with his index finger and she shivered eyes closed eyelashes fluttering sunset light slanting through the Venetian blinds in bars showing the contour of her breasts and the rumpled sheets outside the sound of the surf and someone playing a radio

the doctor lifted his daughter's hand on the tips of his fingers and drew him closer and pointed to the newborn's pinky so tiny so perfect the fingernail so miniscule you needed a magnifying glass to see it but perfect nonetheless and he said see this finger dad and Dan worried said yes what is it and the doctor said that's the finger she is going to have you wrapped around and later he would put his own finger into his baby daughter's hand small pink soft and the hand gripped his fingertip so hard that strength of instinct holding on the way we held onto life don't let go Dad Jinny said her voice quavering I won't he said she wobbling down the street on the bike he was jogging alongside holding the seat don't let go she said and he let go and she sped off on her own away from him down the slope faster than he could run pedaling now and at the end of the street she stopped awkwardly gripping the handlebars and shouted back her face glowing with triumph I did it

on the third move his hand slipped and his left foot lost purchase and he fell not so far ten feet maybe but he missed the pad and came down wrong and the snap in his ankle the sound more than the pain told him this would be it for rock climbing and in some way he was relieved Dan are you all right Mickey his partner said everyone in the gym stopping and coming over looking up into their faces that pretty girl he always watched her when she climbed and it wasn't just the shape of her ass though that had something to do with it couldn't remember her name that was spring of '98 or was it '99 he couldn't remember smell of sweat in the air the throbbing pain now they helped him up awkwardly icepack and over the PA some song heavy fuzz bass and organ that reminded him of a sixties song he'd heard on his brother's transistor radio in the back of the pickup on the way to Green Lake

his brother's hands on the sides of the cargo deck what was his name he had two brothers and one of them started with an L or was it W how could he forget something like that but he didn't feel bad about it right now he felt calm it was okay they were going to take care of him it was easier to forget because trying to remember only made him anxious and now he wouldn't have to be anxious anymore and the person beside the bed holding his hand let it go

SLY WAS SCOUTING eBay to see what the latest bids were on his merchandise when he got the call.

"Hello," she said. "Is this Sylvestre Wesley?"

"Who wants to know?"

"New Life Choices gave me this number," the woman said. She sounded tired. "You did some work for them concerning my husband, Daniel McClendon. You cleaned the house for us."

Sly remembered McClendon. The item he was checking bids on was one of McClendon's radios. That was more than a month ago. "Yes, I did. Did I miss something?"

"No that's not it at all. Actually, I need you to—to bring some things back."

"Bring things back? That's not what I do, Mrs. McClendon."

"Nonetheless, I need you to bring them back."

Sly's job was making things disappear, and he was good at it. He was a contract employee at New Life, erasing files, destroying records, pulling government documents, and sweeping clients' homes of objects that would remind them of things they had paid large sums to have erased from their memories. It was a lucrative sideline, but not his day job. Normally he was a software engineer.

When they had called him and told him his next assignment was Daniel McClendon, the name seemed vaguely familiar. Then, when they sent him the files, he realized that he had taken a computer engineering class from McClendon a decade before.

Professor McClendon had been the strangest prof Sly had ever seen. Middle-aged, a little slow-moving, he conveyed the sense that the math he was so good at was just an elaborate game. In the middle of an explanation he would recite limericks about DRAM, or tell a funny story about the real reason the cell phone was invented, or sing some silly song. He had little patience for the slow-witted. He did complex calculations in his head, barely giving the students time to keep up.

Once a student had asked him to repeat an explanation, and he replied, "Look, I'm not going to repeat it. It's as simple as two plus two equals four."

"Can't you at least write it on the board?"

"Sure," McClendon said. He picked up his marker, turned to the white board and wrote:

$$2 + 2 = 4$$

Sly thought McClendon was a hoot. His attendance was not faithful, but he was good on the tests. As he listened to Mrs. McClendon's request, he realized it probably wasn't any treat to be married to him.

"They told me he would be an Alpha Package cleaning," Sly said. "That he'd wake up in the hospital and be told he had been in a car accident and suffered a concussion. That you wanted everything related to the family removed from the premises."

"Whoever told you that was wrong," she said. "He knows some things are missing, and he wants them back."

Sly was going to have trouble recovering everything. He was supposed to destroy it all, so it could not ever turn up again, but he had been supplementing his income by selling the more valuable items. "What things?"

"He wants his books. His Draper Prize trophy. The stuff from his workroom: his tools, his radios. His teaching notes."

"He's still teaching?" Reuben had told Sly that the guy was having more erased than anyone in his experience.

A bitter irony crept into her voice. "He can't remember my name, but he's back teaching at the university.

"I'll see what I can do." Sly had to get onto retrieving the radios right away. Those vacuum tubes, some of them eighty years old, were irreplaceable. The only source for them nowadays was when someone occasionally discovered a cache in some decaying Soviet warehouse.

A week later he showed up at the McClendon house with the back of his Jeep packed with junk. He'd gotten the tools and some of the old radios and the framed photos. He parked in the drive of the old craftsman bungalow and sat smoking a cigarette. Mrs. McClendon had told him to wait; she didn't live there anymore.

As he waited outside, the front door of the house opened and McClendon came out onto the porch. He looked a lot the way he did back when Sly was in school, maybe a little heavier, less hair. He squinted at Sly, then waved him over. Sly got out of the jeep.

"Got my stuff?"

"Yes sir."

McClendon stared at him a little longer than was comfortable. "You're Sylvestre Wesley. ECE 530, Physical Electronics. You missed too many classes."

"Yes sir."

"And see—see what you ended up doing? Bring my things in."

While he was ferrying boxes, Mrs. McClendon drove up in her Beamer. She saw that he was already almost done. Her husband, sitting in a wicker chair on the porch, was fiddling with an ancient 8-track tape player. He looked up, noticed her, and went back to the tape player.

Mrs. McClendon hesitated, standing by her car. There was a hurt expression on her face.

Sly didn't want to see them together. He interrupted McClendon. "Where do you want these boxes?"

McClendon put down the tape player. "Follow me." He took Sly into the house, down the steps to his workroom, and had him heft the unwieldy box full of coils and transformers onto the bench. McClendon sat on a stool and began unloading the items, slowly, examining each as he took it out. Sly went back upstairs.

Mrs. McClendon was in the living room looking over the only box of personal items that Sly had retrieved. "You needn't have bothered with these," she said. "He doesn't remember us at all. I don't know if what they did to him has changed him, or only wiped the fog off the glass so we can see clearly what's inside him. What's inside him is nothing."

Sly didn't need this. "He's had his memory wiped. You can't blame him."

"I can't?" Mrs. McClendon picked up a framed photograph from the box. It showed her husband and her and a little red-haired girl standing on a beach, squinting into the sun. Her husband had one arm around her, his other hand resting on the little girl's head.

"In that picture you look happy," Sly said awkwardly.

She put it on the mantle over the fireplace. "Let him try to figure out what it means." And she walked out.

After she left he finished moving the things in. He hesitated, then went down to tell McClendon he was done. The professor was still hunched over the tubes and wires, old resistors and condensers looking like foil-wrapped candies, wirewound pots, rheostats, worn schematics telling how it all fit together so it might work again, on fragile paper turned brown around the edges. "I'm finished," Sly said.

"That's good," McClendon said softly.

Sly couldn't just leave. "You know I wasn't the best student, but I liked your class. I liked all those stories you would tell.'

McClendon turned and looked at him. "Stories? I don't—I don't know any stories."

THREE MONTHS IN Cambridge had not helped Jinny to deal with the aftermath of her father's erasure. She had avoided calling home, had refused any attempts Elizabeth made to contact her, erased her emails unread, refused the phone calls, wiped out any voicemails without listening to them. Then, in a casual conversation with her cousin Brittany, she heard that her father was back teaching at the university.

"What? How can that be?"

"Apparently he was able to keep all his intellectual abilities."

Jinny called her mother. "No, he doesn't remember us," her mother told her. "He's as awkward as a grad student with Asperger's, can hardly carry on a conversation."

"But he can still do his work?"

"He made a bet that he could keep the electrical engineering and still beat the Alzheimer's," her mother said. "Looks like he won." She sounded remarkably philosophical about the whole thing, not the bitter woman she had been when they lived together. "But everything else is gone. He peeled his memory back to before you were born, to before he ever met me. He reminds me of what he was like when we first met. He acts like a young, poorly socialized man."

"I'm coming to see him."

The line was silent for a moment. "If you have to. But honey, I don't know if it's going to make you feel any better."

"I have to."

Jinny talked to her mother for an hour. Elizabeth tried to alert her about what to expect. Then Jinny booked a flight for that weekend; the plane touched down at four in the afternoon on Friday, and she rented a car and drove straight to the house.

She hesitated on the porch, considered knocking, and rang the doorbell. She heard sounds from inside, and through the glass in the door saw him come toward her. He opened the door wide and spoke to her through the screen door. "What do you want?"

Physically, he looked good. He had lost some weight. He was clean shaven, his hair brushed back from his high forehead. He had his shirtsleeves rolled up and a pair of needle-nosed pliers in his left hand.

"May I come in?"

"You're my daughter, are you?"

"Yes." Her voice caught in her throat. "You remember me?"

He opened the door and let her in. "They told me I had a wife and daughter. The woman comes around sometimes. I'm working. If you want to talk you have to come down with me."

They went downstairs. He had a big RCA cabinet radio half taken apart on the floor. The thing must date back to the 1940s; it was an elaborate set, with AM and shortwave reception and a built-in record player with a 78-rpm turntable. The cabinetry was beautiful, inlaid chevrons of dark and light wood. The turntable was dismounted, exposing the wiring.

She sat on a stool next to him, held a light so he could see as he worked his narrow hands into the interior of the cabinet. She could not think of much to say, overwhelmed by his physical presence, the smell of the solder in the hot, musty basement. His sinewy arms and intent, old man's face. He made no attempt to put her at ease.

She asked him questions about the radio set. When he realized that she could tell a capacitor from a resistor, he let her help him. She took off her sweater and got down on her knees to be closer.

"Why do you like these old radios?" she asked him. "It's hard to get parts. They can't even pick up FM, let alone satellite. Nothing but political rants and holy rollers."

He did not look at her, concentrating on the work. "They're simple," he said. "I can understand every piece of them. I can take them completely apart and put them completely back together again. A modern circuit you can't see without a microscope. I know how that works, too, but I can't put my hands on it. If it breaks, you can't fix it—you just throw it away. This light isn't getting in there. We have to turn this cabinet around. Help me."

He started to get up, his legs failed him, and he had to make a second attempt before he got to his feet. "I'm old," he said. "I keep forgetting."

Together they wrestled the bulky radio around so that the bench light was more useful. Her father exhaled sharply and drew his forearm across his forehead. "Do you want a coke?"

"Sure."

He got two old-fashioned glass bottles from the basement refrigerator and popped the caps, handed one to her. Jinny took a drink. She watched him lean down into the cabinet again, squinting.

"Would you like to hear a poem?" she asked.

"A—a poem?" Her father lifted his head and looked at her, eyebrows arched.

"It starts like this: 'There are strange things done in the midnight sun, by the men who moil for gold—'"

"Moil? What does that mean?" he asked. He looked so trusting, like a child of eight.

Jinny moved in closer so she could see into the cabinet. "It means to work hard. Like we're doing now."

Another Orphan

And I only am escaped alone to tell thee.

—Job

ONE

HE WOKE to darkness and swaying and the stink of many bodies. He tried to lift his head and reach across the bed and found he was not in his bed at all. He was in a canvas hammock that rocked back and forth in a room of other hammocks.

"Carol?" Still half-asleep, he looked around, then lay back, hoping that he might wake and find this just a dream. He felt the distance from himself he often felt in dreams. But the room did not go away, and the smell of sweat and salt water and the stink of something rotting became more real. The light slanting down through a latticed grating above him became brighter; he heard the sound of water and the creak of canvas, and the swaying did not stop, and the men about him began to stir. It came to him, in that same dreamlike calm, that he was on a ship.

A bell sounded twice, then twice again. Most of the other men were up, grumbling, and stowing away the hammocks.

"What ails you, Fallon?" someone called. "Up, now."

TWO

HIS NAME WAS Patrick Fallon. He was thirty-two years old, a broker for a commission house at the Chicago Board of Trade. He played squash at an

415

athletic club every Tuesday and Thursday night. He lived with a woman named Carol Bukaty.

The night before, he and Carol had gone to a party thrown by one of the other brokers and his wife. As sometimes happened with these parties, this one had degenerated into an exchange of sexual innuendo, none of it serious, but with undertones of suspicion and the desire to hurt. Fallon drank too much wine and said a few things about Carol that he immediately wanted to retract. They drove back from the party in silence, but the minute they closed the door it was a fight. Neither of them shouted, but his quiet statement that he did not respect her at all and hers that she was sickened by his excess managed quite well. They had become adept at getting at each other. They had, in the end, made up, and had made love.

As Fallon had lain there on the edge of sleep, he'd had the thought that what had happened that evening was silly, but not funny. That something was wrong.

Fallon had the headache that was the residue of the wine; he could still smell Carol. He was hungry and dazed as he stumbled into the bright sunlight on the deck of the ship. It was there. It was real. He was awake. The ocean stretched flat and empty in all directions. The ship rolled slightly as it made way with the help of a light wind, and despite the early morning it was already hot. He did not hear the sound or feel the vibration of an engine. Fallon stared, unable to collect the scattered impressions into coherence; they were all consistent with the picture of an antiquated sailing ship on a very real ocean, all insane when compared with where his mind told him he ought to be.

The men had gone to their work as soon as they'd stretched into the morning light. They wore drab shirts and canvas trousers; most were barefoot. Fallon walked unsteadily along the deck, trying to keep out of their way as they set to scrubbing the deck. The ship was unlike anything he had ever seen on Lake Michigan; he tried to ignore the salt smell that threatened to make it impossible for him to convince himself this was Lake Michigan. Yet it seemed absurd for such a small vessel to be in the middle of an ocean. He knew that the Coast Guard kept sailing ships for training its cadets, but these were no cadets.

The deck was worn, scarred, and greasy with a kind of oily, clear lardlike grease. The rail around the deck was varnished black and weather-beaten, but the pins set through it to which the rigging was secured were ivory. Fallon touched one—it was some kind of tooth. More ivory was used for rigging-blocks and on the capstan around which the anchor chain was wound. The ship was a thing of black wood fading to white under the assault of water and sun, and of white ivory corroding to black under the effect of dirt and hard use. Three long-boats, pointed at both ends, hung from arms of wood and metal on the left—the port—side; another such boat was slung at the rear of the deck on the starboard side, and on the raised part of the deck behind the mainmast two other boats were turned turtle and secured. Add to this the large hatch on the main deck and a massive brick structure that looked like some old-fashioned oven just behind the front mast, and there hardly seemed room for the fifteen or twenty men on deck to go about their business. There was certainly no place to hide.

"Fallon! Set your elbows to that deck, or I shall have to set your nose to it!" A short sandy-haired man accosted him. Stocky and muscular, he was some authority; there was insolence in his grin, and some seriousness. The other men looked up.

Fallon got out of the man's way. He went over to one of the groups washing down the deck with salt water, large scrub brushes, and what looked like push brooms with leather flaps instead of bristles, like large versions of the squeegees used to clean windows. The sandy-haired man watched him as he got down on his hands and knees and grabbed one of the brushes.

"There's a good lad, now. Ain't he, fellows?"

A couple of them laughed. Fallon started scrubbing, concentrating on the grain of the wood, at first fastidious about not soaking the already damp trousers he had apparently slept in, soon realizing that that was a lost cause. The warm water was sloshed over them, the men leaned on the brushes, and the oil slowly flaked up and away through the spaces in the rail into the sea. The sun rose, and it became even hotter. Now and then one of the men tried to say a word or two to him, but he did not answer.

"Fallon here's got the hypos," someone said.

"Or the cholera," another said. "He does look a bit bleary about the eye. Are you thirsty, Fallon? D'your legs ache? Are your bowels knotted?"

"My bowels are fine," he said.

That brought a good laugh. "Fine, he says! Manxman!" The sailor called to a decrepit old man leaning on his squeegee. "Tell the King-Post that Fallon's bowels are fine, now! The scrubbing does seem to have eased them."

"Don't ease them here, man!" the old man said. The men roared again, and the next bucket of water was sloshed up between Fallon's legs.

THREE

IN THE MOVIES men faced similar situations. The amnesiac soldier came to on a farm in Wales. Invariably the soldier would give evidence of his confusion, challenging the farm owner, pestering his fellow workers with questions about where he was and how he got there, telling them of his persistent memory of a woman in white with golden hair. Strangely—strangely even to Fallon—he did not feel that way. Confusion, yes, dread, curiosity—but no desire to call attention to himself, to try to make the obvious reality of his situation give way to the apparent reality of his memories. He did not think this was because of any strength of character or remarkable powers of adaptation. In fact, everything he did that first day revealed his ignorance of what he was supposed to know and do on the ship. He did not feel any great presence of mind; for minutes at a time he would stop working, stunned with awe and fear at the simple alienness of what was happening. If it was a dream, it was a vivid dream. If anything was a dream, it was Carol and the Chicago Board of Trade.

The soldier in the movie always managed, despite the impediments of his amnesia and the ignorance of those around him, to find the rational answer to his mystery. The shell fragment that had grazed his forehead in Normandy had sent him back to a Wessex sanitorium, from which he had wandered during an air raid, to be picked up by a local handyman driving his lorry to Llanelly who in the course of the journey decided to turn a few quid by leasing the poor soldier to a farmer as his half-wit cousin laborer. So it had to be that some physicist at the University of Chicago, working on the modern equivalent of the Manhattan Project, had accidentally created a field of gravitational energy so intense that a vagrant vortex had broken free from it and, in its lightning progress through the city on its way to extinction, plucked Fallon from his bed in the suburbs, sucked him through a puncture in the fabric of space and time, to deposit him in a hammock on a mid-nineteenth-century sailing ship. Of course.

Fallon made a fool of himself ten times over during the day. Despite his small experience with fresh-water sailing, he knew next to nothing about the work he was meant to do on this ship. Besides cleaning the deck and equipment, the men scrubbed a hard black soot from the rigging and spars. Fallon would not go up into the rigging. He was afraid, and tried to find work enough on the deck. He did not ask where the oil and soot had come from; it was obvious the source had been the brick furnace that was now topped by a tight-fitting wooden cover. Some of the cracks in the deck were filled with what looked like dried blood, but it was only the casual remark of one of the other men that caused him to realize, shocked at his own slowness, that this was a whaling ship.

The crew was an odd mixture of types and races; there were white and Black, a group of six Asians who sat apart on the rear deck and took no part in the work, men with British and German accents and an eclectic collection of others—Polynesians, an Indian, a huge shaven-headed Black African, and a mostly naked man covered from head to toe with purple tattoos, whorls and swirls and vortexes, images and symbols, none of them quite decipherable as a familiar object or person. After the decks had been scrubbed to a remarkable whiteness, the mate named Flask set Fallon to tarring some heavy ropes in the forepart of the ship, by himself, where he would be out of the others' way. The men seemed to realize that something was wrong with him, but apparently did not take it amiss that one of their number should begin acting strangely.

Which brought him, hands and wrists smeared with warm tar, to the next question: how did they know who he was? He was Fallon to all of them. He had obviously been there before he awakened; he had been a regular member of the crew with a personality and a role to fill. He knew nothing of that. He had the overwhelming desire to get hold of a mirror to see whether the face he wore was indeed the face he had worn in Chicago the night before.

The body was the same, down to the appendix scar he'd carried since he was nine years old. His arms and hands were the same; the fatigue he felt and the rawness of his skin told him he had not been doing this type of work long. So assume he was there in his own person, his Chicago person, the *real* Fallon. Was there now some confused nineteenth-century sailor wandering around a brokerage house on Van Buren? The thought made him smile. The sailor at the Board of Trade would probably get the worse of it.

So they knew who he was, even if he didn't remember ever having been here before. There was a Patrick Fallon on the ship, and he had somehow been brought here to fill that role. Reasons unknown. Method unknown. Way out...

Think of it as an adventure. How many times as a boy had he dreamed of similar escapes from the mundane? Here he was, the answer to a dream, twenty-five years later. It would make a tremendous story when he got back, if he could find someone he could trust enough to tell it to—if he could get back.

There was a possibility that he tried to keep himself from dwelling on. He had come here while asleep, and though this reality gave no evidence of being a dream, if there was a symmetry to insanity, then on waking the next morning, might he not be back in his familiar bed? Logic presented the possibility. He tried not to put too much faith in logic. Logic had not helped him when he was on the wrong side of the soybean market in December 1980.

The long tropic day declined; the sunset was a travel agent's dream. They were traveling east, by the signpost of that light. Fallon waited, sitting by a coil of rope, watching the helmsman at the far end of the ship lean, dozing, on the long ivory tiller that served this ship in place of the wheel with handspikes he was familiar with from Errol Flynn movies. It had to be a bone from some long-dispatched whale, another example of the savage Yankee practicality of whoever had made this whaler. It was a queerly innocent, gruesome artistry. Fallon had watched several idle sailors in the afternoon carving pieces of bone while they ate their scrap of salt pork and hard bread.

"Fallon, you can't sleep out here tonight, unless you want the Old Man to find you lying about." It was a tall sailor of about Fallon's age. He had come down from aloft shortly after Fallon's assignment to the tar bucket, had watched him quietly for some minutes before giving him a few pointers on how the work was done. In the falling darkness Fallon could not make out his expression, but the voice held a quiet distance that might mask just a trace of kindness. Fallon tried to get up and found his legs had grown so stiff he failed on the first try. The sailor caught his arm and helped him to his feet. "You're all right?"

"Yes." Fallon was embarrassed.

"Let's get below, then." They stepped toward the latticed hatch near the bow.

"And there he is," the sailor said, pausing, lifting his chin aft.

"Who?" Fallon looked back with him and saw the black figure there, heavily bearded, tall, in a long coat, steadying himself by a hand in the rigging. The oil lamp above the compass slightly illuminated the dark face—and gleamed deathly white along the ivory leg that projected from beneath his black coat. Fixed, immovable, the man leaned heavily on it.

"Ahab," the sailor said.

FOUR

LYING IN THE hammock, trying to sleep, Fallon was assaulted by the feverish reality of where he was. The ship rocked him like a gentle parent in its progress through the calm sea; he heard the rush of water breaking against the hull as the *Pequod* made headway, the sighing of the breeze above, heard the steps of the night watch on deck, the occasional snap of canvas, the creaking of braces; he sweated in the oppressive heat belowdecks; he drew heavy breaths, trying to calm himself, of air laden with the smell of mildewed canvas and what he now knew to be whale oil. He held his hands before his face and in the profound darkness knew them to be his own. He touched his neck and felt the slickness of sweat beneath the beard. He ran his tongue over his lips and tasted salt. Through the open hatch he could make out stars that were unchallenged by any other light. Would the stars be the same in a book as they were in reality?

In a book. Any chance he had to sleep flew from him whenever he ran up against that thought. Any logic he brought to bear on his situation crumbled under the weight of that absurdity. A time machine he could accept, some chance cosmic displacement that sucked him into the past. But not into a book. That was insanity; that was hallucination. He knew that if he could sleep now, he would wake once more in the real world. But he had nothing to grab hold of. He lay in the darkness listening to the ship and could not sleep at all.

They had been compelled to read *Moby-Dick* in the junior-year American Renaissance class he'd taken to fulfill the last of his humanities requirements. Fallon remembered being bored to tears by most of Melville's book, struggling with his interminable sentences, his woolly speculations that had no bearing on the story; he remembered being caught up by parts of that story. He had seen the movie with Gregory Peck. Richard Basehart, king of the sci-fi flicks, had played Ishmael. Fallon had not seen anyone who looked like Richard Basehart on the ship. The mate, Flask—he remembered that name now. He remembered that all the harpooneers were savages. Queequeg.

He remembered that in the end, everyone but Ishmael died.

He had to get back. Sleep, sleep, you idiot, he told himself. He could not keep from laughing; it welled up in his chest and burst through his tightly closed lips. He sounded more like a man gasping for breath than one overwhelmed by humor: he barked, he chuckled, he sucked in sudden drafts of air as he tried to control the spasms. Tears were in his eyes, and he twisted his head from side to side as if he were strapped to a bed in some ward. Some of the others stirred and cursed him, but Fallon, a character in a book where everyone died on the last page, shook with helpless laughter, crying, knowing he would not sleep.

FIVE

WITH A PRETERNATURAL clarity born of the sleepless night, Fallon saw the deck of the *Pequod* the next morning. He was a little stunned yet, but if he kept his mind in tight check the fatigue would keep him from thinking, and he would not feel the distress that was waiting to burst out again. Like a man carrying a bowl filled with acid, Fallon carried his knowledge tenderly.

He observed with scientific detachment, knowing that sleep would ultimately come, and with it perhaps escape. The day was bright and fair, a duplicate of the previous one. The whaler was clean and prepared for her work; all sails were set to take advantage of the light breeze, and the mastheads were manned with lookouts. Men loitered on deck. On the rear deck—the quarterdeck, they called it—Ahab paced, with remarkable steadiness for a man wearing an ivory leg, between the compass in its box and the mainmast, stopping for seconds to stare pointedly at each end of his path. Fallon could not take his eyes off the man. He was much older than Fallon had imagined him from his memories of the book. Ahab's hair and beard were still black, except for the streak of white that ran through them as the old scar ran top to bottom across his face, but the face itself was deeply worn, and the man's eyes were sunken in wrinkles, hollow. Fallon remembered Tigue, who traded in the gold pit, who had once been the best boy on the floor—the burnout, they called him now, talking a very good game about shorting the market. Tigue's eyes had the same hollow expectation of disaster waiting inevitably for him—just him—that Ahab's held. Yet when Fallon had decided Ahab had to be the same empty nonentity, the man would pause at the end of his pathway and stare at the compass, or the gold coin that was nailed to the mast, and his figure would tighten in the grip of some stiffening passion, as if he were shot through with lightning. As if he were at the focal point of some cosmic lens that concentrated all the power of the sun on him, so that he might momentarily burst into spontaneous flame.

Ahab talked to himself, staring at the coin. His voice was conversational, and higher pitched than Fallon had imagined it would be. Fallon was not the only man who watched him in wonder and fear.

"There's something ever egotistical in mountaintops and towers, and all other grand and lofty things; look here—three peaks as proud as Lucifer. The firm tower, that is Ahab; the volcano, that is Ahab; the courageous, the undaunted, and victorious fowl, that, too, is Ahab; all are Ahab; and this round gold is but the image of the rounder globe, which, like a magician's glass, to each and every man in turn but mirrors back his own mysterious self..."

All spoken in the tone of a man describing a minor auto accident (the brown Buick swerved to avoid the boy on the bicycle, crossed over the yellow line, and hit the milk truck, which was going south on Main Street). As soon as he had stopped, Ahab turned and, instead of continuing his pacing, went quietly below.

One of the ship's officers—the first mate, Fallon thought—who had been talking to the helmsman before Ahab began to speak, now advanced to look at the coin. Fallon began to remember what was going to happen. Theatrically, though there was nobody there to listen to him, the mate began to speak aloud about the Trinity and the sun, hope and despair. Next came another mate, who talked of spending the doubloon quickly, then gave a reading comparing the signs of the zodiac to a man's life. Overwritten and silly, Fallon thought.

Flask now came to the doubloon and figured out how many cigars he could buy with it. Then came the old man who had sloshed the water all over Fallon the previous morning, who gave a reading of the ship's doom under the sign of the lion. Then Queequeg, then one of the Asians, then a Black boy—the cabin boy.

The boy danced around the mast twice, crouching low, rising on his toes, and each time around stared at the doubloon with comically bugged eyes. He stopped. "I look, you look, he looks, we look, ye look, they look."

I look, you look, he looks, we look, ye look, they look.

They all looked at it; they all spouted their interpretations. That was what Melville had wanted them to do to prove his point. Fallon did not feel like trying to figure out what that point was. After the dramatics, the *Pequod* went back to dull routine, and he to cleanup work on the deck, to tarring more ropes. They had a lot of ropes.

He took a break and walked up to the mast to look at the coin himself. Its surface was stamped with the image of three mountains, with a flame, a tower, and a rooster at their peaks. Above were the sun and the signs of the zodiac. REPUBLICA DEL EQUADOR: QUITO, it said. A couple of ounces, worth maybe $1,300 on the current gold market, according to the London fix Fallon last remembered. It wouldn't be worth as much to these men, of course; this was preinflation money. He remembered that the doubloon had been nailed there by Ahab as a reward to whoever spotted Moby Dick first.

I look, you look, he looks, we look, ye look, they look.

Fallon looked, and nothing changed. His fatigue grew as the day wore through a brutally hot afternoon. When evening at last came and the grumbling of his belly had been at least partially assuaged by the meager meal served the men, Fallon fell exhausted into the hammock. He did not worry about not sleeping this time; consciousness fell away as if he had been drugged.

He had a vivid dream. He was trying, under cover of darkness, to pry the doubloon away from the mast so that he might throw it into the sea. Anxiously trying not to let the helmsman at the tiller spot him, he heard the step, tap, step, tap, of Ahab's pacing a deck below. It was one of those dreams where one struggles in unfocused terror to accomplish some simple task. He was afraid he might be found any second by Ahab. If he were caught, then he would be exposed and vilified before the crew's indifferent gaze.

He couldn't do it. He couldn't get his fingers under the edge of the coin, though he bruised them bloody. He heard the knocking of Ahab's whale-bone step ascending to the deck; the world contracted to the coin welded to the mast, his broken nails, the terrible fear. He heard the footsteps drawing nearer behind him as he frantically tried to free the doubloon, yet he could not run, and he would not turn around. At the last, after an eternity of anxiety, a hand fell on his shoulder and spun him around, his heart leaping into his throat. It was not Ahab, but Carol.

He woke breathing hard, pulse pounding. He was still in the hammock, in the forecastle of the *Pequod*. He closed his eyes again, dozed fretfully through the rest of the night. Morning came: he was still there.

The next day several of the other men prodded him about not having taken a turn at the masthead for a long time. He stuck to mumbled answers and hoped they would not go to any of the officers. He wanted to disappear. He wanted it to be over. The men treated him more scornfully as the days passed. And the days passed, and still nothing happened to free him. The doubloon glinted in the sun each morning, at the center of the ship, and Fallon could not get away. I look, you look, he looks, we look, ye look, they look.

SIX

FALLON HAD ASSUMED his sullen station by the tar bucket. There he felt at least some defense from his confusion. He could concentrate on the smell and feel of the tar; he remembered the summers on the tarred road in front of his grandparents' house in Elmira, how the sun would raise shining bubbles of tar at the edges of the resurfaced country road, how the tar would stick to your sneakers and get you a licking if you tracked it into Grandmother's immaculate kitchen. He and his cousin Seth had broken the bubbles with sticks and watched them slowly subside into themselves. The tar bucket on the Pequod was something Fallon could focus on. The tar was real; the air he breathed was real—Fallon himself was real.

Stubb, the second mate, stood in front of him, arms akimbo. He stared at Fallon; Fallon lifted his head and saw the man's small smile. There was no charity in it.

"Time to go aloft, Fallon. You've been missing your turn."

Fallon couldn't think of anything to say. He stumbled to his feet, wiping his hands on a piece of burlap. A couple of the other sailors were watching, waiting for Fallon to shy off or for Stubb to take him.

"Up with ye!" Stubb shoved Fallon's shoulder, and he turned, fumbling for the rigging. Fallon looked momentarily over the side of the ship to the sea that slid calmly by them; the gentle rolling of the deck that he had in so short a time become accustomed to now returned to him with frightening force. Stubb was still behind him. Taking a good breath, he pulled himself up and stepped barefoot onto the rail. Facing inward now, he tried to climb the rigging. Stubb watched him with dispassion, waiting, it seemed, for his failure. Expecting it. It was like trying to climb one of those rope ladders at the county fair: each rung he took twisted the ladder in the direction of his weight, and the rocking of the ship, magnified as he went higher, made it hard for his feet to find the next step. He had never been a particularly self-conscious man, but felt he was being watched by them all now and was acutely conscious of how strange he must seem. How touched with idiocy and fear.

Nausea rose, the deck seemed farther below than it had any reason to be, the air was stifling; the wind was without freshness and did not cool the sweat from his brow and neck. He clutched the ropes desperately; he tried to take another step, but the strength seemed drained from his legs. Humiliated, burning with shame yet at the same time mortally afraid of falling—and of more than that, of the whole thing, of the fact that here he was where he ought not to be, cheated, abused, mystified—he wrapped his arms around the rigging, knees wobbly, sickness in his gut, bile threatening to heave itself up the back of his throat. Eyes clenched tight, he wished it would all go away.

"Fallon! Fallon, you dog, you dog*fish*, why don't you climb!" Stubb roared. "You had better climb, weak-liver, for I don't want you down on my deck again if you won't!" Fallon opened his eyes, saw the red-faced man staring furiously up at him. Perhaps he'll have a stroke, Fallon thought.

He hung there, half-up, half-down, unable to move. I want to go home, he thought. Let me go home. Stubb raged and ridiculed him; others gathered to laugh and watch. Fallon closed his eyes and tried to go away. He heard a sound like the wooden mallet of the carpenter.

"What is the problem here, Mr. Stubb?" A calm voice. Fallon looked down again. Ahab stood with his hand on the mainmast to steady himself, looking up. His thumb was touching the doubloon.

Stubb was taken by surprise, as if Ahab were some apparition that had been called up by an entirely inappropriate spell. He jerked his head upward to indicate Fallon.

Squinting against the sun, Ahab studied Fallon for some time. His face was unnaturally pale in comparison to the tanned faces of the others turned up to look at him. Yet against the pallor, the white scar ran, a deathlike sign, down the side of his face. His dark hair was disarrayed in the hot breeze. He was an old man; he swayed in the attempt to steady himself.

"Why don't ye go up?" Ahab called to Fallon. Fallon shook his head. He tried to step up another rung, but though his foot found the rope, he didn't seem to have the strength he needed to pull himself up.

Ahab continued to regard him. He did not seem impatient or angry, only curious, as if Fallon were an animal sitting frozen on a traffic mall, afraid of the cars that passed. He seemed content to stand watching Fallon indefinitely. Stubb shifted nervously from foot to foot, his anger negated. The crewmen simply watched. Some of them peered above Fallon in the rigging;

the ropes he clung to jerked, and he looked up himself to see that the man who had been standing at the masthead was coming down to help him.

"Bulkington!" Ahab cried, waving to the man to stop. "Let him be!" The sailor retreated upward and swung himself onto the yardarm above the mainsail. The *Pequod* waited. If there were whales to be hunted, they waited too.

Very distinctly, so that Fallon heard every word, Ahab said, "You must go up. You have taken the vow with the rest, and I will not have you go back on it. Would you go back on it? You must go up, or else you must come down, and show yourself for the coward and weakling you would then be."

Fallon clung to the rigging. He had taken no vow. It was all a story. What difference did it make what he did in a story? If he was to be a character in a book, why couldn't he defy it, do what he wanted instead of following the path they indicated? By coming down he could show himself as himself.

"Have faith!" Ahab called. Above him, Bulkington hawked and spat, timing it so that with the wind and the rocking of the Pequod, he hit the sea and not the deck. Fallon bent his head back and looked up at him. It was the kind sailor who had helped him below on that first night. He hung suspended. He looked down and watched Ahab sway with the rolling of the deck, his eyes still fixed on Fallon. The man was crazy. Melville was crazy for inventing him.

Fallon clenched his teeth, pulled on the ropes, and pushed himself up another step toward the masthead. He was midway up the mainsail, thirty feet above the deck. He concentrated on one rung at a time, breathing steadily, and pulled himself up. When he reached the level of the main yard, Bulkington swung himself below Fallon and helped him along. The complicated motion that came when the sailor stepped onto the ropes had Fallon clinging once again, but this time he was out of it fairly quickly. They ascended, step by dizzying step, to the masthead. The sailor got into the port masthead hoop, helping Fallon into the starboard. The Pequod's flag snapped in the wind a couple of feet above their heads.

"And here we are, Fallon," Bulkington said. Immediately he dropped himself down into the rigging again, so suddenly that Fallon's breath was stopped in fear for the man's fall.

Way below, the men were once more stirring. Ahab exchanged some words with Stubb; then, moving out to the rail and steadying himself by a

428

hand on one of the stays, a foreshortened black puppet far below, he turned his white face up to Fallon once again. Cupping his hand to his mouth, he shouted, "Keep a steady eye, now! If ye see fin or flank of him, call away!"

Call away. Fallon was far above it all now, alone. He had made it. He had taken no vow and was not obligated to do anything he did not wish to. He had ascended to the masthead of his own free will, but, if he was to become a whaler, then what harm would there be in calling out whales—normal whales? Not white ones. Not literary ones. He looked out to the horizon. The sea stretched out to the utmost ends of the world, covering it all, every secret, clear and blue and a little choppy under the innocent sky.

SEVEN

FALLON BECAME USED to the smell of the *Pequod*. He became accustomed to feeling sweaty and dirty, to the musty smell of mildew and the tang of brine trying to push away the stench of the packing plant.

He had not always been fastidious in his other life. In the late sixties, after he had dropped out of Northwestern, he had lived in an old house in a rundown neighborhood with three other men and a woman. They had called it "The Big House," and to the outside observer they must have been hippies. "Hair men." "Freaks." "Dropouts." It was a vocabulary that seemed quaint now. The perpetual pile of dirty dishes in the sink, the Fillmore West posters, the black light, the hot and cold running roaches, the early-fifties furniture with corners shredded to tatters by their three cats. Fallon realized that that life had been as different from his world at the Board of Trade as the deck of the *Pequod* was now.

Fallon had dropped out because, he'd told himself, there was nothing he wanted from the university that he couldn't get from its library, or by hanging around the student union. It was hard for him to believe how much he had read then: Skinner's behaviorism, Spengler's history, pop physics and Thomas Kuhn, Friedman and Galbraith, Shaw, Conrad, Nabokov, and all he could find of Hammett, Chandler, Macdonald, and their imitators. Later he had not been able to figure out just why he had forsaken a degree so easily; he didn't know if he was too irresponsible to do the work, or too slow, or above it all and following his own path. Certainly he had not seen himself as a rebel, and the revolutionary fervor his peers affected (it had seemed affectation ninety percent of the time) never took hold of Fallon completely. He had observed, but not taken part in, the melee at the Democratic Convention. But he put in his time in the back bedroom listening to The Doors and blowing dope until the world seemed no more than a slightly bigger version of the Big House and his circle of friends. He read *The Way of Zen*. He knew Hesse and Kerouac. He hated Richard Nixon and laughed at Spiro Agnew. Aloft in the rigging of the *Pequod*, those years came back to Fallon as they never had in his last five years at the CBT. What a different person he had been at twenty. What a strange person, he realized, he had become at twenty-eight. What a marvelous—and frightening—metamorphosis.

He had gotten sick of stagnating, he told himself. He had seen one or another of his friends smoke himself into passivity. He had seen through the self-delusions of the other cripples in the Big House: cripples was what he had called them when he'd had the argument with Marty Solokov and had stalked out. Because he broke from that way of living did not mean he was selling out, he'd told them. He could work any kind of job; he didn't want money or a house in the suburbs. He wanted to give himself the feeling of getting started again, of moving, of putting meaning to each day. He quit washing dishes for the university, moved into a dingy flat closer to the center of the city, and scanned the help-wanted columns. He still saw his friends often and got stoned maybe not quite so often, and listened to music and read. But he had had enough of "finding himself," and he recognized in the others how finding yourself became an excuse for doing nothing.

Marty's cousin was a runner for Pearson Joel Chones on the Chicago Mercantile Exchange who had occasionally come by the house, gotten high, and gone to concerts. Fallon had slept with her once. He called her up, and she asked around, and eventually he cut his hair short—not too short—and became a runner for Pearson, too. He became marginally better groomed. He took a shower and changed his underwear every day. He bought three ties and wore one of them on the trading floor because that was one of the rules of the exchange.

IT OCCURRED TO Fallon to find Ishmael, if only to see the man who would live while he died. He listened and watched; he learned the name of every man on the ship—he knew Flask and Stubb and Starbuck and Bulkington, Tashtego, Daggoo and Queequeg, identified Fedallah, the lead Philippine boatsman. There was no Ishmael. At first Fallon was puzzled, then came the beginnings of hope. If the reality he was living in could be found to differ from the reality of Melville's book in such an important particular, then could it not differ in some other way—some way that would at least lead to his survival? Maybe this Ahab caught his white whale. Maybe Starbuck would steel himself to the point where he could defy the madman and take over the ship. Perhaps they would never sight Moby Dick.

Then an unsettling realization smothered the hope before it could come fully to bloom: there was not necessarily an Ishmael in the book. "*Call* me Ishmael," it started. Ishmael was a pseudonym for some other man, and there would be no one by that name on the *Pequod*. Fallon congratulated himself on a clever bit of literary detective work.

Yet the hope refused to remain dead: Yes, there was no Ishmael on the *Pequod*; or anyone on the ship not specifically named in the book might be Ishmael, any one of the anonymous sailors, within certain broad parameters of age and character—and Fallon racked his brain trying to remember what the narrator said of himself—might be Ishmael. He grabbed at that; he breathed in the possibility and tried on the suit for size. Why not? If absurdity were to rule to the extent that he had to be there in the first place, then why couldn't he be the one who lived? More than that, why couldn't he make himself that man? No one else knew what Fallon knew. He had the advantage over them. Do the things that Ishmael did, and you may be him. If you have to be a character in a book, why not be the hero?

FALLON'S FIRST CONTACT with the heart of capitalism at the CME had been frightening and amusing. Frightening when he screwed up and delivered a

May buy-order as a July trade and cost the company ten thousand dollars. It was only through the grace of God and his own guts in facing it out that he had made it through the disaster. He had, he discovered, the ability to hide himself behind a facade that, to the self-interested observer, would appear to be whatever that observer wished it to be. If his superior expected him to be respectful and curious, then Fallon was respectfully curious. He did it without having to compromise his inner self. He was not a hypocrite.

The amusing part came after he had it all down and he began to watch the market like an observer at a very complex Monopoly game. Or, more accurately, like a baseball fan during a pennant race. There were at least as many statistics as in a good baseball season, enough personalities, strategies, great plays, blunders, risk, and luck. Fallon would walk onto the floor at the beginning of the day—the huge room with its concert-hall atmosphere, the banks of price boards around the walls, the twilight, the conditioned air, the hundreds of bright-coated traders and agents—and think of halftime at homecoming. The floor at the end of the day, as he walked across the hardwood scattered with mounds of paper scraps like so much confetti, was a basketball court after the NCAA finals. Topping it all off, giving it that last significant twist that was necessary to all good jokes, was the fact that this was all supposed to mean something; it was real money they were playing with, and one tick of the board in Treasury Bills cost somebody eleven hundred dollars. This was serious stuff, kid. The lifeblood of the nation—of the free world. Fallon could hardly hold in his laughter, could not stop his fascination.

FALLON'S FIRST CONTACT with the whale—his first lowering—was in Stubb's boat. The man at the forward masthead cried out, "There she blows! Three points off starboard! There she blows! Three—no, four of 'em!"

The men sprang to the longboats and swung them away over the side. Fallon did his best to look as if he was helping. Stubb's crew leapt into the boat as it was dropped into the swelling sea, heedless to the possibility of broken bones or sprained ankles. Fallon hesitated a second at the rail, then threw himself off with the feeling of a man leaping off the Sears Tower. He landed clumsily and half bowled over one of the men. He took his place at a center oar and pulled away. Like the man falling off the building, counting off the stories as they flew past him, Fallon thought, "So far, so good." And waited for the crash.

"Stop snoring, ye sleepers, and pull!" Stubb called, halfway between jest and anger. "Pull, Fallon! Why don't you pull? Have you never seen an oar before? Don't look over your shoulder, lad, *pull!* That's better. Don't be in a hurry, men—softly, softly now—but damn ye, pull until you break something! Tashtego! Can't you harpoon me some men with backs to them? *Pull!*"

Fallon pulled until he thought the muscles in his arms would snap, until the small of his back spasmed as if he were indeed being harpooned by the black-haired Indian behind him in the bow. The sea was rough, and they were soon soaked with spray. After a few minutes Fallon forgot the whales they pursued, merged into the rhythm of the work, fell in with the cunning flow of Stubb's curses and pleas, the crazy sermon, now whispered, now shouted. He concentrated on the oar in his hands, the bite of the blade into the water, the simple mechanism his body had become, the working of his lungs, the dry rawness of the breath dragged in and out in time to their rocking, backbreaking work. Fallon closed his eyes, heard the pulse in his ears, felt the cool spray and the hot sun, saw the rose fog of the blood in his eyelids as he faced into the bright and brutal day.

AT TWENTY-FIVE, FALLON was offered a position in the office upstairs. At twenty-seven, he had an offer from DCB International to become a broker. By that time he was living with Carol. Why not? He was still outside it all, still safe within. Let them think what they would of him; he was protected, in the final analysis, by that great indifference he held to his breast the way he held Carol close at night. He was not a hypocrite. He said nothing he did not believe in. Let them project upon him whatever fantasies they might hold dear to themselves. He was outside and above it all, analyzing futures for DCB International. Clearly, in every contract that crossed his desk, it was stated that DCB and its brokers were not responsible for reverses that might be suffered as a result of suggestions they made.

So he had spent the next four years apart from it, pursuing his interests, which, with the money he was making, he found were many. Fallon saw very little of the old friends now. Solokov's cousin told him Marty was now in New York, cadging money from strangers in Times Square. Solokov, she said, claimed it was a pretty good living. He claimed he was still beating the system. Fallon had grown up enough to realize that no one really beat any system—as if there were a system. There was only buying and selling, subject to the forces of the market and the infirmities of the players. Fallon was on the edges of it, could watch quietly, taking part as necessary (he had to eat), but still stay safe. He was no hypocrite.

"TO THE DEVIL with ye, boys, will ye be outdone by Ahab's heathens? Pull, spring it, my children, my fine hearts-alive, smoothly, smoothly, bend it hard starboard! Aye, Fallon, let me see you sweat, lad, can you sweat for me?"

They rose on the swell, and it was like rowing uphill; they slid down the other side, still rowing, whooping like children on a toboggan ride, all the time Stubb calling on them. Fallon saw Starbuck's boat off to his right; he heard the rush of water beneath them, and the rush of something faster and greater than their boat.

Behind Fallon, Tashtego grunted. "A hit, a hit!" Stubb shouted, and the whaleline was running out with such speed that it sang and hummed and smoked. One of the men sloshed water over the place where it slid taut as a wire over the gunnel. Then the boat jerked forward so suddenly that Fallon was nearly knocked overboard when his oar, still trailing in the water, slammed into his chest. Gasping at the pain, he managed to get the oar up into the air. Stubb had half risen from his seat in the stem.

They flew through the water. The whaleboat bucked as it slapped the surface of every swell the whale pulled them through. Fallon held on for dear life, not sure whether he ought to be grateful he hadn't been pitched out when the ride began. He tried to twist around to see the monster that was towing them, but able to turn only halfway, all he could see for the spray and the violent motion was the swell and rush of white water ahead of them.

Tashtego, crouched in the bow, grinned wickedly as he tossed out wooden blocks tied to the whaleline in order to tire the whale with their drag. You might as well try to tire a road grader.

Yet he could not help but feel exhilarated, and he saw that the others in the boat, hanging on or trying to draw the line in, were flushed and breathing as hard as he.

He turned again and saw the whale.

FALLON HAD BEEN a good swimmer in high school. He met Carol Bukaty at a swimming pool about a year after he had gone to work at the CME. Fallon first noticed her in the pool, swimming laps. She was the best swimmer there, better than he, though he might have been stronger than she in the short run. She gave herself over to the water and did not fight it; the kick of her long legs was steady and strong. She breathed easily and her strokes were relaxed, yet powerful. She did not swim for speed, but she looked as if she could swim for days, so comfortable did she seem in the water. Fallon sat on the steps at the pool's edge and watched her for half an hour without once getting bored. He found her grace in the water arousing. He knew he had to speak to her. He slid into the pool and swam laps behind her.

At last she stopped. Holding on to the trough at the end of the pool, she pushed her goggles up onto her forehead and brushed the wet brown hair away from her eyes. He drew up beside her.

"You swim very well," he said.

She was out of breath. "Thank you."

"You look as if you wouldn't ever need to come out of the water. Like anything else might be a comedown after swimming." It was a strange thing for him to say, it was not what he wanted to say, but he did not know what he wanted, besides her.

She looked puzzled, smiled briefly, and pulled herself onto the side of the pool, letting her legs dangle in the water. "Sometimes I feel that way," she said. "I'm Carol Bukaty." She stuck out her hand, very businesslike.

"Pat Fallon." She wore a gray tank suit; she was slender and small-breasted, tall, with a pointed chin and brown eyes. Fallon later discovered that she was an excellent dancer, that she purchased women's clothing for one of the major Chicago department stores, that she traveled a great deal, wrote lousy poetry, disliked cooking, liked children, and liked him. At first he was merely interested in her sexually, though the first few times they slept together it was not very good at all. Gradually the sex got better, and in the meantime Fallon fell in love.

She would meet him at the athletic club after work; they would play racquetball in the late afternoon, go out to dinner, and take in a movie, then spend the night at his or her apartment. He met her alcoholic father, a retired policeman who told endless stories about ward politics and the Daley machine, and Carol spent a Christmas with him at his parents'. After they moved in together, they settled into a comfortable routine. He felt secure in her affection for him. He did not want her, after a while, as much as he had that first day, those first months, but he still needed her. It still mattered to him what she was doing and what she thought of him. Sometimes it mattered to him too much, he thought. Sometimes he wanted to be without her at all, not because he had anything he could only do without her, but only because he wanted to *be* without her.

He would watch her getting dressed in the morning and wonder what creature she might be, and what that creature was doing in the same room with him. He would lie beside her as she slept, stroking the short brown hair at her temple with his fingertips, and be overwhelmed with the desire to possess her, to hold her face between his hands and know everything that she was; he would shake with the sudden frustration of its impossibility until it was all he could do to keep from striking her. Something was wrong with him, or with her. He had fantasies of how much she would miss him if he died, of what clothes she would wear to the funeral, of what stories she would tell her lovers in the future after he was gone.

If Carol felt any of the same things about him, she did not tell him. For Fallon's part, he did not try to explain what he felt in any but the most oblique ways. She should know how he felt, but of course she did not. So when things went badly, and they began to do so more and more, it was not possible for him to explain to her what was wrong, because he could not say it himself, and the pieces of his discontent were things that he was too embarrassed to admit. Yet he could not deny that sometimes he felt as if it was all over between them, that he felt nothing—and at others he would smile just to have her walk into the room.

REMARKABLE CREATURE THOUGH the whale was, it was not so hard to kill one after all. It tired, just as a man would tire under the attack of a group of strangers. It slowed in the water, no longer able so effortlessly to drag them after it. They pulled close, and Stubb drove home the iron, jerked it back and forth, drew it out and drove it home again, fist over fist on the hilt, booted foot over the gunnel braced against the creature's flesh, sweating, searching for the whale's hidden life. At last he found it, and the whale shuddered and thrashed a last time, spouting pink mist, then dark blood, where once it spouted feathery white spray. Like a man, helpless in the end, it rolled over and died. Stubb was jolly, and the men were methodical; they tied their lines around the great tail and, as shadows grew long and the sun fell perpendicularly toward the horizon, drew the dead whale to the *Pequod*.

EIGHT

DURING THE CUTTING up and boiling down of the whale that night, Fallon, perhaps in recognition of his return to normality as indicated by his return to the masthead, was given a real job: slicing the chunks of blubber that a couple of other sailors were hewing out of the great strips that were hauled over the side, into "bible leaves." Fallon got the hang of it pretty quickly, though he was not fast, and Staley, the British sailor who was cutting beside him, kept poking at him to do more. "I'm doing all the work, Fallon," he said, as if his ambition in life were to make sure that he did no more than his own share of the work.

Using a sharp blade like a long cleaver, Fallon would position the chunk of blubber, skin-side down on the cutting table, and imitating Staley, cut the piece into slices like the pages of a book, with the skin as its spine. The blubber leaves flopped outward or stuck to each other, and the table became slick with grease. Fallon was at first careful about avoiding his hands, but the blubber would slide around the table as he tried to cut it if he didn't hold it still. Staley pushed him on, working with dexterity, though Fallon noted that the man's hands were scarred, with the top joint of the middle finger of his left hand missing.

His back and shoulders ached with fatigue, and the smoke from the try-works stung his eyes. When he tried to wipe the tears away, he only smeared his face with grease. But he did a creditable job, cursing all the time. The cursing helped, and the other men seemed to accept him more for it. When finally they were done, and the deck was clean the next day, they were issued a tot of grog and allowed to swim within the lee of the stationary ship. The men were more real to him than when he had sat and watched from the outcast's station of the tar bucket. He was able to speak to them more naturally than he had ever done. But he did not forget his predicament.

"Ye are too serious, Fallon," Staley told him, offering Fallon some of his grog. "I can see you brooding there, and look how it set you into a funk. Ye are better now, perhaps, but mind you, stick to your work and ye may survive this voyage."

"I won't survive it. Neither will you—unless we can do something about Captain Ahab."

Bulkington, who had been watching them, came by. "What of Captain Ahab?"

Fallon saw a chance in this. "Does his seeking after this white whale seem right to you?"

"The whale took his leg," Staley said.

"Some say it unmanned him," Bulkington said, lower. "That's two legs you'd not like to lose yourself, I'll daresay."

Fallon drew them aside, more earnest now. "We will lose more than our balls if we do nothing about this situation. The man is out of his mind. He will drag us all down with him, and this ship too, if we can't convince Starbuck to do something. Believe me, I know."

Friendly Bulkington did not look so friendly. "You do talk strange, Fallon. We took an oath, and we signed the papers before we even sailed a cable from shore. A captain is a captain. You are talking mutiny."

He had to go carefully.

"No, wait. Listen to me. Why are we sent on this trip? Think of the—the stockholders, or whatever you call them. The owners. They sent us out to hunt whales."

"The white whale is a whale." Staley said.

"Yes, of course it's a whale. But there are hundreds of whales to be caught and killed. We don't need to hunt that one. Hasn't he set his sights on just Moby Dick? What about that oath? That gold piece on the mast? That says he's just out for vengeance. There was nothing about vengeance in the papers we signed. What do you think the owners would say if they knew about what he plans? Do you think they would approve of this wild-goose chase?"

Staley was lost. "Goose chase?"

Bulkington was interested. "Go on."

Fallon had his foot in the door; he marshaled the arguments he had rehearsed over and over again. "There's no more oil in Moby Dick than in another whale..."

"They say he's monstrous big," Staley interjected.

Fallon looked pained. "Not so big as any two whales, then. Ahab is not after any oil you can boil out of the whale's flesh. If the owners knew what he intended, the way I do, if they knew how sick he was the week before he came out of that hole of a cabin he lives in, if they saw that light in his eye and the charts he keeps in his cabinet..."

"Charts? What charts? Have you been in his cabin?"

"No, not exactly," Fallon said. "Look, I know some things, but that's just because I keep my eyes open and I have some sources."

"Fallon, where do you hail from? I swear that I cannot half the time make out what you are saying. Sources? What do you mean by that?"

"Oh, Jesus!" He had hoped for better from Bulkington.

Staley darkened. "Don't blaspheme, man! I'll not take the word of a blasphemer."

Fallon saw another opening. "You're right! I'm sorry. But look, didn't the old man himself blaspheme more seriously than I ever could the night of that oath? If you are a God-fearing man, Staley, you know that is true. Would you give your obedience to such a man? Moby Dick is just another of God's creatures, a dumb animal. Is it right to seek vengeance on an animal? Do you want to be responsible for that? God would not approve."

Staley looked troubled, but stubborn. "Do not tell me what the Almighty approves. That is not for the likes of you to know. And Ahab is the captain." With that he walked to the opposite side of the deck and stood there watching them as if he wanted to separate himself as much as possible from the conversation, yet still know what was going on.

Fallon was exasperated and tired.

"Why don't you go with Staley, Bulkington? You don't have to stick around with me, you know. I'm not going to do your reputation any good."

Bulkington eyed him steadily. "You are a strange one, Fallon. I did not think anything of you when I first saw you on the Pequod. But you may be talking some sense."

"Staley doesn't think so."

Bulkington took a pull on his grog. "Why did you try to persuade Staley? You should have known that you couldn't convince such a man that the sky is blue, if it were written in the articles he signed that it was green. Starbuck perhaps, or me. Not Staley. Don't you listen to the man you are talking to?"

Fallon looked at Bulkington; the tall sailor looked calmly back at him, patient, waiting.

"Okay, you're right," Fallon said. "I have the feeling I would not have a hard time convincing you, anyway. You know Ahab's insane, don't you?"

"It's not for me to say. Ahab has better reasons than those you give to him." He drew a deep breath, looked up at the sky, down at the men who swam in the shadow of the ship. He smiled. "They should be more wary of sharks," he said.

"The world does look a garden today, Fallon. But it may be that the old man's eyes are better than ours."

"You know he's mad, and you won't do anything?"

"The matter will not bear too deep a looking into." Bulkington was silent for a moment. "You know the story about the man born with a silver screw in his navel? How it tasked him, until one day he unscrewed it to divine its purpose?"

Fallon had heard the joke in grade school. "His ass fell off."

"You and Ahab are too much like that man."

They both laughed. "I don't have to unscrew my navel," Fallon said. "We're all going to lose our asses anyway."

They laughed again. Bulkington put his arm around his shoulders, and they toasted Moby Dick.

NINE

THERE CAME A morning when, on pumping out the bilge, someone noticed that considerable whale oil was coming up with the water. Starbuck was summoned and, after descending into the hold himself, emerged and went aft and below to speak with Ahab. Fallon asked one of the others what was going on.

"The casks are leaking. We're going to have to lay up and break them out. If we don't, we stand to lose a lot of oil."

Sometime later Starbuck reappeared. His face was red to the point of apoplexy, and he paced around the quarterdeck with his hands knotted behind his back. They waited for him to tell them what to do; he stared at the crewmen, stopped, and told them to be about their business. "Keep pumping," he told the others. "Maintain the lookout." He then spoke briefly to the helmsman leaning on the whalebone tiller, and retreated to the corner of the quarterdeck to watch the wake of the ship. After a while Ahab himself staggered up onto the deck found Starbuck, and spoke to him. He then turned to the men on deck.

"Furl the t'gallantsails," Ahab called, "and close reef the topsails, fore and aft; back the main yard; up Burtons, and break out in the main hold."

Fallon joined the others around the hold. Once the work had commenced, he concentrated on lifting, hauling, and not straining his back. The Manxman told them that he had been outside Ahab's cabin during the conference and that Ahab had threatened to shoot Starbuck dead on the spot when the mate demanded they stop chasing the whale to break out the hold. Fallon thought about the anger in Starbuck's face when he'd come up again. It struck him that the Starbuck of Melville's book was pretty ineffectual; he had to be to let that madman go on with the chase. But this Starbuck—whether like the one in the book or not—did not like the way things were going. There was no reason why Fallon had to sit around and wait for things to happen. It was worth a shot.

But not that afternoon.

Racism assured that the hardest work in the stifling hold was done by the colored men—Daggoo, Tashtego, and Queequeg. They did not complain. Up to their knees in the bilge, clambering awkwardly over and about the barrels of oil in the murderous heat and unbreathable air, they did their jobs.

It was evening before the three harpooneers were told they could halt for the day, and they emerged, sweaty, bruised, and covered with slime. Fallon collapsed against the side of the try-works; others sat beside him. Tall Queequeg was taken by a coughing fit, then went below to his hammock. Fallon gathered his strength, felt the sweat drying stickily on his arms and neck. There were few clouds, and the moon was waxing full. He saw Starbuck then, standing at the rear of the quarterdeck, face toward the mast. Was he looking at the doubloon?

Fallon got shakily to his feet; his legs were rubbery. The first mate did not notice him until he was close. He looked up.

"Yes?"

"Mr. Starbuck, I need to speak with you."

Starbuck looked at him as if he saw him for the first time. Fallon tried to look self-confident, serious. He'd gotten that one down well at DCB.

"Yes?"

Fallon turned so that he was facing inward toward the deck and Starbuck had his back to it to face him. He could see what was happening away from them and would know if anyone came near.

"I could not help but see that you were angry this morning after speaking to Captain Ahab."

Starbuck looked puzzled.

"I assume that you must have told Ahab about the leaking oil, and he didn't want to stop his hunt of the whale long enough to break out the hold. Am I right?"

The mate watched him guardedly. "What passed between Captain Ahab and me was none of your affair, or of the crew's. Is that what you've come to trouble me with?"

"It is a matter that concerns me," Fallon said. "It concerns the rest of the crew, and it ought to concern you. We are being bound by his orders, and what kind of orders is he giving? I know what you've been thinking; I *know* that this personal vengeance he seeks frightens and repulses you. I know what you're thinking. I could see what was in your mind when you stood at this rail this afternoon. He is not going to stop until he kills us all."

Starbuck seemed to draw back within himself. Fallon saw how beaten the man's eyes were; he did not think the mate was a drinker, but he looked like someone who had just surfaced after a long weekend. He could almost see the clockwork turning within Starbuck, a beat too slow, with the belligerence of the drunk being told the truth about himself that he did not want to admit. Fallon's last fight with Stein Jr. at the brokerage had started that way.

"Get back to your work," Starbuck said. He started to turn away.

Fallon put his hand on his shoulder. "You have to—"

Starbuck whirled with surprising violence and pushed Fallon away so that he nearly stumbled and fell. The man at the tiller was watching them.

"To work! You do not know what I am thinking. I'll have you flogged if you say anything more! A man with a three-hundredth lay has nothing to tell me. Go on, now."

Fallon was hot. "God damn you. You stupid—"

"Enough!" Starbuck slapped him with the back of his hand, the way Stein had tried to slap Fallon. Stein had missed. It appeared that Mr. Starbuck was more effectual than Stein Jr. Fallon felt his bruised cheek. The thing that hurt the most was the way he must have looked, like a hangdog insubordinate who had been shown his place. As Fallon stumbled away, Starbuck said, in a steadier voice, "Tend to your own conscience, man. Let me tend to mine."

TEN

LIGHTNING FLASHED AGAIN. "I now know that thy right worship is defiance. To neither love nor reverence wilt thou be kind; and even for hate thou canst but kill, and all are killed!"

Ahab had sailed them into the heart of a typhoon. The sails were in tatters, and the men ran across the deck shouting against the wind and trying to lash the boats down tighter before they were washed away or smashed. Stubb had gotten his left hand caught between one of the boats and the rail; he now held it with his right and grimaced. The mastheads were touched with St. Elmo's fire. Ahab stood with the lightning rod in his right hand and his right foot planted on the neck of Fedallah, declaiming at the lightning. Fallon held tightly to a shroud to keep from being thrown off his feet. The scene was ludicrous; it was horrifying.

"No fearless fool now fronts thee!" Ahab shouted at the storm. "I own thy speechless, placeless power; but to the last gasp of my earthquake life will dispute its unconditional, unintegral mastery in me! In the midst of the personified impersonal, a personality stands here!"

Terrific, Fallon thought. Psychobabble. Melville writes in a storm so Ahab can have a backdrop against which to define himself. They must not have gone in for realism much in Melville's day. He turned and tried to lash the rear quarter boat tighter; its stem had already been smashed in by a wave that had just about swept three men, including Fallon, overboard. Lightning flashed, followed a split second later by the rolling thunder. Fallon recalled that five seconds' count meant the lightning was a mile away; by that measure the last bolt must have hit them in the ass. Most of the crew were staring openmouthed at Ahab and the glowing, eerie flames that touched the masts. The light had the bluish tinge of mercury-vapor lamps in a parking lot. It sucked the color out of things; the faces of the frightened men were the sickly hue of fish bellies.

"Thou canst blind, but I can then grope. Thou canst consume, but I can then be ashes!"

You bet.

"Take the homage of these poor eyes, and shutter-hands. I would not take it..." Ahab ranted on. Fallon hardly gave a damn anymore. The book was too much. Ahab talked to the storm and the God behind it; the storm answered him back, lightning flash for curse. It was dramatic, stagy; it was real: Melville's universe was created so that such dialogues could take place; the howling gale and the tons of water, the crashing waves, flapping canvas, the sweating, frightened men, the blood and seawater—all were created to

444

have a particular effect, to be sure, but it was the real universe, and it would work that way because that was the way it was set up to work by a frustrated, mystified man chasing his own obsessions, creating the world as a warped mirror of his distorted vision.

"There is some unsuffusing thing beyond thee, thou clear spirit, to whom all thy eternity is but time, all thy creativeness mechanical..."

There is an ex-sailor on a farm in Massachusetts trying to make ends meet while his worried wife tries to explain him to the relatives.

"The boat! The boat!" cried Starbuck. "Look at thy boat, old man!"

Fallon looked, and backed away. A couple of feet from him the harpoon that was lashed into the bow was tipped with the same fire that illuminated the masts. Silently within the howling storm, from its barbed end twin streamers of electricity writhed. Fallon backed away to the rail, heart beating quickly, and clutched the slick whalebone.

Ahab staggered toward the boat; Starbuck grabbed his arm. "God! God is against thee, old man! Forbear! It's an ill voyage! Ill begun, ill continued; let me square the yards while we may, old man, and make a fair wind of it homewards, to go on a better voyage than this."

Yes, yes, at last Starbuck had said it! Fallon grabbed one of the braces; he saw others of the crew move to the rigging as if to follow Starbuck's order before it was given. They cried, some of them in relief, others in fear, others as if ready at last to mutiny. Yes!

Ahab threw down the last links of the lightning rod. He grabbed the harpoon from the boat and waved it like a torch about his head; he lurched toward Fallon.

"You!" he shouted, staggering to maintain his balance on the tossing deck, hoisting the flaming harpoon to his shoulder as if he meant to impale Fallon on the spot. "But cast loose that rope's end and you will be transfixed—by this clear spirit!" The electricity at the barb hummed inches before him; Fallon could feel his skin prickling and smelled ozone. He felt the rail at the small of his back, cold. The other sailors fell away from the ropes; Starbuck looked momentarily sick. Fallon let go of the brace.

Ahab grinned at him. He turned and held the glowing steel before him with both hands like a priest holding a candle at mass on a feast day.

"All your oaths to hunt the white whale are as binding as mine; and heart, soul, and body, lung and life, old Ahab is bound. And that you may know to what tune this heart beats; look ye here! Thus I blow out the last fear!"

He blew out the flame.

THEY RAN OUT the night without letting the anchors over the side, heading due into the gale instead of riding with the wind at their backs, with tarpaulins and deck truck blown or washed overboard, with the lightning rod shipped instead of trailing in the sea as it ought to, with the man at the tiller beaten raw about the ribs trying to keep the ship straight, with the compass spinning round like a top, with the torn remains of the sails not cut away until long after midnight.

By morning the storm had much abated, the wind had come around, and they ran before it in heavy seas. Fallon and most of the other common sailors, exhausted, were allowed to sleep.

ELEVEN

THE ARGUMENT WITH Starbuck and his attempts to rouse others to defy Ahab had made Fallon something of a pariah. He was now as isolated as he had been when he'd first come to himself aboard the *Pequod*. Only Bulkington did not treat him with contempt or fear, but Bulkington would do nothing about the situation. He would rather talk, and they often discussed what a sane man would do in their situation, given the conflicting demands of reason and duty. Fallon's ability to remain detached always failed him somewhere in the middle of these talks.

So Fallon came to look upon his stints at the masthead as escape of a sort. It was there that he had first realized that he could rise above the deck of the *Pequod*, both literally and figuratively, for some moments; it was there that he had first asserted his will after days of stunned debility. He would not sing out for the white whale, if it should be his fortune to sight it, but he did sing out more than once for lesser whales. The leap of his heart at the sight of them was not feigned.

They were sailing the calm Pacific east and south of Japan. They had met the *Rachel*, and a thrill had run through the crew at the news that she had encountered Moby Dick and had failed to get him, losing several boats, and the captain's son, in the process. Fallon's memory was jogged. The *Rachel* would pick up Ishmael at the end of the book, when all the others were dead.

They met the *Delight*, on which a funeral was in progress. From the main-mast lookout, Fallon heard the shouted talk between Ahab and her captain about another failed attempt at the white whale. He watched as the dead man, sewn up in his hammock, was dropped into the sea.

It was a clear steel-blue day. The sea rolled in long, quiet swells; the *Pequod* moved briskly ahead before a fair breeze, until the *Delight* was lost in the distance astern. The air was fresh and clear out to the rim of the world, where it seemed to merge with the darker sea. It was as fair a day as they had seen since Fallon had first stood a watch at the masthead.

Up above the ship, almost out of the world of men entirely, rolling at the tip of the mast in rhythm to the rolling of the sea swells, which moved in time with his own easy breathing, Fallon lost his fear. He seemed to lose even himself. Who was he? Patrick Fallon, analyst for a commodities firm. Perhaps that had been some delusion; perhaps that world had been created somewhere inside of him, pressed upon him in a vision. He was a sailor on the *Pequod*. He thought that this was part of some book, but he had not been a reader for many years.

Memories of his other life persisted. He remembered the first time he had ever made love to a woman—to Sally Torrance, in the living room of her parents' house while they were away skiing in Colorado. He remembered cutting his palm playing baseball when the bat shattered in his hand. The scar in the middle of his hand could not be denied.

Who denied it? He watched an albatross swoop down from above him to skim a few feet above the water, trying to snag some high-leaping fish. It turned away, unsuccessful, beating its wings slowly as it climbed the air. There was rhythm to its unconscious dance. Fallon had never seen anything more beautiful. He hung his arms over the hoop that surrounded him, felt the hot sun beating on his back, the band of metal supporting him.

This was the real world; he accepted it. He accepted the memories that contradicted it. I look, you look, he looks. Could his mind and heart hold two contradictory things? What would happen to him then? He accepted the albatross, the fish, the sharks he could see below the water's surface from his high vantage point. He accepted the grace of the sea, its embrace on this gentlest of days, and he accepted the storm that had tried to kill them only days before. The *Delight*, reason told him—let reason be; he could strain reason no further than he had—the *Delight* might perhaps have been a ship from a story he had read, but he had no doubt that the man who had been dropped to his watery grave as Fallon watched had been a real man.

The blue of sky and sea, the sound of the flag snapping above him, the taste of the salt air, the motion of the sea and earth itself as they swung Fallon at the tip of the mast, the memories and speculations, the feel of warm sun and warm iron—all the sensual world flowed together for Fallon then. He could not say what he felt. Joy that he could hardly contain swelled in his chest. He was at one with all his perceptions, with all he knew and remembered, with Carol, wherever or whatever she might be, with Bulkington and Daggoo and Starbuck and Stein Jr. and the Big House and Queequeg and the CBT and Ahab. Ahab.

Why had Fallon struggled so long against it? He was alive. What thing had driven him to fight so hard? What had happened to him was absurd, but what thing was not absurd? What thing had made him change from the student to the dropout to the analyst to the sailor? Who might Patrick Fallon be? He stretched out his right arm and turned his hand in the sun.

"Is it I, or God, or who, that lifts this arm?" Fallon heard the words quite distinctly, as if they were spoken only for him, as if they were not spoken at all but were only thoughts. God perhaps did lift Fallon's arm, and if that were so, then who was Fallon to question the wisdom or purpose of the motion? It was his only to move.

A disturbance in the blue of the day.

Why should he not have a choice? Why should that God give him the feeling of freedom if in fact He was directing Fallon's every breath? Did the

Fates weave this trancelike calm blue day to lead Fallon to these particular conclusions, so that not even his thoughts in the end were his own, but only the promptings of some force beyond him? And what force could that be if not the force that created this world, and who created this world but Herman Melville, a man who had been dead for a very long time, a man who had no possible connection with Fallon? And what could be the reason for the motion? If this was the real world, then why had Fallon been given the life he had lived before, tangled himself in, felt trapped within, only to be snatched away and clumsily inserted into a different fantasy? What purpose did it serve? Whose satisfaction was being sought?

The moment of wholeness died; the world dissolved into its disparate elements. The sea rolled on. The ship fought it. The wind was opposed by straining canvas. The albatross dove once again, and skimming over the surface so fast it was a white blur, snatched a gleam of silver—a flying fish—from midflight. It settled to the ocean's surface, tearing at its prey.

The day was not so bright as it had been. Fallon tried to accept it still. He did not know if there was a malign force behind the motion of the earth in its long journey, or a beneficent one whose purpose was merely veiled to men such as himself—or no force at all. Such knowledge would not be his. He was a sailor on the *Pequod*.

UPON DESCENDING, FALLON heard from Bulkington that Starbuck and Ahab had had a conversation about turning back to Nantucket, that the mate had seemed almost to persuade the captain to give up the hunt, but that he had failed.

Fallon knew then that they must be coming to the end of the story. It would not be long before they spotted the white whale, and three days after that the *Pequod* would go down with all hands—save one. But Fallon had given up the idea that he might be that one. He did not, despite his problems, qualify as an Ishmael. That would be overstating his importance, he thought.

TWELVE

HE WOKE SUDDENLY to the imperative buzzing of his alarm clock. His heart beat very fast. He tried to slow it by breathing deeply. Carol stirred beside him, then slept again.

He felt disoriented. He walked into the bathroom, staring, as if he had never seen it before. He slid open the mirrored door of the medicine chest and looked inside at the almost-empty tube of toothpaste, the old safety razor, the pack of double-edged blades, the Darvon and tetracycline capsules, the foundation makeup. When he slid the door shut again, his tanned face looked back at him.

He was slow getting started that morning; when Carol got up, he was still drinking his coffee, with the radio playing an old Doors song in the background. Carol leaned over him, kissed the top of his head. It appeared that she loved him.

"You'd better get going," she said. "You'll be late." He hadn't worried about being late, and it hit him for the first time what he had to do. He had to get to the Board of Trade. He'd have to talk to Stein Jr., and there would be a sheaf of notes on his desk asking him to return calls to various clients who would have rung him up while he was gone. He pulled on the jacket of his pinstriped suit, brushed back his hair, and left.

Waiting for the train, he realized that he hadn't gone anywhere to return from.

He had missed his normal train and arrived late. The streets were nowhere near as crowded as they would have been an hour earlier. He walked north on La Salle Street between the staid, dark old buildings. The sky that showed between them was bright, and already the temperature was rising; it would be a hot one. He wished it were the weekend. Was it Thursday? It couldn't still be Wednesday. He was embarrassed to realize he wasn't sure what day it was.

He saw a very pretty girl in the lobby of the Board of Trade as he entered through the revolving doors. She was much prettier than Carol, and had that unselfconscious way of walking. But she was around the corner before he had taken more than a few steps inside. He ran into Joe Wendelstadt in the elevator, and Joe began to tell him a story about Raoul Lark from Brazil who worked for Cacex, and how Lark had tried to pick up some feminist the other night. And succeeded. Those Brazilians.

Fallon got off before Joe could reach the climax. In his office Molly, the receptionist, said Stein wanted to see him. Stein smelled of cigarettes, and Fallon suddenly became self-conscious. He had not brushed his own teeth. When did he ever forget that? Stein had an incipient zit on the end of his nose. He didn't really have anything to talk to Fallon about; he was just wasting time as usual.

Tigue was sick or on vacation.

Fallon worked through the morning on various customer accounts. He had trouble remembering where the market had closed the day before. He had always had a trick memory for such figures, and it had given him the ability to impress a lot of people who knew just as much about the markets as he did. He spent what was left of the morning on the phone to his clients, with a quick trip down to the trading floor to talk to Parsons in the soybean pit.

Carol called and asked him if he could join her for lunch. He remembered he had a date with Kim, a woman from the CME he had met just a week before. He made his excuses to Carol and took off for the Merc.

Walking briskly west on Jackson, coming up on the bridge across the river, he realized he had been rushing around all day and yet could hardly remember what he'd done since he had woken up. He still couldn't remember whether it was Wednesday or Thursday.

As he crossed the bridge with the crowds of lunch-hour office workers, the noontime sun glared brightly for a second from the oily water of the river. Fallon's eyes did not immediately recover. He stopped walking, and somebody bumped into him.

"Excuse me," he said unconsciously.

There was a moment of silence, then the noise of the city resumed and he could see again. He stood at the side of the bridge and looked down at the water. The oil on the surface made rainbow-colored swirls. Fallon shook his head and went on.

Kim stood him up at the restaurant. He waited a long time by the cashier. Finally he made the woman seat him at a table for two. He looked at his watch but had some trouble reading the time. Was he due back at the office?

Just then someone sat down opposite him. It was an old man in a dark suit who had obviously undergone some great ordeal. His face held a look of great pain or sorrow—with hate burning just beneath it. Though his hair was black (and quite unforgivably unkempt for midtown Chicago, as was his rough suit), a shock of white fell across his forehead, and a scar ran from the roots of that white hair straight down the man's face, leaping the brow and eye to continue across the left cheek, sinewing down the jaw and neck to disappear beneath his shirt collar.

He looked strangely familiar.

"It won't work," the man said. "You cannot get away. You have signed the articles, like the rest, and are in for a three-hundredth lay."

"Three-hundredth lay?" Fallon was bewildered.

"A three-hundredth part of the general catastrophe is yours. Don't thank me. It isn't necessary." The old man looked even more sorrowful and more wild, if it were possible to combine those seemingly incompatible emotions.

"To tell you the truth," he said, "I wouldn't hold you to the contract if it were strictly up to me." He shrugged his shoulders and opened his palms before him. "But it isn't."

Fallon's heart was beating fast again. 'I don't remember any contract. You're not one of my clients. I don't trade for you. I've been in this business for a long time, mister, and I know better than to sign..."

The wildness swelled in the man. There was something burning in him, and he looked about to scream, or cry.

"*I have been in the business longer than you!*" He swung his leg out from beneath the table and rapped it loudly with his knuckle. Fallon saw that the leg was of white bone. "And I can tell you that you signed the contract when you signed aboard this ship—there's no other way to get aboard—and you must serve until you strike land again or it sinks beneath you!"

The diners in the restaurant dined on, oblivious. Fallon looked toward the plate glass at the front of the room and saw the water rising rapidly up it, sea-green and turbid, as the restaurant and the city fell to the bottom of the sea.

THIRTEEN

ONCE AGAIN HE was jerked awake, this time by the din of someone beating the deck of the forecastle above them with a club. The other sleepers were as startled as Fallon. He rolled out of the hammock with the mists of his dream still clinging to him, pulled on his shirt, and scrambled up to the deck.

Ahab was stalking the quarterdeck in a frenzy of impatience. "Man the mastheads!" he shouted.

The men who had risen with Fallon did just that, some of them only half-dressed. Fallon was one of the first up and gained one of the hoops at the main masthead. Three others stood on the main yard below him. Fallon scanned the horizon and saw off to starboard and far ahead of them the jet of mist that indicated a whale. As the whale rose and fell in its course through the rolling seas, Fallon saw that it was white.

"What d'ye see?" Ahab called from far below. Had he noticed Fallon's gaze fixed on the spot in front of them?

"Nothing! Nothing, sir!" Fallon called. Ahab and the men on deck looked helpless so far below him. Fallon did not know if his lying would work, but there was the chance that the other men in the rigging, not being as high as he, would not be able to make out Moby Dick from their lower vantage points. He turned away from the whale and made a good show of scanning the empty horizon.

"Top gallant sails!—stunsails! Alow and aloft, and on both sides!" Ahab ordered. The men fixed a line from the mainmast to the deck, looped its lower end around Ahab's rigid leg. Ahab wound the rope around his shoulders and arm, and they hoisted him aloft, twisting with the pressure on the hemp, toward the masthead. He twirled slowly as they raised him up, and his line of sight was obscured by the rigging and sails he had to peer through.

Before they had lifted him two-thirds of the way up, he began to shout.

"There she blows!—there she blows! A hump like a snow-hill! It is Moby Dick!"

Fallon knew enough to begin shouting and pointing immediately, and the men at the other two masts did the same. Within a minute everyone who had remained on the deck was in the rigging trying to catch a glimpse of the creature they had sought, half of them doubting his existence, for so many months.

Fallon looked down toward the helmsman, who stood on his toes, the whalebone tiller under his arm, arching his neck trying to see the whale.

The others in the rigging were now arguing about who had spotted Moby Dick first, with Ahab the eventual victor. It was his fate, he said, to be the one to first spot the whale. Fallon couldn't argue with that.

Ahab was lowered to the deck, giving orders all the way, and three boats were swung outboard in preparation for the chase. Starbuck was ordered to stay behind and keep the ship.

As they chased the whale, the sea became calmer, so the rowing became easier—though just as backbreaking—and they knifed through the water, here as placid as a farm pond, faster than ever. Accompanying the sound of their own wake, Fallon heard the wake of the whale they must be approaching. He strained arms, back, and legs, pulling harder in time to Stubb's cajoling chant, and the rushing grew. He snatched a glance over his shoulder, turned to the rowing, then looked again.

The white whale glided through the sea smoothly, giving the impression of immeasurable strength. The wake he left was as steady as that of a schooner; the bow waves created by the progress of his broad, blank brow through the water fanned away in precise lines whose angle with respect to the massive body did not change. The three whaleboats rocked gently as they broke closer through these successive waves; the foam of Moby Dick's wake was abreast of them now, and Fallon saw how quickly it subsided into itself, giving the sea back its calm face, innocent of knowledge of the creature that had passed. Attendant white birds circled above their heads, now and then falling to or rising from the surface in busy flutterings of wings and awkward beaks. One of them had landed on the broken shaft of a harpoon that protruded from the snow-white whale's humped back; it bobbed up and down with the slight rocking of the whale in its long, muscular surging through the sea. Oblivious. Strangely quiet. Fallon felt as if they had entered a magic circle.

He knew Ahab's boat, manned by the absurd Filipinos, was ahead of them and no doubt preparing to strike first. Fallon closed his eyes, pulled on his oar, and wished for it not to happen. For it to stop now, or just continue without any change. He felt as if he could row a very long time; he was no longer tired or afraid. He just wanted to keep rowing, feeling the rhythm of the work, hearing the low and insistent voice of Stubb telling them to break their backs. Fallon wanted to listen to the rushing white sound of the whale's wake in the water, to know that they were perhaps keeping pace with it, to know that, if he should tire, he could look for a second over his shoulder and find Moby Dick there still. Let the monomaniac stand in the bow of his boat—if he was meant to stand there, if it was an unavoidable necessity—let him stand there with the raised lance and concentrate his hate into one purified moment of will. Let him send that will into the tip of that lance so that it might physically glow with the frustrated obtuseness of it. Let him stand there until he froze from the suspended desire, and let the whale swim on.

Fallon heard a sudden increase in the rushing of the water, several inarticulate cries. He stopped pulling, as did the others, and turned to look in time to see the whale lift itself out of the water, exposing flanks and flukes the bluish white of cemetery marble, and flip its huge tail upward to dive perpendicularly into the sea. Spray drenched them, and sound returned with the crash of the waves coming together to fill the vacuum left by the departure of the creature that had seconds before given weight and direction, place, to the placeless expanse of level waters. The birds circled above the subsiding foam.

They lifted their oars. They waited. "An hour," Ahab said.

They waited. It was another beautiful day. The sky was hard and blue as the floor of the swimming pool where he had met Carol. Fallon wondered again if she missed him, if he had indeed disappeared from that other life when he had taken up residence in this one—but he thrust those thoughts away. They were meaningless. There was no time in that world after his leaving it; that world did not exist, or if it existed, the order of its existence was not of the order of the existence of the rough wood he sat on, the raw flesh of his hands and the air he breathed. Time was the time between the breaths he drew. Time was the duration of the dream he had had about being back in Chicago, and he could not say how long that had been, even if it had begun or ended. He might be dreaming still. The word *dream* was meaningless, and *awake*. And *real*, and *insane*, and *known*, and all those other interesting words he had once accepted without questioning. Time was waiting for Moby Dick to surface again.

The breeze freshened. The sea began to swell.

"The birds!—the birds!" Tashtego shouted, so close behind Fallon's ear that he winced. The Indian half stood, rocking the whaleboat as he pointed to the seabirds, which had risen and were flying toward Ahab's boat twenty yards away.

"The whale will breach there," Stubb said.

Ahab was up immediately. Peering into the water, he leaned on the steering oar and reversed the orientation of his boat. He then exchanged places with Fedallah, the other men reaching up to help him through the rocking boat. He picked up the harpoon, and the oarsmen stood ready to row.

Fallon looked down into the sea, trying to make out what Ahab saw. Nothing, until a sudden explosion of white as the whale, rocketing upward, turned over as it finally hit the surface. In a moment Ahab's boat was in the whale's jaws, Ahab in the bows almost between them. Stubb shouted, and Fallon's fellows fell to the oars in a disorganized rush. The Filipinos in the lead boat crowded into the stern while Ahab, like a man trying to open a recalcitrant garage door, tugged and shoved at Moby Dick's jaw, trying to dislodge the whale's grip. Within seconds filled with crashing water, cries, and confusion, Moby Dick had bitten the boat in two, and Ahab had belly-flopped over the side like a swimming-class novice.

Moby Dick then began to swim tight circles around the smashed boat and its crew. Ahab struggled to keep his head above water. Neither Stubb nor Flask could bring their boats close enough to pick him up. The *Pequod* was drawing nearer, and finally Ahab was able to shout loudly enough to be heard, "Sail on the whale—drive him off!"

It worked. The *Pequod* picked up the remnants of the whaleboat while Fallon and the others dragged its crew and Ahab into their own boat.

The old man collapsed in the bottom of the boat, gasping for breath, broken and exhausted. He moaned and shook. Fallon was sure he was finished whale chasing, that Stubb and the others would see the man was used up, that Starbuck would take over and sail them home. But in a minute or two Ahab was leaning on his elbow asking after his boat's crew, and a few minutes later they had resumed the chase with double oarsmen in Stubb's boat.

Moby Dick drew steadily away as exhaustion wore them down. Fallon did not feel he could row any more after all. The *Pequod* picked them up, and they gave chase in vain under all sail until dark.

FOURTEEN

ON THE SECOND day's chase all three boats were smashed in. Many of the men suffered sprains and contusions, and one was bitten by a shark. Ahab's whale-bone leg was shattered, with a splinter driven into his thigh. Fedallah, who had been the captain's second shadow, was tangled in the line Ahab had shot into the white whale, dragged out of the boat, and drowned. Moby Dick escaped.

FIFTEEN

IT CAME DOWN to what Fallon had known it would come down to eventually.

In the middle of that night he went to talk to Ahab, who slept in one of the hatchways as he had the night before. The carpenter was making him another leg, wooden this time, and Ahab was curled sullenly in the dark lee of the afterscuttle. Fallon did not know whether he was waiting or asleep.

He started down the stairs, hesitated on the second step. Ahab lifted his head. "What do you need?" he asked.

Fallon wondered what he wanted to say. He looked at the man huddled in the darkness and tried to imagine what moved him, tried to see him as a man instead of a thing. Was it possible he was only a man, or had Fallon himself become stylized and distorted by living in the book of Melville's imagination?

"You said—talking to Starbuck today—you said that everything that happens is fixed, decreed. You said it was rehearsed a billion years before any of it took place. Is it true?"

Ahab straightened and leaned toward Fallon, bringing his face into the dim light thrown by the lamps on deck. He looked at him for a moment in silence.

"I don't know. So it seemed as the words left my lips. The Parsee is dead before me, as he foretold. I don't know."

"That's why you're hunting the whale."

"That is why I'm hunting the whale."

"How can this hunt, how can killing an animal tell you anything? How can it justify your life? What satisfaction can it give you in the end, even if you boil it all down to oil, even if you cut Moby Dick into bible leaves and eat him? I don't understand it."

The captain looked at him earnestly. He seemed to be listening, and leaping ahead of the questions. It was very dark in the scuttle, and they could hardly see each other. Fallon kept his hands folded tightly behind him. The blade of the cleaver he had shoved into his belt lay cool against the skin at the small of his back; it was the same knife he used to butcher the whale.

"If it is immutably fixed, then it does not matter what I do. The purpose and meaning are out of my hands, and thine. We have only to take our parts, to be the thing that it is written for us to be. Better to live that role given us than to struggle against it or play the coward, when the actions must be the same nonetheless. Some say I am mad to chase the whale. Perhaps I am mad. But if it is my destiny to seek him, to tear, to burn and kill those things that stand in my path—then the matter of my madness is not relevant, do you see?"

He was not speaking in character.

"If these things are not fixed, and it was not my destiny to have my leg taken by the whale, to have my hopes blasted in this chase, then how cruel a world it is. No mercy, no power but its own, controls it; it blights our lives out of merest whim. No, not whim, for there would then be no will behind it, no builder of this Bedlam hospital, and in the madhouse, when the keeper is gone, what is to stop the inmates from doing as they please? In a universe of cannibals, where all creatures have preyed upon each other, carrying on an eternal war since the world began, why should I not exert my will in whatever direction I choose? Why should I not bend others to my will?" The voice was reasonable, and tired. "Have I answered your question?"

Fallon felt the time drawing near. He felt light, as if the next breeze might lift him from the deck and carry him away. "I have an idea", he said.

"My idea is—and it is an idea I have had for some time now, and despite everything that has happened, and what you say, I can't give it up—my idea is that all that is happening..." Fallon waved his hand at the world, "...is a story. It is a book written by a man named Herman Melville and told by a character named Ishmael. You are the main character in the book. All the things that have happened are events in the book.

"My idea also is that I am not from the book, or at least I wasn't originally. Originally I lived a different life in another time and place, a life in the real world and not in a book. It was not ordered and plotted like a book, and..."

Ahab interrupted in a quiet voice: "You call this an ordered book? I see no order. If it were so orderly, why would the whale task me so?"

Fallon knotted his fingers tighter behind him. Ahab was going to make him do it. He felt the threads of the situation weaving together to create only that bloody alternative, of all the alternatives that might be. In the open market, the price for the future and price for the physical reality converged on delivery day.

"The order's not an easy thing to see, I'll admit," Fallon said. He laughed nervously.

Ahab laughed louder. "It certainly is not. And how do you know this other life you speak of was not a play? A different kind of play. How do you know your thoughts are your own? How do you know that this dark little scene was not prepared just for us, or perhaps for someone who is reading about us at this very moment and wondering about the point of the drama just as much as we wonder at the pointlessness of our lives?" Ahab's voice rose, gaining an edge of compulsion. "How do we know anything?" He grabbed his left wrist, pinched the flesh and shook it.

"How do we know what lies behind this matter? This flesh is a wall, the painting over the canvas, the mask drawn over the player's face, the snow fallen over the fertile field, or perhaps the scorched earth. I know there is something there; there must be something, but it cannot be touched because we are smothered in this flesh, this life. How do we know—"

"Stop it! Stop it!" Fallon shouted. "Please stop asking things! You should not be able to say things like that to me! Ahab does not talk to me!"

"Isn't this what I am supposed to say?"

Fallon shuddered.

"Isn't this scene in your book?"

He was dizzy, sick. "No! Of course not!"

"Then why does that disturb you? Doesn't this prove that we are not pieces of a larger dream, that this is a real world, that the blood that flows within our veins is real blood, that the pain we feel has meaning, that the things we do have consequence? We break the mold of existence by existing. Isn't that reassurance enough?" Ahab was shouting now, and the men awake on deck trying to get the boats in shape for the last day's chase and the *Pequod*'s ultimate destruction put aside their hammers and rope and listened to his justification.

It was time. Fallon, shaking with anger and fear, drew the knife from behind him and leapt at the old man. In bringing up the blade for the attack he hit it against the side of the narrow hatchway. His grip loosened. Ahab threw up his hands and, despite the difference in age and mobility between them, managed to grab Fallon's wrist before he could strike the killing blow. Instead, the deflected cleaver struck the beam beside Ahab's head and stuck there. As Fallon tried to free it, Ahab brought his forearm up and smashed him beneath the jaw. Fallon fell backward, striking his head with stunning force against the opposite side of the scuttle. He momentarily lost consciousness.

When he came to himself again, Ahab was sitting before him with his strong hands on Fallon's shoulders, supporting him, not allowing him to move.

"Good, Fallon, good," he said. "You've done well. But now, no more games, no more dramas, no easy way out. Admit that this is not the tale you think it is! Admit that you do not know what will happen to you in the next second, let alone the next day or year! Admit that we are both free and unfree, alone and crowded in by circumstance in this world that we indeed did not make, but indeed have the power to affect! Put aside those notions that there is another life somehow more real than the life you live now, another air to breathe somehow more pure, another love or hate somehow more vital than the love or hate you bear me. Put aside your fantasy and admit that you are alive, and thus may momentarily die. Do you hear me, Fallon?"

Fallon heard, and saw, and felt, and touched, but he did not know. The *Pequod*, freighted with savages and isolatoes, sailed into the night, and the great shroud of the sea rolled on as it rolled five thousand years ago.

Consolation

LESTER

GIVEN LAST month's denial-of-service attack on the robocar network, I was surprised when, over the streetcam, I saw Alter arrive in a bright blue citicar. As it pulled away from the curb toward its next call, he tugged his jacket straight and looked directly up into the camera, a sheen of sweat on his forehead. 1142 AM, 5 November, the readout at the corner of my pad said. 30 C. Major rain in the forecast.

Alter was forty, stork-like and ungainly. He stuck his hands into his pockets and approached the lobby, and the door opened for him.

I set down the pad and got up to open my office door. Alter was standing with his back to me, peering at the directory. "Mr. Alter," I called. "Over here."

He turned, looked at me warily, and then came over.

"Right in here," I said. I ushered him into the office. He stood there and inspected it. It looked pretty shabby. A bookshelf, a desk covered with papers, a window on the courtyard where a couple of palms grew and a turtle sat on a log, a framed print of Magritte's *La reproduction interdite*, two armchairs facing each other. Like an iceberg, nine tenths of the office was invisible.

"No receptionist," Alter said.

"That's right. Just you and me. Have a seat."

Alter didn't move. "I thought this would be a government office."

"I work for the government. This is my office."

"You people," Alter said. He sat down. I sat across from him. "What's your name?" he asked.

"It's uncomfortable, isn't it, working in a state of incomplete knowledge. Call me Lester."

463

"I like to know where I am, Lester."

Everything in his manner, in the way he sat in the chair, in the timbre of his voice, screamed sociopath. I didn't need some expert system to tell me where he fell on the spectrum: I had been dealing with men like Alter—always men—for long enough to read them in my sleep.

"You're in Canada," I said. "In Massachusetts, to be specific. You're in my office, about to tell us what you've done."

"Us?" he said. "Do you have a hamster in your pocket?"

"Think of 'us' as the rest of the human race."

Alter's eyes narrowed. "'Us' like the U.S. You're a Fed."

"There are no Feds anymore. That's a Sunbelt fantasy."

"You know I'm not from the Sunbelt. I'm from Vermont. You've been invading my privacy, surveilling me. You're going to dox me. Turnabout is fair play. Eye-for-eye kind of thing. Very biblical."

"Do you always assume that everybody else is like you?"

"Most people aren't." He smiled at that, quite pleased with himself.

"Doxing only works against a person who has something to lose. Friends. A family. A valuable job. A reputation. You're dox-proof, Jimmy. All we want is for you to explain what you've done."

"You already know what I've done. That's why I'm here. You violated my privacy, my personhood."

"Yes, that's true. Why do you think we did that?"

"Why? What I wish I knew was how. No way you should have been able to trace me." He looked around my office. "Certainly not with anything you have here."

"You aren't here for *me* to tell *you* things, you are here for *you* to tell *me* things. So let's get on with it. We'd like you to say what you've done. We need to hear you speak the words. Imagine it's so we can measure your degree of remorse."

"I'm not remorseful. Everything I did was right."

He was beyond tiresome. His pathetic individualism, his fantasy of his uniqueness, his solipsism. I wanted to punch him just so he might know that what was happening in this room was real. "So tell us all those right things you did."

464

"Well, I turned up all the thermostats in the Massachusetts State House. Sweated them out of there for an afternoon, anyway."

"What else?"

"I inventoried the contents of all the refrigerators of government employees with a BMI over thirty. And the bathroom scales, the medical interventions, the insurance records. All those morbidly obese—I posted it on Peeperholic."

"Is that all?"

"I scrambled the diagnostic systems in the Pittsfield New Clinic. I deflated all the tires in the Salem bikeshare—that one was just for fun. At UMass I kept the chancellor out of her office for a week and put videos of her and her wife in bed onto every public display on the campus."

"Is that all?"

"That covers the most significant ones, yes."

"I know you don't believe in law, but I thought you believed in privacy."

"They don't deserve privacy."

"But you do."

"Apparently not. So here I am."

"You resent us. But you object to your victims resenting you?"

"Victims? Who's a victim? I was punching up. The people I troubled needed to be troubled. Here's what I did—I punctured their hypocrisies and exposed their lies. I made some powerful and corrupt people a little uncomfortable. I managed to tell some truths about a pitifully few people, to a pitifully small audience. I wish I could have done more."

I'd been doing this too long. One too many sociopathic losers with computers, broken people who didn't know how broken they were. The world churned them out, full of defensive self-righteousness, deformed consciences, spotty empathy, and a sense of both entitlement and grievance—bullies who saw themselves as victims, the whole sodden army of them out there wreaking havoc small and large without a clue as to how pathetic and pathetically dangerous they were. A sea of psychopathy, with computers. The mid-21st century.

Thank god I didn't have to deal with the ones carrying guns. That was another department.

Alter was still going on. I interrupted him. "Why don't you tell me about Marjorie Xenophone."

"Funny name. I don't believe I know that woman."

"You knew her well enough to send her STD history to her husband. To tell her car to shut down every time she turned onto her lover's street."

"That's a terrible thing to do. But I never heard of the woman before you mentioned her name."

"So you don't know she killed herself."

"Suicide, huh? She must have been one messed-up lady."

"You turned off her birth control implant and she got pregnant. Her husband left her, she lost her job. She was humiliated in front of everybody she knew."

"Some people can't deal with life."

"Mr. Alter, you are one bad, bad pancake," I said. "You worked with her at Green Mountain Video Restoration."

Alter's eyes slid from mine up to the Magritte painting. A man is looking into a mirror, the back of his head to us. The mirror shows an identical image of the back of his head.

When Alter spoke, his tone was more serious. "What went on between me and that woman was private."

"Privacy was an historical phase, Jimmy, and it's over. Nobody had a right to privacy when they were indentured servants or slaves. For one or two hundred years people imagined they could have secrets. That was a local phenomenon and it's now over. Your career is evidence of why."

"So why is it a crime when an individual does it but perfectly fine when your social media platform or service provider or the government does? People sign away their privacy with every TOS box they check. If they get upset when I liberate publicly available materials, too bad. Maybe they'll get smart and stand up to people like you."

"Well said. Where were you born, again?"

"Burlington, Vermont."

"Right. Burlington. South Burlington—the part that's in Texas."

Alter didn't say anything. I had never seen a man look more angry. "Indentured servants and slaves," he muttered.

"Did you really think you could create an identity that would get past our friends at MIT?" I said. "And then have the arrogance to pursue a career as a troll? Where did you go to school? Texas Tech?"

"That's a lot of questions at once."

"We already know the answers."

Outside, thunder sounded. Fat raindrops began to fall into the court-yard, moving the leaves of the palms. The turtle remained motionless. "Where were you born?"

After a hesitation, he said, "Galveston."

"Sad about Galveston, the hurricane. How long have you been a refugee?"

"I'm not a refugee."

"An illegal immigrant, then?"

"I'm a Texas citizen. I just happen to be working here."

"Under a false identity."

"I pay your taxes. I pay as much as any citizen."

"Don't like our taxes, go back to Texas." I smiled. "Could be a bumper sticker."

Alter looked straight at me for a good five seconds. "Please, don't make me."

"But we're persecuting you. The jackbooted thugs of the totalitarian Canadian government."

"You're no more Canadian than I am. You're an American."

"Check out the flagpole in Harvard Square sometime. Note the red maple leaf."

"Look, I get it. You have power over me." Alter rubbed his hands on his pants legs. "What do you want me to say? I'll sign anything you want me to sign."

"What about Marjorie?"

"You're right. I went too far. I feel bad about that." Alter's belligerence had faded. He shifted in his chair. "I'm sorry if I got out of line. Just tell me what you want and I'll do it."

"I got the impression you didn't like people telling you what to do."

"Well...sometimes you have to go along to get along. Right?"

"So I've heard."

"How many sessions are we going to have?"

"Sessions? What sessions?"

"Because of the court order. You're supposed to heal me or certify me or something, before I can go back into the world."

"It's not my job to heal you."

"Maybe it's punishment, then."

It was a pleasure to see the panic in his eyes. "This isn't a prison and I'm not a cop. I'll tell you what we will do, though. We'll send you back to the hellhole you came from. Hope you kept your water wings."

Just then I noticed something on my pad. It was raining hard now, a real monsoon, and the temperature had dropped 10 degrees. But in the middle of hustling pedestrians stood a woman, very still, staring at the entrance of my building. People walked by her in both directions, hunched against the storm. She wore a hat pulled low, and a long black coat slick with rain. She entered the lobby. She scanned it, turned purposefully toward my office, reached into her coat pocket, and walked off camera.

"I don't think anything I've done's so bad..." Alter said. I held up my hand to shut him up.

The door to my office opened. Alter started to turn around. Before he could, the woman in the black coat tossed something into the room, then stepped back and closed the door. The object hit the floor with a solid thunk and rolled, coming to rest by my right foot. It was a grenade.

ESMERALDA

THE BLAST BLEW the door across the lobby into the plate-glass front wall, shattering it. By then I was out on the sidewalk. I set off through the downpour in the direction of the train station.

Before I had walked a hundred meters the drones swooped past me, rotors tearing the rain into mist, headed for Makovec's office. People rushed out into the street. The citicar network froze, and only people on bikes and in private vehicles were able to move. I stepped off the curb into a puddle, soaking my shoe.

Teo had assured me that all public monitors had been taken care of and no video would be retrieved from five minutes before to five after the explosion. I walked away from Dunster Street, trying to keep my pace steady, acutely aware that everybody else was going in the other direction. Still, I crossed the bridge over the levees, caught a cab, and reached the station in good time.

I tried to sleep a little as the train made its way across Massachusetts, out of the rainstorm, through the Berkshires, into New York. It was hopeless. The sound of the blast rang in my ears. The broken glass and smoke, the rain. It was all over the net: Makovec was dead and they weren't saying anything about Alter. Teo's phony video had been released, claiming responsibility for the Refugee Liberation Front and warning of more widespread attacks if Ottawa turned its back on those fleeing Confederated Free America.

Outside the observation window a bleeding sunset poured over forests of russet and gold. After New England and New York became provinces, Canada had dropped a lot of money on the rail system. All these formerly hopeless decaying cities—from classical pretenders Troy, Rome, Utica to Mohawk-wannabe Chittenango and Canajoharie—were coming back. If it weren't for the flood of refugees from the Sunbelt, the American provinces might make some real headway against economic and environmental blight.

Night settled in and a gibbous moon shone. Lots of time to think.

I was born in Ogdensburg back when it was still part of the U.S. There'd been plenty of backwoods loons where I grew up, in the days when rural New York might as well have been Alabama. But the Anschluss with Canada and the huge influx of illegals had pushed even the local evangelicals into the anti-immigrant camp. Sunbelters. Ragged, uncontrollable, when they weren't draining social services they were ranting about government stealing their freedom, defaming their God, taking away their guns.

My own opinions about illegals were not moderated by any ideological or religious sympathies. I didn't need any more threadbare crackers with their rugged-individualist libertarian Jesus-spouting militia-loving nonsense to fuck up the new Northeast the way they had fucked up the old U.S. We're Canadians now, on sufferance, and eager to prove our devotion to our new government. Canada has too many of its own problems to care what happens to some fools who hadn't the sense to get out of Florida before it was inundated.

The suffering that the Sunbelters fled wasn't a patch on the environmental degradation they were responsible for. As far as I was concerned, their plight was chickens coming home to roost. Maybe I felt something for the Blacks and Hispanics and the women, but in a storm you have to pick a side and I'd picked mine a long time ago. Teo's video would raise outrage against the immigrants and help ensure that Ottawa would not relax its border policies.

But my ears still rang from the blast.

It was morning when the train arrived in Buffalo. The station was busy for early Saturday: people coming into town for the arts festival, grimly focused clients headed to one of the life extension clinics, families on their way up to Toronto, bureaucrats on their way to Ottawa. In the station I bought a coffee and a beignet. Buzzing from lack of sleep, I sat at a table on the concourse and watched the people. When the screen across from me slipped from an ad for Roswell Life Extension into a report on the Boston attack, I slung my bag over my shoulder and walked out.

I caught the Niagara Street tram. A brilliant November morning: warm, sunny, cotton ball clouds floating by on mild westerlies. They used to call this time of year Indian summer back when it happened in mid-October, when the temperature might hit 70 for a week or so before the perpetual cloud cover of November came down and Seasonal Affective Disorder settled in for a five- or six-month run.

Now it was common for the warmth to linger into December. Some days it still clouded up and rained, but the huge lake-effect snowstorms that had battered the city were gone. The lake never froze over anymore. The sun shone more and the breezes were mild. The disasters of the late 20th and early 21st centuries had passed, leaving Buffalo with clean air, moderate climate, fresh water, quaint neighborhoods, historic architecture, hydroelectric power beyond the dreams of any nuke, and a growing arts- and medicine-based economy. Just a hop across the river from our sister province Ontario.

The tram ran past the harbor studded with sailboats, then along the Niagara River toward the gleaming Union Bridge. Kids in LaSalle Park were flying kites. Racing shells practiced on the Black Rock Canal. A female coxed eight, in matching purple shirts, rowed with precision and vigor.

None of those women had blown anybody up in the last 24 hours.

The tram moved inland and I got off on the West Side. I carried my bag a couple of blocks, past reclaimed houses and a parking lot-turned-community garden, to the Fargo Architectural Collective. Home. We'd done the redesign ourselves, Teo and Salma and I, fusing two of the circa-1910 houses with their limestone footings and cool basements into a modern multi-purpose. It had earned us some commissions. In the front garden stood a statue of old William Fargo himself, looking more like a leprechaun than the founder of separate transportation and banking empires.

Teo greeted me at the door and enveloped me in a big bear hug.

"Esme," he said. "We've been worried. You're okay?"

"For certain values of the word okay." I dropped my bag. Salma poked her head out of her workroom. She looked very serious. "What?" I said.

"Come have some tea," she said.

The three of us sat down in the conference room and Teo brewed a pot of mood tea. "Am I going to need to be calmed down?" I asked.

Salma leaned forward, her dark brow furrowed. "Our friends in Boston screwed up. Turns out not all of the video cameras were disabled. There may be some images of you approaching the building."

"Shit."

"The fact you're not from Boston will help," Teo said. "You have no history. We're boring middle-class citizens; none of us are known activists."

"That should slow them down for about thirty seconds," I said. I sipped some tea. We talked about the prospect of my taking a vacation. Vancouver, maybe, or Kuala Lumpur. After a while I said, "I didn't sleep last night. I'm going to take a nap."

I went up to my room, sat on the bed, and unlaced my shoes. The right one was still damp from the puddle in Cambridge. I lay down. Outside my window a Carolina wren, another undocumented immigrant from the torrid South, sang its head off. Teo's tea was good for something, and in a few minutes I drifted off to sleep.

It was late afternoon when I woke. Salma came in and lay down beside me on her side, her face very close to mine. "Feel any better?"

"Better." I kissed her. "It was awful, Salma."

She touched my cheek. "I know. But somebody has—"

I forced myself up. "You don't know."

Salma sat up and put her hand on my shoulder. "If you're going to be a soldier for change, then you have to accept some damages. Try not to think about it. Come on, take a shower, get dressed. We're going out."

I swung my legs off the bed. I had volunteered, after all. "Where are we going?"

"There's a party at Ajit Ghosh's. Lot of people will be there."

Ghosh was a coming intellectual voice. An aggregator, a cultural critic, the youngest man to hold a named chair in the history of UB. He lived in a big state-of-the-art ecohouse with a view of Delaware Park, Hoyt Lake, and the Albright-Knox. The neighborhood was money, new houses and old occupied by young, ambitious people on their way up. I didn't like a lot of them, or who they were willing to step on in order to rise, but you had to give them points for energy and creativity.

I did not care for the way they looked down on people whose roots in WNY went back to before it became trendy. The party would be full of people who came here only when living in New York City got too difficult, the Southwest dried up and blew away, and the hurricane-battered South turned into an alternating fever swamp and forest fire.

I didn't think I needed a party. But Ghosh's house was a Prairie School reboot with a negative carbon imprint. It was better than lying around with the echo of an explosion in my head.

"All right," I said.

SCOOBIE

I'D SPENT THE last three days at Roswell Park getting my tumors erased, and now I was out on the street ready to do some damage. I headed toward the restaurants on Main Street, walking past the blocks of medical labs, life extension clinics, hospitals, all with their well-designed signage and their well-trimmed gardens and their well-heeled patients taking the air. Most of them looked pretty good. Pretty much all of them were doomed.

They treated their ailments and told themselves that nobody lives forever. But I would. An immortal living in the world of mortals—one of the few. The ones who committed to the task and made the best choices. Rationalism. Certain practices, investments, expectations. Habits of living.

There's an industry devoted to anti-aging, a jungle of competing claims and methods. Most of it is garbage, pretty pictures papering over the grave. Billions wasted every year.

Not me. I didn't invest in a single platform, but maneuvered between the options. Of course you could not always know the best choice with certainty. If you went the T+p53 route, you entered the race between immortality and cancer. You had to boost your tumor suppression genes to counter the increased telomerase that prevented chromosome erosion. Hence my visit to Roswell. There was SkQ ingestion to reduce mitochondria damage. A half-dozen other interventions and their synergistic effects, positive and negative. To keep on top of this you needed as much information as possible. Even then you could make a mistake—but that was the human condition for us early posthumans.

I had backups: a contract to be uploaded once they had worked out the tech. A separate contract to have my head cryogenically preserved once the brain had been uploaded. Some other irons in the fire, depending on the way things broke.

I grew up in Fort McMurray, Alberta, in the destroyed landscape of bitumen strip mines and oil sands, with its collapsing economy and desperate gun-toting mountain people. When the U.S. broke up and the northeastern and Pacific states joined Canada, freedom-loving Alberta took the opportunity to go the other way, ditching the arrogant bastards in Ottawa to join in a nice little union with Montana, Wyoming, and Idaho. Big skies, free men. Petroleum fractions. Though it had its charms, I had things I wanted to do, and not many of them could be done in Calgary.

It was a beautiful day, a good day to be alive. I felt very young. Though this latest treatment would blow a hole in my savings, I decided to spend some money. At Galley's on Main I ordered broiled salmon and a salad. I had not eaten anything like this in a year. I let the tastes settle on my tongue. I could feel the cells in my body exploding with sensory energy. The crispness of the lettuce. A cherry tomato. It was all astonishing, and I let it linger as long as I could.

A man leaving the restaurant glanced at me and did a double take. It was Mossadegh.

"By the fires of Ormazd!" he said. "Not expecting you in a place like this. How's it growing, brother?"

"Germinal," I said. My connections with Mossadegh were mostly business. He knew a lot of women, though. I waved at the chair opposite. "Sit down."

"Haven't seen you much," Mossadegh said. "Where you been?"

"Out of town for a few days. Clients." I didn't advertise that I was going to live forever.

Mossadegh was a pirate. He said it was principle with him, not self-interest: freedom of information, no copyright or patents. That was how I got to know him, and on occasion he and I had made some money together. I would never let Mossadegh know anything about who I really was, though. The free flow of information is essential to posthumanism, but I didn't want anybody in my business.

I don't belong to any of those cults. No Extropians. No oxymoronic libertarian socialists. Most of all, I don't want any connection with any-body—anybody human, anyway. That might get you some information others didn't have, but it's too risky. The most vocal ones make the most idiotic choices.

"Got anything working?" he asked.

"Making some phony archives," I said. "Mostly boring—famous places, New York City, Beijing. Last week somebody wanted an event set in Kansas City in the 1930s, and I just about kissed his hand."

Mossadegh flagged down a waiter and ordered a drink. Alcohol—he wasn't going to live forever, I can tell you that. "I know somebody who used to live in Kansas City."

"Really? He got out before it happened?"

"Get this: he left one week—to the day—before."

"You're kidding," I said.

"Truth is truth."

As the afternoon declined we went on about nothing particularly important. Mossadegh rubbed his long jaw with his long fingers. "Say, you want to come to a party?"

"When?"

"Right now, brother! Maryam's been taking some grad classes and this rich prof's throwing a blowout."

"I'm not from the university," I said.

"But I am, and you come with me. Stout fellow like you's always welcome."

Mossadegh was no more from the university than I was, but I had nothing better to do. We caught a citicar up Elmwood. The setting sun reflecting off the windows of the houses turned them into gold mirrors. We passed a public building where somebody had plastered a video sign onto the side: "Go back to Arkansas... Or is it Kansas?"

The party was in a new neighborhood where they had torn out the old expressway, overlooking the park. It was twilight when we got there, a little chill in the air, but warm lights glowed along the street. The house looked old-fashioned on the outside, but the inside was all new. A big garden in the back. Sitting on the table in the living room they had a bowl of capsules, mood teas, bottles of champagne and a pyramid of glasses. I passed on the intoxicants and drank water.

The place was crowded with university students, artists, and various other knowledge workers. The prof who owned the place, dark and slender, wore all white; he held a champagne coupe in his hand, his palm around the bowl and the stem descending between his fingers in an affected way that made my teeth hurt. He had long, wavy dark hair. He was talking with two young women, nodding his head slightly as he listened. People sat in twos and threes, and there was a group in the sunroom talking politics. Lots of them seemed pretty lit.

All of these people were going to die while I stayed alive.

I stood at the edge of the political talk. A woman was speaking with emotion in her voice. "The people you can fool all of the time are dumber than pond scum, and it isn't exactly a matter of fooling them—they want to be fooled. They'll fight against anybody who tries to pull the scales from their eyes. The hopeless core of any politician's support."

She looked to be about thirty. She wore a loose white shirt and tight black pants and she spoke with an intensity that burned, as if what she said wasn't simply some liberal platitude. This college-undergrad cant mattered to her.

"But fooling all of the people has become harder. Any conflict of interest, hypocrisy, double-dealing, inconvenient truth gets out as soon as somebody with skills addresses finding it, and too many people have the skills. A politician's best bet is to throw sand into people's eyes, put enough distracting information out there that the truth will be buried. You can make a career as long as people are blinded by ideology or just can't think their way through your crap."

I didn't want to get into these weeds. I wasn't the kind of person they were. But she was right about ideological blindness, even if she didn't realize that it applied to her, too.

I thought about my last three days in the clinic. Four tumors they'd zapped out of me this time. Prospects were that cancer treatments would get better, and if they didn't I could go off telomerase life extension and try something else. But I had to admit that staring at the ceiling while the machines took care of something that in the old days would have killed me in three months was not pleasant. And there was nobody I could tell about it. Not anybody who would care, anyway.

The next time I passed through the living room, I poured myself a glass of the champagne. What the hell.

It tasted good, and unaccustomed as I was to alcohol, I got a little buzz on right away. For an hour I wandered through the house listening to snatches of conversation. I got another glass of wine. After a while I went out into the garden. It had cooled off considerably, and most of the people who had been out there were back inside now that it was full night. Balls of golden light shone in the tree branches. It was pretty.

Then I noticed somebody sitting on a bench in the corner of the garden. It was the woman who had been ranting in the sunroom. She ignored me. Leaning on one arm, wine glass beside her, she looked as if she were listening for some sound from a distant room in the house. I drifted over to her.

"Hello," I said.

She looked up. Just stared for a moment. I noticed that her earrings, bright against her dark skin, were golden rectangles containing Fibonacci spirals. "Hello," she said.

"Sorry to interrupt," I said. "Do you live here?"

"No."

"Friends with somebody who does?"

"Salma is my sister. She's one of Ghosh's girlfriends."

"Who's Ghosh?"

She looked at me again and smiled. "This is Ghosh's house."

"Right. Do you mind if I sit?"

"Knock yourself out."

I sat down and set my glass next to hers on the bench. "Political, are you?"

"Politics is a waste," she said. "Like this thing in Cambridge yesterday—what are they trying to prove?" The anger I had heard in her voice earlier came back. "It's just killing for killing's sake. The things that need changing aren't going to be changed by blowing people up. It's in the heart and the head, and you can't change that with a hand grenade."

Maybe the wine was working in me, but I couldn't let that go.

"Lots of things are decided by hand grenades," I said. "Most things, in the end, are decided by force. Hell, politics is just another form of force. You figure out where the pressure points are, you manipulate the system, you make it necessary for the ones who oppose you to do what you want them to do. You marshal your forces, and then you get what you want."

She looked unconvinced. I liked the way her black hair, not too long, curled around her ear. "You're not from around here," she said. "The accent. You a real Canadian?"

"Alberta."

Her eyebrow raised. "An immigrant?"

"Technically, I guess. It's not like I wasn't born and raised in Canada."

"What's your name?"

"Scoobie." I could smell her faint perfume.

"Esme," she said, holding out her hand. I shook it.

"So what do you think that bombing accomplished, Scoobie?"

"Not much. People don't even know who it was aimed at, and for what reason. No way was it some pro-immigrant group. That's a false-flag move. The two guys they blew up aren't particularly influential. They have no power, not even symbolic power. They might as well have been hit by lightning."

"Sounds like you agree with me."

"If you think it was done stupidly, then I agree with you."

She looked down at her feet. She wore black canvas slippers. "I agree with you," she said. "It was done stupidly."

We sat in silence awhile. I picked up my glass and drained the last of my wine. Esme took up her own.

"So why did you emigrate?" she asked me.

"I came to Toronto for the work, at first. I have an interest in the medical professions. The big clinics, the university. Then it was McGill for a few years. Then I came here."

"Do you get any flak? Lots of people don't like immigrants. Alberta is pretty hard right."

"I don't care about that. I guess you could say I'm apolitical. The differences between the Canadian government, Texas, and the Sunbelt states mean nothing to me. I suppose you could call me a libertarian—small 'l.' Certainly I'm for free information, but it all seems petty to me."

"Petty?" The edge came back into her voice.

"This is just a moment in history. Like all political debates, it will pass. What's important is staying alive. You don't want to get caught between two crazy antagonists. Or get connected up with one side or the other."

"Do you seriously believe that?"

I don't know why I should have cared what she thought. Something about the way she held her shoulders, or the slight, husky rasp in her voice. It was the voice of somebody who had cried for a long time and was all cried out. She was arrogant, she was wrong, but she was very sexy.

I tried to make a joke. "Singularity's coming. All bets are off then."

"The Singularity is a fantasy."

I laughed. "What are you, a religious mystic?"

"I'm an architect."

"Then you ought to know the difference between the material world and fairyland. Is there something supernatural about the human brain? Is it animated by pixie dust?" I was feeling it now. Humanists, with their woo-woo belief in the uniqueness of the "mind."

"They've been talking about strong AI for eighty years. Where is it?'

"Processing power is still increasing. It's only a matter of time. It's just the architecture—"

Esme laughed. "Now you'll tell me about the architecture. Listen, no Jesus supercomputer is going to save you from the crises around us. You can't sit it out."

"I can and I will. The fighting between Canada and the Sunbelt is completely bound to this time and place. It doesn't matter. It's just history, like some war between the Catholics and Protestants in the 14th century."

"How can you say that! People are dying! The future of our society depends on what we do today. Immense matters hang in the balance. The climate! Whole species! Ecosystems! Women's rights! Animal rights!"

"You know," I said, "you're hot when you get angry."

Her hand tightened on her glass. I could see the muscles in her forearm; her skin was so brown, so smooth. For a second I thought she was going smash the glass into my face, then she tossed it away and hurled herself onto me. She bit my neck. I fell over and hit my head on the trunk of a tree, went dizzy for a second. The grass was cool. She had her legs around my waist and we started kissing. Long, slow, very serious kisses.

After some time we surfaced for breath. Her eyes were so dark.

"There were no Protestants in the 14th century," she said.

ESME AND SCOOBIE waited in a restaurant at the Toronto airport. Their flight for Krakow left in an hour. They were traveling light, just one small bag each—"getting out of Dodge," Teo called it—and Esme was persuaded. Scoobie knew somebody at the university there, and there was some clinic he wanted to visit.

Both of them were nervous. Neither was sure that this was a good idea, but it seemed like something they should do. At least that was where they were leaving it for now.

"Can I get you something from the bar?" Scoobie asked. "Something to eat?" For a person whose social skills were so rudimentary, he was quite sensitive to her moods.

"No," Esme said. "Maybe we should get to the gate."

Scoobie got up. "Gonna hit the men's room first."

"Okay."

For three days, since that moment in the garden, they had spent every minute together. Inexplicably. He was a cranky naïve libertarian child, afraid of human contact. His politics were ludicrous. But politics—what had politics ever given her besides migraines? Scoobie was so glad to be with her, as if he'd never been with anyone before. Their disagreements only made her see his vulnerabilities more clearly. He had some terribly stupid ideas, but he was not malicious, and he gave her something she needed. She wouldn't call it love—not yet. Call it consolation.

It didn't hurt that on no notice whatsoever he'd managed to get her the subtle tattooing that could deceive facial-recognition software. Teo had produced credentials for them as husband and wife, and their friends had created a false background for them in government databases. They had a shot at getting out of the country.

Up on one of the restaurant screens a news reader announced, "Authorities offer no new information in the hunt for the woman who threw an explosive device into the Cambridge, Massachusetts, office of Lester Makovec, consultant to the New England provincial government's Bureau of Immigration."

The screen switched to scenes of the aftermath of the Cambridge blast: a street view of broken windows, EMTs loading a body zipped into a cryobag into their vehicle.

"But there's an amazing new wrinkle to the story: Makovec, pronounced dead at the scene, was rushed to Harvard Medical School's Humanity Lab, where he underwent an experimental regenerative treatment and is reported to be on the way to recovery." Image of a hospital bed with a heavily bandaged Makovec practicing using an artificial hand to pick up small objects from the table in front of him. The chyron at the bottom of the screen read, "Lifesaving Miracle?"

"Accused terrorist and illegal immigrant Andrew Wayne Spiller, a.k.a. James Alter, who escaped the blast with minor injuries, has been moved to

Ottawa to undergo further interrogation." Image of Spiller, surrounded by security in black armor, being escorted into a train car.

"Meanwhile, Rosario Zhang, opposition leader, has called on Prime Minister Nguyen to say what she intends to do to deal with the unprovoked attack by what Zhang calls 'agents of the Texas government.' The prime minister's office has said that the forensic report has not yet determined the perpetrators of the attack, nor, in the light of denials from the Refugee Liberation Front, have investigators been able to verify the authenticity of the video claiming credit for that group."

Across the concourse stood an airport security officer in black, arms crossed over his chest, talking with an Ontario Provincial Police officer. The airport cop rocked back on his heels, eyes hooded, while the OPP spoke to him. The airport cop had a big rust-colored mustache; the OPP wore his black cap with the gray band around it.

The airport security man turned his head a fraction to his right, and he was looking, from ten meters away, directly into Esme's eyes. She had to fight the impulse to look away. She smiled at him. He smiled back. Esme considered getting up and moving to the gate—she considered leaping out of the chair to run screaming—yet she held herself still.

It took forever, but finally Scoobie returned.

"Time to go?" he said. He looked so cheerful. He was oblivious to the cops.

She kissed him on the cheek. "Yes, please," she said.

They slung their bags over their shoulders, she put her arm through his, and they headed for the gate.

The Baum Plan
for Financial
Independence

—for Wilton Barnhardt

WHEN I picked her up at the Stop 'n Shop on Route 28, Dot was wearing a short black skirt and red sneakers just like the ones she had taken from the bargain rack the night we broke into the Sears in Hendersonville five years earlier. I couldn't help but notice the curve of her hip as she slid into the front seat of my old T-Bird. She leaned over and gave me a kiss, bright red lipstick and breath smelling of cigarettes. "Just like old times," she said.

The Sears had been my idea, but after we got into the store that night all the other ideas had been Dot's, including the game on the bed in the furniture department and me clocking the night watchman with the anodized aluminum flashlight I took from Hardware, sending him to the hospital with a concussion and me to three years in Central. When the cops showed up, Dot was nowhere to be found. That was all right. A man has to take responsibility for his own actions; at least that's what they told me in the group therapy sessions that the prison shrink ran on Thursday nights. But I never knew a woman who could make me do the things that Dot could make me do.

One of the guys at those sessions was Radioactive Roy Dunbar, who had a theory about how we were all living in a computer and none of this was real. Well if this isn't real, I told him, I don't know what real is. The softness of Dot's breast or the stink of the crapper in the Highway 28 Texaco, how can there be anything more real than that? Radioactive Roy and the people like him are just looking for an exit door. I can understand that. Everybody dreams of an exit door sometimes.

I slipped the car into gear and pulled out of the station onto the highway. The sky was red above the Blue Ridge, the air blowing in the windows smoky with the ash of the forest fires burning a hundred miles to the northwest.

"Cat got your tongue, darlin'?" Dot said.

I pushed the cassette into the deck and Willie Nelson was singing "Hello Walls." "Where are we going, Dot?"

"Just point this thing west for twenty or so. When you come to a sign that says Potters Glen, make a right on the next dirt road."

Dot pulled a pack of Kools out of her purse, stuck one in her mouth, and punched the car's cigarette lighter.

"Doesn't work," I said.

She pawed through her purse for thirty seconds, then clipped it shut. "Shit," she said. "You got a match, Sid?" Out of the corner of my eye I watched the cigarette bobble up and down as she spoke.

"Sorry, sweetheart, no."

She took the cigarette from her mouth, stared at it for a moment, and flipped it out her window.

Hello window. I actually had a box of Ohio Blue Tips in the glove compartment, but I didn't want Dot to smoke because it was going to kill her someday. My mother smoked, and I remember her wet cough and the skin stretched tight over her cheekbones as she lay in the upstairs bedroom of the big house in Lynchburg, puffing on a Winston. Whenever my old man came in to clear her untouched lunch he asked her if he could have one, and Mother would smile at him, eyes big, and pull two more coffin nails out of the red-and-white pack with her nicotine-stained fingers.

One time after I saw this happen, I followed my father down to the kitchen. As he bent over to put the tray on the counter, I snatched the cigarettes from his shirt pocket and crushed them into bits over the plate of pears and cottage cheese. I glared at him, daring him to get mad. After a few seconds he just pushed past me to the living room and turned on the TV.

That's the story of my life: me trying to save the rest of you—and the rest of you ignoring me.

On the other side of Almond it was all mountains. The road twisted, the headlights flashing against the tops of trees on the downhill side and the cut earth on the uphill. I kept drifting over the double yellow line as we came in and out of turns, but the road was deserted. Occasionally we'd pass some broken-down house with a battered pickup in the driveway and a rust-spotted propane tank out in the yard.

The sign for Potters Glen surged out of the darkness, and we turned off onto a rutted gravel track that was even more twisted than the paved road. The track rose steeply; the T-Bird's suspension was shot, and my rotten muffler scraped more than once when we bottomed out. If Dot's plan required us sneaking up on anybody, it was not going to work. But she assured me that the house on the ridge was empty and she knew where the money was hidden.

Occasionally the branch of a tree would scrape across the windshield or side mirror. The forest here was dry as tinder after the summer's drought, the worst on record, and in my rearview mirror I could see the dust we were raising in the taillights. We had been ten minutes on this road when Dot said, "Okay, stop now."

The cloud of dust that had been following us caught up and billowed, settling slowly in the headlight beams. "Kill the lights," Dot said.

In the silence and darkness that came, the whine of cicadas moved closer. Dot fumbled with her purse, and when she opened the car door to get out, in the dome light I saw she had a map written on a piece of notebook paper. I opened the trunk and got out a pry bar and pair of bolt cutters. When I came around to her side of the car, she was shining a flashlight on the map.

"It shouldn't be more than a quarter of a mile farther up this road," she said.

"Why can't we just drive right up there?"

"Someone might hear."

"But you said the place was deserted."

"It is. But there's no sense taking chances."

I laughed. Dot not taking chances? That was funny. She didn't think so, and punched me in the arm. "Stop it," she said, but then she giggled. I swept the arm holding the tools around her waist and kissed her. She pushed me away, but not roughly. "Let's go," she said.

We walked up the dirt road. When Dot shut off the flashlight, there was only the faint moon coming through the trees, but after our eyes adjusted it was enough. The dark forest loomed over us. Walking through the woods at night always made me feel like I was in some teen horror movie. I expected a guy in a hockey mask to come shrieking from between the trees to cut us to ribbons with fingernails like straight razors.

Dot had heard about this summer house that was owned by the rich people she had worked for in Charlotte. They were Broyhills or related to the Broyhills, old money from the furniture business. Or maybe it was Dukes and tobacco. Anyway, they didn't use this house but a month or so out of the year. Some caretaker came by every so often, but he didn't live on the premises. Dot heard the daughter telling her friend that the family kept ten thousand dollars in cash up there in case another draft riot made it necessary for them to skip town for a while.

So we would just break in and take the money. That was the plan. It seemed a little dicey to me; leaving piles of cash lying around their vacation home did not seem like regular rich people behavior. But Dot could be very convincing even when she wasn't convincing, and my father claimed I never had a lick of sense anyway. It took us twenty minutes to come up on the clearing, and there was the house. It was bigger than I imagined it. Rustic, flagstone chimney and entranceway, timbered walls and wood shingles. Moonlight glinted off the windows in the three dormers that faced front, but all the downstairs windows were shuttered.

I took the pry bar to the hinges on one of the shuttered windows, and after some struggle they gave. The window was dead-bolted from the inside, but we knocked out one of the panes and unlatched it. I boosted Dot through the window and followed her in.

Dot used the flashlight to find the light switch. The furniture was large and heavy; the big oak coffee table that we had to move in order to take up the rug to see whether there was a safe underneath must have weighed two hundred pounds. We pulled down all the pictures from the walls. One of them was a woodcut print of Mary and Jesus, but instead of Jesus the woman was holding a fish; in the background of the picture, outside a window, a funnel cloud tore up a dirt road. The picture gave me the creeps. Behind it was nothing but plaster wall.

I heard the clink of glass behind me. Dot was pulling bottles out of the liquor cabinet to see if there was a compartment hidden behind them.

I went over, took down a glass, and poured myself a couple of fingers of Glenfiddich. I sat in a leather armchair and drank it, watching Dot search. She was getting frantic. When she came by the chair I grabbed her around the hips and pulled her into my lap.

"Hey! Lay off!" she squawked.

"Let's try the bedroom," I said.

She bounced off my lap. "Good idea." She left the room.

This was turning into a typical Dot odyssey, all tease and no tickle. I put down my glass and followed her.

I found her in the bedroom rifling through a chest of drawers, throwing clothes on the bed. I opened the closet. Inside hung a bunch of jackets and flannel shirts and blue jeans, with a pair of riding boots and some sandals lined up neatly on the floor. I pushed the hanging clothes apart, and there, set into the back wall, was a door. "Dot, bring that flashlight over here."

She came over and shined the flashlight into the closet. I ran my hand over the seam of the door. It was about three feet high, flush with the wall, the same off-white color but cool to the touch, made of metal. No visible hinges and no lock, just a flip-up handle like on a tackle box.

"That's not a safe," Dot said.

"No shit, Sherlock."

She shouldered past me, crouched down, and flipped up the handle. The door pushed open onto darkness. She shined the flashlight ahead of her; I could not see past her. "Jesus Christ Almighty," she said.

"What?"

"Stairs." Dot crawled forward, then down. I pushed the clothes aside and followed her.

The carpet on the floor stopped at the doorjamb; inside was a concrete floor and then a narrow flight of stairs leading down. A black metal handrail ran down the right side. The walls were of roughed concrete, unpainted. Dot moved ahead of me down to the bottom, where she stopped.

When I got there I saw why. The stairs let out into a large, dark room. The floor ended halfway across it, and beyond that, at either side, to the left and right, under the arching roof, were open tunnels. From one tunnel opening to the other ran a pair of gleaming rails. We were standing on a subway platform.

Dot walked to the end of the platform and shined the flashlight up the tunnel. The rails gleamed away into the distance.

"This doesn't look like the safe," I said.

"Maybe it's a bomb shelter," Dot said.

Before I could figure out a polite way to laugh at her, I noticed a light growing from the tunnel. A slight breeze kicked up. The light grew like an approaching headlight, and with it a hum in the air. I backed toward the stairs, but Dot just peered down the tunnel. "Dot!" I called. She waved a hand at me, and though she dropped back a step she kept watching. Out of the tunnel glided a car that slid to a stop in front of us. It was no bigger than a pickup. Teardrop shaped, made of gleaming silver metal, its bright single light glared down the track. The car had no windows, but as we stood gaping at it a door slid open in its side. The inside was dimly lit, with plush red seats.

Dot stepped forward and stuck her head inside.

"What are you doing?" I asked.

"It's empty," Dot said. "No driver. Come on."

"Get serious."

Dot crouched and got inside. She turned and ducked her head to look at me out of the low doorway. "Don't be a pussy, Sid."

"Don't be crazy, Dot. We don't even know what this thing is."

"Ain't you ever been out of Mayberry? It's a subway."

"But who built it? Where does it go? And what the hell is it doing in Jackson County?"

"How should I know? Maybe we can find out."

The car just sat there. The air was still. The ruby light from behind her cast Dot's face in shadow. I followed her into the car. "I don't know about this."

"Relax."

There were two bench seats, each wide enough to hold two people, and just enough space on the door side to move from one to the other. Dot sat on one of the seats with her big purse in her lap, cool as a Christian holding four aces. I sat down next to her. As soon as I did, the door slid shut and the car began to move, picking up speed smoothly, pushing us back into the firm upholstery. The only sound was a gradually increasing hum that reached a middle pitch and stayed there. I tried to breathe. There was no clack from the rails, no vibration. In front of us the car narrowed to a bullet-nosed front, and in the center of that nose was a circular window. Through the window I saw only blackness. After a while I wondered if we were still moving, until a light appeared ahead, first a small speck, then grew brighter and larger until it slipped off past us to the side at a speed that told me the little car was moving faster than I cared to figure.

"These people who own the house," I asked Dot, "where on Mars did you say they came from?"

Dot reached in her purse and took out a pistol, set it down on her lap, and fumbled around in the bag until she pulled out a pack of Juicy Fruit. She pulled out a stick, then held the pack out to me. "Gum?"

"No thanks."

She put the pack back in the purse, and the pistol, too. She slipped the yellow paper sleeve off her gum, unwrapped the foil, and stuck the gum into her mouth. After refolding the foil neatly, she slid it back into the gum sleeve and set the now empty stick on the back of the seat in front of us.

I was about to scream. "Where the fuck are we going, Dot? What's going on here?"

"I don't have any idea where we're going, Sid. If I knew you were going to be such a wuss, I would never of called you."

"Did you know about any of this?"

"Of course not. But we're going to be somewhere soon, I bet."

I got off the seat and moved to the front bench, my back to her. That didn't set my nerves any easier. I could hear her chewing her gum, and felt her eyes on the back of my neck. The car sped into blackness, broken only by the occasional spear of light flashing past. As we did not seem to be getting anywhere real soon, I had some time to contemplate the ways in which I was a fool, number one being the way I let an ex-lap dancer from Mebane lead me around by my imagination for the last ten years.

Just when I thought I couldn't get any more pissed, Dot moved up from the back seat, sat down next to me, and took my hand. "I'm sorry, Sid. Someday I'll make it up to you."

"Yeah?" I said. "So give me some of that gum." She gave me a stick. Her tidy gum wrapper had fallen onto the seat between us; I crumpled the wrapper of my own next to hers.

I had not started in on chewing when the hum of the car lowered and I felt us slowing down. The front window got a little lighter, and the car came to a stop. The door slid open.

The platform it opened onto was better lit than the one under the house in the Blue Ridge. Standing on it waiting were three people, two men and a woman. The two men wore identical dark suits of the kind bankers with too much money wore in downtown Charlotte: the suits hung the way no piece of clothing had ever hung on me—tailored closer than a mother's kiss. The woman, slender, with blond hair done up tight as a librarian's—yet there was no touch of the librarian about her—wore a dark blue dress. They stood there for a moment, then one of the men said, "Excuse me? You're here. Are you getting out?"

Dot got up and nudged me, and I finally got my nerveless legs to work. We stepped out onto the platform, and the three people got into the car, the door slid shut, and it glided off into the darkness.

It was cold on the platform, and a light breeze came from an archway across from us. Instead of rough concrete like the tunnel under the house, here the ceiling and walls were smooth stucco. Carved above the arch was a crouching man wearing some kind of Roman or Greek toga, cradling a book under one arm and holding a torch in the other. He had a wide brow and a long, straight nose and looked like a guard in Central named Pisarkiewicz, only a lot smarter. Golden light filtered down from fixtures like frogs' eggs in the ceiling.

"What now?" I asked.

Dot headed for the archway. "What have we got to lose?"

Past the arch a ramp ran upward, switchbacking every forty feet or so. A couple of women, as well dressed as the one we'd seen on the platform, passed us going the other way. We tried to look like we belonged there, though Dot's hair was a rat's nest, I was dressed in jeans and sneakers, I had not shaved since morning, and my breath smelled of scotch and Juicy Fruit.

At the top of the third switchback, the light brightened. From ahead of us came the sound of voices, echoing as if in a very large room. We reached the final archway, the floor leveled off, and we stepped into the hall.

I did not think there were so many shades of marble. The place was as big as a train station, a great open room with polished stone floors, a domed ceiling a hundred feet above us, a dozen Greek half-columns set into the far wall. Bright sun shining through tall windows between them fell on baskets of flowers and huge potted palms. Around the hall stood a number of booths like information kiosks, and grilled counters like an old-fashioned bank, at which polite staff in pale green shirts dealt with the customers. But it was not all business. Mixed among people carrying briefcases stood others in groups of three or four holding pale drinks in tall glasses or leaning casually on some counter chatting one-on-one with those manning the booths. In one corner a man in a green suit played jazz on a grand piano.

It was a cross between Grand Central Station and the ballroom at the Biltmore House. Dot and I stood out like plow horses at a cotillion. The couple hundred people scattered through the great marble room were big-city dressed. Even the people who dressed down wore hundred-dollar chinos with cashmere sweaters knotted casually around their necks. The place reeked of money.

Dot took my hand and pulled me across the floor. She spotted a table with a fountain and a hundred wine glasses in rows on the starched white tablecloth. A pink marble cherub with pursed lips like a cupid's bow poured pale wine from a pitcher into the basin that surrounded his feet. Dot handed me one of the glasses and took one for herself, held it under the stream falling from the pitcher.

She took a sip. "Tastes good," she said. "Try it."

As we sipped wine and eyed the people, a man in a uniform shirt with a brass name pin that said "Brad" came up to us. "Would you like to wash and brush up? Wash and Brush Up is over there," he said, pointing across the hall to another marble archway. He had a British accent.

"Thanks," said Dot. "We just wanted to wet our whistles first."

The man winked at her. "Now that your whistle is wet, don't be afraid to use it any time I can be of service." He smirked at me. "That goes for you too, sir."

"Fuck you," I said.

"It's been done already," the man said, and walked away.

I put down the wineglass. "Let's get out of here."

"I want to go see what's over there."

Wash and Brush Up turned out to be a suite of rooms where we were greeted by a young woman named Elizabeth and a young man named Martin. You need to spruce up, they said, and separated us. I wasn't going to have any of it, but Dot seemed to have lost her mind—she went off with Martin. After grumbling for a while, I let Elizabeth take me to a small dressing room, where she had me strip and put on a robe. After that came the shower, the haircut, the steambath, the massage. Between the steambath and massage they brought me food, something like a cheese quesadilla only much better than anything like it I had ever tasted. While I ate, Elizabeth left me alone in a room with a curtained window. I pulled the curtain aside and looked out.

The window looked down from a great height on a city unlike any I had ever seen. It was like a picture out of a kid's book, something Persian about it, and something Japanese. Slender green towers, great domed buildings, long, low structures like warehouses made of jade. The sun beat down piti-lessly on citizens who went from street to street between the fine buildings with bowed heads and plodding steps. I saw a team of four men in purple shirts pulling a cart; I saw other men with sticks herd children down to a park; I saw vehicles rumble past tired street workers, kicking up clouds of yellow dust so thick that I could taste it.

The door behind me opened, and Elizabeth stuck her head in. I dropped the curtain as if she had caught me whacking off. "Time for your massage," she said.

"Right," I said, and followed.

When I came out, there was Dot, tiny in her big plush robe, her hair clean and combed out and her finger and toenails painted shell pink. She looked about fourteen.

"Nice haircut," she said to me.

"Where are our clothes?" I demanded of Martin.

"We'll get them for you," he said. He gestured to one of the boys. "But for now, come with me."

Then they sat us down in front of a large computer screen and showed us a catalog of clothing you could not find outside of a Neiman Marcus. They had images of us, like 3D dolls, that they called up on the screen and that they could dress any way they liked so you could see how you would look. Dot was in hog heaven.

"What's this going to cost us?" I said.

Martin laughed as if I had made a good joke. "How about some silk shirts?" he asked me. "You have a good build. I know you're going to like them."

By the time we were dressed, the boy had come back with two big green shopping bags with handles. "What's this?" Dot asked, taking hers.

"Your old clothes," Martin said.

I took mine. I looked at myself in the mirror. I wore a blue shirt, a gray tie with a skinny knot and a long, flowing tail, ebony cuff links, a gunmetal gray silk jacket, and black slacks with a crease that would cut ice. The shoes were of leather as soft as a baby's skin and as comfortable as if I had broken them in for three months. I looked great.

Dot had settled on a champagne-colored dress with a scoop neckline, pale pumps, a simple gold necklace, and earrings that set off her dark hair. She smelled faintly of violets and looked better than lunch break at a chocolate factory.

"We've got to get out of here," I whispered to her.

"Thanks for stopping by!" Elizabeth and Martin said in unison. They escorted us to the door. "Come again soon!"

The hall was only slightly less busy than it had been. "All right, Dot. We head right for the subway. This place gives me the creeps."

"No," said Dot. She grabbed me by the arm that wasn't carrying my old clothes and dragged me across the floor toward one of the grilled windows.

No one gave us a second glance. We were dressed the same as everyone else, now, and fit right in.

At the window another young woman in green greeted us. "I am Miss Goode. How may I help you?"

"We came to get our money," said Dot.

"How much?" Miss Goode asked.

Dot turned to me. "What do you say, Sid? Would twenty million be enough?"

"We can do that," said Miss Goode. "Just come around behind the counter to my desk."

Dot started after her. I grabbed Dot's shoulder. "What the fuck are you talking about?" I whispered.

"Just go along and keep quiet."

Miss Goode led us to a large glass-topped desk. "We'll need a photograph, of course. And a number." She spoke into a phone: "Daniel, bring out two cases... that's right." She called up a page on her computer and examined it. "Your bank," she said to me, "is Banque Thaler, Geneva. Your number is PN68578443. You'll have to memorize it eventually. Here, write it on your palm for now." She handed me a very nice ballpoint pen. Then she gave another number to Dot.

While she was doing this, a man came out of a door in the marble wall behind her. He carried two silver metal briefcases and set them on the edge of Miss Goode's desk in front of Dot and me.

"Thank you, Daniel," she said. She turned to us. "Go ahead. Open them!"

I pulled the briefcase toward me and snapped it open. It was filled with tight bundles of crisp new one-hundred-dollar bills. Thirty of them.

"This is wonderful," Dot said. "Thank you so much!"

I closed my case and stood up. "Time to go, Dot."

"Just a minute," said Miss Goode. "I'll need your full name."

"Full name? What for?"

"For the Swiss accounts. All you've got there is three hundred thousand. The rest will be in your account. We'll need your photograph, too."

Dot tugged my elegant sleeve. "Sid forgot about that," she explained to Miss Goode. "Always in such a hurry. His name is Sidney Xavier Dubose. D-U-B-O-S-E. I'm Dorothy Gale."

I had reached my breaking point. "Shut up, Dot."

"Now for the photographs..." Miss Goode began.

"You can't have my photograph." I pulled away from Dot. I had the brief-case in my right hand and my bag of clothes under my left.

"That's all right," said Miss Goode. "We'll use your photographs from the tailor program. Just run along. But come again!"

I was already stalking across the floor, my new shoes clipping along like metronomes. People parted to let me by. I went right for the ramp that led to the subway. A thin man smoking a long cigarette watched me curiously as I passed one of the tables; I put my hand against his chest and knocked him down. He sprawled there in astonishment, but did nothing; nor did anyone else.

By the time I hit the ramp I was jogging. At the bottom the platform was deserted; the bubble lights still shone gold, and you could not tell whether it was night or day. Dot came up breathlessly behind me.

"What is wrong with you!" she shouted.

I felt exhausted. I could not tell how long it had been since we broke into the mountain house. "What's wrong with me? What's wrong with this whole setup? This is crazy. What are they going to do to us? This can't be real; it has to be some kind of scam."

"If you think it's a scam, just give me that briefcase. I'll take care of it for you, you stupid redneck."

I stood there sullenly. I didn't know what to say. She turned from me and went to the other end of the platform, as far away as she could get.

After a few minutes the light grew in the tunnel, and the car, or one just like it, slid to a stop before us. The door opened. I got in immediately, and Dot followed. We sat next to each other in silence. The door shut, and the vehicle picked up speed until it was racing along as insanely as it had so many hours ago.

Dot tried to talk to me, but I just looked at the floor. Under the seat I saw the two gum wrappers, one of them crumpled into a knot, the other neatly folded as if it were still full.

THAT WAS THE last time I ever saw Dot. I live in St. Croix now, but I have a house in Mexico and one in Toronto. In Canada I can still go to stock car races. Somehow that doesn't grab me the way it used to.

Instead I drink wine that comes in bottles that have corks. I read books. I listen to music that has no words. All because, as it turned out, I did have a ten-million-dollar Swiss bank account. The money changed everything, more than I ever could have reckoned. It was like a sword hanging over my head, like a wall between me and who I used to be. Within a month I left North Carolina: it made me nervous to stay in the state knowing that the house in the Blue Ridge was still there.

Sometimes I'm tempted to go back and see whether there really is a door in the back of that closet.

When Dot and I climbed the concrete stairs and emerged into the house, it was still night. It might have been only a minute after we went down. I went out to the living room, sat in the rustic leather chair, picked up the glass I had left next to it, and filled it to the brim with scotch. My briefcase full of three hundred thousand dollars stood on the hardwood floor beside the chair. I was dressed in a couple of thousand dollars' worth of casual clothes; my shoes alone probably cost more than a month's rent on any place that I had ever lived.

Dot sat on the sofa and poured herself a drink, too. After a while, she said, "I told you I'd make it up to you someday."

"How did you know about this?" I asked. "What is it?"

"It's a dream come true," Dot said. "You don't look a dream come true in the mouth."

"One person's dream come true is somebody else's nightmare," I said. "Somebody always has to pay." I had never thought that before, but as I spoke it I realized it was true.

Dot finished her scotch, picked up her briefcase and the green bag with her old skirt, sweater, and shoes, and headed for the door. She paused there and turned to me. She looked like twenty million bucks. "Are you coming?"

I followed her out. There was still enough light from the moon that we were able to make our way down the dirt road to my car. The insects chirped in the darkness. Dot opened the passenger door and got in.

"Wait a minute," I said. "Give me your bag."

Dot handed me her green bag. I dumped it out on the ground next to the car, then dumped my own out on top of it. I crumpled the bags and shoved them under the clothes for kindling. On top lay the denim jacket I had been wearing the night I got arrested in the Sears, that the state had kept for me while I served my time, and that I had put back on the day I left stir.

"What are you doing?" Dot asked.

"Bonfire," I said. "Goodbye to the old Dot and Sid."

"But you don't have any matches."

"Reach in the glove compartment. There's a box of Blue Tips."

The Dark Ride

"...he appears to be a strange creature of moods, a dreamy, uncanny sort of individual in whom the quality of imagination has been abnormally developed."

"Assassin Has No Moral Sense,"
St. Louis Post-Dispatch, October 6, 1901

SEPTEMBER 6, 1901

O N WEDNESDAY evening, Leon managed to get into the depot at the north end of the Pan-American Exposition grounds, among the crowd gathered for the arrival of the President's train. He tried to move close, but though the public was allowed into the building, police guarded the platform. Precisely at six the train glided into the station. Through a doorway, Leon saw the President's special coach draw up. The glass of its spotless windows reflected ghostly images of the waiting dignitaries on the platform.

They said the coach offered every luxury, a little White House on wheels. Leon wondered how much it cost to run a special train from Canton. Probably more than a laborer in a wire factory could make in ten years. As he moved forward, one of the cops looked his way. The cop stepped toward him, but then somebody called him back to the platform and Leon slipped away into the mass of people.

Outside, as the President and his wife emerged to cheers and applause, Leon hung on the edge of the crowd. He could not see through the forest of parasols and men in derbies. The President and the First Lady climbed into their carriage and rode down the length of the Exposition grounds, surrounded by national guardsmen in bright uniforms. Leon followed for a few minutes, then gave up, made his way off the fairgrounds, and took the street-car back to the saloon where he had lived for the last week.

On Thursday, Leon tried again. In the late morning, McKinley gave his speech on the fair's Esplanade. The President stood at the railing of a big bandstand smothered with flag bunting, holding some papers lightly in his hand as he spoke. "Expositions are the timekeepers of progress," he declared. There had to be fifty thousand people there; the crowd was so great that Leon could not lift his arms, let alone get close enough to manage a clear shot.

Leon was so far away from the bandstand that he was unable to hear everything the President said, or even get a good look at him. Occasionally a phrase would float clear on the summer air. Some lies about free trade. Some lies about peace and brotherhood. It was bitter irony to hear these words from the agent of the plutocrats who ran the country, fat men in waistcoats who ignored the plight of the workers whose sweat generated every penny they squandered on yachts and mansions. When McKinley spoke of "unexampled prosperity," Leon felt dizzy and had to close his eyes. The sun beat on his eyelids and he measured the labored breath going in and out of his lungs.

The President ended with some line about "prosperity, happiness, and peace." More cheering. A brass band played. The crowd thinned; the press of people around Leon let up. McKinley gently helped his invalid wife down the steps of the platform and into her own carriage, made sure she was comfortable, then moved with some others, among the secret service men, to a second. Leon lost sight of him. But then came a break in the crowd and he had a moment's clear path to the men climbing into the victoria.

Leon clutched the pistol in his pocket. He took three steps forward. But *two* men were getting into the carriage. Two stout middle-aged men in silk hats. Which one was McKinley? Leon had never seen the President up close, and the drawings of him in the newspapers did not give him confidence to know which man he was.

As Leon hesitated, the men settled into the carriage and were driven away. The national guardsmen trotted along beside the carriage and Leon faded into the crowd.

So here it was, Friday, September 6th, another hot, sunny day, and his last chance. The papers reported that McKinley would spend the morning at Niagara Falls, but he and his entourage were due back at four to greet people at the Temple of Music. Leon took the Delaware Avenue streetcar up to the Exposition grounds in the morning. The breeze of the streetcar's progress gave a blessed relief from the heat. Along the way he studied his fellow Americans: girls in long white dresses with sashes, carrying parasols; men in straw boaters; children in short pants and caps; dandies in their Sunday best looking to spy a pretty ankle. On the Exposition grounds he regarded the boats on the lake, the reflecting canals, the beds profuse with flowers of red, white, and blue. Along the Midway vendors sold cotton candy, hot dogs and sausages, lemonade, beer. The fountains splashed, another brass band played. At the tops of the ornate Spanish-styled buildings, flags fluttered in the breeze blowing off the Niagara River.

He had hours to wait. He visited the Cuban Pavilion, where he heard again the story of our brown neighbors freed from beneath the bootheel of Old Europe by vigorous Uncle Sam. The beginning of a new American century. Leon Czolgosz was an American, born in Detroit, but what had any of this to do with him? Twenty-eight years old, of fair hair and average height, with clear blue eyes—his best feature, his mother had told him— he did not have an American name, just a stew of consonants that nobody could pronounce, and for a long time he had been a spectator of his own life.

He spent an hour in the horticulture building looking at palm trees and flowers as big as dinner plates. He ate a hot dog and drank some lemonade. The heat rose as the day progressed, and the men on the concourses took off their derbies and mopped their brows. The women in their broad flowered hats and parasols were little better off. Children abandoned their shoes and waded in the reflecting pools.

Leon sat on the edge of a fountain sipping his lemonade, uncomfortably aware of the .32-caliber Iver Johnson revolver in his right pocket. Gaetano Bresci, a New Jersey anarchist, had used the same kind of pistol to kill King Umberto I of Italy the year before. Leon carried a newspaper clipping about the assassination in his wallet.

The last couple of years, living on his father's farm, Leon had gotten pretty good with a pistol. He had not done much physical labor there as the medicines he took made him sleepy. His symptoms might go away for weeks at a time, but he could not seem to rid himself of the feeling that something was wrong.

He couldn't bring himself to do work that used only his body. That was what he was to the capitalist system, a body. He had tried to explain it once to his brother Waldek, back when they were having their discussions about the Catholic Church. Waldek and Leon both felt the church served the rich, but Waldek wasn't political, and never would be.

One of the things Leon did do on the farm was hunt. He'd used a pistol his father had bought years ago, an old Colt, to shoot rabbits. He got so he could hit pretty much anything he aimed at, and he wasn't afraid to fire a gun.

Whenever he shot a rabbit it would leap frantically. Wounded animals spasmed with astonishing energy, as if spending all the additional life that they might have lived in a few seconds of violent motion. He studied their torn bodies. He studied their dead eyes. You could always tell between dead and living eyes.

Strolling along the Midway, Leon came upon a crowd of people waiting at the entrance to one of the attractions. A sign above the arch read "A Trip to the Moon."

The ride was widely celebrated. They said that the men who created this show had already earned back the $52,000 they'd spent building it. Housed in a large, square building, it cost fifty cents, half a day's salary at the wire factory. Leon's money was running low due to his summer of inactivity, but after today he would never need money again. Why not see what the Moon might offer that he had not been able to find on Earth?

He stepped up to the ticket booth.

THE DARK RIDE

INSTEAD OF GIVING him a ticket, for his half-dollar the girl in the booth handed Leon a circular red tag bearing the image of a crescent moon, with a hole at the top and a thread to loop around his coat button. Printed on the tag were the words:

Once thirty tags were sold, the fairgoers were ushered into a darkened auditorium. They were ordinary people: workers on their day off, mothers with children, younger men and their girlfriends. A slender man in a fine suit, gold watch fob across his vest, with his well-corseted wife in a big feathered hat. A foursome, probably college students, the men in straw boaters, carrying their jackets—one fellow had his sleeves pushed up to show his manly forearms. The women were a skinny girl and a stunning strawberry blonde who laughed at something the man said.

Leon thought of Nora. For a long time, he had avoided thinking of her, but he supposed that on the day when he planned to assassinate the President of the United States, he could think about anything he wanted to think about. He'd loved Nora, but she had thrown him over because he had no money. He tried to condemn her, but it wasn't her fault. It was the world that made her abandon him. She thought he was a dreamer. She thought she had too much common sense for him, but she was blind and would follow her common sense to the grave.

He sat in the auditorium under the shadow of these thoughts. Everybody here seemed to be in a holiday mood, eager for this tour of wonders to begin.

The guide from Thompson's Aerial Navigation Company, dressed in a neat blue uniform, stepped into a spotlight.

"Good day, ladies and gentlemen. You are about to embark on a trip to the Moon, to see celestial sights never before seen by human beings, to meet and converse with the queer inhabitants of the Earth's only satellite. As soon as our crew completes preparations for launch, we'll usher you to the Landing Dock where our patented airship the *Luna* is moored. The *Luna* is constructed of that miracle element aluminum, the lightest, strongest metal known to man, to a design patented by Thompson's Aerial Navigation for travel through outer space to other planets. Rest assured that the *Luna* is completely safe, equipped with the latest mechanisms to produce the anti-gravitational force, and manned by our experienced crew of aethereal sailors.

"Once we are aloft, please remain in your seats and refrain from leaning over the airship's rail—we would hate to lose any of you! There may be some strong winds as we reach the upper atmosphere: If your hat blows off, raise your hand like this—" the guide raised his hand, palm open, waving "—and wave goodbye to it, for we shall not land to retrieve it!"

The people laughed.

"When we reach the Moon, keep to our group, as the lunar surface is hazardous. We will be descending below to the underground City of the Moon and the Palace of the Man in the Moon, the Grand Lunar and his court of Selenites. Though they will no doubt appear strange, rest assured that the Selenites—unlike the Filipinos—are grateful for our presence. Why, only yesterday, President McKinley himself journeyed with us to meet the Grand Lunar and confirm US diplomatic relations with the lunar nation."

The people responded readily to the guide's jokes. Leon wondered if the President had actually taken this ride or if this was some fiction aimed at drumming up business. He smiled grimly to think that yesterday he might have assassinated the autocrat on the surface of the Moon.

As if he were going to assassinate anybody. The President would probably not even make it back from Niagara Falls in time for his reception. By that evening, Leon would be in his room above the tavern once more, trying to figure out what to do with his life. Maybe he would travel out west. He could stop in Chicago and seek out Emma Goldman again. He could make it clear to her that he was not some spy, but a man of action.

Except he would only be able to see her if he failed to act. If he did kill McKinley, he would not see Emma Goldman or anyone else again.

He had first encountered the notorious anarchist last May in Cleveland. He'd gone into town from his family's Warrensville farm, telling his suspicious stepmother that he was attending a meeting of the Knights of the Golden Eagle. Instead he went to the Memorial Hall where Goldman was to give a speech for the Liberty Association of the Franklin Liberal Club.

Leon studied her as she came to the platform. She was a woman of about thirty, with a good figure and light brown hair. She wore pince-nez glasses that she let fall on a ribbon to dangle on her breast as she spoke with passion of mankind's nature and how the social structure thwarted it in a hundred ways.

She did not smile, except as a sardonic grin played briefly about her lips, a look of bitter knowledge of the capitalist world's oppression. She waved at the police standing in the back of the hall, sent to monitor her. "Spies," she called them, "the meanest and most despicable creatures in the universe." She explained to the gathered workingmen and women "the galling yoke of government, ecclesiasticism, and the bonds of custom and prejudice" that was responsible for their troubles. She praised men like Bresci, men "unable to stand idly by and see the wrongs that were being endured by their fellow mortals." She called them "martyrs of the deed."

She spoke of love, "the strongest and deepest element in all life, the harbinger of hope, of joy, of ecstasy, the defier of all laws, of all conventions, the freest molder of human destiny. If the world is ever to give birth to true companionship and oneness, not marriage, but love will be the parent."

Goldman radiated a magnetic vitality. She glowed with humor, rage, sarcasm, and passion. These things were not simply ideas to her, they were living, breathing truths. Leon was stunned. Who knew that a revolution could be powered by love?

During the interval, Leon gathered his courage and went up to speak with her, awkwardness evident in his every motion. He had no fine words: all he had was his heart, and he spoke it. "You are... I never heard anything like that, ever."

She looked right into his eyes, as a man might, and helplessly he looked back. Leon felt that she saw him as no one else had. "You must not have heard many Anarchists."

"I'm not an Anarchist," he said. "I've been a Socialist. Can you tell me some things I could read?"

She recommended he read Kropotkin's "Appeal to the Young," and the newspaper *Free Society*, published in Chicago by Abraham Isaak.

Leon told her he would. Then one of the organizers, a man named Shilling who had introduced her, came over. She took the time to tell Leon, "Read those. Someday we'll talk again." And then she was gone.

It was as if her voice had gotten inside his head; he could call it up whenever he needed to. He might need it today.

After the speeches were over, some of the people who had been at Goldman's talk gathered at a nearby tavern. Leon went there, sat, and watched them. He did not speak to anyone. Later, he walked the streets, thinking. Goldman had said, "It is only intelligence and sympathy that can bring us to the source of human suffering, and teach us the way out of it." In the light of her words, Leon realized that he had been suffering, and flailing, in his unfocused way, to find his way out.

In the morning, he rode the trolley to the end of the line and caught a ride on a milk wagon out to the farm. His mind was on fire. Sitting on the hard wooden seat next to the wagon driver, he laughed out loud, spontaneously, and the man looked at him.

"What's so funny?"

Leon just laughed again. "Everything, comrade."

"Conrad's my brother. I'm Rudi."

In the darkened room at the Exposition, a gong sounded. The man from Thompson's Aerial Navigation Company raised his hands to the eager passengers. "That signal tells us it's time to depart on our great adventure. If you will, ladies and gentlemen, follow me through this portal."

Double doors opened and the people crowded up a ramp into a great dark room that contained the dramatically lit green and white metal airship. It was the size of an excursion boat, with twelve red canvas wings, six to a side. As on an excursion boat, the passengers were seated in double rows of deck chairs on either side. In the twilight, once they were settled, buzzing with conversation, there came the rattle of chains as the crewmen cast off. The engines rumbled, and the wings began slowly to beat, then faster. The ship bumped and rose, yawing slightly from side to side. A breeze sprang up. The guide directed their attention down below and the crew shone spotlights as they passed above the Exposition grounds, the city of Buffalo, and the river; the airship banked over the Niagara Falls, its big wings beating the air.

As they ascended, they passed through clouds of mist. A storm arose: The wind increased, lightning flashed, thunder echoed, the airship shook. The young women clutched their boyfriends' arms. The breeze became a gale.

Then they were past the storm and into outer space. Below, Leon could see the outline of Lake Erie shrinking until all of North America was visible. As they continued to rise, the entire Earth shrank to a disk, falling back into the distance.

It was a vision of the world that one never had. The entire human race lived on that one planet. All history, the rise and fall of nations, the great conflicts, the great achievements, had occurred on that sphere. What differences existed between human beings that could compare with the fact that they shared the Earth? Except they didn't share it. Some people owned it, and others did not. Humans had invented ownership, and it had taken over their minds.

He observed his fellow passengers. The bourgeois man held his wife's gloved hand and whispered something into her ear. The two couples were laughing, the fellow with his sleeves rolled up sliding his arm around the blonde's waist.

The clouds began to clear and stars came out on all sides, bright, clear pinpoints in the blackness. Ahead, the Moon hove into view, with the grinning face of the Man in the Moon.

What hokum. Leon shifted in his seat. The pistol in his pocket *thunked* against the frame of his chair. The man seated next to him said, "Excuse me. Did you drop something?"

"No," Leon said.

The disk of the Moon grew larger still. The sailors on the airship began to move about; there came the clanking of an anchor chain. Then, as the ship banked to the right, the spotlights were cast below, revealing a craggy landscape over which the *Luna* soared. The beating of the wings slowed. "Remain in your seats, ladies and gentlemen!" the guide admonished.

The breeze diminished, the *Luna* swayed, and around them rose the walls of a crater. With a bump, the ship landed. The captain announced that they had reached their destination. The swell took the blonde's arm in his and helped her down the gangplank. Leon, among the excited patrons, followed onto the rugged lunar surface. Around them was strange plant life in every shade of blue and green, huge red blossoms, and mushrooms the size of maple trees.

From between two of the giant mushrooms, through dense foliage, an alien creature advanced toward the ship.

It was a tall, green thing with spikes sticking out from its back and its head, arms serrated like a grasshopper's legs. It wore some kind of leather coat and carried a spear.

THE TEMPLE OF MUSIC

LEON CAME TO himself standing outside the exit of the Trip to the Moon, blinking in the bright sun, his eyes tearing up after the darkness of the building.

Among the people emerging behind him was a young swell with a beautiful blonde on his arm. "Would you love me if I were the girl in the Moon?" the woman asked the man.

"Sweetheart," he said, "I'd love you even in Lackawanna."

Leon shook his head to clear his mind. He checked the clock on the Electricity Building. It was one-thirty. People would already be gathering at the Temple of Music.

When he got there, he saw that scores of others had preceded him. After some confusion, the milling crowd resolved itself into a line outside the closed doors of the hall. Leon found a place not too far from the entrance, behind a swarthy Sicilian with unkempt black hair. The big domed building, red and blue and yellow, glistened like a huge candy egg. The sun fell bright and hot on Leon's neck.

People of every description stood in line. Many looked like workingmen who had taken the day off to "do the Pan." Teutonic men with luxuriant mustaches. Mothers with restive children in tow. A few spaces ahead of him, a woman bent down to comb her son's hair with her fingers. Others mopped their brows and necks with their bandanas. After an hour or so, some gave up and left the line to sit in the shade at the nearby Pabst restaurant, where for an outrageous thirty cents you could buy a seltzer and lemon, but more arrived all the time to take their place.

Leon hunched his shoulders, hands in the pockets of his jacket. In his left pocket he had some money, a pencil, and a letter certifying his paid-up membership in the Knights of the Golden Eagle. In his right he felt the pistol, his handkerchief, and something else, small and rubbery, that had not been there this morning. He pulled it out. It was a nipple like that from a baby's bottle. How had he come by it? He had lost the red tag that had served as his ticket. He tried to remember what had happened on the Moon ride. It was queer that he could not. He felt as if he were in a trance. Nervously shifting from one foot to the other, he stared at the doors of the Temple of Music.

Behind Leon in line stood a tall Black man in a dark suit. "It's hard to wait," the man said.

Startled, Leon looked up at him. He was extraordinarily tall, maybe six and a half feet.

"Hard to wait in this heat," the man repeated. He wore a starched collar, a watch chain across his vest, and a soft black hat. He smiled down at Leon. "If you want to step out of line to buy something to drink," the man said in a gentle Southern accent, "I'll keep your place."

"No, thank you," said Leon. "I get out of this line and I won't come back."

He tried to focus on his plan. It was not much of one. When the doors opened and the line moved forward, Leon would take the pistol in his hand and wrap his big white handkerchief around it like a bandage. As he approached the President, he would pretend it was injured—if the guards around the President could be fooled by such a simple ruse.

It would not do to have this Black man pay too much attention to Leon, but during the two hours that they waited in the swelling line, the man insisted on being friendly. He told Leon that his name was James Parker. He told Leon that he was a waiter in the Plaza restaurant but had taken the day off in the hope of meeting the President. He told how in the 1880s he had been a constable for Judge Moses Bartlett in the Fourth Militia District near

Charleston, South Carolina, but had lost that job when the Black magistrates were eliminated.

Why Parker wanted to shake McKinley's hand was a mystery to Leon. McKinley was part of the reason why Parker was no longer a constable. The Republicans had sold out the Blacks in the election of 1896. On an ordinary day, Leon might have explained that. He sympathized. Black men and Poles shared a place at the bottom of the heap.

Leon knew about the bottom of the heap. His mother had died when he was ten, some weeks after his sister Victoria was born. They were right to call childbirth labor: Mary Czolgosz had been a factory for babies, producing seven sons and two daughters. This last birth had been hard, and she did not recover from it. In the weeks after, Leon took care of infant Victoria while his mother languished in bed.

It cost them two dollars to call a doctor. The doctor gave her some pills but could not say what was wrong with his mother. She just weakened and faded away. Every day during those last weeks, Leon sat at her bedside, praying for her to get up. At times, she rose to walk around, giving him hope, but she was not in her right mind. She mumbled to herself in Polish. "My children," she said, "the time will come when you will have greater understanding."

Leon knew she was talking to him. Unlike his brothers, he was a good student. After their mother died, he and his sister Ceceli took care of baby Victoria as best they could. Soon afterward, Paul Czolgosz remarried. Somebody had to cook and clean and Leon and Ceceli were not up to it. Paul's new wife Catarina did not see why a boy old enough to do useful work should waste his time in school and complained that Leon was just lazy. She was an ignorant, hard woman and Leon hated her. He respected his father, but his father was a quiet man who knew nothing much beyond hard work and expected that was what people did. He wasn't going to fight his wife. Catarina won the battle and Leon went to work.

His first job was in a glass-bottle factory. At the factory he carried the new bottles on sticks from the glassblowers to the annealing oven. The glass was so hot the sticks smoked and caught fire, and the heat scorched his face. That was in Pennsylvania, but then the family moved to Ohio where he became a wire winder at the Cleveland Rolling Mill. Leon and his brother Waldek worked there until the panic of 1893 crashed the stock market. The owner cut their wages; the workers went on strike and the factory hired scabs. The brothers were blacklisted.

Waldek and Leon prayed for work. They got a Polish Bible and read it four times together. No work came. They asked the priest about it and the priest told them to pray harder. They prayed harder, but nothing happened. Finally, Leon realized that churches were a fraud. The Pope was the head of a corporation like Andrew Carnegie or William H. Vanderbilt. "The public be damned," Vanderbilt said, and he was right—men like Leon were damned.

As the strike dragged on and the owners refused to give in, Leon went back and applied for work at the mill under an assumed name. Although Leon was on the blacklist, the new shop manager did not know him, nor did the scab workers. He told them his name was Fred C. Nieman and they hired him.

He worked at the mill for another five years, as hard as anybody, but he had grown cynical. He read Socialist newspapers. He read a book called *Looking Backward*, about a man named Julian West who fell asleep in 1887 and awoke in the year 2000. Leon was dazzled by the wonderful future that Edward Bellamy depicted, a society where all men received an equal share of the products of labor, and no man was privileged. Readers of Bellamy's book started clubs, and Leon joined one.

The Pan-American Exposition presented a vision of that bright future. At night the fairgrounds became a fairyland. Nicola Tesla's "City of Light" boasted a half-million electric lamps powered by the new hydroelectric plant at Niagara Falls. At night, 11,000 of them outlined the 391-foot-tall Electric Tower, from whose top a powerful searchlight pierced the skies. Electricity. Incubators and X-ray machines. Electric carriages. Peace and prosperity. Progress. Trips to the Moon. A future so marvelous as to seem a paradise.

But none of this applied to men like Leon. As his mother had predicted, he had gained greater understanding. If his nerves held, if he had the guts to kill McKinley, that might lead to the future that Bellamy described in his book. The one that Emma Goldman talked about. There were men, all around the world, who understood this. Gaetano Bresci, Sante Casario, Luigi Lucheni, Michele Angiolillo. All rulers were their enemies: Kaiser Wilhelm in Prussia, the Russian Tsar, the Empress of Austria, the King of Italy, the President of France, the Prime Minister of Spain. The King of England.

Leon pulled the kerchief out of his pocket and used it to wipe his brow. He looked down at his hand, which trembled a little, and, fumbling, wrapped the kerchief loosely around it. It slid off. He wrapped it around again. He did this three times then stuffed it back into his pocket and resumed his stare at the building. His plan was idiocy. They would catch him the moment he drew the pistol.

He could still step out of the line. As simple as that, it would be over. Buy that lemonade. Go back to the saloon on Broadway. No one was stopping him. So far, he had done nothing. He was just a citizen at the fair.

And then what? McKinley would go back to Washington to serve the rich as he had his entire life. Leon would run out of money, then find work or starve. He might go back to Cleveland, maybe talk to his father—but no, he could not go back to the farm and endure his stepmother's disgust, Waldek's skepticism, and Victoria's worries. He had burned his bridges there.

He couldn't go back to any anarchist meetings, either. Nobody would know that Leon had failed because nobody knew what he'd intended, but Leon would know. It would be in his head whenever anybody talked about the men who had given their lives for the cause.

By four o'clock, the line had grown until it stretched around the corner of the building and up the Esplanade. There was a commotion and a young man came running from the other side of the temple.

"He's coming!"

A buzz ran through the crowd.

"At last," Jim Parker said.

A couple of mounted police herded the people into some sort of order. A few minutes later, two soldiers swung open the big doors on this side of the temple and, after some further bustle at the front, the line began to move. The sound of some classical organ music filtered out of the building.

The people shuffled forward, murmuring. Children bounced on their feet or clutched their mothers' skirts. It was five minutes or more before

Leon approached the door. In no way would McKinley be able to greet all of the people who had waited through the afternoon. Once the President's men figured this out, they would shut the doors and call it a day. Leon would be free. Instead of pressing forward to his chance, he lagged behind the swarthy man in front of him.

Parker nudged Leon. His friendliness had worn thin: With some exasperation, he said, "If you can't go faster, at least let me by."

Leon lurched forward. Once they reached the doors, he saw an aisle had been formed by barriers from the entrance to the reception area. Along this aisle were stationed national guardsmen. There had to be sixty men with rifles crowded into the building.

The organist played on. The citizens shuffled forward in single file under the eyes of the guardsmen. Leon peered ahead at the reception area where, in front of a display of potted plants and flag bunting, McKinley greeted the fairgoers one by one. Whenever a woman presented a child, the President would tousle the boy's hair or say a word to the little girl. Otherwise, wearing a fatherly smile, he used two hands to clasp their outstretched one, gave each a single firm handshake, gently moved them past, and turned to the next person in line.

Among the dignitaries crowded around him were some men in suits whose gimlet-eyed inspection of the well-wishers as they approached stamped them as secret service agents. Leon slid the gun and handkerchief out of his pocket, got the handkerchief wrapped around the pistol, and held it just below his breast as if his hand were in a sling. He tried to look innocuous. One of the guards fixed his gaze on Leon for a second, only to slide past him to look at Parker, a head taller than anybody else in the room.

Another of the agents was preoccupied with the dark-haired man ahead of Leon. As the fellow drew closer, the agent stepped forward and seized him by the shoulder, leaned in, and asked him a question. The man, flustered, shook his head. The agent held on to his arm as he moved the man out of the line and past the President.

Leon's turn came. His heart raced, his lips parted. Five feet away, McKinley looked at him. The President's small, purposeful, professional smile did little to soften his stern features. It was the face of the cop behind the desk at the precinct, of the banker turning down your request for a loan. His belly swelled out beneath what looked like an acre of spotless white waistcoat. A white bow tie and high starched collar constricted his ample neck.

Leon stepped forward. He held out his left hand. McKinley reached out with his own. When he did so, Leon stuck the pistol into McKinley's belly and fired twice. Two small reports, the sound of a ruler slapped on a desk. McKinley's eyes went wide. He rose up on his toes, then stumbled forward.

The handkerchief, on fire from the discharge of the gun, fluttered, flaming, to the floor. A woman screamed.

Leon raised the pistol for a third shot. A blow to his head knocked him sideways.

Jim Parker slammed into Leon, reaching for the pistol, and they tumbled to the floor. Leon lost hold of the gun and Parker kicked it away.

"Get the gun, Al!" somebody yelled.

Guardsmen fell onto Leon. They pummeled him with their fists and the butts of their rifles. One of the secret servicemen yanked Leon to his feet and punched him in the face, knocking him down again.

They might have beaten him to death right there if, through cries and shouting, the President, who had fallen back onto a folding chair, had not gasped, "Go easy on him, boys."

The beating stopped instantly. The secret serviceman seized Leon and jerked him to his feet again. Leon saw the bright, spreading blood on the President's white waistcoat.

"Clear the building!" someone shouted. "Get an ambulance!"

THE MOON MAIDEN

THE SELENITE WAS just a man in a costume with a mask over his face. Leon could see the man's reddened eyes through the holes in the mask. Behind him came a small troupe of little people in green tights and knee breeches, arms padded with rows of spikes down the outside. The Selenite leader held his spear at rest and saluted.

"Welcome to our home, which you call the Moon. We are the royal guard of the King of the Moon. The Grand Lunar is eager to meet you, gentle friends from Earth. Come! Let us descend to the City of the Moon."

The Selenite captain led the passengers between the rows of little soldiers, who bowed deeply, to a cave entrance festooned with elaborate carvings.

Dark at first, the cave grew darker still as they advanced, and the women drew closer to their escorts. Gradually a blue light rose around them. Farther in were lights of crimson and gold. Jewels gleamed in the rough walls. The cave opened into a chamber large enough to hold all of the earthlings. Here were more Selenites, small females whose long hair draped undone over the shoulders of their glittering gowns. A couple of them played stringed instruments. All bowed their heads when the visitors were assembled.

The little males bent sideways and looked up at them. The spiky tops of their heads looked like cactus plants. They smiled and shook hands with the passengers.

All this struck a chord in Leon. Earlier that summer, lying around his rented room in West Seneca through a sweltering July, out of work, spending down his savings, Leon had passed his time reading newspapers and magazines. In *Cosmopolitan* he had read a scientific romance by the British writer H.G. Wells titled *The First Men in the Moon*, about a failed businessman named Bedford and a crazy scientist named Cavor who flew to the Moon in an antigravity ship. Wells' moon had giant fungi on its surface and was honeycombed with caverns where lived insectile Selenites. Clearly the designers of the Trip to the Moon had read Wells' story and turned it into this exotic music hall show.

Although these were midgets and children, and the grotto was constructed of plaster, in the blue light and the play of shadows the faux-rock looked real, and out of the corner of his eye, Leon was startled when one or another of the Selenites moved in a way that no human might move. That one in the corner, bent forward, head wobbling—it looked more like a big drunken grasshopper than a person. But when Leon peered at it, he saw it was just a sideshow midget dressed up in green tights and bloomers.

To the right and left, visible between glowing stalactites, shadowed galleries ran off into darkness, giving the illusion that this complex must reach far below the Pan-American fairgrounds. The air was cool. They followed the guide and the Selenite captain through another tunnel. The floor trembled with a vibration that made Leon think of the machines in the wire mill, and in the distance he thought he heard twittering. As he passed one of the openings he glimpsed some large, pale thing in the darkness, something like a huge slug, heaving along the floor on no legs. Leon stopped and someone bumped into him.

"Keep moving," the guide said.

When Leon looked back through the opening, he saw nothing.

At the end of the underground avenue was the City of the Moon, a cavern where they met more Selenites. Here was a bazaar, souvenir booths selling pins made of aluminum, and mooncraft demonstrations. The Selenites offered the visitors samples of green cheese.

They entered the palace of the King of the Moon. His throne room was like a theater, elaborately decorated, with red pillars, a midnight-blue ceiling painted with the sun and stars, and a figure of the crescent Earth rising over the lunar mountains. A fountain shone with all the colors of the rainbow. At the far end, on his pearlescent throne, strongly backlit, sat the Grand Lunar, bracketed by two giant bodyguards.

The silvery light that surrounded his throne made it hard to discern the details of the Grand Lunar's person. He appeared to be a manlike creature in silver robes that flared out over his lower body. His stupendous crown glittered with jewels that shone as if lit from within. In his right hand he held a glowing staff. He smiled down on the visitors.

"Welcome, people of Earth," he said in a surprisingly high-pitched voice. "We hope that you enjoy your visit and will report back to your home planet that we are friendly creatures who wish intercourse with humans on mutually beneficial terms. Free trade, low tariffs, and brotherhood, we are convinced, will lead to unexampled prosperity, happiness, and peace."

Leon realized after a moment that the King was some sort of giant puppet.

"As a token of our goodwill," he announced, "we present this entertainment, performed by my daughters in the American style!" He lifted his staff and knocked it one, two, three times against the floor.

An unseen orchestra struck up a tune. From a passage behind the throne came a dozen young women, Moon Maidens in sparkling corsets, bloomers, and tights. The music paused. They bowed gracefully, smiling, and when the music resumed began to dance.

There was nothing insectile about these Selenites—pretty girls in sequined costumes of red and green. They swayed in time to the tune, their gold wrist and ankle bracelets shining in the lights, and began to sing.

> "My sweetheart's the Man in the Moon.
> I'm going to marry him soon.
> 'Twould fill me with bliss just to give him one kiss.
> But I know that a dozen I never would miss.
>
> "I'll go up in a great big balloon
> And see my sweetheart in the Moon.
> Then behind some dark cloud where no one is allowed
> I'll make love to the Man in the Moon."

One of the dancers caught Leon's eye. Her dark hair was piled high, her skin fair, her neck slender. Eyes so dark that he could not see her pupils. She looked like a postcard photograph Leon had seen of Evelyn Nesbit.

Though she sang and danced, her brow was troubled. Her eyes flitted toward the guards stationed around the room.

When the song was done, the Moon Maidens turned to leave. The guide from Thompson's Aerial Service called to the visitors to gather near an exit. Leon hung back. His diversion was almost over, and soon he would be standing on the Midway faced only with the prospect of his grim task.

As he hesitated, one of the guards pulled aside the Moon Maiden that Leon had been watching. She struggled in his clawlike grip, looking terrified. No one paid any attention. As she tried to pull away the guard twisted her arm until she fell.

Leon took three steps toward them. The guard did not see him approach; Leon shoved him aside. To Leon's astonishment, his shove propelled the Selenite completely off his feet; he flew three yards through the air, crashed into a pillar, and lay crumpled at its base.

The girl looked up at him. Guards turned toward them, brandishing their spears. Leon, confused by the ease with which he had thrown aside the guard, prepared to face them down, but the girl tugged at his sleeve.

"We must flee!" she said. She pulled him between two of the pillars and Leon stumbled after her.

They entered a tunnel. It twisted to the right, the left, then pitched sharply downward. A flight of stairs descended to another chamber from which four other tunnels branched. Leon felt queasy and his head swam.

He had no time to catch his breath. Two more Selenites entered the chamber. The smooth carapaces of their heads glistened nightmarishly in the faint blue light. They twittered and raised their spears.

"Stop," Leon said, "there's no cause—"

These two were more convincingly alien than the ones he had seen earlier. They moved as if their joints were awry, and their masks covered their entire heads.

One of the Selenites poked his spear at Leon and its sharp point penetrated his pants leg. He was startled by the pain and fell back. But when the other moved toward the girl, Leon ducked his spear and punched him in the side of his head.

Leon's fist broke through the thing's skull as if it were an eggshell. The creature's head exploded like a rotten melon. Bloody pulp spattered everywhere.

The Selenite fell dead at his feet. When the other came at them, Leon seized its spear and yanked it. The Selenite lurched forward and Leon knocked it aside. It flew across the cave as if it were made of sticks, struck the cave wall, and slid to the floor, broken.

Leon stood there, stunned.

"Come," the girl said, seizing his bloody hand. "We must go, now!"

Leon let her pull him down another tunnel. If she was upset at the carnage he had perpetrated, she did not show it. Leon wondered if they could have been mock creatures, some puppets he had destroyed. But they had moved and wielded the spears like living beings. He felt the stickiness of the blood on his hand as they ran through darkness.

The tunnel branched; without hesitation, the girl took him down several byways. How could this network of tunnels have been constructed beneath the fairgrounds? Something was direly wrong.

A channel of glowing blue liquid ran along the side of the tunnel, casting eerie light on the girl's perfect cheek. In this light her mass of dark hair was jet-black.

"Who are you?" he asked as they hurried along.

"I am called Wima," she said. "And you?"

"My name is Leon."

"Thank you for saving me, Leon. The Grand Lunar would have tortured me to reveal my compatriots, and I fear that I could not have held out. You saved more lives than mine today."

"I didn't think I was saving anyone's life. I killed that...person."

"That was no person." She turned to look at him, and when she saw his expression her voice softened. "We don't always know how the things we do will affect others, or whether we bring life or death. But affect them we must, inevitably."

He had no time to ponder her words. The air grew warmer the deeper they went. "Where are we going?"

"To the secret chambers of the Brotherhood of Lunar Workers," she said.

POLICE HEADQUARTERS

THEY DRAGGED LEON, beaten and bloody, into a little room in the corner of the Temple of Music. A couple of soldiers threw him onto a table. Leon's head swam. His cheek was cut and blood spattered his shirt. His ear hurt and his ribs hurt and he tasted blood.

It took him a while to come back to himself, to realize who was there in the room with him, to hear the commotion in the other room. The soldiers guarding him stared at him stone-faced. One of them said, "I'm going to hit him."

"Don't," the other said.

A man in civilian clothes—the secret service agent who had pulled the fellow in front of Leon from the line—came into the room. "What's your name?" he asked.

Leon spat out some blood. "Who are you?"

"You don't need to know my name. Who are you?"

"Fred Nieman. N–I–E–M–A–N."

The man's jaw worked. "Why did you shoot the President?"

"Is he dead?"

The man stiffened but mastered his anger. "You will be if you don't tell me who you are working with."

Another, older man entered the room. In the brief time the door was open, Leon heard competing voices outside. Then came the sound of people pounding on the walls of the building. Leon could hear them crying for "the assassin" to be given to them.

The new man, in a suit and clean-shaven, told the agent, "I'm Colonel Byrne, head of the Exposition Police. We have to get him out of here right away. There's a crowd growing out there that would rather lynch him than breathe."

Three of them stayed to guard Leon while Byrne went back outside. One of the guards looked out of the room's small window onto the crowd beating like surf against the building.

Ten minutes later, Byrne came back with uniformed policemen. They handcuffed Leon.

"We're going to walk through the hall," he told Leon. "Keep your hands down and your mouth shut." They grabbed Leon's arms and pushed him toward the door.

The interior of the hall was still a jumble of soldiers and men in suits. McKinley wasn't there anymore, but Leon saw the chair he had fallen into after he'd been shot, and other overturned chairs where Leon had scuffled with the guards. Marines blocked the doors. They took Leon to a side door; one of the cops opened it and stuck his head out, pulled it back in, and nodded. They dragged Leon out, three quick steps to a closed, leather-topped carriage, and threw him inside like a piece of baggage. The secret service agent climbed in with him, slammed the door, and they trotted off down the

Esplanade. Some of the crowd tried to reach the carriage but were held off by guardsmen.

They took him to the police headquarters and put him into a cell. A big man in a suit who said he was Police Superintendent Bull came in and talked with him. He was remarkably casual. He lit two cigars and gave one to Leon. Leon smoked nervously. He was keyed up, excited. He had done it.

He asked for a washcloth to clean his face. It bothered him that there was blood on his shirt.

Then came another man in a suit. "Mr. Nieman, my name is Frederick Haller. I'm the assistant district attorney and I would like to talk with you."

Now they wanted to talk with him. He was no longer invisible. "I'm hungry," Leon said, "and I'd like a clean shirt. And a handkerchief."

Haller looked at him squarely. "A shirt," he said flatly. "You want a shirt. Who's going to pay for this hypothetical shirt?"

"You took my coat. There's some money in the pocket."

They checked and found $1.54 in his coat along with the pencil, the letter from the Knights of the Golden Eagle, and the rubber nipple.

Haller sent one of the cops out to buy him a new shirt and a handkerchief. Meanwhile, they fed Leon. He was ravenously hungry.

"All right, now let's talk," Haller said.

Leon had not talked to anyone for weeks. He had so much bottled up inside him and felt full of energy. He'd just shot the President of the United Sates—he was a martyr of the deed, and it didn't matter anymore what he did or said. So he told Haller everything he had done since he'd arrived in Buffalo, and before that in Cleveland. Haller took notes. Leon talked about his father and his stepmother and brothers and sisters, about seeing Goldman's lecture in Cleveland, about working in the wire mill and how he'd been living on the farm for the last few years doing nothing but reading and thinking. He told them he believed in free love. He told them he had been in love with a girl once, but she had gone back on him and since then he'd had nothing to do with women.

Haller took it all down and went away. That night at ten o'clock the cops returned and took Leon to a room full of men on the second floor. Bull was there, and Haller, and a man who said he was the district attorney, and the secret service agent who had spirited Leon from the Temple of Music, and a doctor, and a stenographer. A crowd of men smelling of cigars and sweating in the heat of the room. They opened the window. One of the cops lingered there, leaning out.

"There's two thousand people down there wanting to lynch him," the cop muttered to nobody in particular.

They had typed up Leon's statement to Haller. DA Thomas Penney had it in front of him on the table. He said, "Your name's not Nieman, it's Leon Czolgosz. We found it on the letter in your pocket." He spoke with a British accent.

"It's pronounced 'Shol-Gosh.'"

"All right, Mr. *Shol*-gosh. Heaven forbid I should mispronounce your name."

Penney proceeded to ask Leon a lot of leading questions. He treated Leon like he was stupid, coming at the same points over and over, trying to get him to admit to things that were not true. That he was part of a conspiracy. That he had sworn an oath to kill the President. That Emma Goldman had told him to do it. That he had met with some shoemaker in Buffalo named Valetchy. That he had snuck into the Temple of Music ahead of McKinley. That he had planned to escape in the crowd after he shot the President.

Others joined in the questioning. Whatever they had gotten from Haller was all garbled. They weren't really listening. They thought they already knew all about Leon and only wanted him to confirm what they had in their heads. To the degree that Leon resisted, they got impatient. The hatred in their eyes was obvious.

Men came into and went out of the room as the interrogation continued. Through the window Leon could hear the mob outside.

Leon admitted that he had shot the President and that he had intended to kill him. But some of the questions they asked touched on things for which he did not know the answers.

Penney said, "You are not sorry you did it, are you? You would do it over again, would you not?"

Leon hesitated. "I don't know whether I would or not."

Penney put it to Leon that he was willing to sacrifice himself to get rid of the President, that he knew the consequences and realized that he might be electrocuted. And it was true that Leon had told himself those things, but he had not imagined this room full of men questioning him, the mob in the street, the endless worrying over words to describe exactly what he did and did not intend.

When he kept denying things they told him he had done, they asked him to write it down in his own words. They tried flattery. "You've done this great deed for the people's benefit. Write something there that can be published in the newspapers."

Suddenly Leon's hands were shaking. He could not write with all of them watching him. He said the stenographer could write it down and he would sign.

"No," Penney said. "We cannot take his writing. Write whatever you please about what you did."

Leon said, "Can't the reporter write it?"

Penney grimaced. "All right. Make your statement and he'll write it out. Say it however you like."

The room fell silent. Leon didn't know if he could put it into words. "Put on there that I killed President McKinley because I done my duty."

The stenographer's pencil moved over the page.

"Do you want to say anything else to the people?" Penney asked.

"Say I don't believe one man should have so much service and another man should have none."

They wrote it down. Leon signed the statement.

By the time he was back in his basement cell it was after one in the morning, and he was exhausted. He fell into a deep sleep.

Saturday morning he awoke ravenous. He had never been hungrier. They fed him and took him up to Bull's office again. Some doctors came to see him. They measured and weighed him and asked more repetitive questions. Had he ever had sexual intercourse? Had he ever heard voices? How did he decide he needed to kill the President?

Then one of them, Leon thought his name was Crego, asked, "How will you feel if you failed to kill him?"

A shock ran through him. "He's alive?"

"You didn't know that?" Crego said. He looked at Bull in surprise.

"He doesn't need to know," Bull said. "He doesn't—"

Just then came a knock on the door. A detective was there with a man Leon recognized from the Cleveland Liberty Club, Albert Nowak. Nowak was a blowhard who thought he was smarter than anyone else and talked big about a Socialist revolution. What he was doing here Leon could not imagine.

"Go ahead," the detective told Nowak.

Nowak made a little speech, ostensibly at Leon but clearly intended for the cops, about how he had always been Leon's friend, and how Leon had betrayed their friendship. As he went on about this under the detective's skeptical gaze, he realized that maybe it was not so smart to link himself to Leon, so he switched to attacking Leon for disgracing his family and bringing trouble to all the good Polish citizens of the US.

Nowak tried to look indignant, but Leon could see he regretted digging this hole for himself. He finished lamely with, "I'm not a Socialist or an Anarchist. I'm a Republican."

Leon had to laugh. Nowak the Republican.

"Oh, yeah," Leon said. "You're a Republican for what there is in it." He held his thumb and fingers together and rubbed them in front of Nowak's face.

When the cops realized that letting Nowak rant at Leon was not going to produce anything useful, they hurried him out of the room.

The doctors came again on Sunday. It became clear to Leon that they were trying to figure out if he was crazy. On the one hand, they thought that only a crazy person could have shot a man as beloved as William McKinley. On the other, he had to be sane in order for them to convict him.

Leon remembered the chapter in *Looking Backward* that talked about crime and punishment in the future. In the year 2000, there were no prisons and hardly any crime because there was no more wealth or poverty. The future people believed that money—not having enough of it, or having too much of it—was the cause of crime. Once you got rid of rich and poor, the book said, then for the most part people stopped committing crimes. The only people who still did so were sick. They were treated not as criminals but as patients.

But this was not the year 2000. Leon was not a patient and they were not worrying about what treatment to use. The angry crowds were still outside, and the doctors' looks did not suggest benevolence.

On Monday, when for the third day straight they came to ask the same questions, Leon said he didn't remember shooting anyone. What were they talking about?

They got all excited. They argued for half an hour. Then one of them huffily reminded Leon they had a signed statement from him saying he had shot the President, and Leon gave up and refused to answer any more questions.

When he asked whether McKinley had died they wouldn't tell him.

After he refused to talk, they left him more or less alone. There were no other prisoners down in the basement, just Leon. A single guard on the green masonry corridor, one during the day and one during the night. The day guard was Harold, a skinny man with blond hair and bad skin. The night guard was Louis, a stolid, square man with a drooping mustache. They both looked at Leon as if he were an animal in the zoo, but Harold seemed more curious than disgusted.

Over the next days, Leon could not remember ever being as hungry. He ate his three squares and slept. Once a day they let him out of the cell to walk up and down the corridor for exercise. Warily he chatted with the guards. Harold told him things that were going on outside the jail, things he was probably supposed to keep quiet about.

"The reporters are lined up three-deep in front of the building. One guy offered me a hundred bucks if I could get him five minutes with you."

"What are they saying about me?"

"You better hope they keep you in jail. You're the most hated man in America. They say you're going to get at least ten years for attempted murder."

"The President's alive? He didn't die?"

Harold looked chagrined. He lowered his voice. "Teddy rushed into town ready to take the oath, but the old man got better. They say he's going to be all right."

Leon had failed. But his heart leapt at the news. It was a queer mixture of deflation and relief.

"That Black fellow who knocked you over is a hero in all the papers. They call him the man who saved the President. People are bidding to buy the buttons off his vest. It's making the secret service so mad they could spit. You ought to be thanking that boy."

A day or so later Leon was walking the corridor, explaining to Harold how he'd gotten the scar on his left cheek the time a wire snapped in the factory and lashed his face, when Louis came in. His shift was not supposed to start until seven PM.

They stuck Leon back in his cell. He could hear their mumbled conversation outside the door, but not what they were saying. After a minute, Louis went away.

"What's up?" Leon asked Harold through the grate in his door.

Harold was silent for a moment. Then he said, "McKinley's dead."

REVOLT OF THE WORKERS

THE DEEPER WIMA took Leon below the lunar surface, the less gravity he felt. They came to a huge chamber, high and arching, so big that Leon could not estimate how far away the opposite wall was. It was lit by phosphorescent mushrooms ten feet tall. Leon, hurrying after the girl, found that with each step he bounded a couple of yards into the air. Gravity here was a fraction of that he was used to.

The air was warm and dense, like in the iron mill, but ripe with the smell of plants and soil instead of coal smoke and hot steel. The narrow rivulet of glowing blue fluid they had followed through the tunnels broadened to a little stream, and the stone floor yielded to a loamy soil.

The girl slowed and tuned off between the mushrooms. They came to a pool of the glowing fluid. Wima kneeled down beside it and cupped some in her hands to drink.

"Are you thirsty?" she asked.

"What is that?"

"Water."

"Why does it glow?"

"It is infused with a miraculous invigorating element, radium."

Leon washed the blood of the Selenite he had killed from his hands. He scooped some of the glowing water into his palm and drew it to his lips. Despite the light it gave off it was cool. Lots of little mushrooms sprouted in the dirt around them. When he was a boy, his father had taken Leon and Waldek hunting for mushrooms in the woods around Alpena. He taught them the difference between the good ones and the poisonous ones. Some of these looked like purple versions of the morels they had found.

Wima broke off a piece of one and washed it in the water. "Eat," she said. He took it from her. It tasted good.

"I don't understand this," Leon said. "Where are we? Is this the Moon?"

"That is what you call it."

"Those creatures aren't human, but you are."

"The Selenites have always ruled the Moon. Humans, captured from the Earth eons ago, have for centuries been slaves here, the lowest class of workers. Only recently have your people come. When first we saw the humans from Earth, our hearts rose in the hope that you would liberate us from the tyranny of the Grand Lunar. But no: Your government would rather ally with those who keep us in misery. Your President is about to sell the Grand Lunar weapons of war that they shall use against any uprising of the workers. Once that deal is made, we shall never lose these."

She touched the metal bands that encircled her wrists and ankles, and Leon realized they were not bracelets but shackles.

"But why do you dance for them?"

"We dance not for the Grand Lunar, but for you. The Selenites use us to ingratiate themselves with you human visitors. While they hold our loved ones in their thrall, we have little choice but to do their bidding. That is why—"

A noise came echoing to them from the arched roof of the cavern, and Wima pressed her fingers against Leon's lips. She whispered into his ear. "The utmost silence, now."

In the pale light, Leon made out a crowd of figures advancing along the path they had followed. Two by two they marched, leaning forward, over six feet tall and massive, with broad shoulders and narrow heads. Their legs were extraordinarily long, their skulls covered by carapaces that Leon now realized were not clothing but hard exoskeletons. Each carried a long spear.

Unlike the other Selenites Leon had so far seen, whose skin—if you could call it that—was green, these were the hue of a spring rose. They fairly glowed in the gloom.

Leading them was a somewhat shorter being whose head was swollen and knobby, and who had huge ears like those of a bat.

"Who are they?"

"Pinks," Wima hissed. "Keep still!"

When they came abreast of where Leon and Wima had left the path, their leader stopped. It held its head up alertly and its ears, like a deer's, swiveled toward them. The troop behind it halted as if controlled by a single mind. Their absolute stillness sent a shiver down Leon's spine. He slid his hand into his pocket and gripped his gun.

The large-headed leader twittered to the others and they spread out between the mushrooms, moving in a line toward Leon and Wima.

Behind them was only the cavern wall. "Is there another way out?" he whispered.

"No. We must get past them."

The eyes of the Selenites were turned on them. They paused, an arc of menace with Wima and Leon at its focus.

The lead Selenite held up a three-fingered hand and said, "Visitor is lost? Do not listen to bad girl. Come to us, visitor, and we will send you home quick."

"I am not lost," Leon said. He was surprised by the force of his own voice.

"Leave bad girl. Lying girl. We will not harm her. We will teach her better her job."

It gestured slightly toward the pinks, who advanced, tightening the arc that closed them in.

"They won't let you go, now that you have seen the truth," Wima said.

"I know."

Spears thrust forward, the Selenites attacked. Leon pulled the pistol from his pocket and shot the nearest one. The thing's chest exploded into fragments and its body recoiled like a discarded marionette.

The pistol's report, magnified by the roof of the chamber, was deafening. The Selenite captain clapped its hands to its ears and fell writhing to the ground. The others flinched.

In a single bound, Leon was amid them. He swung the pistol into the carapace of the nearest. His hand went right through it and the thing was instantly dead. Leon seized its spear and swung it about him, smashing two more Selenites to flinders. The others fell back. "Come on!" Leon yelled to Wima.

The plucky girl ran to his side, picked up another fallen spear, and the two of them beat their way through the confused soldiers. Leon killed another before they broke free. "This way," she said, tugging at Leon's sleeve.

They raced along the channel of blue water and into one of a row of tunnel entrances. Leon found that, now that he understood his strength, with very little effort he could move much faster than Wima by long, low strides.

"Let me carry you," he said.

Wima nodded.

He shoved the pistol into his pocket, took the spear in his left hand, and Wima climbed onto his back. In the lunar gravity, she was hardly heavier than a cat. The walls of this tunnel were slimy with mold, the stone floor slippery. They hurtled down the passage in twelve-foot strides, Leon working to avoid hitting the tunnel's roof.

"That way," Wima said, pointing to a by-passage. Her arms were around his neck and her scent was lovely.

The passage ended in another cavernous room. Here bloody red light revealed row upon row of metal racks receding into the distance. On them stood ranks of basins. Each basin held a single human infant, naked, asleep. Each infant had a rubber nipple in its mouth connected to a tube that ran up to a swollen lozenge the size of a dirigible that hung suspended from the roof of the cave.

Small Selenites moved along the rows, occasionally stopping to unkink a tube, adjust the flow of nourishment, or spray baby excrement down drains in the basins.

"They won't find us here," Wima said. "Put me down."

Leon did so. "But what of these Selenites? Won't they report on us?"

"These workers are the lowest class. They know and care only for the smooth functioning of the production line. They have no interest in anyone who is not an infant; if we do not disturb them, I would be surprised if they are even aware of us."

"What is this place?" Leon asked.

"This is the child factory," Wima said. "Here the Selenites grow the next generation of human slaves. These infants will soon be on their way to becoming cogs in the Grand Lunar's industrial machine—unless our revolt succeeds."

Wima drew him on to an adjoining room. Here they saw older children, of perhaps a year or two, crammed into bottles with only their arms left free to hang out of a constricted opening. "See what they do to us," Wima said.

Leon recoiled. "What is this monstrous cruelty?"

"These children are meant to grow into machine tenders. Their role will be to spend their lives crawling within the cramped interstices of great mechanisms in order to repair them. The Selenites compress their bodies while stimulating their arms and hands so they may do their assigned work with maximum efficiency."

Leon looked down into one of the bottles, past the extended arms to make out a child's face—he could not tell if it was a boy or a girl—looking up at him, lips slightly parted, eyes half-closed. Leon's heart went out to the poor creature. One of the nipples from the previous room lay on the floor beside the tortured child. He took it up idly, weighed it in his palm, and put it into his pocket.

Wima and Leon wove their way back to a place in the baby factory behind a forest of standing pipes. She touched the stone wall of the chamber and the wall split open to reveal a little room. They entered and the doors closed. The little room hummed and the floor dropped away. For a second, Leon floated into the air. It was an elevator, such as Leon had heard they used in the towering buildings of New York.

Down, down, down they went. Leon felt pressure on his feet as the room stopped moving and the doors opened onto another cave. Wima took him further, always down, through a warren of caves and passages, to an astonishing depth. The only light came from pools of the blue water. Here were chasms and funnels and canyons, lakes and galleries. The Moon, Leon realized, was a great anthill, a sponge of caverns. There were underground cities, though Wima and Leon avoided them and their hordes of Selenites. Eventually they came to a region where escaped workers lived.

Wima took him to a room off one of the caves that contained a pallet, a low table, and an electrical light like those on display at the Exposition, so bright in relation to the relative darkness they had come through that

Leon squinted. She lowered the light's intensity. "We do not use these lights much, since we need to keep our vision adjusted to the Selenites' level. But the human eye is better able to deal with bright light than theirs, and this gives us some advantage."

She fed him a cold stew of mushrooms and some bits of meat. Mooncalf stew, Wima called it. "But now you must sleep. I will tell you more in the morning."

After she left, Leon lay down on the pallet of sponge-like fiber. Terribly tired, but sleepless, he wondered at all he had seen. The horror of shoving his fist through the head of the first Selenite who had attacked. It was a moment out of a nightmare. He could hardly grasp that he had begun the morning in the saloon on Broadway amid the smell of stale beer and the crapper behind the building. The notion of shooting President McKinley seemed like some fantasy he had imagined in another lifetime, though it could only have been hours since he boarded the Trip to the Moon. The celluloid tag still dangled from the button of his coat, spattered now with the blood of one of the Selenites he had killed. He unwound the thread and put the tag on the floor beside his pallet.

In the morning—though in the perpetual darkness of the lunar caves there was no proper morning—Wima brought him to the central committee of the Brotherhood of Lunar Workers. Though there were a couple of older, silver-haired men present, most of the committee were young. There was a Black man among them, and two women. Wima introduced a handsome young man with dark hair and penetrating eyes.

"This is Geron," said Wima.

The man took both of Leon's hands in his and looked him in the eye. "Thank you for saving my sister," he said.

"I only done my duty," Leon said.

"Your duty? But you owe us no allegiance."

"Wima needed help. I couldn't ignore her."

One of the older men said, "You survived a fight with over twenty pinks. No human has ever done that."

"What are these 'pinks'?"

"The lunar police," the gray-haired man said. "They are trained from infancy to be perfectly obedient to the Grand Lunar."

Wima touched Leon's arm. "They are the meanest and most despicable creatures in the universe. They know no mercy, cannot be reasoned with, and take joy in nothing so much as in brutally executing the orders of their rulers."

The older man nodded. He turned to Wima. "We are glad that you are back with us."

"But I failed," she said, lowering her head.

"We shall try again," Geron said.

"What was your task?" Leon asked. "Why did the guards seize you after your dance?"

Wima pulled a knife out of her sleeve. "I was there to assassinate the Grand Lunar."

ALIENISTS

MCKINLEY'S SUDDEN DEATH after he had appeared to be recovering sent the newspapers into frenzies of speculation. The President's doctors were the best in the country; they could not have botched the surgery. There must have been poison on the bullets.

The lynch mobs were back outside police headquarters in full force.

As a precaution, the police moved Leon to the county penitentiary. In order to avoid attracting attention, they took him out the back of the city jail, unhandcuffed, with a single cop as his guard. They climbed into a plain coach. When they got in, the cop hauled out his pistol and held it against Leon's head.

"You move and I'll kill you," he said.

Leon was in the county penitentiary only a few days and then they moved him to a jail across the street from the City Hall. Soon after he was settled in the new cell they dragged him into a courtroom and indicted him for murder. The court appointed two retired judges as his attorneys. One was named Titus and the other Lewis, but Leon had trouble remembering which was which. They might have been brothers except one of them had hair and a beard and the other was bald and clean-shaven. They were both old men. Soon, like Leon, they would be dead.

He had little doubt now that he would be executed. He only wished that McKinley had died in the Temple of Music when Leon had shot him, not eight days later after everyone thought he was recovering. Then Leon would have been spared the confusing emotions that came from thinking that both of them might survive their encounter.

Neither of his lawyers could hide his dismay at being made to defend him. One of them had been in Milwaukee at a convention of Masons when he got the word. They showed up a week before his trial and asked him the same questions he had answered repeatedly before he had stopped talking to the cops.

"We need to know why you shot the President," the bearded one said.

"A new alienist, Dr. Carlos F. MacDonald, a professor of mental diseases at Bellevue Medical College, is coming up from New York City to interview you," the bald one said.

Leon didn't answer. He watched their mouths as they spoke. He had begun to feel increasingly detached from the person they were talking about. This Leon Czolgosz— Fred Nobody—who was he?

Less and less of this seemed to have anything to do with him. He felt like the character Bedford from Wells' story, coming back from the Moon after escaping from the Selenites, weightless and detached. It was as if "Leon Czolgosz" were some trivial thing to which Leon was connected by accident; what happened to "Leon Czolgosz" had nothing to do with him, though he could not deny their connection. Who was Leon Czolgosz? He had always thought that he knew who he was, but everything that had happened since he'd gotten off that ride to the Moon—which he still could not remember—made him wonder. Everyone had a different opinion, from his family to Nora to Emma Goldman to the district attorney and the cops and Harold the guard. What did the murderer of the President of the United States have to do with the boy who had grown up in Alpena, Michigan?

"Czolgosz, we can't mount a defense of you unless you talk to us," said the bald one.

"It is our duty to see that the decorum of the law is maintained," said the bearded one.

Leon said nothing. From his vantage far above the Earth's atmosphere, he saw them clearly. They could hardly stand to be in the same room with him. One of them seemed more disgusted by than terrified of him; the other was more terrified than disgusted. But they both felt terror and disgust.

Two days before Leon's trial was set to begin, Dr. MacDonald arrived, with yet another alienist in tow. The fact that the district attorney gave them his own office in which to interview Leon suggested how likely they were to take Leon's part. Leon turned his back on them and looked out the window at the City Hall across the street, where on Monday the trial would begin.

MacDonald was a man in his fifties with dark hair and a beard. His manner was calm and friendly. The other alienist, named Hurd, was more forbidding. When Leon told them he would not talk about the assassination, MacDonald did not look upset.

"All right," he said. "Let's talk about other things." MacDonald asked him about his family, about his work. About whether he had friends. About where he had lived, and how. He asked if Leon had been alone as much as he claimed, how he spent his time.

"Do you masturbate? Have you any other unnatural practices?"

Leon had masturbated daily when he was an adolescent. His fear that his stepmother Catarina knew about it was one of the reasons he disliked her. "No, I don't do that," Leon said. "Never do that."

"Have you ever had a girlfriend?"

"I had a girlfriend. She threw me over."

"Have you ever had sexual intercourse with women?"

Leon colored. "You don't need to know that."

"That's all right. It does not bear directly on your situation. Perhaps you have never been with a woman?"

"I've been with a woman."

To the church, self-abuse and fornication were equally mortal sins. Worse still, just thinking about a woman in that way was a mortal sin; you did not even have to do anything. Yet Leon had not been able to avoid thinking about women. He was deeply ashamed, and never talked to any girls except for his sisters Cecili and Victoria.

One night in Cleveland more than a year ago, he had gone into the city to a meeting of the Socialist Club. Afterward, as usual, the people went to a tavern. As usual, Leon had his one beer and sat in a corner, listening. The men from the meeting talked about the twenty thousand workers a year killed in industrial accidents, about how the Spanish American War had been fought to distract people from the way that the owners kept them down.

A girl had come into the tavern. Leon had seen her before. She was a streetwalker. A plump girl with red hair and a spray of freckles over her nose. She looked Irish. Her dress had furbelows at the shoulders and hem, and she was tightly corseted; she wore a black sash around her waist.

She looked around the barroom, past the intense men talking, toward Leon. Their eyes met. He looked away, then after fifteen or twenty seconds looked back. She was still watching him. He felt himself color. She passed the bar and came over to stand beside his table.

"You're back again," she said. "You go to these meetings, but you never talk with anyone. Do you know how to talk?"

"I can talk," Leon said, "when I have something to say."

She sat down. "Why don't you buy me something to eat and we can talk."

Leon bought her a beer and a plate of stew. She wolfed it down. He watched her chew and swallow. She was young, not even as old as he was. One of the men at the other table looked over at Leon and winked.

"You dress better than these Socialists," she said.

"I'm a Socialist," he said.

"Always neat and clean. You must have money."

"What's your name?" Leon asked.

"Nora. Yours?"

"Fred C. Nieman."

"Well, Fred C. Nieman, thank you for the meal. Are we going to sit here all night and listen to them whine?"

"What do you want from me?" he asked.

"The question is, what do you want from me, Fred C. Nieman?"

"I don't know you."

"Well, now we're getting to know each other. Would you like to see my room? It will cost you only two dollars."

Leon's smile felt frozen on his face. He tried to look assured, but he could feel the beads of sweat at his hairline. "Show me," he said.

She led him out of the saloon and down the street, around a corner. Rain fell in a fine mist, a chill in the air that would get worse after midnight. There were bars all along the way here. On the corner, under an awning, stood a music grinder with a monkey sporting a tiny green fez. The street was full of horseshit; water ran in the gutters. Other women on the sidewalk leaned against buildings. From the taverns they passed came the sound of loud voices.

Nora took him to a big house on Ashtabula Street with a verandah and lit windows. Behind the tall front door was a foyer and staircase; off to the side an archway opened onto a parlor where a number of other women sat with a couple of men. A fire burned in the fireplace. The place didn't look like a whorehouse; it looked like a good boarding house. Nora led him up the stairs and along a landing; from below Leon heard the sound of laughter. She opened the last door on the landing.

Nora lit a lamp on a dresser. A small window with white lace curtains opened onto the street. Some dresses hung on pegs in a tiny closet. There was a big iron bedstead and a deal table with a pitcher and an enamel bowl of water with a towel beside it.

She asked him for her two dollars and he gave it to her. She sat on the bed, took off her shoes, lifted her dress, and rolled down her black stockings. He stood there uncertainly, shifting from foot to foot. "Don't be afraid," she said. She gestured at the basin. "You should wash."

Leon began to wash his hands.

"Not your hands, Fred," Nora said, laughing. "Here, I'll help you."

She came over to him, unbuttoned the fly of his trousers. His heart beat fast.

After a minute or two she said, "Now, come sit with me."

When he hesitated, she took his hand and pulled him down beside her.

"Kiss me," she said.

He kissed her. He had never kissed a girl.

She smelled of powder. He sat there stiffly. She put her arms around him and pulled him to her. He did not know what to do with his hands. She laid her head on his neck, her hair against his cheek. His erection ached.

She lay back, taking him with her, and they made love. Leon felt miserably embarrassed and ashamed and still desperately wanted her. She saw how inexperienced he was. She said nothing but helped him. She closed her eyes and moved against him.

It was over soon, but Leon could not imagine a greater pleasure. Afterward he lay beside her almost trembling. She probably wanted him to go. He didn't want to go. "If I give you another dollar, can I stay for a while?"

She raised herself onto one elbow, took a cigarette from a box on the table, and lit it from the lamp. She exhaled a plume of smoke. "It will cost you another two dollars, Fred. Do you have another two dollars?"

Leon took two bills from his wallet and laid them on the table. And so they spent that night together.

Leon came to see Nora the next night, but after that he ran out of money and had to go back to the Warrensville farm. He tried staying there but found he was always thinking about her. He had to see her again. He asked his father for some of the four hundred dollars Leon had given him to help buy the farm. But his father said he had no cash—all the money they had was tied up in the farm. What little cash they had they needed for the family. Maybe he could borrow some from one of his brothers. Frank had a good job as a bricklayer. But Frank asked him what he wanted it for and Leon could not make up a good enough lie. Catarina told Frank that if he lent Leon any money she would not feed him, since he had so much he could throw it away.

When Leon considered the privation he had gone through to save such a sum as four hundred dollars on the wages of a wire puller, he felt bitter resentment. He'd foregone meat and eaten boiled potatoes in order to save every cent. For what? He wasn't ever going to get ahead. He'd just end up old and broken like his father. And now he couldn't even get his money back!

After two weeks, Leon begged his father to help him. Paul Czolgosz looked in his son's eyes, made him promise not to let on to Catarina, and gave him twenty dollars he had squirreled away. Leon went back to the city.

He saw Nora again, and again. He made her go out to eat with him. She would not tell him anything about herself. It bothered him that other men were seeing her. It was because of capitalism that women had to sell themselves like that.

But that didn't keep him from buying her favors as often as he could afford.

This was before he learned about Free Love, when he still believed in bourgeois ideas of morality and marriage. He had been seeing her for a month when one night, up in her room, he asked her if she would marry him. "You would never have to do this again."

"Oh, I think you would not like it if I never did this again," Nora said..

"No—you would still do it with me," Leon said.

"But only you."

"Don't you want to?"

"I want a million dollars and a house in the country."

Leon was hurt. "Please. I love you."

"How much money do you make, Fred?"

He hadn't made any money in a year. "I earned a dollar and a half a day at the wire factory."

"I clear twenty-five a week," she said.

When she saw his hangdog face, she threw a washrag at him. "Don't be so glum, Leon. You can visit as often as you like."

"How do you know my name?"

"It was in your wallet."

She would have seen he only had a couple of bucks on him. "Then you know I can't afford to keep paying you."

"Leon, I grew up next to the Toledo city dump. I shared my room with two brothers, a sister, an uncle, and too many rats to count. I'm never going back there."

"But I love you."

"Even if I loved you, which I don't, marrying you would not do either of us any good." She handed him his wallet. "I think you had better go now."

He had gone back to the farm. Where else could he go? He stayed away from her. His health seemed to suffer. He developed a cough. He felt tired. He had a rash. It was then he realized that Nora must have given him a disease.

He went to see a doctor. The doctor examined him and said he did not think there was anything wrong with Leon. But he took Leon's money and gave him some pills.

Through the end of winter, Leon was sick. He coughed and he felt weak. He lay about more than usual. He needed to leave again, but he could not get at the money he had given to the family.

Sometimes he felt better, and his father would give him some of his money, complaining all the time, and Leon would go to the city, but he never returned to the house on Ashtabula Street. If women came along he crossed to the other side of the street, afraid one of them might be her.

Emma Goldman had spoken of Free Love, of men and women living together without being married, as a good thing. Listening to her lifted Leon's heart. When you said something was free, that meant you didn't have to pay to have it. But people used the word in other ways, too. On the farm you dunked the sheep in lye to make sure they were free of lice. Emma Goldman taught Leon what men and women living together without being married were free of. They were free of hypocrisy. They were free of the idea that one can own another person; they were free to be together for the sole reason that they wanted to be with each other. They were together because they loved each other. That was Free Love.

The only love Leon had ever known was the opposite of free. Except with his little sister Victoria, whom he loved without expecting her to love him back—and maybe with Nora, a little. He had seen it sometimes when he looked into her face. She would turn away whenever he caught sight of that, and he would pay her.

All these things had happened to the Leon Czolgosz who had shot the President and who was now sitting in a cell, soon to be on trial for murder. Looking down from his safe place beyond the Earth's gravity, far above the Erie County Courthouse, he was not sure what these memories had to do with him.

CAPTURED

WIMA EXPLAINED HOW she had infiltrated the corps of Moon Maidens. She told of the many indignities she had suffered in the process.

Her dark eyes were hard with righteous anger, but Leon perceived her sensitive soul beneath the rage. His heart went out to her.

The Brotherhood of Lunar Workers asked Geron to acclimate Leon to life among the rebels, and Geron, with the help of his sister, took Leon under his wing. Like a brother, Geron accepted Leon's peculiar Earth ways without judgment.

During his weeks among the rebel humans, Leon learned much about the social structure of the Moon. Spying with Wima and Geron, he observed the myriad types of Selenites. They ranged in size from as small as terriers to as large as bison. He saw the dim-witted, nimble herders who, during the two-week lunar day, led the great mooncalves to feed on the phantasmagoria of strange plants that sprouted in the sunlit craters pocking the surface. He saw the Grand Lunar's attendants, ones with overdeveloped eyes and ears and brains, those suited to memory and those suited to action. He saw the burrowing miners with their dim eyes, sharp claws, and blunt faces.

"In the Moon," Geron explained to him, "every citizen knows his place. He is born to that place, and the elaborate discipline of training, education, and surgery he undergoes fits him at last so completely to it that he has neither ideas, nor mental capacity, nor physical ability, for any purpose beyond it."

"This is horrifying," Leon said. "But how have you in the Lunar Brotherhood escaped this cruel fate?"

"Our fate is more subtly cruel," said Wima. "The Grand Lunar knows that if he wishes to conquer the Earth he must have humans to serve as go-betweens, so, at the risk of having us rebel, some of us—the ones he allows you earthlings to see—are left to grow naturally to adulthood. Even capitalists might balk at making common cause with an insect race that enslaves all humans."

"Though our capitalists also make slaves of the working class," Leon said. "And like the Selenites, they would prefer servants so accustomed to their place that they could not imagine any other."

Wima touched his arm. "You understand us completely," she said.

"But how are you able to recruit others to your cause? You must not be allowed to publish newspapers, to speak in public."

"We recruit from the unemployed."

"The unemployed! Do you have unemployment here?"

"I do not know how your world works," Wima said, "but here there are times when the need for machine tenders is less. During those times when there is no work for humans to do, rather than spend resources on feeding and housing them, the Selenites administer powerful drugs to the workers that put them to sleep. Asleep, they may be stashed in crowded galleries and empty caverns, and so long as they are awakened before they starve they do not need to be fed.

"Then, when some industrial accident kills a few thousand workers—and typically more than twenty thousand die every year—they simply waken an equivalent number to replace them."

Leon could only shake his head in sadness.

"Fortunately," Geron said, "their disregard for humans means that the warehouses of sleepers are not well guarded. So we are able to sneak into them, awaken the workers, and spirit them off to our hiding places. Once they taste freedom and understand their duties to their brothers and sisters, they join our movement."

Leon was moved, his brain set afire.

"Though I have nothing to offer but my hands and heart," Leon said, "what can I do to help?"

"I see you more clearly than you do yourself," Wima said. "Your strength is beyond that of any man among us."

"I'm no stronger than the average earthman," Leon said. "It's your lower gravity."

"It is your heart that is strong," Wima said.

Geron said, "The Selenite hierarchy is like a great pyramid with the Grand Lunar at its apex. If the ruler were exterminated, the entire system would be thrown into confusion, and our revolution might succeed in an hour." The kind-hearted lunar proletarian lowered his voice. "You, Leon, might perhaps prevail where Wima was thwarted. The problem is getting close enough to the Grand Lunar to kill him."

"I have this," Leon said. He pulled the Iver Johnson out of his side pocket.

Geron took the pistol. He tested its weight in his hands. "What is this?"

"It is a fearsome weapon," Wima told Geron, "of the sort the Grand Lunar seeks to purchase from the Americans. I saw Leon use it against the pinks—it blew one of them to pieces."

"How does it work?" Geron asked.

"It fires projectiles at a speed faster than you can see, with a force that can pierce armor," Leon said. "With it I could kill the Grand Lunar. If I could get within ten feet of him, I know that I would not miss."

Geron eyed him soberly. "You would likely forfeit your life. Why should you take up our cause? We are not your people."

"The oppressed of the Earth—and the Moon, too—are my brothers and sisters."

Wima's eyes glistened. "You are our savior," she whispered.

Leon's plan was simple: Wima and Geron and several other members of the Brotherhood would dress themselves in the comic Selenite costumes and infiltrate the performers at the arrival of Thompson's Aerial Navigation ship. Leon would sneak up to the arrival crater, hide among the foliage there, and when the passengers debarked, slip into their number as if he had just arrived with them. When they reached the Grand Lunar's palace, Wima and the others, already inside it, would cause a diversion. In the confusion, Leon would rush the dais and shoot the Grand Lunar.

The Brotherhood managed to steal or fabricate the necessary costumes. They cleaned and pressed Leon's coat and trousers, for which Leon was glad— he was always fastidious about his clothing. Geron carried one of the gold spears. Wima wore a dress that came to her ankles; she had cut a slit in the skirt so that she could slide the knife from the sheath she had strapped to her thigh.

It was a long journey from the remote sublunar caverns to the surface. At last they reached the elevator to the baby factory. When the doors opened on the red-lit scene, they moved quietly out, in ones and twos, slipping along the racks of infants who, should Leon succeed, would live complete and humane lives.

They approached the surface passages. It was time for them to separate, for Wima and Geron to slip past the Selenite guards to infiltrate the dressing rooms of the human performers.

Geron grasped Leon's forearm, and Leon his, in the secret handshake of the Lunar Brotherhood. "May the spirit of the workers be with you," Geron said. "In an hour, we shall be free."

Wima looked so harmless in her silly costume, green makeup, long false eyelashes, and red spots on her cheeks. Her dark hair was hidden by a green cap with spikes. "I don't know if we shall see each other again," she said quietly. "But whatever the outcome, remember that you carry two hearts in your breast: yours and my own." She leaned up to kiss Leon on the cheek.

She and Geron moved off into the darkness.

After they departed, Leon made his way to the crater on the surface. After weeks underground, it was a balm to see stars shine in the lunar twilight, the great blue disk of the Earth low on the horizon. This late in the lunar day, the crater was profuse with exotic plant life. He crouched behind a great orange puffball and watched the sky above the landing stage. Wima had told him how the plants of this crater sprouted, grew to maturity, and then withered and died, all within the two weeks of lunar daylight.

As Leon waited, he recalled how, at the beginning of July, when his father had finally agreed to return his money to him, Leon and Waldek had walked far away from the house to talk where their stepmother could not hear them. She begrudged Leon every cent he asked for from the hundreds of dollars he had contributed to the family. They would have to sell off land in order to repay him, and for that she hated him.

Waldek and Leon stood beneath a sparsely leafed elm smoking cigarettes. They talked about the nights they had read aloud from *Looking Backwards* when they shared a room in Cleveland while working at the iron mill. Leon felt the increasing distance between them. He could tell that Waldek wanted to draw him back into the family.

Waldek asked, "What can you want this money for?" The frustration was plain in his voice.

Leon tapped the ash from his cigarette, like a telegraph agent sending a message. It drifted down to the toe of his boot. His breath came short.

"Look at this tree," he said.

"What about it?" Waldek asked.

"It's dying."

"It looks okay to me."

"No," Leon said. "You can see that it isn't going to live long."

They finished their cigarettes and went back to the house. The next day, Leon's father gave him one hundred and ten dollars and he left. He had not seen any of them since.

After a half hour of waiting, Leon heard the *chuff* of wings and the *Luna* appeared in the distance, trailing phosphorescence in the Moon's dispersing atmosphere. It swung over the crater walls and floated toward the landing, almost hovering now. He could hear the clank of chains and see passengers peering over the side. The great ship glided forward a few feet and settled onto the slip. Gangplanks were dropped and the guide—the same one from Leon's own trip—spun out his spiel about the Moon and the Selenites.

While the crew busied themselves mooring the ship, Leon scuttled into the shadow of a giant mushroom a dozen feet back of the gangplank. The guide led the passengers down and they spread out around the dock, talking excitedly and staring at the lunar forest. Leon stepped around the mushroom's bole and stood casually among them, his hands in his pockets, imitating their gazes of curiosity and astonishment.

There followed the familiar greeting by the costumed human Selenites, and the progress into the cave and the lunar underground. This time around, Leon kept his eyes open. He caught glimpses of true Selenites in the dark hollows of the sublunar galleries, there to monitor the costumed humans and keep them from giving the charade away. How strange that here he was again, hand on his pistol, once more contemplating an assassination, this one of perhaps more consequence even than the assassination of McKinley might have had, if Leon had followed through with it. Someone else would have to take care of McKinley.

They reached the palace. Once more the vendors peddled cheese and moonshine. Once more the dancers came out and sang "My Sweetheart's the Man in the Moon." The tourists from Earth gathered to receive the blessings of the King. Leon drifted to the edge of the group, twenty feet from the dais. The King of the Moon smiled down and waved his scepter benignly.

A commotion arose at the back of the room. Shouts and counter-shouts. Two of the costumed Selenites fought with a much larger one. It was Geron and another Brotherhood member wrestling with a pink.

Leon stepped quickly toward the dais. Though most of the guards were distracted, one of them noticed him and came forward, extending his spear to block the way.

A female figure rushed between them and threw herself at the guard's feet. "Help me!" she cried.

The guard hesitated just long enough for Leon to get past.

He was a dozen feet from the King now. Up close he could see how much of the figure, including his smiling face, was puppetry manipulated by Selenites that sported multiple tentacles rather than arms and hands. They were amazingly dexterous at making the puppet look real. Of course, Leon thought. They had been bred for this purpose.

The lower body of the King, though, was alive—it was really the enormous head of the Grand Lunar. Invisible from elsewhere in the room, the creature's face was crammed into a small space at its bottom, almost as if an afterthought.

But its sagacious eyes were fixed on Leon.

Leon jerked the gun from his pocket, tangling it in the coat. He got it out and pointed it at the great domed skull.

Before he could shoot, a whiplike tentacle shot out and yanked the pistol from his hand. Other tentacles bound his feet, and he fell hard onto his shoulder. More tentacles around his arms, hands, face. One slapped over his mouth.

Out in the room he could see the guard raise his spear over the fallen Wima. Then Leon's eyes were covered, and he could not breathe, and he saw nothing.

CONDEMNED

ON THE MORNING of his trial they shaved Leon, gave him a new shirt and suit, and handcuffed him to guards by both wrists. Instead of crossing the street to the City Hall, they took him down into the basement of the jail and through a dimly lit tunnel that reeked of mildew. The walls of the tunnel were slimy with mold, the stone floor slippery. The passage was so narrow it was hard for Leon and the guards handcuffed to him to walk. He seemed to remember going through a tunnel like this before. It was one of those moments when you would swear that you had lived it already and knew what was going to happen a fraction of a second before it did.

At the other end of the tunnel, they took the stairs up to the second-floor courtroom, directly above where McKinley's body had lain in state not long before. Leon entered the courtroom to a chorus of hisses and boos from the more than two hundred spectators. It was not a big room. The jury box did not even have a rail around it—it was just a six-inch-high platform with chairs on it.

Leon had not spoken to either of his attorneys since a week earlier. The two old men had not seen the inside of a courtroom in years. They made Leon stand up and the DA read the charges against him. The judge asked Leon how he pled.

Leon found it hard to stand in the face of the waves of hatred that came off every person in the room. He did not want to have to go through this farce. He whispered, "Guilty."

That sent everybody into a flurry. The crowd in the courtroom buzzed. It was funny: Everybody in the room knew Leon was guilty but they were startled when Leon said it. The judge explained to Leon that in the State of New York, in a capital case, the defendant was not allowed to plead guilty. They entered a plea of "not guilty."

Did this mean that he might be acquitted? It took him a while to understand that no, this was only about the death penalty. In order to give them the option to execute him, he could not plead guilty.

Once he realized this, Leon stopped paying attention to the proceedings. While the legal show went on around him, he watched the afternoon sunshine that slanted through the high courtroom windows light dust motes that floated in the air. His presence was not necessary: He was there only to witness how legally and morally circumspect they all were. They would not simply pull a pistol on him the way he had on McKinley.

He was in space again, looking down. They were going through a ritual for their own peace of mind. They spent most of the time establishing things that were not in question. They introduced witnesses who testified that they had seen Leon shoot the President. They showed the Iver Johnson pistol and the charred handkerchief. They called on the secret service man and guards from the Temple of Music to describe their heroic capture of Leon. They asked the doctors to explain where the bullet entered McKinley's body and what they had done to try to save him, making sure that everybody knew that their failure to find it, and the fact that they had not used the X-ray machine on display at the fair to help, had nothing to do with the President's death. They established that Leon had shot McKinley and that this shooting was the cause of his death.

He noticed one lapse in their story: They never mentioned the Black man Jim Parker. His part in disarming Leon was left out. The things that Parker had done they asserted were done by some Irish guardsman.

It took some time to go through this. After the prosecution was finished, Leon's lawyers took over. They presented no evidence. They called no witnesses. Instead, each of them addressed the jury. The first said that the only issue was whether Leon was insane, but he made no argument for Leon's insanity. Rather, he pointed out that Leon had tried to plead guilty, so he must therefore have known that what he had done was wrong. He gave a lecture about how the defense in a trial like this was merely a way to ensure that Leon's condemnation and execution would be handled in a legal, orderly, and proper manner. The rest of his speech was a lengthy panegyric on President McKinley, "one of the noblest men that God ever made...a man of irreproachable character...a loving husband...a grand man in every aspect that you could conceive of."

After that, Leon's other attorney stood and said he had nothing to add.

The judge wanted Leon dead. The prosecutors wanted him dead. The jury members, in their answers to the lawyers' questions during selection, had made it clear that they would be happy to see him dead. Leon's lawyers would be relieved once they no longer had to pretend they did not want him dead.

As he listened, Leon wondered if he didn't deserve to die. The lawyers talked about Mrs. McKinley. In his 1896 campaign, McKinley had refused to travel around the country because, he said, he needed to keep close to his Ida. Both of their children had died young. Ida was subject to fainting spells and, they said, epileptic fits, though McKinley never alluded to this malady. It was said that, whenever she froze in her chair at some public dinner, McKinley would take out his spotless handkerchief and drape it over her head like a veil.

Leon had seen how solicitous the President was of her—he might be the most powerful person in the country, with important decisions to make and hordes of sycophants to do his bidding—but in the midst of all that pomp McKinley always had an eye out for his wife, making sure she was comfortable, worried about her being too much in the sun, too cold in the shade. Patient, unceasingly attentive, always at her side.

The papers said she had hand-sewn his satin neckties. Maybe she had sewn the tie McKinley was wearing when Leon shot him. In killing her husband, Leon was killing her as surely as if he had put a bullet in her belly, too. How could that not be an evil thing?

"Go easy on him, boys," McKinley had said. Everybody talked about how Christian it was of the President, seconds after being shot, to call off his dogs. Leon might have pointed out how much power McKinley must have in order, with a word, to stop a crowd of men with their blood up from beating him to death. McKinley's having such power was reason alone to assassinate him. But sitting there in the courtroom, Leon did not feel the force of that injustice as much as he had when sitting in his rented room reading *Free Society*.

After Leon's lawyers came the district attorney. Penney concluded his summation by characterizing Leon as an example of the unsavory refuse who had entered the country with the immigrant influx of the last decades. Leon was a member of "an awful class of people that have no place upon our shores...they must go hence and keep forever from us...they will not be permitted to come here."

Then the judge charged the jury and sent them out to decide on their verdict. Waiting for their return, Leon could not help but dwell on all the things these men had said about him. To them he was a monster, a blankness, a bewilderment. He felt bewildered himself. He did not belong in the same world that they lived in. There was some polite murmuring in the courtroom while the jury was gone, but no one spoke to him or made any effort to remove him while they all waited.

A half hour later, the jury came back with a verdict: guilty of murder in the first degree.

Spectators exclaimed, reporters scribbled in their notebooks. The entire trial had taken eight hours.

They took Leon back to his cell. He did not sleep well that night. With the verdict, his space vehicle had returned to Earth. He no longer floated above himself. He was back inside Leon Czolgosz. This part of the peculiar ritual had come to an anticlimactic end.

In the morning, the guards brought some people to his cell. To his surprise it was his father, his brother Waldek, and his sister Victoria.

Leon was glad to see his father and Waldek, but it hurt him to see Victoria. She ran to him and embraced him, sobbing, "Leon, what have you done?"

He let his hands hang by his sides as she wept against his chest. He looked at his father and Waldek. His father's face was creased with sorrow. Gently Leon separated Victoria from himself. "I must speak with Father," he said.

She turned, still weeping, head down.

Waldek explained that they had arrived the day before but that the police would not let them see Leon. Instead, the DA questioned them about their actions in the last months, trying to get them to admit they were a part of Leon's plan to kill the President. He demanded to know who else was in it with Leon. Only after his family had convinced Penney that they had no part in the assassination did he relent.

Leon spoke to his father in Polish. He told him he was sorry, that he did not want the family to suffer because of him. His father said nothing.

As Leon spoke, Victoria kept sobbing. She looked at him through her tears, and Leon saw that she had become a beautiful young woman. He saw that this was happening not just to him, but to all of them. After he was dead, Victoria would always carry around the fact that her brother had killed the President of the United States. He had branded her, the infant that his mother had left them, whom he had taken care of as a boy. The only three people in his family who gave a damn about him were here in this cell, and there was nothing he could say or do that would take away their grief. They cared about him. He had not grasped that the way he should have.

"Don't cry," Leon pleaded with Victoria. "I can't stand it if you cry."

He gave her his newly purchased handkerchief. Victoria gathered herself together and stopped weeping.

Leon's father still had not spoken. Leon tried to explain to him, in Polish, what had happened, but he found he did not have words for it. This awful reality. He spoke with Waldek in English.

"Who put you up to this?" Waldek said. "Maybe if you tell them they won't execute you. Tell them. Tell them, Leon."

"Nobody put me up to it," Leon said. Standing there, he hardly understood how he had put himself up to it.

He asked them to forgive him for the trouble he had brought them. After that there was not much more to say. His father had not said a word to him, just looked at him with sad incomprehension.

Leon shook hands with Waldek and his father. Victoria kissed him and started crying again. "Goodbye," he told them. They left.

He had fooled himself. He had thrown away his life for no good reason. What did he accomplish? And even if he had accomplished something, was this the way to do it?

The next afternoon, Thursday, the cops came and took him back to court for the sentencing. The courtroom was packed, standing room only. The best show in town. Only one of his lawyers—Titus, that was this one's name, the bearded one—represented him this time. Leon looked for Waldek, Victoria, or his father, but they were not there.

Before pronouncing his sentence, the judge made Leon stand. He asked Leon if he had any statement to make.

Leon could have told them about injustice, about how the rich fed off the poor, about how the rules of society consigned working men to lives of misery, about how for some women it was better to be a prostitute than to be married, about how the church told them to be good and to pray and nothing came of it. He could have talked about how hard it was to breathe in the iron mill, and what it felt like to have a hot wire whip across your face, about men who got their hands cut off in chopping machines, about his father's gnarled fingers and stooped back and the lines on his face.

He didn't say any of this. His voice failed him. He whispered, "My family had nothing to do with it. I was alone. I was alone and had no one else, no one else but me."

"What did he say?" the judge asked, his mask of dignified impartiality broken by annoyance.

Titus repeated what Leon said.

Leon said, a little louder, "I never told anything to anybody about killing McKinley. I never thought of it until a couple of days before I did it."

Dead silence from the crowded room.

After a moment, the judge said, "Anything further?"

"No, sir," Leon said, voice failing again. "That's all."

The judge sat straighter in his black robes. His moment had come. Leon clutched the back of the chair to support himself.

"Czolgosz, in taking the life of our beloved President, you committed a crime which shocked and outraged the moral sense of the civilized world. The sentence of this court is that in the week beginning on October 28, 1901, at the place, in the manner, and by the means prescribed by law, you suffer the punishment of death.

"Remove the prisoner."

OCTOBER 29, 1901

NO ONE COULD say that they had condemned Leon without decorum. The newspapers complimented everyone: the prosecution, the judge, the jury, the officers of the court, the jailers, the mobs in the street outside, and themselves. They heaped praise in particular on Leon's lawyers, who had undertaken "the disagreeable task of protecting the legal rights of the wretched culprit."

It was a concerted effort to erase the shame that Buffalonians felt over the fact that the President had been killed in their city. The funeral and the trial had put quite a damper on the Exposition, but while they lasted, they flooded the hotels and restaurants and railroad depot and telegraph offices with business. It was a pity the execution would not take place for another month, and would happen far away.

The night of his sentencing they hustled Leon off on a train to Auburn State Prison. The sequence of events that had started when Leon pulled the trigger in the Temple of Music had moved forward like this train on its tracks, steady, unwavering, destination fixed. He was a ghost, on a train, and he could not get off.

Somehow the word must have gotten out: When the train stopped in Canandaigua, it was met by a mob with torches and rope and guns. "Sorry, boys," the conductor told them. "Czolgosz ain't on board. The sonofabitch won't leave Buffalo until Saturday."

He got back onto the train and spat at Leon's feet. "Don't thank me," he said.

When they arrived in Auburn at three in the morning, another mob was gathered. They called for Leon's head. The Auburn depot was directly across the street from the prison entrance, not one hundred feet away. Angry men rushed the phalanx of guards surrounding Leon. For the first time since his arrest, Leon was afraid. The DA and the lawyers had wished to make Leon go away, but they had been constrained by their belief in the law. If these men got him he would be ripped to pieces. Amid the shouting and darkness, Leon's legs failed him. A couple of the guards grabbed him by the shoulders and dragged him toward the prison gate. The cops used billy clubs to beat off the mob, and they wrestled Leon inside.

There they stripped him, threw him into a cold bath, weighed and measured him, and put him into a striped prison suit. They stuck him in a cell on death row.

The cells on the death row in Auburn Prison were windowless, eight feet square, and seven and a half feet high. Each cell contained a cot and a shit bucket and nothing else. Three sides were masonry and the barred cell door faced onto a gallery on the west side of the prison. In the cell to one side of Leon was Clarence Egner, an inmate who had killed a guard; on the other was Fred Krist, a married man from Waverly who had murdered a seventeen-year-old girl named Kittie Tobin when her parents forbade her to see him.

Auburn had established the method of holding prisoners in solitary confinement and forbidding them from ever talking with anyone so that they might contemplate their crimes. Leon did not want to talk to anyone. Maybe if he could figure out what had happened to him, and why it had happened, and whether he had made a mistake, and exactly what his mistake was, he might have something to say worth listening to. But for now, he was quiet.

One of the things he thought about in his month waiting for his execution was Emma Goldman. All his time in custody they had badgered Leon to implicate her, but he had refused. Yes, her speech had set him on fire, but he insisted that killing the President was his own idea, nobody else's. Now he tried to understand the degree to which Goldman was responsible for his actions. Was it, as they all seemed to think, her fault?

After her speech in Cleveland he had seen her one other time. It was in July, when he had gotten his money out of the farm. He had heard some members of the Liberty Club say Goldman was living in Chicago. He took the train there and arrived on a muggy evening, got directions, and went to the home of Abraham Isaak, editor of *Free Society*, with whom she was supposed to be staying. As he arrived at the nondescript brownstone, she appeared on the front stoop carrying a valise. A cab drew up by the sidewalk, the horse restive in its traces.

Leon caught her before she could climb into the cab. "Miss Goldman."

"Yes?" she said. She looked at him, at first with some suspicion, and then, when she saw his face in the streetlight, with surprise. "We've met before. In..."

"In Cleveland, in May, when you spoke there."

"Ah, yes. What can I do for you, Mr....?"

"Nieman. Fred Nieman. I wanted to talk with you about anarchy. Some ideas I have."

"Unfortunately, Mr. Nieman, I am leaving Chicago. I need to get to the depot to catch a train for Rochester, where my sister lives."

"May I ride with you to the station?"

She agreed, and they got into the cab together. While the driver drove them through the busy streets to the Lakeshore station, Leon, tongue-tied, tried to explain himself to her. "I wish to do something for the cause," he said. "To help the working people."

"Have you read Kropotkin?"

He had not. "I've read *Free Society* and attended some meetings."

She shook her head. "You need to educate yourself. I can't do it for you."

He told her he wanted to be one of the comrades, to be let in on the secrets of anarchism. She seemed puzzled by both his ignorance and his eagerness. Her hand rested on the handle of the valise between them. He could have put his own over hers. He did not.

They talked. She admitted how, when she first got involved in radical politics, she had known no more than Leon about political theory. She had been moved, she said, by her sense of justice, fairness, and basic humanity. Perhaps, she said, that was enough.

All too soon they arrived at the station, where Goldman was met by some of her anarchist friends, including Isaak. After she boarded the train, Leon felt deflated. Isaak asked him where he was staying. Leon said that he had just arrived and did not have a stopping place. They talked for over an hour; Leon admitted he knew little more of anarchy than he had heard from Goldman's speech in Cleveland and explained how he had been disillusioned by the Socialist Party and their internal squabbles. Leon asked if he could attend the anarchists' secret meetings. Isaak said there were no secret meetings.

"What about plans for action by the comrades?" Leon asked.

Isaak gave him a peculiar look. "We need to find you a place to stay. I can recommend a good, inexpensive hotel."

"I don't have any money," Leon said.

Isaak took pity on him. He accompanied Leon to a hotel and booked him a room, offered to buy him breakfast the next morning, and to help him find a job.

Leon felt bad lying about being broke, and afraid he would make a fool of himself if he had to talk further, so he left early the next morning rather than meet with Isaak. He hadn't gone to Chicago, he realized, to talk about anarchism. He had gone to see Emma Goldman. He had failed to impress her; she thought him a man of no consequence. He was not like her lover, Alexander Berkman, serving fourteen years in prison for shooting Henry Clay Frick, the man who had broken the Homestead Strike.

But what Goldman had said about being moved by a sense of justice was true for Leon as well. She had seen that in him, at least.

He was in Buffalo when the September issue of *Free Society* came out. In it, Isaak published a notice titled "Attention!" in which he called Leon a police spy.

His demeanor is of the usual sort, pretending to be greatly interested in the cause, asking for names, or soliciting aid for acts of contemplated violence. If this individual makes his appearance elsewhere, the comrades are warned in advance and can act accordingly.

The next day, Leon went out and bought the pistol. To what degree was it to prove Isaak wrong, to make himself into one of Goldman's martyrs? Maybe the suffering of the working classes had nothing to do with it. So he had taken a sick woman's husband, a man who, fatally wounded by a bullet in his gut, had worried about the man who had shot him.

The day before Leon's execution, they sent a priest from Buffalo to talk to him. Leon was surprised. The warden had asked him if he wanted a priest and Leon had said no. But there he stood outside the cell in his black cassock and white collar. He was younger than Leon would have expected, a vigorous man in his forties with penetrating eyes and a big nose. He might have been an ironworker himself.

"Who are you?"

"I am Father Hyacinth Fudzinski," the priest said in Polish.

"Speak English," Leon said. "I was born here. I'm an American."

"I've come to hear your confession," the priest said.

"I don't want to confess," Leon said.

"Maybe we can just talk. If we sit for a while, something may come to you. Maybe you have some messages you'd like to pass along to your family?"

The priest was well intentioned. Leon let him in. They brought a wooden stool for him, and Leon sat on the bed. Leon asked the priest to make the guards go away.

"We're not going anywhere, Czolgosz," the guard said. "If you try to harm the father they won't have to fry you tomorrow; I'll put you down right here and now."

The priest said something to the guard and the guard stepped out into the gallery.

The tiny cell, just the two of them, was like a confessional. "Were you raised Catholic?" the priest asked.

"Yes. But I quit the church. I don't believe in the church."

"God hasn't quit you," the priest said.

"What does God know about me?

"He knows the good and the evil in your heart. You have committed a terrible sin, but that does not mean that God won't take you into heaven. If you make a sincere confession, I will absolve you and you will end your life in a state of grace. Tell me your sins and by this time tomorrow night you will be in heaven. If not, you will burn in hell for all eternity."

"That's what you want me to believe," Leon said, "so you can control me. I used to believe that, but I don't anymore."

"Do not harden your heart, Leon. You can be forgiven."

Leon smiled. "Don't worry. You've done your job, coming here. Now you can go home and tell everybody how you tried to save my soul but I refused. Tell them their sorrows are temporary, they can be cured if they will pray. And the poor people will take bread from their children's mouths in order to put money in your basket on Sunday. You'll eat a fine meal, drink some holy wine, and sleep quiet in your bed."

Father Fudzinski paled, but he did not raise his voice. "What I do is not a job."

"It's a job. Even being the Pope is a job, like a shoemaker, except he earns a lot more money. And when you pay the shoemaker at least you end up with a pair of shoes."

The priest sighed. It was dark in the cell, and Leon could not make out his expression. Leon looked out of the cell into the gallery, where the sunset light had turned everything so bright that he had to squint.

"Many things you think you know are wrong," the priest said.

His voice sounded different, sibilant and high pitched.

Leon turned to face him, and everything was changed. The cell was altered, larger, much larger. It wasn't a cell anymore; it was a vast cavern dimly lit with blue light. His cot and his shit bucket were gone. It was foolish even to expect such things in this place, ornately decorated and suffused with a glowing blue mist. Around them stood a horde of misshapen, dark figures. The priest, too, was changed. He did not sit on the wooden stool but on a dais, and it was not the priest at all, but rather some monstrous thing with a huge head and a tiny face. Around it hovered insectile creatures carrying odd devices. One of them sprayed a cooling mist around the monster's great dome of a skull.

"You are about to die," the Grand Lunar said, "but before you do, we would take it as a courtesy if you would answer some questions for us."

Leon looked around the great chamber. There were no barred doors, no cells, no gallery. There were guards, and they were human, but they did not wear the uniforms of the Auburn State Prison. Leon himself wore the clothes he had worn on the day that he had visited the Moon at the Pan-American Exposition. The day he had shot McKinley.

"Why should I answer your questions?"

"No reason. But your attempt to kill me must have been motivated by something, and in order for me to rule justly, it would help if I understood my human servants. You see—" the Grand Lunar waved one of its pitifully small arms at the human guards among the Selenites "—that they remain loyal to me still, despite the revolt of some of their brothers and sisters, whose minds must have become confused. I thought that perhaps you might be able to explain the source of their confusion."

It all came back to him. Leon remembered Geron grappling with the Selenites in the phony palace; he saw Wima's eyes fixed on him as she went down, desperately, before the Selenite guard in order to give Leon the chance to kill the alien tyrant. He had failed them. Tears came to his eyes and, overcome with emotion, he drew a ragged breath.

"They wish to be free," Leon said.

The Grand Lunar's little eyes glittered. "You have seen that we do not have money here. Everything on the Moon is free."

Leon laughed bitterly. "Your human slaves are not. You torture infants from birth, warping their bodies and minds, stunting their abilities in one area and exaggerating them in another, not according to their desires but to what you conceive to be their usefulness. You treat them as objects to be fitted into slots in your machines, used up, abandoned, and replaced without a qualm when they can no longer do their jobs. And they never know another possibility. All the potential they might have had to think, to dream, to live a full life, is squashed down into a bottle with no room for art, love, imagination."

"It is true that we do this. We do this out of our concern for them."

"Concern? You destroy them before they can even know they are being destroyed!"

"Should we rather, as I understand you humans do on Earth, allow them to grow to adulthood with every capacity you so eloquently describe—for art, for love, for imagination—and then force them into a menial job that does not allow them to express those capacities? Let a boy grow to twelve years old, a thoughtful and imaginative child who longs for a larger life, and then thrust him into a glass factory where for twelve hours a day, seventy-two hours a week he carries red-hot bottles to an annealing oven, his hair and eyelashes singed by the heat, ears deafened by the roar of the furnaces, mouth parched, hands blistered, eyes red, feet and back aching, repeating the same tasks endlessly, reduced to a pair of hands and a pair of eyes until he cracks? Here, our workers do not know they are being destroyed. There, you let them realize they are being destroyed, and then destroy them. This hardly seems like a better alternative."

"You drug the workers into unconsciousness when you do not need them, then wake them only when you do."

"Is it better, when there is no work for them, to leave them awake and turn them into the streets to starve?"

Rage rose in Leon's chest. "Freedom means that a person may choose his own fate. You may tell yourself that by eliminating choice you have made your slaves happy, but the fact that they sent me to kill you puts the lie to your sophistry."

The Grand Lunar said, "Your heart is full of anger. Tell me this: What happens when a free human wants something, and another wants the same thing?"

"They share."

"Is this what happens on Earth?"

Leon would not lie. "Sometimes they fight, and one wins and the other loses."

"So the freedom you speak of only means that people will discover reasons to fight one another."

"They have the *ability* to share. No one has to own or be owned. We can preserve good things and make new ones that are equally good. We can give ourselves freely and love one another."

"And that is why you attempted to kill me? You would bring down the order that we have created over generations, which has tamed the lunar world and created this vast number of variegated beings, in order to replace it with a teeming conflict of individuals in the hope that they will not fall to killing each other. They will 'give themselves freely and love one another.'"

"Yes. They will."

"Why, then, is your Earth not a paradise?"

"Not everybody can do it, yet. The powerful ones repress the others. The violent ones insist on imposing their will. There are—"

"Yes, I see. I see one such in front of me." The Grand Lunar slowly closed his eyes and opened them again. He waved a feeble arm at one of his attendants. "Take this one to be executed."

Leon felt himself seized from behind. They pulled a hood over his head and all was darkness. They grabbed his wrists and manacled his hands together. He struggled, but their grip on him only tightened. They marched him forward. The sense of the large space around him changed and he was in a hallway. He heard only the footsteps of his guards. The air grew colder. A metallic clang, the creak of iron hinges, a door opening.

They jerked the hood off him. He squinted against the light.

He was in a room full of men. The warden was there, and some guards, and the alienist Dr. MacDonald whom he had spoken with back in Buffalo, and another doctor, and some other men in suits. On a square rubber mat raised an inch or two above the floor stood a blocky wooden chair with leather straps at the wrists and ankles. Thick cables ran from its sides. A leather helmet dangled above it on a cable from the ceiling. The guards had told him that this was the first electric chair ever built. It used alternating current, the same current that powered the thousands of lights that turned the Pan-American Exposition into a fairyland every night.

They did not let Leon catch his breath; without ceremony they frog-marched him to the chair. This was the end, and he didn't want to let it pass without telling them what he had seen and felt even if he did not know what it meant: that the injustice that had driven him was real, that McKinley was an agent of that injustice, that the events of his life since he heard Emma Goldman speak had been as much fantasy as a trip to the Moon, that he had been born with the capacity to do better but the world had shaped him into a hand holding a gun. That he was a martyr to nothing. It was too much; it would take him a lifetime to say it and his lifetime was done.

As they strapped him in, Leon managed to say, "I shot the President because I thought it would help the working people. I did it for the sake of the common people. I am not sorry for my crime. That is all I have to say."

But as they tightened the straps around his head and chin, he thought of something else. "I am awfully sorry I did not see my father again."

They were all watching him, except for one of the guards whose eyes followed the cables from the chair to the generator. For a moment, Leon wondered why he did this, but then he recognized that the guard was Geron.

The straps would not let Leon move his head, but he could still make out, among the people there, at least three other members of the Brotherhood of Lunar Workers.

The Grand Lunar said to the technician, "Proceed."

The Selenite moved his articulated, three-fingered hand to the mechanism. Before he could close the switch, Geron knocked him aside. The other rebels sprang into action.

"Stop them!" the Grand Lunar shrieked in its whistling voice, but the creature, its body atrophied and mind without resources to understand what was happening, was helpless to do anything without its slaves to command.

And then, dashing into the room came brave Wima, laying about her with her golden staff, knocking Selenites around like ninepins. Within moments the rebels controlled the room. Wima fell on the straps binding Leon. Through his tears he watched her beautiful, determined face. She undid the band holding his head rigid and threw her arms about his neck, sobbing with relief and triumph at this victory over power and circumstance.

Leon struggled from the chair. "Thank you," he said.

Geron embraced him. "Comrade."

Wima took his hand and pulled him away.

"Come," she said. "We have work do."

Story Notes for
The Dark Ride

MANY OF these stories were written for and critiqued at the Sycamore Hill Writer's Workshop, which I founded with Mark L. Van Name in the mid-1980s and ran with him, and later Richard Butner, for about twenty years, and which has continued under Richard's direction since 2005. Sycamore Hill has for me been an extended education in fiction writing and a source of energy for much of my career. I must thank Richard and the many writers over the years who have read and commented on my story drafts, and whose commitment to speculative fiction has inspired me to try to write as well as I can.

I'm likewise grateful to the many editors who have published these stories over the last forty years, in particular Ed Ferman, Gardner Dozois, Sheila Williams, Ellen Datlow, Gordon Van Gelder, Jonathan Strahan, Bruce Sterling, and C.C. Finlay.

Thanks to Kim Stanley Robinson for his introduction, which explained to me things about my stories that I sort of knew but did not.

Finally, my thanks to Therese Anne Fowler. Who knew that being married to another writer could be so much fun?

Not Responsible! Park and Lock It!   1981

While in grad school at the University of Kansas, I made friends with another student named Tim Roth (no relation to the actor), an aspiring writer whose oddball sensibilities were similar to my own. We took a workshop taught by James Gunn. One week Gunn brought a Visiting Famous SF Writer to teach the class, and the VFSFW assigned us the task of writing a story in 24 hours. Mine was a non-sf story called "Home" that became my first published story, appearing in the *Cottonwood Review* in 1975. Tim's was a deconstruction of heroic fantasy, about the kind of young village boy who is often the hero of such tales, called upon to face a brutal villain in single combat over the honor of the heroine and of his home town. Think Frodo. Think Eragon. Think Luke Skywalker. We all know how this story ends: in the climax, the hero, despite the odds against him, defeats the evil warrior and wins the girl.

Except in Tim's story the brutal warrior beats the snot out of the hero, who has no real combat skills, pisses on his prostrate body, leaves him half-dead, and rapes the girl. It's a shocking ending to a story that we think cannot end that way. I thought it was a daring challenge to the assumptions of genre fiction—especially in 1974.

In class the next day, the VFSFW proceeded to savage Tim's story. He spent at least twenty minutes ripping the opening pages apart. He read sentences aloud in a funny voice. He mocked the characters' names. He capered and waved the manuscript in the air and laughed aloud. The rest of us students sat silently cowering. Tim was brutalized. Somewhere in the middle of this rant I realized that the VFSFW had not read past the first few pages, and therefore thought that it was just another clichéd wish fulfillment fantasy.

After that workshop—this is the absolute truth—Tim decided he wasn't any good as a writer, gave it up, dropped out of school, and joined the army. He washed out of basic training, came back to Lawrence, found Jesus and ended up living in a communal home with other born-again Christians. I lost track of him.

Tim had written a different story that I had always admired, "Going Mobile" (side two, track two, *Who's Next*), the story of a boy growing up in a family living in a moving automobile, in a world where everyone lived in automobiles, traveling on an endless highway, never stopping. Tim treated this absurd premise matter-of-factly, with a tone of wistful nostalgia veiling social critique. In its Kafkaesque way it was a deadly accurate portrayal of what it was like to come of age in a middle-class American family in the 1950s.

I couldn't forget this story, and I regretted that Tim had never published it. Some years later, after I had sold my first few stories, I went by the house where he was living with the other Christians. He came out to talk with me. He had cut off all his long hair. I told Tim that, if he was willing to give me the manuscript of "Going Mobile" I would like to rewrite it and we could try to sell it as a collaboration. He told me that his writing was a painful reminder of an earlier life that he was trying to get past, and that he had burned all his manuscripts. I was appalled. I asked him if he would let me use the idea in a story of my own, and he said yes.

So I wrote "Not Responsible! Park and Lock It!" It's not the same story that Tim wrote, but it owes its existence to him.

The title comes from a record by the Firesign Theater, *Don't Crush that Dwarf, Hand Me the Pliers.*

Events Preceding the Helvetican Renaissance   2009

As a boy I liked adventure science fiction. When Jonathan Strahan and Gardner Dozois asked me to contribute to *The New Space Opera 2*, I took it as an opportunity to write something in that mode, unlike what most readers might expect from me.

The inspiration for this story came from an anecdote I'd heard about the poet and fascist supporter Ezra Pound, who during World War II did propaganda radio broadcasts for Mussolini. Reportedly, Pound suggested in a letter that the U.S. should settle its dispute with Japan after Pearl Harbor not with a war, but by ceding the Japanese the island of Guam in return for films of 300 Japanese Noh plays, which Pound suggested could be shown in U.S. high schools to generations of students, to inestimable cultural value. Trading plays for territory: what a great, lunatic idea!

"Helvetican Renaissance" also taps into issues of the existence or non-existence of God, the claims of those who say they are guided by His hand, the place of religion in human life, and the workings of fate vs. chance, things I have pondered from my very devout Catholic boyhood to my decidedly un-devout present state.

Pride and Prometheus

"Critical fiction" is a term defined by Henry Wessells as "a work of art that explicitly declares itself as a critique of another work of literature and explicitly makes use of that earlier source text."[1] Some people call this "fanfic" and I suppose that fanfic can be seen as a form of critical fiction, though I don't know how critical of the original works most pieces of fanfic are.

At any rate, I've been interested in this form of story for a long time, and have tried quite a few versions of it. I'll leave you to decide whether the result is fanfic or literary criticism or just another sort of fiction.

At the 2005 Sycamore Hill Writers Workshop, Benjamin Rosenbaum brought a draft of a story titled "Senseless and Insensible," a wild send-up of Jane Austen. In offering my critique of the story, I happened to mention that though Austen was a generation older, she and Mary Shelley were contemporaries. I had never thought about the fact that Austen's novels and Shelley's *Frankenstein* were published at more or less the same time, and as I said it I got the idea for this story. As soon as my turn to speak was done, right there at the critique table I began making notes.

It took me a while to figure out the story. I read *Pride and Prejudice* and *Frankenstein* again. In *Frankenstein* Victor goes to England for the purpose of creating a mate for his murderous, alienated monster, who follows him. As Victor travels about England he says he began to "collect the materials" he will need to create a female creature. Though he doesn't say so, I thought: one of the materials he will need would be a female body.

On their way to Scotland, where Victor will create this bride, Victor and his friend Henry stop in Derbyshire, at the resort town of Matlock. In *Pride and Prejudice*, Mr. Darcy's estate Pemberley is in Derbyshire, near the resort town of Matlock.

At the end of *Pride and Prejudice*, two Bennet sisters are left unmarried, flirty Kitty and serious, moralizing, plain Mary. What might the two of them be like after ten years, when they are in their late twenties and approaching spinsterhood?

---

[1] From his introduction to *My Man and Other Critical Fictions* by Wendy Walker.

From a certain point of view, aren't *Pride and Prejudice* and *Frankenstein* both about the difficulty of finding a suitable mate?

Once I got going, I found more and more to write about. It was so much fun!

One of the risks of getting into the ring with Jane Austen was that I could not really match her wit—who could? I might do a bit better with the gothic style of Shelley. I tried my best. I think of "Pride and Prometheus" as the story of an Austen heroine who accidentally falls into the middle of *Frankenstein*. One of the reasons I had never considered Austen and Shelley's contemporaneity was that, at least when I was younger, they were never spoken of together: Austen was not a Romantic writer and Shelley was one of the greatest Romantics. Jane is the mother of the novel of manners and Mary the mother of science fiction. They don't fit together. That's one of the things that made this so interesting to write.

My career, in retrospect, has been to cross the sensibilities of literary fiction with those of pulp fiction, and this story is one in which that impulse has expressed itself.

My working title of this story was "Austenstein," but that didn't feel right. At a reading of the story soon after I'd completed a draft, I mentioned that it was titleless, and from the audience F. Brett Cox suggested "Pride and Prometheus."

One last note: I wrote this before the craze over *Pride and Prejudice and Zombies*, a book that I tried to read and found I could not.

Ten years after this story was published, I published a novel version. You should look it up.

The Motorman's Coat   2009

In 2007 and 2008 I co-taught summer fiction writing workshops with Wilton Barnhardt in Prague. As an assignment for our students, we asked each to write a story having something to do with Prague. Under the influence of Franz Kafka and Karel Čapek, I wrote this story. It's one of the saddest I have ever written, and may have the most sudden ending.

The Closet ###### 2010

For Ursula Le Guin's 80th birthday Karen Joy Fowler and Debbie Notkin put together a festschrift, and I was honored to be asked to contribute. Rather than doing a piece of nonfiction, I felt it would mean more if I were to write a story. People have told me that "The Closet" isn't a very Le Guin-like story, and I agree, but I think it comes out my own examination of gender, and I would not have gotten interested in these issues or written such stories if it were not for Le Guin.

"The Closet" also owes something to Theodore Sturgeon's brilliant, twisted story "The Other Celia." You should read it.

Some Like it Cold ###### 1995

After the publication of *Good News from Outer Space*, an apocalyptic, grim vision of the near future, I wanted to do something different for my next novel. I began writing a screwball time-travel comedy, inspired by Lewis Shiner and Bruce Sterling's "Mozart in Mirrorshades," that later became *Corrupting Dr. Nice*. But sixty pages into the book I got stuck (this seems to be a habit with me), and began to doubt whether the time-travel concept I had worked out was viable. I decided to try a short story set against the same background, and that led me to the character of my time-traveling "talent scout" Detlev Gruber.

Once I decided what Detlev did for a living, I needed to find a figure from the past that he might attempt to recruit. I considered several possibilities before I settled on Marilyn Monroe. I read a number of biographies, concentrating on the circumstances of her death, and discovered the hordes of conspiracy theories surrounding that sad event. In this situation, with competing claims offered, I picked what seemed to me a probable sequence of events given what I'd been able to find out. But naturally I had to make some things up and select others with a view to the story I was telling.

Once I got started the story came very rapidly and I was quite pleased with the result, which I managed to sell to Ellen Datlow at *Omni*, a tough market for me. Later Ellen bought a second Detlev Gruber story for SCIFICTION.

But unlike *Corrupting Dr. Nice*, the Gruber stories, though they may be enlivened by Detlev's cynical wit, are not comedies.

One of my little jokes here is that, unlike Detlev, with a little work I could pass for Abraham Lincoln, but for me, Einstein is out of the question.

The Miracle of Ivar Avenue   1996

In attempting a screwball comedy in *Dr. Nice* I had occasion to study the masters of this form and that led me to become fascinated by the life of Preston Sturges, which turned out to be as full of triumphs and pratfalls as any of his films. The several volumes of his screenplays, edited by Brian Henderson, are well worth reading, as is the biography *Christmas in July* by Diane Jacobs.

When I went back to the novel after writing "Some Like It Cold" but still could not get it going, I considered another Detlev Gruber story and came up with "Ivar Avenue."

For this one I turned the plot inside out and buried the science fiction element.

Besides comedy I love classic detective fiction, and this gave me the opportunity to indulge in a Southern California, late 1940s film noir. I researched old Los Angeles street maps, located a copy of the January 6, 1946 issue of *Life* magazine, found out the phase of the moon on May 2, 1948, and hunted down photos of The Players restaurant. I needed a detective, so I invented Lemoyne Kinlaw and his own troubled life.

The only other element required for me to write this story was the change that came over my life with the birth of my daughter Emma. When I wrote "Ivar Avenue" Emma was a year old, and I was acutely aware (as I still am today) of how to have a child is to surrender a hostage to fortune. I have to thank Karen Joy Fowler for telling me the one thing I remember anyone saying about this story at that year's Sycamore Hill Workshop: "You cannot put a time machine and the father of a lost child into the same story and then ignore the implications." Her comment profoundly changed the story, much for the better.

The story originally appeared in *Intersections: The Sycamore Hill Anthology*, which I edited with Mark Van Name and Richard Butner.

Spirit Level   2020

This is the only ghost story I have ever written. I wanted it to have some of the eeriness of classics like Henry James' "The Turn of the Screw" or "The Jolly Corner," and like James use the ghosts to explore my character's psychology.

In some ways it's one of my most personal stories. The haunted house Michael has returned to is the house I grew up in. I have certain points of biographical contact with Michael, and have felt some of the things he has felt, though he is not me and his situation is not mine. In a way I wrote it as a critique of and message to myself.

Stories for Men   2002

I remember watching my daughter as a toddler back in the 1990s in the playground of the day care center and observing what seemed to me to be systematic differences in the playing styles and interactions of the little boys and girls. Even at the age of two, the boys seemed to be running around a lot more, off doing things by themselves, while the girls were more likely to play together quietly. I did not seek to draw any conclusions from this. How much of what I saw was real?

Having grown up in a patriarchal culture of very traditional male/female roles, and learned through feminism to question this, and having observed personally the behavior of men around me, I'd sporadically, in an unorganized way, explored masculinity in my stories. In the late 1990s I began to approach it systematically. We live in a time when traditional ideas about what makes a person female or male are being challenged in a dozen ways. Certainly the feminist movement of the last century sought to redefine womanhood. There are masculinists who claim to speak for what is essentially male. There are also inquiries from anthropology and what is now called evolutionary psychology. I read books on bonobos and chimpanzees and speculations on the evolutionary sources of human behavior. I did not know what I thought about all of these things. I began writing a novel set in a lunar colony whose social structure was based on that of bonobos, among whom females hold the positions of dominance. But the novel got stalled so, as with *Corrupting Dr. Nice*, I tried writing some "proof of concept" stories.

In "Stories for Men" I wanted to deconstruct masculinity. I wondered what might happen if my Society of Cousins were challenged from within by men who felt it to be unjust. Where would a man who had a more traditional vision of masculinity fit in? Certainly, no matter what the political or educational system, there would be men who wanted to revolt. What happens, I thought, if John Wayne is introduced to the Society? In the first draft, my disruptive would-be revolutionary called himself "Ethan Edwards," the character played by John Wayne in the great western *The Searchers*.

But my character wasn't really John Wayne—he was much more of a smartass than any John Wayne character. I thought of Tyler Durden. I do not mean my Tyler to be the same as Chuck Palahniuk's—Thomas Marysson takes this *nom de guerre* without, I think, understanding *Fight Club*. But I wanted my Tyler to have some of the raffish attraction to young men of the "How's that working out for you?" provocateur portrayed by Brad Pitt in the film. It struck me that he might be very attractive to disaffected teenagers like Erno.

The book *Stories for Men* that Erno finds is a real anthology from the 1930s; a copy was given to me when I was twelve by my Uncle Steve, who found it in a house he moved into. The climactic game of chicken played by Tyler and Erno was inspired by an anecdote told me by my father-in-law, the accomplished and deeply humane Col. Robert M. Hall, M.D., about an incident that occurred between him and a French officer during a mortar attack during the Korean War.

I've seen the Society of Cousins described as dystopian, and lots of people have asked me the degree to which I agree with Tyler. Though I gave him intellect and some good arguments, I never meant Tyler to be sympathetic. As for the Society, I did not mean it to be either utopian or dystopian. I do, however, disagree with those who see it as a tyranny. If the Society is a dystopia, then what we live in today is a nightmare of toxic masculinity.

I wrote three other Society of Cousins stories, and later found my way to writing *The Moon and the Other*, a very different novel from the one I'd started in the 1990s. It takes up Erno's story ten years after the end of "Stories for Men."

The Pure Product   1986

"The Pure Product" is the oldest story in this book: I wrote the first draft over the Christmas holiday of 1972. That version was vastly different from what you read here, but at the time I felt quite happy with the result. After many rejections, it was the first story I ever sold, in 1975, to an original anthology titled *Black Holes*. Though I got paid, *Black Holes* was never published, and the rights reverted to me a couple of years later. By that time I could see the story had some problems; I rewrote it and submitted it again. After more rejections it was accepted by Pat Cadigan for the magazine *Shayol*. But a year later *Shayol* suspended publication without printing it, and Pat sent it back to me. I rewrote again, had it rejected some more until it was taken for a new, slick fantasy magazine *Imago*. But their financing fell through and it never appeared.

By now it was the mid-1980s and I had come to call this story my "magazine killer." When Gardner Dozois took over the editorship of *Asimov's SF*, I was in the midst of a debate with Bruce Sterling about the cyberpunk movement and I rewrote it again, gave it a new title, and sent it to Gardner, warning him that the last three editors who had bought it had gone out of business. He took it, gladly, and it appeared in the March 1986 *Asimov's* to a very positive reception. By the time "The Pure Product" was published, it had been rejected more than thirty times over a fourteen-year period. Since then it has been reprinted several times and was the title story of my second story collection.

Most of what I wrote in the 1970s was deservedly abandoned, but for some reason I stuck with this story beyond the bounds of reason. I think it was because this was the story in which I discovered an amoral, active protagonist which I had never written before. Gerald of "The Pure Product" is the father of many other characters, including Richard Shrike in *Good News from Outer Space* and Detlev Gruber from my time-travel stories—though his story still, to my eyes, bears a few signs of the 22-year-old who first wrote it. But maybe that's because I knew him when he was just a boy.

Gulliver at Home   1997

My pal James Patrick Kelly wrote a story called "Glass Cloud", about an architect who is approached by aliens to build the tomb of a god-ruler on a distant planet. To do so the man would have to leave Earth and his family, and because of interstellar time dilation would never see them again. The story ends with him deciding to go. I overheard Jim tell someone that he imagined it to be the story of "Gulliver before he went on his travels."

That got me to thinking: what about Gulliver's wife? She does appear in the brief passages between the four voyages Gulliver tells us about in his book, but she is largely invisible. What was it like to be married to a man who kept leaving her in charge of the children while he sailed off to be reported lost in shipwrecks, more than once presumed dead, only to return home years later with another improbable tale?

Karen Joy Fowler, after reading my story, asked me if I would mind if she wrote a story on the same idea. Her version is "The Travails" and you can find it in her collection *Black Glass*. Is it false modesty for me to say that I think hers is better? But I think I hit a few interesting notes.

Buddha Nostril Bird   1990

One of the nicest things a reviewer has ever said about me was when John Clute called me "an astonishingly savage writer." On some days, yes. I think the world is an absurd place—when not heartbreaking, then hilarious. But some of my stories are more absurd than others.

I have to thank Allen Bloom and his *The Closing of the American Mind* for this one. Bloom's assault on all things modern was a bestseller and intellectual *cause célèbre* in the late 1980s. Dr. Robert Hall, whom I mentioned earlier, a man no more sanguine than I about the state of American civilization, not having read Bloom's book, gave me a copy for Christmas. I hated every word of it.

Rather than write a letter to the *New York Review of Books* explaining why I thought Bloom was an ass, I chose the much more direct path of making him into the hero of a space opera and then tormenting him mercilessly for his wrongheadedness. My Blume would be the quintessential Western thinker, a monster of categorical imperatives, a towering monument to blind egotism, a worshipper of Plato, wrong in everything he thought, said, or did in exactly the way that I saw his inspiration to be wrong in his execrable, narrow-minded screed.

I plotted this story using the *I Ching*, throwing the coins and coming up with a different hexagram for every scene as I moved forward, the way that Philip K. Dick is supposed to have plotted *The Man in the High Castle*. It was a puzzle trying to figure out what the oracle (i.e. my id) wanted me to do, but also a liberation.

The result is maybe the weirdest story I have ever written, one that confused everybody when I brought it to the critique table at Sycamore Hill that year, and that must have seemed equally opaque to readers when it was published in *Asimov's Science Fiction*. But you'll note that since it was published, nobody has ever spoken of Allen Bloom again.

The *I Ching* has subtle powers of influence. In Jonathan Lethem's breakout novel *Motherless Brooklyn*, on page 234 of the hardcover first edition, Jonathan's tourette's syndrome-suffering hero, in the middle of a conversation, shouts out, "Buddha nostril!"

Invaders   1990

If I were forced to pick a single story on which to base my claim to heaven, "Invaders" would be it. Not that there aren't things in here that I could have done better, but the story comes closer than most of what I have written to expressing my feelings about certain aspects of the world's complexity, paradox, tragedy, and their effect on my heart.

If you haven't already, you should see Peter Schaffer's play *The Royal Hunt of the Sun* or the movie made from it. Then read the classic *The Conquest of Peru* by William H. Prescott, and *Conquest of the Incas* by John Hemming.

The opinions stated in this story on science fiction are much harsher than my own opinions. I guess you could say that about most opinions expressed in my fiction—the rhetoric of storytelling causes me to say things I would not say in real life. When, in his essay "Borges and I," Jorge Luis Borges draws a distinction between himself and the man who writes his stories, he is stating a profound truth: "I know the perverse way he has of distorting and magnifying everything."

The Lecturer   1984

I got the idea for this story just after Christmas 1981, when I was riding on the airport bus in New York City one dreary early morning from the MLA convention hotel to LaGuardia in order to fly back to Kansas City. Quite naturally, given that I had just interviewed for a couple of jobs, I was thinking about universities and professorships but was still ambivalent about whether I wanted to pursue an academic career. I had recently read Kafka's "A Hunger Artist" and Damon Knight's story "The Handler." All this mixed together in my mind and the image of the Lecturer presented itself to me.

As a result of one of those MLA interviews, I got hired to teach American literature and creative writing at North Carolina State University. When I moved from KC to Raleigh, I was in the midst of a burst of creativity that had started when I quit my editing job at a wire service the previous May. "The Lecturer" was the first story I wrote while at NCSU, and the first story I ever wrote on a computer, an Apple IIe I borrowed from my colleague Robert Kelton of the NCSU English faculty. Robert was always an early adopter, and I wasn't sure I was ready to make the jump to a very expensive computer when I had a perfectly fine Sperry Remington typewriter.

Ironically, years later when I finally met Damon Knight for the first (and only) time, without any prompting he volunteered that "The Lecturer" was "magnificent." I had the great pleasure of telling him the part that his story played in its inspiration.

Buffalo   1991

I wrote "Buddha Nostril Bird" and "Invaders" and "Buffalo" one after another, just after I had finished my first solo novel *Good News from Outer Space*. "Buffalo," the last of this trilogy, was the one closest to my own life, and seemed to touch people in a way that few of my stories have. It was risky to use personal material in this way—I had played around the edges of such things with "Not Responsible! Park and Lock It!" and "Invaders," but this took it much further.

In a trunk in the basement of our house I later found my father's discharge papers from the Civilian Conservation Corps, which occurred when he hurt his back and was sent to Walter Reed Hospital in D.C. But that's a different story.

In some ways Wells and my dad were my science fiction father and my biological father. They might seem to have little in common in their lives, but they were both engaged with issues of class, and self-improvement, and personal vs. public satisfaction.

Both ended up in a pretty dark place. It's my hope not to end up there. More light!

Clean   2011

This is a sequel to a story titled "Hearts Do Not In Eyes Shine" that I wrote twenty-eight years earlier. I wrote "Clean" at the instigation of my media agent Vince Gerardis, using the bible he and I prepared for a TV series Vince pitched. Vince got the well-known script writer Ron Bass to sign on as show runner and write a script for a pilot. It came within an inch of being produced by NBC. If any of you are interested, give us a call.

I borrowed one element of this story from the life of my friend, multiple award-winning writer Kij Johnson, who when she was a girl used to help her father repair radios. But I want to make it clear that the daughter in "Clean" is not Kij, and the father is not her father (whom I never met).

Another Orphan   1982

I first read *Moby-Dick* when I was a sophomore in an American literature class at the University of Rochester. I did not know what to make of it. Parts of Melville's book bored me to death, but other parts—the obsession of Captain Ahab, the comedy of Ishmael and Queequeg, the adventure story, the speculations about the nature of reality—struck some chord in me. But I would never have called it a favorite. Then, several years later at the University of Kansas, when I took a graduate seminar on Hawthorne and Melville from the marvelous teacher Elizabeth Schultz and read *Moby-Dick* again, I was astonished to see how much it had improved in the interim.

In the late seventies while sampling some oregano I had the idea of stranding a contemporary man in *Moby-Dick*, but I didn't begin writing this story until December of 1979, at which time I was living alone and working at a commodities wire service. I kept at the story off and on throughout 1980, finishing the first draft almost exactly a year after I had started. Though I considered it a genre story, in writing it I let go of most of the expectations that it would find a genre audience. I was working on my dissertation in creative writing, and Elizabeth Schultz was my director. When I showed it to her after I had a draft, she gave me many suggestions, and I did a rewrite over the next four or five months.

Then I tried to sell it to science fiction and fantasy markets. Not surprisingly, it was rejected everywhere I sent it. Finally, I tried *Fantasy and Science Fiction*, which to that time had bought more of my stories than any other magazine. I sent it with a cover letter in which I was so bold as to tell editor Ed Ferman that if he didn't buy it, it was going to go into my drawer, not likely to come out for a long time.

He told me my plea was unnecessary and took it immediately. It came out in September 1982, and received enough recommendations to make the final Nebula ballot. In April 1983 I flew up to New York for the awards banquet and stayed with Jim Kelly at his parents' home in New Canaan, Connecticut. Connie Willis, who was nominated in two categories that year, for "Fire Watch" and "A Letter from the Clearys," also stayed there with us, and we rode the train into Manhattan for the ceremony. At the banquet I was flabbergasted to receive the award for best novella, and Connie won nebulas for both of her stories. We rode back on the train, arrived at Jim's parents' house late at night, and put the three trophies on the kitchen counter. In the morning when we got up, Jim's mother made breakfast for us.

"I knew you were going to win," she told us. "Now how do you like your eggs?"

Consolation   2015

Here's another story of Buffalo.

I write these notes a month after a mob of people, convinced, despite the complete lack of credible evidence, that the 2020 presidential election was stolen, stormed the U.S. Capitol to prevent the results from being certified.

Some of them at least, in what they considered to be justifiable outrage, sought to kill the Vice President and the Speaker of the House.

It strikes me that my opening scene, where Lester Macovic character-izes destructive fools like Alter as "sociopathic losers with computers...full of defensive self-righteousness, deformed consciences, spotty empathy, and a sense of both entitlement and grievance," was prescient. I look forward to a time when this story will seem like lunatic speculation, not reportage.

The Baum Plan for Financial Independence   2004

This one started, as a couple of my stories have, with an exercise I some-times give to my students: Write a grammatical English sentence. Take some element from that first sentence and use it to write a second sentence that follows from the first. Take something from the second sentence and write a third. Keep doing this until you have a story.

Of course what happens is that once you have written a paragraph or two of sentences, you are into a character and situation, and the story takes off from there (or it doesn't, I suppose). I wrote a fair way into this one with no good idea of where it was going, which is very much against my normal practice. I have tended to be a writer who needs to know (or think he knows) where he is driving to before he can start the car. But in recent years that has changed, and I am more willing to get going without a clear destination in mind just to see where I might end up.

In "The Baum Plan" I had gotten Sid and Dot to the door in the back of the closet and was completely stumped as to what they would find on the other side. When I complained about this to my friend and colleague, the wonderful writer Wilton Barnhardt, he told me, "What you find on the other side is the understanding of the class system." That wasn't very specific, but it got me going.

I should mention that I had in recent years read all of the L. Frank Baum Oz books aloud to my daughter Emma, some of them more than once, so I was steeped in Oz magic. But I did not have Oz in mind when I started this, and many of the Oz references—such as Dot's red sneakers, believe it or not—pre-sented themselves unconsciously to me, and I did not notice them until later.

I had the story done and ready to send out but no title—or rather, I had six or seven titles that I didn't like. "The Baum Plan for Financial Independence" came to me at the very last minute, and it is one of my favorite titles ever. As is the story.

The Dark Ride   2021

Despite the fact that it takes place over one hundred years ago, this story draws from points of contact I have with the history described in it: I grew up in a blue collar family in Buffalo, New York, the site of the 1901 Pan American Exhibition; I used to ride my bike on McKinley Parkway; I saw the pistol and handkerchief mentioned in this narrative in the Buffalo History Museum, which began its life as the New York pavilion at the fair. My father, born in 1904, was a Polish immigrant factory worker, and I labored one summer in the 40-inch rolling mill at Bethlehem Steel in Lackawanna, where my cousin Raymond died in an industrial accident when he was nineteen years old.

The Trip to the Moon was an actual ride at the exposition, one of the first true "dark rides" of amusement park history, ancestor of such rides at Disneyland and Universal City. After the Pan American Exposition was over, it was moved to Coney Island and gave its name to Luna Park.

As I was writing an early draft of this story, my wife Therese was writing her novel *A Well-Behaved Woman*—steeped in the Gilded Age—and kindly gave me the quote from William H. Vanderbilt that so annoys Leon in my story. Thanks, dear.